a novel by **Monique van Vooren**

Night Sanctuary

SUMMIT
BOOKS
New York

Copyright © 1981 by Monique van Vooren
All rights reserved
including the right of reproduction
in whole or in part in any form
Published by SUMMIT BOOKS
A Simon & Schuster Division of Gulf & Western Corporation
Simon & Schuster Building
1230 Avenue of the Americas
New York, New York 10020

SUMMIT BOOKS and colophon are trademarks of Simon & Schuster
Designed by Irving Perkins & Associates
Manufactured in the United States of America

1 2 3 4 5 6 7 8 9 10

Library of Congress Cataloging in Publication Data
Van Vooren, Monique, date.
Night sanctuary.
I. Title.
PS3572.A5447N5   813'.54   81–9420
AACR2
ISBN 0–671–40093–2

Permission to reprint lines from the song
"Night Sanctuary" by Sammy Cahn and
Peter Daniels is gratefully acknowledged.

for you

Acknowledgments

I would like to acknowledge the irreplaceable influence Jerry Purcell had on my life and let him know that he has my gratefulness for giving me his faith and support throughout the years.

To my friend Donna McCrohan, my appreciation for her never losing her sense of humor through the long working hours and the frantic deadlines.

To Drew Patterson, my indebtedness for his constant and invaluable guidance during this enormous task, and most of all for directing me in what I believe to be the right path at the right time in my life.

M. v V.

New York City
February 20, 1981

Prologue

To have broken through
and be back at the point one began
at the point one has reached.
—Harvey Perr,
Rosenblum

VLADIMIR/*New York City/Tuesday, September 27, 1966*

Everything about Vladimir was beautiful. His pale skin, his Slavic bones, his awesome body, his terrifying anger. He was a sexual magnet attracting both men and women.

He was a superstar, but he did not bear his celebrity easily.

Vladimir Volodin's fans had already gathered at the stage door of the Metropolitan Opera House when he arrived, just before six. Ordinarily he would have made a reluctant effort, forcing himself to sign the obligatory autographs. But not this time. He rushed past the group into the theater saying, "Not now! Not now!" Even though it was oppressively hot for September, a leather coat was draped loosely over his shoulders.

In the corridor several dancers nodded to him; he greeted no one. Nearing his dressing room, he spied two middle-aged women sitting on a bench, huddled in conversation. At the sound of his approaching footsteps they turned around in unison. One of them, a newspaper reporter, stood up and approached Vladimir to speak with him, but suddenly stopped in her tracks, petrified. The words never passed her lips; they were swatted in mid-breath as Volodin, taut with anger, shouted for all to hear, "You are a vicious, lying bitch! Get out of my sight!" The voice had a slight accent. The command was in plain English.

He entered his dressing room, slamming the door behind him. Loudly and clearly, Vladimir began to swear in his own language. He removed his clothes: a black Nehru suit, knee-high leather boots, a white silk Cossack shirt. Donning his frayed blue robe, he went to the makeup table. Calmly, as if nothing had happened, he seated himself in front of the mirror and, framed in white lights, he started the ritual. He first applied a light foundation, which emphasized his natural pallor. Shading his nose, his temples, his cheeks, he stopped, drew himself back slightly, pencil still in hand, and studied his reflection. It was a look devoid of narcissism, an impersonal evaluation of someone else's face, one that could have belonged to anyone, a stranger. But the face was known worldwide as that of Vladimir Volodin, the most spectacular ballet dancer since Nijinsky.

What was exciting about watching Vladimir dance is akin to what is exciting about watching a sky-diver: a feeling of imminent danger. He brought a total lack of fear to every one of his performances, like a trapeze acrobat flying without a net. He could bring the public to the edge of their seats and, through his own involvement, grab them with every step, pirouette and leap—hitting at the gut and inciting the imagination at the same time. His performances were so highly charged that one expected him to die at the climax of each of them or, if not, then surely at the end. This he achieved seemingly without physical effort. He had no equals, only imitators.

Vladimir leaned closer and began shadowing his eyes. Large gray sad eyes, always seeking something, as if recalling a tragedy that could never be erased. Looking, learning, dismissing, approving, inquiring, mischievous, old, young, sad eyes.

Melba walked in, carrying the lavishly embroidered costumes for the second act.

"Who let that bitch backstage?" Vladimir's voice was toneless.

"What bitch are you talking about?" Melba turned her back to him and began tidying his wardrobe.

"That cross-eyed, lying newspaper bitch who wrote that dreadful article about me in *New World.*"

"You mean *New Time.*"

"You know what I mean. *New World, New Time,* it doesn't matter. How did she get in?"

Melba faced him helplessly. "I was busy, I didn't even know she was here. I'll find out. Should I—"

"You should nothing. Just—oh, never mind. Just shut up and give me my tea."

One might have expected a samovar in the dressing room of so famous a dancer, but Melba made tea in a plain brown English pot that Vladimir had bought at a Woolworth's not far from Covent Garden. He had learned from members of the Royal Ballet Company that the best "cuppa" is made in such a prosaic pot. The one luxury he did allow himself was an electric kettle from Bloomingdale's.

His dressing room was large and comfortable but had taken on the appearance of a Gypsy caravan since he had moved in the day before. Shoes, clothes and various other paraphernalia were strewn about the floor and chairs. Bottles and jars of makeup clogged the table, along with half-empty cups, scripts, books, ballet tights and photographs.

When the tea was ready Vladimir gulped it Russian-style, holding a lump of sugar between his front teeth and sucking the hot liquid through it. He peered at a pile of unopened telegrams and letters. The distinctive handwriting on one caught his attention. The envelope was marked "personal." There were no stamps; it had arrived by private messenger. He ripped it open and read the enclosure at top speed, then again very slowly, his eyes becoming strangely glazed. He fingered the note with the same gesture of tenderness one would the intimate garment of a woman one has loved. Then he folded it carefully and quickly placed it inside the cover of a book, as if holding it a second longer would burn his hands. He remained silent for a long moment, his eyes gazing into the mirror as though a whole portion of his life, unseen by anyone else, were unfolding miraculously before him.

Someone knocked. He snapped at Melba, "I don't want to see anybody."

Two men entered, wheeling a five-foot floral arrangement in the shape of a swan.

"What the hell is that?" he asked with a devilish glint in his eyes.

"It's a white swan, Vladimir," Melba replied. "A white swan made of carnations."

"It looks like funeral wreath to me. See who wants me dead!" His laughter erupted in shades—dark, medium, light—gone. Melba removed a gold-embossed card and was about to read it aloud when Volodin snatched it. He stalked back and forth several times, surveying the unusual offering, like Mephistopheles evaluating the contents of a boiling cauldron, then read the printed invitation.

"In honor of Vladimir Volodin and the Ballet Company of Lincoln Center, Mrs. Sinclair J. MacAlpine requests the pleasure of your company at a reception to be held at the Four Seasons following the benefit performance. Tuesday, September 27, 1966." Handwritten in a familiar script was a personal note: "Best wishes for your success tonight and forever. Love, Denise."

Vladimir returned to his dressing table and was outlining his lips when Frank Wilbur, the company manager, entered. He approached the dancer more obsequiously than necessary. "Do you think, Vladimir—do you think it would be possible to arrange a television interview at your hotel tomorrow morning?"

Vladimir was already shaking his head, but Wilbur continued. "It's very important that the company gets as much—" Vladimir cut him off with a wave of his hand. Wilbur retreated and reached for the doorknob, then ventured, "Monica would like to rehearse some steps from the second act when you start your practice. Could you do it?"

"If Monica doesn't know part by now, no point dancing with her," he replied in slightly choppy English, into which he lapsed when tired or annoyed. The manager said nothing more and departed.

Melba followed. "I'll be back shortly," she said as she exited. "I have to get your cape."

"Why did you forget it in first place?" Volodin asked, scowling. She did not reply, being used to his gruff comments, which she took as a sign of affection.

Melba was a short Italian woman with a nondescript face, ready to obey orders without question. Her face was unmarked. Easy to forget. She was wearing a gingham dress, and her graying hair was pulled into a long girlish ponytail. She was either a young woman looking old or an old woman looking young; it was hard to tell. But she was utterly devoted to Volodin.

From the hallway the frantic rustling of dancers, musicians and technicians tuning up for the evening reached his ears with a crescendo of tension.

Tonight, the twenty-seventh of September, promised to be a gala evening. For the first time in its short history the new Metropolitan Opera House was presenting a ballet company on its majestic stage. It was also the first time the legendary Vladimir Volodin was dancing to his own choreography of *Sleeping Beauty*, with the newly formed Ballet Company of Lincoln Center. The opera house had opened only two weeks earlier, marking the completion of the main portion of the performing-arts complex. The critics had a grand time writing about it. One wag said, "The architecture looks like something Mussolini would order by telephone." On the whole, though, the new theater received the immediate approval of music, theater and dance lovers.

The hot Indian-summer evening vibrated with anticipation, both inside and outside the opera house. By six o'clock hundreds of people were milling around the large central plaza, waiting for the parade of celebrities and public figures to begin. Extra police had been assigned to patrol the area, now being invaded by balletomanes with the determination of an occupation army. As the taxis and limousines began discharging their passengers, it was clear from their dress that while some still clung to summer and its sweet memories, others had plunged headlong into autumn. New Yorkers strained to see their handsome mayor, John Lindsay, and his wife. They greeted the couple with a mixture of cheers, boos and hisses. Paul Newman and his wife, Joanne Woodward, enthusiastic supporters of ballet, received an outburst of applause. Alice Tully, wearing a full-length ermine cape in spite of the heat, passed through the throng unnoticed, although she was one of the Center's most generous patrons, whose name would soon be given to a nearby auditorium still under construction. Clive Barnes, *The New York Times* dance and drama critic, also went unrecognized.

The group applauded respectfully when Lady Bird Johnson and her daughter Lynda, accompanied by Vice-President and Mrs. Hubert Humphrey, arrived, surrounded by a bevy of Secret Service agents. Other prominent guests included Senator Jacob Javits and his glamorous wife, Marion; John D. Rockefeller III, the man most responsible for the birth of the center, his wife, Blanchette, and his brother, Nelson, New York's governor, with his second wife, Happy. They were followed by Jerome Robbins, the brilliant choreographer; Nathan Berger, the notorious attorney, with the beautiful film actress, Angelica Anders; and Rudolph Bing, manager of the Metropolitan Opera Company.

Suddenly a wave of screams and cheers ripped through the crowd of onlookers. It swelled to delirium, exploding with an exuberance that was clearly heard by those inside the opera house. Mattie Maxwell, the celebrated singer and actress, had arrived. Her streaked light-auburn hair, worn in a bouffant style with a chignon, gave her a sophisticated look. She was more striking than ever, the famous nose unmistakable. Her latest film had just opened at Radio City Music Hall, and the critics were already predicting another Oscar. She was escorted by Montgomery Clift. They made a golden couple.

The walk from their limousine to the foyer was long, but Mattie and Montgomery managed to smile and wave, guided by several bodyguards, who provided only the slightest protection from their adoring fans. Both were nearly blinded by the flash of camera bulbs as they finally made their way inside the opera house. Mattie was awestruck by the huge chandelier hanging above the circular lobby, and a press representative felt obliged to explain that the seventeen-foot hand-blown crystal object that had captured her imagination had been donated to the center by the republic of Austria in gratitude for American aid during the difficult years following the Second World War. Mattie Maxwell and Montgomery Clift were then ushered inside the spectacular theater.

Bells sounded repeatedly, urging the glittering audience to take their seats. They poured out of the Top of the Met, the beautifully appointed restaurant, the Opera Cafe, on the ground level, and the Opera Club, near the dress circle. Ushers scurried up and down the aisles to assist stragglers. The lights began to dim. Robert and Jacqueline Kennedy walked hand in hand toward their seats; she wore a high-necked gown, no jewels, and looked starkly understated. Princess Lee Radziwill, her sister, was with them. They were followed by choreographer George Balanchine and Doris Duke. Then Martha Graham, with a large party, made a grand entrance, moving elegantly down the circular staircase. Sol Hurok, the producer of the evening's event, sat alone, two rows from the back. Aristotle Onassis and Maria Callas took their places in a box. The lights continued dimming. A hush descended on the hall.

The retractable crystal chandeliers in the theater auditorium slowly ascended to the high gold-leafed ceiling. The hum of the crowd sustained itself as if buffeted by an invisible wind, lingering on the threshold between sound and stillness. The murmur of the veiled voices, mixed with timid ripples of laughter and studded with an occasional muffled sneeze or cough, sounded like the planned harmony of a gigantic chorus.

The conductor lifted his baton. The sudden outbreak of silence was as deafening as a roar. The orchestra began the overture, and the audience was engulfed in a sea of expectation as the golden-draped curtain rose on the prologue.

Backstage, Melba returned to Volodin's dressing room, carrying the cape. She left the door ajar and announced, "Mrs. Sinclair MacAlpine is here to see you." Before he had a chance to reply, the woman entered with the assurance of an expected visitor.

Denise MacAlpine was in her early thirties, her blond hair pulled back in a French twist. Her simple white lace off-the-shoulder dress was set off by an extraordinary diamond-and-emerald necklace, which had once belonged to the Maharani of Kapurthala, reputedly purchased at Sotheby's for two million dollars. She stood near the entrance anticipating an appraisal of her spectacular beauty and style. There was none. Volodin raised his head but did not get up. "Hello—I didn't plan to see you before the performance." She walked toward him and kissed him lightly on the lips.

"Easy, Denise! I don't think we're using the same shade of lipstick!" he said.

"I don't use lipstick. Mine's lip gloss."

"Whatever it is, it tastes good," he said and winked at her.

She tugged at a chair near his makeup table, pushing a pile of aging sweaters to the floor.

"Why don't you sit down?" he asked with affected graciousness.

"I think I will. Thank you. I thought you'd never ask." She sounded miffed.

Muted voices could be heard in the corridor as well as the sound of doors being opened and closed. The voices rose, grew louder, faded, disappeared. It was quiet again. Denise's eyes darted back and forth between Vladimir and Melba, as if willing the woman to leave the room. Volodin understood. "Melba, fammi un piacere. Will you find Monica and tell her it would be helpful to *me* if she could rehearse some steps of the second act? I'll be warming up shortly." She left.

"Denise, you know I don't like visitors before performance. You know I need concentration. You should be in your seat. Ballet has started."

"I'm only interested in seeing *you* dance. This is just the prologue, and since you don't appear until the first act, I wanted to come by and wish you good luck," she explained. "Everybody in the world is here!"

Vladimir stood up and walked across the room to inspect several pairs of ballet slippers. Denise continued, "It should be the most exciting evening you've ever had!" He didn't reply. Twisting her diamond bracelet, she gazed at her reflection in the mirror and asked, "What do you consider has been your most exciting evening?"

A few seconds passed as he sat on the floor, trying on one pair of slippers after another. "My most exciting evening was never. I've only had exciting moments. Whenever I'm on the stage dancing, that's my most exciting moment. People don't make the event. I am my own event. I don't know who's been screwing around with these," Vladimir said impatiently, hurling a slipper across the room. It landed on the dressing table between a dance belt and a box of tissue paper, knocking over a cup of tea in the process. Denise picked up a towel and mopped the spilled liquid.

"You seem very nervous tonight. *Are* you nervous?"

"Yes, I am."

"More than usual?"

"What is this, an interview? No, not more than usual. As much."

Melba entered the room for a moment. "Excuse me, Vladimir. The German photographer who took your pictures for *Stern* last week would like to know if you've made your choice."

"They're all terrible. I don't want any of them published."

"What shall I say to him?" she asked apprehensively.

"Tell him to go fuck himself."

Melba left, mumbling to herself in Italian. Volodin poured another cup of tea. Denise automatically dropped in five cubes from a little sugar bowl on his table.

"Can we see each other tomorrow afternoon?" she asked.

He looked at her over the rim of his cup as he sipped. "Not tomorrow."

"Why?"

"I have a class, a television show and an interview with *The New York Times*." It was not true. He simply didn't want to see her. Not tomorrow. Vladimir looked at her, saw again how beautiful she was, and knew for certain he no longer desired the body that had given him so much pleasure. He tried to visualize her naked, as he had so many times in the past, but could not. How strange that he vividly remembered the details of every dress he had seen her wear but was unable to recall the movement of her naked body while making love. In a last attempt, he tried to visualize her face, contorted in the throes of pleasure, or pain. It was useless. The magic was gone. If only women could treat the men they love like those they don't. As he watched her sitting in all her splendor he sought to recapture what first had attracted him to Denise. It was the look, smell and texture of luxury, the gestures of the very rich, that pretty hand, her gentle insolence. He had been hooked on the mystery of her, and now it had been solved. More than anything else, he wanted to see her walk out the door.

"I was very sorry to hear about Mariela," she said. "Have you spoken to her?"

"No." Vladimir was going to stop there, and should have. But his voice went on, "I've gotten a letter," and his eyes wandered to the book from which the missive poked out several inches.

"What can I tell you? Who lives by the sword, dies by the sword." Denise spoke with clipped arrogance.

"She's not dead, Denise. Far from it. Mariela's a survivor. I know she's going to pull through it."

Denise listened without responding.

"Are you still jealous?" he asked, glancing sideways.

"Don't be silly. I feel sorry for her."

"But you are jealous." It was a statement.

"I was. I've always been jealous of everyone that mattered to you. Did you ever love her?"

He did not answer.

Love? To Vladimir "love" was a word that had been tossed about recklessly, a word eroded by years of usage. Sex was love. He loved his work, his art, his ambition. He also loved caviar, vodka, long walks and reading. Love? Of course Denise meant love as an all-encompassing emotion superseding every other one. And that he couldn't feel. Emotions? Of course he had emotions, too many, but always hidden behind a façade of callousness and the pursuit of many women. So many women it no longer mattered.

Had it ever? Perhaps long ago. Yes, many years ago. She was older than he. Not beautiful. Better than beautiful. Womanly. And he had loved her. She was his music teacher and his first affair. It was a memory, a pain, a guilt, *a woman*. After her Mariela had come the closest. She was the first woman he had allowed to know him. The first woman he had allowed to walk out on him before he was ready to let go. And for a long time after, he could obtain physical gratification in other arms only by fantasizing about her. Sometimes he still did.

Melba reentered the dressing room. "You'd better go to your practice, Vladimir," she said in a maternal tone.

"Don't be pain in ass, Melba. I'll be out shortly. You know I don't go on until—"

"Mattie Maxwell is here!" Denise interrupted. "I saw her in the lobby. She practically got mobbed."

"Yes, I gave her the tickets. Look what she sent me." He pointed to a balloon in the unmistakable shape of a phallus, which had been fastened to the wall. Denise rose and read the note dangling from a ribbon of orchids attached to it: "You have no competition. Love, Mattie." They both laughed, but if laughter could be described in terms of color, his was bright red, hers a drab yellow.

"It's obvious what kind of competition Mattie is referring to! I'm sure she hasn't seen enough ballet to be a connoisseur!" Denise spat the words with the elegant bitchiness of one who patronizes the world's classier playgrounds. Her voice was vaguely reminiscent of a Tennessee Williams heroine. It was the kind of voice spawned in the South and taken through every fashionable place at the right time—a very American voice trying to sound almost British. "I know she's famous, Vladimir, and talented, but for the life of me, I never knew what it is you see in her."

"She's kind, considerate and loyal—three qualities that you lack entirely." Volodin blurted it out.

"And a good fuck, no doubt," she whispered in his ear. Volodin had intimidated her into speaking freely. He shrugged. "Don't you think you'd better put that thing away, Vladimir?" Denise snapped, her eyes directed at the balloon. "Lady Bird and Lynda are here. Jackie and Bobby Kennedy too. They'll surely come backstage to offer their congratulations."

"It was sent to me. I'm not offended! If they don't like it they can leave. Let's hope that after performance they will come to see me, not the décor."

Denise rose and stood behind Vladimir, grasping his shoulders. She locked eyes with his in the mirror. "Mattie was certainly crazy about you. What did you do for her that no other man could?"

He gave her that slow, searching look that made her feel devoured. "What do I do for you that no other man can?"

She nodded. "What are you looking at?" she asked.

"At your necklace."

"You've seen it before." Her voice was half mocking, half curious.

"I know. I was just thinking." His eyes lit up mischievously, and their humor spread to his sensual features. "I was thinking that object saves a lot of time for prospective suitors. When they see your jewel they know approximately the amount of money they'll need to bid for your affections."

"I never heard you bid."

"I didn't have to bid, Denise. This time *you* were doing the bidding."

Vladimir got up and removed the blue robe that he had worn since his days with the Kirov. Melba caught it before it hit the floor. He was completely nude. Denise tried to avert her gaze, but couldn't. His translucent skin, stretched tautly over the feral body, seemed lit from within. Its incandescence spread to every corner of the dressing room. He was strong, muscular and as beautiful as any of the statues Michelangelo had sculpted of his gods. Vladimir was more slender and incredibly well proportioned. Above all, one could sense his musicality. He was musical in the way he moved his head, reached for a cup of tea, laughed, got up from a chair, held his fingers, touched his face, walked, spoke, danced. When looking at him one thought of music as well as motion. In short, he made it possible to *see* music as well as hear it.

His body was his instrument.

Slowly, Denise moved closer to him. Impulsively she reached for his bare waist, then allowed her hands to follow the contours of his naked buttocks. "Let me get dressed," he said, moving away from her. He stepped into his tattered rehearsal tights and adjusted their straps. "You'd better go now. I must practice. I'll see you later."

Denise said, "After the performance I will go directly to the Four Seasons with my guests and send the limousine back for you. By then you will have seen all of your admirers." She laughed softly and looked up at him. Her eyes were as dispirited as her voice. "But hurry, darling. We'll all be—"

There was a timid knock at the door. A small, ethereal dancer walked in and went straight to Vladimir. They spoke together in Russian. Selecting one of his many bouquets, he presented it to her. She kissed him as a child would and departed with tears in her eyes.

"That was nice of you," Denise said.

"Before the end of the evening I'll give them all away. I do not like cut flowers."

"Why?"

"Their life is too short. I don't like the thought and I don't want to be reminded of it. I like trees and forests."

"Will you give away my swan?" Denise asked, spreading her arms toward the gigantic floral arrangement.

"No"—again the glint. "I'll keep him here during this entire engagement and watch him die slowly in front of my eyes."

Denise turned and left the room without a word. She had no intention of taking her seat in the auditorium. Not just yet. She stepped behind a panel outside Vladimir's dressing room and waited.

Volodin grabbed several pairs of ballet slippers, a couple of towels, his leg warmers and sweaters, draped the old blue robe over his shoulders and started for his grueling practice backstage. At the door he tugged playfully at Melba's ponytail and said, "After I leave tonight, be sure to cut all the cards from the flowers and have someone take them to girls' dressing room." Before he disappeared down the hall he added, "Just keep the swan. . . . Oh, cara Melba, I forgot my tea. Please bring it." Melba followed him hurriedly with a hot thermos bottle.

Slowly and carefully, Denise reentered Vladimir's dressing room. Very slowly and very carefully. She went directly to the book that held Mariela's letter. Quickly she read every word of the letter. She was stunned. She made certain to leave it just as she had found it, and headed for the grand tier.

Melba returned to the dressing room. Vladimir's apparent disorganization was, to him, utter precision. Amidst the chaos of his table he could have located—blindfolded—anything he wanted. Melba knew that she was to touch only the obvious discards. She started clearing away the empty cups from his table, noticed a piece of notepaper protruding from a book and pushed it back inside. Gathering the soiled facial tissues, she glanced once again at the book. She opened its cover, saw the letter lying there and realized it was the one that earlier had occupied Vladimir's attention so totally. She retrieved it furtively, closed the door and read:

Aruba
September 26, 1966

Vladimir,

I am not with you. I won't be. I cannot be. Only forces stronger than my will, out of my control, could have prevented me from being there tonight, cheering you in what I know will be a triumph. Being able to speak to you daily has been of much comfort and help to me in this trying period.

I am not immune, strong, untouchable. I stand still—possessed by a memory of you that can never be erased. I must confess that letting go of you is the only act of unselfish love I've ever given to anyone in my life.

I'll be waiting for you October 9, as promised. I need your strength. I'm so afraid.

It was no accident that these things happened to me. I had suspicions and dismissed them. But now I believe they might be confirmed. Please, hurry!

I need you. To help me. To hold me.

I'm lying low. The oak has become a willow.

As always, as ever, be well,
Mariela

Melba felt a sudden flush of embarrassment and shame. She folded the letter, replaced it where she had found it, sat down and crossed herself.

※

Book One

Getting There

MARIELA/*New York City/Saturday, January 30, 1954*

The burgundy Rolls Royce moved slowly down Park Avenue, its dashboard lit up like a small city. The young woman in the back seat strained to check her makeup in a jeweled compact. Her lips and teeth, reflected in the tiny, shiny circle, took on the almost clinical look of a mouth examined at close range by a dentist. She glanced out the window. It was a bleak Saturday night.

A heavy snowfall had blanketed Manhattan, covering it like a giant tea cosy, muting its usual cacophony and temporarily transforming its filthy streets and sidewalks into pristine arteries. People were walking precariously and huddling in pairs. The atmosphere was eerie and still. One could not only *hear* the muffled sounds of the city but could actually *see* them, as wisps of frosted breath ballooned from the mouths of pedestrians like captions floating from comic-strip characters. The streets were deserted except for an occasional taxi, a few cars grudgingly en route to some uncancelable obligation and an isolated bus plowing through drifts.

The limousine turned up Madison Avenue. As it passed an exclusive shop the woman admired a gown in the window and made a mental note to return sometime during the following week to examine it more closely. She switched on the radio in the mahogany panel next to the built-in bar. Eddie Fisher warbled "Oh, My Papa." The music didn't suit her mood. This was no time for syrupy sentimentality. After trying several other stations she abruptly turned it off. She crossed her legs, and the sound of expensive silk underwear swishing against itself rustled through the car, releasing a sensual whiff of Shalimar perfume as immediate as passion.

The limousine stopped in front of a six-story townhouse on the upper East Side, where the elegantly dressed passenger alighted, telling the white-uniformed chauffeur to return for her by eleven. The young woman touched the doorbell with her gloved hand. An intercom voice requested identification. She replied, "Miss Mariela Koenig."

As she entered the immense marble foyer she heard indistinguishable voices coming from a large drawing room to her right. On her left an

Aubusson tapestry covered an entire wall. In front of it stood a red-and-gold lacquered commode that had belonged to Cardinal Mazarin of France during Louis XIV's reign. Atop it sat a large eighteenth-century porcelain figure.

A butler approached, took her sable coat and said, "Mr. Ravenstein is expecting you in his study."

She hurried toward the elevator, changed her mind, and walked upstairs to the second floor, the thick pile of the carpet muffling the click of her heels. A door to her right was ajar. She opened it farther and stood for a moment in the doorway, a phantasmagoric figure sheathed in a black velvet Ceil Chapman dress that accentuated her flawless white skin. An exquisite diamond necklace with matching earrings completed the vision of total elegance. Mariela Koenig was a strikingly beautiful woman, a regal five feet eight inches tall. Her sensuous face was framed by shining black hair that she wore pulled back in a fashionable chignon.

Karl Ravenstein was seated at his desk behind a bank of five telephones. He was talking into one of them when he noticed Mariela, and waved for her to enter. A heady aroma of Rigaud candles, tuberose, and cigar smoke pervaded the room. Ravenstein was dressed in a black silk robe, white shirt and black velvet pants.

Mariela went directly to the enormous dark green sofa that stretched across the entire length of one side of the library.

"Howard, I've got a heavy night ahead of me," Ravenstein was saying. He looked at Mariela, blew smoke in her direction and smiled. "But I will be in Beverly Hills next Friday. . . ."

Mariela returned his smile conspiratorially and winked. Her eyes flitted from surface to surface. The lush velvet walls were adorned with a Goya, several blue-period Picassos and a number of abstracts. A Giacometti stood in a corner. All were lighted by pin spotlights. She shifted her focus to Karl's desk, made especially for Napoleon, decorated with gilded winged horses and signed by the brothers Jacob. On it was a photograph of a young girl and another of Karl dressed as Napoleon.

"Listen. I put my money where my mouth is and you can believe my money will be there when it's needed—as long as Darlene continues—"

"—to fuck me," Mariela whispered to herself in unison with Karl.

Mariela knew a lot about Karl Ravenstein, as did many others, especially in the financial world. An unauthorized book had already been published on his exploits, *How to Own Everything and Everybody,* and its sales had been huge.

The shelves behind Karl's desk were filled with volumes published in five languages—English, French, German, Russian and Japanese—all of which he spoke fluently. Karl had been called a genius, wizard, scoundrel, rogue, crook, pervert and innumerable variations thereof. But no one denied his intelligence or his success.

Born to great wealth in St. Petersburg, his father had been financial adviser to Rasputin, the mad monk of czarist Russia. By 1918 the family had escaped the Revolution and, with a fortune in jewels sewn into little Karl's knickers, had established itself in England. He was then nine years old.

"Jack's coming in from Canada on Monday and we'll take care of that little cocksucker who thought . . ."

Karl's vulgarity hardly befitted an Eton graduate who had continued his studies at Cambridge. After only three years he had soaked up all the economics the professors could teach him and, at twenty-one, moved to Paris to become the managing director of the Franco-Asiatic Bank. By age twenty-three, Karl had manipulated the French franc into such a tailspin that he was ordered deported. Having made a five-million-dollar profit in the scabrous affair, he took the money with him as a consolation prize when he left the country.

"That fucking Perona. I'll have his ass, that two-bit prohibition boot-legger. Why, he even barred Zsa Zsa from El Morocco two years ago because she . . ."

In London, Karl accumulated more wealth through a succession of shady deals. He eventually went to Japan with a Hungarian charmer, "Countess" Natasha, and in a short while, by wheeling and dealing yen, made another profit, this time some ten million dollars. Faced with the problem of getting so large a sum of money out of the country, Ravenstein had one of his agents pose as an exporter and buy a huge batch of obis, the silk sashes stiffened with cardboard tubing that Japanese women wear around their waists. The notes were stuffed into the tubing, and the shipment whizzed through Japanese customs without a question. Ravenstein unloaded his yen in major United States cities, creating a depreciation in the currency which it took Japan years to recover from.

"Say hello to Ava if you see her. I haven't had a chance to return her call. And take it easy with those planes, Howard. I'm still planning to go flying with you one of these days."

Ravenstein rose as he hung up, parted his sensuous lips and exploded in happy laughter. "Howard is the only man I know who is having as good a time as I am—and making even more money while he's doing it." His tone changed. "Mariela, aren't you late?" He looked at his watch, which indicated 8:40, and walked toward her.

"Sorry, darling. I was waiting for a call from Rome."

"And I was waiting for you," he said, kissing her fingers, eyes boring into hers. Abruptly he let her hand drop, fussed with his cuff links, whirled around and snapped, "Can you believe that Perona is still holding a grudge against me for not canceling my table last month! That bastard has barred me from El Morocco! Goddamn it, I'll buy the building and drive that little wop back where he belongs, herding sheep on some deserted mountain in Italy. In the meantime I promised that creep press agent of his, Danny Gordon, a couple of hundred bucks to smooth things over."

Mariela was accustomed to his moods. What a lot of crap, she thought, but kept smiling. Seconds passed. Karl looked at her intently.

"Christ! You look good! Have some champagne." The Dom Perignon was already uncorked and iced. He filled her crystal glass almost to the brim and sat next to her.

"Aren't you having some with me?" asked Mariela as she sipped slowly.

"You bet I will, and from my favorite cup." He pulled her dress gently down her shoulders to reveal her large breasts confined in a lace and satin bra. "Unfasten it," he ordered.

"Do it yourself," Mariela replied with mock sternness. "It hooks in front. You should know that by now. Do it." It was a command.

Karl rose to his feet and moved silently behind the green velvet sofa. He put his arms around Mariela, and, deftly, subtly, his hands explored the contours of her bosom and soon found the fastening. He purposely delayed exposing her nakedness and the intense pleasure he derived from the sight and feel of her creamy flesh—much as a gourmet waits to savor last the rare truffle on his pâté de foie gras. As her head fell gently backward against Karl's chest, Mariela closed her eyes, then opened them momentarily and caught the look in his. Something indefinable implored her to put him into a mood, the kind of mood that only *she* was able to bring out—the mood that would set the tone for their evening. She was the ringmaster. It was up to her to raise the curtain on their lust. The time was now.

Impatiently Mariela placed her hands on his, guiding them firmly and slowly around her breasts, kneading them together, inch by inch parting the delicate fabric, revealing her incredible voluptuousness, until she was bare to the waist. He found the hardness of her nipples and squeezed them harshly. His fingertips brushed her moist cleft.

Karl came around to the front of the couch and dipped his forefinger in the glass, wet both her nipples, bent down and ravenously sucked the champagne from them. He repeated this procedure again and again and each time a tremor passed through her body.

"Put your tit in the glass," he said huskily. "I'm thirsty, very thirsty." Holding her breast in her hands provocatively, she did as he ordered. "Where is your fur coat?" he asked as he caught his breath.

"William took it when I arrived, but—"

"You know that I want you to wear it," he said with urgency. "I'll ring for it." Karl walked across the room to his desk, picked up one of the telephones and gave the order. Returning to Mariela, he knelt before her, grabbed one of her hands roughly and put it open-palm between his legs, pressing it until he was sure she felt what he wanted her to feel.

Mariela slowly sank to her knees in front of him. She unzipped his trousers and spread his legs apart. "Do you like it?" she asked, intensifying her caresses so he was unable to say yes, but there was no doubt in her mind about his ecstasy. Suddenly she stopped, raised her head, and with the smooth, long fingers of her free hand she stroked the back of his neck. "I heard some voices from the drawing room as I came in," Mariela said in a throaty voice. "What surprises do you have in store for us tonight?" Karl continued to fondle her breasts. "Stop it, Karl. Please—I want to know."

"Two of the girls are from Madame Geraldine's," he said casually. "You've met Bonnie. As I recall, you seemed to like her." Their eyes met, sharing a secret. "The third one was recommended to me today by Sam Goldman. He said she was the best—"

Mariela eased herself backward onto the sofa. She knew Sam Goldman well. A fat, balding man with stumpy legs, he always had a cheap cigar clamped between his discolored teeth. Furrier by profession, pimp by disposition, Sam Goldman had been one of the first people she had met upon her arrival in New York three years earlier. He was notorious, venal and useful. Each Wednesday he gave a cocktail party in his Central Park West apartment, where he gathered the newest and prettiest girls in town, auctioning them off to a few well-chosen and well-heeled men, preferably from Wall Street. None of Sam's girls "gave in" for anything less than five hundred dollars, 40 percent of which went to Sam. If a client took a girl out more than three times, it was understood he would buy her a fur coat.

Sam Goldman had introduced Mariela to Karl two years earlier at Belmont Park. Her voluptuous figure, remote European manner and smoldering sexuality had attracted Karl instantly. She seemed untouchable, a challenge. During the entire afternoon she had hardly looked at him. He bet four races for her, and her winnings exceeded three thousand dollars. She never thanked him—simply said "I'm just lucky" as she folded the money neatly and deposited it in her alligator handbag. After an evening on the town he saw her home. She was about to bid him good night, but when he slipped a thousand dollars into her cleavage, she invited him in for a nightcap.

"Karl, I thought I heard a man's voice when I came in tonight," Mariela said, hoping to extract more details from him about the evening's activities. Karl said nothing. Just as she had fastened her bra and readjusted her dress, there was a knock at the door. The butler entered, laid the sable coat on a chair and left without a word. Karl poured himself a glass of champagne and sat staring at the priceless malachite coffee table laden with Fabergé objects. Slowly, stressing each word, as if explaining the most intricate of business transactions, he told Mariela in his deep and beautiful voice what he expected his pleasure to be that night, how he was going to go about getting it, and what role she was expected to play.

Karl walked to a wall safe behind the Goya and extracted some bills. "Everything is ready upstairs," he said. "Bring our friends to the third floor. Here's fifteen hundred dollars. Take care of them in advance. There's two thousand for you," he said, handing her the money. "That should keep you in nylons for at least a week," he added. "I'll be upstairs shortly."

Mariela went to the small bathroom at the back of the study, repaired her smeared lipstick, smoothed her hair and hurried down the stairs. She felt a pleasurable stiffness in her nipples, and the tingling warmth of anticipation undulated through her body. Arriving in the vestibule, she hesitated for a moment. Now her palms were damp. She felt flushed and was perspiring.

Instead of entering the parlor where the guests were waiting, she stepped into the room adjacent to it, to allow herself time to regain her composure. She touched a wall switch and a gentle light flooded the large oak-paneled dining room, where an extensive part of Karl's art collection was displayed: a Rembrandt, an enormous Gauguin, a Vlaminck and a Soutine portrait of Karl's mother, her wide shoulders draped with a luxurious dark fur. A Persian rug that had belonged to Napoleon spread almost wall to wall. Two crystal chandeliers from the ballroom of Catherine the Great's summer palace gleamed overhead in all their magnificence. The imposing dining table had at one time graced the palace of Cardinal Richelieu.

Mariela seated herself on one of the burgundy-damasked chairs, picked a tiger lily from the floral arrangement in the silver centerpiece and slipped it behind her ear. The butler entered the room so silently that she was startled when he said, "May I fetch you a drink, Miss Koenig?"

"No, thank you, William. Have the guests had something to eat?"

"Yes, Miss Koenig. Mr. Ravenstein ordered a cold buffet set out for them in the drawing room."

The faint sound of the distant doorbell interrupted them. "Will you excuse me please?" he said.

Mariela sat alone for a few more moments, recalling an evening in the spring of 1953. Karl had organized "a dinner party," as he liked to describe it, at which no fewer than ten young women, nude from the waist up, were seated around the antique table. They wore black garter belts and stockings, the highest possible heels and diamond necklaces. Karl had lent them for the occasion.

They were made to appear even more Fellini-esque by the small white-and-black masks they wore. Two menservants, dressed entirely in black leather, poured the champagne and served the poached salmon with such aplomb that Mariela wondered if they had ever waited dinner in normal attire. Some of the girls were uneasy. Mariela was not, for she was the only one present who had previously assisted at Karl's "special parties." The diamond necklace that encircled her neck belonged to her—a gift from Karl—and it gave her a feeling of superiority over the others. Besides, her breasts were the largest in the group, and the tight corset that Karl made all the girls wear caused her bosom to appear to be on the verge of bursting. That pleased Karl immensely. His fetish was known from coast to coast.

Mariela enjoyed Karl's special parties, more than even he suspected, and tonight's promised to be spectacularly erotic. Composed now, she opened the French doors, eager to meet the guests, and stepped into a drawing room filled with icons and massive furniture. Again she smelled the pungent muskiness of Rigaud candles and inhaled deeply.

"My God, I thought you'd never arrive," exclaimed a dark-haired beauty named Bonnie. "Have you just gotten here?"

"No," Mariela replied coolly. "I had some phone calls to make. I hope you weren't bored." She quickly surveyed the other guests, smiled charmingly and said, "My name is Mariela."

"Mine is John," announced a blond young man who remained seated on a suede sofa.

"I'm Susan," volunteered a pretty blonde with her hair piled high and her face layered with too much makeup, "and over there is Donna and . . ." She paused, then said falteringly, "I'm sorry, I didn't catch his name. What's your name, honey?"

The young man turned around and, fixing his cold gaze intently on Mariela, replied, "Just call me Andreas."

"Andreas what?" asked Mariela, holding his gaze.

"Poppidoppolous."

"Andreas Poppidoppolous," repeated Mariela. "Andreas Poppidoppolous. Your name is so difficult that I'm sure it must be hard to forget."

Andreas didn't answer. He just kept looking at Mariela. Mariela thought he seemed familiar. But she knew those male hustlers were all the same, finding their own make-believe heavens only in the admiring eyes of others.

She wasn't giving him that satisfaction. Mariela knew instinctively the evening would be even more pleasurable than she had fantasized.

Karl remained in his study for a while after Mariela had left to greet the guests. He caressed Mariela's fur coat and brushed his cheek against it, stroking it as a man strokes a woman's body, making her ready for love. Then he studied himself appreciatively in a large Regency mirror. Karl bore a strong resemblance to the actor George Sanders. He was over six feet tall, with a strong body, and his youthful, handsome face belied his forty-six years. He had arrogant hazel eyes, dark graying hair (which was dyed every two weeks), full lips and a slightly irregular nose. The scent of Monsieur from Lanvin permeated everything he wore.

He made a phone call to Canada, got no answer, then spoke briefly with someone in Florida. Finally, he lifted the intercom and said to William, "I won't be needing you anymore tonight. Wake me up tomorrow around ten o'clock. I want to sleep late. I have a two o'clock flight to Florida. Good night. Oh, William, don't put on the alarm. I'll see to that later."

"Good night, sir."

Karl picked up the fur coat again, turned off the study lights and went upstairs to his private quarters. An enormous canopied bed occupied an alcove. Photographs of himself with various celebrities, including one signed by Harry Truman, were placed on a small Regency table. Napoleonic memorabilia could be seen everywhere in the room. On the walls hung two Monets, a Fragonard and several Matisses. A Rodin stood on a pedestal in the corner. Against one wall there was an ebony and Japanese-lacquered table that had belonged to Marie Antoinette, on which stood a large bronze clock that once had indicated the hours to Madame du Barry.

The windows were made of stained glass and the streetlamps cast diffused shades of topaz, ocher and sienna onto the pale blue walls and ceiling. Karl pushed a button, which caused the drapery behind the sofa to part, revealing a large glass panel, which was actually a two-way mirror. It enabled him to watch, in complete privacy, the activities in the next room, which he fondly called "the playroom." He made a quick survey of the plates of salmon, caviar, cold roast beef and the variety of salads on a long buffet table, the several silver ice buckets containing bottles of Dom Perignon, and the large box of Havana cigars. He then entered the playroom, which was entirely mirrored, including the ceiling, and contained an extremely low wall-to-wall "bed" covered with a black satin spread. There were erotica everywhere—statuettes, objets d'art, drawings and paintings. Much of it had come from the collection of the late King Farouk, which Karl had purchased from his estate. This was the place where Karl "entertained" and gave full rein to his seemingly unlimited libidinous energy.

Karl faced three chairs before the one-way mirror and from a closet removed several whips, chains, cords, leather masks, studded dog collars and wrist bands, cock rings, nipple clamps and a variety of rubber appliances. From another cupboard he produced an ivory box and examined the contents to make certain there was enough of the precious white powder to last the evening. Taking a gold spoon from his pocket, he tested its quality. He also set out several bottles of amyl nitrite in delicately ornate silver sniffers. Hearing the guests approach, Karl left Mariela's coat on the back of an armchair, reached for a leather object and returned to his bedroom.

He took his clothes off and lay nude on his bed, propped up by several cushions to allow himself a comfortable and clear view of what was happening in the playroom. The three girls, the two boys and Mariela disappeared briefly into a dressing room.

When they returned, Bonnie, Susan and Donna were covered entirely in vinyl catsuits, except for two round openings that exposed their breasts. Their faces were hooded in the same fabric, with slits for their eyes, mouth and nose. They were also wearing very high heels. Their hands were cuffed in front of them.

Mariela ordered the girls to kneel down, and, taking the white powder from the ivory bowl with a delicate spoon that hung on a chain between her breasts, she forced each girl to snort deeply. She took out a tube of lipstick and painted their nipples, then her own, and commanded them to sit on the chairs that Karl had positioned.

Mariela was wearing a black garter belt, a tight waist cincher attached to a strapless push-up bra, fishnet stockings and high-heeled boots. Her black crotch was completely exposed. The diamond necklace adorned her neck. She slipped into the floor-length sable coat. Her costume was now complete.

Andreas and John were clothed in leather jumpsuits cut in such a way that their huge cocks and balls hung out, their enormous erections engorged and prolonged by the cock rings they wore. At Mariela's command they took a length of rope, tied the girls to the chairs and helped themselves to the cocaine. Then Mariela pushed a sniffer containing amyl nitrite to the girls' noses. She picked up a whip from the bed and flogged their exposed breasts with such force that each girl let out a piercing shriek, which merely served to incite Mariela further. She paused long enough to let John attach breast clamps to their nipples, and then she began licking the welts and droplets of blood on their bruised flesh. When Mariela finally stopped, beads of perspiration clung to her forehead, which glistened like freshly oiled marble. She bent down and put her own breasts into the girls' mouths, forcing them to suck her nipples while she fondled them gently. Then she untied Bonnie, laid her on the bed, undressed her hastily, kissed her on the mouth and motioned for the two boys to join them.

Karl was beside himself with excitement. He had moved to the sofa, and he pressed his forehead against the glass wall while he listened to every sound of pain or pleasure as it was amplified through the loudspeaker. The fur coat was on the bed and one of the robust young men lay on it, entering Mariela from the rear. She was spread-eagled on top of him while the other stud took her from the front. Bonnie was on her knees, pleasuring him with her mouth from behind.

Karl heard Mariela cry out, "Fuck me! Fuck me! Fuck me hard! Fuck me harder! You cheap hustler!"

Pinning her down by her wrists, John shouted back, "I'll fuck the sweet ass off you, you stupid bitch!" Both men rammed their cocks into her in synchronized rhythm, gasping for breath. Andreas began caressing her breasts frantically from the back, while Bonnie suddenly lowered herself over Mariela's face as both she and John reduced her to a frenzy of pleasure. The two men were panting. Both Mariela and Bonnie were moaning. The four of them exploded in violent orgasm.

Karl took another snort from his gold coke spoon and burst into the playroom with frenzied anticipation. He was wearing an exact replica of the military jacket Napoleon had worn when immortalized by painter Jacques Louis David. A leather hood was on his head. He approached the bed, mumbling incoherently. Mariela closed the zipper covering his mouth and attached handcuffs to his wrists. She then put a studded dog collar around his neck to which she connected a leash and began to kick him with her high-heeled boots, making him crawl around the floor like a dog for several minutes. Then she chained him to a hook on the wall and untied the two girls from their chairs. She gave each of them a cat-o'-nine-tails, which they used to lash his bare buttocks. Karl emitted a stifled cry when Mariela shoved a popper up his nostrils, which he sniffed greedily. His breath was coming in staccato gulps.

"Andreas, you be first!" she commanded. The young man who had been addressed rolled up his sleeve past the elbow and cupped his fist, which he greased profusely with vaseline. "You filthy dog, spread the cheeks of your ass," Mariela ordered Ravenstein. "Wider! Wider! Andreas, Napoleon is now ready!" The greased fist slowly descended, ready to ram in.

Hours later Mariela descended the circular stairs to the marbled vestibule. Her footsteps echoed eerily in the silent mansion, sending shudders of apprehension through her body. In a nearby room a clock began to chime. Stepping into the street, she glanced around furtively, casually dropped a white glove by the entrance, saw it fall and did not pick it up. Karl's limousine was waiting, with Bertrand, the chauffeur, asleep behind the wheel. She knocked on the window. Apologizing, he left the driver's seat to open the rear door.

She entered the car gracefully and lay back exhausted. Her legs felt weak and her body ached all over. "What time is it, Bertrand?" Mariela asked in the most officious tone she could muster.

"It's twelve-twenty, Miss Koenig," he replied.

Mariela toyed nervously with the one remaining glove, then carefully folded it into her purse. She looked out the window. The curbs were lined with snow-covered cars that reminded her of the igloos she had seen in geography books as a schoolgirl. And her memory took a dizzying ride on the roller coaster of time, stopping in Munich. The year: 1940. She was fifteen. . . .

—�֍—

The teacher said, "Fraulein Chelmsford, what are you reading?"

"My—my geography book, Frau Mueller."

"Your geography book! Would you stand up, please, Mariela Chelmsford, and repeat out loud what I was just telling the class?" Her voice was cold and flat. "Since you were following everything I said so intently in your geography book, it should be very easy."

"Well . . . I believe you said . . . I believe . . ."

"Yes . . . I'm listening. You believe what?" barked Frau Mueller.

"I believe . . . I believe . . ."

"I believe you are lying, Fraulein Chelmsford. Come to my desk immediately and bring me the piece of paper that fell from your lap when you stood up."

Mariela obeyed the order, giving her teacher the letter that had slipped to the floor.

"Let's see what kind of *geography* you were concentrating on," Frau Mueller said menacingly, unfolding the missive. "I will read it for your fellow students.

> My dearest of dearests,
>   Last night was the most beautiful night of my life. I have a pass next Saturday and will meet you on the corner of Maximilian Strasse and Wurzer at seven o'clock.
>   I cannot wait to hold you in my arms again. I kiss your mouth—your skin—your breast—your—"

Frau Mueller's face turned dark with anger and she tore the note into little pieces.

"Now, Fraulein Chelmsford, you will be confined to your dormitory every evening after supper, including weekends, for one month. Class dismissed! Heil Hitler!"

It was so vivid—the humiliation far more excruciating than the pain of the ruler hitting her fingers repeatedly until blood came. . . .

—�֍—

Mariela's mind snapped back to the present and once more she looked through the car window, trying to focus on the passing images outside. But she could not, she simply could not; it was as if for a brief moment her senses had abandoned her. Resting her head listlessly against the cushion and closing her eyes, she reflected upon the last few hours, which were no different from the last few years. She was not looking for an explanation of her behavior. If there was any, it was too deeply rooted in her past, which long ago had closed all possible access to its origins. But she knew this kind of life had to cease; it *had* to—soon! Mariela was so lost in her reveries that it was necessary for Bertrand to call out her name twice when the car arrived at its destination.

"Good evening, Miss Koenig," said Pete, the doorman at her Park Avenue building.

"Good evening, Pete. Do you by any chance have the time?"

"It's twelve-thirty, Miss Koenig."

"It's twelve-thirty already? Are you quite certain?"

"Yes, Miss Koenig. I only came on duty half an hour ago."

"Thank you, Pete, and good night." She attempted a smile.

The elevator stopped at the fourth floor. She took out her key, opened the apartment door, switched on the light without removing her coat, went straight to the telephone and dialed a number.

Mariela waited impatiently for the hotel operator to answer her call. "Mr. Jack Hamilton, please."

"Did you say Hamilton, with an *H?*"

"How else would you spell Hamilton?" Mariela snapped.

"There's no need to be fresh, miss. I'm only trying to assist you. . . . I don't see a Mr. Jack Hamilton registered. I'll give you the front desk." Mariela sighed resignedly.

"Front desk. May I help you?"

"I'm trying to reach Mr. Jack Hamilton. The operator tells me that he's not registered, but I know he has a reservation. Could you check it for me, please?" She paced the room as she spoke.

"Yes, ma'am." The clerk came back on the line. "He has arrived at this very moment. I'll put him on the line for you."

Her impatience and annoyance mounted at what seemed to be an interminable wait.

"Hello. This is Jack Hamilton." The voice was strong and somewhat British. "Who is this speaking, please?"

"It's me. I was afraid that this dreadful weather would prevent you from coming at all."

"It almost did. There was a long delay in Toronto. But all's well. I rang you from the airport but got no answer."

"I only just returned home, and I'm later than I thought I would be, but 'our friend' had quite a time for himself this evening."

"And you, my dear?" he asked. "Did you have quite a time for yourself this evening?"

"Not bad," she said laughing. "Not bad at all." She added, "He's sleeping like a newborn baby."

"Good. I'm just checking in, so let me ring you back once I'm settled in my suite."

"I'm dead, darling, and I've got to get my beauty sleep. Let's meet at the Savoy Plaza around four tomorrow afternoon. I just wanted to let you know that *all* went well."

"Good. I have some business to take care of tomorrow," Jack said, "and I don't know when I'll be finished, so let's play it by ear. I'll call you before noon."

Mariela put the phone down, took off her coat and hung it between the sapphire mink stole and the chinchilla cape in one of the closets of her enormous dressing room. She relaxed in a hot bath, then went to her luxurious all-pink bedroom, lay down and fell asleep waiting for a very special call.

※

MATTIE/*New York City/Saturday, January 30, 1954*

Mattie was alone. Mother, father, family, career, friends—it didn't matter. It had never mattered. Ultimately she was alone, and this was just another lonely time. She arrived by taxi at the Toronto airport, checked her three suitcases at American Airlines and made her way to the departure desk. She felt tired, lonely and anxious to return to New York.

Mattie had just finished a three-week engagement at the Royal York Hotel and was glad to be going home. She had an audition coming up on Monday to understudy the leading lady, Carol Haney, in *Pajama Game,* the smash Broadway hit.

The flight had been due to depart at 8:00 P.M., but bad weather had caused a three-hour delay. From past experience she had learned to telephone the airport before leaving a hotel, thus sparing herself the discomfort of hanging around crowded and anonymous waiting rooms. Mattie leaned against a wall in a special stance that made it appear she was actually holding it up.

Once again, as she had done many times, she thought of Tony Rook and their new romance. He was finishing up a six-week singing tour and would soon be with her. Surely with Tony by her side she would be less lonely. Or would she?

In her mind Mattie tried to reconstruct everything about Tony. She could recall his manner, his walk, his lovemaking, his clothes, the size and smell of his body, but his face was a void. Her mind was playing a trick and had completely blanked out his features, leaving her with an image resembling the cardboard prop used by amusement-park photographers which waits for a customer's head to fill in the hole. Perhaps their sporadic meetings were too far apart. She was desperately eager to see him on Wednesday, reassuring herself that the spark of rediscovery that comes after a long absence would once again work its magic.

For some reason the waiting lounge at an airport at night can seem the loneliest place of all. And right now Mattie's loneliness stung her. To pass the time she counted everything that could be counted around her: wrinkles, pimples, noises, cigarette butts, matches, gold teeth, well-cared-for fingernails, bitten nails, dirty nails. The sadness.

As she had done so many times in the same circumstances, Mattie scanned the crowd and stared into the faces of strangers. Her gaze paused at a woman sitting on a chair, wearing a ballerina-length cotton dress, a pair of Indian moccasins and a brown sweater. Her fingernails were polished silver. Her bare legs appeared to be webbed with varicose veins, but on closer examination Mattie was certain they were mosquito or flea bites. "How can insects survive in subzero weather?" Mattie wondered. The woman was carrying bundles filled with crumpled packages. She seemed worn out, and Mattie hadn't even looked at her face. When their eyes met, Mattie saw in hers the hopelessness of people who have spent too much of their lives saying goodbye to loved ones in depots and airports.

To the left of her sat a man in his early twenties, his stomach overlapping his belt. His shirt, face and hair all were red; only his trousers were gray. "A young boy in a middle-aged body," Mattie remarked to herself. Amid the despair and gloom the only refreshing contrast was the attendant behind the airline counter. He was tall and blond, with a chiseled jaw and golden skin that suggested a recent vacation at some white-sand, blue-water resort. Broad shoulders and thick, strong arms pulled at the buttons of his uniform. Mattie thought *he* was cute.

When Mattie finally boarded the plane, she sat in a window seat, planning to read the Toronto *Globe* for most of the trip. A photograph of the great film star Beverly Langdon, with her husband, Jeremy Rabb, the flamboyant producer who had for some time taken a protective interest in Tony, caught her attention. Jeremy had his arm around his beautiful young wife, who was flashing for the photographers the new fifty-carat diamond ring her husband had bestowed on her as a birthday present. Mattie had just started Walter Winchell's column when a stocky man of about thirty, his blond hair clipped in a crew cut, sat down beside her. She didn't look up, and hoped he hadn't recognized her. From the corner of her eye she watched him remove a bottle of cheap whiskey from a brown paper bag. "Care for a drink?" he asked. His breath reeked of alcohol.

"No, thank you," she said defensively, in the slightly rude tone some women acquire when they live alone. She considered telling him that she drank only wine but realized it would just encourage further conversation, so remained silent. Annoyed, she shifted the newspaper and turned a page, pretending to be engrossed in reading it. The man uncapped the bottle, took three long swigs and quickly placed it beneath his seat. Mattie noticed that his pants were too wide and too long. He abruptly launched into a dizzying monologue about being stranded by the blizzard at the airport for five hours without food and how his wife and kids would be worried. It was idle talk from a frustrated man. Mattie cursed her luck at being seated next to a half-drunk man obviously intent on relieving his own loneliness.

She concentrated again on the newspaper. Olivia de Havilland was having a feud with Robert Mitchum. . . . Helen Hayes was rehearsing *The Wisteria Trees*, which was to open the following Wednesday at the City Center, in New York. She loved the way Winchell made up words: writing of Allison Hayes he referred to "pufflicity." Clever. Clever. . . . Weather in New York was the coldest in twenty years. . . . General MacArthur, speaking on his seventy-fifth birthday, had called on Americans to return to the morality of patriotism. . . . The man beside her chatted mindlessly on, and her annoyance increased.

Some fifteen minutes into the flight Mattie asked the stewardess for a glass of Chianti.

"I'm sorry, miss," was the reply. "We don't serve wine aboard, but you can have any mixed drink you want." Then, with a smile, she added, "Free."

"Oh well, thanks, but no thanks. I never touch hard liquor." Out of the corner of her eye she noticed, as her seat companion took another swig from his flask, that his fingers were stained with Mercurochrome. She theorized unkindly that he must have cut them peeling potatoes. His watch caught her attention. It was large, gaudy, ugly, and, she thought cynically, probably accurate. For some unknown reason she tried to imagine him having sex. It was unthinkable, grotesque. Masturbation, perhaps. Sex with a partner, no. Masturbation. That's it, she told herself. She suppressed a smile as she visualized the hulk of a man jerking off in the bathroom while his wife feigned sleep in the bedroom. The man screwed his face up in an absurd smile and continued his chatter.

"Do you want to hear about it or am I keeping you awake?" Mattie had yawned. Without a word she rose to go to the lavatory. The man scrambled to his feet, in the process spilling part of his bottle, which he was nursing again.

The inevitable question came on her return. "Aren't you Mattie Maxwell, the singer?"

"Yes, I am."

"I knew you looked familiar," he said, slapping her on the knee. "I saw you on a talk show on TV a couple of days ago. Weren't you singing at the Royal York?"

"Yes, I was there three weeks and—"

"I've never heard you sing, but everybody says you sound just like your mother." Mattie's discomfort grew. She turned her back to him and looked toward the window, staring at her own blurred reflection.

"I was a great fan of your mother's. I really loved her—like everybody, I guess. I have all her records. I've seen all her movies at least once, even twice." His voice was getting louder. "I'll never forget the night she sang at Carnegie Hall. I lived in Houston then, and I made a special trip to New York just to see and hear her. Gee, was it worth it! She really made show business history that night!"

It was a familiar and often repeated litany. "I know," Mattie said tersely, turning sharply around. "I was there."

"Tell me about her. She really was my idol."

Mattie tensed visibly. "Please try to understand." She paused, and when she spoke again her voice was cold and impersonal. "I don't feel like discussing my mother. I really don't feel like discussing anything."

The man looked at her in astonished silence. He had finally succeeded in embarrassing himself, and Mattie hoped it would quiet him for the rest of the trip.

Why can't dull men be mute? she thought. How long will I be fair game for every witless clod in sight? I seem to be going through life with a sign in front and back which reads "alone." She sighed. She asked for a glass of water, and held it like a child cradling a cup of milk, letting her newspaper slip to the floor.

The man resumed his boring stories in a voice barely audible, but Mattie no longer heard him. For a fleeting instant she reproached herself for being harsh and insensitive to a perfectly harmless human being. She tried to think of the many ways people had described her: gamine, kook, ugly, unique, sloppy, oversexed, undependable, trendy, selfish, a put-on, generous, a carbon copy of her mother, ambitious and opportunistic.

Mattie Maxwell would soon turn nineteen. Tall, awkward, not beautiful, but striking, she had features that were singularly expressive. She also had what the French call *du chien*. Her mouth was large, her eyes enormous, and her nose too pronounced. She had planned to have that fixed as soon as she could afford it. Long, shiny auburn hair brushed her shoulders. Mattie's impulsive marriage at eighteen to singer Eddie Baker had been dissolved two months after the wedding when she realized that Frank, who was Eddie's accompanist, and whom he had introduced as his brother, was no blood relative at all but his lover.

Her mother was the late Jessica Miller, who had made a great name for herself as a singer and the star of innumerable Westerns. Her father was the famous architect John Maxwell, more famous as a stud than for any of his highly publicized architectural projects. Between her mother and father there were nine marriages and seven children scattered among the various parents. Jessica had died two years earlier from "an accidental overdose" of barbiturates while on a European concert tour. The whole of show business and her legion of fans were shocked, though not surprised. There had been so many previous "accidents" that it was only a matter of time before another one would occur.

When Mattie's mother died, her father's fourth wife was America's sweetheart, Polly Collins. John declined to attend Jessica's funeral because he was honeymooning in Hawaii, but he *did* send flowers. Mattie had made all the arrangements. She had never been close to her mother; Jessica had been too preoccupied with her erratic career, her erratic love life and her precarious health. It was obvious to everyone, including Mattie, that she had never enjoyed motherhood, but it was nonetheless Mattie's intention to pay off the staggering debts that Jessica had left on her death. She understood her mother's desperation, but only after she had died—her inner struggle, her inability to age gracefully. She hoped that this would not happen to her.

The plane was now approaching New York, but had to hold over La

Guardia fully twenty minutes because of the bad weather. As she waited for a taxi, shivering in the freezing weather, she watched a distinguished, well-dressed man get into a limousine and wished she were in his place. But it's coming now, she thought. It won't be long before it's all mine.

"Is this your luggage, Mr. Hamilton?" she heard the chauffeur ask. The distinguished man spoke with an English accent, and she couldn't help noticing the striking resemblance he bore to Lord Bracket, the English peer who had been involved in a homosexual scandal in London with young boys and had gone to prison for it. Mattie had met him once back-stage when her mother was appearing at the Palladium. She liked him, and felt sorry for him, and especially for Elspeth, the girl to whom he was engaged and who waited for him and married him when he came out of jail. Mattie took her turn in the line, which seemed interminable, finally entered a taxi and rode into Manhattan.

It was nearly 1:00 A.M. when she put the key into the lock of the front door. Her apartment was on the third floor of a small converted brown-stone on East Fifty-fifth Street, between First and Second avenues. She liked the location. It was near the Cue Club, on Fifty-eighth Street, where she usually ended up late at night, and not far from her beloved East River. Besides, it was cheap, convenient, and anonymous. As usual, the small elevator was out of order. She had to make two trips to carry her luggage upstairs. "Why do they always have so many steps to climb in places that are inexpensive?" mumbled Mattie.

She switched on the light as she entered the cluttered living room. Mattie always enjoyed coming back to her pad, as she called it; it had a lived-in quality about it. An upright piano stood near the window. The floor was littered with sheet music. Ashtrays were filled with cigarette butts. A wood and stainless-steel coffee table, with a vase holding dead flowers, stood near the leatherette armchair. Next to it a bronze candelab-rum—two hundred and fifty dollars' worth of pretension. Rehearsal clothes were strewn on the couch.

Mattie was a collector of hats—hats from the 1920s, hats from the 1930s, straw hats, broad-brimmed hats, derbies and boaters. They all hung from the walls on hooks, like trophies from a county fair. Next to the display she had tacked an unframed print of Andrew Wyeth's "Christina's World."

Dirty coffee cups, stained glasses and plates were piled everywhere. The carcass of a chicken that had been devoured before Mattie's departure for Toronto reposed on the dining table. The bones were so dry that she was reminded of a relic of some extinct species she had seen at the Museum of Natural History. A defunct Christmas tree, with branches bent low under the weight of the glittering ornaments, stood in a corner. Mattie was in the habit of leaving the tree up until after her birthday, which fell on February 17. Among the books shoved sideways and upside down on her shelves were *Uncle Tom's Cabin, The Prophet,* several Mickey Spillane paperbacks, *Spartacus, Crime and Punishment,* the *Kama Sutra, The Pic-*

ture of Dorian Gray, a volume on the French Revolution, another on czarist Russia, another on Shirley Temple, *Look Homeward, Angel, Las Vegas Today, Of Time and the River,* Lee Mortimer's *Show Business Confidential* and dozens more. Gift-wrapping paper and colored ribbons were tangled on the floor with leotards and tap shoes.

She carefully removed her boots, to avoid soiling the rug, and stepped gingerly over each hurdle toward the bedroom in her stocking feet. The sight of this room made her gasp and turn around momentarily. She muttered out loud, "What a mess. This apartment could make the cover of 'House & Garbage' magazine!"

The bed hadn't been made. Clothes were scattered across the furniture and flowed onto the floor. A pile of shoes, looking like strange animals, lay sprawled in every direction near the radiator, as if ready for a Salvation Army fire sale.

Red candles were everywhere, standing erect like angry phalluses. A lacy bedspread had been draped over one of the windows on her last day in town to make the room "darker and sexier." Towels hung loosely from a pink velvet-upholstered chair. The apartment looked like a cross between an airport lounge, a rehearsal hall, and a tart's boudoir ransacked by burglars who obviously hadn't found what they were looking for.

She called her answering service, scribbling down her messages on a pad stained with coffee. One was from her agent, Harry Ross, who wanted her to do a club date the following Friday at Levinsberg's Hotel, in the Catskills; another from Sylvia Rubins, her theatrical agent, reminding her that *The Pajama Game* audition was for Monday at the Majestic Theatre; a third was from Danny Gordon, her press agent, who had lined up some publicity stunt for her. Mattie went to the kitchen and opened the refrigerator, which was devoid of food except for a half-empty bottle of white wine.

Having filled a tall glass (the only clean one she could find was in the bathroom) with the remains of the wine, she popped three Nembutals into her mouth and gulped them down. Then she returned to the bedroom, took off her clothes, dropped them on the floor and pushed everything from the bed into a heap on top of the clothing. Mattie lay down, exhausted, wondering what time it was. A little electric clock indicated 2:00 A.M., but in Mattie's world it was always 2:00 A.M.

She dreaded the following day. Sundays were the hardest for her to bear. People tend to travel in pairs on Sunday, trailing laughter behind them as they passed. She knew tomorrow would be cold, and she wished for a strong arm to cling to, if only to keep warm. Mattie had difficulty pretending that all was well on Sunday, because when you walk alone on a Sunday afternoon, all is not well. She had seen it written on searching faces and in her own hurried footsteps going nowhere. How she hated Sunday, with its slow music on the radio, antiseptic television shows and the pretense of cleaning up old papers and files, paying bills and taking a long bath, preparing for some event that wouldn't take place. Sundays were especially unbearable if her body had not been made love to the night before. She missed that most of all. She also missed the lovemaking on Sunday morning, with coffee-tasting kisses.

She recalled one Sunday in particular, attending a party on the upper West Side, just before going to Toronto. A young man was standing next to her, with beautiful brown hair and fawnlike eyes that had a haunting, hungry look. She was instantly attracted to this man because he resembled Tony. But his hands were different. Smaller. His body was slighter, and, she found out later, his feet were not aristocratic, his second toe extending beyond the big one. His smile was cruel and a bit forced. He wanted to please her. She slept with him that night, not really wanting to, just to see what it was like. After all, it *was* Sunday, and on Sunday one is not supposed to be alone.

Mattie looked at her clock. Its hands, which seemed to be dragging themselves around the face, indicated 3:00 A.M.

She curled herself into a neat ball and, wishing for Wednesday, when Tony would be in her arms again, fell asleep.

—⁂—

DENISE/*New York City*/*Saturday, January 30, 1954*

"Did you know that Saturday night is 'Jew Night' at El Morocco?" said Sinclair MacAlpine, chuckling, to his obviously well-heeled companions. "Society avoids it!" he informed the woman on his right arm, Frances Vanderbilt, as they entered the New York supper club. Sinclair had spoken sotto voce, or so he thought, but his Texas twang was audible ten feet away. Then he laughed genially while helping his wife, Carolyn, take off her expensive coat.

"*We* are society. What do I care who else is around! When I come here, or anywhere for that matter, I consider it to be 'Escobar Ortiz Night,'" replied Escobar Ortiz, nudging his friend Tyrone Power.

At the center of this group, with all the men clustered around her, was a young woman of rare and classical beauty, draped in a floor-length white mink coat, which she wore with such nonchalance that it could just as well have been a bathrobe. She let the coat drop from her shoulders with the assured aplomb of one who knows from past experience that someone will be there to catch it before it falls to the floor. Photographers followed Tyrone Power wherever he went, and tonight was no exception. Cameras were clicking, and the young woman behaved as if they didn't exist. She was posing all the time. Posing as if from afar. Unconcerned. Unseeing. Aloof. Impatience quivered under her flawless skin. She regretted compromising. It only postponed the inevitable. But Escobar wanted to show her off to New York. All right, New York, here I am, she thought grudgingly. But look fast.

New York officially became aware of Denise Cunningham as she made a grand entrance into the glamorous main room of El Morocco. For months gossip columnists throughout the world had spoken of the fortune Escobar Ortiz, forty years her senior, had showered on this virtually unknown girl, scarcely twenty-one.

Without a doubt, Escobar Ortiz was the largest shipowner in the world, his wealth astronomical. But even more important, Escobar had become the most influential man in Argentina under the Perón regime.

Denise's blond hair was styled in a demure pageboy. Her Christian Dior white silk suit was set off by a single strand of pearls. Her short, well-manicured nails were polished in a natural tone, and the absence of makeup enhanced her large azure-blue eyes. Hers was the look of total simplicity that only the very wealthy can afford and then have the audacity to discard: she wore a diamond of dazzling magnitude on the ring finger of her left hand. All attention was focused on her. She seemed absolutely sure of herself and looked neither to the right nor to the left. She was compellingly feminine. Men and women alike were drawn to Denise, by her elusiveness, astounding beauty, and the caliber of the men surrounding her.

She glided through the room with a bearing that said it all: Here is a woman who can never stumble; here is a woman who will never fall.

Heads were turning. Voices were whispering. "She's an heiress from South Carolina—" "The old man behind her is her godfather—" "I've heard that she has inherited millions—" "Her *father* was a train conductor—" Some of their words found her ears. The rest she could imagine. Let them guess, she thought. Let them envy me. It's of no importance what they think! She was used to it. The best is yet to come.

Even though the place was crowded to capacity, Carino, the maître d', ushered the illustrious group to the very best table in the room famous for its zebra-striped banquettes. Every eye was riveted on them. When Denise laughed, the men laughed with her, obviously enthralled by her beauty. She kept her head bent down, fidgeted with her napkin, opened and closed the menu, opened it once more, pretended to read it but couldn't concentrate, then finally decided not to eat after all. She picked up her champagne glass and sipped slowly, her smile frozen as if by a shot of Novocain. Escobar Ortiz whispered in her ear. An intimate gesture. Denise didn't hear him and only pursed her lips. Her mind was a million light years away. Her eyes saw all and took in nothing.

John Perona, the club's suave, handsome owner, rose from the table where he was sitting with his cronies, straightened his bow tie, flicked a bit of invisible lint from the sleeve of his impeccable tuxedo, and walked toward the impressive party to greet them personally. "What a great honor to have you with us!" John Perona was addressing himself to Escobar Ortiz. "Who could tell that tonight would be like this!" he said incredulously, still fussing with his bow tie. "Seems like New Year's Eve! And with a near blizzard yet! You know what Saturday night usually brings. . . ." He winked. "Nothing but Seventh Avenue types. But just take a look at who's here tonight!" Perona always spoke pompously, as if each word started with a capital letter. With his hand partly tucked in his jacket pocket, he turned to the left and said, "There's the Duke and Duchess of Windsor sitting with Elsa—"

"My dear John," interrupted Escobar, "I think you know most of my friends, but allow me to introduce you to my niece, the most beautiful girl in the world, Denise Cunningham. Denise, this is John Perona. He is personally responsible for making El Morocco the most famous nightclub in America."

"How do you do, Miss Cunningham." John leaned forward to clasp her hand. Not until he touched it did she respond to his presence. His hand felt warm, hers was cold. She looked up with a start.

"How do you do, Mr.—?"

"Perona!" Escobar repeated, his brows arched.

"Mr. Perona. I'm pleased to meet you," Denise said in a soft southern voice. John noticed that she was trembling slightly. "Won't you please join us?" she added graciously.

"I can think of nothing that would give me greater pleasure," John replied, thinking to himself that for all her charm, she seemed uncomfortable. Seating himself next to her on the banquette, he asked, "Is this your first visit to our club, Miss Cunningham?"

"Please call me Denise. Yes, it is. I was in New York briefly three years ago with—with my mother, but I'm afraid to say that El Morocco wasn't on her agenda!" She didn't flinch.

"Where have you been hiding all this time? New York really needs someone like you." John's flattery was sincere. "With your beauty . . . you should be in show business—"

"Show business is not for this young lady," Escobar interjected. "She's been very busy with her art studies at the Sorbonne, and decorating her new apartment in Paris."

"I also have a home on the Riviera," said Denise. "I spend a lot of my free time there."

"Yes, the Château d'Antibes. That was my twenty-first birthday present to my niece," added Escobar, taking her hand. "But we're planning to spend much more time in New York, aren't we, darling?" He kissed Denise's fingertips. "Aren't we?"

She turned her head away without responding, and for a few seconds all three were framed, motionless, as though the reel of a movie projector had suddenly jammed.

John cleared his throat, hoping the awkward moment would clear with it. If Ortiz wants to pretend this young girl is his niece, he thought, what a strange way to go about it! Well, that's none of my business. At a loss for something to say, he repeated his compliment. "With your beauty, Denise, I still think you should be in show business. Haven't you ever given it a thought?"

"Never—my family would have killed me! I come from the South! Very old-fashioned folks!" She said this so fiercely and defensively that John looked up in surprise and started to speak, trying to lighten the mood. "Over there is Hope Bendel . . ."

Denise was no longer hearing. Hope Bendel . . . John Perona . . . Escobar . . . El Morocco—everything faded from her view until only her "old-fashioned folks from the South" remained. She could see them clearly now in stark relief against the black surrealism of memory.

—❋—

The South! Jellico, on the border of east Tennessee and Kentucky, where she was born, may be the Appalachian Mountains but it is *still the South!* Not the South of her make-believe, perhaps, but "South Carolina" certainly sounds better! She thought of her father. He had not been the plantation owner of her fantasy and her publicity releases, just a coal miner, grubby and illiterate. She remembered him as an old man at thirty, defeated by life, getting up before dawn, already fully clothed, washing his face and hands in the kitchen sink, going off to work day after day. No amount of washing could remove the soot that was ingrained in the pores of his skin and coated his dark lashes. It seemed as if the transparent blue eyes were always peering at her from the bottom of a mine shaft. He died of black-lung disease when she was only eleven, and she came to think of him as a failure with dirty fingernails somewhere up in heaven, who had forgotten her.

How well she recalled the day she, her twin brother, Jonathan, and their mother were evicted from their sharecropper's shack. That day Denise was planting flowers. "Delta Mae Cunningham," the stranger said to her mother in a voice parched and ugly, "you've got a week to pay up or move." There were more words. Her mother answered something, something soft, filled with pain. The stranger was gone. Denise felt very tiny, very scared, and stopped planting the seeds.

"Don't bother makin' no holes, Deeny," said her mother. "No flowers ain't never gonna grow in these here parts. No flowers!" The tears were streaming down her gaunt cheeks.

"But, Mama, why does that man want us to go away? Didn't you say Daddy's in heaven, lookin' after us?"

"I dunno, chile. I jist dunno. Maybe he was aplayin' cards today and plum fergot."

They moved to Prairie, near Terre Haute, Indiana, where relatives took them in, more out of a sense of obligation than pity.

—❋—

". . . who's known as the perennial Duchess of Fifth Avenue. . . . Denise . . . Denise . . . ?"

"Duchess of—? Oh, John, forgive me. I'm afraid I wasn't listening. I have a beastly headache—but please, go on."

Perona grinned, gesturing. "As I was saying, that woman there is Hope Bendel. She's known as the perennial Duchess of Fifth Avenue." The elderly lady in question was on the small, cramped dance floor, holding onto what appeared to be a maharaja and struggling under the weight of her jewels. Denise had to laugh when John explained that "the maharaja" was, in fact, a salesman in an Indian fabric shop. Then, assuming a confidential tone and lowering his voice, John pointed to a brassy blonde on the other side of the room. "There's the girl who made headlines not long ago by sitting provocatively on the peacock throne of the Shah of Persia."

And look where she's sitting now! thought Denise. Under a big artificial palm tree. That's what I call a comedown!

". . . And over there . . . and on your right . . . and . . ."

Denise glanced vaguely as John pointed. Her imperturbable eyes opened wide. It was no use. Again she was distracted by images forged in the yesterdays of her life. Without a word she stood and walked across the floor and majestically ascended the stairs to the ladies' lounge, her thin smile evoking the sweet-sour joys of summer lemonade.

She entered the richly appointed powder room and sat at the vanity table, looked in the mirror and smiled. Nothing could alter the beautiful, unblemished face. Nothing could alter the course of her future. Nothing. After all, Denise thought, she had always been able to get what she wanted, and this time would not be any different! Her trance was interrupted by a familiar voice radiating trashy cheer. It was like opening a can or a refrigerator door and releasing a foul odor.

"Well, Jesus H. Christ and call me Magnolia Blossom, as I live and breathe, if it isn't Miz Melanie Wilkes-honey! *In person!*" the voice spoke in an exaggerated southern accent.

Denise turned around and raised her impossible blue eyes, recognizing Lori, whom she hadn't seen since 1951, when they had worked together as show girls at the Chez Paree in Chicago. "Hello, Lori," Denise said calmly, with undisguised indifference.

"The food in this joint sure beats 'chipmunk surprise' and 'marinated possum,' " Lori continued with sarcasm. "Or do you miss the good ole days, honey?" She took a long drag on her mentholated cigarette, sticking out from the end of a gaudy holder.

Denise turned her back, picked up a comb and didn't reply. Her tenuous composure melted into pure liquid rage—fiery, fierce, like molten lava. An impotent rage.

Lori sat down next to Denise, legs straddling a stool, puffing a long, billowing stream of smoke at her garish reflection in the mirror. "Well, hush mah mouth, I must admit the company you're keeping now sure beats that jerk from Terre Haute you used to date," she said, winking at her significantly.

Denise put down the comb. "Well, that jerk from Terre Haute, as you put it, was a book salesman who took me *out* of Terre Haute and *away* from waiting on tables and gave me a job in Chicago." Denise felt a lump in her throat and bit her lip. She wanted to explode.

"You sure got a better job now," taunted Lori. "What kind of books do *they* sell?" She flicked her ash onto the glass counter, breaking up into peals of vulgar laughter.

"Okay, that's enough!" Denise spoke quietly, belying the fury she felt inside. "We're not alone here!"

Lori went on as though there had been no interruption. "I'm sure your parents didn't arrange a li'l ole comin'-out party down on the li'l ole plantation, then introduce you all proper-like to this ole moneybags you're with," she sneered, dropping her cigarette butt and grinding it into the carpeted floor with her high heel.

"You could at least use an ashtray," admonished Denise.

"Fuck it," countered Lori. "I've never won the Good Housekeeping Award for gracious living! Oh, come off it, Duchess, let's face it. If it wasn't for me introducing you to that hundred-dollar South American jeweler in Chicago—what was his name? Reinaldo? Reinaldo . . . oh hell, I can't remember his name—anyway, if it wasn't for me introducing you to him, you would never have gotten to Argentina, and instead of wearing that huge rock on your finger, you'd still be wearing rhinestone-beaded G-strings. *And* you wouldn't know that there's more to life than a shithouse and a square meal!" Lori kicked her satin pump into the carpet for emphasis, and winced. "Oh fuck, my foot hurts! You know, you're lucky I'm not demanding a ten percent commission, fiddledeedee," mocked Lori in a bitter, mean tone as she sprayed herself frenetically with perfume. "Oh, *now* I remember the name of that South American john. *Reinaldo Vega!* See. I got a good memory." Lori mouthed the name as if it were a curse aimed directly at Denise. "Obviously he was good for the money. Was he good at you-know-what?" She leered, rolling her eyes in an obscene parody.

All this ugly chatter was carving another indelible wrinkle in Denise's soul.

"Hey! I'll bet you're wondering what I'm doing here."

There was no reply.

Lori answered herself. "Yeah! I'll tell you what I'm doing here, Miz

Shoofly Pie. I met up with this rich Chink about a year after you flew the coop. He has all kinds of money. Well, not the kind you got hooked up with, but then, I never had your ambition. But who needs it, I got all the money I'll ever want, and I get to come to classy places like this and rub shoulders with broads—excuse me, dames—like you, so—"

Denise didn't hear the end of her sentence. She rose wordlessly, feeling the warmth of her blush. Once more she faced the mirror, and saw there a reconfirmation of her incredible beauty. Only now the image was a few years younger, hungrier, flaunting the overwhelming appeal of her over-exposed flesh.

❈

She was back at the Chez Paree. The scanty spangles of her costume. The brassy chorines filing onto the stage as she hung back, mortified. Lori was last to leave the dressing room. "Think about it, Little Miss Virgin. That South American john is good for a hundred big ones just for a few grunts. He's in the lounge. When you see Reinaldo, tell him I sent you!"

The words assaulted then as they assaulted now. Lori was such a bitch! How dare she! That two-bit whore! A hundred bucks! Why, that's just about enough tip for the ladies' room attendant. . . . I'll make some-thing of myself. I'll show them all. A hundred bucks—I won't be cheap! Never! Never again! Her hand was a frustrated, blue-fingered fist. "I—will —be—very expensive!" There was more to be gotten out of life. Soon. Now.

❈

The memory flashed through her mind and was spent within seconds. Tak-ing a long last look, she saw the reflection of herself flaming with indigna-tion, and left the powder room with concentrated fury, stopping only long enough to leave a hundred-dollar bill for the attendant. "Here's a dollar from the girl in the toilet and ninety-nine from me," Denise said as she walked out. She heard Lori's loud curses from behind the closed door.

Denise's emotions clogged into a dark-brown ball of hatred in the pit of her stomach. She flung herself against the corridor wall. Paralyzed with anger and out of breath, she sought to regain her bearings. "I'm not going to waste my time thinking about that tacky girl—I just won't," Denise mut-tered, half aloud. "As far as I'm concerned, she never existed. I have no past to catch up with me, because my past is what I say it is. Period." This last humiliation suffused Denise like a shot of adrenalin and triggered a reaction that now made her look forward to the inevitable, which would occur tonight. It had to be tonight!

With a casualness that could be achieved only by a severe effort, Denise descended the blue-carpeted stairs of El Morocco. As she walked toward them the men at the table rose as one body for her, and she took her seat beside John Perona.

Almost immediately Denise reached nervously for her compact, opened it and glanced at herself without really trying to see anything. Escobar looked at Denise. He sensed a turmoil, a confrontation that could no longer be avoided.

"I'm sorry I left so abruptly," Denise said apologetically to John.

"Denicita, would you care to dance?" asked Escobar.

"No, thank you, Escobar. Not now. I'm a bit tired."

"Well, I'd better go back to my table," said John, getting up. "I'll see you all again before you leave."

"John, before you go," said Escobar, "let me explain to my niece what an unusual table it is. You see, Denicita, that's the famous 'round table.' Have you ever heard of it?" Without waiting for her answer he went on, pointing discreetly toward the back of the room. "That's Johnny Meyers. He's Howard Hughes's right-hand man. That's Macocco, the famous Argentinian playboy. The man in the middle's Pepe de Albrew, the local eccentric. Can you see that thing on his lapel? It's a live mouse! And that is—" Everyone laughed. Denise merely stared stonily.

Who cares about that table and all these idiots, she thought. Sinclair MacAlpine leaned forward and whispered to Denise.

"Well, I really must leave you now," said John. "I hope everything has been satisfactory."

"Perfect, my dear John, absolutely perfect," answered Escobar. When he turned back, Denise was on her way to the dance floor with Sinclair MacAlpine. Escobar's jealousy increased as he watched her float in MacAlpine's arms, twirling to the rhythm of Chauncey Grey's orchestra playing "Change Partners." He shot an uneasy glance all around him, slapped the table in exasperation, and tried to join the conversation to his left.

Escobar had reason to be jealous. It was on such a night, to the same tune, that he had waltzed Denise away from Reinaldo Vega and into his life.

While Escobar drummed his jeweled fingers nervously against his glass, Denise danced gaily to the lilting music of her unofficial theme song. "Won't you change partners and . . ."

Another recollection, but this time triumphant. It brought Denise back to the smoky lounge of the Chez Paree in Chicago.

—✺—

She waved to Sean O'Malley, the attractive young man at the keyboard, who never failed to delight her with that song. Her favorite. She arrived at the table. A well-dressed man with unruly light-brown hair, much younger than she had anticipated (somewhere in his early thirties) rose and kissed the fingers of her hand.

"I'm Reinaldo Vega," he said with an air of comfort. "And you are Denise?" They spoke. Trite nothings. "Your speech, Denise. It is so gentle. Where were you born?"

There was no hesitation. "Charleston, South Carolina."

"One of those southern belles?"

"Not *one* of those. Definitely not *one* of those!" She smiled. Blue eyes, soft. "The *only* one!"

"I must tell you, querida Denise, that you—how shall I say it?—you do not seem to fit into this ambience of show business."

"Oh, I'm just dabbling. I'm an only child. When my father passed away, my mother remarried a real estate entrepreneur." This last was a word she had just read in John O'Hara's *A Rage to Live*. "They moved to California. I find the worst thing one can do is remain idle, and since I'm going to school in Chicago . . ."

The champagne cork popped. "To you, Reinaldo," she murmured. Her eyes were steady, unblinking, brimming with something too enormous to be contained.

" '. . . won't you change partners and dance with me?' " Sean crooned the words at the very moment Denise had decided to swap the book salesman for Reinaldo Vega. The book salesman who took her virginity in exchange for a secondhand set of encyclopedias.

For Reinaldo it was love at first sight, and for her, the virgin gambler's first big win. Denise made him wait. After a week of ardent courtship she gave herself to him with a heady (if insincere) passion few of his past lovers had displayed. Then the offer came. Denise accepted Reinaldo's invitation to accompany him to Buenos Aires by way of New York. She was well aware that blondes were much in demand south of the border. It was a beginning, and besides, Reinaldo was one of the jewelers who served Eva Perón.

—❋—

Her reverie ended as Lori loomed into view, nodding and muttering conspiratorially to her escort and dancing aggressively in the direction of Denise and Sinclair, trying to edge herself up next to them.

Returning to their table on Sinclair MacAlpine's arm, Denise remained standing and put her hand on the back of Escobar's chair. In a whisper meant to be heard by everyone she murmured? "I'm so tired, Escobar dear. It's been such an exhausting day. I'll just go home, and you can stay with your friends. I'll send the car right back for you."

"Of course not, Denise," insisted Escobar. "I'm very tired as well. We'll leave together." They said their goodbyes to the entourage.

On the way out they passed Stanley Finkelstein, a wool manufacturer and man-about-town, who was hosting a large, jubilant party in honor of Milton Berle and obviously enjoying his first outing at El Morocco.

Escobar shook hands with several acquaintances. John Perona was waiting for them at the door. They exchanged a few pleasantries. Inclining confidentially toward John, Denise said, "Do you see that woman on the dance floor? The one who's making such an exhibition of herself? I hate to be the one to tell you, but . . . John, how can a woman like that get in here? I caught her going through my purse in the powder room when she thought I wasn't looking!"

Perona's mouth dropped. "She—? Denise, why didn't you say something sooner?"

"John, how could I?" Her honey tones oozed. "How could I disrupt such a perfect evening?"

"Oh, thank you for telling me, Denise. We will have her ushered out at once." Immediately he signaled his maitre d' and instructed him firmly in Italian. He then turned back to Denise and Escobar. "That woman will never be admitted to El Morocco again. This I promise you."

"Thank you, John. I thought you would want to know."

Denise and Escobar moved toward the checkroom. Escobar braced himself for the bitter and biting wind, buttoned his sable-lined cashmere overcoat, and helped Denise with her fur coat. They walked into the night and entered their limousine, assisted by a doorman resplendent in a costumy Foreign Legion uniform.

They rode back to their Fifth Avenue hotel. No conversation. Only strained silence. Escobar was the first to speak. "What is going on in your head, Denise? Is there something wrong?"

"Nothing—why?" The lie made no sense. Sooner or later she must confront him. She had wanted to tell him before the theater. Before dinner. After dinner. But there had been no privacy. Now there were only the two of them. Should she tell him tonight? Why wait? What could he do? It didn't matter.

The elevator stopped at the twenty-fifth floor. Ordinarily at such a late hour Escobar would have accompanied Denise to her suite and gone back to his at once, especially since they had both arrived from Paris that morning. Tonight he didn't. Instead he followed her into the vast apartment, which was filled with white flowers. The champagne was open. They were alone together for the first time since arriving in New York. Denise filled two glasses, gave one to Escobar, and walked to the window with him. They both stared out on a sparkling Central Park, which resembled a giant pinball machine left out in the snow.

Denise spoke. "I hate to say what I have to tell you."

"If you hate to say it, why tell me?"

"I think," she said, her back to him, "I think we've come to the end of our journey." Denise took a long swallow of her champagne and moved swiftly to an armchair. Strange. She didn't feel anything. No regrets. No pity. She couldn't feel pity for a grown man. For a kitten, yes. But not for a grown man. A kind of anger? Yes, perhaps, at having to hurt him. She didn't want that, yet there was no other way.

"When did you arrive at this conclusion?"

"Today."

Escobar seemed unable to comprehend. His face sagged. "What made today different from yesterday?"

"Today I knew for certain," she said primly.

"You knew what for certain?"

"That I'm going to be married," she replied almost merrily.

The blood rushed to Escobar's face, darkening the color of the veins in his neck. "May I know the name of the fortunate bridegroom?"

"Prince Francesco Borgia." She wished she could apologize, but for what?

"Why Francesco Borgia?"

"Would it matter whether it was Francesco or someone else?"

"Why didn't you tell me earlier?"

"I didn't know earlier."

"When are you thinking of leaving . . . me?"

"In a couple of days," replied Denise without feeling.

"Don't you think you should wait . . . wait perhaps a week . . . a week so that—"

"I'm not a secretary or a cook giving notice till you can find a replacement." Her voice was a rasp. She knew her words were twisting into his flesh as surely as the sharp point of a knife. She *wanted* to know how far she could go. She *wanted* to bring him to the brink of despair. She *wanted* to see it all. She had never felt this way before and hated herself for it.

Escobar's expression didn't change. "When do you plan to get married?" he said.

"In a month."

"Where?"

"At his castle in Tuscany. But you don't really want to speak about him, do you?" She was toying with her enormous diamond ring.

Escobar refilled his own glass and moved to the fireplace. He looked uncertain about what to do next. "I know, Denise, we have never spoken of eternal love. Nor have we promised anything to one another. But I cannot believe you could treat even the most casual of acquaintances with such total lack of concern." Beads of sweat were forming on his forehead. He looked at her face—a mask of impassivity. "You know that I love you." His voice was subdued. Trying hard to control himself, Escobar was acting as though he had expected all of this, even the pain. He kept on. "You mean to say that whatever was between us isn't anymore? That you just . . ."

"I mean to say that I have never loved you—not now, not ever. I cannot be in love with you or anyone else."

"You said you loved me."

"I lied."

"Why?"

"To please you."

"Didn't I make you happy, Denise? Didn't I?"

She approached and stood only a few inches away from him. Escobar brought his glass up in front of him like a shield, trying to hide the wrinkles that he sensed the unflattering light was cruelly carving into his face. He spoke softly. "I have given you everything, Denise."

"I know."

"I am too old."

"No, Escobar, I am too young."

"You didn't think so when—"

"I was—"

"Let me finish. You didn't think so when we began three years ago."

"I was a different person. I wanted the world. I still do, but I have changed." She touched his shoulder and looked at him with intense determination. "I want a future. Not just a past or even a present. A *future*."

Escobar was sipping his drink in silence. He brushed her hand aside and moved once more toward the window.

"I want a husband, children, respectability. No matter what you give me, Escobar, in the eyes of the world, in my eyes, I shall always be your whore. A kept woman."

"You mean our relationship is unsalvageable?"

"You didn't hear a word I said. Please try to understand. I'm only twenty-one." She raised her voice. "How could you have expected this to go on forever? Everything comes to an end."

Escobar lurched toward Denise, gripping her arm with such force that she let out a cry. "How long have you been seeing this—this man behind my back?" he asked angrily.

"I have seen him three times in my life and always with you present—with the exception of today. Let go of my arm!"

"And you plan to marry someone you have met three times?"

"Someone I have met *only* three times," she corrected him.

"Does he know about us?"

Denise nodded. "I have told him you were . . ."—she hesitated—"my godfather."

"Yes. Why not? You yourself introduced me everywhere as your niece." Escobar moved to the sofa. "Have you made love with him?"

Denise felt uncomfortable. "No. He thinks I am a virgin."

"That's a good one," retorted Escobar with a short, dry laugh. "What if he knew that you've fucked your way up the ladder since you were fifteen? What if he knew you were mine whenever I wanted? Would he still marry you?"

Denise was taken aback. "Don't use vulgarities, Escobar. It's out of character. You make me out to be a tramp. I've only been to bed with four men in my life."

"You told me there were only three."

"I forgot about one. He was so unimportant." She looked at him with sincerity. "Help me, Escobar," she said softly. "Help me." He wouldn't deny her that, would he? He wouldn't.

"Why should I do anything more for you, Denise?" he asked vindictively.

Slowly Denise sat down at his feet. "Because you love me. Because I am sure you want the best for me. Because this is a unique chance being offered to me. Because I want to be Princess Francesco Borgia." She laid her head on his knees and felt him shaking. "Do you want to make love to me now?" asked Denise gently.

Escobar did not answer. She looked up at him. His eyes, deep in their sockets, were filled with tears that overflowed onto his hollow, tanned cheeks. Denise took his hand, which had fallen helplessly by his side, and kissed it tenderly. He was staring straight ahead. Silent. Resigned. Old.

When Escobar left her apartment she lay on her bed concentrating on the carved ceiling. Something inside her felt different. It was nothing she could define. Tonight was the end of another chapter. Tomorrow would be another debut. She wanted to cry, but couldn't.

�֍

MARIELA/*New York City/Sunday, January 31, 1954*

The phone jangled, shattering the darkness of the silent room. Mariela shifted but did not wake up. The ringing continued to jar her slumber. Gradually she opened her eyes and groped for the phone with an unsteady hand.

"Hello," she answered in a voice thick with sleep.

"Better wake up fast! I've got news for you."

Mariela looked up at the gold Cartier clock next to her bed, which read 11:20, and sat up apprehensively.

"All right, take it easy, Jack. I'm still half asleep. In fact, I was in the middle of a beautiful dream."

"Well, here's another beautiful dream for you." The voice came hard and slow. "Our *friend* joined his master in hell sometime during the night, and not the way he intended journeying there either!"

"Stop talking in riddles!" snapped Mariela as she switched on the light.

"Okay, baby. Here it is." Jack's tone changed, stressing each word. "Karl has been murdered. His precious cock was found floating in the aquarium in his bedroom, and his balls cooling off in an ice bucket next to a bottle of champagne."

Mariela gripped the phone. "Jack, please don't make terrible jokes."

"You'd better believe what I'm telling you. I just found out about it accidentally through a journalist friend of mine, who got the news an hour ago."

Mariela felt weak. Her voice took on a new edge. "Tell me it's not true, Jack. It didn't have to happen this way. I feel dreadful." Her hands were moist. "Karl was perfectly all right when I left him. I swear to that." The lump in her throat dropped to her stomach.

"Yes, I know, I know," Jack said.

"I can't understand this. I feel as if it's all a nightmare," Mariela whispered, thoroughly distraught. "I left him about midnight and he was very much alive. When did it happen?"

"The coroner hasn't given a complete report as yet, but it would appear that he died around five this morning."

"What are you going to do?" Mariela's voice sounded parched.

"I'm on my way to the Nineteenth Precinct right now with my attorney. I've had too many business dealings with Karl. His secretary, Lynne, was aware of our meeting tomorrow, and I want to get out of here as soon as possible. In the meantime, some advice. Get in touch with your blue-blood senator and see what he can do to prevent your name from appearing in print. Meet me in the Palm Court of the Plaza at four this afternoon. We have some things to settle. I'll head for the airport from there." He slammed the phone down.

Mariela jumped out of bed and turned the radio on loud. Her brain could do nothing but react with intense terror. The news program was almost over—no mention of Ravenstein.

She looked around her, uncertain where to begin, then dashed to the bathroom while Bill Haley and the Comets' hit record, "Shake, Rattle and Roll," was playing. She washed her face hurriedly, brushed her waist-length hair, put on a dressing gown and sat at the small desk in her pearl-gray living room. There was no reply at the first number she dialed. The second call, to Nathan Berger, went through to him in Connecticut. He answered in the manner of a man accustomed to fending off requests.

Mariela and Nathan were friends. She had known him socially for almost a year, having met him through Karl Ravenstein. A shrewd and experienced lawyer, he was in private practice with the prestigious firm of Berger, Davis and McEvoy.

Nathan spoke; his orders were simple. "As of right now, under no circumstances are you to answer your telephone or doorbell. Meet me at my apartment at two o'clock." He hung up abruptly.

Mariela dialed area code 703, followed by a number she took from her small Hermès pocket calendar. She received no reply and tried area code 617, Boston. Again the insistent snarling of the telephone was all she heard. At long last a familiar voice answered.

"It's me," she said.

"Hi, hot stuff. I'm sorry I couldn't call you last night as promised, but—"

"Glover, I need a very important favor. Is it safe to talk on this line?" Mariela spoke quickly without acknowledging his greeting.

"Now, you know, hot stuff, a politician's line doesn't always guarantee a private conversation." His tone was jovial. "I'll call you back if what you have to say is confidential."

"It's more than confidential," said Mariela. "But I'm not answering my telephone, so let it ring once, hang up and call again. I wouldn't have bothered you on a Sunday, but it really is a matter of life and death. I mean it."

Fifteen minutes later Glover Anderson, bundled up against the inclement Boston weather, called Mariela from a telephone booth, reversing the charges and using the name James Holder.

"Sorry about reversing the charges, Mariela, but I haven't any change. In your memoirs you can mention that a future president of the United States once called you collect!" Glover chuckled.

"Listen carefully." Mariela's voice was urgent. "Karl Ravenstein had a small dinner party last night, and I was the last to leave him, around midnight."

"Don't tell me he got you pregnant," Glover quipped.

"Please be serious and listen. Sometime later, around five in the morning, Karl was murdered. I don't have the details. There's been no news of it on the radio, and there are no evening papers today. I'm calling you for a *favor*," she stressed, pausing a moment. "I use the word 'favor,' Glover, because I wouldn't wish to imply that you owe me anything, nor do I wish to use the word 'demand.' "

He remained silent and waited for her to finish what she had to say.

"The favor I'm asking of you is that my name should not appear anywhere in connection with this affair."

"What about the other guests?"

Mariela could tell from the tone of Glover's voice that he was beginning to understand the seriousness of the situation.

"One girl knows me. The others are total strangers." She faltered. "Listen, Glover. I know it will be impossible to conceal the fact that I attended the party. That isn't what I'm asking. I simply don't want my name spread across the headlines." Seconds passed. "I know it can be done." Glover did not reply, and Mariela went on. "Your sister's name was never mentioned when they raided that after-hours club in New York and found her with marijuana in her handbag."

"That wasn't murder, Mariela."

She continued as if she hadn't heard him. "I'm also thinking of you," she whispered. "It wouldn't do for an aspiring candidate for the presidency of the United States to be associated with the woman who had dinner with Karl Ravenstein the very night he was murdered."

"Who's to know that?" he asked quickly.

"Glover, be realistic. It's common knowledge among many people in influential positions that you have a mysterious brunette flying in your private plane to rendezvous with you every Wednesday, and it wouldn't be so difficult for those same people to discover that her name is Mariela Koenig, and to use that against you."

"Damn it," Glover said angrily. "What a hell of a spot you're putting me in! Don't you know it's Sunday? And my wife's insisting I go to church with her. How the hell am I supposed to find anybody on a Sunday?"

"I found you, didn't I?" purred Mariela.

"I'll see what can be done, goddamn it." He lowered his voice. "I guess this Wednesday will be out for us?"

"That depends upon the turn of events," replied Mariela. "Call me tonight after seven. I want you as badly as you want me," she added seductively. When she put the phone down, she caught a glimpse of her face in the baroque wall mirror. A small but definite smile was on her lips.

※

DENISE/*New York City*/*Sunday, January 31, 1954*

Yvette looked once more at the clock on the mantelpiece, then at her wrist-watch, as if looking at both would somehow accelerate time. Adjusting her white starched apron, she timorously pushed the bedroom door ajar and peeked. Denise was sound asleep in a fetal position. Looking at the watch again, Yvette took a deep breath, steeled herself and entered the darkened room on tiptoe.

"Mademoiselle Denise," she whispered softly. Blond curls moved from one side of the bed to the other. "Mademoiselle Cunningham," she repeated, slightly louder.

Denise tried to open her eyes and groaned, voice full of slumber, words muffled in the pillow, "Why are you waking me?" She yawned noisily. "Didn't you see my note in the living room?" she asked, turning on her back abruptly. "I specifically asked not to be disturbed."

"But Mademoiselle Denise—"

"As I've been telling you for the past two years," Denise began slowly, "when I wish not to be disturbed, *it—means—just—that.*"

"I'm sorry, mademoiselle, but it's eleven-thirty—"

"Eleven-thirty—*so what!*" Denise yelled, flinging herself to the other side of the bed.

Denise couldn't remember when she had finally fallen asleep, but it was long after her call to England at dawn.

"Mademoiselle, Mr. Ortiz wishes to speak with you urgently. He's called several—"

The name Ortiz sent Denise's mind reeling. "Please don't speak of Mr. Ortiz right now," she said crisply.

Yvette picked up an evening dress that had been carelessly discarded on the floor. "You also had a call from Rome, mademoiselle."

"Prince Borgia! Why on earth didn't you wake me?" she snapped angrily. A shaft of light from the open closet fell across the bed, making Denise shield her eyes against the glare.

"But mademoiselle, you left instructions—"

"Shut that door! That light hurts my eyes!" She raised herself with difficulty. "Oh, for God's sake, leave that dress alone and bring me some black coffee—and a couple of aspirins too. I've a terrible headache." Immediately Yvette attempted to plump up a small lace pillow under her mistress's neck. Denise grabbed it and fired it across the room.

"Dammit! Stop all this fussing, will you! Bring me some coffee. My head needs help, not my neck!"

The maid scurried toward the windows and started drawing back the drapes.

"Christ, what on earth's gotten into you today! Leave them alone! Bring the coffee!" she shrieked.

Yvette turned around, startled. Her back hunched, her stomach thrust out, her mouth open, she held one foot over the other. She was transformed into a gigantic question mark.

"Now!"

Yvette stumbled from the room. Denise picked up the phone, and at her request the hotel operator connected her with Air France and then BOAC. The conversations were brief. Yvette returned, carrying a small tray with coffee, aspirins and a white rose pinned to an envelope. White. Unmarked. The identity of the sender more recognizable than if he had scrawled his name in gold. Who else but Escobar! Denise tossed it aside as if it were yesterday's newspaper and welcomed the hot ebony liquid, which she downed in one long swallow.

"I hope you didn't tell the prince I was asleep."

"No, mademoiselle. I told him you were out, as you have instructed me to say when you're not available. He will ring again around noon."

"Good."

"Mademoiselle, is there something in particular you'd like me to do?" asked Yvette, her friendly composure restored.

"As a matter of fact, yes. Pack everything."

"Pack—everything?" Yvette said incredulously. "But, mademoiselle, we arrived only yesterday. I'll—"

"I know perfectly well when we arrived, stupid," said Denise, her voice shrill. Yvette was taken aback, hurt by her rudeness.

"I'm sorry, Yvette. I didn't mean to shout at you. I'm very nervous. I didn't sleep all night." Denise paused. "Will you forgive me?" A sudden switch turned on her smile and the single dimple. "Just do as I say, Yvette. Pack! Here, take this. I'm finished with the coffee," she announced loudly. "We're leaving tomorrow or Tuesday."

"With Mr. Ortiz—on his plane?" Yvette picked up the tray.

"Without Mr. Ortiz and by Air France," Denise said, bristling. "We're going home to Paris. And fill one suitcase with two or three sets of casual clothes," she added, "and keep it separate from the others."

"But, mademoiselle, I don't understand . . ."

"You are not paid to understand. Instead of being so inquisitive, why don't you go about your business?" Yvette was standing, silent, immobile, and looking at her strangely. Denise aimed her gaze very surely at Yvette, as if she were the target in a shooting gallery. "Will you stop gaping at me, please!"

"Oh, mademoiselle, I completely forgot. A Mister Harry Winston called."

"Harry Winston! On a Sunday! Whatever for?"

"I couldn't understand. Something to do with measuring one of your fingers this afternoon," she answered.

Measure my finger? Denise thought, It's probably Escobar making a last attempt to keep me with him. But it couldn't be Escobar. By now his jewelers knew the sizes of *all* her fingers. Harry Winston . . . diamonds bigger than the Ritz. Come on, this is no time to think in clichés. Her mind grasped the implication: What else—who else—but the engagement ring for Denise Cunningham from Prince Francesco Borgia! Princess Francesco Borgia. How melodious. Princess Denise Borgia. That's it!

"I'll see Mr. Winston at four," she announced. "In the meantime I'm out to everyone except Prince Borgia."

"And Monsieur Ortiz?"

Denise thought for a moment. "Tell him I'll be back at five-thirty. Right now, I want to be alone!" Yvette didn't move; her eyes were nailed to her mistress in total disbelief. "Don't just stand there! Please—start packing!"

Yvette left the room, closing the door behind her.

Picking up the envelope by the side of the bed, Denise opened it.

Denise, my dearest

In conveying tragic news, there is no transition. One moment there is a certain relationship; the next it is no more. I was deluding myself; I thought I could hold onto a hand like yours, but one must not tempt the gods. You see, my dear child, I've had a very long and full life and could see the vagaries, the unexpected developments. I fought against the inevitable, and the hopelessness of the situation is choking me.

I have never overlooked the fact that besides possessing incredible beauty and maturity beyond your years, you are a strong and determined person—strong of ambition, strong of will; after all, if it weren't for those qualities, I would never have fallen as deeply in love with you as I did.

Being addicted to your love and to your sexual attractiveness cannot be reasoned away; it can only be repressed or transcended. I'm the spectator at a play, an old actor watching as he acts a part he has written and created for himself.

Time heals all wounds; the sad thing is that I have so little time. And still, I must learn to live as gracefully as birds and realize that to dip with sadness is just as beautiful as to rise with happiness; to fly continually straight is a sin.

I need not be ashamed that you are the only great love of my life. Beyond you there is nothing. I'm thankful for the many things you have given me. What are the joys I would have missed, the pain, if our paths had never crossed? In your quiet moments—and there won't be many—perhaps you'll be able to reflect on these lines and hold dear some memories of our time together.

I have decided to help you in facing the practical side of this issue and will do everything within my power to ease the way for you. Parting is always sad: it is to die a little; for me it is to die a lot. I leave you with my sincerest best wishes for your future happiness.

I am resigned that you are gone, my child. I kiss your eyes, your cheeks, your lips, your hair, your ears, your feet, for legs, your thighs. I kiss you. I kiss you for the last time.

Escobar

Reading the letter had no effect on Denise—no flurried heartbeat, no quivering pulse—only a single thought. "Resignation is a virtue of the vanquished," she sighed. However, there was still one important thing she wanted from Escobar, and she knew she would obtain it easily. Hadn't she always gotten what she wanted? Even against that great bitch goddess Eva Perón?

Still holding the letter, Denise reclined on her white lace pillows, closed her eyes and was back in Buenos Aires in October of 1951.

⁂

Denise was ensconced in Reinaldo Vega's large apartment on Calle Posadas, in Buenos Aires. A far cry from the shabby one-room apartment she had shared with a roommate in Chicago. The place, the people were a dream come true. She knew her whole life was changing, she could feel it. All she had to do was to be patient. It wouldn't be long. Reinaldo made the waiting less lonely by introducing Denise to Milwaukee-born Janet Ortiz, twenty years her senior. Janet Ortiz was a lucky woman. Her husband, Escobar, happened to be the wealthiest shipping magnate in the world, and her best friend was the First Lady of Argentina, Eva Perón.

Their friendship was intimate. On numerous Parisian shopping expeditions Janet would buy expensive and elegant clothes for herself, but made a point of purchasing equally impressive clothing and gems for Eva—the most glittering and showy the couturiers and jewelers had to offer. She was well aware of Eva's preferences, knowing her friend could never appreciate the difference between taste and flamboyance.

These gifts from Janet and Escobar Ortiz ensured the couple's position in the Perón hierarchy—and made it easy for them to take their money out of the country and invest it in Uruguay.

Juan Perón held supreme power in Argentina, yet some said his wife, Eva —called Evita—wielded more power than he did. Her clothes and jewels were legendary.

Denise was truly fascinated by Eva Perón. One night over dinner she begged Reinaldo for one more of the many anecdotes he had collected about Argentina's First Lady.

"Escobar bought each of them a jewel of equal elegance and beauty. I can vouch for it, Denicita. I arranged the sale myself. Eva, of course, was unable to appreciate its quality, as it was not large enough for her, and threw it clear across the room, hitting old Escobar right in the head—"

"Oh, poor Escobar!"

"And Eva shouted like an exasperated fishwife, 'Bury it where you found it! Maybe it'll grow!' " Reinaldo and Denise laughed. "And guess what he did, Denicita? Bought her a life-sized orchid in pure white diamonds, measuring five inches by seven, and worth three hundred thousand dollars."

Denise was too stunned to speak.

From Janet Ortiz she heard other stories about Argentina's queen.

"She has twelve maids around the clock to look after her, you know."

"Twelve maids!"

"Twelve maids aren't so many, considering her obligations and the fact that she changes clothes four times a day."

Denise made a mental note.

"But Eva Perón's a hard worker and is worshiped by all the people, as you've been able to see," Janet continued.

"Oh, imagine if we could get Eva and Eleanor Roosevelt in bed together," said Denise. "We'd all be living in Nirvana." The two women laughed hysterically, until Janet composed herself and warned that one did not make jokes at the expense of the First Lady.

Eva Perón! Never in her life had Denise been more eager to meet anyone!

At Christmas she got her wish. Denise and Reinaldo were invited to attend a reception to be held, not at the official Perón residence in Buenos Aires, but in the suburb of San Vicente. The estate covered forty-five acres and had two swimming pools, one indoors, one outdoors, with machine-made waves. Architects from all over the world had participated in the design of the magnificent mansion and grounds, where flamingos, storks, ostriches and guanacos roamed freely. Dealers had been dispatched to every corner of Europe to adorn the walls with paintings and objets d'art.

December is the height of summer in Buenos Aires. Denise chose a sleeveless white organza dress with a deep flounce at the bottom and a matching floor-length stole; her blond hair cascaded over her bare shoulders and glistened like spun sugar.

Denise, accompanied by Reinaldo, Janet and Escobar Ortiz, walked apprehensively up the stairs of the mansion, through a double row of military cadets, and into the immense mirrored hall, fashioned after Versailles. She was first introduced to Eva's older sister, Bianca, and to Major Alfredo Arrieto, Bianca's lover.

Janet and Escobar took Denise by the hand and introduced her to the President.

"Welcome to Argentina, Miss Cunningham," he said in perfect English. "You are a beautiful young woman, and I am a great admirer of beauty." For an instant they faced each other, her hand in his, her large blue eyes riveted on his narrow brown ones.

"And I am a great admirer of your beautiful country, Mr. President," she murmured.

"Well, seeing you with Escobar and Janet, I know that you are in good hands."

As he held her fingers a fraction of a second longer than necessary, she sensed his real meaning—Juan Perón would love to have her in *his* hands.

Perón's eyes followed Denise as she was led to an adjacent reception area. There a slender, pale-haired, dark-eyed woman of thirty-one stood surrounded by friends. It was Eva Perón, resplendent in a gold lamé strapless dress. She literally glittered, wearing an enormous hammered-gold necklace encrusted with emeralds, several bracelets to match, and an emerald ring the size of a pigeon's egg. Bestowing an all-encompassing smile to the right and left, Eva left her group and embraced Janet warmly. When introduced to Denise, the First Lady greeted her in Spanish with a handshake that was forceful, vulgar, impatient and unnaturally cold.

Although confused, Denise plunged ahead: "I am so pleased and honored to meet you. I've waited a very long time for this extraordinary—"

"Janet!" Eva cried imperiously. "I have something of the greatest urgency to communicate to you. Please come with me."

As they walked away, Eva's jealous glare was fixed on her husband, who was still mesmerized by the young American woman. Denise wondered what they were discussing so heatedly as she watched Eva's reptilian eyes darting at her.

Denise joined Reinaldo, in conversation with the American journalist Fleur Cowles. Dinner was about to be served when Janet approached and took Denise aside.

"Denise, you may not understand this," she whispered, "but you must leave at once, pretending to have a headache."

Denise was silent, staring, unable to comprehend.

"Don't repeat what I shall tell you to anyone, or it could have bad repercussions for Reinaldo. It is *imperative* that you do not sit down to dinner."

"But why?"

Janet looked cautiously around her, took Denise by the arm and walked her toward an open veranda. "Eva cannot tolerate competition. She believes that her husband has been looking at you."

"But I didn't even—"

"Furthermore, she *hates* anyone with the same color hair as hers."

"But I've had this color—"

"I know, but she claims that you've copied hers!" Denise was appalled. Janet pressed her hand and continued. "Before Eva sees you again—and I promise you that she will—you must darken it." Denise looked at Janet blankly, letting go of her hand, taking a step sideways. Janet went on haltingly. "Eva is a very strange and demanding woman."

"Janet, I never—"

"Let me finish. A most beloved actress in Argentina, Paloma Bertad, made the error of copying one of Eva's ball gowns. She had to leave the country because all artistic doors in Argentina were closed to her, since Eva Perón has control over the media and the theaters." Denise couldn't find her voice, but nodded. "Of course," continued Janet, "the fact that Paloma was Perón's mistress when he was still a colonel in the army, and introduced him to Eva when she was a virtually unknown radio actress, may have had something to do with it."

Denise was on the verge of tears. She went to Reinaldo and pleaded an unbearable headache. He wanted to leave with her, but she insisted that he remain.

That night Denise vowed that she would sleep with President Juan Domingo Perón. The opportunity arose much sooner than she had anticipated.

It was not long after the Christmas incident that Denise found herself dining with Reinaldo and some of his friends at La Cabaña, a folkloric restaurant in one of the bawdiest quarters of Buenos Aires. That night every table was occupied. The festive atmosphere was impregnated with the sensual smells of onions, wine, spices, tobacco, garlic and the bitter aroma of maté, a heady green herbal tea, which mingled with the pungent odor of roasting meat as whole sides of beef were slowly charcoaled in open pits. The noise was overpowering. Gauchos in their native costumes of white shirts tucked into black ballooning trousers, with calf-length boots, their slender waists cinched by six inch-wide leather belts heavily encrusted with rows of silver coins, were dancing, heels clicking, feet stomping, sombreros flying to the nonstop beat of guitars and castanets, punctuated by the rhythmic clapping of hands, the clatter of clinking glasses and rattling dishes. With its roughhewn wood walls, the place resembled an authentic cabaña, the rustic habitation of gauchos on the pampas.

As Denise and her party were about to order, a great commotion occurred at the entrance. "What's going on over there, darling?" she asked Reinaldo, taking his hand.

"I don't know," he replied, craning his neck like everyone else in the room. "Some celebrity must have come in, but there are so many people clustering around, it's impossible to get a good look. Wait a minute! It's a woman! I think it's Paloma . . . it *is!*" His voice rose an octave. "It's Paloma Bertad!"

All the diners rose to their feet and burst into spontaneous applause and shouts of "Bravo!"

"Who *is* she?" Denise asked.

"Just the most famous star in South America, that's who!" Reinaldo replied. "Why, she's as big as . . . as . . . She's as big as your Beverly Langdon in the States!" He added, sotto voce, "Paloma was made to leave Argentina because Eva Perón . . ."

Denise stopped listening. Reinaldo's words hung in her mind like a drop of oil. Suddenly it all came back. Her heart skipped a beat. Paloma was the actress Janet had alluded to that Christmas night. The night Denise was humiliated by Eva Perón.

Paloma was an intense woman in her late twenties, with a mass of dark, glossy hair. She had a pretty face, oval and broad, with flared nostrils, brown flashing eyes, and full lips parted in a glistening smile. Wearing a red-and-black print dress generous in décolletage, she teetered on ankle-strap platform sandals with heels so high they were a triumph of engineering. Paloma was overly made up, with a beauty spot drawn to the left of her scarlet mouth. Large gold loop earrings hung at each side of a head that seemed too heavy for the short, stout body. Bracelets clanged with each movement, constantly pushed back by clawlike hands, the nails long and painted crimson. Despite the obstacles she set for herself, her overall appearance was one of uncommon gracefulness and attractive, opulent vulgarity. Paloma Bertad possessed the aura of a superstar.

"Do you know her, Reinaldo?" Denise asked, her curiosity whetted.

"No, I don't, but—"

"*I* do," interjected Dario, a heavy-lidded man sitting across from Denise. "I know her very well. Dolores is a good friend of hers."

"I'm dying to meet Miss Bertad," said Denise with unusual intensity. "Do you think she could be persuaded to join us?"

"I don't know, but let me try," declared Dario as he rose.

Reinaldo looked at Denise quizzically. "Why are you so interested? I thought you didn't even know who she was."

"What in heaven's name are you talking about, Reinaldo?" replied Denise. "I've seen all her movies! Now, really!"

Dario managed to bring Paloma and her escort to the table. The presentations were made.

"What gives us the good fortune to have you in Buenos Aires?" asked Dolores, embracing her old friend effusively.

"I'm only here for the holidays."

Denise insisted that Paloma sit right next to her. "What would you like to drink, Miss Bertad?" Denise didn't wait for an answer. "The champagne, Reinaldo. Pass the champagne, *por favor.*"

Her attention focused on Paloma. "I'm so delighted to meet you, Miss Bertad," cooed Denise. "I've heard so much about you and I'm one of your biggest fans!"

"Please call me Paloma, and you are—?"

"Oh, I'm Denise," she said airily. "I know it must be very difficult to catch names when one meets as many people as you do." She looked up to see Reinaldo scrutinizing her closely, but ignored it. "You know, Miss Ber—

I mean, Paloma, you are extremely popular in the United States. I'm so fascinated by you." She flicked the tip of her tongue around her immaculate teeth, then lowered her voice so her next lie would not be overheard. "I've seen all your pictures several times."

"Come on, Denise, don't monopolize Paloma!" Reinaldo said. "We all want to share her!"

"I'm sure you must be bored to death with people gushing over you everywhere you go," Denise continued, feeling a strange new excitement.

Paloma withdrew a plastic compact studded with rhinestones from a gold, heart-shaped satin handbag. "It's difficult," she sighed, "but I try to bear it. It's the price one pays for being famous." She applied lipstick to her full mouth. "Sometimes I wish I could disappear into the woodwork and be just like the average person."

"How could you ever be like the average person?"

"Believe me, Denise, I try. That's why I tone myself down when I'm out in public."

Denise took another look at Paloma and repressed a smile. Their conversation was interrupted by waiters serving the food. Paloma attacked the contents of her plate ferociously.

"I admire the way you can eat so much and still keep your gorgeous figure. Do you exercise?" asked Denise.

"No, I do absolutely nothing. I guess I'm lucky." She threw back her head and laughed raucously. Denise observed her overflowing bodice and the red welts made on her arm by the fabric cutting into her plump flesh.

"Do you know that we have no one in films like you nowadays?" Denise said calculatingly.

Paloma's olive complexion darkened. "Oh, come on, Denise. How about Beverly Langdon, Jayne Mansfield, Gina—"

"Caricatures, just caricatures!" Denise interrupted. "That's all they are, not real women like you! Everything about the others is fake, even their hair! They wear wigs all the time—underneath, they're bald."

"Bald!" Paloma exclaimed, fluffing out her luxuriant hair. "Completely bald?"

"Completely bald! What is the secret of your crowning glory?"

Paloma momentarily forgot all about her food. "Well, I wash it daily with the yellow of eggs. Then I . . ."

Denise was smiling but not listening, her mind engulfed by a very private thought.

"Have you heard my latest recording?" It was Paloma speaking. She had to repeat the question twice before Denise responded.

"Is that the one you do so well, with the word 'corazón' in it?" Denise had yet to hear a Latin number that omitted the word "heart" in its lyrics.

Paloma hummed a few bars. "It's called 'Amor de Mi Vida.' You like?"

"I love it!" squealed Denise. "I play it at home all the time!"

Paloma stood up, clapping her hands over her head to attract the attention of the guitarists, who enthusiastically surrounded her. Denise sat with her elbows on the table, supporting her head, affecting rapt attention. Paloma and the orchestra produced an anarchy of sound. Denise's instincts were correct. Paloma Bertad was vain and she sucked up admiration like dry sand. Denise flooded her with flattery. By the end of the evening they had exchanged telephone numbers. What's more, Paloma had accepted an invitation for lunch at Denise's apartment the following day. It never occurred to her that Denise had any other purpose than to seek a new friendship. Paloma Bertad was wrong.

It was one-thirty precisely when Paloma, overdressed, overjeweled and overweight, rang the bell at Calle Posadas. Denise cheerfully opened the door of her apartment and the two women embraced warmly. "What punctuality! I'm very flattered! Come in!" exclaimed Denise. Hips swaying, Paloma followed her inside the spacious and cool living room. "Amor de Mi Vida" was playing in the background. Denise had purchased it that very morning.

"What a pretty place, Denise! You have no idea how hot and humid it is outside!" She removed a large black straw picture hat, its brim encircled by red silk poppies, with green streamers trailing down the back. "It's so difficult for a star to go unnoticed in the streets of Buenos Aires!"

"Oh, Paloma! How I sympathize with you! It must be murder!" Denise led the way toward the veranda overlooking a garden alive with waves of red, yellow, blue and white flowers. The foliage of an oak tree, more somber than jade, screened them from the brutal sun.

"Won't you sit in that wicker chair, Paloma? You'll be more comfortable there."

"Thank you, Denise." A large revolving fan hummed overhead.

"What a beautiful frock you're wearing, Paloma! Wherever did you get it?"

"I'm glad you like it." Paloma smoothed the silky fabric of the green-and-white polka dot dress over her generous thighs. "I bought it in Rio last month."

Denise leaned over the edge of the balcony, plucked a flower, and presented it to her guest. "Just smell this rose! Isn't it luscious? And what a coincidence! It's just the color of your lipstick!" The blossom was pink, Paloma's lips fuchsia. A wasp came between them for a moment; Denise waved it away.

"Goodness, the maid is so nervous because you're here, she forgot the champagne. I'll go get it." Denise returned shortly with a bottle in one hand and a glossy eight-by-ten photograph of Paloma in the other. "Could I impose upon your good nature to autograph it for me?" she said, pursing her lips with saccharine sweetness. Denise put the photograph, also purchased that morning, on a glass table and handed Paloma a pen. Paloma, with a grand gesture, wrote: "Usted es mi mejor amiga, con mucho estimación, Paloma Bertad."

"Thank you, Paloma. I'm so proud that you're calling me your best friend." They spoke about Paloma Bertad's favorite subject—Paloma Bertad. The champagne flowed. By the time lunch was served in the dining room they were giggling like schoolgirls.

It was after dessert that Denise timidly confided how Eva Perón had humiliated her at the Christmas party. "I wouldn't mind teaching Eva Perón a good lesson," Denise said jokingly. "After all, if one has the name, one might just as well play the game!"

"What do you mean by that?"

"Well, since Eva Perón accused me of being interested in her husband, I might just as well be."

"Be what?"

"Be . . . interested. Get the opportunity . . . to be *really* interested. You know what I mean." Paloma understood perfectly. "I see it this way, Paloma. Revenge is a dish that can be eaten cold, and I'm very hungry!" They both chuckled.

Denise was waiting for Paloma to take the initiative. She did. Jumping to her feet, she asked, "Where's your telephone?"

"It's right over there in the living room, by the sofa, but if you want more privacy, there's an extension in the bedroom." Surely she would want more privacy.

"Does Juan Perón know your name?"

"I think he remembers it. I'm sure he recalls our meeting. Why?"

"Oh, nothing. I'll be back in a moment."

Denise was still seated at the dining room table when Paloma returned, hands on hips, head slightly crooked to one side, a vindictive smile on her lips. "I have good news for you, Denise."

Rising slowly, Denise poured one glass of champagne and gave it to Paloma. "What kind of news, dear?"

Paloma took her time. "Perón will call you within three days." Denise didn't respond. "Aren't you pleased?"

For a brief instant Denise reflected on the shoddiness of it all, but dismissed the thought. Paloma continued. "I think that's the best revenge you could take, believe me."

Never for a moment had Denise thought otherwise. "That's wonderful," she said. "But . . ." She hesitated. "Reinaldo's here in the evening."

"I'm way ahead of you, Denise. I told the President you're available only in the afternoon."

"That's fantastic! Just fantastic!" Denise exclaimed. "Let's drink to the merit of wicked women!" She poured champagne into her own glass, and a sparkle, just short of a glint, shone in her blue eyes. Impulsively she took off a gold charm bracelet she was wearing and put it around Paloma's wrist. "It looks beautiful on you. I would consider it an honor if you'd wear it."

"I love it, but why are you giving this to me? Why? she repeated, fingering the unexpected present.

"Because I want you to remember me," insisted Denise. She almost added, "When I'm with Perón, I'll be remembering you. After all, didn't he dump you for Eva?"

It was dusk, and a rumble of thunder could be heard in the distance when Paloma finally took her leave. "We'll get together soon. I want to know all about it! Enjoy!"

Closing the door, Denise let out a deep sigh of relief. Everything had fallen gently into place. Returning to the veranda, she picked up the photograph of Paloma, walked regally to the bathroom and tore it into several pieces, eyes wide as she watched half a mouth, mascaraed lashes, a nose with part of a cheek, a ripped bosom, the signature, disappear slowly into the swirling water of the flushing toilet.

Denise had no intention of ever seeing Paloma again.

Everything worked out as Denise had planned. Within two days a limousine pulled up in front of 15 Calle Posadas. She got in and was driven to an estancia near Cañuelos, south of Buenos Aires. It was actually a hunting lodge surrounded by an immense private park.

As she was being helped from the car by a military man she noticed two other uniformed guards standing by the entrance. Juan Perón himself opened the door. He looked extremely handsome and imposing, wearing a yellow sweater, matching slacks and holding the leash of a huge yellow mastiff with yellow cowlike eyes. He ushered Denise into the large rustic living room, furnished in various shades of yellow; even the grand piano, brick fireplace and curtains were in tones of yellow. The lodge had an unlived-in look, like a furnished house shown by real estate agents to prospective buyers. There were no personal touches, no photographs or magazines, not even a flower. Denise repressed a smile and thought to herself, Eva obviously isn't doing *her* fooling around in this place!

Denise draped herself across the yellow couch. Perón offered her a glass of spring water, which she accepted, disappointed that her fantasy of a champagne fountain had not materialized. Perón sat next to her.

"Denise. May I call you Denise?" asked the dictator as he took her hand.

"Why, yes—that's my name," she said, crossing her legs at the knees while coquettishly reaching for the heavy yellow gold medallion that hung around his neck. Fingering it. Turning it. Appraising it inwardly. On one side Perón's zodiac sign—Libra. On the other the profile of Evita. Denise raised her eyes in question.

"It's a birthday . . . gift from my . . . from my wife."

"Oh, how nice," she said, releasing it. "And now—what should I call you?"

"Call me Juan," he said softly, inching himself closer to her. "You look stunning, Denise. I must admit that I am flattered that such a beautiful girl as yourself took the initiative to be with me." He fumbled for words, stabbed out his cigarette. "What do you do in life, Denise, besides being beautiful?"

"I do as I please." She picked up her glass and lifted it in a mocking gesture.

Perón laughed heartily. "What I mean to ask is, how do you earn a living?"

"I invest in people."

Perón's eyes opened wide, as eloquent as a question.

"I invest *my time* in people," Denise amended.

"I don't want you to ever *waste* your time with people." His breath quickened. "With me you will never waste time, Denise. I wish you would buy yourself a present to remember me." Perón took several large bills from his shirt pocket, pressing them into her hand.

She looked at the amount and smiled. "You misunderstand me completely, Juan," she said with a lilt in her voice, placing the money on the table. "I'm not here for money. Money does not interest me. I'm here for you, only for you."

Without another word he took her by the hand and led her upstairs to a bedroom that looked like the rest of the house—unused. They embraced, and the knowledge of the man's power excited her tremendously. Some of the great names in history paraded through her mind—Napoleon Bonaparte, Genghis Khan, Julius Caesar, Henry VIII, Mark Antony and Louis XIV.

Caressing her hair and shoulders, Perón was flushed and perspiring. "Do you think you can be yourself with me?"

"I'm always myself."

"It must be very difficult for a man to know you."

He guided her to the bed. She folded her hands behind her neck and let him touch her body. Watching one of the most powerful men in the world, on his knees, kissing her all over, caused her to tremble. She felt like a queen. Denise's glance swept quickly around the room and stopped, riveted, on a portrait of Eva Perón, in all her regalia, staring at her from the wall. Eva's eyes appeared to be following Denise's every movement. She marveled at Eva's gentle smile and also at the size of the aquamarine earrings. At least forty carats each, she thought, maybe fifty. Abruptly Perón stood up and said, "Take your clothes off." Direct. Commanding. An order. She quickly removed her things and let them fall to the floor. Perón did likewise. He was more exciting clothed than naked, she thought, remembering her fantasy about him making love to her while wearing his uniform.

Denise had no way of knowing the opinions of others; as for herself, Perón proved a poor lover. While inside her, he kept pleading anxiously, "Do it to me! Do it to me!" She had no idea what he wanted done to him. As his movements accelerated with his passion, so did the swing of the heavy gold medal around his neck. The pendant hit her chin with the regularity of a metronome and the sting of reality. Denise glanced again at Eva's eyes in the hope that they might provide an answer. Perón was still pleading, "Do it to me! Do it to me!," his massive body nearly crushing hers, when out of nowhere the huge yellow dog suddenly jumped on the bed with such force that Denise and Perón fell to the floor with a crash. The great Perón called a recess, and the dog was banished from the room. Unfortunately for Denise, the fiasco resumed.

Somehow the dog got into the room once again. Panting, running about wildly, snarling. The big yellow dog was tearing at something. Denise bit her lips to avoid laughing. Perón was totally oblivious to the antics of the animal.

"That's it, Denise. Now you're doing it to me. . . . That's it. . . . You're doing it now. Keep doing it!"

Denise had absolutely no idea what she was *now* doing that so excited the dictator.

After she faked one of her better orgasms, Perón lay back exhausted. "That was good," he said. "It was so good. And for you?"

"The best!" she sighed. "The best. But I knew it would be."

The whole episode had lasted less than fifteen minutes and had reconfirmed her belief that men will go to any lengths to possess an illusion.

"We better get going," said Perón, walking toward the bathroom. "I have an important political meeting in a couple of hours."

Denise began looking for her clothes, which, to her dismay, had been partially torn and chewed by the dog. Her stockings were in shreds. Unable to find a wastepaper basket in which to discard the now useless hosiery, she stuffed it in her handbag. While she and Perón were embracing and saying their goodbyes, the dog charged between Denise and the dictator, holding something in his mouth. What was it? Her stockings, of course, which the animal had retrieved from her purse. Denise looked with despair at the still serenely smiling portrait of Eva.

In an effort to corner the dog and his quarry, Perón ran down the stairs, a large towel wrapped around his waist.

An equally anxious Denise followed. "I want to leave," she pleaded. Perón, however, insisted that she remain until they had recovered "the evidence." They continued chasing the dog. Perón's towel fell to the floor. The beast changed gears, dropped the tattered stockings, and galloped upstairs, dragging the yellow towel in his mouth.

Denise was exhausted, though not from His Excellency. They both collapsed on the couch.

"Querida Denise," said the naked Perón, kissing her hands. "I cannot believe what a beautiful gift you granted me. I insist that you allow me to present you with—with a token of my gratitude. Please, querida, anything. I'll give you anything."

"Anything?"

"Si."

Her eyes fell once again on the gold medallion. She reached for it. "So your birth sign is Libra."

"Yes, I was born October eighth at the—"

"Since you insist, I will accept the medallion."

"The . . . the . . .?" He stammered, swallowed, blanched. "But this . . . it is from . . . it . . ."

"Didn't you say *anything?*"

"No . . . yes . . . I mean, it's just that . . . it is known. If you wore it, it would be recognized as a present that Eva—"

"Then I won't wear it. Only cherish it as a memory, a memory of this day that I will never, *never* forget."

"Neither will I. Never." Without hesitation he unfastened the clasp of his chain and dangled the pendant between his fingers, suspended above her open palm. The gold medallion slid easily into her hand. She transferred it to her purse with care, as though it were a precious, frail butterfly.

"Thank you, Juan."

An expression as vivid as light on water danced on Denise's face. The expression of a vanquisher.

On May 20, 1952, Denise and Reinaldo, along with a dozen other guests, were invited by Janet and Escobar Ortiz to travel on their private plane to Montevideo and spend the weekend at Janesco, their sumptuous and spectacular mansion. It had three swimming pools, all Olympic size, an eighteen-hole golf course, its own nightclub and a gigantic motion picture theater. An international film festival had been held there recently. Among the Escobars' guests were such film celebrities as Tyrone Power, Lana Turner, Betty Grable and Grace Kelly, who bore an uncanny resemblance to Denise in appearance and manner.

Late Sunday evening they were all seated at a lavish supper, the tables laid in exquisite taste with vermeil dinner service, magnificently set off by Alençon lace tablecloths and Baccarat crystal.

Suddenly Denise felt Escobar's eyes on her, and as his gaze grew more persistent, she became distinctly uncomfortable. Each time their eyes met she averted hers, but she couldn't ignore him when he lifted his glass to her, silently mouthing the words "To you." When Escobar rose, she knew he would ask her to dance.

Escobar guided her toward the patio, gradually allowing his arm to encircle the suppleness of her willowy body. "What perfume are you wearing, Denise?" he asked. It was clear that he was having difficulty controlling his breathing. "It's called Night Sanctuary," she replied in her most cultivated voice, adding with a note of irony, "Do you like it?" She *knew* he liked it. She *knew* he liked her. "Oh, they're playing my favorite song,"

Denise said to Escobar. It was true. She hummed softly in his ear. "Won't you change partners . . . la la la . . . you may never want to change partners again. . . ." She could feel his heart pounding against her breast.

"I'm going to Paris in a couple of weeks," he whispered in her ear. "There is nothing in the world I desire more than to meet you there. Is it possible? I will make all the arrangements through Armando Cellis, my personal secretary." Escobar spoke quickly, making one long uninterrupted sentence as if the phrases had been overrehearsed and would lose their aura of spontaneity in the process of being uttered. Although Denise felt an inner excitement, her large blue eyes showed reproach.

"How can you even suggest such a thing?" she asked. "You must be aware that Janet has become my closest friend."

"I understand that," Escobar said, pausing and imperceptibly brushing his lips against an earlobe, "but please try to understand that Janet is my wife in name only." Denise listened without responding as Escobar continued haltingly. "Since you and Janet are such good friends, surely she has told you—"

"Janet has told me that you have other interests besides her, but nothing important enough to disrupt your marriage. She's well aware that you have your own life."

"It's not my life. What did she tell you about hers?"

"What about Janet's life?"

The music had changed rhythm, and Denise had trouble following Escobar, who was not a very good dancer.

"Didn't you know that my wife is far more interested in Eva Perón's welfare than that of her own husband?"

Her eyes wide. Innocent. Trying hard for an astonished look, she retorted, "You should be very proud of the support Janet gives to the wife of the President of the Republic."

Escobar smiled strangely. "Her support goes above and beyond the call of duty."

Denise studied him a moment. People were looking at them, and she forced a smile. "I hope you'll forgive me for saying this, Escobar, but I think you're being very ungrateful." Denise held her smile.

"What do you mean by that?"

"Thanks to Janet's friendship with Eva Perón, you have benefited enormously, not only politically but socially and financially."

"That is only partially true, Denise. I was a very rich man before Perón came to power." He led her to a less crowded part of the patio and continued. "I have paid dearly for this friendship."

"In what way?"

"Surely you must know by now what is common knowledge."

"I don't know what you mean."

"That friendship has cost me my wife."

Denise stared at him in bewilderment.

"Janet and Eva are lovers," he confessed in a tone of quiet resignation. "That is but one of the many reasons I want you to go away with me. I would like you to leave Buenos Aires within a week. Listen to me, Denise, I beg you. I have loved you from the first, from the day I met you. Go to Paris and wait for me. You will never regret your decision as long as you live."

Denise stopped dancing. She couldn't move. Escobar led her toward the pool and helped her onto a chaise longue. Escobar took off his jacket and draped it around her shoulders. Her expression was vacant.

"Say something," Escobar whispered.

Denise's heart was beating wildly. She suddenly understood as if someone had drawn a diagram. "You have been very honest with me, Escobar. You have made your position quite clear. Now I must be equally honest with you and clarify mine." She looked up at him. "You have not taken into consideration Reinaldo, and, to be brutally frank, he is my only source of security." She wondered for an instant if she hadn't been too frank, played her cards too openly, showed a price tag. After all, whores didn't change the course of history; courtesans did.

"You don't love him," Escobar said impassively. It was a question.

"No," she replied quickly. She didn't mean to be so blunt, but she lacked any emotion, and it would have been too difficult to explain that she had never loved anyone in her life.

"I need you."

"Why?"

"I'm trying to find the reason for my need."

"And have you found it yet?"

"Not yet. It takes time, but I want to discover it with you. I want to show you the world. . . ."

"What do you expect of me?"

"Only to be yourself. And I will *give* you the world. If you agree to meet me, I'll deposit fifty thousand dollars in your name in a bank in Switzerland."

Denise felt a tightening in her stomach. She lowered her eyes for just a moment, then raised them very slowly without moving her head and locked her gaze into his. She took his hand and squeezed it gently. Escobar understood.

A week later Denise and Reinaldo attended a party marking Eva's birthday at the Perón's official residence, the old Palacio Unzue, which stood on the river's bank. Josephine Baker was performing for the occasion.

Eva, paler than usual, was making her way through the evening with considerable effort, smiling, being charming to all. At one point Eva saw Dr. Zarwarski, her private physician, huddling with Perón. She approached the two of them and, with arms crossed on her bosom, she demanded, "What are the two of you discussing?"

"I have been warning His Excellency that your condition is serious and that you must not continue working so hard."

"I told you that you were not to discuss my health with the President," she cried loudly. The voice that had incited the worshiping masses to frenzy was now harsh and ugly.

She picked up a wineglass from a nearby table and threw its contents into the doctor's face, then swept from the room like some great bird in flight, with Dr. Zarwarski following, wiping his dripping face with a napkin.

Denise and Janet, who had been chatting when the outburst occurred, were stunned at Eva's behavior. Perón approached them. "I hope you will forgive Eva. I'm afraid she is sick. Very sick. And refuses to admit it."

"I know," replied Denise. All three locked eyes knowingly. Eva Duarte de Perón was fighting terminal cancer. Fighting a losing battle.

May 29 was the day of Denise's departure. Everything had been prearranged to the most minute detail. With the exception of a small carry-on bag, her suitcases had been picked up the night before while she and Reinaldo dined at the presidential palace.

Denise felt her heart beat faster as she opened for the tenth time the small jewelry box containing the twenty-carat solitaire. Armando Cellis, Escobar's secretary, had brought it to her along with a numbered account from a reputable bank in Geneva, registering a fifty thousand-dollar deposit. She kissed the stone with a little squeal, creating a small cloud that momentarily obscured the glitter of the gem. With the phone cradled under her chin, breathing on the diamond, and polishing the jewel against the silky fabric of her blouse, she dialed Reinaldo at his office.

"Querido, Reinaldo . . . Hawh, hawh"—she breathed on the diamond again—"we're still meeting at the Alvear Palace bar tonight at eight-thirty? Hawh, hawh . . ."

"What is wrong with you, Denise? You seem out of breath."

"Ay, Dios mio! Why should I be out of breath, Reinaldo? I'm sitting right here at home. Hawh, hawh . . ."

"Of course, Denicita, we are still meeting tonight, and I will tell you where I think we . . ."

Denise was skimming the note once again that had accompanied the spectacular gift. It read: "It is your birthday in five days, and I want to be the first to . . ."

"Why, of course, Reinaldo, I'm listening to you."

". . . wish you all the happiness you should and will have. . . ."

"What was that, Reinaldo? Oh, yes, yes! That's a wonderful idea, Reinaldo! I love it! I'll see you later!"

". . . fondly, Escobar."

She sat down and wrote Reinaldo a short note, tore it up and wrote another, and another. On her fourth attempt she was finally satisfied, and sealed it in a plain white envelope.

Denise penned a second letter in Spanish:

Doña Eva Duarte de Perón   May 29, 1952
Palacio Unzue
Buenos Aires

Dear Señora Perón,

Please accept this modest gift as an expression of gratitude for the marvelous hospitality I have received in your country and in your home. I hope the Eva Perón Foundation can perhaps auction it off, and the proceeds be given in my name to your special division for the rehabilitation of wayward women, which cause I know to be closest to your charitable heart.

I am deeply proud to have met a woman such as yourself, who will surely be remembered in history along with Mrs. Eleanor Roosevelt and Madame Chiang Kai-shek, both of whom have done so much to alleviate the suffering of the underprivileged.

I wish you every success in your candidacy for the Vice-Presidency. May I respectfully ask you to convey my kindest regards to the President, truly one of the great men in the world.

Most sincerely,
Denise Cunningham

From the drawer of her Louis Philippe desk she took the gold medallion that Juan Domingo Perón had so generously given her at their first amorous encounter. She glanced once more at the profile of Evita etched on one side and the Libra scales on the other. She inserted the medallion, along with the letter, into an envelope, addressed it and marked it "strictly personal." She slid her tongue slowly over the glue of the flap and sealed it with a crafty smile.

It was noon when Denise entered the limousine. Winter was coming in Buenos Aires, but her excitement was such that she hardly felt the coolness of the air. Her first stop was the Alvear Palace Hotel. Denise left the white envelope with the concierge to be given to Reinaldo Vega that evening. She made another stop. At the presidential palace, leaving the letter for Eva with a guard.

The limousine continued down the wide Avenida Alvear through Palermo Park along the river, made a left turn onto the highway and sped toward the airport.

—✳—

Denise's thoughts were interrupted by a loud, impatient knocking at the door as Yvette cried excitedly, "Mademoiselle, Mademoiselle! Prince Borgia on the line!"

Denise's face lit up. She reached for the telephone, curbing her eagerness as she clutched it.

"Oh, darling Francesco. It's so good to hear your voice! What an unexpected pleasure," she said with affected surprise. "You did? . . . When? . . . Yvette never mentioned a word of it. I've been shopping for you all morning." In a flash she realized her error. So did Francesco.

"In New York many stores are open on Sunday!" Denise let out an inaudible sigh of relief. "Harry Winston? No, not yet. The Junker diamond! Francesco! The most spectacular diamond in the world! Your name was all I wanted, my beautiful darling—"

Her fingers released Escobar's letter, which fell to the floor, weightless, with the imperceptible rustling of a dead leaf fallen from an autumn tree.

MARIELA/*New York City/Sunday, January 31, 1954*

Nathan Berger was the best criminal lawyer money could buy. He wielded great power. His dramatic courtroom manner generally disconcerted his colleagues. The brilliance he concealed behind a vaguely baffled demeanor had earned him respect and envy.

It was Nathan Berger who had saved the famous movie star Georgina Royal when her gigolo lover was found in her bed, a knife plunged between his shoulder blades. And although it was proved beyond a shadow of a doubt that more than three hours had elapsed before police were notified, Berger succeeded in persuading the jury to believe Miss Royal's testimony that a stranger had entered her apartment while the two of them were asleep, murdered her young lover and then raped her. The publicity ended Georgina Royal's career but established Nathan Berger as one of the most gifted trial lawyers in the nation. Thereafter it was common knowledge that, when in trouble, one should hire West Coast ace attorney Geisler, but if in hopeless trouble, Berger was the man. He knew the right people and how to use them. His friends included alleged Mafia bosses, important politicians, scores of show-business, literary and sports celebrities.

An inveterate collector of memorabilia from the old American West, Nathan dressed at all times in the manner of a prosperous gambler in the booming days of Virginia City: a well-cut suit with a brightly colored lining, vest, handkerchief, string tie, custom-made alligator cowboy boots, and a red carnation always in his lapel.

Mariela arrived at Nathan Berger's apartment shortly after two o'clock. She was expecting to see him in his usual attire. Instead he met her at the door wearing a heavy gray wool sweater and corduroy pants, contrasting markedly with his customary flamboyance.

"Let's go to my study," he said without even a hello. "It's the only half-way comfortable room. This whole place is a mess. I'm redecorating."

Nathan's apartment was empty of furniture. Swatches of fabric and carpet samples were scattered everywhere. There was a pervasive odor of fresh paint. The study was a large and cozy room with a stone fireplace imported from England. Above it, a Frederic Remington bronze—four cowboys on horseback—sat on the mantel. Hundreds of books lined the shelves, lay in stacks on the desk and tables, were piled on the floor. Near the couch, on a large wooden crate that served as a temporary coffee table, two books were prominently displayed—*The Roman Code Viewed by a Common Law Addict,* by Nathan Berger, and *The History of Crime in the Old West,* also by Nathan Berger.

Berger sat next to Mariela on a dark-green leather chesterfield. Without any preliminaries he said, "Well, I've come all the way from Connecticut on your account, left my guests, was in the midst of cooking—which you may or may not know is one of my favorite pastimes—so the story better be a good one! Go ahead!"

Mariela squirmed and asked for a drink.

"What can I get you?"

"Vodka on the rocks," she said, removing her mink coat.

"Vodka it shall be." Nathan moved toward a turn-of-the-century teller's counter from a Carson City bank, which had been transformed into a cabinet bar.

"You'll join me, won't you?" Mariela asked.

"I've got no minor vices, Mariela. Not drink, anyway!" Nathan handed her the glass, walked to his imposing desk and sat on its edge. "Okay, Mariela, spill it. I want the truth, whatever it is, because only then can I advise you properly."

He studied her surreptitiously.

She sipped her drink, set the glass on the table and leaned forward cautiously. "You know about Karl Ravenstein?"

"Of course," Nathan replied. "Frankly, I'm glad the bastard finally got what he deserved, though, personally, I thought the penis in the aquarium was a bit Grand Guignol! I know you don't bite that hard!"

Mariela did not smile. She picked up her glass, cleared her throat of imaginary phlegm, tucked in her chin and, with studied directness, related the bizarre events of the previous evening. Nathan listened without stirring.

"What happened before you departed?"

"The three girls and the two men left first," Mariela said in a voice devoid of inflection. "I personally closed the front door behind them."

"Why you?"

Mariela's discomfort grew. "Karl asked me to. My role was to act as . . ."

She paused, searching for the right word. ". . . to act as his hostess," she continued. "Besides, the servants were either out or asleep. I returned to the playroom. Karl was stretched out on the bed. When I came in, he asked me to bring him some champagne. He was thoroughly exhausted."

"I'll bet he was!" Nathan observed cynically. "I'm exhausted just hearing the details of that intimate little party."

"Both of us," Mariela continued, "cleared up the mess. We returned to his bedroom and had some more smoked salmon and caviar. Karl mentioned that he was going to Miami and would be back on Monday morning. Then. . . ." She hesitated.

"Then what?" asked Nathan impatiently. "We haven't got all day!"

She fidgeted, apparently annoyed at his brusqueness. "When Karl was in the bathroom I emptied the contents of three Seconal capsules into the champagne. He drank it all and said he was too tired to see me out. I kissed him good night and waited until he was sound asleep, then went out of the house, leaving the front door unlatched."

"But why?" inquired Berger.

Mariela grew tense and slightly pale. "I was to get Karl's keys, or, if I couldn't find them, leave the front door unlatched. I couldn't find the keys." She waited for a reaction. There was none. Nathan was looking at Mariela with cold intensity. Her mouth was dry and she took a sip of her drink. "The signal was for me to drop a glove on Karl's doorstep when I left the house, and make a telephone call the moment I got to my apartment, to indicate that the door was open. I did both."

"Who answered your call?"

"No one did. No one was supposed to. It was merely a signal that the coast was clear, so to speak."

"What would you have done had you found the keys?"

"I'll come to that in a moment." She took a cigarette from her purse and lit it with a gold lighter.

"Mariela, stop telling the story your way," he demanded impatiently. "I want to hear it my way." He repeated the question. Mariela nodded apologetically.

"I would have put them in a large box wrapped in Bergdorf Goodman paper and left the box with my doorman with instructions about its being picked up. I would then have telephoned yet another number to establish that I had the keys."

"In other words, you set him up."

She slammed her glass on the table. "Certainly not to be murdered or even harmed," she asserted with vehemence.

Nathan raised his eyes slightly and stared at a small pattern on the wallpaper. "Who is the mastermind behind this plot?"

She sipped some of her vodka and said rapidly, "Jack Hamilton, a very highly placed businessman from Canada." She was disappointed when this revelation failed to produce a response.

Berger had succeeded in keeping the surprise from his face. "I know him. I drew up the contracts when several of his publishing companies in Europe, Canada and the States were amalgamated. What was the purpose of your, shall we call it . . . venture?"

Mariela glared at him defensively. To emphasize the secrecy of what she was about to disclose, she stood and closed the half-open door, then took a chair opposite Berger. She lowered her voice almost to a whisper. "It started a year ago. . . . Karl Ravenstein threw a large cocktail party. Jack Hamilton was one of the guests. He seemed very interested in me. I gave him my telephone number, and the following day we made a date. Jack took me to dinner at a small out-of-the-way bistro, for which he apologized, explaining he couldn't afford to be seen in my company, since he was married."

"Weren't you Karl's exclusive girl?" asked Nathan.

"Karl had many girls, and although he enjoyed me more than any other, we certainly didn't have a definite agreement. I saw other men."

"Always men of substance, naturally," said Nathan with a trace of contempt.

Mariela ignored the comment. "To my surprise, Jack never tried to get intimate with me. Nevertheless he gave me five hundred dollars each time we met."

"How many times did you meet?"

"Four or five times. Then, a month ago, he asked me if I was interested in making a lot of money with very little effort. 'It depends on what you mean by very little effort,' I said. 'All you'd have to do is arrange a small party at Karl's house when his help has the day off, and'—"

"Was Jack Hamilton aware of the kind of party Karl enjoyed best?"

"Yes," answered Mariela hurriedly. "I never hid my relationship with Karl, or the fact that we both enjoyed the same things. In any case, Jack told me that it would only entail my making sure Karl was asleep before I left the house. That's all. 'Completely harmless,' as he put it."

"Weren't you curious about his motives?" asked Nathan.

"Naturally. He told me Karl was a crook and had falsified several documents, which he held in his safe. Jack made me understand that he'd lose a great deal of money if these documents could not be retrieved. I was assured Karl couldn't complain about it to the police without admitting his own guilt in connection with these papers. Jack simply wanted to get back at Karl for his shady business practices. I gave it some thought and . . . of course, the money seemed quite a lot for so small a risk." Slowly Mariela lit another cigarette while Nathan remained discreetly silent. "About two weeks ago Jack Hamilton called me from Canada. 'Now is the time,' he said. 'Arrange this—this party for Saturday the thirtieth.' "

"Call it by its proper name," interrupted Nathan. "It's 'orgy,' isn't it?" He left his desk, gave a slight poke to the fire and perched himself on a stool.

"Well, whatever you call it. As Hamilton requested, I suggested it for that Saturday, and Karl more than willingly agreed."

"What about the signal?"

"Jack explained the way in which I should leave the house, slip Karl the Seconal, drop the white glove; he gave me the numbers to call. But I've already told you all about it." When Mariela finished her account of the events of the previous night, they were silent for a few moments.

Nathan asked, "How much did you get for this?"

"Ten thousand dollars. That was a month ago, when I agreed to the scheme. I'm supposed to get another fifteen thousand . . ." She hesitated.

"Meaning when?"

"Meaning today."

"What does Hamilton have to say about all this?" He posed the question skeptically, staring at the wallpaper.

"I don't know. I can't make out if it's an act or the truth, but he sounded genuinely surprised and shocked at the turn of events. I'm going to meet Hamilton at the Plaza after I leave you and—"

The sudden ring of a telephone interrupted their conversation, reverberating in Mariela's ears like a loud noise in a cathedral. She jumped, spilling some of her drink.

"Take it easy, it's only a phone in a lonely man's apartment," said Nathan with a dry humor that only irritated Mariela further. "Excuse me, I'll only be a moment."

Nathan walked to the other side of the room, sat again on the edge of his desk and picked up the phone. "Hello. . . . Why, Joyce baby, what gives me the pleasure of hearing from a 'long-stemmed rose' on Sunday?" Like a chameleon, his whole demeanor changed abruptly—the way he relaxed his body, the insouciance of his voice. "Well, if the Mighty Billy's out of town I'd be more than delighted to take you to dinner this evening —after all, what do I have to fear? I'm five eleven and he's only five four, and that's with his elevator shoes on!" He laughed, shifting the phone. Mariela noticed for the first time that the little finger on his left hand was missing. "Kidding aside, Joyce, you don't mind if Jack Dempsey tags along, do you? I've already made plans with him for tonight. . . . Good. I'll pick you up at eight sharp and we'll go to Luchow's. That's always fun on Sunday nights."

He hung up and wheeled around, the interruption already out of his mind. "Now, listen to me," said Nathan to Mariela, plunging again into a serious, businesslike tone. "You came to me for advice because you know I'm the best. Listen to me carefully." And as though to give her time to prepare herself for what he was about to say, he got up and placed another log on the fire. "Do you have any witnesses who can testify as to the time you returned home?"

"Yes, two," she answered.

"Perhaps you can be a little more specific."

"The chauffeur picked me up at twenty past midnight, and the doorman knows that I entered the lobby of my building at half past midnight"— Mariela shifted her gaze—"because I deliberately asked him the time."

"Fortunately for you, you're unknown in New York. You've been leading a prosperous—"

Mariela raised her hand and was about to speak.

"Shut up, Mariela, and let me finish! You've been leading a prosperous, discreet and anonymous life. That's in your favor. I'll help you—in fact, I'm the only one who can. But it will cost money." Nathan glanced at her. "Remember this as long as you live: favors received free prove in the long run to be the most expensive. I shall not do you any favors. Some people will have to be paid off as well." He sat in the chair behind his desk.

Trying to camouflage her apprehension, Mariela purposely modulated her voice. "How much?"

"You've already gotten ten thousand dollars. Correct?"

"Correct."

"You're about to receive another fifteen. Right?"

"Right."

"That makes twenty-five grand in all. Yes?"

"Yes."

"My fee will be half of that in cash. Agreed?"

"Agreed."

"Have you spoken about this to anybody besides myself and Jack Hamilton?"

"Yes," she said. "On Jack's advice I made a telephone call to a . . . ah . . . a powerful political figure."

"Don't play charades with me, Mariela. We don't have time to waste. Would I be wrong in assuming your powerful political figure is a senator with the initials G.A.?"

"How did you know I was friendly with Glover Anderson?"

"It's my business to know. That's why I'm the best. Personally, I can't stand the whole Anderson family. They're all involved with themselves, from the father up!" Nathan continued. "What is it you wanted from Glover?"

"I asked him to use his influence to keep me from getting adverse publicity."

Nathan leaned back in his chair and roared. "Well, 'adverse publicity' is putting it mildly. Before you prevent adverse publicity, you have to prevent yourself from being arrested."

"Could I possibly be arrested?"

"*Possibly?*" he said. "It's a certainty. You're an accessory to murder."

"But how? I was used. It was involuntary!"

"Mariela, you may know a lot about sex, but you know nothing about law! There is no such thing as *involuntary accessory to murder*. Your case is similar to one in which a murder is committed during a robbery. Even if no murder was intended, all the robbers in such a case are *guilty* of accessory to murder, or felony murder, which is to say, *murder.*"

Mariela felt slightly sick. "What do I have to do?" She got up awkwardly, went toward the bar, refilled her glass, and came back to her seat.

"First we have to find the right district attorney and see how much influence Glover Anderson has with him."

"How can I find out?"

"Don't ask such idiotic questions, Mariela. That's my department! I believe I've got our man. I should get a definite answer shortly. Just go to your meeting with Jack Hamilton, get your money—"

"But . . . I don't understand," faltered Mariela.

Berger continued, oblivious to her words. "Call me as soon as you get home. I'll see you in my office at nine tomorrow morning. My secretary will put you down in the book under your maiden name." Nathan paused briefly. "It's Lady Chelmsford, if I'm not mistaken."

Mariela's eyes showed how amazed she was.

"Well, isn't it?"

"But—but nobody knows that," she whispered. "How did . . . ?"

"I know a lot more," he interrupted. "A *lot* more!"

"Why use the name Lady Chelmsford?" she asked.

"I know what I'm doing," said Nathan. "In case the press should get wind of Mariela Koenig and Karl Ravenstein, at least no one would connect you with Lady Chelmsford."

"But you led me to believe there would be no publicity," she said haltingly.

"I certainly did not mislead you. I simply want to cover all eventualities. When will you be in touch with Glover again?"

"He's calling me tonight."

"Good! Be sure to get back to me after your conversation with Hamilton and I'll give you the name of a certain district attorney who will be indispensable to us. I'll count on you to have Glover exert the right pressure on him. Of course I have my own methods for exerting a little pressure as well." His dark eyes were now mere slits. "But I'll tell you my plan later."

Nathan stood up, putting an end to the meeting. Mariela finished her vodka hurriedly and looked at the clock on the mantelpiece. It was 3:40. She had time to walk to the Plaza for her appointment with Jack Hamilton.

Nathan opened the door to let her out, his hand resting on the gleaming doorknob. "I will help you as I said I would," he assured her, "because I assume you've told me the truth. Please don't misunderstand me. I have made a great career defending people who I knew were guilty, but only because they admitted it to me was I able to evaluate which course of action I had to take."

He grabbed Mariela's wrists and looked intently into her eyes. "Do not make a fool of me, Mariela. You could not afford the repercussions." His voice was abrasive and she detected a hint of mistrust.

"I've told the truth, Nathan. Don't you believe me?" Her voice broke. "I swear it. . . . I swear it."

"Where did you say Jack Hamilton is staying?"

"I didn't say." She looked at him in surprise. "Jack's at the Hampshire House."

When Mariela reached the lobby she paused to pull up her fur-lined snow boots and put on her gloves.

Outside, the bitter cold and piercing wind engulfed her with sobering force. She clutched her fur coat closer to her body, still determined to walk the eleven blocks to the Plaza Hotel. Her stride was brisk.

But just as brisk was the stride of the two heavily dressed men who trailed Mariela.

The doorman at the Plaza, dignified and resplendent in a navy-blue overcoat trimmed with maroon, guided Mariela up the slippery steps of the hotel's Fifth Avenue entrance. The overheated foyer jolted Mariela with a blast of hot air, taking her breath away like the unexpected sight of a welcoming lover.

Once inside the lobby, her eyes were drawn to an ornately carved table. On it, in an Oriental vase, was an arrangement of tiger lilies so like one that had decorated Karl Ravenstein's dining room the previous night that it startled her.

She draped her fur coat over her shoulders and stamped her boots to remove the snow. Behind her, the two heavily dressed men entered on the Central Park South side of the hotel. They too shook the snow from their boots and removed their overcoats.

Mariela glanced quickly to her left at the placard in front of the darkened Persian Room, noting the current attraction: Kay Thompson and the Williams Brothers. She quickened her step. The entrance she made into the Palm Court was as red paint spilled on an old, faded masterpiece: all eyes turned to her and conversations fell to whispers.

Jack Hamilton had not yet arrived. Mariela nervously looked at her wristwatch. Ten past four. Could she have been mistaken? Perhaps he had meant the Edwardian Room. She walked impatiently toward it, looked inside, but he wasn't there either. No point going to the Oak Room; women weren't allowed.

Returning to the Palm Court, she sat down at a small round marble-topped table with a wrought-iron base and fingered the single bloom in a crystal rosebud vase. Artificial sunlight, filtered through the wheat-colored glass roof, flooded the court—a genteel garden of antiquity, glass and mirrors in which baroque green, delicate gold, muted beige and faded pink melted like a special bouquet, the kind one rediscovers in an attic, recalling a luminous memory. It did nothing of the sort for Mariela, however. The European elegance of the surroundings merely intensified the darkness of her mood.

Most of the clientele were elderly ladies, young children with governesses, honeymooners, schoolboys on vacation with their mothers, rich tourists and blank New York faces hiding from each other. Noel Coward and Gertrude Lawrence huddled discreetly at a corner table. In homage to the star of *The King and I,* two musicians played "Hello, Young Lovers." The violin's grating strings increased Mariela's anxiety. She moved her chair sideways, the better to scrutinize each new arrival.

"Excuse me," a cultured voice asked, "do you by any chance have a match?" Mariela turned toward the sound to see a suburban lady sitting at the next table. She wore a flowery hat designed by someone who had heard of flowers but obviously had never seen any.

"I haven't a match, but allow me to offer my lighter," she replied distractedly.

"Thank you very much," said the lady. "You are most kind . . ." Her gaze had shifted slightly to the right. Mariela whirled around to see Jack Hamilton sitting next to her.

"You're late!" Mariela sounded accusing.

"Late! Only a few minutes. Why even mention it?" He removed a cigarette from his case. "I've had one hell of a day and I must tell you—"

"It hasn't been particularly easy for me," she snapped.

"Have you spoken with the senator?"

"Will you lower your voice! Yes, I have spoken with him, and Glover will—" A waiter dressed in black trousers, white waistcoat and green cummerbund approached carrying a pastry tray.

"Can I take your order, please?"

"A Scotch and soda," Mariela replied, selecting the richest piece of cake.

"Make it a double for me," Hamilton said. "No cake."

"Glover will help me, and I've just seen an attorney who pulls a lot of weight in New York."

"Don't tell me! By any chance, could it be Nathan Berger?"

"Precisely."

"You don't find them any more crooked than that!" he sneered. "He's a master at dirty pool."

"It depends which side he's fighting for. Like partisans in the underground. If we agree with them, they are freedom fighters; if we don't, we call them guerrillas. Nathan's the same. If he's on your side, he's a genius. If he represents the enemy, you call him a crook. He wins. That's what matters." She was lighting her third cigarette.

"You're right, Mariela. You're absolutely right," Hamilton said acidly.

The drinks arrived and the two fell into uncomfortable silence. Mariela drank down the amber liquid and immediately ordered another.

"I don't blame you for being nervous. We're in a lot of trouble," Hamilton said.

"I don't know what you mean by *we*," she whispered. Her fingers twitched at the stem of the glass. "*We* never had a partnership to commit murder, and if for one moment you thought so, *do* accept my resignation." Despite her composure, there was a note of fright in her voice.

Jack Hamilton bent forward ominously and, placing his arms on the table, continued slowly and forcefully. "But wouldn't it be fair to assume that you're somewhat involved, and that the term *we* is certainly apropos?" he asked, taunting her.

"Jack, there's a lot to clear up, and I expect truthful answers." She eyed him nervously. Everything within her was waiting for something to happen.

"I'll be as truthful as you are, my dear," he replied with mock kindness. "There are a few things I'd like to ask you as well."

Mariela's gaze wandered toward the entrance. She noticed two stout men, their overcoats over their arms, standing between the Corinthian marble columns. Their shabby dark suits and wool caps contrasted with the elegantly dressed patrons of the Plaza. Spotting Mariela, they whispered to each other and departed awkwardly.

"First things first, Jack," she said stiffly as she slowly, delicately took a mirror from her purse, as if she were handling a precious relic. "Wouldn't you agree that in this . . . this project, I've been most . . . meticulous?"

"Of course, of course," said Jack. "But—"

"We had a bargain, didn't we?" She raised her head, looking straight at him.

"I've never reneged on a deal."

"I think I've earned—" She wiped the corners of her mouth and repaired her lipstick. "I think I've earned the balance."

"You don't have to go any further," he said, opening his attaché case and handing her a manila envelope. "It's all there. If—"

"I trust you." She didn't. "You realize that a great deal of this money will now have to be spent on other people." Her voice quavered. "I had nothing to do with murder!"

"Unfortunately, Mariela, our relationship *cannot* be terminated. Far from it." Hamilton spoke carefully, like a knight advancing on a chessboard.

"I . . . I don't know what you are talking about," she stammered, suddenly engulfed by a black tide of apprehension.

"Needless to say, things have not worked out as we had planned."

"At this point I am not at all sure what *you* planned. And stop this *we* business. I only followed your instructions, which were supposed to have no really harmful results. All I know is that I'm through!" She swallowed hard on the remainder of the pastry.

"Don't play games, Mariela. Don't." He gave her a forced smile and continued. "We got the papers we wanted from the safe, but—"

"Well, what's the problem, then?" Mariela asked with a look of surprise. "I thought all you were interested in was retrieving those contracts Karl had." The violinist strolled by playing his version of the "Blue Danube."

Hamilton hesitated. "The problem is that a million dollars are missing."

"A million dollars!" she exclaimed incredulously. "Is this your idea of some crazy practical joke?" His defiant glare was her answer. "But Jack, how would you know he had that kind of money in his house?" she gasped, touched by panic.

"Because, Miss Wide Eyes," he said sarcastically, "we knew that on Saturday, Ravenstein would make a cash transaction at his mansion, at about six o'clock in the evening, and we know for a fact that nobody on his staff left his place afterward. The money *had* to be in the safe."

"I hope you're not intimating I had anything to do with having it opened!" she hissed.

"I'm not intimating any such thing," he said calmly. "The safe was already open when my people arrived at his house." He gulped his drink.

"Then you *are* a liar, Jack! You weren't just after some documents."

"What we were after is none of your business, my dear. Or could it be that you felt underpaid after seeing the money?" He hurled the last words at her. "What time did you say you left Ravenstein, Mariela?"

"I never said when I left. But, if you remember, we spoke on the telephone about twelve-thirty, when I'd just gotten home and you were checking into your hotel. I have witnesses to prove it. I know nothing about the money, and I had nothing to do with the murder."

"Well, I wouldn't exactly—"

She continued. "The awful thing about all this is, believe it or not, I liked Ravenstein. We spoke the same language."

"I doubt if he paid you as highly as he did merely for your conversational skills!"

She attacked in a low voice, looking around to be sure no one was listening. "You know very little about me, Jack. Nor does anyone. That's how it should be. Listen to what I'm going to tell you." Her voice took on an intimate tone. "Sex is cheap, vice is not. It travels almost exclusively in the upper echelons. It is refined, varied, exciting, enjoyable and expensive."

"In other words, you make a lot of money out of it!"

"That shows how naïve you are, Jack! Money has nothing to do with sexuality." Her hands were damp. "I don't know why I'm opening myself to you at a time like this." Her discomfort grew as Jack remained silent. She felt frightened. "I would never have been a partner to murder! Money has never been a catalyst for me."

Thrown off by this sudden confession, Hamilton took out his handkerchief, pretending to cough into it. "Now let me tell you a few things," he said very quietly. "Ravenstein was the most despicable person who ever lived. The ink on any contract he signed didn't have time to dry before he welshed on the deal. After his father died he cheated his own mother and let her die in poverty."

"How can that be?" asked Mariela. "I've seen the glamorous portraits of her at his mansion."

"All done before his father died. Each one painted before he was able to grab every penny she had!" His calm suddenly changed to savage rage. "He screwed me out of millions when we merged some of my companies. Millions!" he repeated. But I'll say this for the rotten devil, he was bright! Yes, goddammit, he was brilliant! And oversexed! But I did not have him killed." Lowering his voice to a menacing whisper, he said, "Mariela, *we* will find out who has the million dollars. I mean *I* will find out—and soon! I just hope for your sake that it isn't you."

They were suddenly very quiet.

"Mariela, I need you for one more thing." His face was expressionless; it was like an empty room. Mariela flashed a look of dismay. He continued. "We have obtained Karl's Swiss bank account number, as well as certain papers necessary for access to it. I cannot involve any more people in this . . . affair. I wish to transfer some of the funds to—"

"To your account, no doubt!"

He ignored her remark. "There's a lot in it for you. What do you say?"

She took one of his cigarettes, lit it, and raised her eyes to him. "I refuse to participate in any swindle. I categorically refuse."

"Mariela, you don't understand." Solicitously he moved the ashtray closer to her. "You really have no choice in the matter. No choice whatsoever." He finished the rest of his drink. "You *will* be leaving for Europe soon." He spoke without fear and with utter determination.

"I have no intention of—"

"Of what?"

"I have no intention of going to Europe at this time," she said assertively, blowing the smoke uncomfortably near his face.

"Perhaps you'll change your mind, Mariela. I think you will."

"Jack, you don't seem to realize what kind of trouble I'm in."

"I don't believe you have to worry about a damn thing. Your good name won't be dragged through the mud. They'd be too scared of frying you because of your powerful friends. The FBI must be aware that your connections go all the way up to—"

"I know how far they go," she snapped angrily, then was taken aback by the loudness of her own voice.

"I hope I'm not interrupting," a throaty voice rasped behind Hamilton. Turning around in his chair, he saw it was Carla, the so-called Gypsy fortune-teller, legendary at the Plaza, strolling among the tables in the Palm Court. Rumor had it that Carla lived in a penthouse apartment on Sutton Place. "Perhaps you'd allow me to tell the beautiful lady's future?" Without hesitating an instant, Jack wisecracked, "The beautiful lady is my wife. She has no future!" Mariela laughed her deep, sensual laugh. Marveling at his self-possession, she said, "How can you make jokes at a time like this!" Carla slunk away.

Hamilton twirled his empty glass pensively. "By the way, Mariela, how's your father?"

She turned nine shades of white. "Why . . . why do you ask that?"

"Oh, nothing. I was merely inquiring after His Lordship's health." She stared at him in a mute trance.

"Still living in the south of France, eh? Unable to return to the homeland? It's really a shame! After all, the war is far behind us, and political beliefs should be forgiven. Have I said something wrong, Lady Chelmsford? You look as if you've seen a ghost. Dear Mariela, I wouldn't divulge your secret for the world. . . . Not unless I *have* to." Jack radiated the heat of bad faith and anger. "How soon do you think you can conveniently leave for Switzerland?" He looked at her with cold pleasure.

Mariela was virtually in shock. "I need another drink," she said.

"I was just going to suggest it," he said, motioning the waiter for another round. She was still trembling.

"I have to call my attorney as soon as—"

"Don't be so fucking formal! His name is Nathan," Jack said, raising his voice now.

Mariela told him what little she knew of Nathan's plans. Hamilton reflected for a few seconds. "Goddammit, that Nathan is a clever son of a bitch. Clever son of a bitch!"

The drinks arrived. "Here's to Switzerland," he toasted mockingly. Mariela kept her glass on the table. "We'd better not leave together," he said. "Otherwise I would gladly drop you off in my car."

"I thought you were going back to Toronto tonight."

"There are too many things to take care of, Mariela, including the small matter of a million dollars." Jack Hamilton paid the check. "I'll call you within the hour," he said, rising abruptly. "I want the name of everyone who attended your—soirée." He hesitated. "Anyway, be prepared for the shit to hit the fan when the papers come out." He kept on. "You didn't respond to my irresistible offer about Switzerland. It should be lovely this time of year. Your complexion would rival the snow."

"I won't be going, Jack."

Hamilton departed without another word.

Mariela remained another ten minutes, exhausted and listless, smoking mechanically. Drained of all energy, she desperately focused her concentration on analyzing the situation. After a short while the awful throbbing in her throat seemed to quiet. One ominous thought remained. *Jack Hamilton needed her and would not hesitate to use blackmail to achieve his aim.*

It was nearly six o'clock by the time Mariela left the hotel. Freckles of rain had been falling. The city was lighting herself for the night, donning her jewels, gem by gem, and wrapping her cold shoulders in a somber cottony fog.

Mariela was fortunate to find a taxi waiting at the stand outside the Plaza. Arriving at her building, she paid the fare, automatically peering up to her fourth-floor apartment. The living room lights were on. She saw it as reassurance. Good! The maid hadn't left yet! But her pleasure was short-lived; the maid *didn't* work on Sunday. Mariela raised her eyes again. Perhaps I've been looking at the wrong window, she thought. But there had been no mistake. Could I have forgotten to turn off the lights? she wondered, trying to quiet her apprehension. The question answered itself. She had left the apartment at one-thirty in the afternoon. Broad daylight! Distraught, Mariela entered the building.

"Gabe," she said to the doorman, profoundly agitated, "is there some reason why the superintendent would have gone into my apartment today?"

"I don't believe so, Miss Koenig. The super's been out since early this morning and won't be back till late tonight. It's his day off." Going behind the desk, he continued jovially, "But I have a package for you." He reached for what appeared to be a large bouquet of flowers in a vase, wrapped in pale-green tissue paper. "Why don't you go to your apartment, and I'll have it sent up."

Her fingers trembled as she inched the key into the lock. Mariela always left her flat double-locked. It was not double-locked now. She entered tentatively, then muffled a cry. The living room had been ransacked. Papers and books were strewn about, and the contents of a mother-of-pearl escritoire had been flung on the floor. Fright and sickness clutched at her.

She ran to the bedroom and put the light on. The closets had been turned inside out. Furs and dresses were piled in a heap. The drawers of the dressing table and chest were emptied. Mariela's specialist wardrobe of leather and rubber, including all the accouterments of a dominatrix—whips, chains, padlocks, handcuffs, straps, masks and truncheons—were scattered. The wall safe had been forced open, but its contents, including the jewels worn the night before, were untouched. The portrait of her father, Lord Chiselhurst, twelfth Duke of Chelmsford, by Augustus John, which usually concealed the safe, was leaning against the fireplace. The picture had been crudely slashed. A dildoe was stuck through it, dripping with what looked like blood. A photograph of a smiling teenaged boy, framed in silver, its glass defaced with a scrawled, mocking inscription, *Oliver = Bastard,* lay on the floor. Several bottles of her favorite fragrance, Golden Amber, had been broken, and its scent intermingled with a vaguely familiar smell that sickened her.

Mariela, unnerved, invaded by indescribable terror and revulsion, did not know what to do or where to look first. The putrid odor nauseated her. She looked timorously to the right and to the left without moving. Her eyes surveyed the room, the bed, the chaise longue, the vanity table, the bed again. She was aghast. She could not believe her eyes. Someone had emptied his bowels, in a pile, right in the center of her pink bedspread. She barely made it to the bathroom, fell to her knees, and vomited into the toilet. Then she turned on the tap and splashed her face and neck with cold water.

Mariela rushed to the living room, got as far as the liquor cabinet, and picked up the brandy. Unable to find a glass, she gulped four times from the bottle. She fell into a chair and fumbled a cigarette out of a box. The doorbell and the telephone rang simultaneously. She took another drink from the bottle before picking up the phone.

"Hello . . . hello . . . ," she answered dully. Perspiration was running down her flushed face. The cigarette she held in her quivering lips fell on the rug. Bending down to retrieve it, she dropped the phone, and it banged loudly on a small marble table. The doorbell rang impatiently. It took all her strength just to stand up.

"Hell . . . hello." There was no sound at the other end of the line. "Who is this? Hello. Who is this?" she repeated, trying hard to sound as natural as possible. The doorbell rang again, more insistently. She heard a click and slammed the phone down.

Mariela went to the door. It was the handyman with her package.

"Shall I bring this in for you?"

"No, no!" she insisted. "I can manage!" The very last thing Mariela wanted at that moment was for anyone to enter and view the suspicious disarray. "I'm sorry, I haven't got any change, George. Bring me the early-morning papers as soon as they arrive, and I'll take care of you later." She dismissed him hurriedly.

Mariela placed the bouquet on the alabaster credenza. Panic returned in fresh waves as she cautiously peeled back each layer of the crisp paper. Finally the contents spread in full glory before her. It was an elaborate arrangement of tiger lilies. Frenetically she looked for the sender's card. There was none. A long white envelope was attached by a ribbon to a stem. It was bulky, and Mariela ripped it open. It was a glove—the white glove she had dropped the night before on Karl Ravenstein's front step.

⁕

MATTIE/*New York City/Sunday, January 31, 1954*

Mattie needn't have worried about feeling lonely on Sunday afternoon and evening, because she slept almost until midnight. In a quarter of an hour it would be Monday. She felt terrible. Her mouth was parched from the Nembutal and she had a slight headache.

Above all, she was hungry, but halfway to the refrigerator she remembered that it was empty. Slipping on a pair of jeans, a sweater that she retrieved from a heap, boots and her mother's last mink coat, she walked briskly to the Third Avenue Pizzeria, where she ordered a pizza with "everything on it." Then she stopped at the Fifty-third Street all-night newsstand

and got *Variety* and the *Daily Mirror*. The headline glared at her: "Karl Ravenstein Slain at Fifth Avenue Mansion." She had never heard of him, but what captured her imagination was a photograph of a man entering the Sixty-seventh Street Precinct. The same elegant man whom she had seen on Saturday night getting into a limousine at La Guardia. His full name, she learned, was Jack Hamilton.

Mattie returned to her apartment, searched everywhere for matches and found some under the bed. "El Borracho" was printed on the matchbook cover; she couldn't remember ever being there. After lighting the oven to warm up the pizza she returned to the living room, piled up the rehearsal clothes, set them aside, lay down on the couch and propped up her feet. The Ravenstein murder captured her imagination like a detective story. "Most Unwanted Man in America Meets Brutal Death," read one headline. Before continuing, Mattie reached into her bag for a leather pouch, rolled a joint and settled back to relish the details. "Financier Found Dead by Butler."

"Just like in the movies," she said to herself as she read that Ravenstein's body had been discovered nude, lying on its back, beaten and mutilated. His arms and legs had been trussed with a cord from his own Venetian blind and his mouth had been sealed with adhesive tape. He had also been stabbed seven times, and his bedroom was found ransacked, along with his second-floor study, where the safe had been forced open.

According to columnist Herman Lorn, Karl Ravenstein had had so many enemies—made through his various shady business schemes—that the list of suspects "had been narrowed down to ten thousand."

Lorn reported that the police had discovered several personal address books containing hundreds of names, among them those of politicians and virtually every call girl and madam in town. Mattie was enthralled. A police official was quoted as saying that "although robbery would appear to be the motive, none of the priceless objects that filled the lavish mansion had been touched. Consequently, it could have been a crime of revenge: Ravenstein might have been killed by extortionists as a result of a shakedown that he reneged on."

Suddenly the room filled with smoke. Mattie rushed to the kitchen and discovered it was coming from grease that had spilled onto the oven before her departure for Toronto. She turned off the oven and opened the kitchen window wide. Removing the pizza and pouring the remainder of the wine into a glass, she consumed both standing by the sink. She called the liquor store to order another bottle of wine, received no reply and banged down the phone, realizing it was almost one A.M.

Mattie picked up the script of *Pajama Game* and read the scene in which the leading man, played by John Raitt, tries to date Gladys, the secretary, the role Mattie hoped to land. She rehearsed a few steps of "Steam Heat," then sat at her piano, playing and singing "Hernando's Hideaway," which was one of the hits of the show. Her last *Olé* was interrupted by someone on the floor above banging heavily on her ceiling with what sounded like the handle of a broom. A couple of more *olés* and she stopped.

After cleaning the ring around the tub Mattie took a bath, changed the sheets and stuffed the old ones into the overfilled hamper. She put some Sinatra and Sammy Davis records and the first Tony Rook album on the stereo. Her hair in rollers, she washed down a Nembutal with a shot of whiskey, the taste of which she detested. Then she called her service and requested a wake-up call for ten o'clock that morning.

Mattie lay on the bed, still groggy from the drugs of the previous night, and hoped that sleep would soon transport her to oblivion. But she wasn't tired. She thought of Tony and his hard body, his beautiful mouth, his incredible lovemaking. Suddenly Mattie felt an infinite sadness. Let's face it, she reflected, my life is really a mess. She got up and went to the bathroom, picked up an eyebrow tweezer and plucked out some stray hairs. Returning to bed, Mattie closed her eyes the better to imagine Tony.

He appeared to her in different sizes, tall when he entered her apartment, medium as he sat in the armchair with a drink in his hand and his knees spread apart, his eyes watching her quietly like a cat stalking a bird. Nothing, she thought, is more eloquent in a man than silence. Tony always appeared smaller to her in the mornings when she awoke and looked at him as he slept.

They had met in New Orleans eight months earlier when he was performing at the Blue Room at the Roosevelt Hotel and she at the Golden Lily on Bourbon Street. Their encounters were short and far between. She could hardly wait for Wednesday, when Tony would be in town for a week, and she anticipated all the things they would enjoy together. She knew he liked the jazz groups at The Embers or Eddie Condon's, and getting a ringside table at the Copa, where his pals Dean Martin and Jerry Lewis were now appearing. They would have some Chinese food and make love. "Oh, boy!" she thought. "Will I make love to him!" She was determined to drive him crazy, so that when the name of Mattie Maxwell was mentioned to him he would shudder with pleasure and something akin to love would inundate him in a warm glow.

Of course the affair couldn't last. She knew that. Too many things kept them apart. They really knew so little about each other. Their time together was devoted to making love and sitting in clubs watching other entertainers. There was much she wanted to tell him about herself and learn about him, but there was never an occasion. Tony's career was just taking off, his first L.P. album having been personally financed by Jeremy Rabb. Whatever the cost, Mattie was determined to take her own career to the height of the profession, even though at times she sensed that nothing was more important than love.

But love was a lie—a lie she enjoyed believing. She seldom had time for soul-searching and thought to herself: I'm a lie that always tells the truth. Suddenly her eyes popped open and she giggled as she said aloud, "What a good title for a song—'A Lie That Always Tells the Truth.'" She tossed restlessly until, at last, the drugs blurred Tony's image. It was nearly four o'clock in the morning when she finally fell asleep.

She expected to dream about Tony, but instead she dreamed about Jack Hamilton, the suave stranger at the airport whose picture was all over the papers. He was waiting for her in white tails in the lobby of her building. "Oh, Miss Maxwell, how ravishing you look," Jack told her as she breezed out of the elevator, which was working for a change. Her waist-length hair had been coiffed like Rita Hayworth's in *Gilda,* and she wore a skin-tight purple sheath with opera-length gloves to match. Impulsively she launched into a raunchy rendition of "Put the Blame on Mame, Boys," also from *Gilda.* Hamilton applauded and helped her into the purple velvet interior of his limousine.

"Now, Miss Maxwell," he said, brushing her shoulders with his lips, "what will be your pleasure tonight?"

"El Morocco of course," she replied imperiously.

"Anything the star of *Pajama Game* desires."

At El Morocco the chauffeur opened the car door, and she swept to the entrance of the club, only to see a large sign, *Closed for Renovation.* She turned around. Jack Hamilton, his white tails, and the limousine had vanished. Desolate and famished, she ran to a Nedick's fast-food stand on the corner and asked grandly for the Orange Room. The other patrons started to laugh at her, and the laughter became louder and louder until Mattie awoke from her strange dream.

***

VLADIMIR/*Leningrad*/*Monday, February 1, 1954*

It was six o'clock in the morning in Leningrad and still dark. The four hundred drawbridges over the Neva were down again and already taking traffic. On Peace Square the statues were covered by wooden boards to keep them from being split by the bitter winter frost. Number 20 Sadovaya Street was a peculiar shade of green—almost the green of a crushed avocado. It still bore naked holes made by the shellfire of World War II.

On the third floor Vladimir Volodin took a quick look at his cell-like room. Everything was in order: the iron bed, its brown blankets neatly folded over the thin mattress. To his left a chair piled with books. One small table with a metal washbasin. An unshaded bulb hanging from the ceiling. He shut off the light, went out and closed the door.

Varvara Pavlovna Volodin was dressing next to her mahogany bed. "Volik," she shouted through the wall, "don't go back to sleep. It's already six-thirty. If you have classes at eight—"

"I'm up, Mamushka." He was listening to the beautiful voice, now slightly deepened with age. Vladimir glanced at the night vapor still misting the small kitchen window and rubbed it with his sleeve. It was cold in the room. His mother walked in and silently gathered kindling to light the iron stove. Mouth tight, teeth clenched, Vladimir helped her by shaking down the gray remains of yesterday's warmth.

They sat at the rectangular pinewood table and had breakfast: tea and black bread spread with a thin coating of fat sprinkled with sugar. As usual, his mother was talking to him about the ugliness of life. Every morning she gave him the same terrible gift: mistrust and suspicion. "Volik, don't waste your time with girls. All of them are without hearts and will only use you! It is their only goal—to use you!" She crossed her arms on her bosom. "Keep your mind on your studies, Volik. Don't make any mistake about it. Beneath her clever wiles, it's really the woman who pursues the man. Yes, yes, it is really the woman. You mustn't stop and listen to their lies. Always walk faster, always walk alone. Always faster, always alone." Vladimir was the receptacle of her grief, rage, love. An ocean of goodwill receiving a river of mistrust and suspicion.

Absentmindedly, Vladimir was thumbing through a copy of Dostoyevsky's *The Adolescent*. His mother gave him a look. He understood its meaning as clearly as if she had spoken. "You are not paying attention, Volik!" And yet he was. He understood all the pictures she painted. And he would never forget.

Vladimir Mikhailovich Volodin, only fourteen, was once again undergoing her ordeal. Ever since he could recall, his mother suffered in the past tense as well as the present. No one could surpass Varvara Pavlovna Volodin in courage. Unconcerned about ice, wind, hunger, war, she simply could not forgive another woman for still having a man of her own, for still desiring a man, when destiny had taken from her the only one she had ever loved. Mikhail Nikolaevich Volodin.

She was so very brave during the nine hundred days of the Leningrad siege, when she worked day and night to get scarce food for her family. Varvara, her old mother, Nina, one-year-old Vladimir and his eleven-year-old brother Alexei occupied a single room in a huge communal apartment at 42 Sadovaya Street. Varvara was still ashamed when she remembered the way they had survived during those famished years. Their neighbor was a warehouseman from a pastry factory. A stern, unsociable man, who came home every night loaded with gingerbread and biscuits carefully concealed in his specially designed pants. The edible trophies were preserved in a large locked suitcase. Once Varvara found where the keys were hidden, she started stealing the invaluable delicacies, exchanging them for frozen cabbage and artificial milk. When her theft was discovered, Varvara, undaunted, started hunting rats. Thus all survived. Except Mikhail Nikolaevich Volodin.

He was killed during the first month of the war on the Leningrad front. The letter announcing his death arrived only at the end of '44. Until then Varvara never lost hope that her Mikhail would return. She was expecting a miracle, but he was gone. Forever. Her life lost all gaiety, and ever since her early widowhood all her love for the lost Mikhail was concentrated on Vladimir and Alexei.

She forbade herself even the thought of a new marriage; the photographs of Mikhail, covering most of the wall in the new two-room apartment, seemed to watch vigilantly over her every step and impulse. Anyway, what kind of marriage was possible after the war, when there were hardly any men to be found on the deserted Leningrad streets? Besides, she didn't want her sons to have a *step*father. When her mother, Nina, died and Alexei went away to Kiev University, Vladimir became the center of Varvara's life.

"Now hurry, Volik. Do you have your hat, your rubber boots, your scarf? Let me help you with your coat." Vladimir was by the door. "Kiss your father goodbye." She brought to his lips, as she did daily, a framed picture of her smiling Mikhail in a greenish uniform. "What time will you return, Volik?"

"Around nine."

"Why nine if school finishes at six?"

"I have a rehearsal and I want to stop by the library."

Since the age of seven Vladimir had read incessantly, grabbing from the shelves volumes of Tolstoy, de Maupassant, Chekhov—whatever remained of the once large home library, which was burned, like the rest of the furniture, in the iron stove during the ferocious blockade winters.

Vladimir walked briskly on the icy street past Peace Square, which, like his mother, he persevered in calling Haymarket Square, its name in the old days of St. Petersburg. In his imagination he could still hear the sounds of the extinct bazaar where Russian peasants and merchants purchased hay and harness for their horses, drank vodka and enjoyed themselves. Now the area stretched in front of Vladimir like an asphalt pancake, mutilated by the streetcar lines going down Sadovaya toward the noble austerity of Nevsky Prospekt.

He hopped on bus No. 13, which, as usual, was filled to overflowing, and stood there pressed from every side, his feet trampled on mercilessly. Vladimir got off in front of the public library, a severe, gray building where he'd spent hours and hours going through old magazines on ballet and art. Behind this sanctuary of knowledge the Alexandrovsky Garden unfolded its frozen, white beauty. In its center stood a bronze statue of Catherine the Great holding her scepter in regal solemnity, surrounded by a throng of statesmen, half of whom, at least, had enjoyed the bed of the lusty czarina.

Damp, heavy snow began falling, and the pernicious wind pierced his coat, his jacket, his sweater, his body, right to the marrow of his bones. He hastened his steps.

Against the silver-gray morning sky, the golden dome of St. Nicholas Cathedral sparkled like a thousand shiny promises above the white-powdered rooftops. It was only a block to the majestic Kirov Theatre, the temple of Russian ballet. There a cranky Frenchman, Marius Petipa, created his dance miracles. Though he had lived sixty years in Russia, he had never learned the language, but instead, in collaboration with Lev Ivanov, had given the world an immortal legacy: *Bayadère, Don Quixote, Sleeping Beauty, Swan Lake* and *Nutcracker*.

Someday, thought Vladimir, I too will walk out onto the stage of that theater and show its blasé audience what I'm able to do. So far this glorious future was as distant as the moon. "But," he told himself, "it will come, this day. It will come as sure as my name is Vladimir Mikhailovich Volodin."

On Rossi Ulitza, the most beautiful street in the world, lay the core of Vladimir's realm: the Kirov's Leningrad State Academic Vaganova Choreographic Institute, named after its unforgettable soloist, who, along with Pavlova, Ulanova and Kchessinska, would be remembered forever as one of the unchallenged goddesses of ballet history.

The ballet had been his own choice, though Vladimir was never able to remember what route brought him to the great doors of the world-famous choreographic school. A huge poster announced: APPLICATIONS NOW BEING ACCEPTED. That evening at the dinner table he simply said to his mother, "Mamushka, I want to study ballet. Take me to the Kirov School."

Varvara Volodin dropped her knife and fork. "Volik, what ballet, what Kirov? Last year you were dreaming of becoming an engineer like me, like Dad. . . ."

It wasn't the first time Vladimir had mentioned ballet. When he was a very small boy, whenever someone asked him, "What will you be when you grow up?" his answer was always the same—"A dancer." At his insistence his mother, Varvara, and his grandmother, Nina, had taken him to the Kirov Theatre when the company opened its first season in liberated Leningrad. By the middle of *Sleeping Beauty* Vladimir had become impatient, and he tugged at his grandmother's sleeve. "Babushka, let's go home. What a bore! This princess is a real fool. She was forbidden to touch a spindle. Why did she take it? Good for her. Let her sleep forever. What idiot prince would want a girl so stupid?"

"Don't you remember, Volik?" said his mother. "We went with Babushka and—"

"Yes, I remember, but it's different now," said Vladimir. "I was young then."

Vladimir always startled his mother. When he was only four years old she showed him the alphabet. All alone he had learned how to read and write. He couldn't wait to start school. But once classes began, it was sheer agony. He dawdled, was cloddish, preferred to play soccer in the backyard with urchins. Then, without any reason, Vladimir suddenly changed and started to attack books feverishly, sometimes reading till five in the morning.

His mother never put pressure on him. She knew his mercurial character and how one moment he could be overwhelmed by wild despair and the next moment he would be shaking with wild laughter.

A few months later Vladimir threw aside the books and became infatuated with American movies, smuggled from defeated Germany. They flooded the Soviet puritanical screen: *One Hundred Men and a Girl* with Deanna Durbin, *Destry Rides Again* with Marlene Dietrich, *Camille* and *Queen Christina* with Greta Garbo. For almost a year he remained loyal to these beautiful ladies, bought their pictures on the black market, tacked them on the walls. Then one morning he impulsively threw his collection of movie queens into the wastebasket and was back into books and school.

And now it was ballet again. Let him try it, his mother thought, knowing the more she argued the more he would persevere.

Perhaps at first it was pure challenge to Vladimir, challenge that served to annoy the urchins in the backyard, yelling at him "Sissy, sissy" and wiggling their feet. But he gradually came to love dancing with a passion. He loved to torture his body, force it to hold the different positions, exhaust himself at the barre. He didn't know yet that ballet masochism runs in the blood of every real dancer. And when Vladimir started to learn the grammar of classical dancing—jumps, turns, beats—his whole being seemed to be filled with new energy and vigor, testing his young muscles beyond endurance, attacking dancing steps as a young tiger attacks its first victim.

In June 1951 Vladimir passed his dancing examination brilliantly, showing such prodigious technique, executed so effortlessly, that he easily won first prize. After the competition, Pëtr Ivanovich, the best men's teacher in the world, came backstage to congratulate him. "Not only do you leap higher than anyone I've ever seen," he said, "but you leap with your soul. I would like you to be my student." Vladimir skipped a year and Pëtr Ivanovich became his teacher. Overnight Vladimir's irrational behavior ceased and he was soon Ivanovich's best pupil. The teacher reminded him of the father he had never known. For him Vladimir wanted to excel. For him he wanted to step beyond boundaries.

It was just eight o'clock in the morning when Vladimir entered through the great doors of the Kirov School. He looked at the large calendar pasted on the left wall and noted the date—Monday, February 1, 1954. He bounded up the enormous staircase to the third floor of the five-story building. Realizing he was one floor too high, he made a great leap to the floor below, landing in front of Dmitri Sobolev, the school director. Vladimir's gray eyes looked at him unabashed.

"Jumping like a frog will only get you into a pond, Volodin," said the director. "Come into my office."

Vladimir followed him. Sobolev was an obese, dwarflike man always panting, perspiring and wiping his forehead with a handkerchief. His face was blunted and indistinct, like the head on a worn coin. The graying hair was cut in the stiff pompadour worn by Russian officials. Sobolev was accustomed to letting his power speak for him, but when he did speak his tone was raucous, as if hoarse from self-congratulation.

"Vladimir Volodin, you skipped math class yesterday. Last week you missed fencing and history. What is your excuse this time?"

"I went to the Kalinka Concert Hall to get a ticket for Brahms's Third Symphony and—"

"And you don't even have the good sense to be humiliated," Sobolev thundered. "Let me warn you, Volodin. If you take off from school again without permission I'll let you pursue your pirouettes in the street once and for all. Did you hear me?"

Vladimir glowered at him.

"Did you hear me?" Sobolev repeated. "You heard me well, didn't you, Vladimir Mikhailovich Volodin?" A heavy silence separated them. Sobolev stretched the slit of his mouth into a smile. A smile that could cut ice. "I want you out of here," he said slowly, enunciating each word distinctly. "G-e-t o-u-t!"

Vladimir strode out of the office, leaving the door open. How he hated this man—his manner of speaking, his sweaty hands, and the furtive, voluptuous glances enveloping Vladimir's boyish slenderness like sticky paper. The hell with Sobolev, that filthy old creep, with his rules and regulations! How could he have any conception of my life, my secret thoughts and dreams? Is it my fault if they start selling tickets only in the afternoon? Is it my fault if it coincides with math class or history class or shit class? Anyway, what is more important—Richter playing Brahms or the crap about math and history? Was it his fault if he was so infatuated with music that the mere thought of last Sunday's Tchaikovsky concert brought back the actual physical burning sensation shivering down his spine and the ecstasy that made him dig his nails into his palms?

Vladimir ran to the dressing room, where the other boys were already in tights and ballet shoes—the uniform and harness of the merciless training of their chosen life.

"Did Sobolev get you again?" teased Nikolai Gonzov, one of the fifteen students in Vladimir's class.

"Yep."

They laughed and left the room, their happy chatter punctuated by high-pitched giggles. When Vladimir was ready, he walked out through the gallery leading to the classroom. The gallery was lined with pictures of all the important dancers who had trained in this famous school in the past century. As always, Vladimir stopped at the portrait of Nijinsky. His eyes lingered over the defenselessly long neck, the passionately open mouth, all ardor and inspiration.

"Aren't you tired of looking at him?" asked Gennady Liepka, one of his classmates.

"No."

"It's too bad that we never had a chance to see him dance," Gennady continued. "Nijinsky was the greatest in the world!"

"Well, you'll have a chance to see *me* dance!" said Vladimir, looking at Gennady wickedly. "I will be the world's second greatest!"

They entered the classroom of Pëtr Ivanovich.

❋

MARIELA/*New York City*/*Monday, February 1, 1954*

"Lady Chelmsford, would you follow me, please?" Mariela, wearing dark glasses, looking chic and confident, got up from a brown leather chair and put down the magazine she had been reading. Throwing her fur coat over one arm and carrying an unlit cigarette in her hand, she followed the receptionist—one of those antiseptic, efficient and unmemorable young New York career women who look older than they are.

They walked along a maze of beige-carpeted corridors, indirectly lit, wildlife etchings beautifully mounted on the walls, and passed several offices, every one identical, with the exception of the obligatory family picture (a photograph of its occupant's wife and children), which adorned each mahogany desk. She had to smile to herself, knowing full well this custom, created to instill an atmosphere of confidence, existed only in the United States. In Italy it's the crucifix! she mused, and thought of the portrait of the queen hanging over her father's desk in Harrogate.

The office complex was a beehive of Monday-morning activity. Lawyers in their uniforms—well-tailored dark suits—were discussing briefs, huddled over the coffee machine and wiping the weekend out of their eyes. Brisk secretaries brushed past them, a plastic cup in one hand, a Danish in the other. Bells rang. Hollow voices came off the Dictaphone. The Telex relayed messages. Typewriters chattered noisily, rudely awakened from their weekend slumber. The noise of life dragging itself slowly to its full volume.

Although prepared by the vast amount of publicity that constantly exposed Nathan Berger's flamboyance, there was no way Mariela could have gone from the stark decorum of the Madison Avenue offices to Berger's private waiting room without being flabbergasted. It was such an anachronism! Styled as turn-of-the-century gold-rush whorehouse, Nathan Berger's love letter to the past was not intended to inspire confidence. He couldn't have cared less. The caliber of his clients was such that he didn't deem it necessary to bolster his already impressive credentials by conforming.

The furniture was heavy, dark Victorian wood, and one high-backed chair bore a brass plaque with the inscription: "Used by King Edward VII." A sparkling crystal chandelier glowed from the ceiling, and red velvet drapes covered all the windows.

"My name's Kathy," said the receptionist, standing behind a massive oak bar from Butte, Montana, which had been converted into a switchboard. "Would you like some coffee, Lady Chelmsford?"

"Thank you, Kathy. Will the wait be very long?"

"Only a few minutes. Mr. Berger's talking long-distance and has one other call on hold. Please make yourself comfortable."

Sitting on an overstuffed burgundy velvet love seat, Mariela was unable to take her eyes off an unsigned portrait of Nathan Berger executed in a nineteenth-century style. Berger was depicted as a distinctly western figure of the period, down to the brocaded vest and riverboat gambler's suit; he was sitting astride a prancing palomino, each hand waving a blazing Colt .45. The background was right out of Wyatt Earp.

Kathy brought the coffee in a cut-glass mug bearing the etched words "Queen Victoria's Diamond Jubilee," and placed the pewter tray on a gaming table from Madame Lulu's of Virginia City.

"Would you like a copy of the morning papers, Lady Chelmsford?"

"No, thank you. I've already read them." Mariela certainly had. From cover to cover. Not a single publication had omitted the news of Karl Ravenstein's murder.

Feeling fidgety and tired, she made an effort to remain poised. Lighting her cigarette from the flame of a perfumed oil lamp, hurricane and predictably period, she rose to her feet, nervously studying the walls. They were covered with flocked crimson-and-gold paisley paper. Scattered over them in gilded antique frames were signed photographs of famous people who had come Nathan's way as friends, clients or both—Mae West, Jack Dempsey, Errol Flynn, Jayne Mansfield, Rocky Graziano, Lana Turner, Mayor William O'Dwyer, Beverly Langdon, Ed Sullivan . . .

Kathy interrupted her scrutiny. "Lady Chelmsford, Mr. Berger will see you now." Quickly and gracefully she walked with a firm stride over the gold-and-red-striped carpet into Nathan Berger's office. Seated behind a Wells Fargo desk, he swung his leg off the arm of the first electric chair ever used in America, a relic with a headrest that read in delicate crewelwork: "Auburn Prison, New York, 1890." Cradling the mouthpiece of a telephone—ingeniously concealed in a conch shell—Berger continued his conversation, and without so much as lifting his eyes, he silently motioned Mariela toward a brocaded couch. She remained standing.

"I'm sorry, Mr. Ortiz," he concluded, "I can't speak with you further at this moment. I'll see you at four." He got up and placed the phone on its rest. Nathan was wearing a gray suit of western cut with red lining, a red handkerchief in the breast pocket, and a fresh red carnation in his lapel.

"You should have that man's problems!" Berger said, laughing jovially. "All he wants to do is pay the gift tax on over a million dollars' worth of jewelry he bought for a girl who's about to marry somebody else."

"I would assume," said Mariela, "that one would seek your services precisely to *avoid* paying tax."

"She's quite clever, this girl. She knows that as an American citizen, she could eventually be in trouble with customs were she to bring back to this country jewelry purchased overseas. There is always a tax to pay, especially when the purchase in question amounts to more than a million dollars." Mechanically he polished his well-manicured nails against his lapel. "She wisely figured, better the donor pay than she."

"But since she's leaving him for another man, wouldn't you expect him to get even by refusing?"

"Obviously the old man is still in love and wants to do what she asks."

Mariela was perplexed. "It doesn't make sense to me."

"Nothing makes sense when you're in love," Nathan replied. "That's why I steer clear of it."

"Who's the lucky bride?"

"Nobody you know, Mariela. She's not from your part of the world. American, but she's apparently made it big in Europe." Nathan abruptly put an end to the subject. "Let's sit down." He showed her to a gray velvet bench along the wall. "How does it feel getting out of bed at nine—instead of getting in?"

Under other circumstances she might have appreciated his attempt at humor. The grandfather clock against the bare brick wall struck once—a quarter past the hour.

"I didn't sleep a second," she stated flatly.

"After you called me last night, I can understand that. Did you speak to—"

"Yes, I spoke to Glover," interrupted Mariela.

"Good girl! Was he surprised when you sprang the name of the D.A. he was to contact?"

"Well, when I first mentioned Vincent Petroni it didn't ring a bell. But when I reminded Glover it was the same D.A. who had helped his sister . . ."

"I'll bet that story rang a few bells! And then?"

"He called me back around four this morning to say he'd finally located Vincent Petroni, who agreed to cooperate and will be expecting your call around noon. I must say, Glover sounded a bit shaken."

"He was probably shaking in his pajamas in a subzero telephone booth. You can be sure he didn't make that call from the house, with the missus listening to his every word."

"I still don't understand your strategy," said Mariela.

"I'm going to call Petroni and tell him that my client has information concerning the Ravenstein murder and would be willing to testify before a grand jury if she is promised immunity."

"Won't that bring on publicity?"

"There's publicity only if you are indicted. But how can you be indicted, since you'll be given immunity?" He paused, "You see my point?"

"How soon could a grand jury be called?"

"With a little greasing of Petroni's palm and pressure from Anderson, it shouldn't take long. And if we have to reach someone higher, we will. I've got more than one ace up my sleeve," Nathan said smugly. "That's why it's very important that you keep in touch with Glover." The phone rang. "It's the last time, I promise," he said, getting up. "I'll ask not to be disturbed again."

She followed him. Absently she ran a finger along the edge of the desk until its path was blocked by a heavily jeweled ermine and gold crown next to several bottles of Hermès cologne and one of English aftershave lotion. At the base of a Tiffany lamp was an assembly of paperweights. A *No Smoking* sign from an old train was prominently displayed. Intimidated, Mariela stubbed out her cigarette in a bronze cast of Lillian Russell's foot—the only ashtray in sight.

"I have to go to Japan in a couple of weeks," Nathan was saying into the phone. "I'll meet you on the twenty-sixth at the Peninsula Hotel in Hong Kong." Mariela gave Nathan a "How long are you going to be?" look. He winked at her a "Don't worry, this'll only take a minute" reply. "I was planning to leave tonight or tomorrow, but something came up and I had to postpone my trip. Listen . . . I'm all packed." She noticed his Mark Cross suitcases on the floor with airline tags on them.

Mariela studied the room, moving away from the desk. In a glass-enclosed case were dozens of tiny faded costumes, tiny shoes, tiny pants, intermingled with huge costumes, huge shoes, huge pants. A yellowing poster dated June 1901 proclaiming: SOLOMON BERGER PRESENTS THE AMAZING BUTTERFLY TWINS was hung behind the case. Amazing indeed, as one stood barely three and a half feet tall. A midget. The other towered above him at over six feet. Not until their deaths was the shocking truth revealed. They were not twins at all but husband and wife. The wife had been the tall one. Nathan had inherited the sideshow collection from his great-grandfather, the first showman to exhibit freaks in New York City. His establishment on Union Square was now a landmark.

A large wooden fan revolved overhead next to a hangman's noose, reputedly the one that helped Jack Bennet of the Wild Bunch pay his debt to society in 1898. Three turn-of-the-century chandeliers flooded the room with light. The highly polished wood floor, exuding an odor of fresh wax, was covered with bearskin rugs. Petrified palm trees stood round the periphery of the room.

"Good to hear from you, old boy. See you soon—my regards to the missus." Nathan rose as he hung up and followed Mariela's gaze.

Framed newspaper accounts of famous cases Nathan had won were mounted on the walls. The remaining space was covered by a zebra skin, a large copper pot and Chinese masks. A pair of shabby boots stood in a corner. According to Nathan Berger, they had belonged to Jesse James. An entire wall was devoted to books, and a red-lacquered ladder leaning against them enabled him to reach the upper shelves. Nathan Berger had elevated clutter to an art.

"I've never seen so many books in such a small space."

"Books are a joy, and women another."

Mariela was now glancing at a photograph of Nathan holding hands with a young girl. "I thought that you above all others would avoid the inevitable family snapshot I find in every professional man's office in this country!"

"Mariela"—his voice was half mocking, half curious—"what else do you see in this picture?" He picked it up and brought it closer for her inspection.

She removed her sunglasses. "It looks like a lamb."

"Good for you! You win on the sixty-four-thousand-dollar question! The photo was taken on Bali, where the custom is to sacrifice a virgin lamb on your wedding day. I keep the photograph here strictly for the lamb. It's the only *virgin* framed in these offices!" He laughed, pleased with himself.

"Nathan, I didn't know you're married!"

"I was, dear Mariela, I was." Having enjoyed his little joke, he carefully put on tortoise-shell glasses and continued. "Now, let's get down to serious business. Did you bring—"

"Oh, yes." She extracted a large envelope from her purse. "It's exactly twelve thousand, five hundred dollars."

"Thank you. I believe good accounting makes for good friendship." His face tightened. "Mariela, you told me on the phone that Hamilton insinuated you were responsible for the disappearance of a million dollars." He leaned on his desk, studying Mariela carefully. "Was Hamilton's insinuation correct?" She merely looked at him. "Don't lie to me, Mariela. Was he right?"

It was a moment before his words sank in. "No!" she said harshly. Anger suddenly swept through her and propelled Mariela into the armchair across from him, fists clenched tightly.

"No point getting excited, Mariela. It was merely a question." Berger took the carnation from his lapel and sniffed it. "Do you know if this money is in any way related to drugs?" he asked nonchalantly.

She was taken aback. "I don't know. I've never thought about it. Karl used a lot of cocaine, but I doubt if he ever trafficked in it."

"It's very strange that in all the newspaper reports there was no mention of drugs being found on his premises. Very strange indeed." He squirted a glass of soda water from a siphon embedded in a ceramic Indonesian elephant and offered it to her. "Would you rather have—?"

"No, nothing, thank you."

Nathan drank the water as if tasting a brand-new wine. "I told you I had more than one ace up my sleeve." He opened a drawer and took from it what appeared to be a deck of cards. "I believe I'm holding the ace in my hand."

"Looks like a complete pack to me."

Closing the drawer with affected slowness, Berger said, "Take a look at these, Mariela." He flung them on the table face down. "I think you'll find these most interesting."

One by one, she picked up the cards, studied them, and gasped. "But that's the mayor of . . . the mayor of . . ."

"How perceptive, my dear," Berger interrupted sarcastically.

"The mayor and—and me! It's me!"

"You bet it is!"

"But I haven't seen him in three years! I didn't even know you then!" Mariela seemed anesthetized. She couldn't say anything more. Her eyes fell once again on the photographs.

"Are you all right?" asked Nathan solicitously. "Get hold of yourself, Mariela."

She waited for a moment and her composure returned. She still couldn't find words.

"Politicians on the way up should be very careful, Mariela." She rose and went toward the small bar. He continued: "Frankly, I don't believe Mr. Big would have a chance of keeping his job if one of his political opponents got his hands on these . . . these exclusive photographs. As for Bob Harrison of *Confidential*—he'd give his right arm!" Mariela poured herself a shot of straight vodka. "Do you by any chance know the name of the young man having such a good time with the two of you?" Nathan asked, pretending tact.

Mariela returned to the desk, sat once more, and studied a couple of the photos. She replaced them on the table. "I don't believe so."

"Mariela, after viewing these *unusual* photographs, it is quite understandable why you didn't have the opportunity to look at his face, let alone remember it. I doubt if you'd recognize him by his ass, but take a look at one of the head-on shots." She took her time, glanced at Nathan, then back at the pictures. Some flickering memory caught fire.

"I believe it's the same young man who was at Ravenstein's Saturday night." She glanced once again.

"His name?" he asked starkly.

She hesitated briefly. "Andreas."

"What else do you know about him?"

"Nothing. He arrived late." She breathed more heavily. "I do remember asking his last name. It was something like . . . Pop . . . Poppo . . . Poppidoppolous. Something like that. No one seemed to know who he was. For a brief moment I had the impression that I'd seen him somewhere but dismissed it."

"Where did Karl get his boys from?" The carnation was now crumbled between Berger's manicured fingers.

"A service that specializes in boys. Do you want that information?"

"Yes, I most certainly do." She wrote it down on a piece of paper.

"This is my second ace and the most valuable. Just name one illustrious city that can handle a degenerate faggot as its leader!" He stopped. Smiled for the flick of an instant. Picked up one of the pictures. Then, casually, let it drop back. "Would there be any way Andreas could have remained behind after the others left?"

Mariela paused for a moment. "He did return, come to think of it. He had forgotten his scarf."

"Did you see him out again?" Nathan pressed.

"I saw him—I saw him go to the door. I was already on the staircase."

"Did you hear the door close?"

"I can't . . . ," she stammered, "I can't recall. I was tired."

"I'll bet!" he sneered. "Was the door closed when you let yourself out?"

"Yes."

"But not locked?"

"No. As I told you yesterday, the servants were off. And—Nathan—I don't understand why you are so rough with me. I'm your client, not your adversary."

"As I said before, I want to make sure you are telling me the truth."

"You really don't trust me."

"I don't trust anyone."

"Still, I am your client, and there is no reason for you to treat me with contempt."

"You're not exactly Mother Cabrini, Mariela. I'm doing you a favor by taking your case."

It suddenly occurred to Mariela, as she looked at the pictures still lying on the desk, that doing her a *favor* was Nathan Berger's least concern. She felt like a pawn. And pawns have to be moved. Who were the players?

"Anyway," said Nathan, "since you have witnesses who can testify accurately as to the time you left the mansion and got home, I believe, my dear Mariela, that this will be the end of your involvement in this matter, especially with Glover Anderson looking out for you." He paused. "When are you seeing him again?"

"He'd like to see me on Wednesday, as usual," she said with almost childish pride. "But I'm really not up to it."

"Not up to it! By all means, Mariela, meet him. Glover is indispensable to you. The sooner the grand jury convenes, the better it will be for all concerned." Nathan shifted the pictures dextrously and stacked them neatly. "Besides, he's missing from my rogue's gallery," he said sarcastically. "His addition will make it a full house!"

"But that's blackmail!" exclaimed Mariela.

"Is that what they call it in Yorkshire?" He smiled at her. A queer smile. "I call it a gentleman's agreement." He rubbed his hands together. "Come back here at two o'clock. I will have spoken to the district attorney and will probably know when we'll be able to make our deposition before the grand jury. Needless to say, my dear, when you do so, by all means omit the sordid details."

"Like what?"

"Like drugs and leather, the glove, and—and Jack Hamilton. It is really unimportant."

"Jack Hamilton," she said, faltering. "But I don't understand. What are these 'revelations' I'm supposed to make to the grand jury?"

"Oh, you can mention you had a little sex. And perhaps that Andreas Popo . . . was acting a little peculiar, the number of people there, their names, and that Karl let you out himself."

"But that's not true."

"If they don't believe you, let them ask Karl if it's true or not," he said. "Are you paying me to get you off or to be found guilty?"

"*I am not guilty,*" she shot back, emphasizing each word.

"All right, all right, excuse me, I got carried away."

He escorted Mariela to the back door, his arm paternally around her shoulder. "What are you going to do about Switzerland?" Berger asked without expression.

"As I told you, Nathan, I don't want to be involved any deeper than I already am."

"I disagree, my dear. The mountain air would do you a world of good, and since the man is dead anyway . . . We'll speak about that later on. But don't dismiss it, Mariela. Opportunities like these come but once in a lifetime. See you this afternoon at two. Do not go to your apartment yet. Try to do without sex for a couple of hours. Do anything . . . get a facial!" He laughed without wickedness.

Mariela turned sharply and walked out. She crossed Madison Avenue, making herself walk faster. Stopping at a Longchamps restaurant, she caught a quick reflection in the glass of the same two eerie men she had seen at the Plaza. They were sitting in a car across the street. She would find out who they were. Soon. Very soon. Shakily pushing the revolving door, Mariela moved forward and entered the restaurant. She went straight to the telephone booth and dialed Glover Anderson's number.

❋

MATTIE/*New York City*/*Monday, February 1, 1954*

Before Mattie's ten o'clock wake-up call, Augustine, the cleaning lady, rang the doorbell. After Mattie let her in, Augustine surveyed the disheveled apartment and concluded that Mattie was preparing to move out. Learning otherwise, she declared that it would take at least a week to put the place in order, working around the clock.

"Don't worry about the suitcases," Mattie said, trying to be helpful. "I'll unpack them when I come home. Now I've got to get ready for a twelve-thirty audition."

Since the part called for a girl of about twenty-five or older, Mattie applied her makeup carefully and more heavily than usual. She shadowed her eyes to make the most of what were her best features, grabbed some dancing clothes and shoes and shoved them into a large "gypsy" pouch.

She arrived at the backstage door of the Majestic ten minutes before her audition time was scheduled. Despite the bitter cold, Sylvia Rubins, her theatrical agent, was waiting outside and greeted her effusively, taking her arm. "Mattie you look great, just great. You've lost weight!"

"I'm glad you can tell. I've lost two pounds!" Mattie answered, more than willing to believe that her weight loss was visible. She pushed open the stage door.

Sylvia was a large, heavy woman, a former actress who took on only a few select clients to whom she was devoted.

"You know you have a good chance, a very good chance of getting this part," she continued. "They've been holding auditions for two weeks and this is the last day. Carol Haney hasn't got an understudy."

"I've never felt more sure of myself," Mattie chirped. "I've worked my ass off for the past ten days while I was in Toronto. Oh, Sylvia, I did great in Toronto! I'll show you the reviews later."

Several girls were waiting inside for their turns, each one filled with the same dreams and ambitions. Then came Mattie. A bare bulb hung from the ceiling, making the empty stage seem like a Christmas tree in daylight, with all its wires showing. Mattie realized again that nothing is lonelier or more frightening than being on an empty stage, knowing that people are out there, people whom you cannot see, people whose names you seldom know, people who pretend to have the knowledge to judge in five minutes —ten if you're lucky—talent and personality it took a lifetime to develop.

The stage manager introduced her: "Miss Mattie Maxwell." She walked on. The theater was cold. She felt nervous but managed a semblance of calm. A male voice that sounded both familiar and strange resounded from the depths of the auditorium.

"Hello, Mattie baby." It was George Abbott, the producer-director. "I guess I shouldn't call you 'baby' anymore. You're grown up now. I can hardly believe it, sweetheart. Would your mother be proud of you! What are you gonna do for us?" Before she had a chance to reply, Richard Adler, the composer, came toward the pit, his dachshund tucked under his arm, introduced himself and offered his encouragement. She gave her music to the pianist and sang one number, "By Strings Attached," with her very own natural gestures: fingers fanned on hips, eyes straight ahead.

"Thank you, that was very good," said the choreographer Bob Fosse. Approaching the ramp, he asked, "Did you bring any dance clothes with you?"

"Yeah—yes," replied Mattie anxiously. She hurried to a dressing room, changed into a black leotard and Capezio dancing slippers and returned to the stage. A kind of dread was building up in her. Fosse quietly explained the sequence he wanted her to do, showed her some routines. She went through them twice and found herself sweating profusely. There was applause, quite unusual at an audition. Mattie just stood there. She was now relaxed and in total command. John Raitt, the leading man, went over a scene with her, the one on which she had worked so hard. The whole audition lasted fifteen minutes. Mattie said goodbye to everyone, feeling elated. Then she put on her street clothes and headed for the exit with Sylvia.

"We'll call you, Miss Maxwell." It was the stage manager. "We have your number, I believe." She couldn't tell if it was a question or a statement.

"Yes, you do, but I'll give it to you again." She wrote it on his pad. "And you also have the number of my agent, Sylvia Rubins, but I'll put it down again."

"You'll be hearing from us." He was smiling. A good sign, thought Mattie. "Thank you and goodbye."

"Goodbye, goodbye," she replied almost breathlessly. Mattie left with Sylvia. They made a dash for Downey's, on Eighth Avenue, and took a seat in the first booth to the left. For a moment they faced each other without speaking. Mattie broke the silence.

"When do you think we'll know something?"

"Maybe this afternoon. They have to make up their minds today."

A waiter came by to take their order. "Give me a salad with lots of gook on it," Mattie said in a giddy voice, "and a glass of white wine. No ice, please."

"Martini and a turkey sandwich on rye with mayo for me." Looking at Mattie, Sylvia said, "I'm proud of you."

The conversation was gay and optimistic. "You were great, Mattie. You're so talented. I know you don't want to capitalize on your mother's name, but I'll tell you something. Being the daughter of Jessica Miller doesn't hurt at the box office."

Mattie winced visibly. They toasted *Pajama Game*. They toasted Mattie. They toasted Sylvia. Sylvia's voice was cheerful. "Didn't you feel good about it?"

Mattie was exuberant. "Yeah, yeah. I must say I did. And I know how lousy I can be at auditions. But this time, Sylvia, it was different. How can I say it? I felt I belonged on that stage. Yeah, I did well." All the while she was fumbling in the depths of her overstuffed bag, and finally took out a bunch of wrinkled newspaper clippings. "Take a look at those reviews, Sylvia. They couldn't be better if I'd written them myself."

Sylvia read carefully: "Mattie Maxwell will be the next big star to explode in the firmament . . ." "Mattie Maxwell's voice is nothing short of electrifying. She belongs on a concert stage . . ." "Today people are applauding Mattie Maxwell for her incredible artistry and because she's the daughter of Jessica Miller. Tomorrow they will applaud even louder, and Jessica Miller will always be remembered of course, but as the mother of Mattie Maxwell . . ." Sylvia didn't lift her eyes. "I know you're on the threshold of everything, Mattie, and I feel comfortable about today, very."

Sylvia paid the check. They bundled up and left Downey's. Thin black clouds dragged themselves through the jagged skyline like shreds of a tattered gown. The snow was melting in brown patches and the cruel wind tightened like a vise around their faces. They had a difficult time finding a cab. Mattie arrived home around three o'clock after depositing the check from her Toronto engagement and buying groceries, liquor and a black nightgown. The apartment was much tidier. Mattie started unpacking her suitcases with Augustine's help. She was about to go out again for cigarettes when the telephone rang.

"Yeah, yeah, Sylvia, any news? Tell me!" Mattie was almost screaming as she straddled the small stool. After the brief conversation she slowly hung up the phone and rose unsteadily; her legs had turned wobbly, her stomach was mush. She poured herself a glass of wine and slumped into a kitchen chair. Mattie's eyes were wide, staring. Tears welled up, then trickled down her cheeks. She let out a deep sob. No, Mattie hadn't gotten the part. They had chosen an unknown dancer, Shirley MacLaine.

"Damn it!" she cried out loud.

Dazed with the pain of rejection, she ran out of her apartment, feeling alternately numb and angry. On the street she passed an acquaintance who tried to engage her in conversation. Mattie pretended not to see him and reached into her pocketbook for sunglasses to hide her tear-stained face. "Who the hell is Shirley MacLaine?" she asked herself. "And why did that phony bunch at the theater pretend to like me? Maybe my mother was right. *I never will amount to anything!*" She bought some cigarettes and crossed Third Avenue against the red light, oblivious to the honking and the shouts of one driver: "Hey, stupid, whaddya think you're doing? Take those sunglasses off—wait for the sunshine to play star! Whyncha get a seeing-eye dog!"

Mattie continued to Lexington Avenue, not knowing exactly where she was heading, and stopped outside a pet shop, where a few people had gathered despite the bitter cold. Little puppies were frolicking in an enclosure in the window, next to three beautiful pedigreed kittens that were sleeping on top of one another. Instantly she forgot her tears, broke into a rapturous smile and impulsively went into the store. The shelves were covered with cages housing birds of myriad colors, and a pen in the center of the room was filled with delightful ducklings, small, fragile and covered with soft yellow down. One of them looked at Mattie as if hypnotized. She came closer. "Do you sell these?" she asked one of the clerks. "I thought they were only popular at Easter?"

"We sell more of them at Easter," answered the clerk, "but we sell them all the year round. People have country houses, you know, and—"

Mattie didn't let him finish the sentence. "How much is this one?" she asked, pointing to the still mesmerized fledgling.

"We can't sell one. You have to buy at least six."

Mattie stared at him bewildered. "Why is that?"

"It's a New York State law designed to discourage people from buying a single duckling on the spur of the moment, only to let it loose on the streets when they've lost interest. Having to buy six of them forces people to be more responsible."

"I'll buy six, then!" Mattie was about to add, "Wrap them up!" but stopped herself in time, even though she didn't know how one was supposed to carry ducks around. As she paid, the clerk told her what to feed them. She left the store with the small cardboard box filled with paper shreddings and immediately put her woolen scarf over it. She hurried home and ran up the flight of stairs in a state of great excitement. Augustine opened the door.

"What in tarnation have you got there, Miss Mattie?"

"Can't you see that they're ducks!" she snapped. *"Really!"*

"I know them are ducks, chile, but when is you planning to cook them?" She let out a guttural laugh.

Mattie was not amused. She set her lively package on top of the refrigerator while she filled a glass of white wine. With drink in one hand, ducks in the other, she returned to the living room and deposited the box in the center of the floor. One by one she removed the ducklings, holding each in the palm of her hand, covering them with kisses and nuzzling their little wings. To her amazement they were mute. "Quack, quack," she said to them, trying to get a response. Maybe a little wine would make them talkative, she decided. She took a big gulp of wine, and without swallowing it, grabbed the smallest of her charges and put its whole head into her mouth, inundating it with wine. "That should liven you up," said Mattie. Having put him back with the others, certain that he had enjoyed it, she repeated the procedure with the remaining five.

The ducks did side steps in the box, tumbling over each other as they strained their necks to see Mattie. She turned them all upside down, trying to determine their sex, but was baffled. Well, in time, she assured herself, *something* will grow.

Augustine's voice boomed from the kitchen. "No, Miss Mattie. I'll clean up after you, chile, but I ain't cleanin' up after no ducks, no sirree!"

Mattie ignored her and closely studied the six faces, trying to identify the one who had originally caught her eye in the pet shop. "Which one are you? How shall I ever tell you apart?" She sprang up and exclaimed, "Of course, why didn't I think of it before?" She hurried to the bedroom, took from a drawer a batch of colored ribbons for wrapping Christmas packages and went back to the living room.

Mattie decided to name each of her unisex flock after characters in plays and musicals in which she had appeared with stock companies. She labeled different colored ribbons with a black marker and tied one around each of their delicate necks, and this is how Boris (*Can-Can*, Cambridge, Massachusetts), Sally (*I Am a Camera*, Brunswick, Maine), Appopolous (*Wonderful Town*, Flint, Michigan), Bianca (*Kiss Me, Kate*, Milwaukee, Wisconsin), Ali Hakim (*Oklahoma*, Canal Fulton, Ohio), and Azuri (*Desert Song*, Boston, Massachusetts) entered Mattie's world and took possession of her bathroom.

※

DENISE/*New York City*/*Tuesday, February 2, 1954*

It was late Tuesday afternoon when the Mercedes-Benz crossed the Triborough Bridge, leaving the city behind. The vague, low sound of New York was like the distant hum of a mighty engine.

Denise looked up. The sky, color of sorrow, drab and melancholy, reflected her own mood. The immediate apprehension she felt was replaced by a force too overwhelming to define—not fear, but an utter determination to accomplish what she had set out to do.

"Yvette, where did you put the suitcase I asked you to keep separate?"

"It's in the back, mademoiselle, with the others."

"How can it be *separate* if it's in the back with the others?"

"It's the only one with a red tag on it, mademoiselle."

Drops of rain were falling and beading the windows like wasted tears. At that moment Denise made a resolution not to let any thoughts fret her, but in the next moment she realized that was impossible. The car made its way through the heavy rush-hour traffic on the Long Island Expressway, moving from lane to lane, starting, stopping, in jerky, irritating spurts.

When would she see New York again? There was no doubt in her mind that she would. Denise would do *everything* she ever dreamed of—yet the trip she was about to make had never been part of her plan.

At this moment Denise couldn't help remembering the very first time she had ever visited New York—October, 1951. It was *not* with her mother.

—❋—

She and Reinaldo Vega boarded the *Twentieth Century Limited* in Chicago and stopped in New York two days, on the way to Buenos Aires.

From their base at the Astor Hotel Denise took the best of what the city had to offer. She drank in the sights—the shops, theaters, museums, restaurants and clubs—which she viewed as lovely toys. She moved through the streets feeling not only welcome but *expected,* and knowing that no matter what the future brought, New York ultimately would be her home and she would be one of its most prominent residents.

—❋—

And now, three years later, she still felt the same way.

Denise realized they were arriving at Idlewild Airport. The International Building. She got out of the limousine amid a jam of taxis, chauffeur-driven cars, jaywalking tourists with umbrellas, Indian women in saris, cars, children and buses. A mélange of accents and a variety of languages greeted her ears. Skycaps with handcarts descended on them like bees on pollen.

"Where you-all headed for, miz?" one of them asked.

"Paris." The acrid smell of diesel fuel made her choke as an airline bus pulled alongside, disgorging its herd of passengers, cameras and binoculars slung over shoulders and hung around necks like medals won in some forgotten war.

"Which airline, miz?"

"Air France," Yvette volunteered.

As the luggage was being whisked away, Denise called over the din. "Give the suitcase with the red tag to another porter! Please!"

"Sho 'nuff, miz."

Yvette, astonished but silent, followed Denise into the terminal. Oblivious of all stares, Denise walked toward the check-in counter, swathed in furs, like the heroine of a Tolstoi novel on her way to some mysterious and secret meeting.

With an air of genteel hauteur she said, "Could I speak to Mr. Poulin, please? I'm Miss Cunningham."

"I'm Mr. Poulin," a man in his early thirties replied. "I'm very pleased to meet you, Miss Cunningham. I've been asked to put myself at your disposal. But," he continued, "aren't we a little early?" He was unable to take his gaze off her. She smiled.

"Your flight doesn't . . . doesn't depart until . . . until eight o'clock, Miss . . . Miss Cunningham."

"I know, I know!" Denise answered icily. "I'm not going to Paris. Madame Yvette Bougardier will be traveling alone."

"But, mademoiselle—" protested Yvette.

Denise ignored her and continued. "Please take good care of Madame Bougardier." She dismissed Poulin with a wave of the hand.

Leading Yvette aside, she put her arm intimately around the woman's shoulders. "Now I can tell you, my dear Yvette," she whispered in a confidential tone. "As you may have guessed"—she hesitated briefly—"I'm not going to Paris."

"But where are you going, mademoiselle?" Yvette asked, trembling slightly.

"I cannot tell you now, but, believe me, there is nothing to worry about. Eugene will pick you up at Le Bourget." Then holding both Yvette's hands, she went on, "If anyone should call, anyone at all, and especially Prince Borgia," she emphasized, "tell them I'm still in America and will return in about"—she thought quickly—"in about ten days."

"And Monsieur Ortiz?" Yvette asked cautiously. "Won't he be calling?"

"I doubt it, Yvette, but if he does, tell him"—she paused for a moment—"tell him I'm in the country somewhere outside Paris." She smiled reassuringly. "Don't worry. Everything will be all right. All right, indeed." Yvette relaxed. "Have a good trip," Denise said jauntily. She kissed Yvette on both cheeks and disappeared into the throng. The porter who had been standing nearby picked up the single suitcase and followed Denise to the BOAC area.

Flight 326 for London was boarding. Soon a faint, steady roar obliterated all other sound as the giant plane lifted itself off the ground, and Denise abandoned herself to the protective sanctuary of the approaching night.

***

MATTIE/*New York City*/*Tuesday, February 2, 1954*

Mattie intended to stay in that evening. Ed Murrow would be interviewing Jeremy Rabb and Beverly Langdon in their southern California home during his *Person to Person* TV show. She knew how much Rabb meant to Tony and how helpful he was to his career. Mattie had never met Rabb, but felt him to be an intimate part of her life. Besides, the magazines and newspapers regularly published lavishly illustrated stories about Rabb and his famous bride. She didn't know who fascinated her more, Jeremy Rabb or Beverly Langdon. Together they embodied all the glamour that the star-struck millions associated with celebrities, flitting from luxury to luxury like agile cats from roof to roof.

Mattie went to the kitchen and began supper: scrambled eggs and sausages and finely chopped lettuce. Not for herself, but for the ducklings. She had decided such a diet would be far more nutritious than the mush recommended by the pet store. While feeding them in the bathroom she noticed that although they still were not quacking, they had made ample use of yesterday's newspapers.

At 10:00 P.M. she hauled them into the living room and, wrapping Boris in a large towel, sat him on her lap. She lit a joint, blowing smoke repeatedly into Boris' beak.

"Calm down," she said to the duck. "Don't fret so much. In a little while you're going to feel very relaxed! Take my word for it!" She switched on the television set, and while waiting for the picture to materialize, listened to the sound of the announcer's voice.

"The first part of our program is presented by Noxzema. And now, tonight, live from Hollywood, California, your host, Mr. Edward R. Murrow." The image of the celebrated newscaster came into focus.

"Good evening, ladies and gentlemen. Welcome to our program. Tonight we will take you to the home of Mr. and Mrs. Jeremy Rabb. Mr. Rabb is the eminent producer, and his wife the incandescent and beautiful actress, Miss Beverly Langdon. I am now sitting in their living room."

The camera panned to a pensive dark-haired man whose face seemed carved from granite, with a rough cast reminiscent of John Garfield. He sat relaxed in a California-style open shirt, a large diamond ring shining on his left hand. The thick, masculine fingers of his right hand balanced a cigar.

"Good evening, Jeremy."

"Good evening, Ed."

"Thank you for inviting our viewers into your home."

"It's my pleasure, really. I like big gatherings."

"Well, this is a large one, Jeremy. I believe about eight million people are with us tonight. Can you accommodate us all?"

"The more the better." His laughter was raucous and down to earth. "Or do they say 'the merrier'? I ain't too educated, you know." More laughter.

"That's what you'd like us to believe," Murrow replied with a soothing voice. "Now, before we show our viewers around your palatial estate, I would like to ask you a few questions."

"Shoot." Just as the camera moved in for a closeup, Rabb exhaled smoke, clouding the small screen, blurring his features. It reminded Mattie of the billowing Times Square billboard ad for Camel cigarettes.

Morrow continued in his oratorical style: "It has been reported that your latest film, starring your beautiful wife, Beverly Langdon, cost the all-time high of three million. Am I correct?"

"That's right, Ed. But every inch of the film is worth twice that. We've been in production for almost two years, and I am sure this is going to be a biggie—the biggest box-office grosser in history. It might even outdo *Gone with the Wind*."

Beverly entered the room as if she had accidentally opened the wrong door. A large Afghan hound trailed after her.

Goddammit! What a good actress! Mattie thought to herself. She's probably been behind that door since yesterday waiting for this moment!

"Oh, I hope I'm not interrupting anything." In contrast to her husband's casual dress, she wore a floor-length clinging jersey sheath. She had jewels on her ears, on her fingers and wrists. The camera shifted briefly to Murrow's face, which, for a fraction of a second, reflected unmistakable awe, mixed with reverence for the lucious blond beauty considered the sex goddess of the world. Her success was attributable to the fact that in spite of the undulating flesh and moist smiles, she was able to tread the very thin line between flagrant sexuality and offensive vulgarity.

The famous tousled white-blond hair moved softly as Beverly sat down next to her husband. Mattie had read in a movie magazine that it took an untold amount of time to make it appear as if Beverly had just gotten up from an unexpected, passionate roll in the hay and had barely regained her composure. Total artifice made natural.

Mattie refilled her glass with one hand, curled up in the big armchair, thoroughly engrossed in the program.

Jeremy and Beverly spoke further about the film. Mattie was sipping her wine slowly, mesmerized by the two people who had captured the world's imagination by openly indulging in every whim and luxury. There was talk about private planes—his and hers—white and black Rolls Royces, hairdressers, press agents, large diamonds, love and the future.

"If I may be so indiscreet," Murrow concluded, "the fact that you both have been married several times—does it make you fearful that this too might not last?"

"Ed, this is forever," Rabb asserted. "You can bet your"—he paused, searching for an acceptable word—"bottom dollar this is forever." He coughed on the smoke of his cigar.

Mattie glanced at Boris. He was peculiarly still.

"Let's look at it this way," Rabb continued. "I'm forty-two, and Beverly is almost twenty years younger, but as far as we are concerned, there is no age difference."

"Not at all, not at all," Beverly chimed in, shifting her hips. "And we cannot bear to be apart. We've been married one year and we haven't spent a night away from each other since we met, eighteen months ago. We do *everything* together." She articulated the word in a way that made it slide suggestively out of her glistening mouth.

Trying to change the subject, Murrow quickly asked, "How about your film schedule, Miss Langdon? Doesn't that interfere with your personal life?"

"Well, I am in the midst of a new film right now with George Barker, but my contract calls for me to finish shooting every day promptly at four P.M. so I can come home to my husband," she whispered in her famous little girl voice.

"Do you cook for him?"

Jeremy roared. "Her talents, I am afraid, do not belong in the kitchen. We have a cook. I want Beverly to relax when she is not working. She is not made for hot stoves."

"Yeah, no doubt she's made for hot beds!" Mattie said to herself.

Once more the couple gazed into each other's eyes. Mattie was envious, watching two people so obviously well mated.

Puffing on the cigarette that had become his trademark, Murrow inquired, "Does his constant cigar-smoking ever disturb you, Miss Langdon?"

"No, I love it!" She crossed her legs, her limpid eyes looking squarely into the camera. "I love to watch the way he blows."

"Do you hope to have children?"

"We are trying all the time," cooed Beverly. Same look. Straight as an arrow. Not a hint of double-entendre.

"You have such a magnificent home—which we will shortly show our viewers. Could you tell us now how you spend your evenings?"

Beverly emitted a barely audible girlish giggle, but the camera was on Jeremy, who replied: "We have a small circle of friends, good friends, mainly in our business—writers like Arthur Lowen, studio bosses—Jack Warner, for instance—actors like George Barker, Monty Clift, Tony Rook." At the mention of Tony's name Mattie stood up, dropping Boris to the floor and cheered, "That's my man! That's my Tony! Yeah, baby, you're a star!" The sight of a towel apparently ambling by itself toward the television made Mattie laugh out loud as she scooped up her favorite duck and put him back on her lap. With rapt attention she heard Jeremy Rabb continue speaking of Tony.

"My wife and I have sort of adopted him, and I predict a big future for that young man. He'll be in my next film project, but it's too soon to go into that now. Tony is a big talent, the biggest in years."

"He can cook too," observed Beverly in a small voice off camera.

"Don't you think all the luxuries you and your wife surround yourselves with are perhaps signs of unreasonable self-indulgence?"

"I have worked all my life," barked Rabb. "I was eight years old when I started selling newspapers in Brooklyn . . ."

Newspapers! That reminded Mattie that she would need fresh papers on the bathroom floor before going to bed.

". . . the money is mine. I earned it. I do what I damn well please with it. If the people are jealous—tough! It's mine and I'll spend as much of it on any broad I want. This is *my* wife and *my* broad, and it's my pleasure to spend it on her."

Beverly looked admiringly at Jeremy and said in her little-girl voice, "I feel I am an extension of Jeremy and Jeremy an extension of me." They held hands for all America to admire. Languidly she leaned over to touch the Afghan, which lay stretched out at her feet. Quickly the camera cut from the forbidden cleavage to the exotic dog. As Beverly stroked the Afghan, Mattie noticed the much-publicized fifty-carat diamond ring. The dog wore a jeweled collar.

Mattie peered at her ducks in their cardboard box, still wearing their dime-store ribbons. Reflexively, she bent down and stroked them gently, trying to emulate the elegance of Beverly Langdon's gesture. She lifted the towel to look at Boris. His eyes were wide open. Opaque. Unfocused. He was stoned.

"Jeremy, you are such a good golfer," Murrow was saying, pointing to a nearby cabinet holding scores of golfing trophies. "If your time weren't so occupied with your show-business career, you could probably turn professional and have a brilliant career there as well, don't you agree?"

Jeremy patted his wife affectionately on the knee. "I guess I could. But it's my old lady here who brings me luck." At that point they rose and walked toward the trophy display. Beverly's lush body undulated without mercy as they neared the cabinet.

"Miss Langdon," Murrow probed, "what is your secret for bringing such luck to your husband? How did he, for instance, win the U.S. Amateur Golf Championship this year?"

"Well"—she exhaled, her breath almost fogging the camera lens—"whenever Jeremy competes in a tournament there's a special good-luck charm I put on him . . . all my own."

"Give us the secret, Miss Langdon," Murrow said.

"Before he tees off," Beverly sighed, "I always kiss his balls."

Mattie fell back on her seat, writhing with laughter, dropping Boris to the floor once again. The TV screen suddenly went blank, then streaked, jittered, flashed, until it finally collapsed into a momentary void. From its depths came a voice of muffled officiousness: "Due to technical difficulties we have had a brief interruption. Our program will continue in just a moment." A saccharine rendition of "Tea for Two" sprinkled its sugar across the lull, then faded out.

The interview resumed.

"How long have you had this fabulous home, Jeremy?"

"Well, Ed, about a year. I gave it to my bride as a wedding present, and we love it. It's got everything. Name it and it's here."

"Don't you find it rather vast for just the two of you? How many rooms do you have?"

Turning to his wife, Rabb asked, "How many rooms do we have, honey? I've never really counted."

"We have seven bedrooms—I know that. Each one a different color. Ours is pink, all pink."

"Why do you have so many bedrooms?"

"Oh, we change rooms sometimes," Beverly answered, shaking her blond tresses, each bouncing curl resembling cotton candy. "It makes us feel like we're going to a motel. You know what I mean, Mr. Murrow?"

The genial and relaxed Murrow became slightly agitated and put on a wary smile as the picture dissolved to a commercial.

Mattie extinguished her joint in an empty yogurt cup. Impulsively she popped up from her seat, ducks in tow, and deposited them in the bathroom.

The phone rang.

"Who? . . . Oh, Harry . . . Harry Ross! No, no, not at all. I'm delighted. Besides, when an agent calls at this time of night, it's always good news. . . . I'm telling you, Harry, you didn't bother me at all. I was just watching it too. Wasn't that great what Jeremy had to say about Tony? . . . Yeah, that's my boy . . . but Beverly Langdon can really give a girl a complex, if you know what I mean. . . . Oh no, no Harry, I'm sorry, go right ahead. I've already seen all I want to see. I was about to turn it off anyway. What's up? . . . Wait a minute, hold on, if you said what I think you said I'd better be sitting down." She dragged a chair across the floor, straddled it and sat in a single motion. "Did I hear you right? The . . . the . . . the Copa . . . for two weeks? You mean the Copa right here in New York? Oh, Harry, that's fab! Are you sure? Boy, I really needed that boost after missing out on that damn Broadway show! When do I open? March eighth? Why, that's just around the corner. . . . Who's the headliner? . . . Joe E. Lewis! I can hardly believe it! . . . Sure, Sunday night . . . that will be fine. I'll be at the Copa lounge at ten sharp. . . . Oh, Harry, are you coming with me Friday to Levinsberg's? . . . Oh, that's okay, nothing to apologize about, I can manage. Perhaps I'll take Sylvia with me. . . . Thanks again, Harry. I'm gonna work like a sonofabitch for that Copa opening. First of all . . ."

❊

The nanny, wearing a starched white pinafore over an iron-gray uniform and a matching headdress, looked out of place, in sharp contrast to the other children's nurses in Nugent-Strong Botanical Gardens on Key Crescent. The closed black leather English perambulator with large wheels, a red balloon fastened to its handlebar, was creating much attention, like a Ferrari among Chevrolets and Fords.

A gray-haired blind man in tattered clothes accidentally stumbled in the buggy's path, hitting it with his white stick. Putting the brake on, the nanny let him pass, nodding apologetically, and, bending down, cooed, "Is my precious baby feeling the heat today?" It was in the high seventies, not unusual for the Florida Keys. "We don't want the little darling getting prickly heat, do we?" she simpered, fussing with the blanket. The baby gurgled as they passed a spouting fountain in the pond near the Japanese rock garden.

Kids were sailing their toy boats and running helter-skelter, rambunctiously throwing rubber balls. A noisy bunch of them were excitedly shoving each other as they stood on line to buy hot dogs and sodas from a scruffy man with a greasy cart. All around the nanny, old men and women justified their existence by occupying small spaces on benches in the late-afternoon sun.

A religious fanatic with a prophetlike face passionately exhorted his small flock of devout followers from an empty crate. "The Lord is waiting for you! The Lord is giving you life! The Lord wants your salvation! Hallelujah!"

"Hallelujah!" echoed the transfixed apostles.

"The Lord forgives you!"

"Hallelujah!" they chanted.

A drunk lying semiconscious in a ditch rose laboriously. "The Lord screws you! Hallelujah! Yeah! Yeah!" He took a swig from a bottle of cheap wine. All heads turned. Shocked into silence. He took another swig, seemingly unconcerned, even bored at this unexpected attention. Then the drunk smiled proudly to no one but himself, mistaking recognition for importance.

Bicycles pedaling furiously through clouds of dust. Lovers embracing shamelessly—making promises.

"My goodness!" a female voice exclaimed behind the nanny. "What a big baby carriage! Do you have twins in there?" It was one of the other nurses.

They were all sitting on benches, smoking, gossiping and laughing loudly among themselves, neglecting the children in their care.

"Is it an antique?" the woman persisted, slightly irritated at the lack of response. Nanny gave her a look of utter disdain and moved on toward the Chinese Pagoda.

"Well, be that way then!" the woman said. "I suppose you've got the Queen of England in there!"

"Or King Kong!" said another.

"Maybe both!" the woman sneered.

They all tittered contemptuously, eyeing the nanny as she disappeared swiftly down the path.

She passed towering tropical vegetation and fruit trees indigenous to the Keys, providing a lush backdrop to a quaint round wooden pavilion where a brass band was playing military music.

"Does the pretty baby want to listen to the music? Does Mama's boy want to march?"

"Kiss, kiss!" a small voice chirped.

"Later, you naughty little boy!" The nanny chastised her charge with make-believe sternness. "Just wait till we get home, and the baby can have all the kisses he wants before beddie-byes."

Lowering the hood slightly, she took his hand in hers, and tracing a finger in circular motions over his palm, hummed: "Walkie round the garden like a teddy bear . . ." The baby laughed uproariously, antici- pating what was coming. "One step, two step . . ." He dissolved in a fit of giggles. "Tickle the baby there!" And she tickled him under the arm. He fell backward. Legs up in the air. Feet covered in pink-and-blue booties. "Now, now!" she reprimanded gently, helping him back to a sitting posi- tion and adjusting the hood. They entered one of the vast greenhouses, a feat of nineteenth-century engineering, constructed of intricately molded cast iron and glass. "I'm going to teach the baby the names of all the flowers. And I want the baby to repeat them after me. Amaryllis. Ama-ryllis. Am-a-ryl-lis."

"Amar . . . amar . . . amra-will . . ."

"No, no! Try again. Amaryllis. Am-a-ryl-lis. Am-a-ryl-lis."

"Amaryllis."

"Nar-cis-sus," she pronounced carefully, touching the white flower.

"Nar-cus . . ."

"No, no, no. Nar-cis-sus. Pay attention! Or Nanny's going to have to smack baby's paddy."

"Nar . . . nar . . . narcus."

"Naughty baby!" she scolded, and produced a twig, smacked the back of his hand. Hard.

The baby cried loudly. "Narcissus . . . narcissus . . . narcissus!" he blubbered, suffocating with tears.

"Now, that's a good baby. Spare the rod and spoil the child. That's what I always say."

"It's none of my business!" said an outraged woman with a soft Jello profile. "But you shouldn't hit that poor child just because he can't pronounce the difficult names of those flowers! Why, I can't even—"

"You were right the first time!" spat the nanny, controlled as ice. "It's none of your business!" Tying the baby's blue lace-edged bonnet and blowing his nose, she speedily pushed the perambulator out of the glass and metal palace into the open air.

Suddenly the nanny jumped. For no explicable reason the red balloon attached to the handle of the carriage burst with a bang, sending the baby into a paroxysm of blind rage. She spoke slowly and softly and with feeling. "I'm sorry, my little darling. We'll be home soon. We'll be just in time for Captain Video." Billowing clouds of baby's audible contentment were the answer to the fluting of her voice.

For a hurried second the nanny squinted at the sun and noticed how tiresome the sky was in its monotonous purity. It was nearly five-thirty in the flowing unreality of that stodgy community, and crowds of workers, smelling from their dull jobs, inundated the park.

The nanny felt a great urgency to leave. Fast. As she eased the perambulator down the curb a policeman came to her assistance. "That's a pretty big baby carriage you've got there, ma'am. I ain't never seen nothin' like it. Lemme give you a hand."

"I can manage!" she said haughtily. "Thank you very much indeed!" dismissing him with a shake of the head.

"I was only tryin' to be neighborly, ma'am."

"I know perfectly well what you're trying to be!" She forced a smile. "Thank you very much for your trouble," she added with artificial politeness.

With difficulty she lowered the perambulator over the curb and pushed it up the hill. Like a desperate swimmer at last gaining the shore, she breathed gratefully on reaching Franklin Delano Roosevelt Avenue.

She hurried on, but was forced to stop when the baby gleefully threw his rattle on the ground. "Who's being a naughty baby?" she snapped, picking up the toy. They had not gone more than a few more yards when the child threw it on the ground again. "Baby's going to bed tonight without his supper if he doesn't watch out!" she admonished, raising her voice. The next time he threw the rattle, she confiscated it and hit the tips of his fingers brutally with the twig. He emitted a desperate wail. In a few minutes she calmly announced, "We've arrived," and almost as if the words were magic, his heartrending cries were replaced by happy sloshing babbles.

The Happy Hideaway Motel was pure Americana. If it weren't for the drooping palm trees surrounding it and the balmy weather, you could just as easily be in Cleveland or Kansas City, the nanny thought. She raised her eyes to the neon billboard that listed the amenities—*Dancing Every Saturday Night, Free Drinks for Ladies—5 to 7, Sunday Brunch Served All Day—All You Can Eat, Only $2, Swimming All Year Round.*

On the roof of the motel was a light-blue banner emblazoned with a smiling black whale straddled by a girl in a crimson bathing suit and the words *Button Manufacturers of America, Welcome to Key Crescent* in gold letters.

Pushing the carriage through the parking lot full of cars from all over the country, she carefully avoided the people who were emerging from them. A sign on the back of one auto read "Just Married"; old shoes and tin cans were attached to it by grimy white satin streamers.

The nanny pushed the carriage through the back door. She rang for the service elevator and waited an interminable length of time for it to reach the ground floor. "Don't fret," she consoled the whining baby, touching the pink cheeks gently, noticing he was perspiring heavily. "It won't be long now."

The doors slid open. A black maid with pickaninny braids shifted her cart a bit and complained, "Why you doan take the front elevator like them decent folk do?"

"Because there are steps in the front. That's why!" Nanny's eyes flashed coldly.

The elevator stopped at the third floor.

"Move your cart out of the way," demanded the nanny imperiously, "and help me with the carriage, please."

"I's jist do rooms, miz. I doan push baby buggies!" The maid yawned lazily, looking like an unmade bed, as if the mere mention of work summoned the sandman.

"I'm not asking you to push the buggy," the nanny said. "Here's five dollars. Just let me pass!"

"Ye-e-e-e-s, ma'am!" The maid understood money.

If anything from the twentieth century is to be added to a time capsule and preserved for posterity, it should be an efficiency motel room: the double beds with their chenille spreads and ammonia-smelling sandpaper sheets, the immovable table lamps without bulbs, the shag rug (a mixture of unhealthy browns and suspicious reds, with strange green spots), the television set with sound or picture, but never both, drawers that don't open, uncomfortable armchairs at opposite ends of the room, the closets lacking hangers, the postcards advertising its ugly façade in grainy, garish colors, the always ignored *Don't Disturb* sign, the telephone that doesn't work, the inevitable Gideon Bible, the flimsy flowered drapes that do not quite close and miss the floor by inches, the cardboard reproduction of Van Gogh's "Sunflowers" nailed to the paper-thin wall, a menu with strange calligraphy scribbled in the margin by a previous occupant, a fully equipped kitchenette with everything in working order—except the stove and refrigerator; a bathtub for midgets, towels too small to wrap your head in, enough wrapped soap to wash one pair of legs, a toilet seat with its "sanitized" paper band begging someone with blasphemous scissors to declare it officially open, the bathroom glass gift-wrapped in cellophane, daring society to lift it to its lips, a half-used tube of toothpaste or blunt razor blade abandoned by a former inmate; potbellied displaced conventioneers, tags on their lapels shouting the names of their anonymity, haunting hallways, barging into each others' always open rooms, and moving to the desperate tune of raucous laughter, their masklike faces cemented into a pretense of prankish, boyish joy. The ice machine grinding loneliness into every pore of one's being. The motel. The American motel. A shrine to impersonality and bad taste. The amorous locale that law-abiding citizens choose for their pursuit of clandestine sex.

The perambulator barely made it through the narrow door of the two spacious adjoining corner suites. The first bedroom had been transformed into a deluxe nursery, replete with toys, stuffed animals, blocks and balls of all sizes, a rocking horse, a tricycle and a large playpen. The nanny immediately closed the curtains. The baby was calm.

The nanny cranked the pram down to the level of the large bed and easily rolled the baby onto it. He whimpered, and she leaned her head on his chest, hearing a quickening heartbeat.

Turning the light on, she lifted him slightly, carrying the weight of his head on her shoulder. His hand took hers with the avidity with which sand absorbs water.

Wrapping him warmly in the white softness of her arms, she laid him down gently. He was wearing skin-colored rubber pants over diapers and a little blue jacket decorated with Donald Duck designs. "Who's been a naughty baby?" she asked, feeling the wet seat of his pants. "Never mind. Nanny's going to forgive him this time." She sounded gruff but unmenacing. He was crying docilely while being divested of his garments steadily and methodically. Spreading his legs apart and arching them in the air, she sponged and dried him lovingly with a fluffy monogrammed towel. "Poor baby! Who's got a bad case of nappy rash?" she sighed indulgently, massaging him with Johnson's Baby Oil. "That'll make him feel better—boo, boo, boo!"

"Mama, mama!" he gasped, holding tightly onto his teddy bear.

"Nanny will give the good little fellow his bath later on, and we'll watch Captain Video."

"Yes, yes. Please, please, Nanny!" he begged.

"Patience, my sweet one, patience . . ."

He savored each of her sentences as if finding gold within.

"Is the baby hungry after his long walk in the fresh air?" she asked soothingly, lowering the front of her pinafore and unbuttoning her gray frock. "Has all that exercise given our little man a great big healthy appetite?"

"Hmmmmmmm," the baby mumbled greedily.

"That's a good boy."

She removed the left cup of her nursing brassiere and an ample breast spilled over the baby's face. The nanny held its fullness. The paleness of the long, tapered fingers were her only jewels.

"Hmmmmmm," gurgled the baby, immensely comfortable in all his rosy skin.

"What a little sweetheart!" she said encouragingly, cradling him, guiding and allowing the distended pink nipple to slip between the waiting, rapturous lips. He sucked voraciously, passionately. The thick white sap ran down his chin mixed with his own saliva.

He kneaded the breast harshly with his hands.

"Easy, baby. Don't hurt Nanny!" she commanded. The baby ignored her and in his impetuosity nearly choked, gasping out incoherent mutterings.

"I told you to take it easy!" she repeated. The baby continued coughing and slurping until the nanny pulled away. He mouthed the air, his lips forming a gaping hole, his fingers clawing her warm, sweet flesh. Pressing him over her shoulder, she patted rhythmically, burping him assiduously. Eventually he belched. A stream of warm white milk, putrid-smelling, trickled down the nanny's back. She went on till all the air was released.

Spreading the fresh, sweet-smelling toweling on the bed next to the rubber pants and large safety pins, she looked at him suspiciously.

"Listen to me," the nanny said with a frightening kindness. "Did you look at any other ladies in the park this afternoon?" He stopped his cooing abruptly and pivoted his head. "Well—did you?" Avoiding her eyes, the baby trembled slightly. "Answer me, you wicked boy! Did you?" A toughness crept into her face.

"No, no," he sniveled, just above a whisper.

"Yes, you did!" she accused harshly, taking hold of his head in both hands as Madame Defarge would a freshly decapitated one. "I can always tell when you're lying! Tell me the truth!" she demanded, turning him on his stomach. "Did you? Did you look at any other ladies in the park?" she asked savagely, producing a wooden paddle from the perambulator.

"Yes, yes, I did," he finally admitted with abject humility. "Forgive me, Miss Fortescue, forgive me," he implored humbly. "Forgive me!" He started to say that none of them were as pretty as Nanny, but his words were stifled as she brought the paddle down hard on his bottom.

"I'll forgive you all right, you ungrateful brat, but not till you've been well and truly punished for your willful ways!"

"Punish me, Miss Fortescue, punish me!" he blubbered. "I deserve it, I deserve it!" She struck him again and again. The tears streamed down his face, the shrieks stifled by a pillow. His agony made him squirm. She put her knee in the small of his back, pinning him down, and flung the teddy bear diabolically across the room.

"Have you been punished enough?" she snarled cruelly.

"No, no! Miss Fortescue, I deserve it!" he bawled. "I deserve it!" Perspiration ran down his flushed face. With all her force she brought the paddle down once more. His buttocks were now swollen, red and sore. Grabbing him furiously by the hair and the waist, she rolled him on his back. With difficulty he lifted his torso. And the strong hairy arms of Senator Glover Anderson wrapped around Mariela as, trembling with excitement, he burst screaming into ecstatic orgasm.

Rivulets of salty-tasting sweat and tears zigzagged down the well-known square-jawed face. Rivulets of pain and pleasure. Those indistinguishable twins. Sharing the same contortions, ecstasy, cries, entreaty, sadness, anguish, joy. Both wearing the same crown. The pleasurable crown of thorns and roses.

She rested her head on the shoulders strong enough to carry a bale of cotton, her finger tracing the outline of his muscular inner thigh. Glover Anderson, at forty-nine, was one of those exceptional men who improve with age.

Glover locked both his hands behind his neck, leaning against the headboard, naked, eyes half closed. "Miss Fortescue . . . Miss Fortescue . . . hmmmmmmmmmm?" he mused. "How old would she be now?" Although forty years had gone by since she was his governess, it was simply impossible for Glover to visualize Miss Fortescue being older than twenty-six or twenty-seven. She would *always* be twenty-six or twenty-seven . . . just like Mariela. Glover would *always* be five years old when he was with her. Mariela . . . Miss Fortescue . . . Miss Fortescue . . . Mariela . . . He couldn't differentiate. He thought of his mother.

—※—

Mercedes Talmadge Anderson had been born on the largest plantation in Americus, Georgia. The family had grandiose expectations for their beautiful only daughter, and this precluded a nouveau riche alliance. Against her parents' wishes, Mercedes was courted by Glover's father, Keller Anderson, and they eventually married. A year later a child was born, retarded, and died. Mercedes experienced the first of several carefully concealed breakdowns. Glover came next, and lived in his adoring mother's shadow. She insisted on breast-feeding him till age three. Soon afterward his father became besotted with Rachel Dewhurst, queen of the silent screen. As a result, Mercedes became desperately ill and unhappy. Gradually, imperceptibly, his mother counteracted her vulnerability by pretending toughness, which soon crystallized into sternness. Glover was often left in the care of nurses, and detested each of them. The exception was Miss Fortescue, an Englishwoman from Woking, Surrey, who bore a striking physical resemblance to his mother.

They could have been sisters. Both were tall and stately, with the same translucent complexion and gray-green eyes like those of a cat blinded by the headlights of an automobile. His mother wore low-cut dresses emphasizing the deep cleft of her extraordinary, full bosom, which had fascinated Glover since he was a baby. Miss Fortescue's severe uniform concealed her voluptuous figure, just as the starched headdress covered the dark hair, which, like Mercedes, she wore pulled into a bun at the nape of her neck. Miss Fortescue delighted in giving him regular spankings whenever he wet his pants or found himself incapable of repeating certain words and phrases after her. Glover, afraid Miss Fortescue would be dismissed, never reported this to his mother. Then came the turning point. He began anticipating Miss Fortescue's punishments. He started to relish his distress.

※

Mariela, showered and perfumed, returned sheathed in a deep purple negligée, her long glossy hair flowing over her shoulders. She found Glover in the living room, wrapped in a brown terrycloth robe, sitting cross-legged on the floor, smoking a Camel in a cloud of tobacco smoke, a drink in hand. She curled in the armchair above him. Glover was suave, serious, not quite comfortable with his own emotions, silent. He began to stand up.

"Stay put, Glover." Mariela was sparkling. He offered her a cigarette from an elaborate gold case.

"What have you done about my—my problem?" she asked.

"I've made several inquiries."

"Inquiries? Is that *all* you've done?"

"Mariela, I've suggested very strongly that they forget your involvement in the case; I've assured them you're innocent." He looked up quizzically. "You *are* . . . innocent, aren't you?"

The way the question was phrased angered her. A dusty memory rose to consciousness. "I hope you've exerted half as much energy for me as you did clearing your sister Joanna when she was found in a San Francisco motel with a professional ice skater smoking reefers. Didn't it cost you two hundred thousand dollars to squash that story, Glover?" He rose. His walk was slow, hunched, as if he carried a load of guilt. His back was turned.

"Don't bullshit me, Glover. Look at me. Who's the most important person you've contacted?"

"The mayor of New York."

"The mayor of New York. . . ." She thought, reflecting on the pictures Nathan had showed her. "And what was the outcome, may I ask?" she said sardonically, meeting her drink halfway.

"I finally spoke to him on Monday, and had the distinct feeling somebody had gotten to him first. Really, Mariela, I've done all I could."

"Why didn't you speak to him on Sunday?" she asked, slightly irritated.

"It was with great difficulty, as you know, that I found the district attorney on Sunday. Sunday isn't easy for me, with my wife around . . ."

Glover's marriage at twenty-one to a wealthy and socially prominent Bostonian had won the immediate approval of his self-made multimillionaire father. Compensation for the background Keller Anderson lacked was essential to the presidential plans he had for his son. He was eager to ensure not only money but the proper breeding for his heirs.

Cornelia Vandevere was educated and beautiful. Her three occupations in life, however, were clothes, horses and making sure that none of her long nails broke. Everything else bored her—politics, friends, sports, theater, and especially sex, which put her to sleep. To dissipate her boredom she had tried her hand at photography and had made a small reputation in that field. In fact, it was Cornelia who had taken exclusive photographs of the Prince of Wales embracing an American girl at a navy party in San Diego during the future king's 1926 North American tour. Cornelia Vandevere's pictures were printed on the front pages of most newspaper and magazine covers throughout the world. Their value increased vastly ten years later when the lady in question became the Duchess of Windsor.

"Are you with me, Glover?" asked Mariela, noticing his distraction as he dragged on an unlit cigarette.

"Why, of course, hot stuff." He smiled apologetically. "Why do you ask?" He brushed a lock of rebellious hair from his eyes. It was clear to Mariela her problem had now fallen out of the realm of Glover Anderson's interest. Her eyes strayed to a large bouquet of tiger lilies. She turned full on him. "What are those flowers doing here?" she said in a panic.

"How the hell should I know? 'Courtesy of the Management,' I suppose! Who cares?"

"I've never known them to send flowers," Mariela said, hoping he was right. She pleaded breathlessly, "Get rid of them—immediately! Glover. Please." Bewildered, he carried them to the kitchenette, closed the door behind him, and pulling up a stool, joined her at the bamboo-and-glass bar near the terrace.

"Glover, there's something I have to say to you." She looked at him regretfully. Outside, the afternoon was slowly merging into night, casting long, portentous shadows. "What would you say, Glover, if I told you that our little . . . *session* today has been filmed?" He stared at her, not comprehending. "Do you think it would affect your Ozzie Nelson image?" The boyish face, complacent in the lazy twilight, collapsed into a mass of wrinkles. Mercilessly she continued. "Do you think it might affect your chances as a presidential candidate if the wrong people got hold of this film?"

He looked at her numbly. "I . . . I don't . . . I don't quite understand what you're saying. Could ya repeat it?" Under stress he regressed to his southern drawl.

"*Avec plaisir*. I'll repeat it gladly," she whispered. "Do you think it might affect your chances as a presidential candidate if this film fell into the wrong hands?"

He followed the movements of her lips as if viewing a silent movie. He was seeing but not hearing. It finally sank in. "I . . . I don't believe it! Not . . . not from you!" he began slowly. "Mariela! You above all!" he gasped helplessly, taking her hands in his. "I . . . I've always made it a point to know everything about the people I associate with. *I know* who you are, Mariela, I *know* where you come from. But I refuse to believe you'd behave like a common, blackmailing tart!"

"Allow me to quote from Kipling," she snapped. " 'The Colonel's Lady an' Judy O'Grady are sisters under their skins.' "

He looked furiously about. "Where . . .? How . . .? How was it made? He raced madly around the room inspecting ceilings, corners, mirrors, floors, opening doors, slamming them. Defeated, he leaned heavily against the bar, where Mariela sat munching peanuts—slowly placing them into her warm moist mouth, savoring each one as if it were a gourmet's delight.

"I always knew the power you held over me. You were the first person in my life who could fulfill my fantasies. I had to have you. There's an expression that explains exactly how I felt when I first met you. I was drawn to you like . . . like 'salmon swimming upstream to spawn.' I . . . I . . .'" He lost the train of his thought and faltered hopelessly, wiping his forehead with the back of his hand in one of the gestures that had become his trademark. "What was I talking about?"

"You were talking about salmon spawning." Her tone was passionless, cold. She tossed another peanut into her mouth, catching it like a trained seal. She never missed.

"Mariela, please tell me it isn't so! I simply can't believe it! I've always given you money! And much more than you ever—"

"Come on, Glover, quit it!" she scoffed. "You *insist* on paying, *insist* on being debased! Money expiates your guilt, doesn't it? Well, doesn't it?" she repeated. His eyes avoided hers. "Look at me when I'm speaking!" she ordered.

Without lifting his head he complied and said weakly, "Mariela, what is it you want from me?"

"You haven't done all you can to save me," she stated flatly. "I told you yesterday that I need someone higher up to intercede on my behalf and have the grand jury convened as soon as possible."

"But I arranged to have Vincent Petroni handle the government's case. Surely he can—"

"No, Glover, he cannot." She got up. "I sincerely believe somebody's setting me up, somebody who thinks I'm in the way and know too much. I'm sure I'm being followed."

"I've already spoken to the mayor."

"You can go higher than the mayor's office."

"But, Mariela, wouldn't—"

"Mariela nothing!" she shouted angrily, harsh lightning filling her eyes.

"But, Mariela, I went as high as—"

"As high as your father did when your mother committed suicide?"

"I . . . How do you know about that?"

"As high as your father went to have the coroner return a verdict of 'death from natural causes'?" Mariela was bristling. "I didn't murder, I didn't steal, and I don't intend to die!" She lowered her voice several tones. "Glover, this is an ultimatum. I want to stop being followed, intimidated and frightened. It's in your power to arrange this. If anything happens to me, you'll go down too."

Breathing shallowly, Glover refilled his drink. "Mariela, this is a nightmare."

She opened the terrace door, listened intently to the foaming song of the ocean, then turned abruptly and said, "If you choose not to help me, *Miss Fortescue* will disappear forever."

He swallowed hard. "Please, Mariela. I have done—"

"Let me repeat. You *can* go higher than the mayor's office!"

"Yes."

"Then do it."

"I will."

"Now!"

"I'd feel self-conscious with you around. I—I'd better make the call from the other room."

"You'll do nothing of the sort. You'll make the call right in front of me!"

"What about the film?" he asked meekly.

"We'll talk about that *later*. Make the phone call *now*."

Mariela sat on a couch across from Glover and heard him dial seven numbers before reaching the State House. She listened carefully to every word.

When Glover had finished his call to Albany he joined her, arms crossed on his massive chest. "Well, Mariela, you've heard it all. He promised me it would be done."

"Promises . . ." She shrugged her shoulders cynically.

"He doesn't give promises! He gives orders!" he assured her. "Now, the film, please," he said with contained rage.

Mariela turned to him. "Glover, there never was any film." His eyes searched her blank features. "I never had any intention of cooperating with Nathan Berger—"

"Nathan Berger?"

"He was eager to get his hands on some very personal footage of you today."

"How the hell did he know we were meeting?"

"I made the mistake of telling him, but I called back to assure him you'd canceled out. Glover, my life is in danger, but no matter how grave, I would never blackmail you!"

He relaxed for the first time, went to the bar and poured the two of them drinks. Stiff ones. His poise somewhat regained, he smiled his famous smile, which began with shrewd understanding, opened a little wider into irony, then shrank back to self-satisfaction. Then, as if struck by a thunder-bolt, he whirled toward her, the smile disappearing. "Shall we speak about fathers, hot stuff? Do you really believe I became the candidate of my party just because of money? Just because of my father?" His face became male-volent. "I'm their greatest hope because of balls, hot stuff! Yes, balls, with a capital *B!* And I'm not afraid of a third-class whore masquerading as a first-class one! Shall we go on about *fathers?*" He gulped his drink to the bottom. "I understand yours did a great job organizing that little tea party between Hitler and the Windsors at Berchtesgaden!"

"What did I—"

"What were you going to say, hot stuff?"

"What did I have to do with all that?"

"Poor Little Miss Goody Two-Shoes!" He swaggered around the room. "Isn't Lord Chiselhurst your father? Wasn't he one of the heads of the British Nazi party? Or have you renounced His Lordship as well?" He advanced closer to her. Mariela could feel his breath. Warm, menacing. She tightened the belt of her robe, looking everywhere for a cigarette. "Here, hot stuff Take this." He threw a pack into the air. She tried to catch it, but it landed on the floor. Mariela picked it up. His gold lighter hit her on the back of the neck as she was about to rise.

"You son of a bitch! How dare you!" she shouted.

He ignored her. "Are you proud of his friendship with the Germans even after the war broke out? What do you think of his role as would-be king-maker in Lisbon? He came pretty close to altering history, didn't he? Where do you think he might have fitted in, with Prince Charming roman-tically restored to his throne? Who knows, Mariela, you could have been in Buckingham Palace right now, bowing and scraping to Queen Snow-Slush instead of playing Nanny in Florida.

She threw the lighter, missing his face by inches. It crashed into a mirror behind him. Glover continued venomously. "Both your father and his side-kick the Duke of Windsor would have been shot for treason if the king hadn't personally intervened to save their necks."

She was immobilized by his words.

"For the sake of variety shall we move to you?" The atmosphere was heavy with his vindictiveness. "I could have had you deported any time. I know a lot more about you, *Lady Chelmsford*. Or have you had enough? I'm sure you're not too eager to inherit your father's title. Isn't that how it works in England? But the old man is still alive, isn't he, so there's no point talking about that. And how much did you have to pay that GI, John Koenig, to marry you so you could come to this country anony-mously, safe from the stigma of the Chiselhurst name?"

"You're a fine one to speak of morals!" she shouted.

"We're all slaves to our infancies, Mariela—but that's another story." He paused momentarily, striking a caustic note. "What's His Lordship up to these days? Harmlessly plotting the demise of the Michaelmas daisy in the south of France?"

"Stop, Glover, stop!"

"So . . . we didn't star in a film production after all!" he ventured, smiling. "That's too bad, hot stuff!" he teased. "You gave one of your better performances this afternoon!" But his cruelty was not calculated to hurt. Unconsciously he was enjoying all this too much to bring the little game to an end.

"No, Glover. I could never have done it!"

"Well, Mariela, I've got some news for you too." She looked at him, intrigued. "I could never have done it either!" he said.

"What couldn't you have done?" she asked, confused.

"Made that phone call to Albany, hot stuff!" Like one of the great actor-managers, his timing was impeccable.

"But I heard you," she protested, bewildered.

"You heard only my side of the conversation!"

Her mind raced. Their eyes met. Controlling her voice, she asked, "But why?"

"I never did take to blackmail, hot stuff."

"Stop talking like a boy scout, Glover," she snapped.

"Temper, temper, my dear Mariela!" he chided. "Besides," he added, letting her off the hook, "I made the call yesterday."

"Why didn't you tell me?"

"I don't have to tell you everything, Mariela. In fact, I don't have to tell you a goddamned thing! I just wanted to see how far you were capable of—"

"I'm sorry," she said in a small voice, and, for the moment, Mariela felt whipped. She sat and looked at him in silence.

"Do you really believe, Mariela, that Glover Keller Anderson III is a horse's ass?" They stood facing each other, defiantly. Mariela sensed an orgy of dangers surrounding her. She perceived a slight rising in the mound between his legs under the terry-cloth robe.

"Get over here, hot stuff!" he rasped hoarsely. "Let's see those big tits!" She moved toward him. "Stay where you are . . . under the light. Open your robe. . . . That's right . . . all the way. . . . More . . . Now drop it to the floor!"

His dressing gown rose visibly as he caressed his groin. He looked at her, loving her severe beauty. He approached, closed his eyes and held her face between his hands. He felt her soft skin on his forehead, on his cheek, on the other cheek, on his eyelid, on the other eyelid. He kissed her mouth. Her saliva wet his teeth as he drank it. The arrows of fire once again pierced his belly with the heat of a volcano. She started tracing arabesques with her hand and mouth.

"Put your tongue out," she commanded. He obeyed. She squashed the lighted butt of her cigarette on it, slowly extinguishing the red glow. He didn't move. Nothing. She offered his pain no relief and felt a cold pleasure.

Muzak was dribbling its syrupy rendition of "Laura," reminding Mariela of elevators, lobbies, doctors' waiting rooms, airport lounges. And the present.

Glover stared at her lips, smoother than oil. *Miss Fortescue* spoke.

"I believe, Glover, that you should be punished for your recalcitrance," she said sternly.

The lines on his face dissolved into a childish innocence, his eyes blinked. "Oh, no, Miss Fortescue. I promise to be a good boy," he cried in a little waif's voice. Allowing his robe to fall to the floor, he cleaved to her naked womanhood, glistening in the semidarkness.

"Promises are not enough, Glover. You know that I like actions!" she tormented. Provocatively, she cupped her breasts with her hands, pushing them up. Legs apart. Her spectacular figure was silhouetted in the doorway. They stalked each other. Two angry, familiar animals. "Go and stand in the corner at once, you naughty, wicked boy!" she snarled.

"Oh, no! Not that, not that!" he pleaded, running into the foyer and hiding, crouched under the table. Mariela closed the terrace doors so his howls could not be heard. Reaching for a cane, she followed him.

—⸙—

MATTIE/*New York City/Wednesday, February 3, 1954*

Mattie was pacing the floor, compulsively checking herself in the mirror each time she passed it. She was wearing the clingingest of Pucci dresses, bought on sale at Saks. Time crawled by. Tony was more than an hour late. He had called her in the morning on his arrival from Miami to say he was going straight to the Gotham Hotel with his luggage and then on to New Jersey to visit his widowed mother.

"I gotta eat some of her lasagna, Mattie, before anything else, or she'll kill me." He assured Mattie that he would be at her apartment no later than five o'clock that afternoon.

It was 6:10. She had already drunk several glasses of wine and nervously tweezed more hair from her eyebrows. Each time the iron gates of the elevator opened or closed on any of the six floors of the apartment house, Mattie heard them, like a blind man with an acute sense of hearing.

Mattie had piled her hair on top of her head à la Brigitte Bardot, her favorite actress. When dressing, she had noticed that one of her brown shoes was a bit scuffed at the toe, so she had filled in the bare spot with her eyebrow pencil. Mattie had splashed herself with White Shoulders, then dabbed Chanel No. 5 behind her ears and between her breasts—a combination of fragrances she thought irresistible.

The bedroom had a bordello look, with its crimson walls and crimson bed cover. Both lamps on the end tables were hooded with dark-green scarves, and she had exchanged the white bulbs for red ones. A picture of herself with her mother and one with her father hung above the dresser; they had been taken when she was "young," as she was fond of telling friends. There was a plaque next to them given to her by Leo Shull of *Show Business* magazine for being "the most promising performer of 1953." Near her bed was an eight-by-ten glossy of Tony inscribed "Let me be your water wings. Love, Antonio."

Although she'd planned to appear deeply absorbed in a feigned phone conversation when Tony arrived, the long-anticipated ring made Mattie drop all pretense and sent her rushing frantically to the door. It was Tony, tall, dark hair, a full mouth and extraordinary green eyes. He closed the door behind him and without a word they melted into each other's arms, kissing passionately.

"I want you now," Tony urged as he caressed her. "Let's go to the bedroom," she said, gently tugging at his sleeve. "Right here," Tony insisted. "Right now." He unbuttoned his shirt. She held his strong shoulders and rested her cheek on his bare skin. "I've missed you so, Tony. I've never missed anyone so much in my entire life." As she started to unzip her silk chemise dress he stopped her. "No, let me do it." She felt the soft fabric slide against her body. He held her close and laid her down on the carpeted entrance hall by the front door, searching her mouth with his tongue, caressing her taut breasts with his hands. He knelt, took off one of her shoes, then the other, pulled down her panties and began kissing her body softly.

"Please, Tony, I can't wait any longer," she pleaded urgently. "Please, Tony, take me."

"Wait, darling, wait, my baby," he said, kissing her nipples. "You're more lovely than I remember." Tony removed his boots and peeled off his tight jeans, throwing them on the floor. He knelt between her legs, then, lowering himself, entered her with such force that she cried out with pleasure.

"I've missed you so, Tony." Her words turned to moans, which inflamed him further, and he deliberately forced himself deeper into her.

"I have too, baby." He was guiding her up and down the crest of frenzy, his tongue darting into her mouth as he reveled in her enjoyment. Her body was writhing beneath his, and she experienced a climax that made her forget where she was. He scooped her up in his arms and carried her to the bedroom. Her mouth and tongue kissed his body avidly. Her eyes met his, but she said nothing and again opened herself to him, ceasing to be aware of anything except his need of her.

"Tony, don't leave me, don't ever leave me." She wanted him to fill her forever and memorize every inch of her body.

"Oh, baby, I won't, I won't! How I've missed you!" They kissed, tongues tracing each other's lips. Slick and hot.

They were, in turn, gentle and fierce with each other, perfectly attuned. After a while the storm abated and they rested peacefully in each other's arms. The only sound they heard was the harmony of their heartbeats. She took a deep breath, moved out of his arms and reached for a joint, knocking over the telephone in the process.

Leaning on her elbow, she looked at Tony and started talking, mainly about herself. Talking about herself was Mattie's way of getting to know another person better. She spoke of her good heart, her great sexual fantasies, her audition, Toronto—everything.

Tony could hardly get in a word. And when he did, he spoke of his new clothes and Jeremy Rabb, his career and Jeremy Rabb, his new songs and Jeremy Rabb. And Beverly Langdon's beauty.

"Tony, I have to work at Levinsberg's Friday night. We can stay there for the weekend. Jenny Levinsberg will be thrilled if you come with me. Red Buttons is going to be there. And Steve and Eydie. It should be fun."

"As long as I can spend twenty hours a day in bed with you, I'll go anywhere." Tony kissed her on the mouth, and felt an uneasy stirring. "But I have to be back in the city on Sunday. I'm doing the Jack Paar show with Geneviève and Dodie Goodman. Jeremy Rabb may fly in from the coast. He has a new plane."

"Why, that's great, Tony. It'll work out perfectly. Listen, Harry Ross called me last Sunday. I'm opening for Joe E. Lewis at the Copa in four weeks. He'll be in town Sunday night and wants to meet me. I'll only be tied up an hour." Without inhibition, she arose naked from the bed, went to the kitchen to fetch some wine.

Tony switched on the radio. The news was on.

". . . it has been discovered that three weeks before his death Karl Ravenstein was beaten on Fifty-sixth Street late at night. The financier refused to give any information about a motive for the assault. He was offered police protection, but he turned it down, declaring that it would interfere with his private life."

"Did you know Karl Ravenstein?" Tony shouted as he twirled the dials looking for some music. He settled on Rosemary Clooney singing "This Old House."

"No," Mattie answered, coming back into the bedroom with two glasses of white wine. Her voice assumed an important tone as she added, "But coming back from Toronto, I saw a man on the plane who I believe was implicated in his murder. I recognized him from the newspaper photos.

Anyway, to hell with Karl Ravenstein! Let's drink to us!" Mattie kneeled on the bed, they clinked glasses and drank the wine.

"Good God!" she exclaimed, looking at the small clock on the night table. "It's almost eleven. How time flies!" She laughed deliciously. "Are you by any chance hungry?" Mattie asked, moistening her lips with her tongue.

"Are you kidding! I'm starved. But let's eat at home. I'm too weak to walk anywhere. How about some Chinese food?"

"Great idea! There's a place near here that delivers till midnight." Mattie dialed Sung Fung Hoo and expertly ordered with the knowledge that she had acquired on the road. "You can't go wrong with Chinese food" had become Mattie's credo, the way some people are firm believers in the maxim "Eat where the truck drivers eat." Hesitantly she added, "Could you also bring a copy of the *Journal-American,* please?" She sounded almost like a child asking for an extra lollipop.

"Did I bore you so much that you want to read?" Tony asked mockingly.

"Of course not, silly, but my agent told me my picture is in it—a publicity shot I did for the Red Cross Blood Donor Program."

"I could use a transfusion myself," said Tony, pulling her back on the bed to lie beside him.

"Oh, Tony, you make me so happy. But I'm the one who needs a transfusion," she giggled. "Right about now I'm beginning to miss the blood I've given away."

"I'll take care of that," he said softly, sliding on top of her. "I'll take care of that . . ."

Twenty minutes later the doorbell rang and continued ringing impatiently. Extricating herself from Tony's arms, Mattie scurried to the door, grabbing her purse and robe en route.

Rising from the bed, Tony yelled, "Take the money out of my wallet. It's in my pants pocket."

"I don't know where they are," she said, dismissing his suggestion.

He laughed. "In the hallway where I left them."

But Mattie ignored him and rummaged through her purse. She sifted through loose cigarette tobacco, various eyebrow pencils, a topless tube of lipstick, and several notes and papers with names and numbers she couldn't recall jotting down, and finally retrieved a crumpled five-dollar bill with a pair of false eyelashes stuck to it like a dead spider. When she had paid for the food, she deposited the paper bag on the dining table as if it were laundry to be unwrapped at a more convenient time. Foremost in her mind was locating her picture. She found it on page two but did not like it at all. She studied the nose, thinking it was entirely too large, although she had taken great care to be photographed from her best angle, the one that minimized its proportions. She was even less satisfied with the caption: "Mattie Maxwell, the daughter of the late Jessica Miller, is seen at the 23rd Street Red Cross Blood Donor's Center, which . . ."

Why the hell does my name always have to be tied to Jessica Miller's? she thought. Haven't I paid my dues yet?

Mattie recalled the last time she had seen her mother alive. It was in London in the fall of 1953.

※

Jessica Miller had rented a small house on North Audley Street and was living there with her new husband, Ralph Cummings, whom she was introducing as a scenarist, now involved in all her projects. Actually Ralph's "writings" had consisted of proofreading the sports section of the *Daily News* in New York. They had met the year before at P. J. Clarke's, where she had fallen to the floor screaming, "I'm Jessica Miller, and I want a drink!" Ralph, who happened to be standing at the bar with a group of his buddies after having finished the late shift at the *News,* believed her. No one else had those haunting eyes. He had helped her to her feet and offered to take her home. She accepted and told him she was staying at the Waldorf.

The rest was well known. He had married her within two months, had nursed her back to some semblance of health, and tried desperately to curb her drinking, without much success. Jessica Miller was addicted to alcohol and to almost every kind of pill.

They had been married for a year when Mattie, at her mother's urgent request, flew from America to appear with her at a Royal Command Performance at the Palladium that would be filmed for an American television audience. It was one of the first public events that young Queen Elizabeth would attend after her coronation. Mattie and Jessica rehearsed an entire week, mainly at night, since Jessica was an insomniac and rarely rose before five in the afternoon. On the day of the much-publicized event Jessica had awakened at three in the afternoon, earlier than usual. Ralph was not at home, having gone to the theater to make certain that all of his wife's demands would be met before her arrival. The dressing room had to be lit with pink bulbs. Two bottles of cold gin were to be on hand. Her hairdresser had to be at the theater an hour and a half before the performance. Her makeup table was to be arranged with various containers of creams and powders in a sequence specified by Jessica, always the same.

Mattie heard her mother scream from the bedroom and was afraid that something terrible had happened to her. "Who the fuck hid my bottle of gin?" she shouted as her daughter entered the room.

"I don't know, Mother."

"How often have I told you not to call me Mother! You make me sound so old. My name is Jessica."

Mattie was used to such outbursts and calmly went to the refrigerator to fetch the iced gin that her mother seemed unable to do without. She had grave reservations about providing her with liquor so soon after she had awakened, but she also knew that not giving it to her would provoke one of Jessica's infamous outbursts. Mattie made a quick decision. She took the gin bottle, poured half of it into the sink, refilled it with water and brought it to her mother.

Jessica took the bottle from Mattie and drank from it greedily, seeming not to notice that anything was amiss. Mattie was delighted that her ploy had worked. Later she helped her mother dress and was able to bring Jessica to the theater in a relatively sober state.

The Palladium had seldom seemed more glamorous. The excitement could be felt everywhere, most of all when the royal family arrived. Bob Hope, who was emceeing the event, finished his first monologue to a standing ovation. On cue, he announced: "Your Majesty, ladies and gentlemen, a very unique young lady." Mattie came onstage. Her first words were: "My name is Mattie Maxwell. I'm proud to be the daughter of Jessica Miller, and I welcome you to this very special evening!"

She began her first song, "Let the Wind Blow My Way," and when she had finished, the usually reserved and undemonstrative British audience wildly applauded this girl, barely seventeen years old, who had belted out a song with a voice that indeed reminded them of her mother as she had sounded ten years earlier. Jessica was supposed to make her entrance immediately after Mattie's song, but her mother was not ready, and Mattie stayed on for the two additional songs she had planned in case Jessica needed a little more time to sober up. Jessica Miller came onstage while Mattie was still singing. The audience cheered madly, rising to their feet. Mattie stopped, accepted a gentle embrace from her mother and exited into the wings.

Although Jessica's voice had long passed its peak of perfection, the audience simply did not care on that history-making night. Jessica sang for over an hour. Toward the end she beckoned Mattie to join her, and together they performed a duet that brought the house down while they tap-danced and sang "Anything You Can Do, I Can Do Better," from *Annie Get Your Gun*. Jessica did several encores. After the curtain came down Mattie headed for her mother's dressing room, anxious to receive her praise and approval. She burst in without knocking. Ralph looked at her, surprised.

"How did you like it, Mother?" she asked breathlessly. Jessica, seated before her mirror, made no effort to turn around, nor did she reply. "How did you like it, Mother? Was I okay?" Then, tentatively, "Jessica?" Mattie approached the dressing table and grabbed her arm. When her mother did not respond, she tugged at her arm again. Suddenly Jessica sprang up, whirled around and slapped Mattie sharply across the face. Then, pushing Ralph aside, she shouted at the top of her lungs, "Don't you ever try to steal the spotlight from Jessica Miller again!"

The sting of the slap and its unexpectedness pained Mattie so deeply that she failed to hear the warning. But she did catch Jessica's next words, snarled between clenched teeth: "Get out of this room and get out of my life. You'll never amount to anything."

Mattie ran out of the theater fighting back tears. Her throat felt constricted and she was biting her lower lip. When Ralph went searching for her, she was standing numbly on the corner amid the theater crowd, looking for a cab.

"What can I say, Mattie?" He gulped and tugged at his collar as if it had suddenly gotten too tight. "You know her better than I do. She doesn't mean it." Mattie was mute, still trying to hold back the tears. He searched in his pockets. "Here. Here's two hundred pounds. Do what you have to do."

Mattie returned to the house, packed her bags, reserved a room at the Savoy Hotel and checked in within the hour. Alone in her room, she threw herself across the bed and sobbed hysterically. She wanted so much to make Jessica proud of her, to do something to earn her love, to make her love her. But Jessica not only couldn't love her daughter, she couldn't even accept love from her. Mattie thought of her father. The last she had heard, he was going on his honeymoon with his fourth wife. There was no point in trying to contact him, even if she had known where he was, John Maxwell had nothing to offer, neither money nor love.

As she lay on the bed cradling herself she thought of what to do to ease the pain. She got up and stood before the mirror in the bathroom, appraising herself. "I'm ugly," she said out loud. "That's why nobody loves me." At that point she resolved: "My talent will make me beautiful and that will bring me love. If only I can keep my sanity." Now she was more determined than ever to leave a mark, to amount to something. She was Mattie Maxwell.

She dried her tears, washed off her stage makeup, leaving the false eyelashes on, and went down to the hotel lounge, knowing instinctively that she would find someone to love her, even someone to pretend. At that moment, as far as she was concerned, there was no difference.

As Mattie entered the American Bar she noticed a man sitting by himself. From the back, he could have been her father. She wondered what his face looked like. She sat in the shadows at a small table, and when he turned around, he noticed her. She returned his gaze with an enticing smile. He made love to her that night in her room, and all the while she wondered what her mother had felt when Mattie's father was on top of her. The stranger left an hour or so later, after she told him, "I can never sleep with anyone all night. I have to sleep alone." After the man was gone Mattie realized that she didn't even know his first name. And that she didn't care.

❋

"Mattie, Mattie, what's going on in here!" Tony shouted at the top of his lungs in the bathroom, but Mattie was so deeply engrossed in her thoughts that she didn't hear him. "Mattie! What the hell are you doing in there? Get your ass over here and forget about the goddamn food!" His cry was a cross between a command and a plea.

Still in a daze, like someone regaining consciousness, Mattie rushed toward him as he wrapped himself in the only towel he had been able to find.

"I can't believe it, Mattie. The floor is covered with duck shit!" he yelled.

"Oh, Tony! How could I have been so dumb? I meant to tell you that I bought some ducks, but you didn't give me time. Aren't they cute, especially Boris?"

"Boris? Which one is that?"

Mattie walked toward the bath, followed by Tony. The ducks were floating in rainbow swirls of water, the color of the now pale ribbons. The yellow plumage of the birds' Long Island ancestors had acquired the hues of exotic birds from faraway lands. Mattie took the ducks out of the tub and carefully placed them in their box by the sink. The box had been lined with the same crimson fabric that covered her boudoir walls and was now badly stained.

"You know, Tony," she continued, "I've only had them two days and already they've grown." She paused. "How big do you think they'll get?" Tony detected a note of apprehension in her voice.

"Big enough to make a meal, if that's what you want to know. And big enough to stink up your whole place. Whatever came into your head, baby? Whoever heard of raising ducks in a New York apartment?"

Mattie looked at him dispiritedly. "I fell in love with Boris and had to buy all six of them."

Tony held her by the shoulders, shook his head in disbelief, brought his palms to her face and kissed her gently. "You're a nut. A beautiful, wonderful nut," he said, gazing at her pensively. He led her to a chair, sat and pulled her down onto his knees. He could feel her naked weight underneath the thin robe as she shifted on his naked lap. "I love you, Mattie, but I won't share a bathroom with a bunch of ducks," he said, as though reprimanding a capricious child.

She held onto him, tears brimming in her eyes. "I love you so much, Tony. I've never loved anyone else before. I feel so helpless. I just don't know what to do anymore."

"I'll help you," he said, having no idea what he would do. He wiped her tears away with his hand, saying, "Come on, don't cry, baby. Ducks need space, and when you build your big mansion in the Hollywood hills, you can have a pond and as many ducks as your little heart desires. I'll tell you what," he added thoughtfully. "We'll take them to Jenny Levinsberg's tomorrow. They'll be in paradise there. You can visit them whenever you like." She nodded, attempting a smile. He looked round. "How come dinner isn't ready yet?"

"It is, it is," Mattie cried, pointing to the paper bag.

"Marron!" he exclaimed. "You'll never make an Italian wife, and that's for sure." He kissed her left shoulder.

An Italian wife, maybe not, she thought to herself and added out loud, "There's nothing wrong with the Irish, you know."

"Where are the plates?"

Mattie readjusted her robe and helped Tony set the table. They were ravenously hungry. Mattie had bought an enormous jug of wine, and the price was still stuck to it—$1.10. She retrieved two glasses from the bedroom—the only two in the house that matched—and poured the wine into them.

Toward the end of the meal Tony said, "I promised June Christie I'd catch her last show at Eddie Condon's tonight. How about it?"

"I hope I can stay awake," replied Mattie, stifling a yawn.

"That's no problem. I've got something for you, baby." Tony got up and walked to where his pants lay. From a pocket he extracted two green capsules and handed them to Mattie. "Take these and you'll feel your day is just beginning."

Mattie recognized the Benzedrine. She could recognize almost any pill; her mother's bathroom cabinet had made her an expert. She swallowed the capsules with wine and within minutes began to feel energized, more alert than she had been in hours. Tony was right.

Mattie was dressing in her bedroom when the telephone rang—one, two, three rings. "Who the hell would be calling at this time?" Mattie grumbled. "Why isn't the service picking up?" Four, five, six, seven times. "Dammit, they're supposed to pick up after three rings!" The ringing finally stopped. She stepped into her dress. Then the phone rang again, more insistently. "I've got to change that lousy answering service. As usual, they're asleep." She picked it up. "Yeah? . . . Who? . . . Yeah. I'll get him. Just a moment please." She went toward the bathroom. The door was open. "Call for you, Tony. Could you zip me up please?" She turned her back to him, holding her waist tightly with both hands to make the procedure easier. "Who knows you're here, darling?"

"I left your number at my hotel in case of emergency. Stand still, Mattie, or I'll never get you zipped. Who is it?"

"I didn't ask. It sounds like long distance."

Tony shuffled into the living room. "Don't be long," Mattie yelled. "It's really getting late, if you want to catch that show."

Tony lifted the extension. "Hello. This is Tony Rook."

For what seemed an eternity there was no sound. Mattie became apprehensive and peeked at him from the bedroom. She saw him holding the phone. He wasn't speaking. His back was hunched. Then she heard him swear and begin to cry all at the same time. The sounds spewed forth with uncommon strength and fury. They reverberated through the room in fragments, slicing and shattering the silence like pieces of plate glass hitting an empty stage.

"When did it happen? . . . I don't believe it . . . Since when? . . . Over where? . . . I don't believe it . . . plane . . . immediately . . . Why? . . . The new plane . . . Jeremy . . . killed . . . I can't believe it. . . . Goddammit it . . . and Beverly? . . . Thank God. . . . I will. . . . Jeremy dead . . . Goddammit it . . . tonight . . . right away."

The phone hit the wall with the sound of a shotgun blast and fell to the floor like a small body. White plaster scattered, leaving in its place a large discolored blotch resembling newly splashed blood. Mattie saw Tony's knuckles, hard and white, by his sides. He stood, legs unsteady, as if unable to bear the weight of his sorrow. His back was still hunched. And then she heard the wrenching sobs.

—✳—

DENISE/*London, England/Wednesday, February 3, 1954*

"What is the purpose of your visit, Miss Cunningham?" asked the passport inspector, his eyes looking impersonally into hers. Denise hesitated a moment, turned slightly to the left as if to get reassurance from the people behind her; for a flickering instant she seemed to wince. Then she erased the expression quickly with a dazzling smile, which had no effect on the bureaucrat.

"Miss, the purpose of your visit, please?" he repeated.

Denise managed to put on a regal pout as she replied in measured tones, "Friends—I'm visiting friends. And sight-seeing—but mainly friends."

"How long will you be in England?"

"Ten days. Maybe less."

"Your address in the United Kingdom, please?"

The same hesitation while she opened her purse and read aloud from a small address book. "The Hall."

"The hall? What hall?"

"Yes," she replied quietly, "The Hall. That's the name of the place. North Downs, in the county of Kent. Between Tunbridge Wells and—"

"Yes, miss, thank you. I know where North Downs is located. Have a pleasant stay."

She passed through customs with her single suitcase, and just beyond the gate noticed a uniformed man, with a round, chubby face and tiny, muddy eyes. He was carrying a placard bearing her name. "Are you Perkins from The Hall?"

"Yes, I am. Perkins is the name," he replied. "Miss Cunningham, I presume? Have you had a good trip?"

"Yes, Perkins, but exceedingly long. Thirteen hours in all."

The porter lifted her luggage into the trunk of the Bentley, and they left Heathrow Airport. The apprehension Denise had felt as the aircraft lurched through alternate layers of nearly opaque grayness and wispy silver strands was dissipated as the smell of England—an indefinable mixture of moist lavender and old leather, overwhelmed her. The gentle aroma gave Denise a sudden exquisite sense of well-being.

Remembering such movies as *Brief Encounter* and *Maytime in Mayfair,* Denise tried unsuccessfully to imagine what London would look like. "How long will it take us to get into London?" she asked excitedly.

"I'm afraid we're not going to London, Miss Cunningham. We're taking the Guildford Road to Kent."

She was disappointed, and it brought her back to the reality of her visit. Just as well too, she reflected. I wouldn't have time to sight-see anyway. Absentmindedly she observed the people along the motorway. They seemed shabby, especially the women, in their ill-fitting tweed suits and thick knitted wool stockings. Denise closed her eyes, allowing her body to sink into the depths of the leather upholstery as she cuddled herself cozily in her nutria coat. Am I doing the right thing? she wondered. Well, it's too late now. It must be done. It's my own decision, my own secret. Like a thousand ants, her thoughts swarmed in her mind, biting at her self-confidence, crawling amidst her fears. Her anguish was mounting.

Perkins' voice broke into her absorption. "We're in the center of Reigate, miss." In no time at all they had left the medieval clock tower, the plaster-and-timber Tudor houses behind them. Denise was engrossed with the image of Francesco. Francesco . . . What if he calls New York before I have a chance to phone him? Will the hotel remember my instructions? The idea was disquieting. Suddenly she recalled the size of the tip she had left the switchboard operators. Five hundred dollars has a way of improving the memory, she reasoned cynically. Money speaks, money listens, money lies and money buys.

"Have you noticed the ancient walls, miss?"

"Ancient . . ." The name "Sir Reginald Findlay" flashed on the screen of her subconscious and a thought swirled up. I hope he isn't too old, she thought. Of course, on the telephone it's hard to tell. No point dwelling on it now. I'll find out soon enough. Her breath misted the window; she didn't bother to wipe it off. Denise made an effort to take an interest in the picturesque stone walls separating the fat fields. "Yes, Perkins, they look very old," she said distractedly. "Do you have the time?"

"They are very old indeed, miss," he explained. "Some of them go back before the Napoleonic Wars. The stones have been—"

"Perkins, the time please," she interrupted briskly.

"Sorry, miss. It's nearly three o'clock," he replied, quickly adding, "The stones have been collected over the years—"

"By . . . ?"

"Farm laborers, miss—shale and slate mostly. They're fitted together like pieces of a jigsaw puzzle; they don't use any cement to hold them together—"

"Do we have much farther to go?"

"It's a dying art, miss. They can't find anybody nowadays who knows how to do it!" He laughed inexplicably.

She stared as if she had shut her ears.

"You'd think they'd fall over, wouldn't you, miss? And they . . ."

She was looking at Perkins through the rearview mirror. Come on, Denise, she chided herself. There's no excuse for weakness. Once you allow it, you're lost.

The car sped into the heart of the North Downs, with its undulating verdant hills and its sharp curves. How much longer, for Christ's sake, will it take? Denise felt a sudden chill, but it wasn't cold; she was afraid and felt slightly nauseated. I can't stand it in here another minute, dammit! She leaned toward the glass partition. "Are we nearing The Hall, Perkins?" she asked wearily.

"We should be there in about five minutes, miss."

In no time at all they had passed the village pub, and conveniently close, the parish church, with its lofty Gothic spires. The car drove through an imposing wrought-iron gate. Denise sat up, readjusting her hat, and felt beads of perspiration on her forehead.

Although it was winter, the grounds had an autumnal look, and the tires, skidding over dead leaves, made a crisp sound like crunched popcorn. Through the window Denise saw—snowdrops still in bloom, crocuses stretching their lush yellow colors, trees bursting with green, sticky buds, daffodils and tulips making their way through the soft earth.

"Perkins," she said, "I'm totally confused about the season we're in. It's February, we're in the middle of winter, and yet the growing flowers and dead leaves give me a sense of autumn and spring combined."

"Ah, Miss Cunningham, one can see you don't know England!" He adjusted his cap at a different angle, proud of the chance to once again display his knowledge. "At this time of year what you see is typical of our beautiful countryside. Oh yes, there is no place like it. You won't find this kind of nature anywhere else!"

The car halted in front of an enormous Elizabethan mansion. Its black gable roof and tall red brick chimneys stood out starkly against the sky. A trout stream, yellow and turbid, sidled up against a weeping willow.

Denise was ushered into the drawing room by a butler in full livery. Immediately warmed by the huge logs in the open fireplace, she seated herself on an overstuffed sofa and barely had time to observe her surroundings when Mrs. Grantham, the housekeeper, a red-faced, jovial lady, entered the room and introduced herself.

"Goodness gracious, Miss Cunningham. Don't tell me Dexter hasn't brought you a cup of tea!"

"I—" Denise began as she got up, but Mrs. Grantham cut her short.

"In England, Miss Cunningham, we don't do anything until we've had a cup of tea! And speaking of England, please allow me to welcome you." Mrs. Grantham shook her hand robustly.

"I would like to—" Denise said hesitantly.

"We serve high tea in the dining room promptly at five," continued Mrs. Grantham firmly, "but I'll have a hot cup brought to you straight away." She moved toward a braided satin cord with sufficient force to rustle the air. The ferns swayed almost imperceptibly. "And I'll see to it that—"

"If it isn't too much trouble," Denise broke in acidly, stopping Mrs. Grantham midway, "I would like to know—"

"Goodness gracious, Miss Cunningham. *Of course* you would prefer to have tea in your room. How thoughtless of me! I'll arrange for Gladys to carry a tray upstairs at once. Come with me."

They walked out into the large entrance hall. Denise stopped. "I wasn't speaking of tea, Mrs. Grantham," she said impatiently. "I don't want any tea or a tray, and I'm not interested in high tea or whatever you call it." Ignoring Mrs. Grantham's astonished look, she went on. "I don't drink tea. I don't like it. All I want to know is how soon I can see Sir—" She hesitated and rephrased her question, feigning nonchalance. "When will it be possible for Sir Reginald Findlay to see me?"

Nervously Mrs. Grantham smoothed her double chins, looking at her manly oxfords in embarrassment as her mouth slackened, appalled at such uncouthness. "Sir Reginald will call on you directly before high tea." The gasping sounds emerged from her throat as if her breath had been sucked away. She thought to herself, No tea indeed! Another rude American! You can tell *she* hasn't had a decent upbringing! No bloody tea indeed!

The furniture in the room that had been assigned to her was certainly ugly and nondescript, Denise thought, but at least it was comfortable-looking. In the distance some bells rang, out of tune and harsh. The maid was there, already unpacking her suitcase. Denise switched on the BBC.

"That's the Light Program, mum," Gladys said. " 'Ave you seen *The King and I,* mum? With Valerie 'Obson?" Denise loved her Cockney accent.

"No," she said absentmindedly, trying to put a title to the music. It was "I Whistle a Happy Tune." There was a knock at the door. Gladys opened it and curtsied her way out as a short, distinguished man with a cane entered the room. The eyes were pale and watery with a glance that moved slowly. His very presence compelled silence, and as automatically as she had turned on the radio, Denise turned it off.

"I'm very pleased to meet you, Sir Reginald," she murmured in a timid voice.

"Thank you. The feeling is mutual, I assure you."

Denise shook his hand, which was dry and cold. He sat down on a bedroom chair beneath a family portrait by Sir Joshua Reynolds, while Denise stood with her back to the fireplace.

"Please be seated, my dear. Try to relax. And please treat this house as your home." Sir Reginald removed his spectacles, breathed on the lenses, polished them with a corner of his handkerchief, held them at arm's length and replaced them on his nose at a slightly different angle. Denise sat on a chair, her body stiff and erect, crossing and uncrossing her legs. Despite his assurances, she felt very uncomfortable indeed.

"Dear child. Please," repeated Sir Reginald, placing his hand on hers, "please do try and put yourself at ease. It is most important."

"Thank you very much for fitting me into your very busy schedule," she said. Her voice trailed off into a barely audible murmur.

"In England we say 'shedule,'" he said, laughing. Denise laughed too, staring distractedly out the window.

The fire gave a crackling pop, as though punctuating an important sentence. Leaning forward, Sir Reginald confided with solemnity, "I must be truthful, dear Miss Cunningham. The very generous donation you made to the Great Ormond Street Hospital for Children was indeed a factor in accepting you on such short notice." He rose and paced the room as he continued to speak. "Although we've had excellent results in the past in cases such as yours, it still represents an extraordinary challenge to me, as I am the only person, the only one, who can be of help to you at this time." He stressed each syllable by knocking his cane against the leg of a small Jacobean dresser. "This new technique is still, so to speak, in its infancy."

Denise felt dizzy and clutched both arms of the chair. "How long will I have to remain here . . . at The Hall?" She had now turned completely around, facing Sir Reginald.

"It all depends. A week perhaps. I can tell you much more tomorrow, Miss Cunningham. My office is on the ground floor. Please be there at eight o'clock in the morning. Do not eat or drink anything after midnight. I will send in a nurse shortly to take the necessary specimens," he said, closing their interview. Sir Reginald was almost at the door when he added, "Make yourself comfortable, young lady. And by the way, if you feel up to it, I'm particularly proud of our croquet lawn. You should definitely see it before it gets too dark."

Denise felt intimidated. She didn't want to see the croquet lawn or any lawn. She didn't feel at home. Standing a foot away from Sir Reginald, she blurted out, "Will it hurt a lot?" How she wished she could cram the tense words back into her mouth! Sir Reginald replied, almost paternally, "No, Denise, no. You may be uncomfortable for two or three weeks afterward, but that's all." He smiled knowingly. "I'm sure it will prove to be well worth it to you."

After Sir Reginald had departed, Denise straightened her back, walked to the telephone on the night table, and requested a number in Rome. "Make it station-to-station, please. And be sure not to mention that the call is coming from England. I want it to be a surprise. Is there a very long wait?"

"Unfortunately, there is, miss—about two hours. I'll ring you as soon as I get a connection."

She threw herself on the bed. Distant voices, footsteps, doors opening and closing kept bringing her back to the moment. She was in a trance when Gladys brought a silver tray laden with cucumber-and-cress sandwiches, nestled on pale Doulton china, fresh, flaky scones with rich, clotted Devonshire cream and a pot of tea beneath a purple quilted cosy. She tried to dismiss every thought from her head, but how could she? Francesco. Princess Francesco Borgia . . . The dream of 1952 was becoming a reality in 1954.

⁂

On August 14, 1952, the Château D'Antibes on the Riviera had been transformed into a paradise of flowers, flaming torches, balloons, streamers and jack-o'-lanterns.

Under a tent woven of thousands of white orchids and magnolias, flown in from Brazil, a lavish supper was being served around the pool. A young man appeared with dramatic suddenness, causing a buzz of recognition among the glamorous assembly. He descended the steps slowly, smoking elegantly, with a romantic and unmistakable air of fine breeding. Insinuating. Irrevocable. Disturbing! Like a warm whiff of sirocco. Dressed in black silk pajamas, he presented a marked contrast to the animated colors of the other guests. A raven perched on his shoulder.

Regarding this spectacle with a tingle of delight, Denise rose very slowly to greet the latecomer. Walking as a queen might have approached the throne that would soon be hers, she looked blandly welcoming. She smiled politely and extended her hand.

"Welcome, Prince Borgia. How nice of you to join us for coffee," she said glibly. "My name is—"

"Yes, I know," he interrupted. "You are Denise."

She raised an eyebrow, amused.

"I might as well call you Denise. I'll be doing it anyway before the night's over! Am I very late?"

"Of course you are! But how were you to know that everyone else would be punctual?" she mocked. "Besides, punctuality is the politeness of kings."

The gold-flecked brown eyes looked boldly into Denise's. "Then I should be excused automatically. I'm only a prince," he chided with a smile impossible to forget.

Francesco Vittorio Borgia, a Roman prince whose ancient title dated from the ninth century, was one of the world's most eligible bachelors. He possessed everything—youth, good looks and inestimable wealth. The illustrious Borgia family had produced three popes, kings in Tuscany, queens in Spain and Portugal, and boasted of an ancestral link to all European royal lines. Prince Francesco Borgia answered to no one. At twenty-five he wore all of his attributes shamelessly, brazenly, like a shining coat of arms. Besides owning the fastest speedboats, racing cars and horses, he was an accomplished athlete who brought a feverish quality to each of his pursuits—the determination to win. Francesco Borgia felt excluded from the fate of ordinary men.

Denise looked at him once more. He was the most handsome man she had ever seen, tall as any cliché and darker than an enigmatic dream. His hair, long and curly, grew thicker around the neck. His mouth, full, with sensual lips, conveyed both humor and sulkiness.

The contrast of the two of them by the pool—she in all her seeming innocence, he with the unmistakable marks of experience about his eyes— brought to everyone's mind a powerful image of carnality and decadence.

"Didn't you read the invitation?" Denise asked. "Everyone has followed the suggestion to dress in either red, white or blue—except you!"

"Black is my favorite color." He laughed. "What's over there?" he asked, pointing to the right.

"A terrace overlooking the Mediterranean."

"I would like to see the view," he said, chaining the bird to a large potted tree.

Denise, pirouetting: "Follow me, Black Prince."

They seated themselves on the veranda amidst a lush jungle of scents. The night seemed like a stranger. Waiting. Now she felt his hand lightly over hers.

"Oh, I'm chilly." She rose suddenly, and he followed her into a small room adjoining the terrace. She closed the door and stood against it invitingly, contemplating the red light of his cigarette in the darkness. Seconds passed. He looked up. Commandingly, he walked toward Denise and gazed into the innocent eyes.

She did not stir. He discarded his cigarette. With a movement at first timorous, his arms gathered around Denise. Her body tightened and shuddered. For one quivering moment he held her closely and fiercely, then, without preliminaries, kissed her voluptuously. In voiceless consent, the enticing, moist lips parted. Through the thin fabric of her dress she felt his hardness pressed against her loins.

Their fingers were interwoven in the first matchless moment of mutual attraction.

"I want you, Denise." His voice was faint, almost unrecognizable. "Please," he begged, "let's get away from here! I want you."

"I have no intention of leaving. This is *my* party," she said crisply. "It's all for me." At that precise moment the fireworks began, the most extravagant ever held on the Riviera. A shower of sparks burst in the sky, raining diamonds and rubies and illuminating their impassioned faces.

"I must leave you," she announced. "I must attend to my other friends."

Clutching her arm: "Would it be possible to see you later?" he asked slightly baffled.

"It's out of the question. I'm sure there will be other occasions." Her voice was icy calm.

Francesco hastily tried another line of attack. "Would you care to lunch on my boat tomorrow? It's called *The Raven* and it's anchored at Ville-franche."

Denise didn't reply. Her body tingled.

"Please . . . tell me you'll come. Please . . ." Denise watched Francesco descending, one by one, the frustrated steps of his disappointment. Then she brushed past him, paused a moment at the door, turned around—"Don't forget your raven, Francesco!"—and was gone.

She sauntered over to a group of friends on the other side of the pool, waved from a distance to Rita Hayworth, dancing dreamily in the arms of Prince Aly Khan, exchanged a few words with playboy Porfirio Rubirosa, in deep conversation with international model Darvina, whom she had met on several occasions in Paris. Denise thought that, outside of herself, Darvina was the evening's most beautiful guest. She continued to circulate, using everyone's name with casual familiarity.

"There you are, my dear," said Escobar, his voice startling her. "I've looked everywhere for you! Where have you been?"

"Taking a walk into the future," Denise answered quietly. And her eyes danced.

—※—

The insistent ring of the telephone brought Denise back to The Hall and back to the frightening present, Wednesday, February 3, 1954. The room had sunk into complete darkness. Dazedly she put on the light and picked up the phone.

"We have Rome for you, Miss Cunningham," the operator announced.

"Oh, Rome—yes, thank you. Prince Francesco Borgia please," said Denise. Her throat was dry. After a short wait his voice came on the line. "Pronto. Pronto."

"Darling Francesco, it's Denise." She giggled nervously.

"Where are you, darling? I've tried your hotel in New York so many times, but you're always out. I even tried at two-thirty this morning and was told you were not to be disturbed. I was just about to call you again." He paused. "Denise, is everything all right?"

"Yes, Francesco. I'm so happy. It's almost all arranged. My godfather is still a bit reluctant. He believes all those rumors about your wildness. In fact, he calls you the ultimate playboy." She giggled again softly. "But I know you love me, and I love you, and it'll work out, I know it will." Denise sounded as if she were trying to convince herself.

"I love you madly, Denise. I've waited for you my whole life."

"When are you leaving for Argentina?" she asked, trying to conceal her apprehensiveness.

"In two days. The polo ponies have already gone."

"Who'll be on your team?"

"Aly Khan, Rubirosa, Michael Butler, Philip Mountbatten . . . But who cares? I'm on the team!" he exclaimed, laughing. "I'll bring back the trophy for you! How's the weather in New York?"

She coughed and faltered. "It's . . . it's very cold and . . . cold and slushy, but . . . but I'm quite busy. There are . . . there are so many things to take care of."

"Denise, it's hard to keep this happiness to myself, but you made me promise to keep it a secret until Escobar gives his consent, and I'm doing just that. How much longer do you think it will be?"

She coughed once more as her discomfort grew. "About . . . about a week . . . yes, one week. By the time you return from Argentina all will be settled and I'll be waiting for you in Paris."

"I recall so vividly the first time you agreed to dine with me, Denise. I wanted you so much. I wanted you more than anyone in my entire life. When I finally asked what it was I had to do to have you—because I had to have you—can you remember what it was you replied?"

She paused a moment. "The Church." Her voice was almost a whisper.

"That's right. The Church. It made me love you even more, Denise. The idea of being the first man to possess you finally drove me wild! But do you know who said that before you?"

"I thought I was the only one."

"Madame de Montespan said the same thing to Louis XIV."

"And what happened?"

"He married her."

There was a silence. Denise had indeed read it in *The Memoirs of Louis XIV,* by the French historian Saint-Simon. At the time she thought it sounded good. It still did.

"When shall I call you, Denise?"

"Let me call you. It's much easier for me to get a good connection in America than it is for you in Argentina." Casually she asked, "Where will you be staying in Buenos Aires?"

"At the Alvear Palace Hotel. Do you know it?"

"No, I've never been there." She could barely mutter, "I'll call you in three days. At seven in the evening, your time." She nervously switched the phone from one hand to the other while fingering her string of pearls.

"Fortunately I don't have a family to consult, Denise, but I'm dying to tell everyone! *Io!* Francesco Borgia getting married! Who would believe it! There isn't a mother in the world who hasn't thrown her daughter at me, and I fell for a girl who wasn't even interested!"

"Very soon, Francesco," Denise said huskily, "I'll be yours. In the meantime take care of yourself. Don't fall off your horse. I don't want a lame bridegroom."

"I won't be lame, Denise," came his reply. "My advice, darling, is to get plenty of rest. Maybe some fresh country air. And eat lots of that terrible American dish."

"What dish are you talking about?"

"That mushy breakfast dish that supposedly gives you lots of energy."

"Oh, you mean Wheaties!"

"That's it, Denise. Eat lots of Wheaties. I kiss you everywhere, my beautiful darling. What time is it there now?"

Denise felt her pulse racing and made a quick calculation, deducting five hours from her watch, which was running on English time. "It's one o'clock, darling. Just one o'clock. I'm about to go to lunch—with Escobar!"

When she had replaced the phone, Denise felt unable to move. She was sweating profusely. "It *must* work! I *must* marry him!" She repeated those words out loud several times. She got up, took off her clothes, put on a robe and switched on the BBC. But she couldn't concentrate. What a twist of fate! she thought. Of all places, Argentina! She was in a state of great agitation. No, nothing can alter my plans! Nothing! After all, money buys its own legitimacy—when there's enough of it. Pouring the tea into the handbasin, she reflected: With a young, titled, handsome and rich husband, the world will kiss my feet! For Denise the mills of life ground fast and exceedingly fine. The nurse walked in.

※

MARIELA/*New York City*/*Thursday, February 4, 1954*

Mariela stepped off Glover Anderson's private plane at the Butler Terminal of La Guardia Airport in New York. A steward helped her down the steps with her single suitcase. It was Thursday morning. The icy wind and freezing cold slapped her face, in sharp contrast to the balmy breeze she had left only three hours earlier in Key Crescent, Florida.

Raising the collar of her mink coat over her ears, she looked around for Stanley, Glover's New York chauffeur. He was nowhere in sight. A large Cadillac limousine with smoked windows and an aerial on its roof was on the landing strip. A strange-looking man approached, wearing an ill-fitting toupee, which looked as though it had been glued to his head. "Are you Miss Koenig?" he asked sheepishly, cap in one hand, an umbrella in the other. She nodded cautiously. "My name is Norman and I've been asked to take you to your destination." She raised her sunglasses in surprise. "Stanley's had an accident," he explained, anticipating the question.

"Nothing serious, I hope."

"Oh, no. He was just shaken up a bit. He'll be all right by tomorrow." It started to rain hard, and Norman sheltered her. Quickly Mariela got into the limousine, noticing it was more spacious and comfortable inside than the usual one. Without a word Norman started the engine, and they drove off.

She fiddled with the buttons, searching for music. "Could you turn the radio on, please?"

"I'm sorry, Miss Koenig, but the radio is out of order."

Mariela picked up a copy of the *Herald Tribune* from the seat, anxious to bring herself up to date on Karl Ravenstein. There had been an extensive police investigation. She was shocked to see a picture of Andreas Poppidoppolous staring at her from the third page. *Poppidoppolous.* A name so hard to remember that one could never forget it. And she hadn't. Mariela recalled vividly speaking those same words to the young man on the fatal evening. And how could she forget that face? There was no doubt about it, Andreas was the moody young man who had participated in the revelries at Karl Ravenstein's last Saturday. He was also the third person in the compromising photos Nathan Berger had showed her at his office. Andreas had been found shot to death in his Greenwich village apartment, an apparent suicide. According to District Attorney Vincent Petroni, "there is a definite connection between this suicide and the Ravenstein murder. Andreas had been the prime suspect. Some valuable objects belonging to Karl Ravenstein were found hidden under his bed. . . ."

Mariela was so engrossed with the details of the account, reading carefully to be sure her name wasn't mentioned anywhere, that she didn't realize the car was heading away from the city. They were now on the Triborough Bridge, going northeast. Mariela knocked on the glass partition separating her from the driver. She couldn't remember closing it. The driver ignored her. She pushed the button to open it. It wouldn't budge. She tried the phone. It was dead. She tried to lower the windows. They didn't work. She pounded on the doors. To no avail. She made desperate signs to other vehicles. They seemed not to see her. Lurching around the back seat like a butterfly in jar, she shouted again and again, "Let me out! Let me out!"

The driver's voice came over the intercom: "There's no point shouting, Miss Koenig. This car is soundproof. There's no point making signals. You can't be seen from the outside. May I suggest that you sit back and enjoy the ride?"

Mariela felt an invisible, terrorizing presence.

Panic gnawed at her entrails like a huge rat. She felt invaded. Submerged. Her head was filled with conflicting thoughts.

Who could be responsible? No one knew her whereabouts. Except Glover

Anderson. Could Glover Anderson . . . ? She banished the thought. But it came back. Heavy. Insistent. Glover Anderson. Why not? His political career mattered more to him than anything in the world. Why wouldn't he want her out of the way? Jack Hamilton? No. He had explained to her on their last meeting at the Plaza how much he needed her to help with Karl Ravenstein's Swiss bank account. *He needed her.* It couldn't be Jack Hamilton. Andreas? How stupid of her! He was dead—hadn't she just read it in the paper? Mariela couldn't believe he had died by his own hand. *Someone must have killed him.* The suicide was probably a cover-up. If only she could get in touch with Nathan Berger! She was certain Nathan would have an answer. Nathan Berger? But wasn't he the one who had urged her to continue seeing Glover Anderson in this difficult period? She had made a point of telling him Glover had changed the Wednesday meeting and could not see her this week, so how could Nathan—or anyone—expect her arrival this morning from Key Crescent? Her suspicions returned to Glover Anderson.

There was a lingering scent in the car. She had difficulty identifying it, like a half-forgotten ballad one recollects in snatches. She knew the smell. What was it? The automobile turned off the highway onto what seemed to be a deserted road, picked up speed as the tires screeched, the wheels spinning off gravel. Mariela clung to the armrest. She held her breath. Words rose to her lips but died in her throat, strangulated by fear.

The limousine came to a halt in front of a large two-story Colonial house. The back door of the car opened just as Mariela identified the permeating odor—carnation.

Nathan Berger helped her out.

He was in his usual flamboyant attire, the red carnation in his lapel. He took her arm and escorted her up the pebble-patterned steps bordered by clumps of shrubbery, still covered with last week's snow, and led her into the house.

"Well," said Mariela, "I've heard of ambulance-chasing lawyers, but this is absurd."

"No more absurd, my dear, than your lying to me about Glover Anderson canceling your—shall we call it—'appointment'?"

She ignored his sarcasm. "Nathan, I hired you as my attorney, not my baby-sitter." He ushered her into a large combination kitchen-living room, one end dominated by a huge fieldstone fireplace. Copper pots, pans and kettles hung over an ultramodern stove.

"May I offer you a drink?"

"Yes, if you promise not to poison it."

"It's vodka on the rocks, isn't it?"

She took off her coat, dropped it on the arm of a large early American sofa, and sat down, her eyes still scanning the room: a pair of rustic bent-willow settees, antique hickory armchairs, a group of massive raw silk-upholstered furniture around a lacquer and leather table, a quantity of books filling the built-in birch shelves, an abundance of green plants and cacti, a pair of carved ebony antelopes, warm, earth-toned Mexican tile floor, high, wood-beam ceiling, and, on the whitewashed walls, rugged western paintings by Robert Schulz.

He brought the drink to her. "I assume everything worked out all right?" said Nathan.

"Since you seem to know everything, I'm sure you already have that answer. What is the purpose of all this?" Her eyes lifted to Nathan, studying him carefully. When he didn't say anything, she continued speaking with more assurance. "I may be whatever you may think me, but I'm not a blackmailer, and I'm sure that between Glover Anderson's influence and your unusual resources I'm, shall we say, in good hands. I simply didn't see the purpose of blackmailing Glover Anderson. Why have you gone to such dramatic lengths just to speak to me?" By now Mariela was regaining her full composure. "I certainly believe you owe me an explanation. The way you've brought me to your house reminds me of a B movie." Slowly Mariela turned around as the door opened and in walked Jack Hamilton. She was incredulous, but concealed it. Jack Hamilton looked at her for signs of amazement. She gave none.

"Very good to see you again, Mariela," said Jack.

"The pleasure is not mine."

"You really have no idea why we've had to do this?" Nathan asked.

"None whatsoever. But I can tell you that everything you're doing is a waste of time."

Nathan took a seat opposite Mariela, then waited for Jack to return from the bar with his own drink before speaking. "I have good news for you, Mariela," he said as Hamilton joined them. "Your appearance before a grand jury is scheduled for tomorrow morning. I will rehearse you thoroughly on what questions to expect and how to answer. That is the good news." Seconds passed.

"I also have some unpleasant news," Jack Hamilton said. Mariela did not respond. "You're going to Switzerland tomorrow afternoon and will complete the final phase of this matter, which we have already discussed."

Something about the tone of his voice must have lacked conviction because Mariela smiled. "All you're doing is a waste of time," she repeated. "I have already made my position clear. . . ." She let the sentence hang itself in midair.

"Mariela, don't be foolish," Jack said.

"Andreas is dead," she said in a toneless voice.

"Well . . . he's dead. What's it to you?"

"I now believe you're capable of doing anything to get what you want."

"You're right, Mariela," Nathan said. He got up from his chair and paced the floor.

"Then I guess you'll have to kill me too. As of tomorrow the matter is finished for me, Nathan. I paid you to do your job. If you didn't want to take my case, you should have said so when I came to you. As for you, Jack, you tricked me into participating in something which, had I known the consequences, I would never have agreed to."

Her defiance aroused Nathan's anger.

"We *will* use you to serve our aims. *We will!* And you will obey to the letter. Tomorrow afternoon you'll be on your way to Switzerland. We have your British passport under your maiden name, Lady Mariela Chelmsford. Someone will stay with you until your departure. And your share will be two hundred and fifty thousand dollars. Cash. You will be accompanied in Zurich by a Mr. Teppler."

Mariela lay back on the couch, her head on the cushion. "My life is worth more than—"

Nathan dragged his chair closer to her. Instinctively she moved away. As he spoke he lifted his head. "The answer is in your hands. Or should I say, on your expensive lips? . . . What's this all about anyway?" He slapped his knee. "It's wasting precious time!" He got up, turning his back on her. "I will say one word, Mariela, *one word only* that will make you come to your senses."

"What could you say to me that you haven't said before?" she asked. "What other lies or pretenses could you add?"

"The word, Mariela, is *Oliver*." He uttered it, enunciating, rolling, extending, stretching each letter until that grizzly truth made of that one word a whole unbearable story. Something irrevocable had been spoken.

"Oliver!" She screamed a primeval scream and lurched toward him. "What's happened to Oliver?"

"Nothing yet, Mariela. But who knows . . . ?" he snarled. "How does it feel to be the prey instead of the predator?"

Mariela tried to dull her mind, pretending it was all a big, childish game, a familiar ritual being reenacted for an invisible audience. A nightmare! The word resounded in her head. *Oliver! Oliver* in her ears . . . in her skin . . . in her guts . . . *Oliver! Oliver! Oliver!!* Louder and louder. She felt weak and nauseated. A carnation fell on the floor. Nathan Berger and Jack Hamilton walked out of the room.

Mariela knew she would be going to Zurich.

—❈—

DENISE/*London/***Thursday, February 4, 1954**

Denise was given the first injection at dawn. Numbness crept up her body as she was wheeled soundlessly on a stretcher through long, dimly lighted corridors and into a green room. Lowering the protective railings, two nurses effortlessly lifted her onto the operating table. Through the drowsiness she could hear the clink of steel instruments being set up, reminding her of her waitress days at the awful diner in Terre Haute. The days she was forever trying to forget. Realizing where she was helped obliterate the memory, at least temporarily. She recognized the anesthetic mask connected to aluminum tanks by black corrugated rubber hoses.

"Daddy," she mumbled, lightheaded. "Daddy." The hospital smells were all too familiar—disinfectant, alcohol, ether—it was the same when her father died. "Daddy," she whispered. "Daaaddy . . ."

Someone spread her legs apart, wide, feet in stirrups. Denise's eyes turned questioningly toward the large overhead spotlight. A face, immense, but dim, appeared, mostly concealed by a white mask.

"Are you all right, Denise?" asked the familiar voice. She looked steadily but didn't answer. Seeing the pale-yellow translucent rubber gloves and feeling a lubricated finger probing the inside of her vagina, she clutched at the hand, lost, frantic. A shot of sodium pentothal pulled her into a dark abyss.

She regained consciousness to find the filtered, blurry faces of Sir Reginald Findlay and a nurse hovering over her.

"Well, how do you feel, Denise?"

There was almost supplication in the look she gave both of them. "I don't know. Did it go well?" She moved her head slowly. "I mean, is everything all right?"

In the distance she could hear the sonorous tones of Sir Reginald's kindly voice. "Yes, I believe all is very well, Denise. Very well, indeed." He took her hand. "Do you have any pain?"

Her other hand instinctively crept slowly along her naked thigh, ending between her legs, where it touched a large bandage.

Denise still couldn't believe what had been done. She scanned the recovery room. Gradually everything came into focus and she broke into a weak smile.

Sir Reginald Findlay, the most famous plastic surgeon of his time, had made Denise Cunningham a virgin again.

※

"Maxwell . . . Maxwell . . . with one *l* or two? With two *l*'s, right?" Mattie nodded. Standing beside her, Sylvia Rubins bobbed her head up and down.

"Maxwell," lisped the stocky woman with blue rinsed hair behind the counter. "Let's see now . . ." Wetting a stubby finger, she turned the pages of the guest register. "Ah, here we are at last!" she announced triumphantly. The rhinestone rings on the puffy fingers flashed. Mattie shifted uncomfortably from one foot to the other.

"Ruth Maxwell—here it is!"

"No!" Mattie denied impatiently. "It's not Ruth, it's Mattie!"

"You ought to know," Sylvia Rubins interrupted. "Miss Maxwell is performing tonight in the Casino Room!"

"Oh, so you're the entertainer!" she exclaimed excitedly to Sylvia, fingering the gold brooch on the mink collar of her blue angora sweater.

"No," Sylvia corrected, "I'm *not* the entertainer. Miss Maxwell is," she emphasized, pointing to Mattie, who looked as bewildered as a newly adopted child in the commotion of the lobby.

"The entertainment director is who you should see," the woman said with authority. "I'll page him." She picked up a microphone and began calling in a nasal drawl, "Mr. Green, Mr. Green, Mr. Sol Green. Wanted at the front desk . . . Mr. Green," she explained to anyone who happened to be listening, "is our entertainment director. . . . Mr. Green, Mr. Sol Green, wanted—" Her announcement was interrupted by a gravelly voice trying to be suave. "Ladies and gentlemen, F.T. is finished. F.T. is finished, ladies and—"

"What the hell is F.T.?" Mattie asked.

"How the hell am I supposed to know?" Sylvia answered. "I only just got here too, remember?"

"F.T."—the room clerk adjusted her rhinestone-encrusted harlequin glasses and explained with the efficiency of an expert—"stands for 'free time' and it happens every day between—"

The public address system was bending under an avalanche of names. "Miss Janet Margolis . . . Miss Janet Margolis . . . Telephone! . . . Miss Becky Weinstein, it's time for your private mambo lesson . . ."

"Ladies and gentlemen," the loudspeaker continued, "Lou Goldstein is waiting for you in the front lobby with your favorite audience-participation game. Ladies and gentlemen," the voice encouraged, "it's time for—

wait for it, ladies and gentlemen—it's time for—you guessed it, it's time for . . . *Simon Sez!*" he shrieked.

"Simon what?" Mattie exclaimed.

"Simon Sez!" the desk clerk explained.

"Miss Goldman . . . ," the public address system ground on. "Sorry about that, it's Mister Goldman. You're wanted in the coffee shop."

"For those of you who aren't in the mood for Simon Sez," the loudspeaker rasped, "lectures are being held in the conference room on foreign affairs and kosher French cooking. In the lower lobby, free classes in pottery, sculpture, jewelry making, flower arrangement, scuba diving and oil paint-ing—it's all done by numbers nowadays, ladies and gentlemen! That's right, boys and girls, painting with numbers. Just like bingo, only prettier."

"Sounds like instant culture to me!" Mattie snickered.

"Don't knock it, sweetheart!" said Sylvia knowingly. This wasn't her first trip to one of these mountain resorts.

"And speaking of bingo, folks, we'll be waiting for you in the game room at three-thirty. And at four-thirty, auction of antiques in the gym-nasium—real old antiques, folks!"

"It's almost like being in kindergarten!" Mattie joked, not quite knowing where she fitted into the schedule.

"You'll get used to the routine after you've been here a while." The mascara-laden false eyelashes flapped like a broken window shade. "In fact," the desk clerk said enthusiastically, "you'll *love* it!"

Mattie was beginning to feel relieved that she wouldn't be there long enough to get used to the routine, let alone love it, when a crowd stampeded past, knocking to the floor her makeup case, which had been perched precariously on the counter. For the most part short, and representing all ages, the women, with teased hair in various shades of champagne-pink, were clutching mink stoles over tight pedal-pushers in pastel colors, wear-ing costume jewelry in abundance. The men were garbed in wide-bottomed gabardine trousers and loud printed shirts, open as far as their paunches would allow, in the latest Harry Belafonte style.

"What are they invading?" Mattie asked, taken aback.

"The lobby for Simon Sez!, I bet." Sylvia said.

"What time is it?" asked Mattie anxiously.

"Two-thirty," Sylvia replied. "We have plenty of time before rehearsal."

"Put your hands over your neighbor's head, Simon Sez! . . . Bend over and touch your bottom, Simon Sez! . . . Turn around in a circle and —Whoops, honey, you in the polka dot shorts, you're out!" The room resounded with squeals of laughter, and an overweight miss of indeter-minate years sheepishly walked toward the side, her yellow wedgies squeak-ing. "Sounds like she's got ants in her pants, don't it, folks!" The shy miss blushed to the dark roots of her beehive and picked up a straw shoulder bag with *Aloha!* written across it. Everybody was falling about, helpless with hilarity, tears streaming down their cheeks. "Rub your tummies, Simon Sez! . . . Stand on one foot, Simon Sez! . . . Stick your arm . . ."

Mattie and Sylvia walked over to the double glass doors that led to the grounds. Seen from inside, the alabaster countryside was beautiful. A black dog was romping in the distance. The word for today is snow! Mattie said to herself. White, drifting, towering snow! A blessing for cherubs and kids, but a pain in the ass for the rest of us! . . . Blow, snow get lost! she thought. Loneliness seized her like a wave in mid-ocean. Her reveries trailed off. Mattie was trying to find a means of dealing with the panic of being without Tony. It hit her hard. What a good day, she reflected sadly, to bite my nails, skate on a lake, fall in a hole and curse the very day my mother lay down for me. . . . "What time is it now, Sylvia?" she said out loud.

"You just asked me that. It's a quarter to three. Why?"

"Tony said he'd call at four—our time."

"Well, Mattie, you have an hour to rest or look around."

"I think I'll stay in the room. I don't want to miss his call."

"You won't miss a thing. Can't you hear how they're paging people nonstop? Anyway, you do what you want. The rehearsal isn't until five. Why don't you try and take a nap? You didn't get a wink last night—"

Before Sylvia could finish the sentence she was interrupted by a tubby, pear-shaped man with greased-back, copper-red hair and a wispy mustache. "I believe you were looking for me. I'm Sol Green, the entertainment director," he added, jovially, as if those facts could be overlooked. He wore a name tag on the lapel of his baggy brown suit which spelled it out: *Sol Green, Entertainment Director*. "And you're Mattie Maxwell!" he said effusively, with an imitation of feeling that experience had taught him was effective. "I couldn't very well miss that up-and-coming profile!" Sol beamed good-naturedly, exuding the stale odor of herring all over them. Stale herring and an emergency overdose of Listerine that fought with it, but lost. Stale herring, Listerine, plus a strong lacing of Old Spice splashed liberally if hurriedly around his face and neck.

"That breath's enough to frost glass!" Sylvia quipped out of the corner of her mouth.

"A real wallpaper-peeler, right?" Mattie whispered, giggling. Trying to control her schoolgirl mirth, she added aloud, "And this is my . . . my theatrical agent, Sylvia Rubins."

"What about Harry?"

"He couldn't make it," Mattie replied simply.

"Pleased to meet you, I'm sure!" he bubbled. They shook hands all round. "Harry Ross sent me your reviews. I hear you're great, kid! The audience will love you! They'll just eat you up, honey! Being Jessica Miller's daughter's enough! And if you've got talent on top of that . . ." Sol was so enthusiastic he didn't notice Mattie's wince. "We're booked solid tonight—"

They were interrupted by two attractive girls in their mid-twenties shyly coming up to them.

"Oh, excuse us, Mr. Green. I hope we're not disturbing you. My name's Luba, and this is my friend Georgina. We're so excited! We've just heard that Marilyn Maxwell's in the show tonight! Is that so?" she asked breathlessly.

"No, no, no, you two gorgeous creatures," he said, smiling benevolently, "*Mattie* Maxwell is in the show, not Marilyn Maxwell!" Taking their hands in his, he went on, "And let me introduce you to her."

"Mattie Maxwell?" Georgina asked, unimpressed.

"As you know," Sol went on, "Mattie is the daughter of Jessica Miller, and just you wait—"

"The daughter of Jessica Miller!" Luba gasped.

"Wow!" Georgina cried.

"Can we have your autograph?"

"Now, now, now, you two ravishing beauties! Mattie's only just arrived. Why don't we give her a little time to unwind and—"

"That's okay, Mr. Green. I hope you girls are having a good weekend." Mattie looked at them graciously, as if she really cared.

"Oh . . . oh . . . oh . . . ," Luba commented.

"Yes," Georgina finished weakly.

"Let's see what I have," said Mattie, fumbling in her pocketbook for a pen.

"Here's an envelope," Sylvia said, "if you're looking for something to write on."

"That's great. Thanks." Mattie scrawled her name on it.

"All right, you two lascivious lovelies," Sol boomed, "we've got work to do." The girls took the autograph, thanking Mattie profusely, and went off down the hall, oohing and aahing in their red-and-white calisthenics outfits and matching sneakers. "Now, where were we, Mattie?" Sol asked, rubbing his hands.

"If it's all the same to you, Mr. Green—"

"Just call me Sol, kid."

"If it's all the same to you, Sol kid—"

"Great sense of humor you've got there, kid." He guffawed, slapping her on the back.

"Yeah, ain't it the truth!" Sylvia remarked.

Mattie went on carefully, choosing her words with deliberation, "I wish you wouldn't mention my mother when I'm introduced for the show."

"Not mention your mother, doll baby!" Sol was dumbstruck. "Why not?" he asked with a look of genuine surprise. "Come on, let's go get something to eat," he said, grabbing both girls by the shoulders. "Food's our trademark here. It's great. You'll love it. We'll eat, we'll talk about it." He addressed himself to Mattie. "Don't you sing 'Whenever the Moon Shines?' That was your mother's trademark and the best western film—"

"No, as a matter of fact, I don't," said Mattie, stopping in her tracks.

"You know 'Hava Naghila' of course."

"No, I don't. And I don't sing any Irish airs either!"

"Oh . . . ," he said, obviously disappointed. "But you *can* sing 'Yes, We Have No Bananas,' can't you? It's a big hit here! They love it, and—"

"No, I'm sorry, Sol, I don't play to the crowd. I only sing words I can identify with, and I don't identify with a . . . a . . . a banana," she said firmly. "When I'm onstage I let the audience come to me . . ." She trailed off. "Do you by any chance have a cigarette?"

"Here, take my pack," Sylvia said, pleased to change the subject.

"But you *do* wear a low-cut gown that shows a little . . . a little cleavage?" he asked, squeezing his own chest and shaping a topless gown with his clasped hands.

"I'm sorry to disappoint you, Sol," Mattie said, sighing almost sadly. "I wear a one-shoulder dress." Mattie and Sylvia exchanged apprehensive looks. "However, Sol, I do something onstage that you'll like very much."

"What's that?"

"I'm good," Mattie answered with assurance. "I'm damn good!"

"I'm sure you are, kid. I'm sure you are. I bet that great talent of your mother's runs through your veins."

"What time do you have, please?" asked Mattie anxiously.

"It's three-ten." They stood warily while Sol Green perused Mattie from head to foot. "Oh, kid," he said suddenly "I almost forgot to tell you how sorry Jenny Levinsberg is that Tony Rook won't be coming. She's very fond of him. Wow, what a tragedy, the death of Jeremy Rabb . . . It's hard to believe! I know Jeremy was very close to Tony. Well, that's life. That's life! Come on, let me get you two girls something to eat. . . . Oh, just before I came down to meet you I heard on television that they've found Jeremy's body and his plane some where in the Rocky Mountains."

"They have?" Mattie said with a heavy heart.

"And I've known Beverly Langdon ever since she was a hatcheck girl. It's too bad. Real bad. They were so in love! Everyone here's upset about it! Terribly upset! . . . Are you all fixed up for rooms?" He patted Mattie on the back with great familiarity.

"No, actually," Sylvia volunteered, "we were waiting for you. The desk clerk couldn't find our names in the register."

"That dizzy broad. She must be in love again," he said, laughing. "I'll take care of that right away. And then we'll get something to eat. Where's your luggage?"

"In the maroon station wagon," Sylvia offered.

"I have a box of ducks on the back seat."

"You use *ducks* in your act?" Sol's eyes opened wide.

"No, no, they're pets."

"Oh, Christ, Mattie, don't tell me you've brought pets. They don't allow pets in the room!"

"They're not for the room," Mattie explained. "Jenny Levinsberg is going to take care of them. I spoke to her about it this morning." Mattie was taking off her fur coat.

"Hey! Keep your mink on your shoulders, kid. It looks good! That's fine. The bellboy will take care of everything. Just leave it all to me." He rubbed his hands together again. "And then we'll get a bite to eat!" Sol disappeared for a minute.

"He talks an awful lot about food."

"Mattie, here you eat three times a day six times a day!"

"Bet you love that!" teased Mattie with an eye on Sylvia's ample figure. "I'm so thankful you came with me—you'll never know . . ."

". . . and the winner of Simon Sez is—what's your name, dearie?—the winner is Miss Pandora Rosen. That's great! Step right up, Dora. . . . Let's give her a big hand, ladies and gentlemen." A black-haired, black-eyed beauty with tangerine lips and a curvaceous figure stepped forward, bored with boredom, amidst admiring whistles and applause. She received the first prize, a great big stuffed rabbit with a blue-and-white pennant bearing the single word *Levinsberg's!*

Sol came back and grabbed Mattie by the arm. "Have you seen our fabulous premises? 'Levinsberg's—Twice the size of Monaco!' " Sol announced with pride.

"I only had time for a quickie look."

"Let me show you the indoor swimming pool. It's Olympic size."

"Okay, Sol," said Mattie. "But I've got to stop at the desk first. I'm expecting a long-distance phone call—Tony, actually—and I don't want to miss it."

"Sure, sure, kid. Love is great!"

"Yeah, great for losing weight!" Mattie said plaintively.

They made their way to the desk, relaying the message to the clerk, who by now was busy straightening the seams of her navy-blue stockings, embroidered with a heart on the outside of the leg.

"Don't forget to give us a page when Miss Maxwell's call comes through, Pearl," Sol instructed. "We'll be by the pool."

The pool was the largest Mattie had ever seen, the water the clearest. Not a soul swimming. However, the tranquillity of the pool was amply made up for by the abundance of activity around it. One end was decorated like a Spanish patio. Rose and smokey-gray synthetic tiles on the floor simulated Moorish paving. The roof of the bar was thatched to create a bucolic atmosphere. Leather bottles hung on the walls. Baskets of fruit and cheese platters; their contents half-eaten, were laid out on tables covered with red-and-white-checked cloths under green umbrellas. Candles in waxed-dripped Chianti bottles, and ashtrays that said "Cinzano" and "Pernod" gave the impression of a still life painted by a demented European of dubious origin.

Tito Puente, all corseted Latin charm, and his orchestra were in full swing. Voluptuous Olga and reed-thin Sanchez were putting their mambo class through their paces. "One, two, cha-cha-cha! You're getting it!" Sanchez exclaimed enthusiastically to a tall and busty lady in a black taffeta ballerina-length dress. She teetered on high-heeled yellow alligator sandals with ankle straps, and tripped intermittently on a silver-threaded white mohair stole.

"One, two, cha-cha-cha! Watch your stole, dear. One, two, cha-cha-cha!" intoned Olga frenetically. "Start with your right foot, Sarah! And Paul, start with your left! One, two— Your left, Paul! Your left!" Olga bellowed.

"Sylvia, it's four o'clock!"

"Please stop already announcing the time—just watch the fun!"

"All right, Tito, one more time, please! 'Cherry Pink and Apple Blossom White!' "

The song was intermingled with the never-ending stream of messages blasted over the public address system. "After the Latin hour, boys and girls, it's 'Get Acquainted Time' in the cocktail lounge. Hot hors d'oeuvres will be served free of charge."

"One, two, cha-cha-cha."

"One, two, cha-cha-cha."

"Miss Maxwell, telephone. Miss Maxwell, telephone."

Mattie squealed out loud with excitement. "Where can I speak privately?" She stumbled nervously over her words.

"Follow me"—Sol came to the rescue. "Don't run, kid, it's slippery! You'll fall in the water!"

They walked into a small, dreary office, its entrance bearing a sign, *Hernando's Hideaway,* in keeping with the rest of the Latin décor. Sol left her to rejoin Sylvia.

Mattie picked up the phone, her hand trembling. "Hello, operator, this is Miss Maxwell." Her palms were damp with anticipation. She tried to get hold of her emotions. "Yes, yes, this is Miss Maxwell!" She waited. Every second that flew from the wall clock seemed like an hour. Suddenly she felt apprehensive. But she knew Tony would banish all her doubts. Yes, he would. She knew it. "Hello, hello," she finally shouted, exasperated. "Hello, hello," she repeated frantically. "Who, who?" she asked, subdued. *"Ruth* Maxwell? You said *Ruth?"* She sat down on a swivel chair, limp with disappointment. "No, I think there's a mistake. You've got the wrong Miss Maxwell." Slowly Mattie cradled the phone. She looked up. It was 4:30. Crossing her arms on the table, she lowered her head and cried unashamedly.

"I'm Mattie Maxwell, operator. I'm sorry to bother you again, but are you sure no one's called for me?"

"Are you almost ready?" It was Sylvia shouting from the living room.

"Yeah, yeah! Just a minute!" She replaced the phone. "I'll be ready when I find my goddamn shoe." Mattie scratched in her drawer like a dog flinging dirt from a hole, everything landing pell-mell on the floor. "I got it!" she shouted victoriously, sitting on the bed. "I need a drink, Sylvia. Is the wine bottle in there?"

"Listen, baby, you've had enough to drink. There's no need to be nervous. You'll be great!"

"This is no time for pep talks, Sylvia. Just get me a glass. I *am* nervous. It's almost nine o'clock and not a word from Tony . . ."

While Sylvia was pouring the wine into the glass Mattie went to her purse and, making sure Sylvia wasn't looking, popped two of the little green capsules from the bottle Tony had left behind in the apartment.

Sylvia walked into the bedroom. Standing behind her in front of the mirror, she stared at Mattie's reflection for a moment. Mattie's visage seemed brittle, as if about to break.

"Sylvia, it's strange. When I'm not onstage I have no confidence in myself. None!" Mattie finished spraying her hair and replaced the can on the dresser.

"Come on, Mattie, what are you talking about?"

"It seems that until now my whole life has been fucked up by one thing or another, mainly lousy men who always dump me."

They both sat on the edge of the single bed. Sylvia's weight made the mattress sink at her end, raising Mattie as though they were on a seesaw.

"Mattie, you are—"

"Listen to me, Sylvia. I want a career. I want to be good. I want to be *me!* Not a copy of my mother! Can you think of the son or daughter of any famous star who made it? I can't. I'm determined to get there. I haven't figured out how yet, but I'll make it! I just hope it won't be too late."

"You're going to be a big star, Mattie. As vivid and flashing as lightning."

"You make me sound like a comet," she said giggling.

"Mattie, be serious." Sylvia got up. She braced herself against the window. "Mattie, I'm ready for a big gamble. I'm willing to make a sure bet that if I concentrate exclusively on you and your career and become your manager, within a year, give or take a few months, you'll be the biggest star in the country."

Mattie stubbed out her cigarette and grabbed the headboard.

"If you listen to me," Sylvia continued, "with the talent you have and my belief in it, give me five years—no, give me four years, and the name of Jessica Miller will never be compared with yours again."

Mattie drank the remainder of the wine. "Give me one more for the road, will you, Sylvia?"

"Why don't I just bring the bottle in? There's hardly anything left in it anyway."

Mattie's melancholy had never been more heroic or more withdrawn. "Where is Tony now?" She wondered aloud. "Why didn't he call?" If only she knew where to reach him . . .

Sylvia returned with the bottle, emptied the rest of the wine into Mattie's glass and sat at a dressing table, crossing her heavy legs. "Until now I've been only your theatrical agent," she continued. "But, if you're willing, from now on I'll handle *everything*. You need a manager to guide your career. Even though your contract at the Copa isn't my doing, it's your *most* important engagement to date, Mattie—and only two weeks away."

"I know. Joe E. Lewis promised me that if I do well, he'll take me to Vegas in a month."

"That's why, baby, you've got to concentrate on being the biggest smash in New York. This is your first job of any consequence. Nothing else should matter. Nothing! People love achievers, and when they accomplish something better than anyone else, the crowd puts them on a pedestal and worships them. It goes for beauty, talent, genius and money. That's life."

Mattie walked over to Sylvia and they clinked glasses.

As in every place Mattie had ever worked, the access to backstage was through the kitchen. There were lots of shouts and whistles in a variety of languages from the staff as she tiptoed carefully, lifting the hem of her gown so it wouldn't trail on the greasy floor.

The curtain had just gone down on Olga and Sanchez. They came off the stage perspiring. Olga and Sanchez would never be stars. That was evident from their costumes. Tonight Olga had metamorphosed into the spit and image of Carmen Miranda—oversized loop earrings, castanets, turban, plastic bananas, and all. Sanchez with his gleaming lacquered hair faintly resembled Ricardo Montalban. But no amount of disguise could alter the fact that he was bowlegged, and the trousers, in addition to being too tight, were also too short, exposing the run-down three-inch Cuban heels on his pointed-toe boots.

The master of ceremonies was on, cracking the perennial jokes about wives and mothers-in-law. Mattie couldn't help hearing, "My mother-in-law was saying just the other day that . . ." The audience laughed. He had stuck his tongue out at them, and the false flower in his lapel had spewed ink in the conductor's face. "My mother-in-law was saying just the other day that time has stood still for her. What she probably meant to say—what she probably meant to say was that her face would stop a clock!" Ha-ha-ha! Drum roll! "Oh God," Mattie thought. When will it end?"

It wasn't ending yet. The jokes came fast and furious. Some funny. Some just vulgar. Ethnic jokes. Jokes about garbage. Old jokes. And anniversary announcements.

"Let's give a big hand to Mr. and Mrs. Al Freedman, celebrating their silver anniversary. They met at Levinsberg's twenty-six years ago. And another big hand for Mrs. Irving Cohen of the Queens chapter of Hadassah, who will be honored with a commemorative plaque in the coffee shop right after the show."

The MC came off to polite applause, which immediately died down. He was ecstatic. "Boy! What an audience! What a response! They're really great! Can you hear them?" All that could be heard was an interminable drum roll. "They're just terrific!"

"That drum roll is so long the audience'll think I'm going to do a trapeze act!" Mattie protested.

"Get out there and introduce her!" Sylvia ordered, pushing the MC from the wings.

The audience didn't seem too happy to have him back. "Ladies and gentlemen, it is with great pleasure that Levinsberg's presents tonight a little lady with a lot of talent. You probably haven't seen her before, but she's known to all of you, and she's dear to your hearts. Ladies and gentlemen, it's Jessica Miller's daughter, Miss Mattie Maxwell!"

"Go out and lay them in the aisles, Mattie. You've done it everywhere else!" urged Sylvia. "Go and kill them, baby!"

The orchestra played the first chords of her signature number, "By Strings Attached." She crossed herself covertly—a gesture of habit more than belief. Mattie skipped nimbly onstage, in a plain one-shoulder red crepe dress. A pink spotlight hit her from the front. Two steel-blue ones squeezed her from the sides. Overhead, the lavender pinspot bathed and clearly framed her, making Mattie shimmer as if wet. She stood for a moment, arms close to her body, eyes straight ahead, allowing the audience to wrap her in welcoming applause. She remained motionless. The music stopped. There was a murmur in the audience. Slowly she started to sing, with only the piano. "Not to be alone . . . you gather with your friends . . . people build cathedrals and hang onto a cross they've never known . . . But I have never seen a coffin built for two . . ."

She sang of birds, empty rooms, unrequited love, puppets, poetry, loneliness, the joy of walking free. She pressed her notes, squeezing them, twisting them into a scream of angry childhood, which erupted in her strong, high register as a shiny flying ribbon. Mattie evoked sympathy because she didn't beg for it, which made her oddly attractive. She moved, she talked, she joked, she had a way with her hands and arms unlike anyone they had ever heard or seen before, including Jessica Miller. She created an irresistible momentum and never surrendered it. The audience knew what was happening. So did Mattie. In front of their very eyes the chrysalis of the starlet was maturing into the butterfly of a star.

Mattie was living her songs, and her slightest wish was translated immediately into the most impressive musical reality. Her ability to race from wit to tragedy had them all laughing while drying their tears. The orchestra was excellent, and cloaked her with magical sound, as a man would with his body. It was in turn soft, gentle, pressing, hugging, holding, letting go—like an impassioned affair played between two lovers—discovering, admiring, rejoicing, stroking, caressing, sustaining, anticipating each other. The pianist who had seen her music for the first time that afternoon was one with her. The violinists became part of her soul and brought tears to all eyes.

Mattie came offstage after her first bow to thunderous applause. She went back for an encore, feeling as though she had just begun; her features erupted into a full candlepower smile. Wherever she looked she met unwavering stares of admiration. Mattie had sung for thirty-five minutes—so simply, so beautifully, so excitingly, that you could almost hear the lights changing intensity. When it was all over, Jenny Levinsberg stood up. The rest of the audience followed suit, giving Mattie a standing ovation. "More, more!" they shouted. "Bravo! Encore!" Then, distinctly, someone at the back called out, "Sing 'Whenever the Moon Shines.'" Suddenly the audience grew silent, both from embarrassment and curiosity. "Sing 'Whenever the Moon Shines,'" bellowed the voice. Every eye was on Mattie. The hall echoed with silence. Finally Mattie broke the barrier with a calm, steady voice. "I'm afraid that one's already been sung." The audience burst into delirious applause. When she came offstage, her body was drenched, trembling with excitement.

Sol Green was the first to grab her. "Kid, you're everything Harry Ross said you were—and more! We haven't had a talent like yours since . . . since . . . in ages! From now on, consider Levinsberg's your home. I'll give you a return engagement whenever you like."

"You'll have to speak to my manager, Sol," Mattie said self-consciously, mopping her face with the towel he had handed her. She looked around, but Sylvia was nowhere to be seen.

"I hope that as soon as you've rested, collected your music and changed, you'll join us for a little bite to eat in the coffee shop. You must be starving!"

"No. Sol, I'm really thirsty."

Sylvia trundled toward them. Her face was creased in a beatific smile.

"I was just telling Mattie that the two of you should join us for a little bite to eat."

"I'm afraid not, Sol. We have to go back to the city."

"Oh . . ." His voice trailed off, disappointed. "In fact, I just sent a hamper of food to your room. Fruits, pickled herring, lox, bagels . . . I thought you were spending the weekend."

"No, I couldn't do that, Sol," Mattie explained. "Boris needs looking after."

"Boris? You have a kid?"

"No. I have a duck." Sol raised his cheerless brown eyes questioningly.

"I gave five of them to Jenny, but I kept the best of the . . . the . . . litter for myself."

He laughed. "In other words, the two of you are going all the way back to New York for a duck! Oy vey!"

"Not exactly," said Sylvia, beaming. "I was just on the telephone, and Mattie's booked for the Jack Paar show on Sunday night."

"Jack Paar!" Mattie screamed.

"That's what I said, Mattie! The Jack Paar show!" The two of them gasped, screamed, shouted, jumped up and down, held each other, kissed, and cried.

"The Jack Paar show!" they sobbed in unison.

"One, two, cha-cha-cha! One, two, cha-cha-cha!" They were dancing. Olga opened the door of her dressing room and gave them a cold-fish look.

Sol Green was beside himself with excitement. "I hate to admit it, Mattie, but that beats Levinsberg's any time! You'll be seen by ten million people! That's great! Real great!"

"Here I am on the Jack Paar show and I don't even have a manager," quipped Mattie, keeping a straight face.

"What do you mean, you haven't got a manager, dummkopf?" Sylvia needled.

"Just what I said. I have *an agent*. But no manager . . . or do I? Do I? Oh, Sylvia, will you be my manager? If you become my manager, I promise I'll make you proud of me."

"Manager!" Sylvia shrieked. "You mean you've made a decision? You mean . . . ?"

"That's right. From now on *you* are my manager." Mattie put her arms around the older woman, singing a few bars. "I'll get by . . . as long as I . . . have you . . ."

Their merriment was interrupted by Red Buttons, passing on his way to the stage. "You were great!" he exclaimed. "I always told your mother she had a star on her hands."

"Oh, Red! Thanks—thanks!" she said, taking his hands in hers. "I wish she could have been here tonight."

"In a funny kind of a way she is, and that's how you have to look at it."

"Thanks, Red, thanks." Beaming, Mattie turned to Sol Green. "And I want you there for my opening at the Copa."

"Me? You're inviting me! That's real sweet of you!"

"Please say yes."

"Why, yes, of course!" he said, hugging her. "And after that, we can go—"

"Get a bite to eat—"

"At Lindy's!"

"On one condition, Sol."

"Huh?"

"Dinner's on us!"

⁂

It was not the ideal place for a funeral. Too many onlookers. Even though it was a simple one, there was no way of knowing if this was how he would have wanted it. But this was the way it had to be. The earth was hastily replaced in the grave with a simple marker bearing the name of the deceased and the date: "Boris—February 7, 1954."

Mattie left Central Park feeling overwhelming loneliness. She carried a toy shovel, which she pitched behind a shrub before hailing a cab on the corner of Fifth Avenue and Sixty-fourth Street.

She blinked her eyes as she entered the Shun Tang Garden Restaurant— its outside a drab storefront, the inside a temple of glaring lights and formica. The walls were red on red, with Chinese scrolls, and intaglio snaking its way around the room. Mattie stood by the door and looked around. She was the only customer. She noticed a group of waiters seated near the kitchen door, chopsticking away to the accompaniment of Chinese music blaring from a radio. "Hello," she said, walking inside the room, waving at them timidly. "Excuse me. Sorry to disturb you. Is there a long wait for a table?"

In unison the waiters lifted their inscrutable faces from their plates and looked at her with utter indifference, then went back to their food and music. Mattie sat down at a table near an illuminated glass bar, supported by carved black-lacquer-and-gold-leaf dragons sitting on their haunches and spewing fire. The pink linoleum floor was the color of lobster Cantonese sauce. It was three in the afternoon. Tony wanted to make certain his privacy would be ensured. Well, this is perfect, thought Mattie. I bet "Tony Rook" is hardly a household name here. She tried to attract the attention of one of the waiters, first by calling, then by tapping a knife against a chipped glass, but to no avail. She stood up, gesticulating wildly with her arms and repeating, "Senta! Senta!" She stopped her efforts, remembering that "Senta" was the Italian way of summoning a waiter and was having no effect in this pure Chinese heaven. A blasé waiter approached her table, or so she thought. He continued to the bar for a bottle of Coca-Cola, and Mattie had to stop him bodily as he passed by her on his return.

"Could I have some saké, please?" she asked very loudly, in the manner of foreigners who do not speak the language of a country and who think that by shouting they will be understood. Her request drew a blank stare. She repeated it, enunciating carefully and miming her desire. "Saké—sa-ké, sa-ké," she said, lifting an imaginary glass to her lips.

"No eat-ie, no sa-ké," the waiter pronounced dictatorially.

"Oh, yes!" Mattie exclaimed. "We eat!" She raised make-believe chopsticks to her mouth. "I wait for friend. Mi amigo. Comprendo? Amigo? Si?"

"Chicken close soon."

"No, no. I don't want any chicken," she replied.

"Chicken! *Chicken!*" He nervously pointed toward the kitchen door.

"Oh, kitchen!" She laughed, finally comprehending.

"Specialty house, Peking duck. Good! Take time."

"Oh, no, no, please, no duck!" she cried, remembering Boris, so newly laid to rest in the wilds of Central Park. The waiter looked as if he were about to petrify with boredom before her very eyes. "Saké. Please. Now," Mattie said, impatiently. When the waiter returned with the wine, she pointed to the evocative Chinese characters on the wall. "What do they mean?" she asked, trying to be friendly.

"Talo duck, plum duck, mock duck, loast duck," he recited in a monotone.

"That's *all* it means?" She was disappointed, having expected a wise saying of Confucius.

"Good duck here! Specialty, bar-be-cue duck . . . I order!"

"No!" Mattie protested. "I told you I don't want any duck."

"Duck-liver sausage. Loast duck—"

"No, no thank you! Merci. We—food—order—later on," she said slowly, struggling good-naturedly. "Prego. Auf Wiedersehen."

He disappeared behind a beaded curtain, much in the manner of Peter Lorre exiting for a clandestine rendezvous with Sydney Greenstreet.

The roar of a vacuum cleaner filled the room. Mattie nervously looked around, fidgeting with her tattered napkin. She glanced anxiously at her watch. Where is Tony? she wondered. Late as usual! To pass the time she consciously memorized the entirely forgettable room. Chop suey revisited. Large blown-up photographs of Niagara Falls, the Coliseum, the Sphinx, and a scenic view of Lake Como. The window was dirty; a cat stretched among tired-looking geraniums and dust-covered philodendrons. This must be the garden! was her mischievous thought. Lanterns hung from the ceiling, from which also were suspended bits of glass that clinked together in the slightest draft. It set her teeth on edge.

After she had been sitting for fifteen minutes Tony walked in, less dapper than usual, a grin spread lazily across his mouth. Mattie tried to remain calm while he kissed her. "Hi, baby, it's good to see you," he said somewhat absentmindedly, grabbing a chair, which grated across the linoleum-tiled floor like fingernails on a blackboard.

She stared at him narrowly. "Well, Tony, I've been waiting for your call since last Friday, and today is—"

"Monday," he interrupted. "You don't seem to realize, baby, what I've been through! I haven't had a minute's sleep since—"

"Wednesday," she interrupted. "The last time I saw you was Wednesday." Mattie poured him a cup of saké. "What I want to say, Tony . . . I want to say . . . Oh, dammit, I don't know how to say it."

"Say it!" Tony looked at his watch.

"I want to say that I understand. You know what I mean. I understand your sorrow and . . . and the terrible loss of your best friend and . . . Well, it's natural that under such stress you would forget to call me."

"Mattie you can't understand—"

"Don't explain, Tony. I understand. I am so sorry for you. I know how it is to lose someone you care deeply about. I mean, someone who's irreplaceable. And me—well, I'm around, you know, and I'll be waiting for you, Tony. I'm always around."

"Mattie, I appreciate your—"

"Forget it, Tony. It's only normal. I know you'd do the same for me." She spoke faster to make sure there would be no answer. "I know you love me, Tony, and that's all that matters. I only wish I could be more helpful. I feel sorry for Beverly—"

"Yes, poor Beverly—she's a total wreck."

"Oh, Tony, give her my sympathy, please. . . . Well, no, don't give her my sympathy. She doesn't even know I exist. But she has it, I swear it, Tony. She has it. Oh, Tony, I so wish I could do something for you."

"Mattie, you are doing it by being understanding. I thank you for it. What time is it? I wonder if my watch is right."

"It's three-twenty," replied Mattie, glancing at her own watch. "Here, have some more saké. It'll make you sexy! It always does that to me." She took a sip and put her cup down abruptly. "Oh, I'm sorry, Tony, I didn't mean to say that. I know it's no time to speak or think of sex." Nervously she started to make a party hat out of her napkin. "Anyway, I want to thank you for getting me on the Jack Paar show," she added hurriedly, annoyed with her nervousness. "How did you do it?"

"Well, when Jeremy—when I had to cancel my appearance, I suggested to my manager that he have Paar's office contact you."

"Did you see me on it last night?" she asked hopefully.

"How could I, baby?" he whined apologetically. "I mean, for Christ's sake, Mattie, I was on the plane back to New York, with Beverly in the front and Jeremy's body in the back. How did you do on the show?"

"I must have been okay because they want me back next Sunday. I sang—"

"Shall we order something to eat?" he cut in. He threw a glance toward the bar, and a waiter sidled over with a stained mimeographed sheet that served as a menu.

"Let me order!" she said. "When it comes to Chinese food, you know, I'm an expert and my Chinese is very good. You didn't know that, did you?"

Opening her handbag, she took out a card and ostentatiously showed it to the waiter.

"What does that say?" Tony asked.

"It's written in Chinese," she explained. "It says, 'I am a friend. Give me the real Chinese thing.' It works wonderfully on the road." From the waiter's expressionless face, however, it appeared that it wasn't working in New York.

"We'll have number twenty-four and number nineteen," Mattie ordered affectedly, as if she were at Maxim's. Bending down to Tony, she explained knowledgeably, "Number twenty-four's pike and nineteen is shredded pork and beef with hot pepper and garlic sauce."

"No! Not take! Too hot! Too hot! You no like!" the waiter warned.

"Oh, it's never too hot for me!" giggled Mattie.

"Too hot! Too hot!" the waiter warned. "No good, I say. You no like!" Mattie insisted. "I like it hot."

"Too hot!" he flushed. His tone rose. "Too hot!" Picking up a bottle of Tabasco sauce, he shook it in front of her face as if to make her understand. "Too hot! Too hot!" he shouted, shoving the bottle under her nose and banging it so hard on the table that some saké spilled out of Mattie's cup.

"You can tell he's been to charm school!" said Tony.

"Two dish—only two dish!" the waiter protested. "You take big table—two dish!" he said, calculating something on a pad.

"I can understand his point of view," snapped Tony, "considering the vast crowd in here!"

Apologetically, Mattie said, "Bring us some hot hors d'oeuvres and jasmine tea to begin with." The waiter disappeared, muttering in Chinese.

"I don't have much time, Mattie. Do you think it'll take long to be served?" He glanced restlessly at his watch.

Her amber eyes snapped. "Tony, I've been desperate to see you." She dabbed at the spilled saké. "You . . . you don't know how much I've waited for your call. I've been sick with worry, and now you tell me you haven't even time to—"

"Mattie," he cut in, "please try to realize I'm going through a difficult time—the most difficult time of my life, in fact. Poor Beverly! I think you should make an effort and understand that."

"Tony, I can understand anything. But I've got to tell you the truth. I'm having anxiety attacks around the clock! I only hope you're not mad that I was the one who tracked you down at the hotel in New York. *Would you have called me?*"

He ignored the question. "Speaking of phone calls," he said, his eyes darting left and right, "I've got to make one."

"But, Tony, you've only just arrived!"

"Beverly is with a nurse, under sedation. I wanna make sure—"

"Make sure of what?"

"Stop it, Mattie!" he snapped. "I know what I have to do." He made his way toward the phone booth. Her eyes followed him.

The hot hors d'oeuvres arrived. They were cold. "Four clock, four clock!" the waiter insisted, pointing to the clock over the fire exit. The time didn't matter. Those hors d'oeuvres were a mistake at any hour.

"Oh, I forgot to order fried rice," Mattie said.

"Flied lice?"

"Yes, that's right. Flied lice." She suppressed a smile.

Tony came back to the table. Her eyes raked him and she marveled inwardly at his graceful and elegant proportions. "How is Beverly?" she asked, affecting genuine interest.

"She's still resting, but I want to be there when she wakes up."

"Why? To feed her pablum?" Mattie said wide-eyed.

"Shut up, Mattie. This is no time for jokes." Tony shook his head in annoyance. "Beverly depends on me now. So I'm taking care of her the best way I know how, and that's that. I know Jeremy would want me to." He nibbled at a sad shrimp. "This morning was just awful."

"Yes, I know," said Mattie. "I saw it on television. Personally, I liked the part where she snatched her little gold Star of David from her throat and threw it on the coffin."

"Yeah, it was heartbreaking."

"I think she was real smart."

"How?"

"Well, it was probably the smallest piece of jewelry she owned. I didn't see any of her big rocks flying into that grave!"

"Mattie, for Christ's sake! Don't be a bitch. This isn't like you. Shit! For me, losing Jeremy was like losing my father, my brother and my best friend all at the same time."

"Try and look on the bright side of it. You've gained a mother and a sister." She attempted a weak smile.

The statement inflamed him. "Mattie, how can you be so insensitive?"

"I'm sorry, Tony." She stared straight into his face, seeing the anger there. "I didn't mean—"

"Goddamn it!" said Tony. "That's why I wasn't sure about seeing you when you called—I knew you'd never understand."

"Oh, Tony, but I do, I do understand—not all of it, but I understand." They sat in silence for a long time. "What are your plans, Tony?"

"I'm going back to California tonight with Beverly, and I'll stay with her until she's herself again."

"Was she ever herself?" Mattie swallowed her breath.

"Please, Mattie."

"What about the tour you were going to start this week to promote your album?"

"It'll have to wait."

"God, I wish I had a friend like you!"

"Mattie, you wouldn't want friendship to be proven this way—I guarantee it. You don't know what hell Beverly's going through. She needs—"

"You. She needs you. Isn't that it?" A new sorrow invaded her.

"Yes, she does," he admitted softly, avoiding her gaze.

"I'd like some champagne," she suddenly announced with false gaiety, and shouted to the waiter, "A bottle of your best champagne, *garçon!*"

"Why do you want to drink so early in the day? There's really nothing to celebrate."

"Oh, I think there is," she said, motioning to a waiter. "Let's just say . . . we're celebrating your leaving me. Because you *are* leaving me, aren't you?"

"Come on, Mattie, stop being childish. The situation's only temporary. You would love Beverly. She's some helluva girl."

"Why is it you've never introduced me?"

"You can figure that one out for yourself. She hasn't been in New York in over a year, and you haven't been to California." Tony's attention wilted.

"What about now?" insisted Mattie with a lump in her throat.

"Now is hardly the time. She doesn't want to see anyone but me. I've got to stick close to her. If she didn't have me by her side right now she'd crack up!"

"What about me?" Mattie's voice quavered. "Don't you worry if I'll crack up?"

"No, Mattie. You haven't had a tragic loss, and you're strong. A lot stronger than you think. Concentrate on your work. Your opening at the Copa is just around the corner. That's the only thing you should be thinking of right now. You'll make it with or without me." Tony sounded belligerently neutral and noncommittal.

The champagne arrived. It foamed with the delicious sound of the ocean as it was poured.

"You know, Tony," Mattie reminisced, lighting a cigarette, "I remember all the things you liked about me. You said I was childlike! Wonderful! You thought me mysterious. Great! I was exciting. Wow! But now—well, you'd think I was yesterday's garbage. You can't dump me fast enough—or have you dumped me already?"

"It isn't like that at all, baby. Please give me time, just give me time." He took her hands and held them for a second. They were icy cold.

The pork and beef arrived, together with the pike platter. The latter could easily have taken first prize as the ugliest Chinese dish in New York. It looked like a hairy fish with some teeth missing. Missing too was one of its eyes, which had been replaced by a sliver of black mushroom pierced by a tiny toothpick topped by a miniature paper umbrella. It was hard to believe that what lay on the platter had actually begun life as a pike. Mattie took a bite and grimaced. "Hmmmmmm. Strange taste . . . That fish has a very fishy taste," she told the waiter, who was standing at attention nearby.

"Fish suppose taste like fish!"

"Ask him if the sauce's supposed to taste like a priest's old socks!" Tony suggested, snickering.

A variety of vegetables of dubious oriental origin arrived in breathtaking technicolor—they too tasted like fish. They started on the pork.

"Too hot! I told you so! Too hot!" shrieked the waiter. Mattie was unmoved as the waiter attacked again. "Too hot! I told you! Ha! Ha! Too hot!" he repeated with glee, standing on the side, ready to pounce at the first sign of rejection. A request for chopsticks simply drew a blank stare. "Too hot! See! Too hot!" the waiter continued.

"Oh, no—perfect! Wonderful!" lied Mattie in an effort to placate the waiter, who retreated to a table and buried his head in a Chinese newspaper. Mattie's and Tony's tongues burned as they alternately drank champagne, saké and water to relieve the fire of the dish. Both were silent. Both were lost in their separate thoughts. Both were thinking of the present and the future. Mattie was hoping against hope that perhaps everything would be all right again. That's it, she thought, time! Just give him time! The radio had long been turned off. There was absolute quiet. A long moment passed before they resumed the conversation.

"The funeral has taken everything out of me today," said Tony.

"I had a funeral today too."

Tony poised the chopsticks in midair, forming an arrow, and looked at her. "What the hell are you talking about?"

"Boris died last night."

"Boris who?"

"Did you say Boris *who?* . . . What do you mean, Boris *who?* Have you forgotten already? Boris, my duckling . . ."

"Oh, *that* Boris!"

"Do you know another Boris?"

"What did he die of? I hope it was constipation!" he said, remembering the ducks' uncontrollable behavior in Mattie's bathroom.

Mattie smiled sadly. One of her crooked smiles. "Oh, Tony, I'm so sad!" she blurted. Her lips moved in a voiceless plea and a tremor she could not still passed through her body. "Oh, Tony, don't leave me . . . I'm so alone. I'm all alone. And I love you so much. Come home with me, Tony. Please." She reached for his arm. "I won't touch you—I won't do anything! I promise. After all, I'm not a recent encounter, or a pickup. I want to share your sorrow . . . please" Her words mingled with tears. "I just want to be near you!"

"I can't, Mattie, I can't. I must take care of my obligations. I don't want to—"

"Be with me anymore. Isn't that it?" All the restaurant lights went out at once. Mattie heard a waiter announce, "Chicken close!" and she burst into tears.

"Baby, please, try to behave. We're in public." Tony spoke in hushed tones. Mattie folded her hands in her lap. The tears streamed down her face. "Don't baby, don't. I think—"

"I think you're being very selfish. You don't care at all."

"Mattie, please believe me. I care. I care."

"I thought you loved me." She stared straight into his face and sighed, long, fat tears edging down her cheeks.

"Mattie, don't cry, please. Not here."

"Where, then?"

"Just not here," he repeated. "People will think I've done something terrible to you."

"What people?"

"The waiters. I should be the one who's crying."

"Then why don't you?"

"Stop it, Mattie!"

He looked at her as if she were a child lost in a department store. "Let's get the check," he said impatiently. As Tony counted the money on the table he casually mentioned, "I'm going to have one of the starring roles in the movie Jeremy was about to produce just before he . . . he . . ."

"Oh, that's wonderful, Tony!" Mattie exclaimed as they both got up to leave. They walked out into the street and were attacked by the bitter cold. She hung onto his arm.

"I've got Beverly's limousine. Can I drop you somewhere?"

"Yeah, let's go to your house. I haven't been there before!" She tried to sound funny, but her heart was heavy. She knew an episode of her life was over. Tony didn't respond. "I was only kidding!" she added. "As a matter of fact, you can drop me off at El Borracho. When will I hear from you?"

"I don't know, Mattie," he replied as they entered the car. "I just don't know. Don't pin me down. I don't know what I'm doing from one hour to the next. But you'll hear from me."

"Can't I call you somewhere?" Mattie was swimming in despair. "Don't you have a number?"

"I'm staying at Beverly's house, and I can't give that number out." He sounded uneasy. "Where's that place you wanted me to drop you? Seems I've heard the name before."

"You probably saw it on a matchbox in my apartment last Wednesday. It's on Fifty-fifth Street, between Park and Madison."

"Are you meeting somebody there?" he asked.

"Yeah, I've got an appointment with a handsome swain. I need a good frolic!"

"Mattie, you'll never change!"

"I'll change, don't worry. What do I have to lose but my old habits?"

The car stopped in front of a canopy spotted with large pairs of ruby-red lips. "Well, Tony . . . I guess it's . . . it's toodleoo . . . and good luck!" she said.

"Mattie, take care of yourself. I'll be in touch. Soon. I promise." He kissed her on both cheeks. She kissed his neck. "Be a good girl. You'll hear from me."

She could feel the tears welling up in her eyes again and hurried out of the car, leaving the door open.

El Borracho was the ultimate in East Side chic. The bar and banquettes were crowded with smart executives and young models. A combo was playing. The sound of voices hummed like the unintelligible moaning of a prayer to some unseen god. The owner, Nicky, greeted her. "May I help you, young lady?"

"Yeah, as a matter of fact, you may." She emphasized the word "may," and that gave her a kick. "I'm waiting for my date. Could I have a table, please?"

"Please follow me. . . . Will your escort be long?" he asked as she sat down. "Because unescorted ladies are not allowed here."

"No. He should be here shortly," she lied.

"You look very familiar," he said inquiringly. "Oh, weren't you on Jack Paar's show last night?"

"As a matter of fact, I was."

"Now I've got it," he exclaimed excitedly. "You were wonderfully funny. You're Mattie Maxwell!"

"That's right!" She smiled.

"You're Jessica Miller's daughter? I've got something to show you that might interest you. Just follow me." Nicky led her into the main part of the lounge, its walls entirely covered by framed lip prints that had been autographed by their famous owners. "I want yours too!" Nicky said. He pointed to a pair of red lips that bore the famous signature *Jessica Miller*. It never failed. Chills ran up and down Mattie's spine. "Just excuse me for a minute," Nicky said apologetically. "I'll get some paper—and in the meantime would you put on some more lipstick?"

Mattie took a mirror, a tube of "Cherries in the Snow," and applied the color carefully. Nicky came back and put the imprint of her lips on a piece of white paper. A camera clicked. Her extra-long lashes cast a deep shadow on the pallor of her face. This was still new to her, and she was excited by the commotion she was causing. Several people were standing at their tables and most of the occupants at the bar had leaned forward to gape. She could hear their comments: "Who is it? Mattie who? Maxwell." Oh, yeah, she was on Jack Paar last night. Sure, she was the wacky kid who talked about ducks. . . . What a voice . . . as great as her mother's!"

A familiar figure, slightly hunched, in a well-cut Ivy League suit, tugging at his tie from force of habit, came toward her.

"Excuse me, Miss Maxwell. I want to congratulate you. I happened to catch the tail end of the Paar show last night and you were simply delight-ful! Very funny. However, I missed your singing. Would you mind calling me tomorrow at my office," he said, handing her a card, "and we'll set up an audition. I hear you have a great voice besides being a terrific wit. If you're as good as they tell me, I want you on my show. My name is Ed Sullivan."

※

MARIELA/*Zurich*/*Monday, March 15, 1954*

"I want to be certain my fitting will be ready for Thursday," said Mariela, stroking the three-quarter length silver fox jacket. "I'm leaving for London Saturday and I would love to take it with me."

"Natürlich, Lady Chelmsford. We always keep our word," replied Kurt Reenweg.

The fitter, in a white smock, tape measure snaking around his neck, helped Mariela into her own sable coat. The manager bowed respectfully. "Auf Wiedersehen, Lady Chelmsford. Have a good evening. We'll be ex-pecting you the day after tomorrow, anytime after one."

She left the Reenweg Fur Salon, heading for Bahnhofstrasse, turned right and walked briskly toward her hotel, oblivious of the crisp March air and the bustle of afternoon shoppers. Passing the gray edifice housing the First International Bank of Zurich, she noticed a familiar figure—a short, balding man with glasses and a florid complexion. She waved at him from across the street, remembering how helpful and efficient Mr. Küller had been in ac-complishing the transfer of funds from Karl Ravenstein's numbered ac-count. The fortune now rested under a different number. Only its owner knew its code. Who was its real owner? Or owners? Mariela recalled every detail—telling Glover goodbye at the Key Crescent airport in Florida, know-ing he would never dare accuse her without the fear of retaliation—calling Berger by phone from Zurich a couple of days after her arrival to report the successful completion of her assignment. Auf Wiedersehen! Case closed and final.

How many people had been involved in this plot? Considering its rami-fications, Mariela was certain there were others. But what others? She had already spent so many sleepless nights trying to figure out who those *others* could be, each time swearing never to give it another thought.

It was no use.

Zurich! The mountains kissed the sky and the air was pure as the day the earth began. Yet for Mariela, Zurich was prison. Exile. A searing reminder for her that people with not even a portion of the money she had could see the stars, while she was blinded to the beauty of the world because her own little realm was so ugly.

Would she be doomed to this life forever? Could she change? Should she run? Run where? Could she hide? How? She was utterly alone except for her enemies. But what enemies? Who could benefit from wanting her out of the way? Why fear? Yet how could she not?

Once again she reviewed the past events to boost her confidence, if only momentarily: The Ravenstein case—officially closed with the "suicide" of its prime suspect, Andreas Poppidoppolous.

Glover Anderson—not a threat, because his political ambition could ill afford exposure in a case in which his personal involvement had already gone well over his head. Jack Hamilton—an unprincipled bully. Nathan Berger—an uncompromising snake. But what could they gain? She had gone along with them every step of the way. Besides, she didn't know any more today than she did on the terrible night of January 30, when it had all happened.

Now nothing in the world was more important to Mariela than to turn her life around. And nothing in the world seemed more impossible.

She felt out of her time, out of her place. Ancient Rome, not Zurich, would have been her natural habitat. There her full-blooded sensuality could have been unleashed. No limits. No shame. The Roman emperors Nero and Caligula could have been denizens of her private hell. She felt unclean. Unfit for human companionship. Unfit to be Oliver's mother. And yet she *was* his mother.

One thing Mariela was sure of: as a result of her participation in the sordid plot she now had two hundred and fifty thousand United States dollars in an account of her own, which enabled her to provide for her son Oliver on a grand scale.

She stopped at Meister Chemist to purchase a vial of Dexedrine. Anticipating a long and pleasurable night, she didn't want to find her energy waning. "Madame Elsie" had reserved the services of a group of Mariela's *special* playmates, and the promise of one or two new faces would prove intriguing. With the brothel at her private disposal for the evening, Mariela wanted to make the most of it.

A sudden cold breeze wafted off the lake and chilled her. She walked on more briskly and entered the stuffy splendor of the Hotel Baur-au-Lac through its revolving doors, going directly to the front desk.

"Good afternoon, Lady Chelmsford," the concierge greeted her.

"Do you have any messages for me?"

"Yes, just a moment please, I'll give them to you."

There were several. She took her key and messages and moved away, easing herself into one of the comfortable, tapestried chairs in the sumptuous marble-and-glass lobby. She opened the first envelope. An invitation to a vernissage, to be followed by a supper party. She read the second note quickly, but it was confusing: "Your daughter Genevieve called from Gstaad. You can pick her up after classes tomorrow afternoon at four o'clock." The message made no sense. It didn't apply to her. Refolding the piece of paper, she glanced at the small envelope. It was addressed to Mr. Curtis Lodge III.

The name rang a bell. Several bells, in fact. Everyone in the world knew Curtis Lodge III.

She returned to the reception desk. The concierge was busy talking to a man. Mariela couldn't avoid overhearing their conversation.

"Excuse me, but this message isn't for me," the man was saying.

The man was an American. There could be no mistake about that, from the way he used, or as Mariela thought, misused the English language.

"It's addressed to Lady Chelmsford. He pronounced it "Chelemsford."

Mariela approached him. "Are you Mr. Curtis Lodge?"

He turned around to face her. "Yes, Curtis Lodge, that's me," he answered with dry precision. The well-publicized president of Curtis Lodge Motor Company, in Detroit, was much better-looking than he photographed, she thought.

"Apparently you have my note," she said, smiling. "I'm Lady Chelmsford. Do you happen to have a daughter named Genevieve?"

"Yes, I do have a daughter named Genevieve."

She laughed. "I'm afraid our messages got confused, and I've read yours before realizing it didn't belong to me."

"If anyone is to read my messages by accident, I couldn't ask for a better choice than a tall, dark, beautiful woman," he answered with a pleasant grin and a broad midwestern accent.

"Genevieve will be waiting for you tomorrow afternoon in Gstaad," Mariela continued, ignoring the compliment.

"And your real estate agent will be waiting for you this afternoon at six," he said with a twinkle. "Are you English?"

"Yes, but I'm now planning to live in Switzerland."

"If I may, I would like to introduce myself properly," he said, taking off his homburg and gloves. "Curtis Lodge the Third, at your service." He kissed the hand she proffered, keeping his eyes on hers. "And you are Lady Chelmsford," he stated, using the proper pronunciation this time.

"The one and only." She laughed her unique laugh—deep and sensual. "But I don't have the advantage of a number after my name."

"You don't need a number. You should be the only one. You're too beautiful to be reissued."

"Thank you. It's worth a mix-up to hear such pleasant words."

They moved away from the desk.

"Perhaps . . . ," Curtis said hesitantly, removing his furlined black cashmere coat, folding it over one arm, perhaps . . . I could persuade you to have a drink with me in the lounge? If you're not terribly busy, that is." He looked at his Patek Philippe watch. "You do have almost an hour left until your real estate agent arrives. My next appointment isn't until seven-thirty."

Why not, thought Mariela. "All right," she said, noticing how he radiated vigor and magnetism.

Curtis Lodge III was in his early fifties, ruggedly handsome, with graying hair, more than six feet tall. His clear blue eyes reflected a rare blend of toughness and humanity, arrogance and sensitivity. Curtis was so impeccably American! So impeccably rich-American! So impeccably old-moneyed, rich-American! A pillar of strength. His Savile Row tweed suit accented his powerful frame. But oh, that tie! In what concoction had it been dipped to reproduce all those colors on such a small piece of fabric? She suppressed a smile.

They crossed the lobby, descended the small staircase to the right and entered the cocktail area. A large, oak-paneled room, warmly lighted by bronze candle chandeliers and clusters of tiny wall lamps. Muted green-and-orange French Provincial armchairs were placed around white marble tables, each decorated with a bouquet of fresh-cut flowers. A rich, thick carpet, woven in a geometric pattern, covered the floor. Mirrored French doors reflected a huge porcelain vase filled with red and yellow gladiolas and mums.

Mariela and Curtis had the place almost to themselves. They took their seats near the entrance, beneath the mammoth portrait of a man Mariela assumed to be the founder of the hotel. A waiter in a black tailcoat with gold buttons approached them and took their orders.

"Did you come to Zurich just to get your daughter?" Mariela asked, draping her coat over an empty chair.

"No. I've been here, or rather in Europe, for several weeks on business. We are opening a plant in England. Genevieve is attending the Vidamanatte School in Gstaad. I'm taking her home for Easter vacation . . . Lady Chelms . . . ford."

"Please call me Mariela."

"Okay, Mariela," he said heartily, as the waiter returned with their drinks. "How long have you been in Zurich?"

"About two months," she answered, playing with the straw in her spritzer. "I like it here. It's close to every big city and yet it gives me a feeling of tranquillity. But I detest living in hotels, no matter how luxurious they are."

Mariela was very conscious of the way Curtis' eyes kept caressing her face and body. She shifted her position to display her magnificent breasts to their best advantage.

"I need to find a place of my own," she declared.

"We should all have a place of our own. Several, if possible," he quipped. "Have you found anything you like yet?" He took a large gulp of his Scotch on the rocks.

"I believe the chalet I'm seeing again today may be the right one."

"But being English, Mariela, wouldn't you prefer London? What do you have against living in London?"

"Nothing. I love London. But there's only one house there that I'd settle for."

"What house? Buckingham Palace?" He winked.

"No, nothing so grand." His shoulder touched her shoulder. "It's on Belgrave Square and was in my family . . ." She hesitated.

"And—?"

"And right now the house isn't available. That's all." Mariela knew the answer to the next question but asked it anyway. "Isn't your wife traveling with you?"

"I've been a widower for six years. My wife died of cancer in 1949."

"Oh, I'm sorry."

"There's no need to be sorry. Life has generally been pretty good to me. I would say pretty good indeed, and . . . and I must admit," he continued, "the Lodge Motor Company has been my main mistress ever since. I really—"

"Excuse me, Mr. Lodge," interrupted a bellboy, approaching the table. "It's an overseas call, sir."

"Thank you, young fellow." Curtis handed the bellboy a large bill. "Don't go away, Mariela," he told her with the assurance of a man for whom the world was one big "yes." "I'll be right back."

Mariela observed Curtis as he picked up the telephone near the bar. What had he said? The Lodge Motor Company his main mistress? Mariela knew better, and wondered how Rosemary Hansford, the ex-manicurist from Chicago who had been Curtis' traveling companion for the past two years, would have reacted to this statement. Also, his "main mistress" must have languished painfully during his notorious pursuit of Faye Larson, the actress renowned for her plunging necklines.

"I'm sorry for the interruption." Curtis sat down agin. "No matter where I am, my office can always track me down! They must have radar! Waiter, another round of drinks, please." Mariela and Curtis talked of many things. Pleasant things. Happy things.

"I'm afraid I'll have to say goodbye," Mariela said, looking at her watch. "The agent is due any minute."

"Is it six already?" Curtis motioned for the check, and helped Mariela into her coat. "I have an idea," he said buoyantly. "Would you mind if I accompanied you? I'd love to see the chalet. Do you mind?"

She could see no reason for refusing. Mariela and Curtis settled comfortably into his chauffeured limousine. Following the agent's car, they traveled east on Bellerive-Quai, passing the Langdustelle Theater toward Seefeldstrasse. The lake was deep blue in the low-angled light of the late afternoon sun, contrasting spectacularly with the snow-encrusted Alps.

The chalet was exquisite. Its white stucco façade, with large wooden beams and carved oak shutters, a slanted ancient tile roof, and balconies filled with blooming flowers like hanging gardens, gave it the picturesque appearance of a set right out of *The White Horse Inn* operetta. They walked inside the house. Each of its twelve rooms had a majestic view of either Lake Zurich or the mountains.

"Isn't it a dream?" said Mariela eagerly taking Curtis' arm.

"What do they want for this place?" he asked.

"Two hundred thousand Swiss francs. How much is that in U.S. dollars?" She knew the answer, but it didn't hurt to defer to the American motor magnate.

"Eighty thousand dollars. It's a bargain."

"Do you like it, Curtis?"

"It's beautiful. Just like its new owner."

"How can you tell who the new owner is?" Her slow, dark, distinctive voice enveloped him like the tang of an expensive perfume.

He paused. "I have a feeling that whatever you *want* will be yours. And the way you've been looking at this place tells me that you want it."

"You are right, Curtis. I do want it! It's perfect for me, just perfect. I love it! You've helped me make up my mind. . . . Would you excuse me a moment," she said cheerfully. "I'll be right back."

Mariela took the agent aside diplomatically. A few minutes later she returned. An ecstatic radiance flushed her face. "Well, Mr. Lodge the Third. I'm now the owner of the Chalet Bienvenue."

"That means 'welcome,' doesn't it?" he asked. "The name alone is auspicious!"

"I didn't know you were such a linguist."

"Mariela, you've got the wrong guy for languages. The only thing I know is how to make money!" Curtis' laugh was raucous, self-mocking.

Their ride back to the hotel was bright and bubbly.

After some time Curtis said, "Now that I've accompanied you on your mission, I think it would only be fair if you gave me the same courtesy."

The superb green eyes looked at him questioningly.

"My day would be perfect tomorrow if you were to accompany me to Gstaad. What do you say? We'll fly in my private plane."

"That seems like a reasonable request." She felt the night chill and drew closer to him. "I'd be delighted to pick up your daughter with you. How old is she?"

"The little lady is eleven."

"I have a nephew about the same age."

"In London?"

"No, Oliver—that's his name—Oliver lives with his grandparents in Germany. My sister and her husband died years ago."

"Oh, I'm sorry to hear that," Curtis said with compassion.

"How long do you plan to stay in Zurich?" Mariela asked.

"We're going to play it by ear. I also want to show Genevieve Rome and London."

"London!" exclaimed Mariela. "I'm going to London this weekend."

"Well, I'll be damned!" he boomed happily. "We should be in London about the same time. Now, you see? The message mistake wasn't a mistake at all, but destiny. One never knows what life has in store." Curtis took her arm and squeezed it gently. "I believe we should celebrate the finding of your dream house . . . and of each other. Let's have dinner together, Mariela. And, by God, I won't accept anything but yes for an answer. What do you say?"

She hesitated as long as she dared. "Well, I won't allow anything unacceptable to spoil the perfection of the day." Mariela smiled. "Of course I will. I'd be delighted." He put his large hand on hers.

They arrived at the Baur-au-Lac. The liveried chauffeur held the door open.

"It's seven-fifteen now," said Curtis. "I have an appointment at the Zurich Banker's Club on Paradeplatz with an old friend from Texas, Sinclair McAlpine. We were at Harvard together. Besides having the biggest yacht afloat, Sinclair knows as much about planes as I know about cars. Yessirree, he's a helluva guy with a helluva company! You're probably too tired and want to refresh yourself, otherwise I'd ask you to come with me now. No, on second thought, I'd better not introduce you to Sinclair. Only a fool would give himself competition. I'd rather have you to myself. What time shall we meet? Is nine o'clock all right? You know this town better than I do. Where would you like to go this evening? Just tell me and my secretary will make the reservation." He spoke nonstop. Wide-eyed, like a child on Christmas morning.

"Let me think. . . . Let's go to La Mouette. It's in the old part of town. The food is delicious and I believe you'll like it."

"I'd like any place if you were with me." He still held onto her hand and said very quietly, "Nine o'clock at the bar—I'll be waiting. . ."

"See you at nine," said Mariela as she floated out of the car and into the lobby.

Mariela got to her peach and brown suite overlooking the private park of the hotel, took off her coat, sat at the small desk and dialed.

"I would like to speak to Madame Elsie, please."

"This is Madame Elsie," a distinguished voice replied.

"Oh, good evening, Elsie, this is Lady M." Mariela tapped her nails nervously on the porcelain ashtray. "I'm terribly sorry, but something has just come up and I'm afraid our appointment this evening will have to be postponed."

"But—but I've already made all the arrangements, Lady M. It's too late to change them at this hour. I could have had other clients for the services of—"

"That's all right, Elsie, don't worry about that, I'll take care of everything anyway. Just consider this evening as a paid holiday for your boys and girls and yourself. We'll make it another night. Very soon."

Mariela walked to the other room. Twilight had given way to darkness. Exhausted, she kicked off her high-heeled brown alligator shoes and collapsed onto the peach-and-gray-striped satin cover of the king-size bed. Automatically her right hand reached for the knob of the built-in radio of her night table. Julie London's breathy rendition of "Cry Me a River" was soothing. She closed her eyes.

Curtis Lodge was smitten. Very. But did *she* mesmerize him or was it Lady Chelmsford? Would he have treated her with the same respect had he known of her past? Of course not. But the past was buried forever. She was Lady Mariela Chelmsford of Zurich and London. The beautiful and very proper Lady Chelmsford. No one else.

Mariela was filled with strange and contradictory emotions. She remembered the words Curtis had pronounced in the chalet—"I have a feeling that whatever you want will be yours." Mariela sensed that he meant more than just the chalet; their lives could be inextricably bound together. It was up to her.

Maybe *this* was what she had been waiting for.

Maybe her life would change after all. Maybe *she* would change. Maybe. Mariela was ready. And if it was to happen, nothing would ever be sufficient to express her boundless gratitude.

Anyway, Curtis Lodge III—wealthy, powerful, socially secure, completely respectable—could be the miracle to make it all come true.

It was certainly worth a dinner to find out.

Besides, she could have an orgy at Madame Elsie's anytime.

—✳—

MATTIE/*Las Vegas/Monday, April 26, 1954*

The taxi pulled up in front of El Rancho-Vegas at four-fifteen in the afternoon. Mattie stepped out, followed by Sylvia carrying a quilted hang-up bag.

The temperature was over ninety in the shade—dry but overpowering.

"Wow! I can't believe it's so much hotter here than in L.A.!" said Sylvia.

They were forced to stop dead in their tracks by a herd of drunken Shriners brandishing beer cans and hip flasks, shirttails and good cheer flying, spinning around like kids in the revolving door.

"Hey, Mattie!" one of them shouted, recognizing her. "How about an autograph for my kids!" His boyish face looked like the map of Ireland. He approached Mattie bashfully and politely. The China-blue eyes lit up. "We're all from Wichita, Kansas. The folks back home would sure appreciate it if we got a picture. Would you mind posing with us all underneath the marquee?"

"Okay, fellas!" Mattie said, giggling girlishly.

"But you've got a radio interview with George Gobel at five-thirty," interrupted Sylvia.

"For heaven's sake, relax, Sylvia. This won't take but a minute!" She arranged herself in the middle of the Shriners while glancing proudly at the marquee: *El Rancho-Vegas Presents Joe E. Lewis, Mattie Maxwell — Musical Director, Cy Bender — and the Don Mitchell Orchestra. Opening May 10, Eartha Kitt.* Turning to her left, she asked, genuinely interested, "What's your name?"

"Steve McEvoy, ma'am," he answered. The black tassel on his red fez caught in his mouth, choking off his words.

"Okay, fellas, here it goes!" Mattie bellowed. "Say cheese, everybody!" she laughed, putting her arm around Steve's shoulder. The camera clicked. It was over in an instant. "Okay, fellas, that's it! I've gotta go! But don't forget to catch my show tonight!"

"We already saw it Saturday, ma'am, and you were fantastic! And me and the missus are big fans since we saw you on the Sullivan show!" he shouted in ecstatic satisfaction. Mattie and Sylvia disappeared through the revolving door.

"You know, Mattie," observed Sylvia, "that was real nice of you. Those guys'll never forget it. You really made their day!"

"Yeah, but I've made up my mind, Sylvia, to give being a bitch a try—it saves time, believe me!" Mattie joked.

"You never could!"

"Just watch me," she said, "Just watch me!"

The air-conditioned darkness of the lobby hit them like a brick wall.

"Sylvia, why don't you give that bag to one of the bellhops—if you can find one who isn't playing the slot machines. In the meantime I'll go to the desk and get my messages."

"My, my, aren't we anxious!" teased Sylvia. "You won't have an answer on your screen test that soon!"

"Don't be silly! I wasn't thinking of that! I might have some other messages. I'm getting pretty popular here, you know!" She closed her lids halfway and sucked in her cheeks, affecting a mocking air of pseudosophistication. "I'll meet you in the lounge. I really do need a drink. After that plane ride, who wouldn't? I don't know why the studio insisted on giving us a private plane—whose service, may I add, compared unfavorably with Chicastegano Airlines!"

"Where's Chicastegano?"

"It's in Mexico, and makes Tijuana look like Paris!" They both laughed. "Find a table, Sylvia, and order me a Tom Collins," Mattie said.

"Do you need another drink, Mattie? I don't want to sound like a Mother Confessor, but—"

"Then don't," Mattie snapped, stalking off.

The lobby was a mélange of humanity in its most outlandish forms of attire and behavior, grasping instant excitement and forcing laughter and good times at four o'clock in the afternoon. Gaudy but pretty hookers and their amateur competition mingled with housewives, widows, divorcées and young women from all parts of the country, wearing what passed in their home communities for chic and sophisticated outfits.

There was no way to reach the desk without passing through part of the gambling area. An air-conditioned Baghdad glittering coolly in the sweltering desert. And there it was: the floor carpeted, the booze on the rocks, the girls available, the food free, the smoke thick, and the action fast and furious. Sounds rose from the green felt crap tables like the litany of a masochistic ritual: "Snake eyes, goddammit . . . lost again . . . Come on, baby, come on . . . the point is four . . ."

Mattie went by a little old lady wearing workman's gloves and relentlessly feeding the insatiable one-arm bandits, two at a time. The incessant clatter brought a demonic gleam to her lackluster eyes. Hundreds of slot machines! Hundreds of demonic gleams! Hundreds of lackluster eyes!

"Jackpot! I've got three cherries!" yelled the little old lady, looking as if she had just devoured her last young. The machine vomited noisily, reluctantly giving back some of its profits.

Mattie took in the faces, the smiles, the shouts, and loved it. Loved it all! The vulgarity, the momentary joy, the hicks, the unsophisticated gapers, the baggy-eyed tourists, the scrutinizing stares, the vapid compliments, the gentle words of appraisal, the recognition. Her name on the billboard in the lobby. Fame creates its own standards. She inhaled and embraced it.

"Anything for me?" asked Mattie at the front desk.

"Here are your messages, Miss Maxwell," said the clerk.

Mattie grabbed the handful of paper and glanced briefly at the notes. She walked toward the lounge, weaving her way among tables occupied by tourists, entertainers and a mixture of high-priced hookers and pit girls waiting for a live one. The captain led her to Sylvia. Mattie slumped in her seat, subdued and silent, a hard, fixed gaze in her opaque eyes.

"What's up, Mattie?" queried Sylvia, her hand full of peanuts. "You look like you've seen a ghost."

"I have." She was still holding onto the piece of paper bearing the hotel message.

Sylvia snatched it from her. "Who the hell's Vinny Pisciotta anyway?" she asked, munching the nuts.

"The PR man for the Riviera Hotel."

"Oh, yeah, I remember him. Nice guy. What does he want?"

"We're invited there after my second show," Mattie said with controlled matter-of-factness. "Did you order my drink?"

"Yes, I did. It's coming." Sylvia looked over her shoulder in the direction of the bar. "I thought you wanted to see Bela Lugosi at the Silver Slipper."

"I think I'm going to like the Riviera show a whole lot better." Mattie was utterly shaken, making a big effort to conceal it.

"Is somebody special performing?"

"Yes, I'd say so."

"Since when are they doing a third show at the Riviera?"

"They're not! Tonight's the opening of this one." For a moment Mattie's voice seemed to fail her. "Where's that drink you ordered me, for Christ's sake?" she snapped, nearly breaking.

"It's on its way now, Mattie. Take it easy! You sound like an alcoholic." A spectacular waitress approached wearing an outfit inspired by the gay nineties—a one-piece number cut like a Victorian corset—her breasts, the nipples barely covered, straining the wire-reinforced push-up bra; her firm bottom was exposed. Black fishnet stockings and spike-heeled shoes completed the costume, except for a bit of nonsense that sat on her head—like that of an upstairs-downstairs maid in nineteenth-century London—in the form of white pleated lace and black velvet streamers.

"Okay, so what gives? Spill the beans!" said Sylvia, picking at the popcorn. "My curiosity's giving me hunger pangs!"

At that very moment the most famous showgirl on the Strip, who was known as Yellowbird, brushed past their table and stopped. "Oh, Mattie," she said, "I watch you from the wings every night. You are the greatest! Bye now!" she chirped, slinking off gracefully on exceedingly high heels. The air was tattooed with the unmistakable aroma of Mitsouko. Mattie's eyes followed her exit with absentminded interest.

"Now are you going to tell me what's going on," Sylvia practically screamed, "or do I have to hit you over the head with this goddamned glass?"

Mattie purposely forced herself to speak lightly. "About an hour ago Beverly Langdon announced that she's getting married. She and the future bridegroom are flying in for the ceremony late tonight at the Riviera. Can you guess who the lucky bridegroom is?"

"Don't tell me! I can't believe it! It isn't—it isn't Tony, is it?" Sylvia gripped her arm. "It isn't Tony Rook?"

"Yes. It is." Mattie said flatly, her eyes filling with sudden tears.

"Are you kidding, Mattie?"

"Would I kid about a thing like that?" Her husky voice was infinitely gentle.

"Mattie, I *am* sorry! It really *is* hard to believe! I know there were rumors —but, my God! It's only three months since Miss Hydraulic Hips was getting ready to throw herself in the grave!"

Their conversation was interrupted by a thunderous roll of drums and the flat midwestern voice of the MC. "Ladies and gentlemen, the treat you've been waiting for all day! Straight from the Blue Angel in New York! And by kind courtesy of MGM in Hollywood! The incomparable Templeton Twins!"

"Are you sure you want to go to the wedding?" Sylvia asked as the Templeton Twins two-stepped across the stage dressed entirely in white: white suits, white shoes, white shirts, white ties and white teeth—too many of them arranged in permanent Ipana smiles.

"You bet I do!" Mattie tried to readjust the false eyelash that was slipping from her moist right eye. "Tonight, Sylvia, I'm going to give the best performance I've ever given! And then I wanna go watch that two-timing wop getting hitched up! Oh, Sylvia, why didn't he love me a little! Just a little!" She sighed. "That goddamned wop!"

"I'll drink to that!" Sylvia lifted her glass and took the last pull on her drink. "Let's get out of here!" Mattie signed the check.

The Templeton Twins were well into "Thou Swell" from *Connecticut Yankee* as Sylvia and Mattie left the lounge.

That night, in her dressing room, Mattie felt unusually attuned to that very special sound of the audience's anticipation. The euphoric nightclub sound. Hundreds of forks scraping dinner plates, ice cubes clinking against glasses, champagne corks popping, the sensuous swish of soda bottles being opened, chairs changing places, lights dimming.

Mattie hit the stage, propelled by sheer desperation, and could feel something going for her as she never had before. She had the audience presold by word of mouth, and she came across like an exploding Roman candle. She gave an absolutely flawless performance. Mattie was drenched in the exhilaration an artist feels when she has given her best. The burst of applause built into a monumental roar, followed by a wild standing ovation. The ultimate reward. The aphrodisiac joy of success wrapped and penetrated every molecule of her being.

Sylvia and Mattie got into a taxi at a quarter to one. Mattie was resplendent in a red jersey strapless dress with a matching hip-length jacket. A gold duck with ruby eyes was pinned to her lapel.

"I've never seen that brooch before," said Sylvia.

"Tony gave it to me on my birthday. February seventeenth, to be exact."

"I thought you never saw him again after the day of Jeremy Rabb's funeral."

"I didn't. Tony sent it to me with a note. 'Wish it could be diamonds. Will speak to you soon.' That's the last time I heard from him in any way, shape or form."

"Are you sure you want to go through with this?" Sylvia was apprehensive. "It seems like an unnecessary ride to the guillotine. Why hurt yourself, Mattie?"

"I know what I'm doing! Just shut up!"

They drove along the Strip, a grotesque Disney World. Frontier Rococo and Miami Renaissance hotels competed with each other to produce the most staggering display of glittering marquees in the Western Hemisphere. Truly a fairyland, where the light was so bright one would think it was day. In a business characterized by shooting stars that burn out overnight, nowhere else in the world was so much talent concentrated in one place. Mattie read the names: Judy Canova at the Sahara, Jimmy Durante and Eddie Jackson at the Dunes, Ben Blue and Peggy Lee at the Flamingo, Howard Keel at the Last Frontier, Carmen Miranda at the Desert Inn, Frank Sinatra at the Sands, Eastman Fletcher, Jr., at the Tropicana.

She popped a pill into her mouth and took a cigarette out of her handbag.

"What was that pill you took?"

"It's a headache pill—I have a headache," answered Mattie curtly. "Oh, Sylvia, my case is not unique. I've cried, that's true, and the tears have taken up much time, too much of my time." Her lighter clicked. "In a way I'm glad this is happening!" She blew a stream of smoke through the slit of the open window. "In the back of my heart there was always that smidgen of hope—and now I know exactly where I stand with Tony. All I'm concerned about at the present moment is my career."

"Why didn't you think along those lines before?"

"I'll tell you something, Sylvia. In school I was voted the girl most unlikely to succeed, and it automatically took a lot of pressure off my ever trying to do anything. Needless to say, my mother was no help at all. I got accustomed to failure, and now I'm getting accustomed to success, and the taste is beautiful! Absolutely beautiful!"

They arrived at the Riviera and entered its crowded lobby through a battalion of TV and newsreel cameramen and reporters and a barrage of photographers' flashbulbs. A reporter shoved a microphone under Mattie's nose. "Mattie Maxwell, ladies and gentlemen! Here we have Mattie Maxwell! The brand-new star burning up the boards, currently appearing at El Rancho-Vegas Hotel." Mattie self-consciously fingered the curls of her new upswept hairdo. "Can you tell viewers of Channel Five your opinion on Beverly Langdon's sudden decision to marry Tony Rook," begged the interviewer.

Mattie pondered the question for a moment. "It's a union made in—made in Hollywood. Tony will make the perfect husband. He can cook—and I'm sure Jeremy Rabb would have wanted it that way," she replied gleefully.

The interviewer seemed totally nonplussed. "Thank you, Miss Maxwell," he said nervously. "I'm sure we all wish the newlyweds the best of luck! Miss Maxwell, are you a personal friend of the happy couple?"

"I've never had the pleasure of meeting the—the blushing bride, but I've sampled the groom's cooking on a number of occasions." It was difficult not to hear the snickers and snorts of muted laughter. "In fact, I can vouch for it," Mattie continued. "It's nothing short of sensational! And now, if you'll please excuse me—" She moved on, her newly found authority accompanied by a cultivated little gesture of impatience.

"I must say, you were divinely bitchy just now," Sylvia said.

"I told you earlier today that I was thinking of becoming a bitch. And you didn't believe me. I just said what I felt. I'm tired of draping myself in false costumes."

Mattie and Sylvia were ushered to the Penthouse with its richly appointed rooms. The largest had been transformed into a chapel. Banks of white flowers—lilacs, camellias, roses, carnations, lilies of the valley, gardenias and orchids—were arranged in the shape of a huge heart. A white satin banner draped around the walls bore the silver words *Beverly and Tony. Forever.*

The reception was already in full swing. Columnists had flown in from all over the country—Earl Wilson with his B.W., Hedda Hopper, Louella Parsons, Lee Mortimer, Ed Sullivan, Irv Kupcinet, Walter Winchell, Louis Sobol. Mattie was warmly greeted by them all. Compliments flew at her like confetti. She basked in the flattery. Guy Lombardo, whose orchestra would be playing later, handed her a glass of champagne. The lights flashed on and off, a signal for the guests to move into a room transformed into a chapel.

Mattie and Sylvia took chairs on the aisle. A hush came over the crowd as if a curtain had suddenly gone up. Mattie's legs felt rubbery and a small hammer pounded against her temples.

Tony finally appeared and stalked down the aisle with his wide grin, tall, slender, well built, his curly black hair cut shorter than before, slicked tightly against his head.

Oh, Jesus, Mattie prayed to herself, if you just let me shine tonight, and if you just let Tony come and speak with me, I promise to go to church every Sunday. I swear it, Jesus. Please let him come over and speak to me. *Please.* She mumbled the word "please" several times like a mantra. She crossed herself almost apologetically and visibly collected her energies. A specially imported organ sounded the opening bars of Mendelssohn's wedding march, and a radiantly beautiful Beverly Langdon floated down the aisle on the arm of Harry Cohn, head of Columbia Studios and her mentor. Mattie cringed in spirit and trembled in body.

Like a true sex goddess, the bride wore a gown worthy of her fame, with a neckline worthy of its claim. A vision in pale pink peau de soie hand-embroidered with tiny seed pearls, the whole overlaid with delicate lace, she glowed like the famous diamond that nestled in her matching head-piece of seed pearls and lace. Everyone knew Jeremy Rabb had given her the precious jewel, but where, Mattie wondered, had she gotten a gown like that on such short notice? Did movie queens keep such extras in their closets? A leftover, perhaps, from a previous wedding? As the object of her thought continued down the aisle, Sylvia whispered, "Edith Head designed that concoction for her next film. There's a wedding scene in the picture. The studio just gave it to Beverly as a present."

Mattie whispered back: "I hope they didn't have to provide all her wedding dresses. If they did, they'd probably have gone broke!"

Mattie focused once more on the spectacle, and what a spectacle it was! Beverly was followed by bridesmaids—at least, at first glance they appeared to be bridesmaids, but were more likely chorus girls chosen at the last minute and dressed for the part. Beverly moved slowly to the altar. Tony came to her side. She turned around and raised her eyes adoringly to his. He responded by taking her arm and sliding his fingers to her wrist. Holding her gently and lovingly.

"Antonio Valerio Rocca, do you take as your wedded wife Beverly Martha Langdon, for . . ." Mattie could no longer hear the words. The clouds in her mind were greyhounds racing back to a shabby walk-up apartment on East Fifty-third Street in New York. How cozy and warm it had seemed with Tony there. . . . Empty now, she reflected on what she had once been filled with. At that moment she hated Tony intensely. She felt acid tears mounting. They wouldn't fall.

The vows had been spoken. The newlyweds exchanged a chaste kiss. Crowds parted as they walked up the aisle, hands, arms entwined. They were as much a symbol of domestic legitimacy as any couple who had ever marched up the aisle at St. Patrick's. For an infinitesimal moment Tony's magnetic eyes locked into Mattie's, registering genuine surprise.

The throng moved to the next room to a reception larger than life, louder than life. The crowd of onlookers would have seemed more at home at a crap table. The couple looked lovingly into each other's eyes to the unromantic tune of popping flashbulbs and directives: "Smile . . . move a little to the left . . . no, that's too much, Tony, you're covering Beverly . . . Kiss her . . . that's it . . . once more . . . bend down . . . again . . . closer . . ."

"That's all for now, boys!" someone commanded officiously. "You'll get plenty of shots when we get to the cake. . . . And now the cake—here it is!" The entire wedding was summed up in that cake! So layered! So leveled! So whipped! So pink! So big! In fact, it was the largest cake in the history of Las Vegas. Of course it *had* to be! For Tony and Beverly it had to be the biggest. Everyone talked about it! Lawford, Sinatra, McGuire, Fletcher, Entratter, Feldman, Bennett. All with cake in their mouths. Everyone was eating it up. Everyone wanted to be connected to the newlyweds, to the cake. No one really cared about the taste. It had none. But by the time the jewels, the cigar smoke and the glitter had moved on to the ballroom, everybody knew it was the biggest. The biggest cake in the history of Vegas.

"Some more champagne, Mattie?" She swirled around and there was Tony. Her thoughts went tumbling, senseless, a shambles, rolling through the big hollow she had inside, fusing together into one magnificent roar of silent joy that filled every inch of her being. A joy that went on and on. Tony had come to *her*. Hallelujah! Her prayer had not been in vain.

"Why not? I'll have some more champagne. Thanks." She took the glass he offered her, playing the game. His game. "Congratulations, Tony. That was a very beautiful wedding. All the luck in the world!" She raised her glass to him. "It certainly surprised everybody." She lowered her eyes. "And me more than anyone. I *am* glad."

"Mattie, I'm sorry if you're hurt. But you are the one who insisted on treating a buried love as if it were still alive. I'm really—"

"Come on, Tony, this is a time for rejoicing. What's past is past. I wish you all the best. I think you made the right choice. Beverly is beautiful, and you make a gorgeous couple."

Too bad Tony couldn't have waited for her, Mattie thought to herself. He was greedy for the glamour, and he wanted the orgasmic success right now. He saw it in Beverly. She could provide it all. In Beverly he had it all. But it wouldn't last! It couldn't last! How long would it be before Beverly tired of him? From far away Mattie heard him ask her how long she'd been in Vegas, but she wasn't sure Tony had even spoken.

"Why don't you answer, Mattie?"

"I'm sorry, Tony, I didn't hear you. What were you saying?"

"I was asking you how long you've been in Las Vegas. I saw your fabulous reviews in the *Hollywood Reporter,* but I didn't know you were still here."

"Yes, I'm still here—until the ninth."

"And what after that?"

"It depends. I just got back from Hollywood this afternoon. I left last night after my show and took a screen test at Vista."

"I'm very happy for you, Mattie. Really happy. I hope you get the part. You deserve everything."

"You can say that again." Her tone was cool.

Beverly minced toward them. Tony began to shift uncomfortably. "Oh, darling, I've got to take you away," Beverly gushed. *"Life* magazine wants to take another picture of us near the cake." Her words erupted in a marsh-mallowy froth.

"Oh . . . oh . . . Beverly." He hesitated. "I want you to meet Mattie Maxwell."

"Pleased to meet you, Miss . . . Miss . . . uh . . ." Beverly extended her hand with polite indifference, exhibiting a simple gold ring. The other hand was wrapped around Tony's arm. It sported an impossibly huge square-cut diamond that was now known as the Langdon Diamond. Jeremy Raab had ensured that he'd be well remembered.

"Do you know my husband?" she enthused. "I'm so glad Tony's found a friend. He hardly knows anyone here."

"Miss Langdon—I mean Mrs. Rook, your husband and I are not friends." She shrugged modestly. "We're merely acquaintances. We met long ago. I was just telling him that I'm having a new apartment decorated in New York, and one always has to wait an eternity to have linen monogrammed! Of course"—she paused indulgently—"I envy you. You don't have that problem—an *R* is an *R*."

Beverly ignored Mattie. "Come on, Tony. The photographers are wait-ing." Beverly wriggled away, holding onto Tony. She looked over her shoulder, casting a malevolent glance at Mattie, who waved coyly, her hand tracing tiny circles close to her face. Smiling.

Hank Greenspun and Forrest Duke of the *Vegas Sun* came over to her, cracking jokes that were passé even by vaudeville standards. She laughed without mirth and left the group, approaching Sylvia, who was diving into her third slice of cake. "Who's that man talking to Frank across the room?" she asked.

"His name's Eastman Fletcher, Junior. His recording of 'Alabama Nights' went gold and he's appearing in the lounge of the Tropicana. Why?"

"He's been looking at me. I find him attractive. I think I'll go over and meet him."

"Are you out of your mind, Mattie? You can't do that! It isn't done!" Crumbs fell out of Sylvia's mouth.

"Why not?"

"It just isn't done, that's why! Do I have to spell it out for you?"

"Just watch me!" Mattie said defiantly as she stalked boldly across the room in the direction of Eastman Fletcher, Jr.

It was five o'clock in the morning when Mattie entered her hotel room. She opened the window, and admitted a gust of air. The irresistible blaze from the Strip was dimming. Daylight was beginning to show. She undressed and got into bed. Why do they say hotel sheets are cool and crisp? Tonight they were hot and sticky. She wrapped and unwrapped herself in a jumble of sheets, flinging her body from one side of the bed to the other with the frenzy that only abysmal loneliness can produce. The enormity of what had happened, the shock, hit her in retrospect. Her anguished fever spread like the effects of a disease contracted on a tropical island.

She closed her eyes. They spelled Tony's name. She could hear it. She could see it. She could almost touch it. Mattie turned on the light, took another pill, got up, went to the window, staring hopelessly into the silvery dawn, went back to bed and fell into fitful sleep, only to wake up with a start ten minutes later. A sudden resolution buzzed through her brain. A thought emerged, colliding unapologetically with her sorrow. She took a long swig from the bottle on the night table, and it soared through her chest. She picked up the telephone. "Get me the Tropicana, would you, please?" While she waited Mattie bit her cuticle nervously, drawing blood. "Oh, hello, is this the Tropicana? Could I speak with Mr. Eastman Fletcher, Junior, please? . . . Oh, I see—I didn't think of that. Would you happen to know where he *is* staying? . . . Thank you and good night—or should I say good morning?" Mattie flashed her own operator and asked for the Vegas Colonial, on Westwood. She lit a cigarette. "The Vegas Colonial? Good morning. Could I speak to Eastman Fletcher, Junior, please? . . . Hello, Eastman, am I waking you? . . . It's Mattie. Mattie Maxwell. I can't sleep—Oh, I'm glad to hear you're a night person too! How would you feel about having breakfast with me? . . . How about over here? . . . Oh,

I see—I never thought of that. Well, then, I'll come over to your place. Is that all right? . . . What room are you in? . . . I'll ring you from the lobby. I'll be there in about fifteen minutes. See you then."

She put on her makeup with the carefulness of hope and a dress with the carelessness of lust. She inserted her diaphragm and left.

⁕

MATTIE/*Hollywood/Wednesday, May 19, 1954*

Mattie felt exhilarated as she drove in the bright California morning sunshine through the gates of Vista Films. She had rented the convertible a few days earlier, on moving into the Sunset Marquee Hotel in Hollywood, after her Las Vegas date had terminated. The top of the car was down and a light breeze, heavy with the perfume of mimosa, kissed her cheeks, blowing through the soft wisps of curls swept into a Gibson Girl knot. It was hard to believe that behind the conglomeration of pretty pink-and-white stucco bungalows situated around a courtyard stood one of the biggest studios in Hollywood. To the left was the sound stage where she had taken her screen test three weeks earlier, on a deserted Sunday afternoon; now hundreds of extras in makeup and costumes were milling around.

For Mattie, the past two months had been like a fairy tale. First there were the two enthusiastically received appearances on the Jack Paar show, where her unique talent was seen for the first time by an audience of almost fifteen million. Then the spot on the Ed Sullivan show, where her performance was so impressive that Sullivan promptly signed her to five more shows. After that came the Copacabana, in New York, with comedian Joe E. Lewis, where she transformed her second-billed opening slot into one with the caliber usually found in starring acts. A three-week engagement at El Rancho Hotel in Las Vegas followed, then the successful screen test, the ensuing contract, the move to California, and now, at last, a summons to meet the big boss himself, Morris Altman, by far the most powerful man in Hollywood. Trailing behind him were the likes of Harry Cohn, Jack Warner, Darryl Zanuck and Joe Schenck. Vista Films was his domain; Culver City his empire.

Altman was not an ordinary man, but a complex force of nature, a mass of contradictions—brutal, violent, cruel, selfish, mean, egotistical, yet capable of inexplicable acts of generosity and kindness. Both an astute businessman and a sensitive artist, he was strong, ambitious, determined, dedicated, and, above all, gifted. He understood what the public wanted before they even knew it themselves, and was infallible in choosing the stars and stories to

satisfy them. His sense of timing was uncanny. His talent for successfully presenting a new theme or a new personality on the screen was incontestable. He knew the movie business better than any other producer in the history of Hollywood. Strangely religious, Altman was a compulsive flirt and an unashamed fornicator. Hard-working, hard-playing, he could be as warm and charming as he was vicious and vengeful. His powers to destroy were frequently and malevolently used; his influence was such that if he dismissed anyone, that name was added to a private black list, and no other studio would dare hire his discards for fear of repercussions. Dane Clark, the brilliant actor, was a perfect example of this venomous practice. Mogul, tyrant, willful child, he was hated, feared, loved, a legend in his lifetime. Morris Altman was all that and much more.

Kathryn Hutton had been scheduled to play an aspiring young hopeful in *Kick Up Your Heels,* a million-and-a-half-dollar Vista show-business musical set in the twenties. Altman had axed her at the last minute. "Too old for the part!" he ruled. Mattie hadn't seen herself on the screen yet, and neither had Sylvia. But the studio heads and Morris Altman *had.* Several times. They agreed unanimously that here was more than just another new face. In the short scene she had performed for her test, rarely had the shadings of anguish, humor, uncertainty been so aptly expressed through look and gesture. The memorized script came so naturally to Mattie that it seemed she had written every word of the speech herself. Every movement she made was instinctive, important and right. She had timing. She was funny. She was vulnerable. The camera captured every nuance of the emotions that played across her face as subtly as breezes ruffling a pond. Her protruding nose redeemed her profile from perfection. Her hazel eyes mirrored intelligence. It was as if she were in some kind of costume all the time. A costume of attitudes. She commanded attention. She couldn't be pinpointed in any specific period.

When she sang she pulled out all the stops. All the pent-up passions, all the destructive frustrations came from the heart without any self-pity. She produced a sound never heard before. She was a fireball of energy. She was innocent. She was mother earth. A child. The woman about to bloom. The girl who lived too fast. She could be anything she wanted. She resembled no one. She was unique.

Mattie Maxwell had gotten the part in place of Kathryn Hutton. A newcomer landing a plum role like this one had to set Hollywood on its heels. Louella Parsons and Hedda Hopper filled their columns with the story. The gossips speculated. Mattie was scared but excited. Her heart seemed never to stop palpitating.

She parked her car next to a brown Rolls Royce backed into a space marked with a sign that read *Morris Altman* and followed the arrows that read *Reception.* Her walk was joyful, she had smiles for everyone. A girl was sitting behind a long, low desk free of anything that resembled work, except for an appointment book. She wore a hairpiece, meticulously combed

into her own heavily sprayed honey-colored tresses, lots of skillfully applied makeup and an embroidered white off-the-shoulder peasant blouse that displayed ample cleavage. She sipped lemonade through a straw, taking care not to smudge her lipstick, as she read a movie magazine.

"Do you have an appointment?" she asked when Mattie approached.

"No," Mattie replied. "I've come to check out the plumbing."

"The plumbing?" The girl looked up stupidly, her wide baby-blue eyes oozing vapidity.

"Yeah," Mattie said. "Mr. Altman's toilet's backed up."

"Oh, my," she whined.

"Look, I was only kidding," Mattie said. "I've got a meeting with Mr. Altman at ten-thirty."

The receptionist confirmed the appointment on the phone and pointed to an elevator separate from the others, attended by a man in a navy-blue and maroon uniform covered with medals and gold braid. "That's Mr. Altman's private elevator," she said. "It will take you straight to his offices on the second floor."

Thanks for nothing, Mattie thought to herself, sauntering past the uniformed attendant. "I'm here to see Mr. Altman," she announced proudly as he pushed the button. She felt ten feet tall. The elevator made no sound as it rose to its destination. Mattie stepped into Morris Altman's reception room.

The secretary here struck a sharp contrast with the dumb blonde downstairs. She was in her middle fifties, handsome and austere, her brown hair cut severely short. Wearing little makeup, she was attired in a long-sleeved, high-necked black sheath.

"You're Miss Maxwell of course." Her voice was deep and warm. "Mr. Altman's expecting you." The room was expensively furnished and decorated, just like a subdued movie set. "Make yourself comfortable, and Mr. Altman will see you shortly." Mattie sat on one of the black leather and chrome sofas and took a pack of cigarettes out of her handbag. "Perhaps you'd like a cup of coffee?"

"Yeah, yeah," Mattie answered with gauche nervousness. "That would be great, real great."

The secretary disappeared into another room.

An illuminated aquarium full of green plants and colorful tropical fish was set into the wall, and pinspots, flush with the ceiling, cast shafts of light. Mattie browsed through the magazines spread on a glass-topped table, mostly *Photoplay, Life* and a few trade papers, with items about Vista Films heavily red-penciled. A color photo of Beverly Langdon and Tony Rook was splashed across the cover of *Look* with the caption, "Picking Up the Pieces—The Newlyweds!" Mattie had already seen it. She pushed it aside, reached for a copy of the *Hollywood Reporter* and read, "Barney Balaban, of Paramount Pix, Declares a $7 Million Profit for 1953. . . . Beverly Langdon Inked for *The Gentlemen Will Oblige* . . ."

Mattie barely heard the secretary come back as she moved softly over the charcoal-gray carpet.

"There you are, Miss Maxwell." She placed the coffee on the table.

"Thank you very much."

"This is your first time in Hollywood, isn't it? That is, working in Hollywood." The secretary was making small talk in the hope of helping Mattie relax.

"No, I was here for a screen test a few weeks ago."

"Yes, yes, I know, but apart from that—"

"Yeah. This is my first movie."

"You must be very excited!"

"Oh, I am."

"I was a great fan of your mother's, Miss Maxwell. She was very kind to me when she was here at the studio. In fact, I owe her a debt of gratitude, so if there's ever anything I can do for you, I hope you'll let me know. My name is Alice Blumensteil."

Mattie felt like hugging the older woman. "That's very nice of you. Please call me Mattie," she blurted. "I really appreciate that and I'll just . . . just . . ."

"Pop right up and see me!"

"That's right! I'll pop right up and see you!"

"In any event, best of luck on *Kick Up Your Heels,* Mattie. I know you're going to be a big hit! . . . Would you excuse me for a moment?"

The walls were covered with large blow-ups of past and present Vista Films stars, including Rita Hayworth, Kim Novak, Robert Montgomery, Rosalind Russell, David Niven and Gloria DeHaven. There were framed posters advertising the greatest of the Vista Films productions: *Queen Boadicea,* starring Claudette Colbert and Claude Raines; *An Affair in Barbados,* featuring Greer Garson and Ronald Coleman; and *The Farmer Takes a Wife,* with Loretta Young and Dana Andrews. Her mother also stared down at her from *Whenever the Moon Shines,* still considered Jessica Miller's greatest screen triumph.

Mattie was unable to take her eyes off the massive oak door of Morris Altman's office. It bore neither a knob nor a keyhole and could be opened only from the inside, so it seemed. Presently the phone rang, and Miss Blumensteil answered it softly, then quietly replaced it in its cradle, like a nurse. "Mr. Altman will see you now." As Mattie stood up, she heard a buzzer, and the door to Morris Altman's office opened as if by magic.

Mattie stepped inside. The door automatically closed behind her with a click of finality. She felt as if she were entering a Gothic cathedral. The vastness of the room sapped her cheerfulness instantly. The first thing that caught her eye was a marble nave containing an impressive display of Oscars. Noticing three doors, Mattie wondered which connected his office with the deluxe dressing room occupied, according to rumor, by those of his stars who were the current "favorites." One wall of the office was solid glass, and the three others were almost completely lined with mahogany shelves crammed with leather-bound volumes. The floor was covered with a pale-gray carpet on which rested a large Persian rug. The office was a virtual garden: an entire length in front of the plate glass window was planted with trees, interspersed with flowering shrubs and myrtle. The setting included a stone birdbath, a sun dial, a weather vane and an oversized couch. A white wicker cage housing a pair of lovebirds hung from the ceiling. This was the inner sanctum where Altman made directors, writers, producers, stars and starlets alike tremble. Mattie looked at the couch suspiciously.

It was in icy silence that she timorously made her way toward the gigantic desk, which stood on a raised platform, an idea borrowed from Mussolini. Dominating its polished top was a large round clock, the hours set in diamonds. It had been built into the Vista Films logo: a globe of the world supported by a man's hand holding that of a woman. A quarter of the desk's surface was covered with photographs of all sizes in exquisite silver frames. One was of Altman's second wife, Ruby Matthews, the famous dancer of the thirties, whom he had married many good times ago. Several others were autographed "To Morrie with love," and showed him wining and dining at the Mocambo, Ciro's or the Brown Derby with such famous stars as Norma Shearer, Jessica Miller, Kay Francis, Jean Arthur, Mary Astor, Frances Farmer, Joan Crawford and Betty Grable. The most prominent photograph showed him with two homely girls, his daughters, Estelle and Sandra. There were also pictures of his palatial estates in Beverly Hills, Palm Springs and Santa Monica; as well as of his yacht, the *Bella Vista,* moored down in Newport. Standing loyally in attendance was a cavalcade of telephones connecting Altman to the outside world and by direct lines to sound stages, directors' offices and stars' dressing rooms. So engrossed in paper work was Altman that he seemed not even to notice her presence. Mattie didn't know whether to sit or stand. She stood. Plaques, hung on the wall behind him, were inscribed "Citizen of the Year" and "Outstanding Moviemaker"; she wondered where he kept his "All-Time Stud" award.

Suddenly Morris Altman opened a Dunhill humidor, took out a cigar, smelled it, rolled it between his fingers, listened to its gentle crackle, and severed its end with a gold cutter. But didn't light it. The silence was broken by his strong, clear voice.

"Hello, sweetheart!" He stood up, holding his unlit cigar pointing in the air. Mattie noticed that he was soberly attired for a Hollywood executive. Dark suit, white shirt, burgundy tie, inconspicuous cuff links, no rings, no flash. To Mattie he was more representative of a Wall Street banker about to enter a board meeting, although the nearest she had come to seeing a Wall Street investment banker was Walter Pidgeon in some late, late movie, the name of which escaped her. They shook hands. His piercing blue eyes fixed her hypnotically.

"I wanted to meet you, sweetheart, and I'm glad you paid me this courtesy call." Mattie thought it was hardly a courtesy call; it was more of a command performance. She had been told by the publicity department to be at Morris Altman's office promptly at ten-thirty—*without* Sylvia.

"I'm glad you're aboard our ship," he continued. "We're one big happy family here, and I just wanted to make sure everything's okay. Is everything okay?"

"Oh, yes, Mr. Altman!" she simpered, giving him the sunshine of her smile. "Everything is simply wonderful! I've already begun rehearsal on the musical numbers, and costume fittings will—" Mattie rattled on with girlish enthusiasm.

Morris Altman wasn't interested. "That's nice, real nice" he muttered, somewhat preoccupied. "Have a seat." His voice had the crisp sound of authority. "Can I offer you anything? Something to drink perhaps?"

"Oh, no, no!" she protested, sitting down on one of the four green leather wing chairs facing him. "Not this early in the morning! Besides, I hardly drink at all," she lied.

"Good, good! Glad to hear it! Drink's been the ruin of more than one good career, and it's terrible for a woman's skin. You don't want to spoil yours, do you, Maxwell? Cigarette?"

"I'm trying to give them up," she said, laughing nervously. "But not with very much success!" He came around the desk with a gold case and opened it. She took out a cigarette, which he lit with a solid silver lighter shaped like the Vista Films trademark. Altman put his cigar in his pocket, patting it lovingly, as if it were his wallet.

One of the phones rang. "Goddammit!" he bellowed. "When will that woman ever learn? How many times do I have to tell her I don't want to be disturbed?" He returned to the high-backed brown leather chair. "Sorry about that, sweetheart, it's one of my private lines! Can't do a thing about it."

"Hello . . . Charlie! How's the best goddamned agent in the business?" he asked with booming affability. He listened in silence. The amiable countenance gradually changed. Altman's geniality vanished. "Well, if the bitch insists on that clause, I've got the right solution. Get her out of my studio!" he exploded. The lines in his face deepened, the brow creased, and the eyes narrowed. "Just get her out of my studio!" he shouted. "Now I don't want her at any price! What do you think of that, hah! Did you hear what I said, Charlie? Not at any price! Besides, she's a bad lay!" he said. "Rank can have her back, and her phony Hungarian accent as well." Mercurially, he suddenly softened his tone. "Keep in touch, buddy. See you on the golf course Saturday." Morris Altman took out the cigar from his pocket and put it between his teeth. He hung up with irritation and turned to Mattie.

"What a dumbbell that broad is! All these nobodies I've made stars of! If it weren't for their good looks and laying the right people, they'd be back slinging hamburgers in Dullsville, U.S.A." Now he was holding his moistened cigar at arm's length. "I'll teach her a lesson . . . just one word and she's through!"

"What one word, Mr. Altman?" Mattie asked numbly.

"The word, Maxwell, is 'out'! O-U-T, out!" he ranted, pounding the cigar repeatedly as he spoke. When he arrived at the letter *t*, it broke in two, as if on cue. He ignored it.

The intense blue eyes were riveted on her. "Oh, Mr. Altman . . . I don't know the whole story," she offered, getting up in astonishment, "but it just seems so unkind to . . . to . . ." She groped to finish the sentence, but couldn't.

"You don't have to be *kind* in this business, Maxwell! I didn't get where I am today by being *kind!*" he said autocratically. "I started from nothin'! Kindness is not a per . . . a persit . . . a pre . . . requisite," he stammered, "to running a major studio. Besides, you don't have to be *kind* on your way up when you know you ain't never comin' down!" He stared Mattie back into her seat. "The trouble begins when they start believing their own publicity!"

"Well, some of them have a lot of talent, Mr. Altman," she proffered helplessly.

"Talent, my ass!" he spat scornfully. "Talent you find thirteen to the dozen! It's all publicity. I'll bet, with the right promotion I could make a star out of my old-maid aunt."

"Well, with my mother it wasn't—"

"With your mother it wasn't what?" he snapped viciously. "Wasn't publicity? Whaddya mean?" he yelled. "Your mother woulda been a nobody without publicity! Don't think for a moment she was irreplaceable!"

"Then why didn't you replace her if she was so replaceable?"

"We needed an army of flacks to prevent her disgusting conduct from getting into print—and we weren't always too successful. That's what killed her!"

"What do you mean, Mr. Altman, it killed her?"

"With Jessica, there was one problem after another. If she wasn't drinking, she was pilling herself to death or screwing the elevator boy!" Suddenly Altman remembered his manners. "Sorry about that, Maxwell," he grunted. "I got a little carried away there. For a minute, sweetheart, I forgot she was your mother." He grinned weakly.

"Yes, she was my mother." Her voice broke almost imperceptibly.

"You've got spirit, sweetheart! I like that! Despite everything, your mother had spirit too! And that's why you're here today."

"Oh . . . ?" Her eyes shone bright with innocence.

"But hang on," he said, getting up. "I've gotta take a piss." Mattie automatically stood up.

"Where you goin', sweetheart? You don't have to come with me!" he joshed. She sat down, her spirits wilting away.

"I'll be right back." He walked through a door directly behind the desk and didn't bother to close it. "Leo Sherman, who's producing the picture you're about to make, thinks very highly of you." A stream of urine hit the water in the toilet. He raised his voice so she could hear him. "As you know, he's the one who caught your act in Vegas and got you the screen test. I had the final approval of course. I had already seen you on the Sullivan show. Even your nose has a certain quality we can package."

"I was thinking of having it fixed, Mr. Altman."

"I can't hear you, sweetheart, whaddidya say?"

"I said I was thinking of having it fixed," she repeated, louder.

"From now on, you don't even change your bra without our permission, so forget about changing your nose. . . . You're pretty good too, but, as I said before, nobody's irreplaceable. Take a look at Ingrid for instance. Once the toast of Hollywood, and now Rossellini's got her operating the wind machine on some island out in the middle of the ocean."

"But she was involved in a scandal. I've never been involved in a scandal."

"And that's why you're here today, sweetheart." The toilet flushed, and on the pretext of making himself heard better, Altman came back and stood in the doorway, his penis fully exposed. "I just want to make absolutely certain you *don't* get involved in a scandal."

"I . . . I . . ." Mattie was at a loss for words. Her jaw dropped. She could feel the blood rushing to her face. Her head reeled with embarrassment.

"I can make you a big star if you play ball with me . . ."

Mattie didn't know where to look. The couch loomed ominously before her. The harder she tried to avert her eyes from his penis, the more inexorably they were drawn to it. He studied her reaction carefully. She was smarting with humiliation, but mustered all her strength to keep from falling apart.

He continued mercilessly. "Or I can break you, Maxwell. Never forget that. I'm the boss, and what I say goes." Slowly he pulled his zipper up. He walked toward her ponderously, the flinty eyes never leaving Mattie, and sat down on a chair next to hers. "Are you by any chance prejudiced?" Morris Altman asked out of the blue, with no trace of levity in his voice.

"I don't know what you mean, Mr. Altman. Are you asking me if . . . if I like or dislike . . . ," she faltered. "You want to know how I . . . how I feel about . . . about Jews?"

"Yeah, how do you feel about Jews?"

"Well, I'm Irish, as you know, and I hate to say it, but most of my friends are—"

"Most of your friends are Jews, right?"

"Well, that's not exactly how I wanted to put it, but I do have a lot of Jewish friends."

"Glad to hear it, sweetheart! Wonderful people, Jews!" Altman pronounced. "Know how to make money, know how to cook—that's what I always say. Remind me to invite you to my place sometime, Maxwell. Mrs. Altman makes a real mean borscht."

"Oh, Mr. Altman!" Mattie simpered. "I'd just love to whenever—"

"How do you feel about niggers?" he interrupted.

"I beg you pardon?"

"You heard what I said! Don't play Babe in the Woods with me." He bolted from his seat. "I said 'niggers.' Goddammit! How do you feel about niggers?"

"I . . . I don't know a lot of colored people."

"You don't know a lot of colored people. You don't know much, do you, sweetheart?" He paced the floor. Hands locked behind his back. "Do you know how much it costs to finance a film? This one, for instance, in which you, an unknown, are starring?"

"Well, I don't really know. I . . . I . . ."

"You dumb broad!" he ranted with an electric force. "You mean you never thought about the financing of a movie? Here we are, paying you twenty-five hundred bucks a week! That money you take is conscience money! Let me tell you something else, sweetheart. We've got a million and a half invested in this venture. In other words, I'm gambling on you."

"I want you to know how much I appreciate—"

"Cut the crap, Maxwell. I don't want your appreciation. I want your cooperation. Just listen to me." He sat down behind his desk, reached for another cigar and clipped it defiantly. Pushing himself back in the leather swivel chair to create greater distance between himself and Mattie, he lit the cigar, clamping his lips around it tightly. He went on. "What would you do if you had a million and a half bucks invested in a project? Would you try to protect your investment or would you leave it all up to divine providence?"

Mattie ventured cautiously, "I . . . I would do all I could to protect it of course." Nervously she extinguished her cigarette in the large silver ashtray on the desk.

"That's right, Maxwell. And that's just what I'm doing. I've got stockholders to answer to, investors, a board of directors. You're damned right I'm gonna protect my investment! And that's why I asked you the question in the first place." He moved his ashtray closer to himself. "How many niggers do you know?"

"I don't use that word, Mr. Altman. I call them colored people."

"Niggers, colored people, whatever you want to call them—how many would you say you know?"

Mattie hadn't expected this. A severe sinking sensation in the pit of her stomach warned her she was in dangerous waters. Aware of the importance of preserving an illusion of self-confidence, she casually took a cigarette out of her handbag, lit it and slowly dragged on it. Turning her head to the left and affording Altman a generous view of her right profile, which she knew was her better one, Mattie languorously blew a fine stream of blue-gray smoke into the air-conditioned and leather-perfumed room. She turned back to him arrogantly.

"How many would you say you know?" he repeated, looking coldly into her eyes, defying her apparent calmness. She adopted a look of innocent concentration as the telephone rang.

"Goddammit!" he stormed. "How many times do I have to tell that woman! Hello, hello!" he answered angrily. "Oh, all right then! Put him on." He changed his tone. "Glad you called back so soon, Burt. I wanna ask you somethin'. Got a copy of the script handy? Good!" Altman picked up his copy, leafing through it rapidly. "Turn to page twenty-seven, Scene Two. Are you with me, Burt? . . . Good! Marjorie—right in the center of the page—Got it? Okay. Marjorie is supposed to say, and I'm reading it to you just like it is, 'Time will beat us all to a pulp.' Then Robert answers, 'Aren't you sagacious, darling.' All I wanna know, Burt, is, what the hell does 'sagacious' mean?" He listened, flicking the ashes off his cigar. "Well, if it means 'smart,' goddammit, then why don't you say it that way! Don't fuck around with words I don't know, Burt, because if I don't know the word, neither does mid-America. And that's where I'm selling my pictures. To mid-Americans, not to college professors! Got me? So rewrite those lines the way I tell you. This ain't supposed to be a quiz show. It's a fun film. You hear, Burt—fun!

"By the way, how's your divorce coming along? . . . Let her go back to Mexico! They deserve each other!" He laughed cruelly. "Yeah, yeah! That's right, Burt. I'll be in the Springs early Friday afternoon. Meet me on the first hole—say, around five. See you then." He put the phone down and slowly faced Mattie again. "Where were we, sweetheart? Oh, that's right. Niggers. We were talking about niggers. You like niggers, sweetheart?"

"Why, Mr. Altman, that's such a difficult qustion to answer."

"Why's it a difficult question to answer? Either you do or you don't. Now, in your case, do you or don't you?"

"All the colored people I know are performers. And they're good performers." There was a tremor in her voice.

"Yeah, sweetheart, I agree with you. They're good performers. They can sing. They can dance. They can play music. And that's what they should keep doing. Singin', dancin' and playin' music. Now, you see Napoleon and Josephine?" He pointed at the two lovebirds in their wicker cage. "They're two of a kind. They're both birds, and they come from the same background. It would never occur to Josephine to screw with a crow, and Napoleon wouldn't ball a raven. They can sing too, and, as you can see, they're both white."

"They're lovely, really lovely," she mouthed.

"Let me ask you somethin', Maxwell. When you see a white girl walking down the street with a nigger, what's the first thing that comes into your mind? Do you find it a normal, everyday occurrence? Or do you turn around and stare? What is your . . . your . . . what is your *opinion* of that?"

Mattie collected her thought as best she could. "It's unusual to see a white girl out with a colored man, I agree, and since most people believe she has to be a whore to do it, even though she isn't, I think . . . I think it takes guts on her part."

Mattie could see his anger mounting. "You say she's got guts because people would say she's a whore if she steps out with a nigger! If she steps out with a nigger, sweetheart, she *is* a whore! No broad goes out with a nigger to hear him sing and dance. If she wants to hear him sing and dance, she goes to a club. She doesn't have to walk down the street with him. What do you tink o' dat?"

"I . . . I . . ."

"Yes?" He waited for her reply, coiled lethally.

She broke into a cold sweat and could feel the perspiration running down her sides. "Well, the colored people I know do more than sing and dance, Mr. Altman. One is a writer—"

"A published writer?" he interrupted pointedly.

"Yeah, he gets his stuff published, but nobody knows he's a . . . a . . ."

"Nobody knows he's a nigger, right?"

"That doesn't detract from his ability. It only proves—"

"It only proves that you're a dumb broad!" His vitriolic voice rose. "I won't let you ruin your reputation and my film—"

"Mr. Altman, I really don't know what you're talking about."

"I won't let you ruin your reputation and my film," he repeated loudly, "just because you like screwing a *great big black cock!*"

"Mr. Altman!" cried Mattie, aghast.

"That's the truth, isn't it?" he sneered contemptuously.

"Mr. Altman!" shouted Mattie. "I don't know what you're talking about!"

"You don't know what I'm talking about!" he bellowed. "You know exactly what I'm talking about! And you're a goddamned liar!" He lowered his voice almost to a whisper. "Let me put it another way, sweetheart. What do you think of Eastman Fletcher, Junior?"

Mattie shook her head in shocked disbelief and stood up abruptly, spilling the contents of her handbag on the floor. Bending down, she hurriedly threw everything back into it, including a bird's feather, and moved unsteadily to the window. Her knees were trembling. She focused on the front bumper of a Daimler in the parking lot below and tried to concentrate on it in an effort to control her shaking. The hollow quiet of the room was shattered by the ringing of the telephone.

"Yeah, yeah," Altman answered grumblingly. "Okay, okay. You can go ahead! He's a faggot, but he looks good and keeps it quiet. Besides, Olivia likes him, and it's important to keep her happy. She thinks being in movies has something to do with acting . . ."

The ringing of the telephone was still reverberating in Mattie's ears. She was grateful for the reprieve. It gave her time to steady her nerves. She knew the worst was yet to come.

". . . Now all you have to do is borrow him from Columbia. The bastard'll want more than he's worth, but do the best you can. I'll leave the details to you. Oh, and one other thing—I don't want his mother on the set. Got me? Right! Keep in touch."

The click of the telephone echoed loudly. Once again they were plunged into silence, except for the rustling of paper and the sound of a chair being moved. Altman got up. Mattie walked jerkily toward the door.

"Where are you goin'?" Altman shouted. "You ain't goin' nowhere till I tell you to. Sit down!" he ordered.

Meekly she sat in the chair she had occupied on her arrival. Altman opened the door of the cage and put his arm into it.

"How are my precious babies? Hmmmmmmm?" One of the lovebirds perched on his hand, pecking at his gold watch. "Now, now, leave Daddy's timepiece alone." The other bird took a position on his little finger. "Did the great white bird up in the sky give Daddy's little babies yellow beaks to catch worms with? Hmmmmmmm? But Daddy's little babies don't have to eat worms, do they? They eat caviar, that's what they eat. Hmmmmmmm? They do as they're told! All little birds should do as they're told!"

Carefully jiggling his arm, he withdrew it from the cage, and the birds hopped nimbly onto their perch, facing in opposite directions. Morris Altman went back to his seat. "What do you think of Eastman Fletcher, Junior?" he repeated.

Mattie still hadn't regained her composure. "I . . . I . . ."

"Take your time, sweetheart, take your time! I'm in no hurry!"

"I saw him perform in Las Vegas and thought he was terrific," she said, trying to sound as natural as possible.

"You saw him perform in Las Vegas and thought he was terrific," he mocked, playing with her.

"Yes, terrific!" she repeated, deciding to brazen it out. "I thought he was terrific!"

"Terrific." He softly enunciated the word for its effect as a double entendre.

"Yes!"

"Terrific where, sweetheart?" he fumed. "Terrific onstage or terrific in bed?"

"Onstage of course." Her voice was barely audible.

"I see." He feigned calmness. "Of course you wouldn't know anything about his performance in bed, would you now?" Mattie didn't reply. Her blood was replaced by a flowing, formless hot terror.

"I can't begin to tell you, sweetheart, how relieved I am to hear that!" His tone was sarcastic.

"Why should I—"

"That's what I want to know!" he stormed angrily. "Why the fucking hell should you want to get a reputation as a nigger-fucker when I've got nearly two million bucks riding on you!"

They glared at each other. Altman's face was purple, the veins standing out on his forehead. Mattie was pale, her fingers nervously tapping the side of her chair.

"Hollywood isn't Greenwich Village. Everything gets known here. There've already been some blind items in Louella Parsons, and if the truth comes out, sweetheart, you're finished before you begin! We obey the rules here, and middle America ain't ready for the daughter of Jessica Miller to be fucking a nigger. The country ain't ready for any white star to be fucking a nigger. Let me tell you one more time, Maxwell. I've got real big bucks riding on this picture, and I ain't gonna have some stupid broad blowing it because she don't know what the fucking hell to do with her goddamned hole!"

"Mr. Altman, really! I resent that." Her defenses were falling into disarray. "Must you use such coarse language?"

" 'Mr. Altman, really, must you use such coarse language?' " he mimicked in a namby-pamby voice. He stood straight up. "I'm from the street, sweetheart, and I talk from the street. You ain't Rebecca of Sunnybrook Farm! Your mother had a mouth like a sewer. She made me sound like Shakespeare. Speaking of your mother, she had an unfillable hole too, but goddamnit, she never fucked around with niggers! From what I hear, they've got a hard-on twenty-four hours a day and a prick down to their knees. If that's what turns you on, sweetheart, I can give you a list of white Hollywood studs who'll be happy to oblige." Opening his top desk drawer, he produced a piece of paper. "Here!" he shouted, handing it to her. She looked the other way. "They've all got dicks eight inches long and over. Here!" He thrust the paper at her. "I had this drawn up especially for you."

By now Mattie was sobbing uncontrollably. "Oh, Mr. Altman . . ."

"Don't turn the waterworks on me. It's a waste of time!" he said gruffly. "There's a lesson in this. An inch of protection is worth a mile of . . . of . . ." he groped.

"An ounce of prevention's worth a pound of cure," she wept.

"Don't get smart-alecky with me!" he snapped. "You know what the fucking hell I mean! This ain't no school!" he yelled. "Look, sweetheart, I don't want to upset you. I'm just trying to acquaint you with a few of the realities of this business. Whoever eats my bread sings my song!" He spoke with an intensity that precluded interruption. "You are never to see Eastman Fletcher, Junior, again. If you like his voice that much, buy his records, but as long as you're under contract to this studio, you don't even attend his performances. Just consider yourself very lucky a scandal's been avoided. As for him, he's been taken care of."

"Taken care of? How . . . ?" she cried aloud.

"It's really none of your business, but seeing it looks like you're gonna cooperate, I'll let you into a little secret. Within a week Eastman Fletcher

Junior's getting married . . . to a girl of his own race. Romantic, ain't it? If he wants to keep on walking, that is!"

"What are you talking about?"

"If he doesn't stop seeing you, or vice versa, Fletcher'll find himself with two broken legs, that's what I'm talking about! Then his cock'll reach all the way to the ground and not just to his knees."

"How could you do a thing like that, Mr. Altman?" Mattie was horror-stricken.

"I can do anything I like, and anything I say goes. Isn't it strange how all these nigger motherfuckers want to become big stars, and the minute they do, they leave their neighborhoods and move into ours, get the biggest, flashiest cars money can buy, and still aren't satisfied until they've fucked our women, too? Not on my time they don't, and not with a girl who belongs to my studio and who's got my money riding on her! That's how it is, sweetheart. I've told you the way things are." Altman stood up. "What are your plans for the rest of the afternoon, sweetheart? Blow your nose."

"I . . . I . . . I've got a costume fitting before lunch."

"If I had a little time, maybe we could fool around a little, huh? Although you're not quite my type. But, unfortunately, I've got a conference, and a lunch date." Mattie stood in silence, utterly humiliated and defeated.

"Well, it's been nice talking to you, sweetheart. I sincerely hope I never have to bring the subject up again, because, if I do, you're out of the picture! And that, Maxwell, means out of Hollywood! Nobody touches what I let go." He led her toward the door, which swung open as he pushed a buzzer on the wall.

Morris Altman put his arm conspicuously around her shoulders with paternal concern. "Mattie, sweetheart, what a great pleasure it was seeing you today! You all remember Jessica Miller's little girl!" he announced to the assemblage in the reception area. Three clerical assistants, a messenger boy carrying studio mail, the secretary, Altman's personal chauffeur, and an entourage of script writers, editors, assistant directors and high-level technicians stood to attention. "Used to bring you around, Maxwell, when you were no taller than a grasshopper! Such a devoted mother she was!"

Mattie couldn't remember any of the faces gawking at her.

"Never hesitate to pop in and see your Uncle Morrie any old time you like! Keep on the way you're going, and who knows? Maybe next year I can add another Oscar to my collection! And all because of you, sweetheart! I'll let you know when we can have lunch next week. Show Miss Maxwell out, will you, Miss . . . Miss . . ."

"Blumensteil," the woman prompted in a resigned voice.

"That's right, Miss . . . uh . . . yeah . . ." Miss Blumensteil had been with Morris Altman for twenty years and he still couldn't remember her name.

Suddenly the elevator doors opened, and Rita Hayworth, all Hollywood glamour, stepped out, escorted by the singer Dick Haymes. Mattie, tears in her eyes, rushed past, bumping into them. "Oh, I'm so sorry, Mr. Hayworth!" she mumbled contritely. "I'm so sorry, Mr. Hayworth."

The debonair Haymes turned around and spoke gently. "Call me Mr. Welles, young lady. Anything! But I'm *not* Mr. Hayworth!" Mattie felt herself redden to the roots of her hair.

"Rita, honey!" Mattie heard Morris Altman exclaim. "Great to see you! And the lucky bridegroom too! Step right inside! I'm so—"

The elevator doors closed behind Mattie, cutting off the sound of the hypocritical chatter. She went downstairs, past the uniformed guard, past the reception desk, past the dumb blonde, into the cardboard world of blue skies and palm trees, and walked to her car in a daze. So that's what Hollywood was all about! All those stories she had heard were true! Opening her handbag, she withdrew a small enameled vial and popped two yellow capsules into her mouth.

When she arrived at the costume department, a newfound determination flashed like hot wires across the screen of her mind. She felt the beauty within her. It had to be fulfilled, this hunger to express it. This beauty had to flow from within just as the heart must beat. Her mind was made up. One of Altman's arrogant pronouncements stuck in her gut. "You don't have to be kind on your way up when you know you ain't never comin' down!" She would not come down! Whatever the cost, no matter what it took, she would be a star! The biggest! Beyond beauty, beyond looks, beyond age, beyond talent. The biggest of all. Mattie Maxwell, the superstar!

※

VLADIMIR/*Leningrad*/*Thursday, June 23, 1955*

Simone Belville was a Russified Frenchwoman, gaunt, neatly dressed. An ageless lady, somewhere between fifty and seventy. And when she claimed to have danced the premiere of Fokine's *Les Sylphides* along with Pavlova, people believed her. She ran the ballet museum affiliated with the Kirov School, taking loving and diligent care of its humble treasures. Simone Belville was a talkative lady. She was fond of Vladimir, for he was a very good listener.

"Oh, Madame Belville, please tell me more about Diaghilev."

"Mon petit Voldemar, I've told you everything I know! I've shown you all of his pictures, I've lent you all the books." She put her hand on his shoulder. "Let's speak about you. Why does such a handsome young man spend so much of his precious free time with an old woman like me? Don't you have a little girl friend, Voldemar?"

He looked up, his eyes untroubled by the question.

"Come on, come on," she continued. "Tell me the truth. You know that you can trust me."

"I don't have time for girls. Girls are so boring, so silly, so brash! They want to wear the pants. My mother always says, 'Fewer girls, fewer troubles.' "

Simone laughed, an old laugh, the kind that has survived many tears. "That is rubbish!" she admonished him. "You are sixteen now."

"Tomorrow."

"All right, tomorrow. And not every girl is stupid! Why don't you—?"

"When would I have a chance to see girls? I dance all the time," Vladimir interrupted. "I study twelve hours a day, sometimes more. I don't have many friends. I don't need many friends. Only *you* Madame Belville, my mother and Pëtr Ivanovich."

Vladimir was right. He didn't need many friends, especially if one of them was Pëtr Ivanovich. Much of his spare time was spent in the home of his teacher and his wife, Tamara. How he loved their cozy living room, decorated with the ancient mahogany odds and ends that remained from the old furnishings. There was always a bed for Vladimir when he rehearsed too late to go home. Together they listened to music, discussed ballet or the books Vladimir had recently read. He had entered a new phase. By chance Vladimir had come across a biography of Lord Byron by André Maurois at the public library. The mysterious figure of the arrogant lord thrilled him. He began to read Byron's poetry translated by Samuel Marshak and Boris Pasternak. Now he could speak of practically nothing but the loves and feuds of his new infatuation.

"Voldemar, Voldemar!" said Simone Belville. "What are you dreaming about now? You probably haven't heard a word I've said in the last five minutes." She touched his shoulder gently. "But I understand. I understand."

Vladimir looked at the clock on the wall. "Oh," he exclaimed, jumping to his feet, "it's nearly two! I cannot be late for my piano lesson. I'll come by and see you tomorrow, Madame Belville." He bowed and kissed her blue-veined hand.

"All right, mon petit Voldemar. What do you have under your arm?" she asked, lifting a pair of steel-rimmed glasses from the bridge of her nose to her forehead.

"It's—"

"No, no, no. Don't tell me. I know! I know!" She closed her eyes girlishly. "It's something . . . something by Byron," said Simone Belville as though she had just received a psychic message.

"You are right, madame. It's—"

"You see! I knew! I knew!" she interrupted, replacing the glasses on the bridge of her nose. "I'm amazed that he has held your interest for so long. Byron was not a dancer."

"It's very much the same, madame. He danced with his words and I write poems with my body."

"You are right, Voldemar. You are right! I would like an opinion, mon petit. Dites-moi . . ." Her finger motioned for him to come closer. In a conspiratorial tone, she asked, "Do you think Lord Byron had an affair with his sister Augusta?"

"In my mind, *always*," Vladimir answered mischievously.

She threw her head back and laughed in high giggles. "You'll be all right, mon petit Voldemar. You have imagination. C'est très bien. Très, très bien. I'll see you tomorrow. And thank you again for the beautiful rose. You are such a thoughtful young man."

He ran to the next floor and was about to enter the classroom. Irina Shatilov grabbed his arm.

"Well, Vladimir," she said, "have you made up your mind?"

"About what?"

"About what?" she said, offended. "Don't you remember saying you would take me to the movies tonight?"

"I said maybe."

"So you see, you do remember."

"Yes . . . yes, I do." He smiled. "Now I remember that, unfortunately, I must tell you no."

"But why?"

"I'm busy. I forgot I was invited to dinner by Pëtr Ivanovich."

"I'm surprised you didn't give me the excuse that you *have* to walk your dog. As you did last week!"

"Actually, I do *have* to walk my dog before I go to dinner. And Lieka is not an excuse. Lieka *has* to be walked." Everyone had seen Vladimir frequently walking his fluffy, husky dog with pointed ears and a long tail along Sadovaya Street, muttering something to her as she looked up at him with gray, unblinking eyes, seemingly absorbing each word of his. Lieka was his friend too.

"Can't we walk Lieka together?" persisted Irina.

"Not tonight."

"Why can't I walk with you? Is your conversation with your dog so private that I would be in the way? Or . . . is it that you just don't want to see me?"

"Irina, you had it right the first time. Now please let go of my arm. You look like a fool." He entered the room.

Irina's eyes welled with tears. What an idiot she had made of herself. She had been warned, and still had fallen victim to Vladimir's cruelty. Nearly every girl who flirted with him had been the butt of his caustic remarks. He now had the reputation of being a savage. He was resigned to the fact and didn't give a damn.

Vladimir would never dream of missing music class. It had a lot to do with his teacher, Ludmilla Fedorovna, or Lucinka—"little Lucy"—as her colleagues called her. For the past three years she had been the only person who had excited his imagination. Ludmilla Fedorovna was about thirty, fair-haired, with an unusually well-developed bosom, a total lack of priggishness, a shining femininity and a radiant smile. In the spring a tiny bunch of violets was invariably pinned to the lapel of her strict English tailleur. She entered the classroom bringing an aura of throbbing life, genuine charm and human warmth. The students rose.

"Good morning, everyone. Or should I say, good afternoon? You may sit down. Now, those of you who did not learn Scarlatti's sonatina are excused. You don't want to steal time from a busy woman, do you?" No one moved. "Well, don't just sit there like zombies!" Her eyes scanned the room. "You mean all twelve of you have done your homework?"

A chorus of *da*'s exploded from various parts of the room. Everyone adored Lucinka.

"I'm very pleased," she said quietly.

Lucinka was like a gulp of fresh air. Vladimir found himself under her tutelage in the fourth year of school—having passed an ordeal with Alla Rassadin, an old spinster with a crooked, dried-out, rubberlike face that she invariably shaped into terrible grimaces, as if constantly suffering from an abominable toothache. Alla Rassadin seemed to know merely one phrase, which she parroted at least four times each lesson: "Hold your back, put your elbows close to your body, and don't let the sounds disappear between your legs. Don't let the sounds disappear between your legs. . . ."

"Well! Volodin," said Ludmilla Fedorovna, "come to the piano and let's start with the Bach fugue. By the way, did you know that he wrote it for the harpsichord?"

Vladimir didn't know. "Of course I do," he answered, intrepidly confronting her glance.

Lucinka was a puzzle to him. Always gay, smiling, elated, as if her life was woven out of perpetual joy and excitement.

After class Vladimir remained behind, dispiritedly gathering papers. Lucinka approached him. "Is something wrong?" she asked. He felt the gentle pressure of her hand on his wrist.

"No . . . yes . . . it's my birthday."

"When?"

"Tomorrow."

"Oh. How old will you be?"

"Sixteen."

"Well, you're a man now! It's your last year of study. You're going to be a soloist at the Kirov! The youngest soloist! You should be very happy. What could I do to cheer you up? I'm sure you already have made plans for tomorrow."

"No. No, I haven't!"

"That's hard to believe!"

"But it's true! My mother is in Kiev," he lied, "and I haven't told anyone about my birthday."

"But you cannot become sixteen and not celebrate!" she said, sitting on the edge of a desk. "I'll tell you what. Do you like Gilels?"

"Oh, yes, Ludmilla Fedorovna! He's my favorite pianist!" This wasn't the time to tell her that he didn't particularly like Gilels' slightly reserved, academic manner and actually preferred Richter.

"If you *really* have nothing to do, Vladimir, I have two seats for Gilels' recital at the Philharmonic tomorrow night. I was planning to call an old friend, but you have worked very hard this year, and this will be my present to you." She wrote something on a piece of paper and gave it to him. "This is my phone number. If you want to go, just give me a call this evening." Vladimir seemed to detect something in the look of her gray eyes, as if they were penetrating him, or perhaps it was just his imagination.

That night, after having seen *Camille* by himself for the hundredth time, Vladimir gathered all the courage he could muster to call Ludmilla Fedorovna. He hesitated . . . dialed . . . hung up before completing the number . . . redialed . . . Finally it was ringing on the other end.

"Hello." It was she.

After they had exchanged a few words, Vladimir felt at ease and eagerly accepted her invitation for the concert.

He was back home now. His mother had retired. Vladimir was sitting on a large windowsill, his legs crossed in the Turkish way, avidly gulping the refreshing night air. It was late, very late, but during the white nights Leningrad seemed to forget about sleeping and kept the day going around the clock. The beige and gray buildings framing the square, enshrouded by a milky, glittering, almost transparent haze, were so fairylike they could have been the setting for a still unknown ballet.

What time is it, he wondered. The deserted Sadovaya Street immediately prompted the answer. Four o'clock in the morning! It must be four— the belated streetcars rambling away, the green lights of taxi cabs—very few—some tipsy wanderers returning home by foot. He was thinking of Lucinka.

Throughout the next morning and afternoon Vladimir remained in a trance, until he met Ludmilla Fedorovna in front of the Philharmonic promptly at a quarter to eight. She looked so fresh and seductive in her blue silk dress. As they sat together in the balcony he could not keep his eyes off her profile, not really beautiful but so strong, yet vulnerable, classic and desirable. The Rachmaninoff concerto moved Lucinka to tears. After the concert Vladimir gallantly offered to see her home.

She beamed acceptance, impishly raising her eyebrows, and took his arm, suggesting a little walk along the Nevsky Prospekt. The famous boulevard was very wide and very straight, with houses on either side. It had an unfinished look about it. Yet the ancient façades were timeless and alive. The dense crowd flowed ceaselessly—a good-natured crowd, easygoing and patient—peasants in their native garb, men and women speaking loudly, soldiers, young people with vague dreams of the future, old people lost in memories of the past.

Walking on the Nevsky one could see all the great characters from Russian novels, the passions of their souls written plainly on their faces. The songs and the strumming guitars resounding from the Neva banks were splitting the night, tinging its white splendor with joy. Gaiety filled the air.

Vladimir radiated pride in having beautiful Lucinka holding his arm. When he first started to think about her, his only desire was to walk with her in silence. Now they were walking in silence and he was racking his brain for something to say.

She started to speak. Their conversation was forced and unnatural. "Where will you go on vacation?"

"Oh, I'm not taking vacation this year. I'm preparing for the Moscow Competition."

"Why, that's wonderful! And then?"

"When I win it . . ." It was said without pretension, in the same manner he would have stated his age or his name.

"What do you mean, *when* you win it?" She laughed, squeezing his arm a little. "Where is your modesty?"

"I guess I don't have any." He looked at her tenderly. "I just know I'll win it!"

There was silence again.

"I hear you'll be doing your first *Sleeping Beauty* this fall with Dudinskaya."

"Yes, I'm very lucky that she asked me to be her partner. Outside of Ulanova, there is no one better."

"Do you mind . . .," Ludmilla started hesitantly, "do you mind that she is so much older than you?"

"Why should I mind? Dudinskaya is a beautiful dancer. Besides, she obviously doesn't mind appearing with someone as young as I."

They had arrived at the Palace Square and the golden Admiralty Spire. Lucinka lived near Petrogradav, across the Neva. They took streetcar number 7 over the Anichkov Bridge. On both sides of the river ancient palaces flaunted their beauty: a symphony of pale pastels and burnished patina—dreamy blues, dying roses, creamy yellows—as though each hue had been obtained by grinding time with solid gold. Around them the trees with their lush, opulent greens, had a luminous quality against the ancient palaces and sky.

They got off at Gorky Street and walked to Kirovsky. Vladimir felt a strange excitement. For the first time in his life he was seeing a lady home. They stopped in front of the iron gates of an old St. Petersburg building with white columns.

"Thank you very much, Ludmilla Fedorovna. It was a beautiful evening and the concert—"

"Would you like to drop by for a minute to see my little castle?" Lucinka offered merrily.

"Oh, yes," he said. Some anxiety drifted across his face like the shadow of a bird over a lawn.

"My relatives have lived here for a hundred years," she said. "Before the Revolution the whole building belonged to my grandfather, and now his granddaughter occupies one small room in a huge communal apartment on the seventh floor. On the highest one . . . closer to God. Isn't it funny?"

Vladimir was slightly dazed as they entered a dark corridor. She put her hand in his. He felt a warm current running back and forth between them. It was after midnight, and in the apartment, which resembled a huge dormitory, everybody slept. Lucinka pressed her finger to her mouth, cautioning him not to speak. She shook her tousled hair and gently ushered him into her room. The room was decently furnished: a marble figurine of Mozart on the piano, bookshelves, an old mahogany sofa beneath an ornate hanging lamp with cupids on its lacquered sides, once lit by kerosene but now adapted for electricity, framed photographs on the wall, and a large round Victorian table covered with a heavy fringed cloth.

The table had been set for two. The candles, in old silver holders, seemed to be expecting him. Suddenly Vladimir felt a strong desire to run away. An inner voice started to whisper something frightening.

"Why do you seem so lost, Vladimir? Make yourself comfortable," Lucinka said in a voice full of promises. "I'll fix some tea. And since it's your birthday, we'll have some wine." She disappeared into the kitchen. He didn't know where to turn. His anxiety was mounting.

Mechanically he began to inspect the photographs. His attention was drawn to an old-fashioned picture of a lad, apparently in his late teens, in a military uniform hugging a girl of about the same age. He recognized Ludmilla's features. The face of the young man looked somehow familiar. He *knew* him. *He'd seen him.* But where? Suddenly Vladimir burst out laughing. Of course he'd *seen* him somewhere! The man resembled him! Him! Vladimir! It was an uncanny likeness—the same almond-shaped eyes, strong neck, sandy hair, high cheekbones, full, sensual mouth. Lucinka came into the room carrying a teapot.

"Who's the fellow?" he asked.

"Oh! This is . . . he . . . he was my fiancé. His name was Viktor. He was killed on the Leningrad front. . . ." She lowered her eyes for a moment, then brightened. "Come on, let's eat and enjoy ourselves."

Vladimir wanted to tell her that his father too had perished in the same battle, but held back. There were so many stories similar to theirs.

"Come and sit down, Vladimir," she said coquettishly. "You must be famished." While he had been preoccupied with the photographs, Ludmilla had heaped the table with cold borscht, ham, sprats in olive oil, a bottle of good Georgian wine, and much to his surprise, a little birthday cake. "Well," she said, with a heartwarming smile, "the first glass is to you, your prosperity, to my future Nijinsky!"

"I . . . I've never had wine before!"

Lucinka was enjoying his confusion. After the first glass he forgot his anxiety. After the second he felt great elation. After the third his head started spinning. Vladimir somehow became conscious of himself feeling the full female arms entwining his neck, inhaling the sensuous scent of gardenia perfume mixed with old lace and frangipani, kissing soft lips gently pressed against his mouth. There were no more thoughts of Gilels, the white nights, or the Nevsky. He was naked on a bed, blinded by myriad lights, sparkling, bursting from a painful surge of lust and passion, caught in the grip of Ludmilla's sultry body, clinging to him with her smooth, fresh-smelling skin, tempting and thrilling. She brought his hand to her breast and his mouth found the hard nipples. She helped him enter her, tossing about between his legs like a brook trout caught in a net. "Oh, Viktor, Viktor, I love you, I love you!" Her voice rose with the heavy pounding of her heart. "Viktor!"

In the diffused whiteness that poured through the window he saw only her face, distorted by delight. Delight and anger. It appeared to him vindictive and sinister, as if she were sucking him in, absorbing him, swallowing him whole. He was afraid he would drown in this abyss. There was no longer "little Lucy." There was an unknown, fair-haired female animal, digging her claws into his back, tearing him apart.

"Viktor . . . Viktor . . . ," she repeated, moaning, gasping, her eyes wild and frenzied.

He kept on riding her like an unbroken mustang, feeling both fright and hatred.

"Oh, Viktor, I'm coming . . . now . . . !" she screamed.

Finally everything was over.

He remained quiet. Bewildered. Arresting emotions filling his whole being. Vladimir felt an enormous sadness. How he loved Lucinka! But he was just a replacement. A replacement for Viktor, whom she could no longer have. He felt used. Yes! He had been used. Was that what sex was all about? So fast? So impersonal? So nothing? Vladimir jumped out of bed, wiping his groin with a towel, got dressed and rushed to the door. Naked, she flung herself at him.

"Where are you going, dushka? Stay with me. There are no buses, no cars until five. The subway won't start until—Where are you going?" The question was almost a shriek.

And again he felt the rain of gentle kisses falling on his face and her arms around his neck. Savagely he pulled free and pushed her violently away. "My name is not *Viktor!* he hissed in blind hatred. "I am not Viktor! I am Vladimir! Vladimir!" How he wanted to hurt her physically. He wanted to slap her beautiful face, to shatter that gentle and compassionate expression. He wanted a whip in his hand, to lash her until her smooth skin was covered with welts. He wanted . . . he wanted . . . he wanted . . . and walked out.

Vladimir started the long trek home. Thick tears ran down his cheeks. He felt dizzy, nauseated, feverish, dazed. The bridge, its two parts uplifted, was hovering in the dawn. He waited two hours before its gigantic claws connected, then caught the first streetcar—and went directly to the Kirov School, where he found an empty room. He practiced frenetically until class officially began.

The following afternoon he missed Ludmilla's lesson. He ran into her in the school corridor. She gave him an inquisitive, mocking glance, which he ignored. Shortly thereafter, by his request, Vladimir was transferred to the "hold your elbows against your body and don't let the sound disappear between your legs" old spinster, and seduced Irina . . . Eugenia . . . Xenia . . .

✳

MATTIE/*Hollywood/Wednesday, March 21, 1956*

VARIETY   Wednesday, February 1, 1955
Donald Ferry, spokesman for Morris Altman (prexy and chief exec of Vista Films) announces completion of final script of *Life Is a Dream.*
VARIETY   Wednesday, February 8, 1955
Mattie Maxwell, under contract to Vista Films, being tested for femme lead in *Life Is a Dream.*
VARIETY   Wednesday, February 15, 1955
Producer Gregory Thompson inks Kirk Flynn and Mattie Maxwell to co-star in *Life Is a Dream,* pic skedded to roll immediately. This marks Miss Maxwell's second commitment under present contract with Vista.
VARIETY   Wednesday, May 15, 1955   *"New York Sound Track"*
Insiders who have had a peek at *Life Is A Dream* rough cuts, starring Kirk Flynn and Mattie Maxwell, directed by Roger Taylor, predict flick will be the boffo sleeper of the year and Mattie Maxwell will emerge a major star.
VARIETY   Wednesday, July 12, 1955
The much ballyhooed *Life Is a Dream,* the new Roger Taylor pic, premiered July 10 at New York's Radio City Music Hall. The opening brought out a galaxy of celebs. Among them were: Arlene Dahl, Fernando Lamas, Dore Schary, Tallulah Bankhead, Norman Mailer, Mary Martin, Montgomery Clift (escorting Mattie Maxwell), David Merrick and New York Mayor Robert Wagner.

VARIETY Wednesday, July 12, 1955 *"Film Reviews"*
Life Is a Dream (Radio City Music Hall—N.Y.C.)
Gregory Thompson film, directed by Roger Taylor and based on Harry Schneider's best-selling novel, opened to an SRO audience July 10. This is an unusually well made and engrossing film, telling with talent and intelligence the story of a struggling writer (Kirk Flynn) fleeing the neurotic adoration of a homely girl (Mattie Maxwell) he bedded once and whom he now cannot get rid of, driving her to near suicide by his disdain. This pic is full of surprises. Foremost is the outstanding and memorable performance of Mattie Maxwell in her debut in a nonsinging role. Miss Maxwell is simply extraordinary in the female lead and proves to be a deft comedienne with rare depth of emotion, bringing to the screen a magnetic presence and a sweeping range of awesome perfection and strength. Her impressive natural skills stamp her as a dramatic actress often reaching sublime heights. Mattie Maxwell can do no wrong. The singer/actress is unique and has no peer that I can think of today. She is completely convincing. Her instinct for what is right has something magical.

Another plus is the title song, "Life Is a Dream," penned by tunesmith Sammy Cahn, which makes full use of La Maxwell's haunting and glorious voice. Come Oscar time, her performance could snare Mattie Maxwell the female thesp nod. In short, she is remarkable and so is the film. Aced casting and top credits make *Life Is a Dream* a winner and Mattie Maxwell a star with a capital S. Clean editing and lensing contribute much . . .

VARIETY Wednesday, July 19, 1955
Life Is a Dream BLOCKBUSTER, HITS BIG, RAKING 300G IN 1ST.
VARIETY Wednesday, December 20, 1955
Cinerama Holiday (January) grosses 10 million for the year, followed by late entry *Life Is a Dream* (July) with a terrif hefty total of 8.5 million.
VARIETY Wednesday, January 24, 1956
Life Is a Dream IS LEADING THE FIELD!
The film that captures the hearts of audiences from coast to coast is heading into spring with a phenomenal box office gross of $10,255,640.
VARIETY Wednesday, February 28, 1956
Mattie Maxwell cops one of the 5 Best Actress nominations for her crafty performance in *Life Is a Dream*. Oscar winner Sammy Cahn slated to run again for Best Song with hot flick theme tune "Life Is a Dream."

Mattie Maxwell, on the arm of a very drunk Montgomery Clift, made her way through the thousands of people still lingering outside the Pantages Theatre. Mattie was late as always. Her nomination for Best Actress in *Life Is a Dream,* only her second released movie to date, had made her a nervous wreck. She'd taken every pill she could find, smoked a joint, and split a bottle of champagne with Clift in the Bentley, hoping to survive the night in one piece. Mattie's evening gown felt uncomfortable—an outrageous purple-feather creation by Scaasi with a matching boa, clashing incongruously with her personality. George Master had done her hair attractively in the latest angel-cut style. The ceremonies were already well under way. People turned and stared as the couple noisily entered the auditorium and took their seats in the fourth row, beside Nedda and husband Josh Logan, nominated as Best Director for *Picnic*.

John Wayne and Susan Hayward had just presented Helen Rose the award for Best Costume Design for *I'll Cry Tomorrow*. Emcee Jerry Lewis returned to the stage with a goofy grin, doing his well-known imitation of a spastic shuffle. It was received with a rousing silence. He introduced Eydie Gorme, who stirred the audience from its near slumber with her upbeat rendition of "Something's Gotta Give." Next came Best Documentary Short Subject, *Man Against the Arctic,* by Walt Disney, Best Cinematography, Best Screenplay, Best Scoring for a Motion Picture. The list seemed endless. There were so many different categories that Mattie thought they would never reach hers. Discreetly she popped one pill after another. Jane Powell sang "Love Is."

The Best Director award followed. James Mason and Jennifer Jones, a vision of beauty in a pale mauve Christian Dior lace gown, revealed the winner—Delbert Mann, for *Marty*.

Mattie's nerves got more irritated as the night continued. Best . . . Best . . . Best . . .

"Ladies and gentlemen, members of the Academy," Jerry Lewis announced, "to sing 'Life Is a Dream,' my good friend, the magnificent and incomparable Eastman Fletcher, Junior."

A pair of cool blue spotlights picked up Eastman as he glided to center stage in tempo with the first chords of the NBC orchestra. The audience applauded. Ruby-tinted glasses set off the rich chocolate color of his skin. His hair was slicked down, and his white dress shirt was unbuttoned, revealing a tangle of heavy gold medallions. As usual, his fingers flashed half a dozen gold rings set with diamonds and sapphires. Eastman began to sing. He milked the song for every drop of emotion. "How could you leave me feeling this way . . . ?" he sang, eyes closed, arms outstretched, voice soaring, snapping his fingers and bopping around the stage, turning the ballad into a Las Vegas number. He was good but not as good as Mattie. The song needed her delicate, vulnerable touch. Eastman finished and took several bows.

For a moment the song made Mattie forget her nervousness. Her excitement returned, however, when Maurice Chevalier came on as the presenter for the Best Song of the Year award. Mattie leaned against Montgomery Clift, squeezing his arm.

"Once again, the nominees are," Chevalier began, " 'Love Is a Many-Splendored Thing,' 'I'll Never Stop Loving You,' 'Something's Gotta Give,' 'Love Is,' and 'Life Is a Dream.' The envelope, please."

A man stuffed into a tuxedo waddled onstage like a penguin and handed the envelope to Chevalier. He opened it and took out a card.

"And the winner is—'Life Is a Dream'! Accepting for Mr. Cahn is Mattie Maxwell, who sang this unforgettable song in the film *Life Is a Dream*."

The applause was deafening. Mattie clapped her hands in delight, then jumped up and headed for the stage. Her boa flipped across her face and she got a mouthful of feathers. Oh, my God, how tacky, she thought as the cameras panned in for a close-up. Without breaking stride she spat out the feathers and continued to the podium. A few feathers were still stuck to her moist cheek. Mattie plucked them with mock delicacy as one might pick a hair from soup. "I didn't know that it was moulting season," she said into the microphone. "Thank you, ladies and gentlemen, members of the Academy. It is an honor to accept this award for Sammy Cahn. I'm sorry that he couldn't be here tonight, but," she continued with a twinkle in her eye, "Sammy never misses his piano lesson, which unfortunately was scheduled for the same time as tonight's ceremony." Cheers, laughter and bravos erupted. "And I know Sammy would like me to thank my friend and mentor and the producer of *Life Is a Dream,* Morris Altman, the president of the Motion Picture Academy and tonight's event"—Mattie smiled mischievously at Morris, who was standing in the wings with a beatific smile on his face—"for it was his unique and *unprejudiced* insight that brought a great song and a great singer together this evening, making it possible for people throughout the whole world to view and hear Eastman Fletcher, Junior's beautiful rendition of Sammy Cahn's 'Life Is a Dream.' Thank you, Mr. Morris Altman!"

Mattie and Maurice Chevalier sashayed off to a big ovation.

As she reached the wings Morris caught her arm. "Listen, Maxwell," he said, "you made me sound like fuckin' Abe Lincoln." He took out a white Cardin handkerchief, mopped his brow and shaded his eyes from the hot lights.

"Well, it's better than Jefferson Davis," said Mattie, laughing.

"Maybe you enjoy being bedfellows with Eastman Fletcher, Junior, but next time, Mattie, keep me out of it!"

"I'll remember that, Uncle Abe. Oh, wait, there's Eastman," she said out loud for all to hear. "Why don't you two take some pictures together? They're bound to make the front page!"

Eastman Fletcher, Jr., strolled over, shook hands with Morris Altman, and kissed Mattie warmly. A dozen photographers started aiming.

Mattie slid free of Eastman's embrace and out of range of the cameras.

Several pictures were snapped before Morris Altman could get away. Mattie watched with glee, then gave the Oscar to an official for safekeeping and was escorted back to her seat.

The rest of the presentations were a blur for Mattie. One thought alone was in her mind. Would she win? Jack Lemmon won the Best Supporting Actor award for *Mr. Roberts.* Jo Van Fleet was named Best Supporting Actress for *East of Eden,* over Peggy Lee, Betsy Blair, Natalie Wood and Marisa Pavan.

Mattie couldn't stand the tension and took another Miltown. "I'm gonna pee in my pants, I'm so nervous," she told Monty, leaning against him as Marlon Brando and Grace Kelly presented the award for Best Actor to Ernest Borgnine.

Mattie waved to friends scattered throughout the audience, shuffling her hands in the air as if she were tossing cards. Over and over again she told herself that if she didn't win, it would be all right. But she knew different. Mattie wanted that award more than anything in the world.

Finally Jerry Lewis said the words. "And now, ladies and gentlemen, we have come to the eagerly awaited category of Best Actress of the Year. Presenting the award are Beverly Langdon and Clark Gable."

Drum rolls sounded. A moment later Beverly Langdon slithered onstage with Clark Gable. Beverly looked like the ultimate sex symbol in a strapless black sequin gown she had actually been sewn into and which displayed her curves and cleavage magnificently. Clark had to slow his gait, for if Beverly walked any faster her dress would split at the seams. Sporting a pair of six-inch gold spike heels, her blond hair carefully coiffed in her famous "I just got out of bed" hair style. They finally made it to the podium to a delirious reception.

Jerry Lewis leered at Beverly's bosom and said, "It's so hard to outshine two great stars like these." The crowd erupted with whistles and outbursts of admiration and laughter. The television cameras zoomed to a close-up of Beverly's chest, then quickly panned to a couple of ushers in the aisle. "No, I didn't mean those two," Jerry said dizzily.

From her seat in the audience Mattie noted with elation a long run in one of Beverly's stockings.

"I'm so happy to be here tonight," Beverly breathed through her sensual parted lips, painted the glossy bright red that was her trademark. "It's truly an honor for me to present the award for Best Actress. Oh, I'm sorry, Clark Gable is here too." She giggled. "Shall we begin, Clark?"

"All right, honey," he answered. "Why don't you go first?"

"The nominees for Best Actress are: Katharine Hepburn for *Summertime*, Anna Magnani for *The Rose Tattoo*, Susan Hayward for *I'll Cry Tomorrow*, Mattie Maxwell for *Life Is a Dream*, and Jennifer Jones for *Love Is a Many-Splendored Thing*."

Magnani and Hepburn, both seasoned dramatic actresses, were Mattie's main rivals. She was the underdog. A clip of each actress in her role was shown, and Mattie squirmed in her seat as she watched Katharine Hepburn gazing out at a Venetian lagoon. Mattie's scene from *Life Is a Dream* was the last clip. It was a segment of the telephone monologue at the end of the movie, after Kirk tells Mattie that he's through with her and will never leave his old girl and she pleads for another chance. Mattie had already been told her acting equaled that of Luise Rainer in a similar scene, done years ago in *The Great Ziegfeld*, which had gotten her the Oscar.

The auditorium fell deadly silent. "The envelope please," Clark Gable said gravely. The envelope arrived and he handed it to Beverly Langdon. She took her time opening it.

"And the winner is . . ." Beverly paused. Mattie held her breath. "How silly of me. I have the card upside down," cooed Beverly. "And the winner is . . . Mattie Maxwell, for *Life Is a Dream!*"

The audience went wild. Mattie let out a scream. Montgomery Clift leaned over and kissed her. She kissed him back and headed for the stage. She was so excited that she tripped twice going up the steps, discarding the cumbersome boa on the lap of a spectator on the way. Clark Gable handed her the statuette and Beverly Langdon embraced her warmly.

Mattie was so misty-eyed that her left eyelash came unglued. She tried to fix it gracefully, then said out loud, "What the hell, I might as well take the other one off too." She pulled them both loose and stuck them to the microphone like chewing gum. Taking the Oscar and holding it upside down, she examined it closely. "Does anyone know if it's male or female?" she said. "I can't tell, and I usually can."

The audience loved her and gave her a standing ovation.

Mattie took a deep breath and spoke. "If someone had told me two years ago that I would win an Oscar tonight I would have told them they were crazy. But here I am. I can't believe it. If they would have told me to re-member all the people who made my career possible, there would have been only a few. Now I have actually won, and there are still only a few. First there is my mother, Jessica Miller, who gave me a precious gift called talent. Then there is my manager, Sylvia Rubins, who believed in me from the beginning and never gave up. Last and most important are all the people who didn't believe in me. Each and every one of them spurred me on to prove that I could do it. Every heartbreak gave me strength, every disap-pointment another push, every lonely moment the courage to continue. So all I can say is thank you . . . thank you. As long as I can keep on feeling all these emotions I promise you I'll get better and better."

There were tears in Mattie's eyes as she walked toward the wings. She had taken a big step. She was no longer just the daughter of Jessica Miller. Rather, Jessica Miller was the mother of Mattie Maxwell. That in itself was a distinction. She was almost offstage when she realized that she was going the wrong way, into a tangle of cameras, cables, lights and booms.

"Shit, I'm going the wrong way," she said laughing. She turned around and returned to center stage. There she saw Clark Gable still holding her Oscar. In her excitement she'd forgotten to take it. Clark handed her the statuette and they exited stage right. Mattie felt wonderful. It was all a dream, a crazy, beautiful dream just like in the movies.

It seemed as if the whole world were waiting to congratulate Mattie. All of the presenters were there, the photographers, newsmen, producers, per-formers, reporters, Louella Parsons, Sheilah Graham, Hedda Hopper, Morris Altman, Clark Gable, Beverly Langdon, Eastman Fletcher, Jr., and Sylvia. Mattie embraced Sylvia as people crowded around them. Cameras flashed and hands reached out.

"Oh, Mattie, you never looked lovelier," chirped Louella Parsons in her familiar singsong voice. "How does it feel to win?"

"A hell of a lot better than losing," Mattie answered.

Everyone laughed. More and more pictures were taken. At last Mattie was alone with Sylvia for a moment.

"Dearest Sylvia," said Mattie with deep feeling. "My dearest, dearest Sylvia . . . Do you remember the prediction you made to me at Levinsberg's back in 1954."

"Was I wrong, kid? Hell, I knew what I was talking about!"

"There's only one thing about your prediction that didn't come true."

"What do you mean, Mattie? What didn't come true?"

Mattie put one hand on Sylvia's shoulder. "You promised that it would take four years for me to become a star."

"Well—aren't you a star?"

"Can't you see?" Mattie's voice had an edgy intensity. "It didn't take four years—it only took two!"

They exchanged glorious smiles, and a message passed between them as between two drunks guzzling at the same bottle. Once more they embraced each other, then embraced the statuette, wetting its impassive golden face with their tears of joy and victory.

—※—

MARIELA-DENISE/*Greece*/*Wednesday, July 25, 1956*

A tall, distinguished man with a receding gray hairline and a deeply bronzed face bounded from his Bentley and ran through the revolving doors of the Hellenikon Airport in Athens. His tan was the kind acquired only by those who can indulge themselves year-round at the world's finest, most exclusive resorts. Or in this case, resorts of their own making. The man was Sinclair MacAlpine, and from his white sneakers to his turtleneck sweater he seemed anything but America's leading aeronautical magnate. He entered the terminal, checked the arrivals board, and hurried to the ramp of the Continental jet to greet the first of his guests—Curtis Lodge III and his fiancée, Lady Mariela Chelmsford.

"You old horse thief! How good to see you!" said Sinclair, beaming.

"Horse thief! Bite your tongue!" returned Curtis. "My middle name is automobile!"

"Hey, you watch—"

The affection of the two men was abundant and genuine, their smiles wide, their clichés the sort that make sense only between the very closest of friends.

"Just you wait until you see my baby," said Sinclair.

"Carolyn?" asked Curtis. "How is Carolyn?"

"Carolyn . . . she's okay." His face sagged momentarily. "But . . . I . . . I wasn't speaking . . . I wasn't thinking about Carolyn, I meant the love of my life, the *Galveston,* my new yacht. Just had it finished in El Ferrol, Spain. We'll be the first to try her out." Sinclair MacAlpine was referring to his latest three-million-dollar acquisition, which served as a floating palace and office for one of the richest men in the world.

From her position as a forgotten and therefore privileged observer, Mariela had a chance to examine Sinclair from a safe distance. She liked what she saw. Sinclair was obviously a man of wealth, power, a law unto himself. And clearly he was a charmer. A man who could put people at ease no matter who they were, no matter where they were. "Ahem . . ." She cleared her throat.

Sinclair turned to her. "Oh, I do beg your pardon—Mariela. I'm sure glad to meet you at last, honey. I feel as if I know you already, and I've got nothing but admiration for the woman who tamed this wild stallion!" He gave Curtis a playful poke in the ribs.

"I love her so much." Curtis caressed her black hair and adoringly squeezed her waist. "There was only one woman in the world who could do it . . . and I found her."

"I'm real happy for you," Sinclair continued. "Hey Mariela—oh yes, and Curtis—have I got a wing-ding planned for you tonight! I've invited twenty guests and you'll love them all. Besides that, I've mapped out stopovers at the most interesting islands in these waters for our two-week cruise!" He laughed expansively. "Hey, got an even better idea. Why don't you two get married on the *Galveston?* It would be—"

"No, Sinclair," interrupted Mariela, "it's a terrific offer, but we're planning a September wedding. Our hearts are set on being married in Zurich."

"That's where we met," offered Curtis.

"Well, shucks, if your hearts are set—"

"Our hearts are also *set,*" she went on, "on having you for our best man."

"How about that! That's great, great news and makes me *real* happy! Yesiree, *real* happy!"

"Oliver and Genevieve?" asked Mariela. "They've arrived, haven't they?"

"Yes, they showed up with their nurses last night." Sinclair hugged her with one strong arm and Curtis with the other. "They're such swell kids too, Curtis. That daughter of yours—Genevieve—is sure growing up pretty as a picture! And Mariela, congratulations! Your nephew Oliver is a regular little gentleman, yessirree!"

It was noon when Francesco and Denise Borgia landed at the same airport in Francesco's Lockheed Lodestar, which he piloted himself.

With Yvette several paces behind, they were met by an attractive middle-aged lady. "I am Flora Gratzos," the woman said, presenting Denise with a cellophane-wrapped spray of white orchids. "I work for Mr. Mac-Alpine's Athens office and I want to welcome you to our city."

"Wonderful," exclaimed Denise.

"I don't want to hurry you," said Flora, "but it would be advisable to go directly to the ship. I'm sure you'd like to freshen up first or take a swim before lunch, which is served promptly at two-thirty."

They arrived at Piraeus harbor followed by a scrambling train of photographers with flashing strobes, hungry for another story about Europe's most glamorous titled couple. Looming in the distance was the *Galveston!* A monument to money.

"My God! I've never seen anything quite like it!" said Denise. "I thought Escobar had the biggest ship in the world. But compared to . . . to . . . Why, this ship must be the size of a football field!"

"The *Galveston,*" Flora explained aboard the launch, "has a crew of forty. The temperature is strictly regulated to preserve some of the world's finest paintings, which Mr. MacAlpine keeps in his own art gallery. There are thirty telephones, so you can ring for the hairdresser, barber, maids, valets, seamstresses, masseurs, or the kitchen, which is open twenty-four hours a day. And they're in—"

Stepping onto the main deck, Francesco and Denise were greeted by the captain in a resplendent uniform. "Welcome aboard, Prince and Princess Borgia. Mr. MacAlpine has assigned you the Houston suite. Dario, your personal steward for the cruise, will show you the way. Everyone is at the pool having cocktails before lunch. Mr. MacAlpine and his guests are waiting for you there. We'll be weighing anchor any minute."

They took the elevator down one level. Their quarters consisted of a luxurious three-room suite. White flowers were everywhere. A Vlaminck painting adorned the living room wall. Another one, "Femme à la Fenêtre," by Henri Matisse, completely captivated Denise.

A round bathtub of lapis lazuli had fixtures of solid gold. The linens, all Porthault. The rugs, leopard. An authentic Fabergé silver-and-enamel clock graced the mantelpiece of a working fireplace.

Although accustomed to luxury, Francesco and Denise were astonished by every opulent detail. "Almost makes you feel poor, doesn't it!" teased Francesco.

Yvette was still unpacking. Denise put on a white one-piece bathing suit. Although quite aware that the bikini was *de rigueur,* fashion could dictate only so much to her. Besides, a bikini was not consistent with the image Denise had long ago chosen for herself.

She rang for Dario to escort them to the pool area.

Sinclair had assembled a glittering mix of business, show business, and society friends. Some were lounging on large mattresses or deck chairs, others were swimming, floating, or dangling their feet in the large mosaic pool, the bottom of which, intricately worked, represented a map of Texas.

Denise, on Francesco's arm, appeared at poolside wearing a white terry cloth robe with the Borgia crest on its breast pocket, her blond hair hidden beneath a matching white terry cloth turban. As usual, all eyes turned toward her. Denise's uncontrolled vanity demanded the necessary reassurance that once again she would be the undisputed focal point of the whole sparkling occasion.

Leaving his group, Sinclair approached them. "It's such a pleasure to see you again, Denise," he said, embracing her affectionately. "I haven't seen you two since Monte Carlo!" Vigorously he continued, shaking Francesco's hand. "Let me introduce you to some of the gang—but I'm sure you know most of them already."

Effusively Denise and Francesco greeted everyone, and especially their good friends Elsa Maxwell, Darryl Zanuck, with his latest protégée, actress Bella Darvi, Maurice Chevalier, ex-King Farouk, and Mohammed Riza Pahlavi, the autocratic ruler of Persia, with his glamorous wife, Saroya.

And then Denise saw a beautiful white, almost porcelain-skinned, woman of imperious distinction, in a black bikini, leaning near the bar. She was holding hands with a tall, fiftyish man in bathing trunks that revealed a roll around his waistline. Denise recognized him immediately. It was Curtis Lodge III. Which meant that the woman beside him had to be Lady Mariela Chelmsford, whom she'd heard so much about.

Pretty silly, Denise thought. Holding hands at their age—like kids!

"Come on," said Sinclair, "I want you to meet my best friend, Curtis, and his fiancée, Mariela. The party tonight is in their honor." Going over to the bar, he made the presentations, then added, "Curtis, old boy, I hate to do this to you, but right now I want to drag you away from your lovely lady so the gals can get better acquainted. Besides, I want to show you my gambling room, which puts Las Vegas to shame!" The men walked away.

Mariela smiled at Denise from under a floppy black straw hat that shadowed her flawless body.

"How do you do." Denise smiled noncommittally. "I've heard about you. *So much* about you that I feel we're already friends."

"I've heard about you too," responded Mariela cheerfully, "from Curtis and Sinclair. Care for a drink?" As she slid a mimosa across the bar to Denise, the enormous diamond ring on her finger caught the sunlight.

"I don't drink, not this early anyway," replied Denise, pushing the glass back toward Mariela. "And that, if I may say so, is the largest *daytime* diamond I've ever seen." She sat on a stool. "It must be new."

Mariela brightened, basking in the sunlight of what she took to be a compliment. "Yes, it's one of my engagement presents."

"What would my grandmother have said! I mean, she always told me diamonds should not be worn until after dark. I guess I'm a little old-fashioned. But her words impressed me so strongly that I don't even wear my engagement ring until nighttime. Now, isn't that silly?"

Mariela smarted from the blinding change of mood in Denise, and wondered about the bitter track marks on the soul of a beautiful young woman who seemed to have no cause for resentment. "I appreciate your telling me. About your grandmother, I mean. The world is aware of your vast collection of jewelry. But who would guess your family tree goes back so far!"

Denise had no intention of retreating. "You're from England, aren't you? It's so—so Dickensian."

"You make it sound so—so dusty and outmoded," laughed Mariela.

"Far from it. I hear it was called 'perfidious Albion' up until World War I," Denise continued calmly. "And if I'm not mistaken, isn't it also the 'land of trumpets, crumpets and strumpets'? I find that quite amusing. Don't you?"

"I *hadn't* heard," said Mariela stiffly, "but then, I'd have no occasion to hear. Whereas I imagine that if *that's* what interests you, you can find it anywhere."

"Why should it interest me?"

"You brought it up. But no matter, I must have misunderstood. Care for a cigarette?" She offered a thin gold case. Denise shook her head.

Mariela continued. "Let's talk about something else. Are you a movie fan?"

"Not really, but I'm told I look like Grace Kelly."

Mariela agreed. Just like Grace Kelly—cold. "I would have said Lana Turner."

"Really, why?"

"Well, you're dressed just like her in *The Postman Always Rings Twice.*"

"But she didn't have a Borgia family crest on her bathrobe."

"I guess she'd never heard the old slogan 'It pays to advertise.' But I was only kidding, Denise—what would life be without a sense of humor?"

Denise seethed as she eyed the scanty bikini and amply exposed flesh. "With a suit like that, I bet you get a lot of sun."

"I never go in the sun," Mariela replied. "It's bad for my skin."

"That's what I thought—" Interrupting herself, Denise continued, "What's that unusual brass chain you have around your waist? It's so original. Is it . . . something you discovered in an Oriental bazaar?"

"This *brass* chain is *gold,*" replied Mariela unhooking it and holding it up for Denise to examine. "It's Egyptian, over four thousand years old, and has quite a story attached to it."

"It must be fascinating." Denise fingered the thin gold links from which hung a small scarab charm. "Would you mind telling me? I'm really curious."

"Well, all right," began Mariela. "In my home in Zurich I have an Egyptian sarcophagus. Its mummy is called Tarutu and—"

Denise had turned the scarab over and discovered a hieroglyphic inscription. "What does it mean?"

"I—I have never told anybody," Mariela replied secretively.

"Not even Curtis?"

"Not even Curtis."

"Yes, well, you'll tell him before the wedding, I'm sure." She returned the charm to Mariela, who re-fastened it around her waist. "When will it be?"

"In September. It seems such a long way off. But right now we're finding out things about ourselves, about each other."

"But nothing about the scarab?"

"No, it's not necessary for a man to know everything."

Denise lifted her eyebrows. There was a silence and they looked at each other. Motionless, as if caught in a time exposure.

The vessel was rounding the coast of Kaburi in the bright Aegean sun.

"Curtis has a child by a previous marriage, hasn't he?" asked Denise.

"Yes, Genevieve, a marvelous little girl."

"I'm truly sorry for you," Denise said, taking Mariela's hand. "It's always such a problem when a woman inherits a child. It inevitably leads to jealousy, rivalry, it is—"

Just then a young girl of about thirteen ran up to Mariela, hiked herself onto her knees and wrapped her arms around her neck, kissing her affectionately.

"Who is this child?" asked Denise.

"This is Genevieve," said Mariela. "Curtis' daughter."

As she spoke, a boy of about Genevieve's age ran to Mariela. She put one arm protectively around him. "Hast du einen guten Tag?"

"Who is he?" asked Denise.

"This is Oliver, my—my nephew."

"But wasn't that German you were speaking?"

"Yes," Mariela answered curtly. "My sister was married to a German." She turned to the children. "Oliver, Genevieve, say hello to Princess Borgia."

Oliver made a deep bow and was about to speak when he noticed that Curtis, Sinclair and Francesco had come back. He dashed off to hug Curtis, while Genevieve giggled and said, "Nice to meet you, Princess Borgia," and ran away.

"Hot dog!" Sinclair exulted. "I see you girls have been getting along real fine. Chums already. I knew it, I just knew it! Come on, let's all take a dip in the pool."

Dressing for dinner in her cabin, Mariela made casual conversation with Curtis.

"This is all so wonderful. You're so wonderful. We've just come on board and already home seems a million miles away." She lifted her hair high off her neck, smiled, and turned her head toward Sinclair in a beckoning gesture. "Have you seen the papers? Any news of the real world?"

"Nothing important, Beautiful." He nuzzled her neck affectionately and kissed the nape. "Only that the *Andrea Doria* has left port, Eisenhower will undoubtedly be renominated next month, and Jack Hamilton, the hot international businessman, has suddenly died of—"

"Jack—?" Her hands dropped to the vanity table.

"You know him?" Curtis asked, drawing back.

"No, just heard of him." Her eyes darted. "Died how?"

"Heart attack."

"Oh, really?" Mariela didn't know whether to relax or dance or scream with joy, or perhaps do all at once. Instead she slid out of her gown for one more matinee with her husband-to-be.

Twenty guests were seated at the elegant candle-lit dining room table. Through the large open portholes the ripple of the ocean, sounding softly by the hull's side, set a romantic mood.

The pool had been emptied, its bottom electronically raised to form a dance floor, and from a distance the lush, lilting melody of an orchestra could be heard.

Denise was seated between Sinclair and Charles Boyer. "I haven't seen your wife," she said suddenly to no one in particular. "Where is Carolyn?"

"Well, Princess, she's not with us this trip," Sinclair said, laughing uneasily. "Let's just say she had a previous engagement."

"Oh, my dearest Sinclair," said Denise, changing the subject, "thank you for the beautiful flowers. You read me like a book."

"If you weren't married to such a hell of a good-looking devil"—he flirted with crinkly eyes—"I'd like to apply for a card to the whole library."

While the cherries jubilee were being served Sinclair invited the women to open the small beribboned packages that were set out before each of them. Amidst "oohs" and "aahs" the gifts were unwrapped—splendid gold medallions, each set with the birthstone of its recipient. Denise paused and glanced down. Everyone gasped as she held up a heavy gold bracelet in the shape of a ram, its head a mass of diamonds and rubies. It exceeded not only Sinclair's habitual standard of hospitality but completely overshadowed the other gifts.

"Let me help you with that," Charles Boyer volunteered. "Such a lovely wrist deserves a lovely decoration."

Porfirio Rubirosa, the Dominican playboy, leaned over. "Denise," he said, without letting go of Barbara Hutton's hand, "if I didn't know Francesco was your husband, I'd lay odds that you'd won yourself a Texan!"

Sinclair flushed. "There must be a lot of Greeks born under Aries, because I couldn't find anything else in Denise's sign at Zolotas. And Zolotas are supposed to be the best jewelers in Athens."

"Thank you, Sinclair," Denise said, squeezing his hand. "Remind me to spend all my birthdays in Greece."

Everyone laughed with delight.

Now Denise was in her element. It was her moment. In her high-necked white organdy dress she looked as stunning and deliciously sensuous as she felt. Wickedly, she stole a glance across the table to where Mariela was sitting.

Mariela was strong competition. The woman's black hair flowing to the waist, her low-cut green gown clinging beneath the marvelous jet tresses, her face radiant with love that a casual stranger could have read at a glance. Mariela was strong competition.

Sinclair turned to Denise. "Godalmightydamn, I'm so glad that Curtis has found the right girl!"

"She's hardly a girl anymore," Denise said, a little too loudly.

"She's a woman, which is great! Curtis has a great need for happiness, and Mariela seems to have a great capacity for giving and receiving love and joy. Which reminds me," he said, rising. "Everybody—y'all—just hush up for a moment. I have to make a toast." He lifted his glass. "I want to toast Curtis and Mariela, and I want to say that I'm sure when happiness comes to a man late in life, it is an unexpected gift. An overwhelming gift. And in Curtis's hands it is well deserved. I know the man, and he has waited for this a very long time."

Mariela was in a state of euphoria, her face glowing with an expression of total love.

Curtis was the next to stand. "First of all, I want to thank everybody here. Especially Sinclair, for giving us this marvelous evening among such a great group of friends. And on September ninth you are all hereby officially invited to the wedding!" Turning to Mariela, he continued, "Darling, I have to wait until September to marry you, but I don't have to wait to give you this present."

On a prearranged signal, a steward handed him a flat package. There was total silence while Mariela opened the red velvet box and took out a necklace. A necklace of twenty-five perfectly matched bronze-black pearls, each one the size of a marble.

"It belonged to Marie Antoinette," Curtis said smiling, "and now it belongs to *my* queen."

Denise's moment was shattered. Her hands twitched. Her appetite deserted her. Only her anger remained. Anger at having been upstaged! The bracelet that only a few minutes earlier had absolutely enchanted Denise was no longer of any interest to her. Absentmindedly she unfastened its clasp and laid it beside her plate, like a five-and-dime trinket.

"Tomorrow," Sinclair announced to the assemblage, "we stop at Delphi to tour the Temple of Apollo. Then . . ."

Denise was no longer listening. Mariela's head was leaning on Curtis' shoulder. They had eyes only for each other. Once more they held hands. Once more Denise noticed the solitaire on Mariela's left hand. Pear-shaped. Flawless. Larger than her own. Denise closed her eyes and threw back her head in a gesture of extreme irritation.

Couples were on the dance floor now, led by Mariela and Curtis. Denise whispered to Sinclair, "You know, I really want to be able to enjoy tomorrow to its fullest. I have a frightful headache. I'll just leave quietly. I don't want to spoil the party." She rose and turned to leave. "And Sinclair, I want to compliment you on the remarkable Matisse you have hanging in my stateroom. I can't stop looking at it."

"Princess!" called Sinclair. "Don't forget your bracelet."

"How silly of me. And thank you again for such a lovely present." Denise took it and dropped it in her handbag. "Sinclair, you're so dear. How can I *ever* thank you for this absolutely gorgeous gift!"

"By accepting the Matisse, since you like it so much! I'll have it shipped to Rome as soon as we come into port!"

It was 9:30 on the morning of July 26 when the door of Denise's stateroom swung open. Francesco entered.

"I'm not quite ready, darling," she snapped. "Isn't it a bit early anyway to go on deck?"

He didn't answer.

Looking at him in the mirror of her dressing table, she noticed his dazed expression and the misty eyes. She turned to face him. "Is something wrong, darling? Are you ill?"

"Denise, we must leave immediately for America."

"Why?"

"I've just received word"—he blanched, his voice lowering to a whisper—"I've just received word that . . . Donatella . . ."

"What about your sister?"

"Donatella . . . was on the *Andrea Doria* . . . and—"

"And what?" interrupted Denise.

"Sometime last night . . . just south of Nantucket"—with difficulty he controlled himself—"the *Andrea Doria* collided with another ship, the *Stockholm*—" His voice broke.

Denise dropped her brush and held out her hand.

"All passengers . . . all passengers abandoned ship, but only two of the lifeboats could be used." Barely audible through his sobs, he finished his tragic tale. "The *Ile de France* picked up about a thousand survivors. They should be arriving in New York this morning."

"Francesco," she gasped, "it all sounds so impossible . . . are you sure?"

His whole body quivered with sobbing. "It just came on the ship's radio . . ."

"Francesco, please, calm yourself. If they've been rescued, perhaps you're worrying over a trifling—"

"Trifling! My sister, Denise! My sister is not trifling!" He held up his head in pathetic despair. "I can't . . . Just start packing. Please! Just—"

"But, Francesco . . . do you think it's necessary for me . . . I mean, wouldn't I just be one more thing for you to worry about if I . . . Shouldn't I just stay here?"

Francesco lifted her bodily from her stool, grabbed her by the shoulders and shook her. Hard. "Denise, what are you talking about! How can you even consider letting me go through this by myself? We must leave immediately. Sinclair has arranged for his hydroplane to get us to Athens, and his Constellation will fly us to New York. . . . But since it's obvious that you prefer to stay here and enjoy yourself, perhaps I'd *better* go alone." Francesco was almost at the door. "Donatella may be dead! The Hollywood actress Ruth Roman . . . put her little boy in a lifeboat . . . he's been reported drowned."

"Francesco," cried Denise, running toward him, "how can you misunderstand me? I merely thought, knowing how devastated you are . . ." Her voice was very gentle now and self-assured. "I thought you wouldn't want to burden yourself with me. I just . . ." She put her hands on his shoulders. "I just . . ." She searched for the right word. "I thought you'd think I'd be in the way."

"You are my wife!" he shouted. "I need you by my side!"

"I want to help."

"I'm sorry, Denise," he said apologetically, holding her close. "You must excuse me. I'm under such pressure. Ti amo."

"Oh, my dear Francesco, I'm so sorry . . . truly sorry. I wouldn't dream of letting you go through such a terrible ordeal by yourself! I belong with you . . . anywhere. I'm ready to leave whenever you are."

❊

DENISE/*Rome/Tuesday, September 4, 1956*

Princess Denise Borgia was the spirit of the twentieth century itself as she drove her low-slung convertible with roaring abandon down the old roads of history. She circled the huge Piazza Venezia, sending the pigeons whirling into the air for safety, and made a right turn in the direction of the Colosseum.

Every time she whizzed by a slower-moving vehicle—a bicycle, a cart, an automobile—Denise could see the smiles of approval and admiration come over the drivers' faces. "That's really living," they were saying. They were right. She was feeling strong. On top. In control. The way a princess should feel.

The long shadows of the early evening sun stretched their fingers across the Piazza di Spagna. Her powerful white Maserati seemed to blink on and off as it tore through the shafts of light and darkness. The ancient square bristled with great vitality, a swirl of life and colors—brown, orange, pinks melting into the gray patina of old houses.

She caught the September smell of Rome. It was like no other smell in the world—the smell of people, food, love, century-old smells still strong and evocative.

A sailor, in a daze, nearly wandered in front of the car. She swerved, avoiding him by inches. The sight of him caught her off guard. He was about the same age and height as her brother Jonathan.

Jonathan—almost five years to the day since Denise had gone home from Chicago to say goodbye to Jonathan and her mother before leaving for Buenos Aires. It was to be the last time.

※

The cab halted in Prairie, near Terre Haute, Indiana. She rubbed the brightness from her eyes as the sun hit her unexpectedly. Before entering the clapboard shack she took a quick look at the abject poverty of her childhood, vivid as a blinking neon sign, resolving never to witness it again. She pushed the screen door that separated the outside world from the kitchen.

Penury flings itself flagrantly; there is no way of opening or closing the doors of the poor without having to endure the agonizing gnawing, grating rattle of an angry latch.

"Is it you, Jonathan?"

The woman standing in front of the blackened charcoal range was dressed in odds and ends of old clothes. A picture of the Sacred Heart of Jesus framed by dusty palms from some forgotten Lent, frayed and yellow with age, hung crookedly on the wall, hiding the growing stain of rising damp, spreading like an uncontrollable disease.

Denise felt a lump in her throat.

The woman turned. Seeing it was Denise, she gave a small muffled cry, threw thin arms around her. They embraced fiercely.

Denise led her mother to a sagging couch, propped up by a Sears, Roebuck catalogue. She pressed the poor tired head to her bosom. Only the large blue eyes were ageless, the sole remnants of youth and beauty in the deeply lined face.

"Mama, I'm going away for a long time."

"What is a long time?"

"I don't know, Mama, I just don't know."

"Deeny, if you're still messin' with this show business, nothin' but evil will come of it! Believe you me! This very mornin' in church Ah was prayin' for ya, and—"

"Don't pray for me, Mama. Don't waste your time! No one's listening, no one. So please don't go begging for me! Tell me sincerely, Mama, if you had a friend who treated you the way God has in this life, would you still be speaking to him? The only one who will do something about my life is myself—and without the help of God. God is dead! And I'm enjoying the ride without him!"

"Ya are blasphemous, Deeny! Shut your mouth or I'll wash it out with soap!" Her voice was quivering.

The thirty-eight-year-old-woman, who looked fifty, got up with difficulty and went to the stove. She returned. Her broad chapped hands offered Denise a cracked cup. Grimacing, Denise swallowed the syrupy brown liquid, either okra or a blend of bean, barley, rice and bread crumbs which passed for coffee.

"Listen to me, Mama." She got up and marched her mother by the scrawny shoulders to the other side of the room, near the shelf with its small, dusty stuffed toy animals won in a long-ago country fair. "I want to live my life, Mama, not yours or anyone else's! Mine! There is no virtue in poverty; it just makes people coarse. There is no freedom in squalor. Look, Mama, look around you. This isn't the way I want to live. I don't want to wash myself in the kitchen sink. I don't want to wear blankets and coats in the house at night 'cause it's too cold. I don't want to hunt squirrel 'cause there's nothing else to eat—"

"Hush, Deeny, hush! Ah don't wanna hear ya talkin' this way!"

"You won't hear me talk this way again, Mama. . . . I want everything!"

Down the dusty road Jonathan came, his weather-beaten old Ford grunting its age, uttering a wheezing death rattle, a call to the heart.

—⁂—

What a far cry it was from Denise's luscious Maserati. To reassure herself she floored the accelerator. The Maserati's motor purred its abundant power, sleek as a royal cat, taking the rush hour traffic like a horse in a barrel race. There was pure exhilaration in the whir of the engine, a fitting match to the jubilation racing in Denise's soul: the car an expensive bundle of perpetual fury; Denise in easy mastery of the car.

—⁂—

And Jonathan—clunkata-clunkata—behind the wheel in dark-blue overalls, plaid shirt and tight-fitting cap. After supper she and her brother had gone to sit on the front porch—decayed and about to topple, with its dilapidated garden furniture, a sad tribute, a vestige of gentility that never was. They settled into rockers and tried to rock, but the old chairs were broken and only creaked, threatening to collapse completely. It was a cool, almost cold, moist, late-summer evening.

"What do you plan to do with your life, Jonathan?"

"Ah dunno . . . Ah've got a job, Sis, Ah'm okay. Ah'm in the mines all week—you know Ah been there since Ah was fourteen—and on Sundays Ah work extra at a gas station in Andersonville. Besides, Ah'll be drafted before long." His voice trailed off. Then, "What about yourself, Deeny?"

"Oh, Jonathan, I have a big future in show business, you know, and I just signed a good contract with a club in South America."

"Shucks! Ya always were the smart one!" Taking some Bugle tobacco from a cotton pouch, he rolled it skillfully in a thin paper with single-handed dexterity. They were silent for a while, listening to the sounds of dusk descending—the sharp barks of a mongrel yelping a few feet away and suddenly stopping, a jalopy croaking along the dirt road, trying to survive as far as the highway, the persistent notes of katydids linking the night with music. Aside from these, quietness engulfed them, and only leaves falling to the ground disturbed the magical stillness of the moment.

A sudden breeze ruffled the dank and stagnant air, and for a moment clean sheets flapped from a clothesline stretched to a hothouse, its broken panes patched with corrugated cardboard. "I think we'd better go inside, Jonathan. I'll see you in the morning." As Denise entered her mother's room on tiptoe she heard the whistle of a freight train.

It was the best sound she recalled while growing up, because the tracks linked with infinity—and it would make all her dreams come true . . . forever.

-※-

Denise spun down the Via Condotti, turned on Via Bocca di Leone, and slowed down. She was home. The Palazzo Borgia—an entire city block, three stories high, two hundred rooms, dating back to the twelfth century. Parts of it were now rented out to various tenants, such as the British Embassy and two Roman banks.

Denise drove through the great marble portals of the Borgia palace, which opened onto the courtyard and stables, and stopped. The concierge left his enclosed gatehouse, doffed his cap emblazoned with the family crest, and said deferentially, "Buona sera, Principessa Denise."

"Buona sera, Aldo. Please take out my packages and have them brought upstairs."

"Certamente, Principessa." He moved immediately to comply, reaching for a small package in her hand.

"Thank you, Aldo, I'll carry this one myself. Just take care of the large parcels in the back." She pulled into the enormous garage housing the prince's collection of mechanical stallions—twenty in all—and parked her white Maserati next to his black Alfa Romeo. The vehicles made a striking pair. Almost as striking as their owners, Denise thought as she strode to the main entrance. Clutching the small package firmly under her arm, she moved jauntily toward the elevator.

The glass-enclosed iron-work cage rose slowly, allowing a full view of the second floor. But she had long ceased to notice the priceless Renaissance paintings and sculptures lining the great halls. The trappings of wealth were only what Denise felt she had earned. Their artistic and historic merit had lost all consequence except as a reflection of her own rise. She was able to speak about them authoritatively with visitors, but they held no value to her beyond the riches they symbolized. Besides, they couldn't be worn. Neither could the forty servants.

The elevator halted directly before the magnificent carved doors of her private living quarters, occupying fifteen rooms on the upper floor. The palazzo itself had to be maintained in accordance with the historical-monument laws of Italy, but the interior of the Borgias' own apartment was furnished in the latest, trendiest fashion, suiting both Denise's and Francesco's tastes. There were other private quarters, such as those previously occupied by his only sister, Donatella, before she had drowned in the sinking of the *Andrea Doria*. And some of the rooms were still used by a few miscellaneous cousins who were hardly ever visible except when they were accidentally encountered in the halls from time to time.

Denise rang the bell impatiently. "Good evening, Marcello. Is the prince at home?" she asked the white-gloved majordomo.

"Yes, Principessa Denise," he answered, closing the door behind her. "But His Highness does not wish to be disturbed."

"Did he say he wasn't to be disturbed . . . by anyone? Surely he couldn't have meant me? Perhaps the prince is not feeling well. I'll go see."

"I'm sorry, Principessa, but his instructions were quite explicit," continued Marcello hesitantly. "Absolutely *no one* is to disturb him."

"All right. All right," she said, obviously annoyed. "Please tell Yvette to come to my room at once." Denise's high heels clacked determinedly down the black-marbled corridor. Maybe Francesco *was* busy. In spite of the many people in his employ, he did take a personal interest in the affairs associated with his vast wealth. At least from time to time.

She entered her richly appointed oyster-colored damask boudoir.

Yvette was already there. "Did you have a good day, Madame la Princesse?"

"Perfectly wonderful," she said, effusively. The thought of her latest acquisitions from Rome's most exclusive shops restored Denise's good mood. "Best of all, Yvette," she continued exuberantly, "I wasn't hounded by those paparazzi." She laughed. "They must have been on strike!" As the extravagant wife of Europe's richest and handsomest prince, Denise had become one of their most sought-after photographic subjects. Her face on the cover of practically every fashion magazine—and the detailed story of the famous couple in the April issue of *Paris Match,* coinciding with their second wedding anniversary—had done nothing to diminish Denise's reputation as the toast of the Continent.

Rapidly she walked to her Venetian mirrored dressing table, decorated with a fourteen carat gold dresser set that had belonged to Francesco's grandmother, and sat down. Carla, her personal secretary, entered the boudoir. "Any calls for me?" Denise spoke over her shoulder.

"Oh, yes, Principessa Denise. Many. Count and Countess Montevida called to invite you and the Principe for the evening of—"

"Did they mention if it will be a large gathering? With the prince still in mourning . . ."

"Yes, certainly, Principessa. It is an intimate dinner."

"Well, in that case we shall accept. Have you arranged with the florist to have—"

"Yes, the flowers will be delivered on the ninth, on time for Lady Chelmsford's wedding—"

"Carla, I hope you didn't address the card to 'Lady Chelmsford'! Please make certain to use her married name, 'Mrs. Curtis Lodge III.' "

"That's what I did, Principessa."

It was strange, thought Denise, that Mariela insisted on a very private wedding in Zurich. To be marrying Mr. Curtis Lodge III—wouldn't she want the whole world to know? There was something elusive she couldn't quite grasp about this Lady Chelmsford.

"Also, the embassy called and would like you to attend a luncheon on the eleventh honoring Mrs. Mamie Eisenhower. It will be—"

"Make some excuse. I don't care for these boring political luncheons. Is that all, Carla?"

"No, there was one more call. Long distance, from Texas. Mr. Sinclair MacAlpine. He's leaving for Zurich tomorrow to attend the Curtis Lodge wedding but will stop in Rome on the tenth before returning home."

At the mention of Sinclair's name Denise's head snapped around. Sinclair! Was he still as flirtatious as ever? It did wonders for her ego. Hah! Good thing he'd got rid of Carolyn, that inane last wife of his. "No other calls, then?"

"No, Principessa."

"All right, you may leave."

She began to unwrap the package she had been carrying so carefully. She removed what lay inside and placed it around her neck. "Would you help me, Yvette?" The maid came behind Denise and attached the clasp. They were both silent for a moment. One hundred and fifty thousand dollars' world of diamonds sparkled on her neck. Deep sapphires accented the extraordinary gems and reflected the color of Denise's glowing blue eyes.

"Oh, Madame la Princesse!" rhapsodized Yvette. "You have so many jewels, but this is clearly the most . . . the most . . . merveilleux! What is the occasion?"

"It's my wedding anniversary present! I've been waiting for it since April. These sapphires are of such rare quality, it took Bulgari all this time to match them!" She rose, grabbed Yvette and waltzed her around the room. "Oh, Yvette, it's such a shame my husband is still in mourning for his sister. I would have loved to go to Mrs. Lodge's wedding in Zurich—just loved to. But now I won't have a chance to show the necklace properly for several months!"

Denise's eyes wandered to a solid gold clock on the mantelpiece. "Oh, good God! It's already nine! Please get me the prince on the intercom." Denise studied herself intently in the four-paneled beveled screen that gave back her reflection a dozen times. The brilliance of the necklace on her high-necked white jersey sheath was unsurpassed. There was no question whatever—she created a stunning picture. She glanced up at the portrait of herself on the wall. The one painted by Salvador Dali only the year before. Denise never had been sure whether or not she liked it. There was a disturbing coldness about the image.

Yvette interrupted her reverie. "I'm sorry, but the prince does not answer."

"Well, never mind. Draw me a bath. I have only half an hour to get ready before supper, and I want to look spectacular this evening."

"What oil would you prefer in the tub, Madama la Princesse?"

"Night Sanctuary. And use lots of it!" she said gaily.

"Which gown will you be wearing?"

"The Dior taffeta. Oh—and have Guido bring a bottle of chilled Dom Perignon and two glasses. Hurry, Yvette!"

It was nearly a quarter to ten when Denise left for the Giacometti dining room, where she and Francesco had their evening meals when they were alone or when they had fewer than eight guests. She took a deep breath before going in, wanting to make a grand entrance. The room was dark. She switched on the lights. The round glass table had not been set. The elongated Giacometti sculptures lined up against the wall seemed foreboding. She picked up the house phone and pushed the button connecting it directly to the kitchen.

"What is going on, Marcello?" she asked brusquely. "I'm in the Giacometti room. Where is dinner being served?"

"Scusi, Principessa. I thought you knew. Principe Francesco wished to have supper in the formal dining room."

"Why the formal dining room? Does the prince have guests?"

"No, Principessa."

She hung up, completely bewildered, and walked out. At the end of a long carpeted hallway, she smoothed the elegant strapless white gown, her fingers touching again the extraordinary necklace. Denise turned the Lalique glass doorknob very slowly.

The black onyx and chrome table was lit by a large modern silver candelabrum, sculptured by Brancusi, in the shape of a hand. A bouquet of white roses and lilacs stood at its center. The table had been set for two with a Wedgwood dinner service. In the semidarkness a geometric-patterned Georgia O'Keeffe mural in black, white and blue, and another by Chagall in shades of reds and grays, were hardly visible.

Precious objets d'art were silhouetted behind the glass panes of a Carrara marble cabinet of overpowering lines. It contained the real star of the room and Denise's most prized possession. The object, made by Fabergé, was called the Peacock Egg and had once belonged to the Dowager Empress of Russia.

Standing nine inches in height, it shimmered in all its splendor beneath its own tiny spotlight. The priceless museum piece was made entirely of rock crystal, supported on a base of solid gold encrusted with large sapphires and cabochon rubies. Inside the partly open egg a finely wrought many-hued enameled peacock perched on branches of platinum covered with flowers of rare pink and yellow diamonds.

Denise paused before the glittering trophy of her first great conquest—a trophy for all the world to see. A wedding gift from Escobar Ortiz!

She scanned the room.

"Franscesco," she purred, "are you in here?"

"Yes, I am." Francesco's voice came from behind her.

Startled, she turned. And then she saw him—sitting in a gray silk armchair at the far end of the immense room, dressed in black as usual, a mourning band circling his left arm, holding a drink, the pet raven on his shoulder.

"Amore, what are you doing in the dark?" She came toward him.

"I see well enough," he answered quietly, still staring at her and past her, to the Peacock Egg.

"How do I look, Francesco?" Denise pirouetted girlishly.

He took in her exquisite features, the distinction of her bearing, the dress that set off her small waist and high, firm breasts. He focused on the necklace resting on the soft white skin. "You look beautiful."

"What about the necklace? Isn't *it* beautiful? Thank you, my dearest darling. You have such good taste! Isn't it the most beautiful necklace you've ever seen?" she repeated, fingering the jewels.

"Yes," he said simply, stroking the raven.

"Is that all you have to say, amore? Why, it's the most extraordinary—!"

Two liveried butlers appeared with trays. Denise walked to the table holding onto Francesco's arm. He held her chair while she seated herself. "Please take Brutus," he told the butler, lifing the bird from his shoulder and detaching the gold chain that held it to his wrist.

"Just the two of us in this enormous dining room," Denise said, "makes me feel like the heroine of a Visconti movie."

"You are, Denise." His voice had a brooding intensity.

"Why are we dining here?"

"I wanted to celebrate."

"Oh, darling! We must have had the same thought! Having gotten the necklace today, I wanted to celebrate our second wedding anniversary again." She turned her blue serene, innocent eyes on him. "But wouldn't it have been cozier in my . . . sitting room?"

He didn't answer. A footman stood between them, placing and removing dishes quietly.

"Francesco, is something bothering you?"

"I've had a very busy day." He gripped his glass tightly, as though it contained a message not to be read by anyone.

The meal was over and they were both sipping their espresso in strained silence. Francesco was staring across the room. Puzzled by his behavior, Denise followed his gaze, which had come to a halt on the glass-and-marble cabinet. Not just on the glass-and-marble cabinet but unwaveringly on the Fabergé Peacock Egg.

"Would you like a Strega, Signore Principe?" a butler asked.

"No, thank you. That will be all, and good night." Francesco picked a cigarette from a platinum case and lit it with a matching lighter.

Denise sighed. "I wanted this evening to be very special." She reached for his hand. "You still haven't told me how much you like the necklace."

"It's a great pity."

The enigmatic response took Denise by surprise. "What's a pity?"

"That such beauty should conceal such a lie."

"What are you talking about, Francesco? Please, I'm not in the mood for games right now. I feel so happy . . ."

He hesitated before he spoke again. Just enough for Denise to feel uncomfortable.

"I had a visitor this afternoon."

"Yes, I know. Whoever it was must have been important. Marcello told me you were not to be disturbed. Who was it?"

"Someone I believe you know."

"Who?"

"Mrs. Grantham."

"Mrs. Grantham? I don't believe I know a Mrs. Grantham."

"I believe you do," he said. "But perhaps your memory could be refreshed." The patrician face lit up with malice. "Do you have a recollection of The Hall and Sir Reginald Findlay?"

Her high-voltage blue eyes blinked. "Those names don't mean anything to me. Why should they?"

"Because you spent some time with them at The Hall just before we were married. In February 1954 you entered as a slut and came out a virgin—"

"No, it's not I. You're mistaken," she said firmly. "I've never been to England!"

Francesco slipped his hand away from hers. Rather carefully, he put his cigarette out and delicately picked a shred of tobacco from his tongue. He looked straight into her face. "But Denise, I never mentioned the word *England!*"

Unsteadily, she rose and walked toward the cabinet, gripping it fiercely just in time to steady her faltering balance.

"But you *are* right, Denise, it *is* England. I have all the proofs here in my safe—the bills, the X-rays, the admission forms that you yourself signed. Can you deny it? Can you deny that last June when you were supposedly attending the funeral of your 'godfather' in Buenos Aires, you went there again to have our child aborted?" Francesco sprang to his feet, overturning his chair. "A child you never told me about. But I probably flatter myself. Maybe it was not my child. I suddenly realize that the father could have been anyone in the world!"

It had been Francesco's child. Of that she was certain. But the thought of having a child by anybody made her cringe. A creature that would distort her body and require her attention. The abortion had freed her.

"How can you believe these wild stories?"

Francesco's eyes swung to a photograph of himself with Lord Mountbatten, as if to transfer his anger to the population of Great Britain.

"The woman is crazy!" Denise insisted, her radiance suddenly diminished. "Absolutely crazy!"

"Crazy enough to demand one hundred thousand pounds to keep this delightful story out of *Paris Match!* Mrs. Grantham seemed to think it would be a fitting sequel to their April issue glorifying 'The Most Perfect Couple in the World.'" Francesco was gesticulating wildly. "Do you really believe I'd be stupid enough to pay that kind of blackmail money unless I knew for certain that it was the truth?"

"What truth, Francesco?" she stammered. "I don't understand."

"You don't understand? How could you understand the truth! Oh, before our marriage I heard rumors, Denise. I'm not deaf. But I was blind. Blind with love! How could I believe that *you* were a woman who had taken so many excursions to hell and back!" His voice rose in pitch and volume. "You actually trembled on our wedding day! You blushed! You held my hand for strength! A flawless performance that took me in completely! And now—now! Only now do I find out that the American tramp has made a colossal fool of the Roman prince!" His words echoed from the walls of the enormous chamber, harsh and funereal. "How your whoremaster of a 'godfather' must have laughed himself silly when he walked you down the aisle and gave his 'virgin niece' to me!"

"It's not like that at all," she protested feebly.

"It *is*, Denise. It *is*. You are—" His eyes searched her face for a sign of concern but found only the usual sculpted perfection, somewhat paler. "You are . . . like that egg of yours. The most beautiful, most expensive exterior in the world. But a mere shell. Inside you are a preening, unfeeling monster. Under the layers of your fantasies I was hoping to find your real nature. But there is nothing. Absolutely nothing!"

He lurched toward the cabinet. "That jeweled peacock egg!" he continued. "Escobar's wedding present—or was it a final payment? What a joke! A quarter million-dollar joke—on me!" He fumbled at the gold filigree key, but his fingers were wet with sweat and the key fell to the floor, sliding out of reach. In uncontrollable rage, his hand formed a fist. He smashed through the glass pane, his fingers groping for the prize. Denise placed herself between him and the precious Fabergé egg. Francesco pushed her aside brutally.

Now she was against the wall. "I did it *for* you. I love you!"

"Love? You don't know the meaning of the word!" Francesco snarled, the blood streaking his wrist and raining drops on the floor. "You patched-up whore of an Argentine dotard!" He was crying, without noise, without sobs. The way men cry.

With electrifying speed he veered around and once again attacked the cabinet. Furiously his stone fist scraped past the ragged edges of glass as he swatted dementedly at the egg. Again Denise tried to protect it, but this time her efforts only drove his hand to the target. The Fabergé relic flew open. Its jeweled peacock fell to Francesco's feet in erratic movement, spilling forth its jarring music-box sounds. Francesco kicked it. The jeweled peacock was now lying on its side, but the music went on. La, la, la, la-la, LA-LA, LA-LA . . . Denise's Peacock Egg seemed indestructible. The sounds of "The Blue Danube" unremittingly filled the room.

Prince Borgia towered over Denise. The rising full moon cast its glow on her hair, surrounding it with a silver halo, which shattered under the blow from his open right hand.

Her head swam with pain as she saw him run from the room. A few moments later she heard the roar of the Alfa Romeo as it hurtled from the courtyard below.

The car leaped from the palazzo and screamed its way to the Via Appia. The prince drove as though the demons of hell were racing him for his very soul.

He lost. The street was too narrow, the Alfa too fast, the curve too sharp. The massive tree hid itself, its branches blocking the moonlight. The soul of Francesco Borgia left him in an instant as the car wrapped itself around the tree, tortured metal twisting itself and his body into shapeless death. Flares from the exploding gasoline tank ignited the huge cypress, and his funeral pyre illuminated the night sky.

When word reached Denise at the Palazzo Borgia she was in the vast library, trying to concentrate on the last pages of Pearl Buck's *Imperial Woman,* still wearing the white gown. The white gown and the necklace. She broke down and wept bitterly and was left with her grief by sympathetic police officials. The family attorney had been advised, and it was comforting for Denise to know that every detail would be taken care of.

When the household finally retired, Denise threw herself face down among the silk and lace pillows of her bed, weeping uncontrollably once again. From the night table she picked up a picture of herself and Francesco on their wedding day. Taken April 7, 1954, at the fairy-tale Borgia palace in Tuscany—a medieval structure surrounded by verdant countryside and protecting drawbridges. Francesco would be buried there in the family crypt.

"He was everything a woman could dream of. Where will I ever find another man like him?" she cried out loud. Unconsciously her hand clutched at her throat; the necklace was still there. She replaced the picture.

The sobs diminished in violence, melted into barely audible whispers, dissolved into a flux of silent tears. Ceased.

She sat on the edge of her bed. Silent. Fidgeting with the damp handkerchief embroidered with the crest of the house of Borgia, she rose and began looking for her shoes. Slipping them on, she walked across her bedroom and the adjoining sitting room, passed through Francesco's quarters, and entered a corridor that led to his private library. It was dark. Closing the door behind her and securing the latch, she switched on a single light and walked resolutely to a mahogany Chippendale shell-carved chest of drawers. She pressed a button concealed in its ornate pattern and stepped back as the center panel opened automatically, revealing a hidden safe.

Denise swiftly worked the dial, as she had done so many times—four to the left, seven to the right, once around to the left again to fifty-four. Francesco had matched the combination to the date of their wedding, 4–7–1954.

Dropping to her knees, she began to search, her long nails catching on slender jeweled chains, which she brushed aside like cobwebs. The mounds of papers, banknotes, even her own precious gems which filled every inch of space—all made her impatient. Determinedly she searched. Cufflinks—diamond studs—watches—trinkets bought for Francesco over the past two years. More papers—she read each one of them. Marriage certificate—deeds—bonds—passports—bankbooks—more banknotes—more bonds—and finally a fat envelope, through which she riffled quickly. She sighed with relief and put it aside. With the envelope clutched in her hand, she closed the safe, switched off the light and returned to her unwelcoming room, back to the unwelcoming present. To a world that had come to an end.

With a match she ignited a page at a time and flung the damning evidence into the fireplace—X-rays, admittance forms, photographs, prescriptions, invoices marked "Paid in full" . . . Goodbye, goodbye forever to The Hall, to Mrs. Grantham. Burn, yesterday, burn!

Was she wrong? No! Francesco had fallen in love with the image *she* had created. An image created carefully for just such a man as he. Would Francesco have wanted her any other way? But of course not!

Feeling utterly alone, Denise was flooded with the harsh awareness of the problems widowhood would bring. She was twenty-four years old. The home on the Riviera was hers, as well as a fortune in jewels. But there was the palazzo to worry about. And the paintings. And the yacht. And the fleet of cars and the palace in Tuscany. And—and— She was Francesco's only close living relative, but there were all those cousins, distant and not so distant . . . She had to be careful to see that nothing was lost. Besides, all the properties and bank accounts were in Francesco's name.

Who could understand what she was going through? Her confusion? Her distress? Her fear? Whom could she turn to? If only Escobar were still alive, he might listen, understand, advise. But what point in thinking about Escobar? Escobar was dead. Gone, like Francesco. Who . . . who else . . .? "Who?" she cried out loud.

Sinclair MacAlpine came to her mind. A friend since her days with Escobar. Yes, Sinclair was her friend, he cared. Now, if only . . . What was it he had said earlier to her secretary Carla? Oh yes, he'd be in Rome after Mariela's wedding, on the tenth—five days from now. Could she wait that long? No.

Frantically she rummaged through her desk until she found her phone book. She checked the time. It was two-thirty in the morning. Still late afternoon in Texas. Denise placed a call to Dallas. The overseas operator started it on its way and Denise waited out the clicks and buzzes that preceded the rings on the other end. After many intermediaries she was finally connected to Sinclair MacAlpine's private secretary.

"I'm sorry, but Mr. MacAlpine is in conference. Would you like to leave word?"

"No, no. It is very important that I speak to Mr. MacAlpine immediately. Please tell him Princess Borgia is calling from Rome. Please!" Her voice was teary and insistent.

"Just a moment, ma'am—Princess."

"I'll wait." The seconds ticked by interminably.

"All right, go ahead. Mr. MacAlpine is on the line."

"Denise, what a surprise!" the voice boomed with a heavy Texas twang. "I wasn't expecting a return call from the prettiest princess in the world. Anyway, I assume Carla told you—"

"Sinclair!" she interrupted, weeping into the telephone. "Oh, my dear Sinclair. I've just had a terrible tragedy . . ." As Denise recited the night's events her sobbing became more intense. "Sinclair, I'm all alone . . ."

The voice on the other end came back strong and soothing. "Denise, I'm just sorry as all get-out. My poor Denise. But I am flattered you should remember me in such a crisis. I'm the right person to turn to. You'll have a shoulder to cry on by this time tomorrow. I can be on my plane within an hour."

"What about the Curtis Lodge wedding?"

"I'll just leave for Zurich from Rome, instead of the other way around."

"Oh, Sinclair, I'd be so grateful. How can I ever thank you!"

"Oh, forget it, Princess. That's what friends are for."

"Sinclair . . . I also need legal advice about the estate . . ."

"Don't you worry your pretty little head, Princess. I'll bring my lawyer and we'll take it from there."

"Oh, Sinclair, thank you. I just didn't know where else to turn. It's a nightmare. I keep trying to wake up, but I'm *already* awake. Francesco's things are all around me, and he's not here." Her hand stroked the stones around her throat. "I keep waiting for him, and then I realize he won't be back." She sobbed loudly. "I'm sorry that I'm behaving like this."

"Go ahead and cry, honey. Get it all out of your system. It's a terrible tragedy. But I'll help you in any way I can. My yacht is in the Mediterranean somewhere. As soon as the . . . as the funeral is over, I'll put it at your disposal. Go wherever you want. Take somebody along. A close friend or two. It'll do you good. Princess, you did well to call me. You are not 'all alone.' Li'l ole Sinclair will take care of everything."

※

DENISE/*Castello del Nuncio*/*Friday, September 14, 1956*

The frenzied preparation for Francesco's last voyage permeated every corner of the Roman palazzo. All the walls of the immense palace had been draped in black velvet, all works of art cloaked in mourning, with only religious subjects exposed to bear witness to the death of the last prince of the house of Borgia.

Sinclair MacAlpine had arrived from Dallas as promised and had stayed with Denise for two days before the Mariela Chelmsford-Curtis Lodge wedding. He cared. They spoke late into the night. She seemed to him an extraordinarily noble woman, calm and courageous, suffering through her tragedy. A woman who in some mysterious way had apparently suffered before. Sinclair wondered how suffering could even have touched Denise.

Dawn came to the medieval Castello del Nuncio—with its superb gardens, private amphitheater, statuary, columns, cascades, fountains, Etruscan ruins, and drawbridge—which for centuries had been the Tuscany seat of the Borgia family. The funeral day arrived, with all its pageantry, grandeur, and spectacle, and rich and poor joined in the same thought, to pay a last homage to their fallen lord of the realm.

After the festivities of the Zurich wedding Sinclair MacAlpine had flown directly to Florence and driven the sixty miles to Nuncio. He stood at the stone-and-gold door carved by Michelangelo which adorned the family's private chapel. A luxurious carriage, drawn by a pair of dashing bays, came rumbling down the road. When he heard the sound Sinclair held his breath. He would be calm and strong, taking Denise's hand if she held it out to him. She would need him. He would comfort her. He stood waiting for her.

He was waiting for Denise. But not *this* Denise. Not this colorless, sad-faced Denise. Wearing a heavy black dress trimmed with glistening jet and cloudy tulle, she stepped from the carriage, stoically refusing any help.

In a trance she moved through the role cast for her by centuries of tradition. Borgia tradition. Tuscan tradition. The ancient rites and rituals of the region. She followed the coffin, flower-strewn with remembrances flung from the windows and houses it had passed.

As in all funerals of the landed aristocracy of Tuscany, the whole town had filed into the church. The town that had worshiped the Borgias for centuries, had worked their land, had prayed for their families and heirs. As was the custom, they did not weep their sorrow. The hour had not yet arrived.

Papal Envoy Cardinal Antonio Ballestrieri delivered the eulogy. The coffin was eased into the family crypt, where it would rest for all eternity beside Francesco's father, Alessandro, his mother, Loredana, his sister, Donatella.

Denise kneeled and laid a cross of white orchids on the casket. Then the crypt was sealed. With solemn tread the procession withdrew to a hill that overlooked the lands Francesco had loved for twenty-seven years and would walk no more.

Silently each man, each woman, young and old alike, who had ever served or been related to the Borgia household, stood, holding a lighted candle.

Their silence spoke. It spoke death.

From behind her sheer veil Denise observed the faces—Francesco's people and Francesco's friends. No one stirred. Not even the breathing of the children could be heard.

Now—another enduring tradition—the slow steps of the prince's personal valet echoed in the eerie soundlessness. He walked, crunching gravel underfoot, nearing the coachman, who held the reins of four black-draped horses. With a loud, commanding voice that pierced the silence, he spoke the age-old words "Our master no longer needs us!"

This was the ancient signal. As one, the people fell to their knees, their hearts beating in unison, their grief shared. The wails burst forth, wrenching, shrieking, distraught, expressing the simple pagan poetry of anguish. Bells tolled their lugubrious dirge. A thousand souls appealed to the Almighty in their agony, a testimony to the high rank of their prince. A testimony to a man who was still alive in their sorrow as he had once lived in their love.

The mingling of sounds, sights, the total awareness of what had befallen her world, invaded Denise's heart.

This was real. Denise was shaken. She had . . . lost. Lost Francesco irretrievably. Now she was alone. Alone, yet determined not to fall backward in life. She could not.

Sinclair was by her side. Twice she tried to speak, but the dryness of her throat prevented it. Her breath labored painfully through her parched lips. "It's so sad," she said at last hoarsely.

Now they were only inches apart against a smudged horizon.

He expected her to say more. But there was no more. Only that. Sinclair held her arm, and for a few moments Denise leaned on him for support as they entered the limousine. A great darkness closed around her in which she neither spoke nor moved. She raised her veil, exposing the pale face, the trembling lips and the tears dimming her eyes. What was there about this child, this woman, this enigmatic creature, what was it that transcended the ceremony and made Sinclair want to take away her hurt?

They journeyed back to Rome. Sinclair stayed for the next three days. Denise remained numb, silent, distracted, threatened by her own inner sense of loss. When it was time for Sinclair to depart she sat dully in her chair. He leaned over her and kissed her on the forehead. She felt nothing.

"Princess, please. If there's something I can do—I'll do anything—"

"I can't thank you enough. You've done so much already." She smiled wanly. "Really, there's nothing."

"Why don't you take my yacht? It's at your disposal. Please. It will make me happy." He spoke with soft-voiced concern.

"Thank you, but no. The last time I was on your yacht Francesco was still . . ." Her hands fell to her lap. Once more she fell into silence.

"Tell me what you want me to do. I'll make you a promise, Princess. I'll always be there for you if you need me. Please need me . . ."

"Give me time, Sinclair."

"Princess, for you I have all the time in the world."

A faint smile played around Denise's lips.

"What are you smiling about, Princess?"

"Was I?"

She was offering questions for answers, an old protective trick. The cryptic code of the newly alone. Or the unconscious reaction to a very private thought on the way to its full fruition.

—�֍—

DENISE/*Rome*/*September, 1956 to April, 1957*

During the remainder of September and October Denise stayed very much by herself at the Borgia palace in Rome. It never once entered her mind that she had been the cause of all this tragedy. In fact, persuaded that by his reckless driving Francesco had thoughtlessly abandoned her, she felt greatly disturbed. Restless and bitter, she went on a shopping binge, ordering several thousand dollars' worth of hostess gowns by Fabiani.

Sinclair called regularly and saw to it that Denise was supplied daily with fresh white flowers. By the end of October she resumed entertaining intimate friends for lunch and dinner and, with the help of Carla, her secretary, began answering the hundreds of letters of condolence that had poured in from all over the world. A touching note from Mariela and Curtis, postmarked Hawaii, triggered in Denise an intense jealousy at their obvious happiness.

In November, with the invaluable help of Sinclair's attorneys, Francesco's last will and testament was probated. The Tuscano palazzo was bequeathed to the city of Florence with the stipulation that it be preserved as a museum. The prince had done the same with the Roman palazzo, directing, however, that members of his family who were now living there could continue to do so for the rest of their lives.

Denise's apartment and all its furnishings were hers to do with as she wished. She sold the yacht, *Raven,* which she'd never cared for anyway, considering it a man's boat, not very comfortable at all. Francesco's fleet of cars were distributed among his close friends, with Denise keeping her white Maserati, Francesco's black M.G., and the Mercedes-Benz. His saddle horses were piously donated to the mounted guards of the Vatican. The only income allotted Denise was the interest from a trust fund, which would cease in the event of her remarriage.

It was clear to Denise that while only a few months ago she had enjoyed the privileges of being one of the world's richest princesses, she was far from being the world's richest widow.

With her affairs in order, Denise flew to New York in Sinclair's private plane. Staying at his usual headquarters at the Pierre Hotel, he joined her for several innocent dinners at her Fifth Avenue apartment. Whenever Denise ventured out of her building, her picture appeared in major newspapers around the world. The only time a photographer caught them together, Denise bought the negatives to prevent their publication. She sent two prints anonymously—one to Sinclair's estranged wife, Carolyn, another to the Dallas *Morning Herald.*

By December she was back in Paris, having stripped the palazzo of her favorite personal possessions. Home would not be home without their presence. Denise would not be Denise without her Fabergé egg. Although Sinclair was in Japan on business, he had not forgotten her, and at Christmas he gave her the priceless painting "Les Deux Amies," by Courbet.

In January, among the headlines Denise read with keen interest was this one: THIRD WIFE OF SINCLAIR MACALPINE GRANTED $11,000,000, LARGEST SETTLEMENT IN DIVORCE HISTORY. "After a one-and-a-half-year separation, former actress Carolyn Turner retained . . ."

By February, Sinclair was calling Denise daily. She visited for a week at his Palm Springs estate. Their every move was chronicled in the society pages.

March found Denise at the Château d'Antibes. She had reached a time of strange inner peace. She could read or listen to music or simply lie on her bed or a couch with no one else to witness her idleness. Something was over, and the next thing had not begun to happen. Yet.

April came and with it the official period of mourning was ended. Denise shed her widow's weeds. Sinclair offered to celebrate with her in Paris. She accepted.

Sinclair MacAlpine arrived in Paris on April 21 as scheduled. He went directly to his penthouse at the Plaza-Athénée Hotel. It was his birthday. Seeing himself in the full-length mirror, he thought, Let's face it, Sinclair MacAlpine, you are fifty-five! Turn him around, face him sideways, dim the lights, there was no help for it. Then he raised his head high. "Still and all," he told himself, "being one of the richest men in the world has a way of making you feel years younger." He emitted a sound that resembled a chuckle.

Sinclair MacAlpine felt a compulsive need for Denise. Her style, beauty and brains, her whole attitude, represented the unapproachable.

Now was his moment. He had to prove to himself, to everyone, that this remote, beautiful young girl, who could easily pass for his daughter, could love him. He would *make* her love him. He would, at any cost. At *all* costs!

Denise had gotten up at 7:30 A.M. Guillaume arrived promptly at 8:00 to make certain her hair would be freshly done. Her masseur came at 9:00. By 11:00 she was dressed in a white Chanel suit, a silk-and-lace shirt framing her face. She slipped on her Junker diamond and waited. At the gentle sound of the bell she rose and stepped gracefully to the door.

Sinclair MacAlpine stood before her. He wore a navy pinstripe suit, a light-blue silk shirt and a maroon tie. He stepped into the marble foyer, dropping his Stetson on the white console. Denise closed the door.

"Denise, my dearest Denise," he whispered, pulling her toward him. "I have waited so long for this moment. You'll never know how long—how much I need you!" He kissed her on both cheeks, slowly nearing her lips. Denise turned her head slightly to the left and gave him her fingers to kiss instead. He held her hand, inhaling its sweet fragrance.

They moved toward the sunny drawing room. Denise attempted to uncork a bottle of champagne.

"Let me help you with that, Princess," exclaimed Sinclair. "But—how did you know?"

"How did I know what?"

"Well"—he hesitated—"that it's my birthday." He filled both glasses.

"Today! Why didn't you tell me?" cried Denise. "I would have bought you a present. Oh, Sinclair!"

"Princess, you could not have given me a better present than the pleasure of gazing on your beauty." He took her by the shoulders, his face in her hair. She bent down, picked up the glass on the table and sipped, smiling.

"Oh boy, oh boy," he exulted, "have I got a night planned for us, Princess! You've had so much sorrow, so much tragedy, so much to forget. Tonight I intend to make sure you do just that. You'll be my hostess. We'll start with cocktails in my apartment—I've the entire penthouse at the Plaza-Athénée. Then we'll move on to Maxim's . . ."

Denise walked slowly toward the window.

". . . I've invited the Rothschilds, Countess d'Harcourt, Darryl Zanuck with his new flame, Bella Darvi, Aly Khan and Bettina . . . there'll be some of my Texas buddies here on business . . . oh, and two of my best friends, Mariela and Curtis Lodge."

"She too?" she said, less with bitterness than resignation.

"Who—Mariela? Don't you like her? She's a hell of a girl. Besides, she makes Curtis happy, and that's good enough for me. And from what he tells me, I hear she's—she must be doing something right!" He laughed loudly, raucously, slapping his thigh.

Sinclair took out a cigar. "You don't mind cigars, Princess?" Without waiting for an answer he continued. "Roger Vadim will join us. He's bringing his wife, Brigitte what's-her-name—I plan to invest in his films!" He faced Denise and stood quietly for a moment. "Let me take you to lunch, Princess. I'm mighty hungry. Afterward we'll go to Cartier. You can help me select some knickknacks for my guests. I love to surprise them by leaving things in their table napkins. Yes sirree! They sure love that!"

"But, Sinclair," she said girlishly, "it's *your* birthday, not theirs!"

He continued speaking. She was hardly listening, enraptured by the stream of unending delights, all programmed for her. She was about to say something, or she was about to say more, when he placed his finger on her lips and resumed his nonstop account of the itinerary he had planned for their Paris visit.

Sinclair helped Denise into her white broadtail jacket, opened the front door, and stopped. He gently touched her arm and tried once more to pull her close to him. She disengaged herself from his embrace and stepped back. This time his hand was hard on her wrist.

"I'll wait for you, Denise, I will." He lifted her chin. "But still and all, what do you want?"

Returning his studied gaze with innocence, she coolly replied, "I want everything."

He would have taken her in his arms, he would have kissed the hem of her dress, he would have cried that he loved her, this girl who before all the world was beautiful, to be desired. How could he resist her? This was a woman he wanted to worship. But he throttled the madness and simply said, "Will you marry me?"

"Yes," she replied.

❋

It was Saturday, May 3, 1958, when the world's most heralded newlyweds, Denise and Sinclair MacAlpine, along with a retinue of sixteen, arrived at the Havana airport aboard the *Sin-Den,* their luxurious private Constellation jet. They were met by a fleet of limousines that drove right up to the landing strip.

Photographers and reporters poured out of the gates, and Sinclair's bodyguards rushed ahead to keep them at a distance. Denise and Sinclair rode in a custom-made Lincoln Continental, which led the eight-mile parade to the center of the city and their destination, the renowned Nacional Hotel.

More photographers, reporters and local officials had turned out to greet them. The general manager himself escorted Denise and Sinclair through the flower-filled lobby and the mob of gaping tourists, into a private elevator, which ascended directly to the royal suite, which encompassed the entire top floor.

Denise found herself in an immense white drawing room. She smelled fresh paint and guessed that the place had been redecorated especially for her.

"I hope you like the color, Princess," said Sinclair. A wry smile crossed his face. "Nothing's too good for my Princess!"

Crisp whiteness was all around them. Masses of white flowers cascaded in lush array from terra-cotta pots on the tables. White. Abundant. Endless.

An open terrace surrounded the penthouse on all sides. Denise rushed to it, and Sinclair followed, camera in hand, snapping shots of his always perfectly posed bride.

"That's a good shot, Princess. Stand over there, so we can have the Prado Avenue in the background." The superb boulevard came into view. "Stand over here, so we can get the Parque del Maines on the waterfront. . . . Over there now, by the Morro Castle. You know, the Spaniards built the damn fortress in the sixteenth century. . . . Come over here now. See that fancy construction behind you? That's the Convent of Santa Clara, where Christopher Columbus is buried. Anyway, that's what they say. . . . Wait! Wait! Let's get one with La Fuerza, the watchtower. Move to the right . . . more, more, so I can see the weather vane La Habana, shaped like a woman. Did you know, Denise, that's how the city got its name?"

"Sinclair"—she smiled vaguely—"you know so much."

"Yup! I did my homework. I want my little gal to be proud of me. . . . Move closer . . . smile . . . Beautiful, baby, you look gorgeous. One more smile, Princess . . . that's it. Now, come on. Let's go inside. I've shot two rolls of film already. And now . . . I want you to have a cocktail with me."

"Sinclair, dear, must we? Isn't it a little early?"

"Really, I think you'll appreciate *this* cocktail." He beamed. "I just bet you will."

He led her through the doors of another airy drawing room, pointing to a huge crystal receptacle shaped like a champagne glass. It could easily have contained two hundred gallons.

Instead it was a cocktail of quite a different nature. Denise remained silent to conceal her bewilderment. Startled, unable to catch her breath, she wiped her face with the back of her hand several times as if to remove some invisible stain from her cheeks. Unable to restrain herself, she ran across the room and plunged both hands into the glass, scattering its contents around her on the floor.

"Big, isn't it!" Sinclair glowed. "In Texas, when you're big, you do things in a big way! That bowl's from Nieman-Marcus. The only one like it in the world!"

Not listening, Denise waded through the treasures. First was a floor-length ermine coat labeled "Nieman-Marcus" and initialed "D.MacA." Then she pulled out a piece of paper, unrolled it, and looked at Sinclair in amazement. "These . . . these look like architectural plans."

"Right you are, Denise. I bought the apartment next to yours on Avenue Foch in Paris. Now, instead of seven rooms, you'll have fifteen." He chuckled. "I gave Jensen's carte blanche in decorating it, and they promised to have it ready by the time we return to Paris!"

Next Denise came up with two tiny items that she cradled in both hands —a miniature silver Rolls Royce and a small model of a boat. Again she turned to Sinclair, eyelashes blinking. "A boat?"

"Why, yes, Princess. I bought you a speedboat in the south of France so you can go water-skiing whenever you like." Denise was speechless. "And I've even taken the liberty of christening it for you," he said. "Can you guess what I've called it?" There was a twinkle in his eye. "I've named it the *White Lady*. How about that. The White *Lady!*" He was proud of himself.

Denise's eye caught the edge of a large velvet box lying at the bottom of the receptacle. She reached for it, turned it over, and opened it slowly. The necklace took her breath away. Three rows of diamonds and emeralds shimmered from a flexible platinum mount. Dangling from it was a pendant. Flawless. A square-shaped emerald of approximately fifty carats. It made her gasp. Attached to the inside lid was a note: "To my wife. Yours for always. Sinclair."

Denise toasted him with her eyes, her lips smiling.

"What's so funny, Denise?" asked Sinclair. "I mean every word of it."

"It's just that I love you so much!"

Still transfixed, Denise stood up, holding out the necklace to him so he could fasten it around her neck. Silently she was estimating the cost of the gems. Close to a million dollars, she thought.

As if reading her mind, Sinclair explained. "The necklace used to belong to Princess Eugénie of France, then was in the collection of the Maharani of Kapurthala. I got it at Sotheby's, in London. Two million dollars!" He grinned. "But two million is a small price to pay for the smile you're wearing now!"

"I can't believe it . . . it's like some fairy tale . . ."

"The fairy tale you're about to live, Denise, has not yet been written!"

Sinclair pushed a button. Music played. "Change Partners." Her song. Now their song. The song they had danced to the first night Denise saw El Morocco, in 1954. He held her in his arms, twirled her, cheek to cheek. "I'm happy, Princess, really happy." He held her close. "You've given me something money can't buy."

Denise's latest fairy tale was unfolding at an incomprehensible pace. Her mind soared above the jumble of words. "Thank you, Sinclair," she breathed in the soft southern accent she knew to be so appealing. "I can't wait to be in your arms *tonight*," she purred, inching her fingers up his lapel while gently brushing her thigh against his.

"What a pleasure it is buying presents for my Princess! What a pleasure," he said, embracing her once more. "And now—well, President Batista is giving a dinner in our honor this evening. And if we break away in time, I want to take you to Ginger Rogers' second show at the Castilian Room. So—maybe I can grab a short nap. My secretary will show you the rest of the apartment. I better leave you now—or they'll have to tear me away." He kissed her hand and departed, blowing her another kiss from the door.

With a regal stride Denise returned to the terrace to survey the city. Havana seemed to be worshiping at her feet. How she would have loved to go walking through the unknown streets. But the twenty-hour journey had taken its toll, and she decided to pass the time more quietly, with her newest companion. Denise's hands caressed the incomparable necklace.

It sparkled in all its splendor, the sunshine capturing its reflections, contrasting perfectly with the blueness of her eyes. All this, she thought, at such a small price. All it costs is a few minutes of affection, an evening now and then of pretended passion, knowing when and how to stroke the vanity of a middle-aged man. Is it worth it? Oh yes . . . a thousand times yes!

Denise went to her boudoir. Set on the central chest of drawers, a profusion of flowers—in shades of orange, blue and gold—exploded from a massive arrangement in a basket. Nestled among the bright-budded array were papayas, avocados, pineapples, a box of Havana cigars—a bottle of rum! Who the hell sent this horror? she wondered, ripping open the small ribboned envelope. Nothing's missing but the bananas and sugar cane! She read the card: "All our wishes for your happiness. Mariela and Curtis Lodge." I

should have known, she thought. Mariela Lodge may be an English lady—
so was Eliza Doolittle.

During the days following, Sinclair saw to it that Denise savored not only
the beauty of the surrounding area and its magnificent beaches but also all
the epicurean delights the island had to offer: moro crabs at the Floridita,
cuba libres, dulce de leches and banana daiquiris at Fernando's, bean soup
at Manuel's, and observing local celebrities at Sloppy Joe's.

Their last evening was spent at the Tropicana, an outdoor nightclub
bathed in a glow of lavender and pink floodlights. A mild breeze blew in
off the Atlantic. Mammoth palm trees had been incorporated into the décor.
Showgirls looking like Carmen Miranda, with elaborate headdresses, danced
with their half-naked partners to the rhythm of Xavier Cugat's orchestra.

Guillaume, the famous French hairdresser and part of the MacAlpine
entourage, had given Denise a dramatic new style, drawing her blond hair
back severely from the classical face. She looked exotic in a backless white
chiffon gown revealing her bare honey-colored skin. She purposely wore no
jewelry so as not to distract from her beauty.

"You look particularly stunning tonight, my darling Denise. When you
wear jewels, it is *you* who enhances *them*. You are the real jewel." He
radiated pride at being seen with her.

"Thank you, darling."

"I feel like a horse's ass saying I love you in that white dress, because you
never seem to wear any other color, but somehow white always looks different on you. Not that I want you to change your ways, Princess, but is there
a reason why you?"

"Since I was a little girl," she interrupted, "my mother insisted that I wear
white, and I've simply never gotten out of the habit." The blue eyes flickered
toward him, keeping their secret as to her true reason for always wearing
white. A reason never remembered except in bitterness.

—�֎—

It was May 24, 1951, and everything was ready for the graduation photograph to be taken on the basketball court adjacent to the railroad line in
Terre Haute. All the boys, in navy-blue blazers, and all the girls, in pretty
white prom dresses, were lined up on bleachers.

"Who's the blond girl in the front row with the brown dress?" fretted the
photographer.

"Denise . . . ," she faltered, nearly choking with self-consciousness.

"Can't you tell the man your full name, Deeny?" snapped Miss Moore, the
biology teacher.

"Denise . . . Cunningham," she replied, frightened and staring at her
scuffed brown sandals.

"You were all told to wear white dresses today, and you're the only one who didn't! Deeny, it's just too distracting to have you right up front! Now, move to the second row, please!"

Denise hadn't wanted to go to school that day, embarrassed at having to make do with an old dress of her mother's that had been altered. Distraught, she had thrown up before leaving the house.

Now her mortification was complete. She nodded, turning faintly pink, and complied hurriedly with the demeaning order, as if getting there faster would somehow make her magically disappear.

The group of children buzzed with half-suppressed snickers. "Everybody, look at the camera!" the photographer commanded. "One . . . two . . . say 'cheese'—"

He stopped abruptly. "Sorry, Denise," he said with a furrowed brow, scratching his head, "I can still see the brown dress. Tell you what, go to the back, up a piece, and you two kids next to her, stand in front of Denise and cover her best you can, so we don't see the dress no more. That's-a-girl! Now, kids, remember, this is an important day in your lives! This picture is a souvenir forever! So, everybody! Please—I ask you! *A great big smile!*

Bitterness and rage welled up in Denise and she vowed to herself, Someday I'm gonna have closets filled with nothing but white dresses. Hundreds of white dresses! You wait and see. You just wait and see!

—❈—

Now a Spanish group, Los Chavales de España, were serenading Denise and Sinclair with their romantic voices to the accompanying strains of violins.

"It's two o'clock in the morning. Our last day. And . . . many have visited Havana," Sinclair suddenly announced, "but few have *seen* Havana."

"What do you mean, Sinclair?"

"It's an old Cuban saying." He took her hand. "Have you . . . have you ever heard of Superman?"

"Everyone has heard of Superman," she said dreamily. "I used to read comic books when I was a little girl!"

"No, no, Princess. You don't *read* the Superman I'm talking about. You *see* him."

Denise was puzzled. "I—I don't understand." He filled her champagne glass from the third bottle they had ordered. "Have you ever seen a blue movie?"

"No, never."

"Well, Superman acts in live blue movies. He is as much a landmark as President Batista's palace. And much more fun!" Denise was savoring her drink. "Denise, darling, would you like to see him?"

"Who?"

"Superman!"

To his surprise, she agreed. Their limousine sped along the Avenida de Maceo, a four-lane highway, and turned into Lamparilla Street, exiting at the intersection of Manicon and Ventritres. Denise was unprepared for the extent of the degradation unfolding before her. The street was brightly lit, noisy, smelly and crowded. American tourists carrying canvas flight bags mixed gregariously with French, English and German sailors. "You want nice boy! You like two boys!" a midget called out. Most of the shops, bars and restaurants were open, many of the doorways occupied by beggars, cripples and derelicts. Street urchins played in the gutter. "You want my sister! You want my mother! Good fuckos!" they offered in broken English. Stalls had been set up, with vendors selling hot sausages, peppers and Chinese food with a Cuban flavor. Pimps, most of them black, were staked out at the street corners for business. "Girls—any color you want! Marijuana, Marijuana! Posiciones, posiciones! Un peso, un peso!"

"What's posiciones?" asked Denise.

"They're picture postcards that show people making love in different positions," Sinclair explained.

She could see inside the Miranda; bead curtains separating it from the street had been pulled back. In the dim interior, girls were standing at the bar, their well-shaped buttocks invitingly encased in shiny fabric, the bar-stools occupied mostly by servicemen.

They came upon rows of eighteenth-century houses, a woman displayed in each of the ground-floor windows, advertising her wares. There was some-thing for everybody: a schoolmarm in a high-necked blouse, naked from the waist down; a nun, her habit in disarray, revealing red fishnet stockings and green garters; a dominatrix in black leather, brandishing her whips and chains; a half man-half woman, his pendulous breasts every bit as impressive as his well-hung penis; whores in corsets and bustles and paraphernalia of a bygone age competing with choirboys, tattooed men and drag queens.

Stopping in front of what appeared to be a boarded-up house, Denise and Sinclair pushed open a massive oak door with a wrought-iron knocker and heavy hinges. A dimly lit room engulfed them immediately. Pseudo-Oriental rugs covered the cool flagstone floors, and chipped gilded sconces tried for an effect of past grandeur. Women of every size, shape and descrip-tion—black, white and high yellow, tall and short, thin and fat, old and young, blonde, brunette and redhead—were sprawled on sagging couches in the shadows. Some of them were quite beautiful, with eyes that had never seen childhood, but most of them were bizarre, flaunting their rouged faces, haggard in their desperation. To the left, a bar with a broken mirror behind it gave the impression of an enormous insect having been squashed right there on the wall. Men and women laughing, watching, whispering, touch-ing, bargaining. Sailors from faraway places. Local soldiers. Tourists. Middle-aged couples looking uncomfortable and embarrassed and trying earnestly to appear debonair.

Presently the madam entered. A grotesque composition of heavy makeup, kohl-rimmed lids, brocades, rings, velvet and satin, swept together by a fluttering Chinese fan. She clapped her hands imperiously. All the women jumped to their feet and stood in a straight line, waiting for customers to make their choices. Sinclair approached the madam, whispered in her ear and passed several bills into her hand.

Denise and Sinclair were directed along a dim corridor, its wall covered with gold-flocked paper. They were met by a Gypsy woman, whose dark curls, piled high on her head, spilled over a silver bandana. Her large breasts swung freely under a transparent mauve blouse. A garter with an ornate clasp peeked through the waist-high slit of a purple satin skin-tight skirt. Hips swayed, eyes shone. The full lips, sensual and moist, frozen in a crimson gash, spoke. "Pleeze, careful for step. You no want accidan now. Si? My name Lupe." Her mouth melted into a phosphorescent white smile. "You like nice chill sampain, si? Twenty dollar. You like nice señorita? Yes? Only ten dollar. I send if you—"

"No, muchas gracias. I have my lady," said Sinclair, putting his arm round Denise's shoulders.

"Ah, si, si, belinda señorita!" Lupe turned around, addressing herself to Denise. "Good show!" she affirmed. "Good man!" She laughed a raucous guffaw.

Denise was fascinated by the size of the woman's breasts. She hiccuped. "I've never seen anything so . . . so . . ." She hiccuped again. "Do you think . . . I could touch them?"

"Go ahead! Touch anything you want, Princess!" Sinclair looked at her in amazement.

Feeling through the thin fabric with both hands, she gingerly reached for the extraordinary breasts as one would approach an open flame, afraid to be burned. "I've never seen such . . . big . . . big . . . breasts," she slurred, giggling like a child making a naughty discovery.

The Gypsy woman led them to a small arena, the circular stage surrounded by red velvet armchairs, shabby, the seats badly worn, the edges frayed. Gaudy lamé curtains separated them from the other spectators, mostly middle-class tourists.

The show was in progress. Apprehensive, Denise, helped by Sinclair, stumbled into her seat. Her eyes had not yet adjusted to the darkness. Slowly it all came into focus. The spectacle before her made her grab Sinclair's sleeve as if they were about to embark on a roller-coaster ride. Her natural shyness was being replaced by avid curiosity.

The center of the stage was occupied by a small, compact Hispanic-looking man with dark hair and eyes. A broad nose and thick, voluptuous lips suggested black blood. His well-built muscular body was smooth and completely hairless except for thick patches in the armpits. Starting at the navel, a dark matted shadow moved downward in the direction of his penis, which, thick, erect and heavily veined, bent toward his well-defined chest—fourteen inches in length, a good four inches in girth.

"Now you know why they call him Superman!" Sinclair whispered to Denise. "And it's not just the size! It's what he does with it! Watch!"

Denise was stunned. Superman was seated on a stool, his legs spread wide apart. He was surrounded by six females. In front of him a pretty, slender blonde was on her knees, gently biting the huge shaft. In his excitement, the foreskin slithered back, revealing a purple heart-shaped glans glistening with sweat in the blue and pink lights.

The girls were huddled closely together, their legs and arms intertwined with his, screeching obscenities in Spanish.

"Si enterate en el!"

"Singame duro!" cried the blonde.

"No, no! Yo primero," another protested loudly.

Lying on his back now among the cushions, he grabbed the blonde. She straddled him. Very slowly, she lowered herself on the massive member and rocked with powerful movements, backward and forward, in and out. She erupted in cries of ecstasy. Lifting her bodily he ordered the black girl to . . .

Moans could be heard beyond the lamé curtains as well as shouts of encouragement in a multitude of languages from the patrons.

"Donnes-lui la bitte!"

"Meteselo en el culo!"

"That's it! Boy-o-boy!"

Denise's embarrassment had vanished. "How many girls can he do this to?" she asked, trying hard to sound sober.

"As many as he wants. He is indefatigable," answered Sinclair. "If the crowd is large, he gives ten performances like these every evening."

"And on Sunday?"

"Sunday, I suppose, Princess, he spends with his wife. She must want to have some of the action too! Right?" He patted her hand.

Lupe arrived with the champagne and served it, bending down over a cheap reproduction of a sixteenth-century Spanish table. "If you wan Lupe after show," she whispered, "we get room here, and Lupe give you good time! I *like* pretty señoritas." She was looking at Denise. "Let me know!" A trailing laugh left with her.

Denise's attention was now drawn to three girls who had assumed center stage. They were fondling and kissing each other passionately, their pleasure riveting and unfaked. One sank to her knees while the second licked and sucked her avidly, burying her head between hot, wet thighs. The third, on her back, groaned and writhed while reaching up to twist their nipples and stroke their breasts.

Denise didn't feel Sinclair place his hand on her thigh, but unconsciously she had opened her legs to him. Working up the inside of the leg, he gradually slipped a finger inside her panties. She was moist.

Her eyes were riveted to the stage, sprawling with bodies in every possible position, the girls lavishing caresses on each other and waiting their turn, as Superman spent himself again and again. Denise was irrevocably aroused. "Sinclair," she implored huskily, "I . . . I want to return to the hotel. I feel very passionate . . . very . . ."

That night for the first time in her life she made love to a man with genuine lust and abandon, her mind indelibly etched with the sexual scenes she had just witnessed. Sexual scenes of women loving women.

The following morning they set off for Rio, her hangover colossal, her guilt supreme.

—※—

Vladimir Mikhailovich Volodin was conquering the night. He was conquering the night as he had done for the past two weeks, turning the arena of Covent Garden's stage into his own celebration. Roars of uncontrollable delight surged from the crowd as Volodin finished his spectacular solo from *Le Corsaire,* executed with such Dionysian fire and abandon that it stopped the show cold, obliging him to repeat it.

Although listed alphabetically in the program of the immense touring company from the U.S.S.R., with no special importance attached to his name, as far as the public was concerned, the young man with a face out of a Pushkin novel, the gloriously trained muscled body and the physical skill of an Olympic champion, was its incontestable star.

The mercurial boy wonder, holder of prestigious gold medals from both the Varna and the Moscow Dance festivals, more than lived up to his reputation as the greatest male dancer in the Soviet Union.

Vladimir's performance was the difference between a recital and a revelation. He was a primitive power harnessed to a prodigious technique mirroring his untamed nature and raw sexuality, which aroused the public to jubilation, knowing they were witnessing something that happens only once in a century.

Only once in a century was such virtuosity lifted instantaneously into legend.

Everyone was enraptured by his powerful and unsurpassable dramatic presence, visible throughout, from the deathly authority of his walk to a preparation to the incredible series of impossible steps—a *double tour en l'air* into an *arabesque,* followed by a *pirouette,* the unrestrained leaps of a demented tiger, the intricate *cabrioles, écartés, entrechats*—the lingering balances, the grace, the virility, the furious desperation, the elegance, the exultant classicism stamping every move with his very own imprint.

As the heavy brocaded curtain ascended and fell innumerable times on the entire ensemble, the usually undemonstrative crowd shouted over and over again, "Vladimir! Vladimir! Bravo, Volodin! Bravo, Volodin! Bra-

Book Two

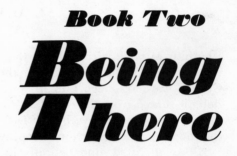

Being There

vissimo!" They leaped to their feet enthusiastically in the exquisite red-velvet-and-gold elegance of Covent Garden, yelling, stamping and applauding, as audiences in Copenhagen and everywhere else had done. Even the Queen stood in the royal box; all members of her party followed suit, including her sister, Princess Margaret, Antony Armstrong-Jones, whom Margaret was to marry the following day, and the Queen Mother.

Vladimir Volodin had pirouetted across the heart of an entire city. As he made his way to his dressing room the rapturous applause reverberated in his ears. Although accustomed to it, having become the darling of Leningrad in his home company, the Kirov, the sound of the audience's adulation never failed to intoxicate him.

"I'll be sorry to leave London," said Sergei Tikhomirov, one of the three dancers with whom Vladimir shared a dressing room.

"Just wait till we get to Paris!" countered Nikolai Vazem. "That'll be even better! I hear its beauty is staggering!"

"And I don't suppose you're talking about the Eiffel Tower!" Sergei said. "I expect you'll be making cultural exchanges every night at the Folies-Bergère!" "Well! Well!" he exclaimed as Vladimir Volodin came into the dressing room. "You've done it again! I don't know if Sergei and I will be able to compete with such stardom!"

"It was all right," Vladimir replied with an air of dissatisfaction. "I could have done better."

"Did you hear that, Sergei! He could have done better! I'm surprised you could dance at all after grand-jetéing all night long! Doesn't it inhibit those leaps?"

"As a matter of fact, no," he said with childlike candor. "It propels them!"

Their laughter was interrupted by a stern voice over the loudspeaker. "Will the company please remain in makeup and go to the stage, where they will be presented to Her Majesty."

"Didn't you hear what they just said?" Sergei asked, noticing that Vladimir was removing his costume.

"I'm not interested in meeting any queens," he replied haughtily. Slipping into a blue robe and wrapping a towel around his head, he began removing his makeup without once looking at his face in the mirror.

"But Leonid Grigorovich insists that everyone must be present!" a shocked Nikolai said. "Aren't you tired of bickering with Grigorovich? Don't you want to meet Princess Margaret? I hear she's very charming."

"Nitchehvoh! I'm very charming too! And I don't care what Blue Beard insists! By now he should know better than to insist!" There was a detached and ironic note in his voice.

The door opened and Gennady Liepka entered, still wearing his Tristan costume. "What! Getting dressed already, and the Queen of England's upstairs waiting to meet you! Such disrespect deserves to be respected!" He grabbed Vladimir by the shoulders. "And don't tell me you are 'otherwise engaged' for the evening! You haven't gone out with us in over a week! Has he, Nicky?"

"I don't really feel like doing anything special tonight. We'll have plenty of time in Paris," Vladimir said with a knowing wink. "I'd rather be alone." His voice faded. His attention wandered.

"You sound like Greta Garbo! You're as annoying as the leaf of a birch, as they say in Siberia. Usually when someone wishes to be alone, it means only one thing—that they've got somebody to be alone *with!* Come on, join us for dinner at the Ivy Restaurant," Gennady urged. "Or, if you like, the Savoy Grill."

"Yes," said Sergei. "We're leaving tomorrow, and none of us has ever been to the Savoy!"

Vladimir gave a faint smile, amused and cold, while removing his dancing shoes and putting on his leg warmers.

"The Savoy? Who wants to go there? It's so stuffy," he said. "I'm not putting on a tie for anybody."

"Oh, well, if you need a tie," Sergei said, somewhat disappointed, "the Savoy's out. I don't even own a tie."

"I don't own one either," said Vladimir. "But if I did, I'd make better use of it."

"How would you use it?" asked Sergei.

Vladimir got up, splashed cold water on his face from the chipped and yellowed marble sink. "To hang Grigorovich!" he said, returning to his dressing table. They all laughed.

Gennady was leaning against the wall a few feet from Vladimir. "Why do you make life so difficult for yourself?" he said softly.

"You talking to me?" Vladimir asked, raising his head. "Difficulty is what makes life interesting! I just can't help myself. When I was born, I suppose a good fairy gave me a passion for the impossible, the unobtainable—what can I do about it?"

"I was reading in the English newspaper—" Gennady went on.

"He can read! He can read!" Nikolai joked in a singsong voice.

"And in English!" said Sergei.

"Come off it, will you, and be serious!" said Gennady gently. "I was reading that our company has been the biggest box office draw since the war. Our past two weeks here have broken all records. That's not bad, eh?"

"I simply can't understand that mentality!" Vladimir snapped. "In Russia they don't measure artistic excellence with box office success." He unscrewed the lid of his thermos bottle and took a mouthful of hot tea, sucking it through a lump of sugar held between his teeth.

The loudspeaker ground out a further message. "This is the final announcement. Vazem, Sorokina, Timofeyeva, Tikhomirov, Volodin, Liepka and Gonzov are missing from the receiving line for Her Majesty. Those whose names have been called will join their comrades immediately. The Queen will be onstage in five minutes."

260

"Vladimir Volodin, if I were you," Nikolai said soberly, "I would put my costume right back on and go upstairs on the double. I have the feeling that if you don't, the situation between you and Grigorovich could get pretty warm!"

"For one who's been in hot water for so long, I can take the warmth! Don't worry about me!"

"We're not worrying!" Gennady said. "We're just warning you! Come on!" he called to the others. "Let's go. Hamlet doesn't need us. He's in search of his own tragedy!" All three left, slamming the door on their laughter.

Vladimir removed his leg warmers and took his robe off, revealing his extraordinary body. His muscles started in his hands, ran through his wrists, twisted and elongated in his arms and exploded around his shoulders like so many rivers. Everything was pliant, strong, beautiful. He was fine-boned, a prince who was a dancer rather than a dancer who was a prince.

He stepped into a pair of brown velvet hipsters he had bought on Carnaby Street as his own private tribute to swinging London and a brown turtleneck sweater picked up in Finland. Sitting down on a stool, he looked for his socks, but could find only one, and grabbed another, belonging to somebody else, that happened to be lying on the floor. It didn't match his own. He then slipped into soft leather Chelsea boots. There was a knock at the door and Natasha Volkov entered—a handsome frail woman in her middle fifties, wearing a simple black evening dress with a low V neck and a string of pearls. Vladimir immediately stood and bowed low to the former dancer who was now the company's choreographer. "You're a strange one, Vladimir Volodin. I've known you now for ten years, since you were a little boy, actually, and although you wouldn't cross the street to help a friend, you never fail to rise when a woman enters the room!"

"I didn't mean to give you such a good impression!" he answered with a twinkle. "Will you please have my seat, madame?"

"Volodin, I have been sent here at the express command of Leonid Grigorovich. He wants you onstage immediately. Otherwise . . ."

"Otherwise . . . ?" Vladimir emitted a mock groan. "I'm sorry, Natasha Volkov," he said with his usual self-assurance, "I've done my duty onstage to the best of my ability, and I'm not prepared to subject myself to the indignity of meeting someone I have no interest in whatsoever. One cannot be all things to all men. I'm afraid I'm not a hypocrite. I have better things to do with my last evening in London."

"I would be careful, Vladimir Volodin," cautioned the ballet mistress. "Grigorovich has often spoken of dismissing you from the company."

"I know. He's always said he wanted to do it, but he has neither the imagination, the energy nor the willpower."

"He is certain you will give him heart failure one day!"

"When Leonid Grigorovich passes on to another world, it will be from an overdose of megalomania."

"I'm sorry, Vladimir Mikhailovich Volodin, you feel that way. I dearly love you and have the greatest respect for your high standards, but tonight you're definitely mistaken. It would take such a small effort on your part, without sacrificing one bit of your independence!"

"I understand. Today a small effort is asked of me, tomorrow a bigger one, and then I'd soon be compromising all along the line. Madame, being what I am, true to myself and my beliefs, selfish perhaps, for me this is true aristocracy. I don't need to gape at royalty." She left the room, voicing her disapproval. He assembled his belongings, folding his robe and placing it in a satchel, along with the ballet shoes, the makeup, the tights and leg warmers, and last, but not least, the thermos bottle and a box of sugar cubes. He slipped into a heavy overcoat and placed a gray astrakhan hat on his head.

The door opened once again. Leonid Grigorovich came in without knocking. He glanced past Vladimir and then stared straight at him. The former great dancer of the Bolshoi was now managing director of the company. Their tour had covered sixteen countries, London and Paris being last on the itinerary. He was a man of medium height who still had great bearing despite the weight the years had added. His graceful hands were those of a man twenty years younger. One of them now held a cigarette between elegant nicotine-stained fingers, the other was buried deep in the pocket of a navy-blue double-breasted suit bought at GUM in Moscow. He was a stern disciplinarian and an intransigent despot, and his outbursts of anger had become notorious.

"I came to see for myself," he bellowed, "what absurdity dances in the dark recesses of your obvious madness. I've had nothing but problems with you on this tour, but this is the final straw! It will not be tolerated! You set a bad example for the rest of the company. Vladimir Volodin, you are aiming at your own destruction, and I—"

"Comrade Leonid Grigorovich," Vladimir interrupted calmly, "I'm sorry if I've displeased you. I've always given a hundred percent to my dancing—"

"You won't be dancing much longer," Grigorovich interrupted, "if you keep on missing practice in the morning. Three times in two weeks! Not to mention the nights you haven't slept at the hotel at all! Furthermore, we aren't pleased that you are constantly in the company of foreigners! And if that weren't bad enough, you've disgraced the entire company by attracting adverse publicity in the newspapers . . ."

Vladimir vividly remembered the incident Grigorovich was referring to. A few nights after the company had arrived in London, a dancer with the Ballet Rambert invited him to go to Ronnie Scott's Jazz Club in Soho, the heart of bohemian London. That night Vladimir slipped out of the theater without being seen and walked along Wardour Street, looking in the windows of pornographic bookstores and strip clubs. He was propositioned several times by prostitutes standing on corners and in doorways.

Not long after his arrival at the club, one of the waitresses recognized him. News of his presence spread like wildfire. Every time somebody would order a drink for himself, he would add, "And one for Vladimir Volodin too!" People lifted their glasses to "Détente!" "Hands across the sea!" and "International understanding!" By the time the musicians went on, Vladimir was quite drunk!

Johnny Dankworth and his band were playing. The vocalist was Dankworth's wife, the young and beautiful black singer Cleo Laine. She couldn't be heard. It was clear the crowd wasn't going to quiet down. Johnny was good-natured about it. "As you all know, ladies and gentlemen, we've got a celebrity with us tonight! Ladies and gentlemen, from the Soviet Union, their second Sputnik, Vladimir Volodin!" Vladimir obliged by getting up on a table. Flashbulbs burst from nowhere. "I understand that Mr. Volodin sings too," Cleo said. "How'd you like to come up here and sing with me, Vladimir?" There were several rounds of applause, punctuated with more flashes, as Vladimir staggered toward the stage. The patrons rose to their feet, singing and pounding their pints on the tables; some of them stood on chairs. Vladimir looked sheepishly at his audience, a grin plastered on his face, a mug in his hand, and slurred the words, "I dance my songs. . . . I sing . . . not so well." The audience cheered. "I sing . . . like a frog . . . I croak. But for you I will croak. It will be bad croak."

When several hours later Vladimir left the premises, more than a dozen newsmen were still waiting for him on the sidewalk. He ran down the street. They followed. He ran faster, and artfully dodged them, or so he thought. Desperate to relieve himself, Vladimir was urinating against a brick wall in Rupert Court when the sudden flash of a camera bulb, recording the event for posterity, surprised him. Turning angrily, he aimed the stream of urine at the photographer. Missed. And soaked his own boots instead. He swore loudly, climbed over the wall, and disappeared.

At four o'clock in the morning the traffic around Trafalgar Square had scarcely dwindled. With difficulty Vladimir wove around the vehicles in front of the National Gallery and crossed the street among the cries of irate motorists. The square was full of tourists, mostly young people, in sleeping bags or playing guitars. Vladimir jumped up on the edge of one of the fountains and danced to the music. Pirouetting, he lost his balance and fell backward into the water with a splash. Someone jumped in after him. Vladimir emerged from the basin soaking wet and holding in his arms a teenage girl with waist-length brown hair. A camera's light blinded him.

The following morning Vladimir's pictures were plastered across the *Daily Mirror,* with the headlines FAMOUS DANCER'S FEET ALL WET and VOLGA MEETS TRAFALGAR AND FINDS MERMAID!

". . . And . . . and . . . And pay attention when I speak to you!" Grigorovich shouted. "Look at me." Vladimir complied. When the echo of the director's shrill voice had died down, there was a silence in the dressing room. "There is no strength without sacrifice," he resumed in a patronizing tone, certain that Vladimir would capitulate, "no efficiency without integrity, and no progress as an artist without discipline."

"But I cannot function as a person in the total absence of freedom."

"There *is* no freedom unless one is prepared to surrender some part of it. You're only twenty-one years old, and while I can tolerate youthful exuberance, I will not suffer insubordination. You're letting success go to your head, and if it proves too much of a burden for you, I can arrange for Soloviev to dance *Le Corsaire!*" He watched Volodin's face. The muscles were knotted, hard as steel. "Then maybe your head will lose some of its swelling. The choice is yours." Volodin smiled at the director, with a glint of schoolboy defiance smoldering around his eyes. An ambiguous, mocking smile.

"Vladimir Volodin, whenever you are onstage, in the street, in a restaurant, whatever you do, you are looked upon as a representative of the Soviet Union that has made it possible for you to become the dancer you are today. You owe your country a debt of gratitude. Do not ever forget that!" Leonid Grigorovich left, slamming the door and leaving a void Vladimir could feel. Picking up his dance bag, he moved toward the stage door.

The narrow street outside the theater was damp and cool, with the perfume of honeysuckle heavy in the air. Patrons drinking pints of bitter on the pavement in front of an old pub underneath a gas lamp watched impassively as crowds of fans waving autograph books and programs surged toward Vladimir like moths attracted to his blazing light. Teenagers in school uniforms stood out in the sedate crowd. Policemen in blue uniforms quietly but efficiently watched over Vladimir, their domed helmets sitting securely on their heads, chin straps resting immediately beneath their noses.

Vladimir graciously signed his name, his letters sprawling, his ink coalblack, muttering "Spahsseebah" each time.

"What's he saying? What's he saying?" a child asked impatiently.

"I think it means 'thank you,'" a housewife whispered.

"Would you like me to hold back the crowd, sir?" a policeman asked.

"Nyet. No, thank you. I'll sign few more first!"

The crowd parted reverently as a black London cab drew up in front of Vladimir. He quickly got into the spacious back seat, and the car disappeared into the night, passing in front of the marquee where the audience was still coming out of the theater, pouring into Bow Street and dispersing around Magistrates Court.

The taxi turned into the Strand, scraping alongside a red double-decker bus. Looking up at its upper level, he noticed two small advertisements extolling the merits of Guinness beer and Brylcreem flanking a full-length poster publicizing his company at Covent Garden. Vladimir winced at the thought that his art was brought down to such a level. The taxi speeded up, then sputtered to a standstill, caught in a traffic jam. Vladimir knew exactly where he was. Paying the fare, he alighted at the top of Villiers Street, near

Charing Cross Station. The smell of gasoline, the fumes of diesel oil, and that special hurried walk of commuters rushing to catch the last train never failed to move him, and brought him back to Privokzalnay Square and the Leningrad Station.

❋

"What will you do when you grow up?" his grandmother asked him, pulling her knitted scarf more closely over her gray head.

"I want to dance, Babushka," Vladimir had answered simply, and his eyes had merely looked ahead at the railroad tracks. He was eight years old and already had the elegance of line intended for a prince.

❋

Struggling through the surging crowd in front of the Lyons Corner House, Vladimir turned left into Whitehall. He walked cautiously, looking over his shoulder several times. He stopped by a plane tree, its yellow mottled trunk disappearing into an iron grill in the pavement. Bending down, he pretended to tie an imaginary shoelace. He straightened up, walked on, and paused in front of the old Banqueting House where Charles I had been beheaded, and then, still apprehensive, made a sudden dash across the street and hailed a cab going in the opposite direction.

Driving toward the lights of the National Gallery, they bore left through Admiralty Arch and drove down The Mall toward Buckingham Palace. The air was sweet. Everyone was in a festive mood for the princess' wedding the following morning. Flagpoles had been erected on both sides of the broad thoroughfare along which the glass coach would take the royal bride on her way to Westminster Abbey.

For the first time since leaving the theater his anxiety dissolved. Closing his eyes and allowing himself the luxury of relief, he pulled out a red and white pack of Avrora cigarettes, lighted one and reflected on what had just happened in the dressing room. There's really no ground, he mused, to support the theory that one should sacrifice one's happiness, even for a moment, for that of others. He felt angry at himself for being selfish, but that was his view. And he felt lonely, so lonely that the feeling swallowed every other thought he had. "Are we very . . . away . . . Belgrave Square?" he faltered, leaning forward.

" 'Ere we are, mate," the driver replied as the cab turned into an elegant Regency square. "What's the number then, mate?"

Vladimir told him.

" 'Ere we are, me ole mate! 'Ow's that for service? Right in front o' the bleedin' door!" Vladimir got out, paying the exact fare. " 'Ey, mate! Wahtcha doin! You fergot me tip!"

"Tips are . . . insult to . . . mankind!" stated Vladimir, lordlier than any lord, challenging the driver's astonished look.

265

"Fuckin' 'ell!" he shouted. "A bleedin' insult to mankind, is it? I'll give ya a bit o' your fuckin' mankind, if that's what ya want! Bleedin' foreigners!" he shouted, and drove off.

Vladimir stepped onto the cream-colored porch of the nineteenth-century brick and stone house. What would a Mrs. Curtis Lodge look like? he wondered as he pulled a cast-iron knob that rang the bell. In the distance he heard a delicate tinkle. Probably an old biddy. As he waited for someone to answer the door he looked up, counting the number of stories in the building. Five floors! Who needs five floors! Such a waste of space! He wished he were spending the evening alone with Genevieve, dining at the Blue Peacock, his favorite Russian restaurant, overlooking Albert Bridge with its little white lights. He thought of Genevieve. Her pleasures were simple, sweet, spontaneous and . . . sexy—the perfect combination. Why has she insisted on introducing me to her stepmother on my last night in town? He rang again impatiently. Well, I'll be persuasive, and we'll soon be out of here and into her little bed!

A butler, wearing gray pinstripe trousers, black jacket and a bow tie under a white wing collar, opened the heavy door slowly.

"I am Vladimir Volodin," said the dancer, dropping his heavy shoulder bag near the entrance.

"Yes, Mr. Volodin. Madame is expecting you." He spoke in rich, sonorous, impeccable English. "Please follow me."

Vladimir was taken aback by the opulence of the hallway. Long and narrow, windowless and exceedingly lofty, it was lit by a fifth-century copper brazier from India which had been electrically wired. An oak staircase rose from the far end of the hallway. The parquet floor was highly polished, partially covered by a single Persian rug in browns and beiges. There was little furniture, but what there was glittered: a small Louis XVI cabinet with chiseled ormolu cabochons and florettes, a black and gold lacquered Korean screen, and an eighteenth-century Chippendale mahogany and gilt mirror. What caught Vladimir's eye immediately was what appeared to be a solid gold Egyptian sarcophagus. Totally in keeping with the luxuriousness was a sixteenth-century Brussels tapestry adorning one wall, which depicted a Renaissance scene in hues of gold, red and blue, its border an interwoven band of flowering branches and fruiting vines.

The butler opened French doors to the drawing room, announcing him.

As Vladimir Volodin strode into the room a beautiful woman seated on a paisley banquette rose to greet him. "Mr. Volodin," she said in a well-modulated British voice, "I am Mrs. Curtis Lodge. Genevieve is my stepdaughter. It's such a pleasure meeting you. An honor, really. I hear nothing but great praise for your unequaled brilliance." Bending low, he kissed her hand gallantly. "I regret to say, Mr. Volodin, I haven't had the pleasure of seeing you perform, and it is indeed my loss, but I've only arrived today from America."

He smiled. Speechless. The flame of her gaze was intense, and Vladimir drew back, intimidated. This was not at all the woman he had envisioned meeting. This was a woman probably in her mid-thirties, aware of her beauty and flaunting it. He gazed at the lace bodice that left her milky white bosom generously exposed, serving as a velvety background for a matchless diamond necklace centered by a huge sapphire.

"Genevieve . . . ," he stammered, awkward and embarrassed, "where is Genevieve?"

"Genevieve will be joining us in a moment, Mr. Volodin. She's in the kitchen playing chef." She laughed. A brief laugh. "Genevieve wants to make certain your steak tartare is just the way you like it. She seems to know exactly how you like everything, Mr. Volodin." She said it simply. Eyes mocking and cool. "It never ceases to amaze me how young ladies go about these things nowadays."

"You are quite young yourself." He lifted his head in invitation. "How do *you* go about those things?"

Ignoring the remark, she asked, "May I offer you a drink, Mr. Volodin?" She went to a Regency commode inlaid with tortoiseshell and mother-of-pearl. A Canaletto hung on the wall behind it. "I know you prefer vodka."

"Yes, thank you. Straight, please. And call me Vladimir."

"But of course—Vladimir." A cut-glass carafe of Stolichnaya stood in an eighteenth-century silver wine bucket filled with shaved ice. "Make yourself comfortable."

The large room was draped with smocked brown fabrics dotted with little flowers of green, orange and beige. Mirrors faced mirrors, recreating and multiplying the images of the lavishly appointed salon. Masses of tiger lilies were everywhere.

Vladimir sat on the banquette and reached in his pocket for a pack of cigarettes. "Do you mind if I smoke?"

"No, not at all. In fact, I believe we have your brand—Avrora." She pointed to a lacquered Thai box on the coffee table. "I give full marks to Genevieve for finding them."

He took a deep drag on his cigarette as she handed him a goblet and sat down next to him. His eyes moved slowly over her face.

"What's the matter?" she asked.

"Nothing. You surprise me, that's all."

"I surprise you? But why?"

"You are so . . . so . . . *krasiva.*"

"What does that mean?"

"It means 'beautiful' in my language."

Her eyes moved from his lips to his eyes, back to his lips.

"Na zdohrov'yeh," she said, raising her glass.

"What is the exact word for that in English?"

"Cheers."

"Cheers, then," he repeated, and they touched glasses.

Genevieve burst into the room with all the exuberance of her eighteen years. Her full skirt flounced above little black high-heeled pumps. Her brown eyes danced as she bubbled, "Why didn't somebody tell me you were here? Why didn't you send word that Vladimir had arrived, Mariela?"

Vladimir stood up, put both his arms around her tiny waist and lifted her in the air. "You've changed your hair style, dushka," he said playfully, putting her down. "It makes you look older. It looks good."

Her long chestnut hair was pulled back into a ponytail and held in place by a gold barrette. She clasped his head in an intimate gesture. "Vladimir, I'm so sorry it's your last night," she said with a distressed smile. "Your performance was extraordinary! You made me cry."

"Dancing supposed to make you happy!"

"I cried with joy. You were so superb. . . . I wish you'd let me wait for you at the theater and bring you here myself."

"You know better, Genevieve. I cannot do it. I must be careful. I am not supposed to be—oh—what is the word?"

" 'Gallivanting' would be the word," Mariela said. "But let's not waste time talking! You must be famished! Genevieve tells me you never eat before a performance!" Mariela didn't wait for Vladimir's reply but took his arm, pressing it against hers as she led the way to the dining room. Desire surged through Vladimir's body as he felt the warmth of her soft, full breast. She sensed his passion but said casually, "I was going to invite a friend, Lady Brackett. She's simply dying to meet you! But I'm afraid you wouldn't have liked her. She's rather tedious. As they say in French, she's a bit 'arrivée.' "

"Then I am very glad you didn't invite her, because the 'arrivées' always arrive a little tired."

"Genevieve," Mariela chastised merrily, "you didn't tell me Vladimir is a wit! And in French, too!"

"French is my second language," he said.

They crossed the hallway. Genevieve whispered, "We must keep our voices down! We don't want to wake up Tarutu!"

"Tara who?"

"Tarutu. That's the name of the mummy," Genevieve said, pointing to the gilded Egyptian sarcophagus standing in the corner.

"I admired it when I came in."

"Yes, it is beautiful, isn't it?" said Mariela. "Tarutu was a singer in the Temple of Amun. The sarcophagus was discovered in Upper Egypt by an ancestor of my father's. He spent a number of years out there, and then, in 1901, his efforts were finally rewarded." Mariela let go of Vladimir's arm. "Do you believe in curses, Vladimir?"

"In my country we are very superstitious. But I'm not."

"According to legend, Tarutu had been disappointed in love and retired to the temple, just as Héloïse entered the convent."

Vladimir stood watching Mariela in brooding silence for a moment, then said, "The love that lasts longest is the one that is never returned."

"That, Vladimir, is typical Slavic melancholy, and I won't hear of it! But let me continue my story. Only in death did Tarutu find the peace she craved. Her lover died at sea shortly thereafter, and the high priest ordained that anyone who disturbed her final resting place would be doomed—as well as that person's loved ones. My father's ancestor, for instance, went insane and had to be locked up, and his wife committed suicide."

"You are not frighten' having Tarutu here?"

"I—I still haven't made up my mind," Mariela answered. "But there's another curse attached to Tarutu. If for whatever reason her sarcophagus should break, unspeakable evil is destined to come to its owner and all who have mocked her."

"What a marvelous story!" Genevieve said, delighted.

They had reached the dining room. Its walls were white with a faint blush of pink. Soft magenta silk curtains framed tall windows. A fire crackled in the white marble fireplace. Gilt brackets over the mantel held a pair of Chinese porcelain roosters.

"Please help yourself to whatever you like." Mariela indicated a sideboard crowned by Sèvres china. It was covered with Russian delicacies: blini with caviar, piroshki, smoked salmon and sturgeon in aspic, steak tartare, cucumber salad, borscht, pickled mushrooms, beef stroganoff, Ukrainian dumplings, fresh cabbage-and-apple salad, wild strawberries in lemon juice, and hot tea. Open bottles of Château Mouton-Rothschild and Dom Perignon stood about.

They sat at a round table covered with a white lace cloth. The centerpiece was a Japanese cachepot that held an arrangement of tiger lilies.

"Tell me, Mrs. Lodge," said Vladimir. "I am curious to know what has brought you to London at this time."

"Please call me Mariela. 'Mrs. Lodge' makes me feel so ancient!" Her leg touched his. Instinctively, he tightened the muscles of his calf. She could feel the pressure and pressed back. He shivered. "I live a small part of the year in London. My husband's business keeps him in Detroit. Genevieve must have told you, he is chairman of the board of the Curtis Motor Company. I'm here for Princess Margaret's wedding in the morning. Do you know the Douglases? He's the American ambassador to England, and his daughter, Sharman—oh, how silly of me! I forgot that's where you met Genevieve— Well, Sharman is also a good friend of Her Royal Highness . . ."

Listening without hearing and looking without seeing, Vladimir barely touched his food. Mariela's perfume warmed his blood. Her napkin fell to the floor. Reaching to pick it up, Vladimir's hand unintentionally brushed against her thigh. As she took the napkin, Vladimir felt the gentle touch of her fingers and the tingling of their warmth. She put her hand in his—an intense current ran back and forth between them. He sensed the yearning that coursed through her, and, fully aroused, he realized that the passion now seizing him sprang not from his but from her initiative. Abruptly she took her hand away.

Words fluttered around and above him. Questions remained unanswered or were repeated.

"Mariela," Genevieve said, yearningly, "Vladimir's dancing *Swan Lake* a week from Saturday at the Paris Opera. Do you think we could go for the weekend?"

"Perhaps."

More words. "By plane . . ." "Wonderful . . ." "You must let me know . . ." "I'll be at . . ." "I will . . ." "Wonderful . . ."

Vladimir could utter only the most ordinary phrases. "Lovely room . . . wonderful blinis . . . I love London . . . Sorry to be leaving . . . Yes . . . No . . . No . . . Yes . . ."

"What time do you have?" he asked suddenly. "I never wear a watch."

"It's a little after one," Genevieve chirped. "The night is still young!"

"Not for me," he said. "I must go to my hotel soon. I don't know our travel arrangements yet."

"Must you? So soon . . ." It was Mariela. "Surely you have time for tea? It's already prepared—"

"I think—"

"—in the Russian style," she added.

"Well, of course . . . I only wanted you to . . . I do not want to overstay my welcome."

They returned to the drawing room, where Mariela poured tea from a vermeil samovar into thick glasses. "How many lumps, Vladimir? One or two?"

"Five."

"Five! My goodness!" she said in mock horror. "So it's true what I read in the papers, that you do nothing in moderation!"

"The newspapers exaggerate and give inaccurate images. It is not—"

"Tell me, Vladimir, does so much sugar sweeten your disposition?"

"I am afraid not! Not at all! We have proverb in Russia. 'Hearts that are delicate and kind and tongues that are not make the best company!' " She laughed. He laughed harder.

"Your command of the English language is so good, Vladimir. Would it be impertinent if I asked you why every so often you drop the articles 'the' or 'a' or 'an'?"

"Simply because they do not exist in Russian. That was the hardest thing in English language for me to learn. How can I explain? They do exist, but not *before* the word. They are added to the end of the word, and then this word is conjugated like a verb. You understand?"

"Absolutely nothing." She laughed. "That's probably why I'll never learn Russian."

"You don't have to, Mariela, since I speak English," he said, looking at her.

"If you're certain to be dancing *Swan Lake* in Paris a week from Saturday," Mariela continued, "why don't you give me a ring?"

"I do not have your number."

"Of course you don't! I'll give it to you!" Mariela walked quickly to a writing desk—a delicate mid-nineteenth-century English mahogany piece, with intricate amber and silver moldings and a floral border of lapis enamel—bringing her calling card, which she placed in Vladimir's hand. She went on: "Then Genevieve and I will come over for the weekend to see you. We can stay with the Baroness de Vuillard at her lovely house on the Île Saint-Louis—"

"Oh, Mariela!" Genevieve gushed, clearly delighted. "Can we really? Oh, Vladimir! Did you hear that?" She sat on his knee. Vladimir wondered if she picked up the scent of his attraction to Mariela. It appeared not. Being just eighteen, Genevieve was at that blessed age when one's soul, inflamed by budding passion, irrationally assumes itself completely loved in return.

Vladimir shifted in his chair—the first sign of his discomfort. His brain was consumed with thoughts of Mariela. He desired her. He could imagine touching her skin, breathing her breath, easing himself inside her. He clenched his teeth with such force that his jaw was outlined on his angular face.

The three of them sat in momentary silence. The tension in the room mounted painfully for Vladimir and Mariela. "Maybe we should go, Vladimir," Genevieve said, toying affectionately with the hair at the nape of his neck. Vladimir nodded agreement and eased Genevieve off his knee. The faintest trace of a smile curled on the edge of his full lips. He stood up quickly.

"It's the last evening for you two children. You'd better run along." Mariela led the way into the hall. "It's getting quite late for you, Vladimir, if you have an early start tomorrow."

Pirouetting mischieviously, Vladimir threw his arms around the sarcophagus, extending his left leg in an arabesque. "Dosvidanya, Tarutu, goodbye," he whispered audibly. "I am not afraid of you either!" Genevieve helped him into his overcoat, handing him his shoulder bag. He turned around. "I want to thank you, Mariela. This was the best dinner I have had in London. I could easily become addicted." Bowing his head, he kissed her long fingers.

"It's better to be addicted to life," she replied. As he raised his head slowly their eyes fixed on each other once more. She stood for a moment in the open doorway, her face transfigured, and was gone without a backward glance.

He whistled for a cab. "Come on, darling, what are you doing?" Genevieve chided. "You know I've got a car!" Vladimir couldn't remember getting out onto the street. The evening had been a glorious dream.

They drove in her Lodge convertible through St. James's, encountering throngs of people leaving Buckingham Palace after a midnight supper and ball.

"Isn't my stepmother smashing?"

"Smashing? What does it mean, 'smashing'?"

"It means fantastic."

"Yes. She is fantastic."

A silence.

"It's such a shame you had to meet her on your last day. You'd have loved her. Everybody does!"

He laughed. Behind his gaiety there was a terrible irony. He already loved her. As they drove up Park Lane, Genevieve's hand rested on his leg, then slowly traveled up his thigh, and stopped at his crotch, softly caressing the mound underneath the cloth. He brushed her hand away. "For heaven's sake, Genevieve, keep both hands on the wheel! You are going to get us killed!"

"Since when are you so concerned with safety, I'd like to know!"

"Where are we going?" he asked.

"To my flat of course, silly!"

"I cannot, Genevieve . . . not tonight."

"But . . ."

"I am disappointed as you are, dushka Genevieve, but there is no way I can stay away from the hotel tonight. I'm in enough trouble already."

"But, Vladimir," she persisted, "I've thought about making love with you all day!"

"Well, you will have to think about it all night!" She drove without speaking. As a guilty afterthought he put his arm around her shoulder. "Dearest Genevieve," he said almost paternally, "life for me is a journey. I told you when we first met, did I not, you should never take me seriously. I am a gypsy."

She tried bravely to conceal her disappointment. "What can I say, Vladimir—you're the boss! I'll drop you off at the Royal Lancaster Hotel, so you'll be home."

"No, no!" he insisted. "You cannot! We should not be seen together! It is frowned upon to be out so late with a foreigner. You know that! My life is not my own! Drop me off at Marble Arch and I'll walk. It is not far down Bayswater Road to my hotel."

She parked the car on Oxford Street. "Now don't sulk," he said, scowling. "You must always look ahead. Why, a week ago I did not exist in your life, and in less than two weeks we'll be together again in Paris."

"I'm not sulking," she said in a childish whimper. "It's just that . . . it's just that . . . I was counting on being alone with you tonight."

"We are full of hopes, Genevieve. Get rid of them as quickly as you can. Now give me a big kiss. Hurry. I cannot bear farewells." He kissed her tenderly and opened the car door.

"Oh, Vladimir . . ." A wan, tearful smile of desire and concern lit Genevieve's face. "Will you call me before you leave?"

"Yes—if I can." Genevieve's eyes misted with tears. "Okay, Genevieve dushka. I've got an even better idea. I'll call you first thing in the morning and give you the time of my departure. Then you can meet me at airport! How's that?"

"Where at the airport?" She sniffed tearfully.

"At the bar."

"Which one?"

"For heaven's sake, Genevieve! I don't know! You will have to look for me. I am very visible!" He took a handkerchief out of his pocket. "Here. Dry your tears, and in the meantime be careful going home."

"Oh, Vladimir . . ."

He kissed her again. "Thank you, dearest Genevieve, for showing me London." She handed the handkerchief back to him. "Keep it!" he said. "Souvenir from mad Russian!" he added, getting out and closing the door.

He watched her drive off. As the car turned into Park Lane, Vladimir walked to the nearest telephone booth, took Mariela's calling card from his pocket and dialed the number. It rang several times. He hung up. Holding the card up to the light, he verified the number and dialed again.

The phone rang, then the ringing stopped. There was a long pause before he heard Mariela's deep voice. "Hello. Hello . . ."

"Mariela." He spoke in a low, hasty tone. "This is Vladimir."

"Oh, yes . . . ?"

He was surprised by the weariness in her voice. "I'm calling because I believe—no, 'believe' isn't the right word—because I hope you feel the same way I do. You are an enchanting mirage. It is ironic that we should meet on my last night. Look—I was thinking I could get in cab and come back to your house—"

"Well, you were thinking wrong, and you're thinking nonsense. Besides, you're only a child."

"No, Mariela, I am not a child. I am a man." He was more excited than ever before. How arousing it was to fantasize about making love to her! "We both have the same emotion, the same passion. I know it. I want you." A pause followed. "Don't you want me, Mariela?"

"Are you asking me to seduce you?" She laughed softly. "Frankly, I'd feel guilty if I were to corrupt your innocence."

"Corrupt me."

"No." Mariela's tone was low and determined. "Vladimir, you have a lot to learn."

"I want to learn."

"Then let me teach you the first lesson. There is great pleasure to be derived from ungratified desire. If something is worthwhile, there is no deadline. It is sometimes good to wait, even if it is painful. I must go."

"Not yet! I have the feeling that if you hang up now, you will disappear in smoke. Will you come to Paris? Will I see you again? I want to see you again. Will I?"

"That depends on how badly you want to. Now, Vladimir, I must leave you."

"Please see me tonight. Please."

"No." Her voice made imploring useless.

"What have I done to deserve this?"

"You misunderstood, Vladimir, simply misunderstood."

"Listen, Mariela, I—" There was a sharp click on the other end of the line. "Hello, hello, are you still there?" She was not. Vladimir held the phone away from his ear and looked at it in disbelief before hanging up. Dumbfounded by Mariela's abruptness, he kicked the wall of the booth with his foot, opened the door and walked out into the street, breathing the cold morning air. Her words resounded in his ear: "You misunderstood, Vladimir, simply misunderstood." How could he have misunderstood? There could have been no misunderstanding. She wanted him. He knew it. Vladimir walked briskly toward his hotel, and just before entering, abruptly changed his mind and crossed Bayswater Road. His steps became more hurried, weaving into the dwindling traffic. He had seen the passion rise in her eyes. Something had passed between them. There had been no mistake. What game was Mariela playing—and why? His disappointment was melting into anger, his anger into fury.

Vladimir began to run—beyond Park Lane, Trafalgar Square, and the Strand. Breathless, he found himself on Bow Street, in front of Covent Garden, and stopped. Moving vans were still being loaded with scenery and costumes from the night's performance. Determinedly he rushed through the side door of the artists' entrance. He climbed a narrow flight of stairs and walked into a long, dark and deserted corridor toward the light at its end.

The stage was empty. Over a network of cables and ropes he approached the ramp, crossed to its center and stood underneath the bare bulb of the working light. He dropped his bag. There was no sound save the muffled voices of a crew of stagehands completing their final chores. The velvet curtain was raised. Vladimir stared out into row after row of empty seats. Slowly out of the blackness figures and forms took shape. Vladimir could still hear the cheers. He took a deep and sweeping bow, as he had done only a few hours earlier. Undying ecstatic applause wrapped him in a cloth of love. In acceptance he raised his head and arms toward the balcony. More love—more cheers. Flowers falling at his feet from everywhere. He bows again. The love is mounting . . . unrestrained . . . pouring . . . drenching every fiber of his being. The public shouts and screams its love— its uncompromising love—louder and louder. "Bis, bis—more, more!" Beads of sweat roll from his forehead down his neck. Pearls of joy. He feels warm. He feels cold. Fire and ice. The crowd is on its feet. One pair of hands beating out a standing ovation. "More, more." A standing ovation! Can you see them? Can you hear them, Pëtr Ivanovich? . . . Mamoushka? . . . Lucinka? It's for me—just me—Vladimir Mikhailovich Volodin! But it's for you that I did it. The shouting is now deafening—delirious—"Encore, encore!" Who cares about you, Mariela? Who cares, when I can drown in this pool of love and adulation every night . . . every night of my life! . . . "Encore, encore!" The pressure becomes unbearable. Vladimir rips off his overcoat, his clothes, his boots. He is naked. His muscles are rippling in anticipation. With a single sovereign hand movement he signals the maestro in the orchestra pit. Vladimir will oblige the demanding crowd, the demented crowd. He will give of himself once again. Walking majestically to the upstage left corner, he readies himself into the position of the first variation. The music shatters his mind. Stravinsky's first chord rises to full pitch, and with an amazing hovering elevation, Vladimir leaps through the imaginary window and into the dream of *Le Spectre de la Rose*. The music plays faster and faster, louder and louder, while he abandons himself to the sounds of the violins and the powerful percussions of his heart, driving his body like that of a dervish propelled from hell. Pirouettes succeed grand jetés, which succeed arabesques, leaps and more pirouettes. The music stops. Vladimir cannot. The applause is deafening. His body writhes with the pain and pleasure of exhaustion and ecstasy. "Oh, this pain and pleasure . . . this ecstasy must never end! . . . it will never end as long as I dance . . . I will always dance. Why won't my company allow me to perform *Le Spectre?* I am ready. Look at me! Nijinsky could not have danced it better!"

The stagehands had ceased their work and neared the wings to watch Vladimir's inspired and maddening spectacle, to witness his genius metamorphosing into the rose. A rose at once passionate, acrobatic . . . sensual . . . possessed. Vladimir stopped. Drained. Contented. Satisfied. Fulfilled.

He reached for his discarded sweater, mopped his face with it, eased quietly into his clothes, picked up his dance bag, and without a word, without a glance, left the theater. The day was already milky bright when Vladimir reached his hotel.

—✾—

VLADIMIR/*London/Sunday, May 8, 1960*

One by one, buses pulled up outside the Royal Lancaster Hotel on the Bayswater Road. Babbling and laughing, members of the Soviet company got aboard, carrying shopping bags, plastic bags, BOAC bags, hanger bags, souvenir bags, shoulder bags and every sort of hand luggage.

"Where's Vladimir?" Gennady asked.

"He was on the telephone in the lobby the last time I saw him," Sergei answered. "I think I'd better go and get him. You hold four seats together. I'll be back in a minute."

Leonid Grigorovich walked angrily toward the bus. "What was that about Volodin? What's he doing on the telephone? We have to be at the airport in two hours, and I'm expected to hold these buses while Vladimir Volodin talks on the telephone!"

A placid Vladimir came out of the hotel. "Good morning, Comrade Grigorovich." He greeted him with cheerful nonchalance.

"Vladimir Volodin, you're late again!" Grigorovich looked at him intently. "I hear you didn't get home until four o'clock this morning! Congratulations! That's very good training for our opening in Paris!" He stared down the young man. They both climbed onto the bus. "Now that Comrade Volodin has terminated his pressing telephone conversation, we can be on our way," Grigorovich announced.

It was a bright, sunny May day and unusually warm for England. The streets were filled with tourists who had come to London especially for Princess Margaret's wedding. A crowd of sightseers, ballet and opera buffs, had gathered around the departing Russians, some of them carrying red flags and shouting messages of good cheer. Across the road several hundred demonstrators had gathered, bearing banners fiercely protesting the treatment of Soviet Jews. "Free the Azimovs!" "Let the Azimovs go!" "Free Natalia and Igor Azimov!" the placards read. The Azimovs were distinguished dancers with the Bolshoi Ballet who had been refused emigration permits to Israel.

As the bus started moving slowly, one of the protesters, carrying a sign at the end of a long stick bearing the words *Liberate Russian Jewry,* shoved it up against the window next to which Natasha Volkov was sitting. She read it thoughtfully and turned to Grigorovich, seated next to her. "Interesting, isn't it, Leonid Grigorovich, how preoccupied they are with matters that don't concern them—"

"And how easy it is," he said, completing her thought, "for them to ignore inequities in their own country."

"Politics has nothing to do with art!" bellowed one woman, running behind the bus as it accelerated. "We think you're just fabulous!" she cried, blowing kisses. "We love you! London loves you!"

Suddenly the bus stopped so abruptly that the dancers lurched forward in their seats. "See what I mean?" Grigorovich complained. The police had closed a stretch of the road to permit a fleet of Rolls Royces, Daimlers and Bentleys to leave the grounds of Kensington Palace. The occupants were formally dressed, the men in black silk top hats, the women wearing jeweled tiaras, their shoulder-length white kid gloves covered with diamond bracelets. "Look at them!" Grigorovich exclaimed. "And you should just see the pitiful way people live in the East End!"

"What's going on?" Gennady asked.

"I don't know," replied Sergei, craning his neck. "I can't see a thing!"

Most of the Russians were now standing, bending, stooping, looking out of the windows at the police-escorted cavalcade of expensive cars bearing flags on the front fenders and coats of arms above the windshields.

"The capitalist pigs are on their way to Westminster Abbey," Grigorovich explained, "to wallow in a cesspool of class privilege and inherited wealth."

"What's going on?" Vladimir wondered aloud over the hum of the idling engine.

"It's that Princess—what's her name?" Grigorovich answered.

"Margaret!" somebody called out.

"They've found a husband for the princess at last!" Grigorovich jeered. "She's getting married today!"

Natasha Volkov's eyes glistened slightly as she watched the impressive procession pass.

"If Comrade Vladimir Mikhailovich Volodin weren't too sleepy to keep his eyes open," Grigorovich spat out viciously, "he could impress us *peasants* with details of the princess' private life!"

Vladimir said nothing and stoically kept his eyes closed, warmly recollecting the evening he had met Princess Margaret.

It was at a Sharman Douglas party, the princess was there with her fiancé, the photographer Antony Armstrong-Jones. Vladimir was escorting Genevieve. Afterward, at the princess' invitation, they joined her at Danny La Rue's. Her party included Prince and Princess Radziwill, Sharman Douglas and Timothy Paisley, a wealthy and aristocratic young man whose name had been linked romantically with Margaret's. Their table was kept separate from the others by a red satin sash attached to brass standards. All eyes were on them.

Danny was the world's foremost female impersonator, and his act was the main attraction at his fashionable Mayfair club. In one dazzling outfit after another he drove the audience wild with a series of impersonations from Jean Harlow to Beverly Langdon. Finally he appeared center stage dressed in the shimmering silver and chiffon costume of his *pièce de résistance,* Marlene Dietrich. "Marlene" sang the inevitable numbers, peppered with Danny's earthy humor. "Marlene" invited any member of the audience to tango with her. Feeling no pain from the champagne and egged on by the others, Vladimir volunteered. He flung "Marlene" around the room, dancing cheek to cheek, and finished their pas de deux in a crescendo of applause and flashbulbs. The following morning a photograph on the front page of the *Daily Express* showed Vladimir in the arms of the famous drag queen. Princess Margaret glowered in the foreground. The caption read: "Margaret Sees Red!"

A policeman standing in the center of the road motioned the driver on. The bus drove through a parade of shops—florists, greengrocers, news agents

—in Notting Hill Gate, gathering speed down a slope into the rundown elegance of Holland Park.

As they headed west toward the airport the hot morning sun poured through the windows. Most of the passengers had drawn the blinds, and those sitting up front wore sunglasses. Some were singing, accompanying themselves on balalaikas. The bus swayed right and left in time with Vladimir's tossing head. He had fallen asleep.

"What a pity you didn't get more sleep last night, Comrade Vladimir Volodin." Grigorovich placed a hand firmly on his shoulder. "You're missing all the beauty of the English countryside." He handed Vladimir an envelope. It was his plane ticket to Paris.

"What's this all about?" Ekaterina, sitting across the aisle, spoke up, bewildered. "That's strange! We've never handled our own tickets before!"

"What difference does it make?" answered Vladimir carelessly, putting the ticket into his pocket. He closed his eyes. Ekaterina was right, he thought. *Never*, but *never*, had they handled their own tickets before. The bus was now leaving Shepherd's Bush, moving into the outer suburb.

"Wake up, Vladimir! Wake up!" Nikolai shook him by the shoulder.

"Take it easy, will you! . . . What's up?"

Grigorovich was moving down the aisle taking back, one by one, the plane tickets to Paris he had just distributed a short time before. Vladimir sensed danger. He focused on the rows of brick terraced houses flashing past the speeding bus.

"Your ticket please, Nikolai Vazem. Come along, Vladimir Volodin! That means you too! Your ticket please." Vladimir looked Leonid Grigorovich squarely in the face. His eyes blank and expressionless, registering no emotion, Vladimir did not betray any sign of his alarm. Grigorovich smiled at him. He smiled back. Vladimir closed his eyes once more. His brain suddenly plunged into hectic thought. Why were they given tickets in the first place? Why were they taken back? How childish! It was a charade. Definitely a charade. But why? For whose benefit was it being played? To lull someone into a false sense of security? What did it all mean? The more he racked his brain, the more certain he became it could mean only one thing: HE WAS NOT GOING TO PARIS.

London was disappearing behind them. The Berkshire hills unrolled their emerald-green carpet, speckled with the yellow of daisy and buttercup. Fear pinched each separate nerve, creating an explosion of panic. He felt alone. He felt sick. All around him happy talk was crackling. Abruptly the bus moved into total darkness. They were in a tunnel. Vladimir tried to reassure himself, thinking back on the events and the special atmosphere woven around him the past few weeks. Copenhagen, Berlin, Athens, Beirut, Cairo, London, yes, London, where he'd spent the most time. The new friends made in the Royal and London Ballet companies. The streets at night, the misty mornings, the pubs, the bridges, the museums, the very special freedom. Perhaps he was mistaken. Perhaps there was nothing amiss.

His deep sense of the dramatic was making him overreact again. But no matter what he pretended, it was useless. His nostrils picked up the scent of impending disaster, spreading like a foul odor through the bus. He took out a cigarette, struck a match, and its hazy glow caught the gaze of Leonid Grigorovich, whose stare remained fixed and indifferent. The sudden light as the bus left the tunnel momentarily blinded him.

"Are you all right?"

"What?" Vladimir was startled.

"I say, are you all right? You seem so pale." It was Nikolai speaking.

"Yes . . . I'm . . . I'm . . . It's just that . . . No, nothing."

"Come on, what is it?" Nikolai persisted.

"I'm afraid of flying."

"Since when? We've flown everywhere on this tour and you've never mentioned it before."

"I'm afraid of flying *even* though I've never mentioned it, Nikolai Vazem." He could not think of anything else to say. "I've always been afraid of flying. There's no point making a big deal out of it!" He put out the cigarette he had just lit.

They were now approaching the airport. In the distance planes could be seen taking off and landing. They came to a halt in front of the International Departure Building. The four buses disgorged their passengers onto the pavement.

"It's now eleven-fifteen," announced Leonid Grigorovich. "We'll all meet in front of Immigration Control in twenty minutes."

The group of Russians dispersed in the direction of the cafeteria, gift shop, newsstand, drugstore and record shop. Vladimir and most of the others headed for the bar for a last drink of vodka before Paris. The bar was packed with journalists and photographers. They descended on Vladimir. "Have you enjoyed your stay in the United Kingdom?"

"Yes, very much. The people are very kind, very friendly, very polite."

"How about the food? Did you like the food?" Vladimir was conscious of the two Russian policemen who had acted as bodyguards during the tour watching him suspiciously from a distance.

"No, not at all. I think English food is not very good. I prefer Russian food, and it is good that I like tea, because you make coffee terrible."

"What do you think of English girls?"

"I like very much. Much better than English food!" Everybody laughed, the cameras clicked, and Vladimir was frozen in the ghostly blue-white of the flashbulbs. The two policemen had moved closer. Then Genevieve came into his line of vision.

"In fact," he said. "I can see my English girl friend now."

"What's her name! Tell us her name!"

"How about a picture of the two of you?"

"Please—she has come to say goodbye. If you will excuse me, please—yes?"

Vladimir hastily walked over to Genevieve, dropping his heavy shoulder bag to the floor. "Keep smiling. Do not say a word. Just listen to what I have to tell you."

"Vladimir, what's—?"

"Shut up! Keep smiling and listen." He spoke with no fear. No excitement. "Pretend I am telling you something amusing! Laugh! Laugh! Louder—more laugh!" They were immediately surrounded by photographers snapping pictures and newspaper men firing questions at them. Vladimir kept smiling and waving to everyone. "We have not got much time, Genevieve. I may be wrong, but I have feeling something terrible is about to happen." Vladimir had spoken in the most relaxed manner, as if he had been whispering sweet nothings in her ear. "Keep smiling, Genevieve, keep smiling, I beg you!" Vladimir noticed three stalwart men he hadn't seen before, talking and gesturing with Grigorovich. The Russian policemen had now stationed themselves at the exit. He ordered vodka—"with ice, with lemon, 'light,' " he specified. Then abruptly he spoke directly to Genevieve. "When we assemble at Immigration Control, I want you to follow me at a distance. If I go through, then all is well and I will be seeing you in Paris. If I don't . . ." He hesitated. Leonid Grigorovich was approaching them.

"And if you don't?" she asked fearfully.

"Comrade Volodin," Grigorovich said loudly, "could I have a word with you privately?"

"We can talk right here. The young lady doesn't speak Russian." Vladimir bowed slightly.

"Vladimir Volodin, I'm not in the habit of frequenting bars so early in the morning."

"What's wrong? What's wrong?" Genevieve asked anxiously.

"Nothing!" Vladimir reassured her impatiently.

"It would be impolite for us to speak in front of your . . . friend . . . in a foreign language. Please follow me."

"Don't worry!" he murmured to Genevieve. "Whatever you do, don't go away!"

The two policemen stepped aside, and Vladimir and Grigorovich took seats in the BOAC lounge. "Vladimir Volodin," Grigorovich said, placing his arm affectionately around Vladimir's shoulders, "we've just had a telegram informing us that you have been chosen to dance tomorrow night at a gala performance at the Kremlin in honor of the President of the French Republic."

Grigorovich's voice tore through Vladimir's body. "But I'm supposed to dance *Swan Lake* in Paris. I've never performed it outside the Soviet Union!" Even though he had expected something catastrophic, this news genuinely flabbergasted him.

"I'm coming to that," replied Grigorovich. "In five days you will rejoin the company in Paris and dance *Swan Lake* as planned." Grigorovich offered him a cigarette and, smiling, lit it for him obligingly. "This is a great honor for you, Vladimir Volodin. In addition to President de Gaulle you will also be dancing before Comrades Khrushchev and Bulganin." Vladimir's eyes narrowed. His head bobbed in comprehension and affirmation. "When am I supposed to leave for Moscow?"

"Almost immediately. Those three men over there," he said, pointing to the heavyset trio Vladimir had observed from the bar, "will escort you to the Aeroflot exit, where a Tupolev is ready for takeoff."

Vladimir felt the blood drain from his face. What a farce! he thought to himself. He had read just the day before that de Gaulle was in Washington! They weren't even trying to be clever about it! In other words, he was going back, not to dance at all! It would mean that the unique passion that invaded his heart, his body, his whole life, would be thwarted. He would be relegated to obscurity, his life would stop before he had lived! Not dance! He would rather be dead!

Making a fast decision, he chose to be amenable to Grigorovich. "Well, in that case, Comrade Grigorovich," he said with a fatalistic shrug, "I'll just go and say goodbye to my friends and pick up my bag—I left it in the bar. Where shall I meet you?"

"That won't be necessary. We'll say goodbye now." They stood up and shook hands. "Your traveling companions will go along with you to collect your things."

As Vladimir walked toward the bar he was joined by the three sinister men. One tried to take his arm. But Vladimir, pulling himself free, spinning violently, ran, raced, reeled, lurched, colliding into other passengers, knocking over luggage, threw himself into the arms of the British airport police.

"Please help!" he implored. "I want to stay, I want to stay!" Pandemonium had broken loose. Cameras clicked and flashed. Reporters anxious for a scoop closed in on him. A crowd gathered.

"I want to stay! I want to stay!" he repeated.

"Vladimir! Are you all right?" Genevieve cried. "Are you all right?" She was weeping and clutching his arm.

The policemen were joined by several others. "He's a Russian dancer," Genevieve explained. "He doesn't want to go back to the Soviet Union. He wants to stay in England, and they're going to make him go back! Please help him!"

The three Russians moved toward Vladimir and the British policemen. "You have no right to kidnap this man! You must release him to us!" one of them bellowed, his face reddening with fury. "Mr. Volodin is a Soviet citizen."

"This is not the Soviet Union. This is England!" declared a policeman. "And this man has come to us of his own free will." Vladimir saw part of his company assembled at Immigration Control. They were silent; some had tears in their eyes. More shouting from the three Russians. "They're arresting him! Mr. Volodin is a Soviet citizen and this is illegal. We will call our embassy!"

Gennady and Sergei tried to reach him in all the confusion. Vladimir saw them. "Goodbye," Vladimir cried out hysterically, "goodbye. Call my brother Alexei in Kiev. Take care of my dog Lieka. She is with my teach—" The rest of his pleas were lost in the melee.

A cordon of police formed around him. "Get back, everyone. Get back! That's an order!"

He couldn't see Genevieve. "Don't do anything that you will regret," yelled Sergei in the background. Everything blurred for Vladimir as he was led to a small whitewashed room furnished with a single table and two straight chairs.

"Mr. Volodin," a somber customs official said, "British law requires that you remain alone for thirty minutes to consider your decision before we can grant you a temporary 'sanctuary' permit. If you decide to adhere to your resolution, we will bring you the necessary papers to sign."

The man left the room, locking the door behind him. Vladimir heard a shouting match between British and Soviet officials going on outside. Then a faint buzzing of voices. Then nothing. He was alone. In front of him a blank wall. Vladimir stared at nothing and everything. He felt weightless. Should he give up his country, the country he loved? Should he give up everything he had ever known? Would his friends and family understand? Never. Would his countrymen understand that it was nothing political? Never. Who but he himself could understand he had to satisfy his unquenchable hunger to see and hear new things? Who but he himself, with his physical vitality, could feed that nonstop hunger? This was the point of no return. If he couldn't dance, life would have no purpose. He grew more confused. He sat down, trembling, covered his face with his hands and began to sob. He hammered the table with his fists. Maybe he would disintegrate in an abyss of loneliness. He felt clammy and miserable, yet when he touched his head he felt no perspiration, only cold flesh.

His mother came to mind. Proud, aging, alone. What about his city, Leningrad, the city he loved? Could it be possible that he never again would walk on Nevsky Prospekt: warm himself in the white nights; marvel at the Hermitage; revel in the massive beauty of the Cathedral of St. Isaac; bask in the gleam of ancient pastel palaces, timeless and alive, clinging to their past; behold the bridges, the canals, Rossi Street, with the Kirov Theatre, the most spectacular in the world; and above all, never again see the Kirov School?

Would he find the strength to compensate somehow for the unique training of the Kirov, which had forged him into the dancer he was and could become? He thought of his teacher, Pëtr Ivanovich, who was like a father to him. Vladimir could not remember his own father, a brave man, dead long ago in the battle of Leningrad. What about his dancing technique? Would he lose it? What about his moral integrity? He would have to reach deep into his Russian roots, seizing their boundless spiritual resources, and make use of the real profundity of his inner life. He *had* to join the great explosion of dance outside his native land. This decision could only be justified to himself if he could endure. He *had* to dance and reach new levels of exaltation. He *had* to. He raised his head. His decision was made. More than the Russia he still loved he belonged to the world of dance. He waited in anxious silence. Part of his soul was steeped in ancient Russia, with its cruelty, generosity, sensuality and hardiness; the other part listened to new worlds beckoning with promises of mysterious and undiscovered horizons.

And all of a sudden he understood many things. It was a time of understanding that could have come to him only at this moment.

The humming of voices started again. The door was unlocked. He rose with a semblance of calm, feeling his decision was something he had made long ago. He was really on his own. Free. He had made his first choice. Right or wrong. Vladimir Mikhailovich Volodin had just taken the greatest leap of his life. The universe opened its gates and he walked in, unaware that it would bring him to the threshold of the most phenomenal career of all time.

VLADIMIR-MARIELA/*London*/*Sunday, June 5, 1960*

It was Vladimir's fourth Sunday as a free man. He had eaten 54 meals and drunk 280 cups of tea; taken 24 dance classes and 56 hours of English lessons; had 138 arguments with various choreographers, dancers, technicians, journalists and photographers; seen 11 plays and motion pictures and 7 different ballet companies; made love 5 times to 4 different women; received hundreds of letters and opened 3; acquired 15 classical records and 2 prints by Erté and Bakst; traveled to 3 different countries; given 14 performances; read 8 books; turned down 3 offers from motion picture companies; been on the cover of 50 worldwide magazines; given 22 interviews and been misquoted 31 times.

Vladimir dried the sweat off his face and hair with a frayed, discolored towel, shoved it with his practice clothes into a bag, dressed hurriedly, waved goodbye to the dancers of his company, descended the three flights of steps of the London Ballet School, crossed the marble lobby and pushed through the revolving doors onto the street.

He hailed a cab. Looking out through its back window, he saw the rain bouncing as it hit the slippery asphalt. It distorted his vision; street lamps, mackintosh-clad pedestrians, the headlights of approaching cars and buses appeared in duplicate.

Vladimir rang the bell of the majestic house on Belgrave Square. Mariela opened the door. She was draped in a flowing gray chiffon hostess gown, her ebony hair falling loosely over her shoulders. "Well, well! Notoriety seems to agree with you!" Mariela spoke in a voice strong, serene, luminous—a voice accustomed to giving orders. Vladimir closed the massive oak door and dropped his bag. With her usual efficiency Mariela swept off his imposing leather coat and deceptively innocent newsboy's cap.

"Notoriety? No, on the contrary, it doesn't suit me at all! It gets in my way, puts restrictions and constraints on my life. I never knew annoyance of publicity. So much publicity. I hadn't bargained for that. I don't know if I can cope with it." He held both her hands. "I'm so happy to see you, Mariela, and *that* I *know* I can cope with." The heavy and sensual fragrance of amber emanated from her.

"Hello, Vladimir! I must say I'm happy too." She gave him a provocative smile. "Why are you holding my hands so tightly?"

Without letting go he said, "I need to cover up my nervousness."

"Don't be silly! With all the excitement about your performances, what could you possibly be nervous about! Your hands are cold and you're wet. Let's go upstairs. It's cozy and warm there."

Reluctantly he released his grasp. "I wish all the excitement I caused had been for dancing!" He giggled. "I just hope that when notoriety dies down, the papers will forget about my private life and concentrate on my dancing."

"You seem to create news just by existing. I doubt your notoriety will ever die down."

"That would be unbearable. As it is, I feel like the bearded lady at the circus." He irreverently patted the Egyptian sarcophagus on its breast. "Dobry v'yehcher, Tarutu! I'm back again, alive and well. You probably brought me luck!"

"I see you've remembered her name," Mariela said, leading the way up the staircase. A heavy scent of amber trailed behind her. "The servants are out," she said, displaying an elegant three-quarter view of herself. "Sunday is their day off. I thought we'd be more comfortable in my sitting room. It's my private little world. . . . Baxter lit a fire before he went off. It's such a miserable day!"

Vladimir saw his reflection in the mirrored wall panels and lowered his eyes, as if not wanting to see too clearly.

Opening a door, Mariela showed him into her "private little world." Chintz slipcovers in a floral pattern! Matching curtains! The decidedly British country-squire air seemed to make the room a veritable parsonage in a palace. Small Victorian overstuffed chairs and a sofa were arranged around an Augsburg center table inlaid in engraved silver with a variety of

Chinese motifs on a dark-brown tortoiseshell ground. A bouquet of tiger lilies and a green jade Ming figure of a water buffalo sat on it. A black bust of a seventh-century B.C. Himalayan love goddess reposed on a stand and quietly but knowingly surveyed them through sapphire eyes; a perfectly shaped pearl of bronze-black color had been set in each breast. Vladimir noticed a gouache-and-pastel drawing that hung over the mantel.

"What a beautiful portrait!" he exclaimed, walking toward it and studying it closely. "Is that you?" he asked.

"No . . . it's my sister." Mariela lowered her eyes. "She died . . . with her husband . . . in an automobile accident years ago."

"Oh, I'm sorry," he said, "but she looks so much like you, I thought—"

"Yes, we did look very much alike," Mariela interrupted, "but she was older than I. It was painted twenty years ago."

"Your sister was very beautiful. But not as beautiful as you." Then Vladimir's eyes shifted to a tulipwood cabinet inset with Sèvres plaques bearing the date 1774. Expensively framed photographs were displayed on its white marble top. "Do you mind if I look?" Vladimir asked.

"Please, go right ahead. They are mostly family pictures. Here is my husband Curtis," she volunteered, pointing to one of herself with an older man, both on horseback. "And this is me in 1958," she said gaily, "accepting the Woman of the Year award."

"And who is this?" asked Vladimir, reaching for a picture of a handsome smiling teenage boy on a bicycle. "Is he your son?"

"No. Unfortunately I have no children," replied Mariela uneasily. "He is my nephew—my sister's son."

"But the painting on the wall . . .?"

"It was done a year before the child was born."

"Ah! He's no longer a child!" Vladimir exulted. "He's almost my age! Where does he live?"

"With his grandparents." Mariela took the photo out of his hand and returned it to its place. "By the way, I should be congratulated," she said, determined to change the direction of the conversation.

"Why?"

"My horse, Night Sanctuary, won the Kentucky Derby last week. His track record is the best for any three-year-old in the last two decades!"

"Why should you be congratulated? The horse ran, not *you*." He looked around him appreciatively. "It is, as you said, a very cozy room. . . . Where were we? . . . Oh yes—but I know nothing about horses." He took a pack of Avrora cigarettes out of his pocket. "Do you mind if I smoke?"

"Not at all, go right ahead." The lighter clicked disturbingly as she held it for him. "Please sit down and let me give you a drink. It's vodka, isn't it?" Without waiting for his answer Mariela moved to a hammered brass Indian tray and poured from a bottle of Stolichnaya. She handed a silver goblet to Vladimir, then cradled her own in both hands.

"Na zdohrov'yeh!" He raised his glass.

"Na zdohrov'yeh!" Mariela drank slowly. She looked at the young man's face with great tenderness. "When will you be dancing in London?"

"I've already started rehearsals on *Swan Lake*." He downed the drink. "I'm dancing with Sybil Parkinson."

"Dame Sybil! I thought she was retiring this year! She must be over forty."

"And looks twenty-five! She's superb!" Vladimir put the goblet down, creating a frosty circle on the surface of the rosewood end table. He erased the mark abruptly with his forefinger. "I remember seeing one of her last appearances in Leningrad. The arm movements and extensions were extraordinary. I must have been twelve years old at the time. My mother took me and—" His eyes closed perceptibly for a moment as if to cloud the scene from his mind. "I'm very flattered Sybil has chosen to make a comeback with me."

"With you as a springboard she can reach greater heights than ever before!"

Getting up, he proprietarily refreshed his drink.

"How do you feel now that you've defected?"

His lip curled slightly with distaste. "I do not call it defecting," he said emphatically.

"What do you call it then?"

"I haven't found the right word yet. It's . . . it's . . . maybe . . . maybe it is artistic exchange . . . expansion . . . I know! It's . . . it's *perfecting*." He sat down.

"Will you renounce your citizenship?"

"How could I do that? I am still Russian. You don't change your nationality just because you are in foreign country." He spoke as if testifying in his own defense. "As an example, take Oscar Wilde—he didn't become French just because he lived in France. Gauguin didn't adopt Tahitian nationality, and Henry James never became British because he lived here. I did not leave my country for political reasons, only to seek and learn—always learn and dance." Unconsciously he kicked at a flowered footstool. It flew against the delicate stand supporting the Himalayan bust, causing it to wobble back and forth on its dainty scroll feet. The Indian statue careened toward the edge and with a mighty crash fell to the floor. Its torso shattered. Vladimir was aghast. "I am sorry, Mariela. I did not mean to . . . I just got . . . I just got . . . carried away. I am so . . . so . . . sorry!" He fell to his knees, picking up the fragments, embarrassed and speaking to himself in Russian.

Then he stared at her in disbelief. He might have expected anger or disappointment, but, no, her smile reflected the opposite. Anticipation. He could smell it, so oppressive was its power in that room.

"You've broken her heart," she said smiling. Wry. Amused. Could she be pleased to be able to criticize, to have the upper hand over this *homme formidable?*

"She never had a heart," he countered, raising his head. "She was a . . . a . . ." He trailed off. "It was a statue made of stone."

But she knew that it was not what he had meant to say at all. What he really had meant was that women have hearts of stone. Would she too break? Mariela didn't know, but she was determined to find out.

"Give me the pieces, Vladimir." She put them carefully into an ivory box.

"Here's a nipple!" He laughed, dropping one of the pearls into her extended palm. "I'll try and find the other one."

Mariela planted a fist on her hip. "If ever I write my memoirs, I must not forget to include the episode in which Vladimir Volodin, on all fours in my sitting room, looked for my second nipple!"

"And if ever I should write mine," he said, "I will never forget that once, in London, I looked on floor for pearl nipple that belonged to the most beautiful woman I have ever seen!" He laughed heartily and rose. "And here is the other pearl."

Her wrists exuded the powerful fragrance of amber, stirring his blood and stinging his imagination like a narcotic. "It's probably all my fault," she said graciously, putting the box away. "I had no business displaying that statue in such a vulnerable place! And besides, how tactless of me to raise an obviously sensitive topic of conversation!" She prodded a log in the fireplace. "People take it for granted—and I'm one of them—" she continued, "that just because you're new in the West, you have no past." She sat down.

Vladimir moved to the window. "Oh. It has stopped raining. That's good." Rain reminded him of snow and snow brought back that faraway place—home! . . . What home? That place—the place he could still smell in his nostrils whenever his country was mentioned.

There was a swishing of silk, a waft of amber. Mariela had crossed her shapely legs.

Vladimir turned around. "You're very beautiful," he said.

"Are you happy now?" she asked, flustered.

"What a question, Mariela! How can I answer? I live on a seesaw of emotions, but . . . sometimes I feel . . . discontent about myself." He sounded almost proud.

"Discontent with oneself is not a virtue, dear Vladimir. It's an infirmity. You seem to have it in excess."

"I suppose going nightly from wild applause to lonely rooms must be part of the reason."

"And of course being Russian makes you a creature of moods and passions," she added delicately.

"Yes, I suppose we are addicted to sacrifice." He sat down again. "It's a known fact there's a great masochistic streak in Russians. So said Dostoyevsky!" His eyes followed Mariela as she leaned forward, lighting the candle in a seventeenth-century brass holder. Her swelling bosom glistened in a pool of soft light.

"I called almost daily to find out when you would be back in London."
His eyes flashed desire at her with suffocating intensity. "Why did you
finally decide to see me?"

"Curiosity, Vladimir," she tossed off indifferently. "Everybody wants to
know about Vladimir Volodin, and I found it rather marvelous to have the
opportunity to learn about him firsthand!" She noticed that the soft bulge
in his pants was stiffening, taking on a thick elongated shape. His brow was
moist. She ran her fingers through her hair. "Are you satisfied with your
decision—with the choice you've made?" she asked shakily.

"I don't know . . ." he faltered. "I really don't know. I have no time to
think. So much to do and see . . . all so new . . ." His train of thought
was momentarily lost. "Only time will tell if, perhaps, I made an irre . . .
trievable error. I have nostalgia. I have spoken to my family by telephone—
to my teacher. They cannot believe what has happened. They are so hurt.
They do not understand. It is very upsetting . . . very upsetting." His
gaze wandered to the fireplace. He felt a huge depression echoing in his
consciousness. "Only dancing makes me forget. . . . I must dance . . .
always dance . . ."

"Let me give you more vodka." Mariela got up. "I've had difficult times
too, Vladimir, but the days spin out. When they've passed, you'll see that
in the long run it's the bad ones that give you the most comforting memories. They are like enemies you have vanquished." He held out his glass
and reached for her other hand. Their fingers intertwined. "We are all
marked by boundaries, Vladimir. You're not alone. I . . ."

He stared at Mariela a long time without speaking. Unlocking their hands
slowly, she walked away from him and leaned on the windowsill. "It's raining again . . ." she began. "It's raining again . . . perhaps you . . ."

He stirred, like a card player about to make his final bid. "Mariela, I
want you more than any woman I've ever known!" The gauntlet was hurled.

The telephone rang in the next room. They stood in silence.

"You're not going to answer it?" His voice rasped.

"No . . ."

The ringing stopped abruptly.

"Do you believe me?" he said. Images ran through his mind. Tongues.
Legs. Breasts. Ten jutting toes. Fingers. To be placed anywhere. With
urgency now! "Do you believe me?"

"Yes."

Suddenly the urge to fling herself at this young man erupted from the
most profound depths of Mariela's being. She moved toward him, and before she could take a breath, Vladimir had crushed her in his arms as if
the two of them could miraculously be merged into one.

He kissed her wildly on the mouth, the neck, the ears, the cheeks. Overcome with uncontrollable desire, Mariela fell backward in his arms, trembling. Clasping her waist, he picked her up, and kicking the door open
with his boot, carried her into the bedroom and laid her on the bed.

Obsessed, he ripped open the bodice of her negligee, kissing her shoulders. Her eyes flashed and widened, her lips parted with moans of protest. "Wait!" she said on his mouth. "Wait!" He didn't listen. His hungry hands caressed her hair, her eyes, her shoulders. Everywhere his fingers went, they came between her vision and the light, cutting off the room, the view, the world. Only the sensual sound of the rain lingered. He unhooked the filmy net brassiere. The luscious breasts spilled out.

Lying now on the bed, supporting himself with one elbow, Vladimir lowered his lips to her creamy flesh. Trailing his mouth across her breasts, he darted his tongue in and out at the beige nipples. They rose to meet his touch. Taking one, then the other, into his mouth, he sucked and teased them with his teeth, gently at first, then harder and harder, until she cried out in the pain of ecstasy. Frenziedly he undressed her. She lay before him in only a garter belt, stockings and satin slippers. A thin gold chain, with what seemed to be an Egyptian scarab dangling from it, encircled her waist. Her flawless body mesmerized him.

Mariela pressed her breasts against him, slowly unbuttoning his shirt, kissing his chest, her tongue on his nipples, under his arms, on his lips, in his hair, on his neck. Her hands helped him loosen the belt of his trousers, and his clothes were soon scattered on the floor. He spread his magnificent nakedness on top of Mariela's, pinning her down with his weight. He raised himself and fell back. She took hold of his head, caressing his neck and speaking fluently to his body with her nails. She discovered the infinity of his flesh. Up and down the back, over the buttocks, between them, down the thighs, between them, across the shoulders, up and down the neck, harder and harder, deeper and deeper, leaving red marks on the rippling muscles, exploring the crevices, ravines and hillocks of this stupendous animal.

Her hand guided his fingers. The hand stopped. The hand went up. The fingers returned, circling, cupping the weight of her breasts. Down again, brushing past her hips, the fingers ended inside her wetness. She guided his hand again, reaching rare tears of pleasure. Her lips quivered. The wounded flesh healed. Love, passion, rose again. Like a drug, the intoxication started at the bottom of her heels. She soared, dreaming. Very softly she began to stroke his hair while his cheek rested on a curve of her breast.

On his back now, Vladimir watched. Slowly, provocatively, sensuously, Mariela unhooked her stockings and rolled them off. With a flick of her hand the garter belt was gone, across the room.

Placing a knee on each side of him, she lowered herself over his body, her breasts caressing his thigh. The dark silk of her hair brushed his abdomen. She explored and caressed. Caressed and kissed. She took his cock in her fingers; it glistened in the soft light. A tremor passed through her body as chills ran through him. He brought his knees up in a quick movement as she forced the massiveness of his thick, heavily veined member into her mouth, stretching her lips to accommodate it. She sucked and massaged it with her tongue, caressing his testicles with one hand. With a finger of the other hand she entered his anus, violating his innocence.

For him Mariel created rivulets of shivers that wound around his feet, his ankles, his thighs, his shoulders. He felt it all. His mind drifted, his eyes sealed—he swam in the turmoil bursting inside him. A gate opened. An emotion. Not just a reverting memory. A new emotion, with its own reason, its own being, its own cry. Obsessed with the desire to bestow her generous body on him, she twisted, slid, pushed herself beneath him. Gripping his shoulders and licking the droplets of perspiration from his chest, she tossed her head in a delirium. Silent, forcing his legs between hers, he entered her savagely. Sliding, ramming, forcing, in and out, moving, bruising, stopping, teasing, starting again with frenetic energy. She squeezed him tightly, enclosing his flesh in hers. He gave himself, eagerly, wildly. She was open to him all barriers down. Her boldness dazed him. Mariela had become the instrument of his satiation. She anticipated each of his demands, responded, accepted, invented, sucked away each new desire. He was her slave. Vladimir was looking for a future in her eyes; she was looking for the next moment in his. A shudder rippled through her arched body. He groaned, gasping for air. She cut off his words, kissing his mouth. They both went limp, drenched in each other's passion.

Crushed by the victor, Mariela took her own triumph modestly, voluptuously savoring her defeat.

Too soon the dawn exposed the lovers to the harsh glare of reality, shrouding their love with the colors of the coming day. Mariela fell asleep, buried deep in Vladimir's arms.

In the wash of a gray light that follows cold morning rain, the amber-scented room revealed its secrets: an ashtray crammed with crushed cigarettes, fur-covered chairs in disarray, stockings and towels on the floor, music playing softly, the acrid odor of burned wax, empty glasses, a window shade pulled askew. The disorder that only lovemaking can produce.

Vladimir Volodin had been here. Now he was gone.

※

DENISE/*Paris*/*Thursday, June 8, 1961*

It was an enthralling day for Denise. She found a small package from Cartier on her breakfast tray. In the package a velvet box. In the velvet box a pair of earrings, each button a flawless five-carat diamond from which hung a ten-carat pear-shaped ruby. With it a short note: "I'll see you tomorrow, Princess. Love, Sinclair."

Her spirits soared as she put on the earrings. Then she became pensive, all enthusiasm dwindling as she reread the note. Tomorrow . . . tomorrow, she thought. Sinclair's timing could not have been worse—the one day I've been able to set aside for having my hair done, for reading, for sleeping late, for enjoying being alone . . . The social whirl of Paris, with its daily rounds of lunch, cocktails, dinners, had taken its toll of Denise. Tonight there'd be still another dinner . . . then Sinclair! He'd want to be entertained. Oh, hell! Why couldn't he have waited a week or so? Denise would have to forget about a peaceful tomorrow. There was nothing to do but hope his international business ventures would keep him from overstaying his welcome. They probably would journey to the Château D'Antibes for the weekend. It made her feel better. The Riviera mansion was the one place Denise felt totally at home.

All her radiance sparkled once more as the mirror returned her stunning reflection, enhanced by the magnificent earrings.

Denise had a five o'clock appointment at the Place Vendôme with an art dealer. Having about an hour to kill, she strolled aimlessly on the elegant Avenue Montaigne, window shopping, appraising, feeling beautiful. A name carved in black marble over a fashionable boutique attracted her attention. *Darvina*. It must be a new place, thought Denise. I was here a week ago, and I'm sure it wasn't . . .

Darvina . . . Darvina . . . Years earlier she had known an American named Carol Davis who was known in the world of haute couture as Darvina. She was Christian Dior's star model, and whenever Denise came in for fittings, they had always exchanged pleasantries and a few laughs. Then Darvina disappeared. "Could it be the same Darvina?" she wondered.

Denise's curiosity finally got the better of her. She entered the plush establishment.

It *was* the same Darvina. She had not changed at all, her red-haired beauty as breathtaking as ever.

The two became reacquainted.

"I'm so flattered, Denise, that you recognize me."

"It's been what—six or seven years?"

"Denise, I remember you even further back—1952 or 1953. You had just arrived in Paris with your godfather. How could I ever forget it! He kept you shopping and shopping. I never saw anyone buy so many clothes, and always white." She laughed good-naturedly. "In those days I wondered if you stopped shopping long enough to breathe!"

"I haven't changed. But whatever happened to you? I go to Dior a dozen times a year—you simply dropped out of sight."

"Oh, Denise." Darvina's color rose with sheer joy. "Luckily for me I realized I couldn't be a model forever. So I went back to America for the necessary financing—tried out a few design ideas—dropped a few names. And presto! Voilà! I was able to come back and open this place. How do you like it?" Darvina twirled around with pride, pointing to the fine and expensive garments, luxurious accessories, the sundry accoutrements of the very rich. "Can I show you a few things? All white of course."

Darvina ignored all her other clients, relegating them to saleswomen. She was devoting her full attention to Denise, bringing dresses of the finest fabrics, the most classical lines, the most exquisite taste, helping her into and out of each, zipping and unzipping. "Can I offer you a glass of wine?"

"Thank you." They both sat down on a gray suede and chrome ottoman.

"Chin-chin," said Darvina, clinking glasses with Denise. "I've read so much about you. I was really sad when . . . when Prince Borgia died. At the time I sent you a letter of condolence, which you answered, but I wonder, with all that was on your mind, if you . . . if you really remembered me."

"Darvina, you are a hard person to forget. I'm sorry that I haven't kept in touch, but my life is so . . . ."

"Nothing to be sorry about." Darvina waved orders to her staff, arranging for Denise's purchases to be wrapped and delivered. "I'm just happy to see you again. Truly happy! You're more beautiful than ever. It's too bad, your being so busy. I probably won't have a chance to see more of —we won't have a chance to see more of each other."

"You've read my mind." Denise giggled. "I'd love to see more of you too." Her excitement was genuine and wholly unexpected.

"I'm sure you could never find the time . . . ."

"Ordinarily I haven't a minute to spare. But tonight," Denise lied, deciding to cancel her plans, "tonight, would you believe it, I have absolutely nothing to do."

"Nothing?" Darvina rested her hand on Denise's elbow and softened her voice. "Since you have nothing to do . . . well, ordinarily I wouldn't ask this, but under the circumstances, I would love to renew our friendship." More assertively, she continued, "Be my guest tonight and let me show you a side of the world—my side of the world. I bet you don't know Saint-Germain-des-Prés. All you have to do is dress very simply."

Denise smiled broadly. "You're talking about a bohemian evening, aren't you?"

"Do you mind?"

"Not at all. You couldn't have asked on a better day." She clasped Darvina's hand with childish enthusiasm and unembarrassed friendship. "I've always wanted to go slumming!"

"But you never had the guts?"

Both women laughed. They set a time for later that evening.

Denise's custom-made silver Rolls Royce stopped in front of a modern apartment house on the Rue de la Tour.

Darvina was waiting in the lobby. "Eight-thirty on the dot!" she exclaimed, entering the car. "Never expected you to be on time." They embraced warmly. "Well, is this your slumming outfit?" Darvina asked.

"I'm afraid I don't have such an animal in my closet," said Denise nervously, smoothing the pleats of her white silk shirtdress. "Until—until the last minute I was still debating as to whether I should—"

"Come on, where's your spirit of adventure?" interrupted Darvina. "Tonight you're going to see a part of Paris that I'll bet is completely foreign to you. It should be a nice change from all your stuffy evenings . . ."

Denise was kneading her forehead as if she were massaging a headache.

"Don't you feel well, Denise?"

"I feel fine. Why?"

"Don't tell me you're still apprehensive." Darvina grabbed her hand impetuously. "Relax! Let's have fun!"

The "headache" was gone.

Gerard drove the two women toward the Left Bank. The lazy traffic crawled, a solid, uninterrupted mass of overheated engines.

Since she wanted to walk from haunt to haunt as inconspicuously as possible, Denise ordered the chauffeur to stop on the Rue de Seine.

She watched the stunning Darvina as she stepped out of the car. She had a look of limitless energy. An attractive, very positive brand of energy. Although redheads don't usually wear the color well, she had on a simple red cotton top with spaghetti straps over her pale shoulders; freckles were an integral part of her charm. Tailor-made black gabardine slacks with low-heeled ankle-high boots completed the image of casualness. The fiery tresses flowed loosely like a mane and the green eyes were devastating. Darvina is really a creature of the night, thought Denise.

Walking arm in arm through the Latin Quarter, past the Church of St.-Germain-des-Prés, they took a table on the terrace of the Café Flore and drank several brandies as they absorbed the street scene: long-haired students in sloppy sweaters and Jesus Christ sandals, boisterous girls laughing, a nostalgic song escaping from an open window, dogs made to order to resemble their masters, American ladies imposing their fur wraps on the balmy twilight, the lusty voice of a street singer, the muted ripple of an accordionist, the jingling of pieces of money falling on plates, women alone or lonely, people calling to each other or simply looking loudly into each other's eyes, vendors barking or whispering their wares—"Birds, holy pictures, umbrellas, flowers, newspapers, etchings, love . . ."—young men looking ancient, old men aping adolescence, the intoxicating smell of coffee and Chanel No. 5, the crinkly wrapping-paper crispness of potato chips, a symphony of automobile horns blaring in different keys, the fat squeal of thick-soled shoes on the sidewalk, the rich aroma of Gauloise, the mellowness of the organ grinder's melodies of yesterday, bringing to mind souvenirs with no past. A hive of murmurs. A Babel of colors. Night descending with the delicate fatality of a bat's wing.

Perhaps an hour passed.

There was a commotion at a nearby table, occupied by a large family gathering. One of the children had said or done something out of turn. The grandfather scolded and struck him hard. Denise was shocked, then surprised, then amused when she observed the child remain stoic as the grandfather burst into tears and fled from the café.

"The French are absolutely wonderful!" Denise marveled. "Absolutely!"

" 'Unpredictable' might be a better word," Darvina responded cynically. "How'd you like some *real* local color?"

"What did you have in mind?"

"This place here is strictly for kids! I'd like to take you somewhere around the corner where the grown-ups hang out."

"What's it called?"

"That's a surprise. Don't you trust me? After all, it was your idea to go slumming."

They walked carefully on the irregular cobblestones of the Rue Jacob, and Darvina took her arm protectively. They stopped in front of a decrepit-looking old building. There was no sign, no window, nothing to indicate that here was the choicest bar-restaurant in Paris, certainly the most expensive.

A long and narrow corridor was lined with couples, embracing, holding hands and whispering furtively. Denise and Darvina entered a crowded bar, gray with smoke, heavy with perfume. Every stool was occupied by beautiful girls and men of movie-star good looks, fashionably attired.

A lean young man in impeccably cut white tails, his 1920s' coiffure black and shiny with brilliantine, approached Darvina. "Bonsoir, Darvina." His tall and supple body bent low as he kissed her fingers. "Why didn't you let me know you were coming? I would have saved you a table!" The somewhat effete voice didn't match the masculine handsomeness.

"We didn't know we were coming—spur-of-the-moment sort of thing, you know," said Darvina with false animation. "Fred, I want you to meet Denise, an American friend of mine."

"Enchanté, mademoiselle," said Fred with admiration in his eyes. Then, turning to Darvina, "There's a famous compatriot of yours here tonight. I'd like to introduce you and Denise to Christine Jorgensen." Denise was about to say something when Fred went on. "Have a drink at the bar. Messaline will take care of you. The floor show's nearly finished, and I'll see that you get a good table." He left with an expansive gesture.

"Who's Fred?" Denise asked nervously.

"Fred's the owner, and she runs the best—"

"*She!*" Denise exclaimed. "What on earth do you mean, *she?*"

"What do you think I mean?" Darvina swung around and ordered drinks from a grotesque drag queen in a copper-colored wig: makeup had gotten into the natural creases, emphasizing the lines in his face; the gown was a vermilion sheath of ferocious gaudiness. The green fingernails unsettled Denise.

"Why does Fred have such a vulgar woman working here?"

"That vulgar woman, as you put it, used to be one of the most famous female impersonators in the world. He's getting on of course, but everyone in Paris who remembers the old days is his friend. Messaline's got a large following, and that's important if you own a club."

As the orchestra went into the finale, velvet curtains separating the bar from the cabaret were drawn apart in readiness for those patrons who would be leaving after the first show. Denise was transfixed by the lineup of gorgeous girls and stunning men.

"Now, before you ask me," Darvina explained, "all the boys are women and all the girls are men."

"Honestly?"

Darvina could see from the look on her face that Denise wasn't comprehending. "Come off it, will ya! This is 1961!" Darvina emitted a naughty laugh. "Where've you been?"

Denise didn't reply.

"For God's sake, Denise, what little game are you playing? Haven't you ever seen two women together?"

"What do you mean?"

"I mean just what I said. Two women together. And I'm not talking about playing tennis. I mean—two women—making love."

"Well, yes," Denise replied shyly, remembering her honeymoon with Sinclair in Havana. "Once."

A mannish female in a black tuxedo, sporting a red carnation, brought them to a table covered with shimmering platinum satin cloth. A round glass globe diffused pink light onto a white placard bearing the number 9 next to an antique ivory telephone.

"What are the phones for?" asked Denise.

"Well, if you feel like calling Princess Margaret, just dial three." Darvina pointed to a large party sitting to their right which included the princess with her husband, Lord Snowdon, Judy Montagu, Sharman Douglas and their escorts. "Or, perhaps," she continued, "you'd prefer number seventeen." Darvina indicated another group, at the center of which sat a beautiful lady covered in silver and gold. "It's Marlene Dietrich," she whispered. Denise squinted momentarily, blinded at the mention of the beloved name. Around them laughter bubbled over, but softly, as if it were bouncing against felt. A sensual sound, being magically sucked out of the room.

The walls were covered in black velvet and adorned with Aubrey Beardsley's erotic prints. One of them caught Denise's eye. It represented two naked women intimately entwined. Darvina's hand had settled on her thigh.

"Come on, Denise, let's dance," she commanded gently.

"But—"

"No buts." Darvina stood up.

Denise was filled with an angry confusion. She looked at Darvina in a quizzical way, a little embarrassed, but challenged, and rose to her feet.

They approached the congested dance floor. Denise noticed the orchestra for the first time. The eight musicians were all women, heavily but exquisitely made up. They wore white ties and tails, gardenias in their buttonholes, and monocles.

"They play only tangos and foxtrots here. This place is right out of the 1920s." Darvina put her bare arm very slowly around Denise, and her little nose, with the arched nostrils, brushed ever so lightly across her velvety forehead.

"This is . . . the first time I've ever . . . danced with a woman," Denise stammered in a hollow voice.

"Well, there's a first time for everything." All eyes were on them. "Gertrude Stein and Alice Toklas used to come here, but we're the most beautiful couple tonight!"

Whirling past a floor-to-ceiling smoked mirror, Denise caught sight of a blonde and a redhead in close embrace, then recognized herself, locked intimately with Darvina.

"Oh!" She stiffened. "I'm no stranger in Paris. Suppose someone recognizes me!"

"Suppose they do?" chirped Darvina, pressing her body against Denise. "They recognize Princess Margaret. They recognize Marlene Dietrich. Why not you?"

"What will they think?"

"They'll think you're damned fascinating—if you'd only stop blushing." Darvina touched Denise's face. "Anyhow—better they see you here than taking out the garbage."

Denise agreed. Suddenly there was a miracle of silence in the noise as a strange new excitement welled inside her.

The Rolls was waiting on the Rue de Seine. Denise and Darvina entered it.

"There's a little bar on the Rue François I," Darvina said, holding on tightly to Denise's hand. "Let's have a nightcap before . . . before you go home. It's really a swell place." She smiled pleadingly. "They have an American pianist who's absolutely the best—"

"Okay, okay, okay!" said Denise excitedly. "You see, I'm not hard to convince. I'm in a great mood!"

The establishment was called Calvados. The two women navigated through the crowded piano bar toward a table in the corner. A flamenco guitarist was concluding his last number. The void caused by his departure was immediately filled by a crescendo of the patrons' raucous and disjoined cackling.

"It's on me this time," insisted Darvina as she ordered champagne.

All of a sudden Denise heard a familiar voice singing at the piano: "Must you dance . . . every dance . . . with the same fortunate man? . . ."

She shot up like an arrow.

"You have danced . . . with him since the music began . . . Won't you change partners—" Only one performer in the world sounded like this: Sean O'Malley, from the Chez Paree—"and dance with me?"

She was not mistaken. It *was* Sean O'Malley. Denise sat down abruptly and glanced at her watch. "Good lord!" she fairly shouted. "I didn't know it was this late! It's after two—I've got to get up early tomorrow." Hurriedly, without another word, Denise rose and began pushing her way through the crowd.

Darvina caught up with her outside the club. "Gee whiz, hold your horses, beauty. It's too late to turn into a pumpkin." She laughed. Denise's chauffeur, who had parked the car outside the club's entrance, got out and opened the door. "Enter your coach, Cinderella," said Darvina.

"Where to?" asked Gerard.

"First we'll drop Mademoiselle Darvina, then home, Gerard," she said as calmly as she could. Denise's face was pale.

"My God, Denise, what on earth came over you? You look as if you've seen a ghost!" said Darvina.

Yes, Denise *had* seen a ghost. A ghost she hadn't seen for ten years. A ghost that reminded her of the early days, the hard days, the cheap days, the nobody days. The days of Denise Cunningham—Denise Cunningham, showgirl, sequined and feathered. Yes, Darvina was right, she *had* seen a ghost. A ghost she certainly did not want to meet face-to-face.

Darvina delivered, Denise continued on in profound silence, solitude, uncertainty. She entered her Avenue Foch home.

Yvette opened the door. "Oh, Madame MacAlpine, Monsieur has arrived."

"Arrived? Here? When? From where? He wasn't expected until tomorrow morning!"

"Monsieur arrived about an hour ago."

"Did you tell him I was dining with friends?"

"Yes, madame. He would like you to ring his room. Monsieur must still be awake."

"Very well," Denise replied blankly as she strode to her quarters—her white room, white even in darkness, white with fox furs and suede and flowers—chaste white, illuminated only by the light above the Fabergé Peacock Egg.

"Perhaps madame would like me to help her get ready for bed?"

"No, thank you, Yvette, I'll be all right. Please see that I'm not disturbed in the morning until I ring for you. Good night."

The door closed behind Yvette.

Denise sat on the edge of her bed. She thought of Sinclair. Fingers poised over the intercom, Denise lifted the phone, then dropped it.

Another thought entered her mind. Warm. Vivid. Immediate. Replacing the phone, she reclined on her bed, reflecting on the unfamiliar sensations rippling through her body.

A single need dominated her thoughts. She felt aroused. She wondered how she would respond sexually to a woman. To Darvina. She raised the white fabric of her dress, letting her hand caress her thighs. Her fantasies became more persistent.

In her mind she watched Darvina enter the room and walk to the side of the bed, where she sat down next to her. Taking Darvina's hand, she placed it firmly over her breast and squeezed it. "Oh, Darvina!" she sighed as her nipples swelled. She gradually lowered the front of her dress and undid her bra, exposing her bare breasts, and continued caressing them until the nipples were completely hard and erect. Slipping her hand into the front of her panties, she could feel her moistness, and as her excitement mounted, she visualized Darvina lowering her body over hers. Finally, unable to stifle the sound of her pleasure, she cried out in ecstasy while arching her back, and fell limp against the bed.

Seconds passed.

Denise wasted no time. Again she picked up the intercom and rang Sinclair. "My dearest Sinclair, what a wonderful surprise! I just got home"—she sighed alluringly—"I was thinking about you all evening. I'm waiting for you . . . hurry . . ."

Slowly the white silk dress slid to the floor.

-❊-

DENISE/*French Riviera*/*Friday, June 16, 1961*

It was a few minutes past five in the afternoon when Darvina, carrying a single suitcase, stepped through the gate of Nice's airport. Denise embraced her warmly. The two young women raced off in Denise's white Ferrari.

They drove along the Promenade des Anglais, passing the famous Hotel Negresco.

"Look!" Denise exclaimed. "This is the exact spot where Isadora Duncan was killed!"

Darvina looked vague.

"Of course you know how the dancer died? Her scarf caught in the wheel of her lover's Bugatti."

"Well, I feel safe," said Darvina. "I'm not your lover and you're driving a Ferrari. Besides, a scarf is so . . . so plebeian. Surely a glamorous dancer deserves a more glamorous death!"

The car sped on in silence.

Although it was still early in the season, Darvina observed that the seafront was teeming with bathers. People clustered under brightly colored umbrellas in small beach-side restaurants. The brilliant blue water spread all the way to the horizon.

"It's just like a movie set!" Darvina exclaimed.

"As Al Jolson was heard to say, 'You ain't seen nothing yet!' " replied Denise.

"There's one thing money *can't* buy," remarked Darvina.

"What's that, pray tell?"

"Poverty!" They both laughed so hard the car veered out of control momentarily, then continued speeding along the Côte d'Azur and into the mountains.

Dazzled by a debauchery of color and light, Darvina strained to see it all. The cliff coastline looked as if it had been sliced by a giant stonecutter. Villas were perched on steep slopes as though a mystical hand had arbitrarily placed them there. Cloud puffs, pale and mute, hung motionless in the infinite sky. At each turn, pine trees and flowers abounded—jasmine, bougainvillea, carnations, roses, orange blossoms—their sweet and exotic fragrances wafting into the automobile.

Half an hour later the Ferrari entered an estate through massive gates, its pillars adorned by larger-than-life-size lions carved from stone, their manes covered in gold leaf. Cypress trees lined the gravel road that wound through the meticulously manicured grounds. They came on the château suddenly. The architecture was Italian rococo, with great balustrades and terraces.

The car came to a halt. A dark-blue-liveried butler waited at the foot of imposing marble steps to meet them.

Denise and Darvina entered a vast hallway that led past an impressive reception area with a floor-to-ceiling window framing the Mediterranean like a priceless seascape.

Denise, bursting with obvious pride, showed Darvina through the maze of rooms.

They ascended a majestic staircase, and walked halfway round the interior balcony to French doors. She opened them to reveal a lavishly appointed white suite.

They passed through the storybook apartment, Darvina in a trance; she had been unprepared for what she had already seen and was unable to imagine what she would see next.

The Art Deco bathroom was circular. Its floor was made of translucent Lalique tiles and was lighted from beneath. In its center stood a magnificent sunken tub carved from a huge block of rock crystal. Two enormous sterling silver dolphins spouted hot and cold water.

"When the tub's not used for bathing," explained Denise, "you can push this button and release a fountain that circulates perfumed water."

Three carved rock-crystal basins, with matching silver dolphins, stood like statuary around the white marble walls. Huge potted plants lined and draped the entire room with their verdant boughs.

Denise led Darvina through a translucent door to a spacious terrace adjoining the sitting room. They stepped out into the warm, late-afternoon air and surveyed the angular shoreline dominating a private beach below.

Beyond the umbrellas, lounge chairs and tables, the shimmering Mediterranean nibbled at the soft white sand. The sun had set, but beautiful shadows lingered. And the palm trees, almost touching the sea, stood dark and shapely against the sky.

"I don't know why you wanted me here when you have all this," said Darvina, still mesmerized.

"Well, I thought we could have such fun together. It's just too bad you can stay only the weekend." Thinking it might serve as further inducement, she continued, "Besides, if you're looking for a rich husband, this is definitely the pond to fish in!" Denise did not feel it appropriate to confess that Darvina had been on her mind often in recent days, and at the most unexpected moments. Each time Sinclair made love to her, she fantasized that it was Darvina's lips that kissed her flesh, Darvina's arms that held and stroked her. Only through fantasy could she endure Sinclair's masculinity.

Eventually Denise had found it impossible to resist, and she had called Darvina in Paris.

—✴—

"Hello. This is Denise," she said as calmly as she could.

"Hello, beauty! How are the rich and famous living it up on the Riviera this year?"

"I'm calling you because I want you to come and join the rich and famous. I feel like new money!"

"And what does new money feel like?"

"Crisp! How soon can you be here?"

"It's the best offer I've had all day, beauty. Let me see now . . ."

"Well . . . ?"

"I could come Friday, but—"

"What time can you leave Paris?"

"Not before three. I'll have to find out what flights are available."

"Nonsense!" replied Denise. "I'll send my plane for you. When I invite someone, I do it in style! What do you think we're running here, a summer camp? My plane will be waiting for you at Le Bourget from three o'clock on."

"You're really living it up, aren't you, what with private planes . . . !"

"I'll meet you at the airport in Nice."

"I can hardly wait."

※

"Come on, beauty, let's go downstairs," said Darvina now.

They strolled to the rose garden. A mosaic-tiled pool shimmered in the late sunset.

No sooner had they sat down than a butler appeared bearing a bottle of Dom Perignon nestling icily in an ornate silver champagne bucket and a large crystal dish brimming with Malossol caviar. He placed them on a white wrought-iron table, where glasses and platters of canapés had been laid out. Silence descended on the garden. The penetrating twilight sounds reverberated against the pink stucco walls of the house.

"It's very peaceful here." Darvina got up and walked to the edge of the pool, where, kneeling, she trailed a long slender hand in the cool blue water. As Denise handed her a glass of champagne she could see Darvina's sensual features reflected, rippling and fragmented on the water's surface. "You must be happy."

"I am."

"And Sinclair?"

"He's very happy too."

"I didn't mean that."

"No?"

"Where is he?"

"Sinclair left yesterday for Germany on business."

"You've quarreled!" she stated sardonically.

"Of course not!"

"So he left you by yourself?"

"I wouldn't say that"—Denise winked—"but it was a close call, and I'd have been by my lonesome!"

"How's that?"

"I mean, if you had been unable to come."

"Were you really concerned?"

She caught sight of Darvina's face, dimly and mysteriously lit. "Yes, very," Denise replied flatly.

Darvina rose. The two women regarded each other silently. Denise turned around and walked toward the table. "Would you like lemon on your caviar?" she asked matter-of-factly, holding a small plate in her hand.

"I'll take anything you give me, Denise."

They both sat on the garden swing, moving backward and forward, basking in the sumptuous gold of the summer evening.

"I sincerely believe, Denise, that you have a lot of merit."

"I'd call it good luck," Denise replied.

"Well," philosophized Darvina, "good luck *always* brings merit, whereas the other way round seldom works out."

"The south of France has been very good to me," Denise agreed, thinking of the first time Escobar had brought her to this fairyland, of his generosity in bestowing this property on her, and, of course, of meeting Francesco Borgia.

"Maybe you should rename it the 'South of Chance'!" Darvina laughed and changed the subject. "What a beautiful night! I'd love to go swimming—how about you?"

"Okay," replied Denise, strangely edgy. "Let's get bathing suits."

"Bathing suits? Why?" teased Darvina, stroking Denise's hair. "Night is the time for nudity!"

"I've never gone swimming in the nude before."

"Never gone swimming in the raw?" chided Darvina.

"Never . . . I . . ."

"I don't believe it!" Darvina laughed, making a face. "Keep your ring on and you'll feel fully clothed. It's big enough!"

"Would you like a *petit* supper afterward?" Denise inquired, diverting her companion.

"What has your restaurant got to offer?" asked Darvina with mocking hauteur.

"What would you say to langouste and champagne?"

"Pourquoi pas, ma chérie?"

They entered the small pool house. Darvina sat down on a linen armchair and lit a gold-tipped black Russian Sobranie. Denise went to the telephone, nervously squeezing the folds of her white crepe dress. Glancing briefly at herself in the mirror, she noticed the blush rising under the glowing tan.

"That's all settled," announced Denise, turning round. "They'll send it up to my apartment right away. . . . I'll give you a terry cloth robe."

She reached into her closet and selected one. "Here," she said. "This one is nice and warm."

Darvina took it from Denise's hand and let it drop to the floor.

Denise's gaze wandered over Darvina's body as she undressed immodestly. Slightly embarrassed, Denise walked to the bathroom. When she returned she saw a shadow run through the doorway. Darvina had left. Denise found her friend in the water, splashing and humming a leitmotiv from a Beethoven concerto. She slipped waist-deep into the pool. Darvina approached silently from behind, delicately cupped Denise's breasts and stared down pleasurably.

"Turn around," Darvina whispered. "You know what I want."

Denise remained motionless, heart pounding. "I'm not sure I do."

"Look at me!" Darvina persisted. Gently turning her around, Darvina placed her lips on Denise's. Parting them and searching the depths of her mouth. Denise found herself impulsively returning Darvina's kisses with ardor.

"Please, Darvina, please! Let's get out of the water!" she implored in a barely audible voice. "Everybody can see us." Darvina wasn't listening.

Lowering her lips to the hard wet nipples, she thrust her naked body against Denise's. "Please, Darvina . . ."

The redhead caressed the blonde with passion, and the blonde surrendered to the redhead with true rapture. The one was force, the other weakness. Hurriedly they put on their robes and ascended the grandiose staircase like two phantasmal shadows. Barely touching the steps.

Entering her apartment, Denise tried to control her breathing without success. "Are you hungry? Would you like some . . . some . . . some cham—" She was about to pick up the bottle when Darvina took both her hands and pinned them behind her back.

"Later, Denise. You're not hungry for food, or thirsty—stop this teasing!"

Denise made a faint attempt to reply, to explain, to rationalize, but Darvina's mouth cut her sentences short, stifled her voice and choked her feeble protests.

"Please . . . no . . . I beg you . . ." She groped for words and gave in euphorically to her long-suppressed desire. Both robes fell wet to the floor. Darvina led Denise to the white couch, put a cushion behind her head and got down on her knees, caressing Denise's body with a gentle touch and kissing her exquisite skin. Starting at the feet and slowly working up the calves of her legs, she kissed them tenderly but with greedy and forbidden intensity. Reaching the inner thighs, Darvina stopped abruptly and moved toward her face. First the neck . . . the shoulders . . . the breasts. Savoring the anticipation before the actual taste. Denise held Darvina by the hair, unconsciously guiding her head. She was sighing audibly, inhaling, exhaling, inhaling again. "Oh, Darvina!" she cried. "Don't—"

"Don't what?"

"Don't stop. I've wanted you so much." Suddenly Darvina grabbed a bottle of champagne and emptied its contents on Denise's nude body. Her mouth pounced as if parched, licking, sucking, gently biting the liquid from every part of her. Denise muffled a cry. Then all was silent.

The barriers of time fell to dust. Hours passed. The flaming sexual excitement wouldn't abate. Morning came with a lingering pleasure.

Alone in bed again, Denise, fascinated by the luxury of her new indolence, stretched like a sensual cat. She rang for morning coffee. It arrived with the papers fresh from Paris and headlines from all over the world: KENNEDY AND DE GAULLE AGREE TO DEFEND BERLIN . . . DOMINICAN CRISIS STUDIED BY U.S. FOLLOWING TRUJILLO ASSASSINATION . . . RUSSIAN DEFECTOR VLADIMIR VOLODIN PARTNERING SYBIL PARKINSON HAILED AS NEW TOAST OF BALLET WORLD . . .

Briefly noting the dancer's photographs, Denise turned to the fashion section, on page four.

❄

The bottle-green Renault 4-L turned swiftly from the Avenue Matignon. The seething steel snake of evening rush hour traffic roared and fumed its way toward the Rond-Point of the Champs-Elysées. Philippe de Chambord pressed his patent-leathered foot on the accelerator, then on the brake, back and forth, playing with the engine and Vladimir Volodin's nerves.

"—Of course her French gives her away, my dear," Philippe said caustically. His long, slender fingers, covered with rings, effetely dripped a Gitane cigarette.

"What do you mean by that?" asked Vladimir. His eyes following sparrows. Sparrows born in Paris.

"If it weren't for her French being so perfect, you'd think she came from a good family!" he said, chuckling bitchily. "But it's too early in the evening, isn't it, love, to be overly malicious? Let's wait till we get to the party for that! Denise throws a good one. Everybody worth dishing will be there!" His tired, pinched mouth puckered; it had lived too long. "Let's give to Caesar what is due to Caesar," he continued. "Besides being a good hostess, Denise is beautiful, exquisite, charming, intelligent and, by God, has the most fantastic record of opportunism I've ever encountered in anyone." The fragrance of Cuir de Russie was overpowering. The rosy skin on Philippe's face suggested the vigorous patting of a hot towel. "Makes you wonder about her interest in the arts—but then, even a rich bitch like Denise is entitled to an occasional redeeming trait. Not many of her sort would bother to endow the ballet in the U.S.—"

Philippe wove in and out of the traffic, stopping and starting, honking the horn incessantly and swearing. ". . . The arts are not subsidized over there the way they are in Europe, you know. Don't overestimate her, Vladimir, Denise is far from altruistic. She simply craves recognition and admiration, and being the one to bring the great team of Volodin and Parkinson to Dallas for the first time—costumes by yours truly—will be another feather in her cap." He punctuated the phrase with an expansive movement toward his head. The massive silver and gold bracelets on his wrist clanked. "Not that she'd ever wear that feather, unless it was diamonds. . . ."

"You make her sound almost interesting." Vladimir looked out the window.

"You misunderstand me, my dear Vladimir. She *is* interesting. *Most* interesting—if you like girls, that is! There are so many stories circulating about her! I can think of one in particular. It's very amusing! Really amusing!" He cackled gleefully. "It's only rumor of course, but rumor is always so fascinating—don't you agree?" The pink silk handkerchief in his breast pocket came out in a flourish of jingle-jangle jewelry. He wiped the moisture from his brow. "Paris is still so frightfully hot and stuffy, don't you think? Did you manage to get away for the summer? . . . Aren't you too warm with those leather boots and that cap?—Now!" he added without stopping for breath or waiting for a reply. "Before Denise became Mrs. MacAlpine she was Princess Francesco Borgia. We're all princesses, are we not? But Denise, dear soul, actually had a piece of paper that said so!" He roared with laughter at his own joke. "They were the darlings of Europe, the world's most ideal couple—young, beautiful and rich! Don't you hate them already?" he shrieked. "I know I did!"

Vladimir caught the beauty of the last glints of velvety sky between the trees.

The light turned red. Philippe was about to go through it. The car in front stopped so abruptly that he was forced to slam on the brakes, which screeched protestingly. Philippe and Vladimir were thrown forward in their seats with such force that the visor over the windshield above Vladimir dropped, depositing a male nude magazine in his lap.

"Sorry, Vladimir. I guess that isn't your cup of tea—or is it?" Philippe laughed and winked, tossing the magazine onto the back seat. "You've got *War and Peace,* sweetheart," he added, smirking, "and I've got *Boys in the Sand!* To each his own, I always say. Now, where was I? Oh yes, Denise . . . On the wedding night Prince Borgia—how shall I put it? The prince dipped his lascivious ladle into her . . . into her . . . how I loathe vulgarity, Vladimir . . . into her steaming saucepot—and wham, bang! She emitted a little cry of pain—poor dear—and blood squirted everywhere! The prince was most impressed with his virgin bride's purity." Philippe's face fell into crevices, lined like a clown's.

"I don't understand," said Vladimir, unamused.

"What don't you understand?" His gimlet eyes were sparkling bitchily. "Denise had managed to have her virginity restored."

"Re—what?"

"To put it plainly, Vladimir, she had had her cherry sewn back into her pouting little pussy!" He laughed viciously. "But you've got to hand it to her! Denise goes for superior human beings rather than inferior ones and shows definite taste, with a capital *T.* And that's really all you can ask from a bitch—that she have taste! Don't you think?"

"How did you find out such . . . such original story?"

"In 1956 I had—dear, dear Vladimir—how *not* to be indelicate? I had a lov—a *friend,* yes a friend, at *Paris Match,* who . . . who . . ."

". . . who obviously shared more than a pillow with you." Vladimir's eyes danced as he caught Philippe at his own game. "Anyway, I must admit that, true or not, it's the best gossip I've ever heard. Now tell me about this party we're going to. Will Denise's husband be there?"

"Her husband! Good heavens, no, Vladimir! You're so old-fashioned. When you have that kind of money, there are always reasons to be apart. Besides, they have opposite, yet complementary, interests."

"Oh?"

"Sinclair devotes himself to making money. She devotes herself to spending it. A perfect combination. Having the old boy around would be a dreadful inconvenience."

Vladimir lifted his brow, uncomprehending.

"Well, you must understand that luxury shopping is very time-consuming. Moreover, there's her social life. They say Denise holds the biggest and most fashionable balls all over the world! And it's true too! Big and hairy!" he screamed, poking Vladimir in the ribs with his elbow.

"I'm awfully glad, Philippe, you don't like vulgarity," Vladimir said, laughing. "Otherwise you could make quite a story out of this!"

"Anyway, Denise detests me ever since—" Philippe was about to continue when a chauffeur-driven Silver Cloud pulled alongside. He recognized a woman sitting in the back seat. "Ursula, darling!" he shrieked. "How are you?" A hawk-faced woman in her forties, overly made up, leaned forward and acknowledged him with a brief wave of the hand. "Wonderful seeing you!" he gushed. "You look marvelous as usual! Simply marvelous! And that little dog of yours is as cute as ever! Dear Ursula, if you haven't seen *Swan Lake,* you must, my dear, you simply must! And tell me what you think of my costumes! You know how much I value your opinion!" The light turned yellow. "I'll give you a ring next week. Maybe we can get together for tea! Bye-bye, darling!" The Rolls Royce set off majestically.

"Fucking bitch!" Philippe sneered. "I wouldn't get together with that whore if she turned out to be Che Guevara in drag! I can remember when she was turning tricks in Monte Carlo for a hundred francs, called herself a German countess, when I know for a fact she was born and raised in Brooklyn! But look at her now! Got some octogenarian multimillionaire American sucker to marry her. And did you see that mutt of hers? At first I thought it was a tall mouse with teased hair! And speaking about that mutt, rumor has it—of course, Vladimir, you understand it's only rumor—"

Vladimir exploded in guttural laughter, slapping his muscular thigh. "It must be great having you as friend." He turned sideways, looking at Philippe's profile. "You see, I love women! I always find something good to say about them."

"Oh, Vladimir, you misunderstood! I don't speak badly about women. Good heavens, no!" He blinked his eyes in mock despair. "I speak badly about everybody!"

The steel serpent crawled up the Champs-Elysées, framed in the distance by the Arc de Triomphe. After a tortuous maneuver they turned into the Avenue Foch. Philippe parked in front of an eighteenth-century building.

"Do you think there'll be many people at the party besides Sybil and me?" Vladimir asked casually, getting out of the car.

"My dear, I must be truthful. Knowing Denise as I do, with you and Sybil as her guests of honor, her drawing room will probably look like the Gare Saint Lazare!" He carried a Directoire cane with a theatrical flourish. "First-class section of course!"

"Parties are something I can endure—provided I don't have to stay too long."

"Well, Vladimir, just remember that they're all rich, but such trash! I'll keep you amused!" Putting a conspiratorial arm around Vladimir's shoulders, Philippe suddenly sounded serious. "Another thing, Vladimir, I know I had to drag you here tonight, but one day you'll thank me. Just keep in mind that if ever you decide to mount your own production of any ballet you choose, the bitch's got the magic wand! When that time comes—just don't forget your good friend Philippe."

They walked to the front door. The concierge buzzed them into a large marble-floored foyer. Vladimir declined to enter the small turn-of-the-century elevator, with its elegant grillwork, pleading claustrophobia.

They ascended the magnificent staircase that curved upward to the next floor.

Philippe rang the bell. The door was opened by a cool, aloof, efficient maid wearing a black uniform with a white lace apron, matching cuffs and a starched cap. "Would you tell Madame," Philippe said, "the Marquis de Chambord has arrived, accompanied by Monsieur Volodin? Thank you."

"Oui, Monsieur le Marquis." She disappeared.

They stood in silence, studying the hall. White, all white. White walls, white ceiling, white marble floor. A single piece of furniture, an Empire table with a white marble top and gold leaf base, stood beneath a mirror of the same period. A huge bouquet of white roses had been carefully arranged in a William de Morgan vase. It demanded reverence.

"Denise is making her first Holy Communion in the morning," Philippe sniped out of the corner of his mouth. "Taking the veil and entering a cloistered world of Sapphic bliss would be more like it—oh, I haven't told you, have I?"

"No, I guess I missed that one."

"How careless of me, dear Vladimir! God knows, I don't want to be bitchy! After all, who am I to talk? A poor, struggling costume designer who sits home nights mending his rags. . . . But rumor has it—of course, it's only rumor—"

The maid returned. "Follow me, please," she said, leading the way.

A babble of voices, punctuated by laughter, wafted toward them as they approached the open French doors. The insidious odor of expensive pleasures —the combination of perfume, cigar smoke, candles, silk and leather—engulfed them. They entered.

The *tout Paris* that one gathers on grand occasions was in attendance, indulging themselves. The first wave included a renowned cubist painter, a publisher, two bankers, several actors, the American ambassador to France, willowy fashion models, movie stars, three ministers, a tempestuous soprano who was making headlines with a Greek shipping magnate, an exiled king, a couple of demimondaines, a secretary of the Comédie Française, grand ladies with their little mouths and large eyes—their sign of nobility, the coat of arms they had already carried in their mother's bellies. Every eye was on Vladimir. His arrival stirred a buzz of recognition. The salon tapered down to silence.

And then he saw her. It had to be her. His gaze followed a beautiful, elegantly slim, fair-haired woman, the portrait of worldly success, drifting happily, effortlessly, toward them.

"How do you do, Mr. Volodin," she said with an engaging drawl. "I'm Denise MacAlpine." Her face lit up and her pelvis pushed forward in some vague gesture of vulnerable provocation. She was dressed in a short white gown, and her long diamond earrings swayed and sparkled, competing with the beauty of her incredible blue eyes. She extended her hand. A fluid hand. Supple. A mist turning to flesh. An enormous ruby of incomparable purity adorned one of her fingers. "Mr. Volodin, I'm delighted you were able to come. And Philippe! How wonderful to see you!" She gave him a distracted kiss without taking her eyes off Vladimir. "My dear Philippe! You have really surpassed yourself with your costumes for *Swan Lake!* They are the talk of Paris."

"My dearest Denise, thank you! Thank you!" He spoke with enthusiasm. "Your ears must have been ringing! On our way over here I was extolling your virtues to Vladimir, telling him all the marvelous things about you! Wasn't I, Vladimir?"

"Oh, stop it, Philippe!" Denise laughed evasively. "I can feel myself blushing!"

"The two of you run along and play, then," Philippe shrilled. "I can see the Duchess de Bethune sitting under a potted palm. Or perhaps I should say, sitting potted under a palm!"

"Philippe can be very amusing," said Denise. "Follow me." She took Vladimir by the arm, her voice near his ear. "I want you to meet my guests."

"I would rather wait. I know enough people. There is plenty of time to be put on display."

She smiled steadily and continued walking as if she hadn't heard him. "My guests are so looking forward to meeting you!"

The high-ceilinged drawing room, decorated and furnished in shades of white, off-white and beige, overlooked the Arc de Triomphe. Everything was genuine, either Louis Quinze or Louis Seize, or contemporary and functional. Masses of white roses everywhere. The green of the potted plants and trees standing in eighteenth-century hand-painted Japanese jardinieres was the only dramatic color.

The crowd of people thickened around them. In the jostle someone spilled champagne all over Vladimir's black silk shirt. He cursed loudly in Russian.

A man approached him and gushed, "I hate doing this to you, Mr. Volodin. I'm working for the *Herald Tribune* in Paris. My little girl wants to be a ballerina when she grows up." The man pushed a napkin into his hand. "Could I please have your autograph?"

"I do not give autographs—but I can use napkin. My hands are wet!" The man left, discomfited.

Denise and Vladimir stopped in front of a Coromandel screen. She took two glasses of champagne from a passing butler. "You *will* have a glass, won't you?" she asked softly, fixing her gaze intently on Vladimir. "You may drink. After all, it's your day off!"

"I drink every day! It's good for my blood!"

She gestured toward a deeply cushioned sofa. They sat. Vladimir shot a quick, canny look at her perfect profile—skin like pale parchment, soft blond tresses reminding him of a magazine advertisement inviting readers to enroll in a drawing course.

Denise crossed her long legs. "The Paris Opéra," she said, "is fortunate to have you and Dame Sybil Parkinson." Vladimir gave her a smile full of promises, twirling the stem of his glass between his fingers and enjoying the mysteries of her flushed and eager face.

"Has Sybil arrived?" he asked.

"Yes, she's in the library, surrounded by admirers." Her voice grew even softer, with a joyful little lilt to it. "But to return to you, Mr. Volodin—I can't tell you how much it means to me that you've agreed to dance for our beautiful theater in Dallas."

Vladimir was looking deeply into her eyes, carried away by their luminescence. He gazed at her like a needy child spellbound by a wonderful toy. A toy unobtainable and desired. Denise had assembled all the contrivances of seduction. She seemed so strong, yet so soft, so pliant—so self-assured, so unyielding, so aloof. Not his type at all, yet irresistible.

"You'll find we have a most appreciative public, and everything will be done to make your stay enjoyable." Her words spilled out to the accompaniment of the bursting bubbles in her glass.

"You are a very beautiful woman," was Vladimir's response. Their lips were only inches away. For a microsecond there was fear in her eyes, but she smiled and smiled. Her color mounted. A butler approached and whispered to her.

"Please excuse me, Mr. Volodin," she said, rising and handing Vladimir her glass. "I'm needed in the dining room. I'll be right back." She smiled with the distant provocativeness that never deserted her and walked away.

Vladimir jumped up and considered how best to avoid the crowd.

"Oh, Mr. Volodin, I saw you dance last night," gushed a stranger. "You were simply—"

"That's nice," Vladimir interrupted, and moved on. The stranger gulped air, lost for words. When the words finally tumbled from his lips, Vladimir was already surrounded by a sea of voices and craning necks. A string quartet was playing, and the musicians, seeing Vladimir, immediately broke into a spirited rendition of "Ochy Chiorn'yeh." The violinist addressed him in Russian, and Vladimir gaily handed him Denise's champagne. They clinked glasses. "Na zdohrov'yeh!"

Soon Denise was back among the guests. Her eyes searched the room. She was looking for Vladimir. She found him. He was standing near a long white-lacquered table covered with photographs. They were mostly of Denise, her narcissism exquisitely framed in silver and vermeil. *Denise* on a yacht with an elderly man. Probably her husband, thought Vladimir. *Denise* in front of what seemed to be an Italian palazzo. *Denise* on skis. *Denise . . . Denise . . . Denise* in a short wedding gown, surrounded by a group of people. From afar Vladimir shot a long look at Denise, who caught it, with the shock of mutual attraction. He smiled, became engrossed in the pictures again, then looked across at Denise once more. Like an elastic band being stretched and relaxed, Denise began to feel ten feet tall each time his eyes were on her, only to find her self-esteem shrinking back to normal when they were not. Feigning casualness, she walked over to Vladimir.

"Who is this beautiful girl?" he asked, holding a picture in his hand.

"She's my best friend, Darvina."

"Is Darvina American too?"

"Yes. She used to be a model here in Paris and now she has a fashionable boutique on the Avenue Montaigne," Denise replied edgily, taking the picture from his hand and replacing it on the table.

Casually, he reached for another frame, talking before he had really looked. "And this—your wedding?"

"Why, yes, it—"

It took Vladimir only seconds to notice what had eluded him at first glance. With false detachment he interrupted pointing to a couple in the wedding party. "Mariela Lodge—you know her?"

"Oh, certainly. Our husbands have been close for years. Curtis was best man at our wedding. But Mariela never mentioned you. How long have you—?" Her mind raced back over the past weeks. How strange. How very strange that Mariela had never mentioned knowing Vladimir, especially since it was only a few days ago that Denise had told Mariela how desperately she was hoping to bring the London Ballet Company to Dallas with Vladimir Volodin! "Have you been friends long? Where did you meet?"

Hastily Vladimir replaced the photo. "London—we met in London. Yes, I know Mariela, but I don't know her well." It hurt him to lie. He hoped he had not lied badly. He hoped, moreover, that Denise and Mariela did not know each other very well. "I've always been nosy about other people's pictures!" he announced. "They tell a lot about a person. Who is this old man? Your father?"

"Almost. He was my godfather, Escobar Ortiz. He passed away in 1955."

As hastily as he had turned from Mariela's picture, he was now drawn to what was obviously a studio photograph of Denise—of course Denise—this time her slender neck encircled by a string of outsized diamond flowers.

"Now, *that* is an extraordinary picture! I'm no connoisseur of fine jewelry, but that must be—"

"Why, thank you, it is—"

"Absolutely regal—befitting a czarina!"

"Why, thank you again. The photo is by Horst, taken when I first came to Paris in 1952. I had just received the necklace from my godfather for—" When she turned to face him, Vladimir had vanished, leaving Denise looking as though she might at any moment deflate like a party balloon.

Denise drifted to a large French window, lingered, and thought of the necklace that had captured Vladimir's imagination.

That necklace—an image her mind automatically associated with Escobar. With 1952.

—❀—

Denise had arrived in Paris a week ahead of Escobar Ortiz. The day of his arrival was the first they really spent alone together. He proudly took her to lunch at Maxim's, then on a mammoth shopping expedition. Several thousand dollars later he had dropped her off at her penthouse apartment at the Hotel George V.

It was six o'clock when Escobar called on her again. He seated himself comfortably on the living room couch and motioned for her to sit next to him.

"What I really came to tell you," he said, "is that I have rented the Château d'Antibes on the Riviera for us, which, with the exception of the Villa Leopolda, is the most exquisite estate in the world. As a matter of fact, I would have taken the Leopolda, but Gianni Agnelli just bought it."

"Oh, Escobar, I am so thrilled!"

The doorbell rang. "That must be the champagne," he said, rising. As the waiter uncorked the bottle, Escobar removed a large blue velvet box from his briefcase.

"We'll help ourselves," he said, dismissing the waiter.

Denise rose from the couch, where she had been pretending not to watch Escobar, and poured two glasses of champagne. "This is for you, Escobar," she said, handing him one.

"And this, Denise, is for you," he said, giving her the velvet box as though returning a small favor.

Denise smiled at him in childish delight, took the case, but said nothing. Her impulse was to run with it to the window. But she controlled herself, walking instead. Escobar's eyes remained fixed on her face as he searched for an expression of emotion. This was the part of gift-giving he most enjoyed: the surprise of the recipient. Denise opened the case to find the ruby-and-diamond necklace she had admired only hours earlier while walking with Escobar along the Rue de la Paix. She had merely said, "Oh, Escobar, isn't it beautiful?" He had nodded as they continued walking. The necklace was dominated by five jeweled flowers the size of silver dollars, each with diamond petals and ruby center. A jewel, she thought, worthy of Eva Perón's envy! "I simply don't know how to express my appreciation," Denise stammered.

She did know of course. And her precise sense of timing told her that the moment to express it had come. Turning from the window, she asked Escobar to excuse her briefly, and walked into her bedroom. Escobar was silently pleased with himself, and while he patiently waited for her return he thumbed through a copy of the *Herald Tribune*.

"Well, how do you like it?"

Escobar lowered the paper, his eyes halting at the point of the voice's origin. He looked up, unable to believe what he was seeing. A solid mass of light had suddenly materialized. Fair, blond Denise stood before him wearing a sheer white negligée, which hung open loosely. Around her throat lay the diamond-and-ruby necklace. Escobar was mesmerized. His desire for her was the strongest he had ever felt for any woman. He had wanted Denise for so long—had wanted to discover what lay beneath her cool exterior. He had to possess it. Haltingly he managed one last question, "Are you sure you want to do this? Are you sure you want me?"

Denise knelt on the couch where Escobar was sitting, slowly took his face in both her hands and kissed him passionately, full on the lips, for the first time.

"I've never been more sure of anything in my life. I want to give you everything I possess, which is only myself." Denise liked what she heard herself saying. Escobar took her hand and led her back into the bedroom.

"What you possess and what you want to give me is a treasure I feel unworthy of," he said. "But I shall do everything within my power to deserve you." With trembling hands he removed her gown and the necklace, marveling at the beauty of her naked body. He guided her to the bed and lightly ran his hands across her firm, delicate breasts, along her narrow waist, and over her hips. Making love to her was even more pleasurable than he had imagined.

Denise acted the part of a sex-starved young girl. She began to experiment on him with her mouth and tongue. Her hands tried new caresses. She was surprised to find how easy it was for her to be bold and aggressive with one for whom she felt no physical attraction whatsoever. Escobar was ecstatic. It was over very shortly. His orgasm burst with a force that almost frightened him. Hers was faked, like all the others in her life. Denise's sense of timing had not failed her, and as she lay there it entered her mind that Escobar was so infatuated with her that it would be easy to marry him. She dismissed the thought.

Denise was aiming far higher.

⁂

Vladimir was on his way to the library, still trying to find Dame Sybil. One face stood out—that of a tall, dark, angular young woman leaning against a Corinthian column.

"Oh, there you are," a voice said. It was Philippe. "Are you enjoying yourself?"

"That's like asking a Christian if he enjoyed the show at the Colosseum." Vladimir swooped a glass of champagne from a passing tray. "Who's that beautiful girl standing over there? I think I've seen her somewhere."

"You've probably seen her picture in all the papers and magazines! Her name's Teresa Santeramo. She's from Costa Rica or Rica Rica—who knows? Anyway, she's living with that English pop star, Buddy what's-his-name. She calls herself a model but hasn't done a stroke of work in her life—except open her legs. A year ago she was working for Madame Claude right here in Paris—"

"Madame who?"

"Claude. She's the highest-class madam in the world! According to rumor —and it's only rumor, I can assure you of that, my dear Vladimir, only rumor—anybody could plug up that hole for whatever the traffic would bear! And now she's one of the beautiful people! Wonders never cease! Oh, Vladimir"—he grimaced—"café society has become so undiscriminat-ing!" He tsk-tsked in disapproval.

"How do you manage to know all the dirt?" Vladimir asked.

"Living twelve years in America was a great help, Vladimir. Gossip is a way of life there. I was a natural!"

Gradually Vladimir became aware of Denise again, at the center of a group of people, looking like a mournful little girl. He stared at her while raising his glass arrogantly. "To you," he mouthed. The magnificent blue eyes glazed with dreamy happiness as she bestowed one of her Pre-Raphael-ite smiles on him.

"Aha! How interesting!" Philippe said mockingly. "I see you've sparked some interest in Little Miss Chastity! There's a certain look in her eyes that makes me glad she doesn't want anything *I* have! Well, Vladimir, you're wasting your time, I can tell you that! She doesn't make a move without checking with her bank manager first."

"But she's rich! What more could she want?"

"Everything—Denise wants everything. And as the song goes, whatever Lola wants, Denise gets. Of course she's had to step on a lot of people to do it, but that's another story, my dear Vladimir, that's another story!"

"I'm sure you'll tell it to me in due course, but in the meantime continue your tale of venom. I love it!"

"Well, rumor has it—and again, Vladimir, it's rumor, only rumor—that occasionally Denise asks some unsuspecting victim to have a look at her Easter egg—"

"Easter egg?"

"A Fabergé egg," Philippe pronounced grandly. "An extraordinary Fabergé egg she keeps on the night table in her modest little cell. It cost her godfather a quarter of a million dollars! I use the term 'godfather' advisedly, my dear Vladimir. No one is quite certain of the precise nature of their relationship, but if Escobar Ortiz was Denise's godfather, then Charles de Gaulle is my aunt!"

"I can see a family resemblance."

"Flattery will get you everywhere, Vladimir, but to return to the egg— her fairy godfather gave it to Denise when she married Prince Charming. And she has been using the line ever since: 'How'd you like to come up and see my egg sometime!' You have to admit, it's quite a line! And, abracadabra, you're in the bedroom! Mind you, the system doesn't work for everybody. If I tried it, for example, I'd probably end up in bed with the Easter bunny! Oh, Vladimir"—he sighed, brushing imaginary lint from the satin lapels of his blue velvet suit—"being beautiful but poor is so—so *trying!*"

"You're so wicked, Philippe. I've been looking for Sybil everywhere— have you seen her?"

"No, but guess who's back in town?" asked Philippe. "The Baron Arnaud de Breuteuil," he said, answering himself, "better known as Chico-Fago, the pillar of French society!"

"Who is the pillar of French society?" asked a regal and striking woman with black hair pulled severely back in a chignon. She fingered a long strand of pearls as she approached them with distinctive gracefulness.

"Sybil!" Vladimir began, giving her an affectionate kiss on the cheek. "I've been looking for you everywhere—"

"You haven't been looking hard enough. Now, Philippe, who is the pillar of French society?"

"The Baron de Breuteuil. And the two of you must excuse me. Arnaud is such an old and dear friend! I must rush over and say hello." Philippe floated away on the river of his own conversation.

"Are you enjoying yourself?" Sybil inquired, smiling.

"Everybody's asking me the same question tonight! If you must know, it's a madhouse and fucking bore!"

"You spoiled brat! You always say the same thing wherever you go, but you're always the last one to leave!"

Vladimir handed Sybil his glass. "Here's some champagne to shut you up."

She pushed it away. "You know I don't drink." She adjusted the black jacket with the red lining over her matching Yves St. Laurent dress. "Have you had a chance to speak to our hostess?"

"Not very much. She's . . . very beautiful."

"Besides that, she's really quite bright. I've known her for some time. I'm so glad Denise has been able to arrange for our appearance in Dallas."

Their hostess approached them, her eyes holding a soft expression, deep, somewhat sad and detached. "I hope you haven't been too bored," she said deprecatingly to Vladimir.

"Actually, I have been. I don't enjoy large parties. I find them a waste of time. Only you, Sybil and Philippe have made it bearable."

A butler approached. "Excuse me, Dame Sybil. You have an urgent phone call from London."

"Oh, it's probably my husband. I left word with the hotel I'd be here. I hope you don't mind," Sybil said to Denise. "Carry on without me. I won't be a moment."

"The buffet will be ready very shortly," whispered Denise as Sybil followed the butler.

"I detest buffets! What an absurd way to eat—standing up!" said Vladimir.

"We're eating at small tables, and for you I have a steak—rare!" Denise gave a small sigh. "Where are you staying in Paris?"

"La Tremoille on Rue—"

"Oh, yes, I know it well. Don't you find it rather . . . rather small?"

"Not at all."

"I have an apartment that I keep permanently at the Plaza-Athénée which is always available for the use of my friends. It would be an honor if you'd let me put it at your disposal."

"Why? Why should I move? All I need is a room. Bed. Bathroom. I get lost in big space. It's not necessary for sleeping."

"You'd be much more comfortable."

"Comfort? Why comfort? It weakens you. I work at the theater maybe ten hours a day. I dine out. I sleep very little. What I need a big, comfortable space for? Waste! Big waste!"

Denise laughed, and Vladimir felt her vanilla breath. Her vulnerability irritated him. Suddenly he was overcome with the desire to make violent love to her, to break open the sophisticated coolness, to shatter the fragile, glossy façade, to bend the slender and pliant body that reminded him of vacuous models one sees in fashion magazines. It wasn't the kind of body that attracted him. An angry urge to see her nakedness welled in his groin.

"Some afternoon, Vladimir—may I call you Vladimir?" He was engrossed with imagining her sex, thinking of ways to humiliate her. "If you can find the time, I would love to show you a most unusual object, truly unique in the world."

"What is it?"

"An Easter egg. A Russian Easter egg. A veritable museum piece." Denise looked at him quietly, shyly. "I'm sure you'd appreciate it." She closed her wondrous eyes for a moment. Her imagination began to stir. His mocking smile made her feel awkward, awakening strange, disturbing feelings in her. She refused to ask herself what it was she sought in him.

"Yes . . . yes . . . ," he murmured, distracted. From across the room Teresa Santeramo had begun her game of conquest. Raising her eyebrows, pouting her sensuous, wet lips, honing her dark beauty on him. "Very soon I'm sure something can be . . . arranged. . . ." Vladimir's voice faded.

Denise's eyes darted to Teresa. Her gracious condescension withered instantly. "Yes, of course, Vladimir. I'd be delighted. And now, if you'll pardon me." Brusquely she removed herself from his presence and walked over to Teresa. "How do you do, Miss . . . ?"

Caught off guard, the young woman faltered. "Teresa . . . Teresa Santeramo. You know me, Denise."

"Yes, I *am* Mrs. Denise MacAlpine. But—how shall I put this?—I've been disturbed all evening by the fact that . . . I simply don't find your name on my guest list." She paused. *"Were* you invited?"

"Denise, my goodness! My husband and I received your invitation a week ago!"

"Your husband . . . ?"

"My husband! My husband, Buddy Henderson! But he's on tour."

Studied recognition dawned on Denise's face. "Of course. I do remember inviting *Buddy*. But those invitations were intended to be strictly personal. I was totally unaware that he was married. How long have you been his wife?"

"We . . . that is . . ." Teresa's whole expression collapsed. "Well, I meant to say we'll be married this winter and—"

"—*and* I must tell you as tactfully as I can, Miss . . . ah . . ." As if chagrined, Denise glanced from side to side, lowered her voice, and continued, "We are here to celebrate an esteemed ballet troupe, to extend them our goodwill, to offer them a foretaste of American hospitality, and I'm sure you understand how little that will leave for you—"

"Madre de Dios, Denise!" She lifted her eyes, numbed with astonishment. "What are you saying?"

"Oh, my dear Miss . . . *Miss.* I'm saying good night. Dress warmly. And when you hit the street, happy hunting. My home is *hardly* the place for it." Triumphantly Denise added, "Of course, if you'd rather leave with a proper escort, I'd be glad to call my security men."

It was sufficient. Teresa had heard enough. "Eso es demasiado! Jamás en mi vida! Eso es . . . eso es . . . !" Flustered, ears ringing, as red as though she had been slapped, Teresa fled in the cloud of her yellow-feathered boa.

Throughout the conversation Denise couldn't help noticing Vladimir's piercing eyes riveted on hers. She gave him a serene smile and rejoined her tiny cluster of guests. Philippe was dishing out vitriol and caviar canapés. Vladimir, devouring both. Dame Sybil, dignified as ever.

"What was that all about?" asked Philippe, unable to contain himself.

"It's so difficult," Denise replied hesitantly. "When . . . when one has

316

a party this size, there are always gate-crashers . . . undesirables. It's just impossible to have eyes everywhere. My secretary should have controlled the guest list better than she did. I'll have to speak to her."

"You mean," prodded Philippe caustically, "that the enchanting Teresa Santeramo wasn't your guest of honor?"

"If you don't mind, I'd rather not talk about her."

"Why, what did she do?" asked Dame Sybil.

"I really hate to talk about all of this. It's so unpleasant. But . . . I think there should be limits to someone's—how shall I call it?—proclivities in another person's home." Feigning dismay, Denise added, "I'm really too embarrassed to continue this conversation."

"Well, I'm not too embarrassed to hear it," said Philippe, cocking his head naughtily. "Go ahead."

Collecting herself, as if her personal virtue had been assaulted, Denise plunged on. "Teresa . . . made an overt pass at my butler!"

"Where . . . where . . .? Which butler? I must have missed him!" Philippe laughed, whisking Sybil away. "Come, dear—I'll need a second opinion."

"What have you got against butlers?" asked Vladimir, taking Denise's arm.

"Nothing at all. But butlers are here to serve my guests," she said, smiling, "not to service any one guest in particular."

His gaze melting into a burning stare, Vladimir gave his full attention to Denise. "I wish," he said, "that all your guests could be made to leave as quickly." His voice was husky and seductive. "You are one of the most beautiful women I've ever seen."

"I consider it a compliment, a great compliment, Vladimir, since your reputation has you surrounded by great beauties at all times." The expression on her face was euphoric.

A maid approached Denise. She spoke inaudibly.

"Supper is served," Denise announced loudly to the assembly. She led the way to an elegant and spacious dining room, extended by a winter garden in full bloom. Dozens of round tables had been set up, each covered to the floor with a white damask cloth and crowned with a centerpiece of white orchids and candles.

Vladimir and Denise approached a table together. She noticed Teresa Santeramo's place card, discreetly slid it into the palm of her hand, crumpled it and dropped it to the floor.

Vladimir held Denise's chair, then seated himself on her right as a waiter brought a steak.

Without a word he cut a piece of meat, impaled it on a fork, and lifted it to his face, pressing it against his cheek.

"I've never seen anybody do that!" Denise laughed heartily. Candlelight played with the classical lines of her face. "Is that a Russian custom?"

"It's my custom!"

"But you must tell me why!"

"I check the temperature, and if it's too hot, it means the steak isn't rare as I like, and I send it back to the kitchen." Vladimir pressed his knee against hers. "Aren't you eating?"

Denise pointed to a line that had formed in front of a long marble-topped sideboard on which the food was laid out. "I'll wait until most of my guests have helped themselves. In that way I can keep an eye on . . . everyone."

"As long as you keep an eye on me," he said.

Dame Sybil was to his right. She rose and walked to the buffet.

No sooner had she left than an overbearing gray-haired woman plunked herself down in the seat just left empty and without any preliminaries launched into conversation. "You don't mind if I have a chat with you, Mr. Volden. My name is Olive Doerflinger." Vladimir nodded with deadly politeness, infuriated by the interruption.

He turned his back on her, his gaze resting suggestively on Denise. "I'm having a little supper at a small, out-of-the-way bistro on Friday night," he said. "Late, of course. Perhaps you'll be available . . . ?"

"I thought you didn't like parties. Will there be many people?"

"Just you and I, Mrs. MacAlpine."

"Please, Vladimir, call me Denise." A small group of violinists wandered among the guests, playing and singing Russian melodies. Denise felt the surge of the Gypsy music between her legs. Suddenly she stood up. "I must attend to my other guests. I'll return in a moment."

Vladimir observed her movement, swan-graceful, from table to table. Images of Denise swelled in him.

Like a shot, Mrs. Doerflinger had insinuated herself from Sybil's seat into Denise's. "Mr. Volden, Horace—that's my husband, Horace Doerflinger—plays with the Cincinnati Philharmonic Orchestra, and he's a friend of your conductor. That's why we were invited. . . ."

Vladimir wasn't listening. His eyes were scanning the room for Sybil, Philippe, anyone, but especially Denise. Then he saw her again. The flawless complexion, the slight dew on her cheeks, the innocent exterior, the detached assuredness, the glowing moisture of her cleavage.

". . . Have you ever been to Cincinnati?" Olive Doerflinger pressed on, chewing noisily on some celery. "It's such a wonderful city, Mr. Volden. Before the night's over I'll give you my phone number, and if you get to Cincinnati, give us a ring. I know what it is to be on the road, and one can always stand a good home-cooked meal! Especially you, with that lean and hungry look." She craned her neck over his plate. "What on earth is that you're eating?"

Dame Sybil returned, noticing Vladimir's newest dinner companion. "Vladimir, you couldn't have gotten tired of Denise so soon and replaced her already?"

"With Denise I am *far* from bored," Vladimir replied. "But *this* woman! This monster of torment! She does not take a hint!"

"Philippe would know how to handle her."

"So do I." Vladimir's eyes glinted like those of a misch. beginning to enjoy the evening. I intend to continue."

". . . And you're so clean-cut and good-looking, Mr. Doerflinger droned on, speaking to Vladimir's back. "You 1. Martian beauty! Oh, and am I glad you left that awful, dreau of yours!" she said, adjusting her girdle. "I was there last year Doerflinger. We couldn't get catsup anywhere. They hadn't even . it! Now, in Leningrad—"

"May I join you?" asked Philippe, sitting down and placing a Lin plate heaped with food on the table. "And you, madame? You are . . .

"Olive Doerflinger—from Cincinnati, Ohio," she rasped.

Suddenly Denise was standing over them. "Is everything all right?" she asked, with her curious talent for making everyone feel significant.

"Oh, Mrs. MacAlpine," growled Olive Doerflinger. "I'm afraid I'm sitting in your chair, but I'll give it back to you in a minute. I'm having such a fascinating conversation with Mr. Volden." Vladimir raised his eyes to Denise in helplessness. She calmly occupied a chair opposite him—the place originally intended for Teresa Santeramo.

". . . So we were staying at the Astoria Hotel in Leningrad," rattled on Olive Doerflinger. "It's supposed to be first-class. Well, they didn't even have a safe for my jewelry! Now, have you ever heard of a first-class hotel that doesn't have a safe for jewelry?" She fingered her rhinestone necklace possessively. "I've heard a rumor—"

"Did you hear that, Vladimir?" mocked Philippe. "Mrs. Doerflinger's heard a rumor . . ."

". . . and it's only a rumor," Vladimir contributed with good humor.

"The melon is wonderful!" exclaimed Philippe, savoring a juicy morsel.

"Mellons! Did somebody say Mellons!" shrieked Olive Doerflinger. "Oh, are they here too? Such a wonderful family! They come from Pittsburgh— but you know that, don't you Mrs. MacAlpine?" Denise stifled a chuckle. "I'm sorry, Mr. Volden, I've never seen you dance," Olive Doerflinger kept on, in a whirlwind of mindless chatter. "I hear you're a great dancer! Mr. Doerflinger and I saw some terrific dancers last night at the Folies-Bergère! We're here on vacation. Maybe we'll get a chance to catch your show too! Do you think you could get us some freebies, Mr. Volden?"

Vladimir turned sharply to her. "The name is Volodin. V-O-L-O-D-I-N," he spelled. "Volodin. Vladimir Volodin."

"Russian is such a strange language, Mr. Voldin! When Mr. Doerflinger and I were in the Soviet Union last year, we were greeted by the word 'Amerikanka' wherever we went. What does it mean, Mr. Voldin?"

" 'American woman,' " he replied impatiently. "It means 'American woman.' "

"How interesting! Which means that they were all conscious of little old me, but not Mr. Doerflinger. I wonder why that was?"

"It also means 'convertible sofa.' "

"Oh, how fascinating, Mr. Voldin! But however does one tell the difference between an American woman and a convertible sofa?"

"I often think, Mrs. Doorclanger, that there *isn't* any difference!" Vladimir's nostrils flared. "Tell me, does Mr. Doorclanger know the difference?
Or is he in the habit of wheeling you into the living room, pulling out your
bottom, lifting your cushions and fucking your springs?" he thundered. The
whole table was aghast.

"Oh, Mr. Voldin," she sputtered, "I don't believe I heard you right. I
. . . I . . . What I really want to know, Mr. Voldin, is this. What do you
attribute your success to?"

There was a painful silence as Vladimir slowly lowered his hand below
the table. He fixed his eyes intently on hers while unbuttoning his fly.
Tense with fury, color flooding his face, he threw the steak, splattering it
all over the tablecloth. Standing up and shoving back his chair, he extracted
his larger than average penis and slammed it on the plate. "My cock, Mrs.
Doorclanger! My cock is basis of my success!" The entire room gasped
audibly. The music was frozen in mid-bar. Denise looked the other way,
amused and appalled. Philippe surveyed the scene with a tingle of satisfaction. Slowly Vladimir put his penis, covered with sauce, back inside his
pants, did up his trousers, threw the plate on the floor, and stormed out of
the room.

"Horace!" Olive Doerflinger screamed frantically. "Horace Doerflinger!
Why are you never here when I need you! Horace!"

"Calm yourself, madame, je vous en prie," Philippe said patronizingly,
placing a hand on the frightened woman's shoulder. "Mr. Volodin has just
introduced you to an ancient Cossack custom."

"What custom? What custom?" Olive Doerflinger sobbed. "We don't have
customs like that in Ohio!"

"Which may explain why I spend so little of my time in your delightful
state," Philippe replied. "But to return to Mr. Volodin's . . . ah . . . ah—
how do you say 'cock' in English? Oh yes, penis! To return to Mr. Volodin's
penis, what he did simply means 'Happy New Year' in Russian!"

They heard the muffled noise of a door slamming.

It was not only Vladimir who left—a part of Denise's heart left with him.
A part of a heart that only hours ago she didn't know existed.

In a room full of people, Denise felt utterly alone.

※

320

VLADIMIR-DENISE/*Paris*/*Tuesday, September 4, 1962*

It was September 4, the day after Denise's party in honor of Dame Sybil Parkinson and Vladimir Volodin. Reluctantly, she lunched with Darvina at the Relais-Plaza, took care of several errands, went to the hairdresser and came home around six o'clock. Many of the previous evening's guests had sent flowers and thank-you notes. Carla handed her a long list of telephone messages. She glanced at them quickly, expectantly, confidently. Then she read through the list again. Vladimir Volodin had not called.

How could he be so rude and ill-mannered? she thought. Not even a word! If they didn't teach him any manners before leaving Russia, surely by now there had been ample time to acquire them! She tried to justify Vladimir's behavior. After all, he probably didn't have time, being constantly on the go and having a performance tonight of *Don Quixote*. But then, so did Sybil, and *she* found time to send flowers and a handwritten note. Perhaps it slipped his mind? Oh no, no, it couldn't have slipped his mind! There was no doubt that she had bewitched him the whole evening—and no one had ever forgotten her! Oh, the hell with that ruffian! He would probably ring her up after the performance. Perfunctorily, Denise made an appearance at a surprise party for Countess Jacqueline Cabrolin, and returned to her apartment after midnight. Still nothing from Vladimir.

By late afternoon on Thursday the sixth Denise still hadn't heard from Vladimir Volodin. She called Philippe de Chambord. Even if Vladimir had made only the vaguest possible allusion to his feelings for her or had casually confided in him, there was no doubt that Philippe would blurt it out with his usual alacrity. Their conversation did nothing to alleviate Denise's anxiety. For nearly half an hour she listened patiently to Philippe's ancient gossip. She canceled her dinner plans and went by herself to the opera house. She sat at the rear, watching with fascination as Vladimir Volodin and Veronica Mason performed *La Fille Mal Gardée*. She slipped out of the hall during the deafening and endless curtain calls.

On Friday the seventh, having slept very poorly, Denise woke up tense and nervous. The date had been circled on her calendar. *Dinner with V.V.* Their words came back: "I'm having a little supper Friday night." "Will there be many people?" "Just you and I, Mrs. MacAlpine." "Call me Denise." . . . What was the name of his hotel? La Tremoille. She went so far as to look up the number but couldn't bring herself to dial.

Friday came and went without a word from Vladimir. This was the *coup de grâce!*

Late Saturday afternoon Denise was strolling aimlessly through the foreign-language department of Hachette, the famous bookstore not far from the Musée d'Art Moderne on the Avenue de Président Wilson.

Vladimir, carrying a tote bag over his shoulder, had just finished a dance class and had entered the shop to browse and cool off. His eyes were immediately caught by a recently published biography prominently displayed in a pyramid on the floor: *The Greatest Love Story Never Told—Diaghilev and Nijinsky*. He bought it.

Denise picked up a copy of an Italian *Vogue* and then went on toward another section, where larger and more expensive publications were displayed. Vladimir followed the impeccable white linen suit. Gold bracelets jangled on her arms as she collected various books.

It was an unusually hot day for September, and although Vladimir could see her only from the back, the elegance of this woman, especially her white gloves, seemed out of place. He wondered what on earth this woman could be doing in Paris on such a hot Saturday afternoon. She showed style and panache. Maybe she was a foreigner. Vladimir was standing a few feet away now. Denise turned suddenly in his direction, and he saw the pure gold of her hair melting into the honey-tinted porcelain of her neck.

"Do you have the latest Gore Vidal?" Denise demanded arrogantly, not bothering to look up. Vladimir didn't answer, hiding his astonishment. She looked up. "Oh!" She giggled, briefly disconcerted, recognizing him. "Vladimir! I thought you were a salesman! Excuse me for being so distracted." Her words erupted like bubbling water.

Vladimir laughed, accentuating his jutting cheekbones, and shook hands in his abrupt manner. Plucking the pile of books from her arms, he motioned to a clerk. "Could you kindly make a large package for madame?" There was a momentary pause. Vladimir turned to Denise, a slow smile breaking on his face. "Will you read all of these?" he asked, waiting for the parcel. "Whatever you do, don't ruin such incredible eyes!" They were a shade of blue Vladimir had never seen except when gazing on a blue sky a long time ago at Yalta. He noticed that her sudden dazzling smile transformed the extraordinary face; it was the smile of an ever so slightly tarnished angel.

The beautiful eyes widened. Denise pressed her hand on his arm. Her grip was firm, and she sparkled. "I'm buying reading matter for the weekend," she said in a purring tone, "since I expect to spend it quietly at home."

Denise let him carry the package, and they left, walking toward her limousine. Nearby, an old man stopped rummaging through a trash can and asked them for a cigarette. Vladimir gave him one. The man promptly put it in his beret and walked away. "That was very nice of you," she said. "The sight of beggars always upsets me."

"I'm always very nice to people I don't know!" Vladimir replied reflectively. "Hey, mister!" he called. The old man turned around. Vladimir threw him his pack of Gauloises. He caught it. "The sight of beggars always upsets me too. They do not exist in my country." Vladimir felt a cold sadness pass over him. He stared at Denise fixedly.

"Look . . . ," she faltered, "I have my car. Can I drop you somewhere . . . ?"

"What time is it now?"

She glanced at her Bulgari wristwatch. "Not quite six o'clock." Her voice was low.

Vladimir looked at the chauffeur standing by the silver Rolls Royce parked at the curb. He was wearing a navy-blue uniform with gold buttons and braid, and the princely crest of the Borgia family adorned the snappy quasi-military cap. Denise had never relinquished her Princess Borgia appurtenances. After all, she had a right to them. For life. Especially since her late husband's title was of papal origin and, not having married Sinclair MacAlpine in the Catholic Church, she was still legally a princess in Europe.

"Where would you like to be dropped . . . *sir?*" she asked in her exquisite voice.

"Where would you suggest . . . madame?"

As if suddenly hit by a brand-new idea: "Well, how would you like to come back with me for a drink?"

"I would like that very much! But I can't stay long." He raised his eyes. "I have a rehearsal this evening."

"Very well," she said, secretly glowing with pleasure at the emerging pattern of events. He gripped her arm tightly as they entered the car. They reclined luxuriously on the off-white leather cushions. "Home, Gerard," she ordered.

Denise took off her gloves. "I'm terribly sorry about yesterday," she said conversationally. "I—"

"What about yesterday? I don't—"

"I know we were supposed to have dinner," she interrupted, "but unfortunately I was visiting friends in the country and totally forgot the name of your hotel so I couldn't—"

"Oh, uh . . . yes, yes, I called you several times, but since you were not home I didn't bother leaving a message," he lied. "And, frankly, I was afraid that after my behavior at your soirée you probably wouldn't want to see me again."

"Actually, I thought what you did was rather"—she hesitated, searching for the right word—"*unusual,*" she pronounced with emphasis, flinging her head back and giggling like a schoolgirl. She caught Vladimir looking at her strangely. Opening her handbag, she put her gloves inside. "I'm always losing gloves," she said. A long trembling sigh filled the air. "How much longer will you be in Paris?" Her eyes were fastened on Vladimir. Everything about him was intriguing.

"Another five days."

"Only . . . and after that . . . ?"

"Brussels. Then I will be making a film in America with Mattie Maxwell."

They rode quietly for some time. Her silence seemed oddly provocative.

Once again Denise became aware of his incredible good looks, now bathed in a wash of fading sunshine. The day was ending, wrapping them both in the flattering light of dusk.

The limousine came to a halt on the Avenue Foch, and Vladimir recognized Denise's house. "Gerard," she said authoritatively, leaning forward, "have the packages sent up. I won't be needing you tomorrow. Be here Monday at eleven sharp."

They went upstairs. The drawing room looked even more spacious and grand without the multitude of people. Once more Vladimir stood near the long white-lacquered table covered with photographs. He reached for the framed picture of Denise's wedding and pointed to Mariela. "When was this picture taken?" he asked.

"I told you," said Denise. "At my wedding."

"Yes, yes, I know that, but what year?"

"In 1958—why?"

"It's just that I saw Mariela briefly in New York about a month ago, and I think she looks even better and younger now than in 1958."

"Yes, she does," Denise said crisply, with that efficient smile she had found so useful while serving on charitable committees. It did not escape Denise that on the night of her party Vladimir had mentioned that he had met Mariela *briefly* in London in 1960. Obviously they had seen each other *briefly* other places as well. Denise made a mental note to investigate these brief encounters of Vladimir Volodin and Mariela Lodge.

"Do you like my house?"

"Yes . . . I like it," he said, replacing the picture. "It is a beautiful and ancient house. I feel like a new wine in an old bottle!"

A maid entered carrying a silver tray with champagne and caviar.

"What makes you think that all I want is caviar and champagne in the afternoon?" From across the room he laughed. A very queer laugh. "Is that what you think of me?"

"I wasn't even thinking of you, Vladimir," replied Denise haughtily. *"This* is what *I* have in the afternoon." She walked toward him and handed him a fluted crystal glass. "What else does one have in the afternoon?" Denise looked like a duchess. At least she looked like the popular notion of a duchess. Her tone softened. "Let's sit down in the bay window. It's so pleasant at this hour. You can watch the traffic going around the Arc de Triomphe without any of the infernal noise." She turned around and led the way. He followed. Denise had left in her wake a perfume reminiscent of the south of France—the fragrance of jasmine, orange blossoms and vanilla.

Vladimir observed this young woman who had an incredible opinion of herself and was sure the world shared it. That strange inner sense of his told him that here was danger. Here was a woman slow to give of herself—if in fact she could ever be brought to yield at all. A challenge! One that already had Vladimir off balance. He had never met anyone who seemed so detached from life. He now wanted her very much. The thought of seducing Denise and making her lose that silvery composure excited him. With a pleasurable sense of anticipation, he dropped into an armchair by the window, leaned back nonchalantly, and lit a cigarette.

She took a seat in the shadows opposite him.

Pity—he couldn't see her face very clearly now.

From her place in the shadow she savored the beauty of his icon face and Viking body. Something was stirring inside of her. Something she couldn't fathom. She moved a little, and the low rays of the sun caught her white suit with an orange splash.

Vladimir was roused from his sexual fantasy by her lovely murmuring voice. "You know, of course, that the MacAlpine Foundation is supporting your appearance with the London Ballet Company in Dallas next spring. . . ."

"I don't know about finance—I know only about dancing. I'm a dancer, not a businessman, so I'll leave the business side of the production to the MacAlpines, their foundation bullshit and tax deduction!" He gave a reckless laugh.

Flushed, Denise rose quickly to her feet. "Let me refill your glass."

"If you don't mind, Denise, I'd prefer vodka. I prefer vodka with caviar."

"Say when." Denise poured from an iced crystal decanter.

"After all, Denise," Vladimir said between puffs, "you're the one who cares about money and power."

She looked at him with supreme indifference and almost ferocious disdain, put the decanter down and slowly returned to her seat.

Vladimir watched her cross her beautiful legs. His eyes blazed. He gave her a penetrating look, which reached into her deeply. She caught his gaze and returned it. A duel of eyes.

"Do you recall, when you were here Tuesday," Denise said, with the air of an actress about to speak her most important line, "I mentioned that I own an unusual Fabergé Easter egg you'd probably be interested in seeing?"

"Yes, yes, I remember that . . ." Briefly, an expression of victory crossed his face. "I was just about to ask you. Perhaps I could see it now."

"Are you sure?" She hesitated, her hands clasped to her breast.

"What do you mean, am I sure?"

"I mean, do you have the time?"

"I can always make the time." The words dripped sensuality, laced with foreboding. "After all—how long can it take to see an egg?"

Denise led him through a labyrinth of corridors, halls, rooms, some with marble floors, others carpeted, all filled with magnificent furniture, pictures and sculptures. Everywhere, white roses, their perfume impregnating her world. She walked almost noiselessly.

Vladimir had pulled the strings of his puppet. Now, like a war-horse, he sniffed the scent of the approaching bedroom, and the strains of Brahms's violin concerto met his ears. Good classical music to fuck by, thought Vladimir. So, it is stud time on Avenue Foch! And I'm the stud! She'll get a stud all right!"

They entered the all-white room, accented with blue Sèvres porcelain. Denise automatically closed the door behind them. A large bed with white crepe de chine sheets and a coverlet of white fox fur dominated the room, beneath Courbet's painting "Les Deux Amies"—two nude milk-and-honey Rubenesque ladies in rapturous embrace. A small writing desk, a few personal photographs, two white suede ottomans, a matching chaise longue, and a long, low bookcase were the only other furnishings. There were no curtains on the windows, and Denise closed the louvered shutters, lacquered a brilliant blue, their color blending with a collection of opaline glass. She lit a pair of Lalique tapers.

"And now let me show you the egg." Denise seemed almost wistful. She approached the priceless object, which rested on an enameled table under a large hand-blown glass dome. She removed it, explaining, "It's called the Peacock Egg and was presented to the Dowager Empress of Russia, Maria Fëdorovna, by Czar Nicholas the Second in 1908. . . ." Desire, like a heavy blanket, was smothering Vladimir. "It's made out of rock crystal—" Vladimir was gazing at her hauntingly.

"Stop it, Vladimir! You should be looking at the egg!" she said without raising her head, talking in her regal drawl. "As you can see, it opens by pushing this button." Denise pressed a twenty-eight-carat Siberian emerald with the majestic sweep of a long, slender finger. The two domes of the egg separated, revealing the enameled peacock. "It's mechanical and musical as well," she continued, removing the bird. "And just look at the eyes! They're diamonds, and the beak is a ruby! I'll take it out and show you." She shut off the Brahms, placed the jeweled bird on the table and started its music box. "And now—"

In an uncontrollable burst, rocked by currents inside him, Vladimir reached violently for Denise. He felt her stir and kissed her, caressing her tongue with his, darting in and out of the soft, wet mouth that opened to him. Her hair hung loose against his cheek. He could feel the warmth of her body. It was shaking and vulnerable. There was more harshness than tenderness in his embrace. Abruptly she disengaged herself, pulling away, and stepped back. He grabbed her by the shoulders. "Do you want me?"

"Yes." She looked straight at him. Her lips quivered. Astonished by her simplicity and passion, Vladimir drew her close, kissing her again—harder. He ran his fingers lightly over the thin silk shirt and cupped one of her small, hard breasts. Her heart was beating on his lips. He kept his mouth over hers. She tried to pull away. He held her firmly. "I'll kiss you till you beg me to stop!" Denise let out a shuddering sigh. She didn't speak. She couldn't. Stilled by his sheer physical presence. His eyes, like arrows, aimed between her legs. "I don't give a fuck about that egg and neither do you. Hypocritical little whore!" he shouted. "Using pretext of historical Easter egg to get yourself screwed!" Brutally he grabbed her hand, thrusting it into his groin. "Get on your knees, bitch!" She remained motionless, frozen. "Down, bitch!" he repeated. He clutched at her, pulled, and half dragged her to the floor. "No! The other way!" he yelled. Terrified, she turned around, presenting her buttocks to him.

"Wait!" she sobbed. "Please wait!"

"When I want something, I don't wait. I don't! I take! It's quite simple!"

With a rough hand he pulled her skirt above her waist and tugged her panties down. He opened her with his fingers. "Don't play games with me, bitch. I know what you want!" Writhing and jerking, she caught her breath with a gasp. Her eyes closed expectantly. She tensed her body as he shoved his foot against the small of her back. One hand was on her neck. "Don't hurt me!" she begged, glancing over her shoulder. "Don't hurt me!" Her childlike face turned perversely demonic. Getting on his knees and unbuttoning his fly, he grasped his long, unnaturally thick organ and rammed it inexorably and viciously inside her without even bothering to lower his trousers. He took her as if craving revenge on life. His face flushed with triumph.

Denise let out a throaty cry, a moan, a scream as a jeweled peacock strutted backward and forward, spreading and closing its many-colored tail to the music-box sounds of "The Blue Danube."

After Vladimir had left, Denise felt a strange elation.

She went to her Fabergé Easter egg. Admired it. Fondled it. And returned it to its place. She sat. She paced. Her thoughts were a strange jumble of memories and longings. "Don't disturb me. I'm in only for Mr. Volodin," she informed her maid.

Denise waited impatiently for his telephone call. Morning came. Nothing.

Denise waited for three whole days and nights, not once closing her eyes to sleep. She simply waited. On the fourth day she rang his room at the Hotel Tremoille. It was very late. Volodin answered. He was home. With whom? She did not speak, only let his voice intoxicate her, and hung up.

Denise could not understand the feelings that had taken over her mind, her body, her breath.

Men who pursued her had always made it their business to assail the impregnable fortress of her heart with their ardor, their stature, their all—from the book salesman who obligingly threw in a set of encyclopedias before making his move, to Sinclair, who offered her a private empire. Invariably the material goods were produced as part of the bargain in exchange for her acceptance of a man who would adore and protect her.

Until now.

Vladimir was different.

This man *had* to belong to her. She *had* to see him again.

On the fifth night she learned Vladimir had left Paris. Vladimir had not called her. The next move would have to be hers.

✵

VLADIMIR-MARIELA/*Brussels/Monday, September 17, 1962*

The train left the Gare St. Lazare while crepuscular murkiness was overtaking Paris. Under the last reddish rays of sun, the silver dome of the Sacré Coeur basilica was a copper silhouette in the distance.

Mariela nervously smoked one gold-tipped cigarette after another. She glanced at her Piaget watch and mentally calculated that the arrival in Brussels would be no later than nine o'clock. She shook her splendid head, half closed her green eyes and blew smoke from her crimson mouth.

A heart-jarring, heartrending whistle, just this side of desperation, pierced the calm of her first-class compartment, causing her to turn reflexively toward the window, becoming deep blue with the coming night. The train hurtled on, gaining momentum, gobbling up distance and space.

Mariela picked up *Town & Country*. The woman gleaming from its cover had a subdued elegance and assuredness drenched with the smell of money. A picture of herself. The accompanying headline read "Grosse-Point: The Home Life of the Beautiful Women and Dynamic Men Who Shape America's Culture and Economy." A spotlight concealed in the ceiling illuminated the glamorous words with a harsh beam. She leafed through the magazine but couldn't concentrate. Restless, she stood, brutally scrutinizing her face in a small oval-shaped mirror on the wall, smoothing her neck in upward motions with the back of her hand. She looked out the window. Her blank, flickering gaze wandered to the dimming landscape, then to nothing at all. She drew the blind. She sat down, fidgeted in her seat, flicked through *Town & Country* again. A full-page photograph of the sprawling Curtis Lodge mansion once more arrested her gaze. Mounted on horses in front of it were Mariela and a distinguished-looking older man with elegantly graying hair and a body and face kept in superior physical condition. The caption read: "Beauteous Mariela Lodge and her husband, Curtis Lodge III, the auto magnate, begin their day with a seven o'clock ride through the grounds of the Lodge estate. Curtis Lodge III has announced his candidacy for governor, a race he hopes will be as successful as that of Night Sanctuary, his prized colt, winner of the Kentucky Derby in 1960."

With a little gesture of discouragement she closed the magazine and lit another cigarette, but it tasted like a bad memory. Impatiently she stubbed it out. In exasperation, Mariela grabbed *Queen,* opening it automatically to page thirty-three. A familiar purplish twinge of jealousy welled up as she gazed for the umpteenth time at a photo of Vladimir affectionately embracing a smiling, large-eyed young woman. A very young woman. With everything youth can lavish on the face and body of a twenty-five-year-old. The caption did nothing to alleviate her feelings: "Vladimir Volodin, the irresistible Sputnik of the dance world, signed for leading film role with American superstar Mattie Maxwell. The dashing couple had eyes only for each other at a party in their honor at the Rainbow Room in New York City."

Slamming the magazine shut, Mariela flung her head back against the seat. A fathomless sensation of breathless falling seized her heart. Oh yes, she needed time to think! That was why she had decided at the last minute to take the late-afternoon express to Brussels instead of going in her limousine. Images of Vladimir succeeded each other jerkily. More than two years since he had entered her life! Names of cities juxtaposed themselves like gleaming pebbles, shining with the patina of pleasure and exquisite bliss— Vienna, London, Spoleto, New York, Paris, Copenhagen—interlaced with the musical strains of Tchaikovsky, Prokofiev, Chopin, Stravinsky. So many furtive meetings, so many ecstatic nights, each stamped indelibly on her memory. She missed Vladimir desperately, longed for him and his wild, devouring, voracious passion. The knowledge that they would soon be together made her quiver in anticipation. Was it really for the last time? It had to be! A gnawing feeling of hopelessness gripped her soul. She tried to dismiss it. It was no use! Her vast capacity for illusion had to face stark reality. Now!

How would she go about breaking up with the only man she had ever loved? How? For days she had thought of nothing else! On the plane across the North Atlantic, Mariela had sat staring out the window like a Gypsy, as if the answer could be read like tea leaves in the deceptive opacity of the white clouds. Passing through London in a trance, she supervised the decoration of her drawing room, dining with friends at Gow's in the Strand, and walking back alone to Chelsea along Cheyne Walk, by the Thames. It was all so pretty and meaningless. Or did she mean petty? All she wanted was to be with Vladimir—forever. That, she knew, was impossible.

Uninvited, a recollection flashed across the years.

Mariela remembered her first crossing of the English Channel in 1939. For a child, barely fourteen, it had been an adventure. She and her parents, Lord and Lady Chiselhurst, had taken the ferry from Dover to France, leaving the pale chalk cliffs behind in a bluish, foggy haze. The sun had been a flaming sphere on the horizon that torrid August evening they sailed into the harbor at Calais, just before the war.

For a moment Mariela thought she would weep. The memory of her mother's frightened face, an omen of the evil days to come, was etched on her memory. She shook her head several times, smiling to herself cynically. Shutting her eyes, she allowed herself the pleasure of languorous fantasy. The soft, gently teasing tones of Sinatra's voice ran through her mind. "Oh, how the thought of you clings . . . these foolish things remind me of you . . ."

Gradually lulled into a fitful sleep by the train's gentle vibration over the rails, Mariela dreamed that she and Vladimir were to meet on a plateau high above some ancient city. In ecstasy they ran toward each other, arms outstretched, their faces creased in beatific smiles. Faster and faster they hurled themselves toward unattainable bliss, never getting any closer to the objects of their desire. After what seemed like an agonized eternity the dream was interrupted by an announcement on the loudspeaker. Mariela woke up, startled. The train was pulling into Brussels' Gare du Nord.

She alighted that chilly, damp September evening feeling the excitement she always felt when arriving in a foreign city. She took a deep breath and walked straight ahead along the quai, pulling her coat collar tightly around her neck. The station was practically deserted at that time of night, and the cold, metallic atmosphere made her shiver. She looked at the half moon ascending the sky. It shone through the grimy glass roof of the terminal, diffusing its light through eddies of dust particles.

Mariela approached the exit as her limousine pulled alongside the station. She entered the car and was driven to her hotel. She rested briefly in her suite before preparing to meet Vladimir after his performance at the Théâtre de la Monnaie. On the front page of the evening edition of *Le Soir* she noticed his picture with Dame Sybil Parkinson. The camera had caught the moment of their final bow, which had now become their trademark: sheer delight on the face of Vladimir, kneeling before a rapturous Parkinson, kissing her hand as she offered him a rose. Another glowing review, written with the uncontained fervor inspired whenever the heralded pair danced together. Only the words were different: "Dame Sybil was the essence of regal poise, with a vulnerable radiance of her own, dancing with her heart as well as her feet, and balanced to perfection with the stellar magnetism and reckless dynamism of Vladimir Volodin, the intense, impulsive rebel. She grows younger and younger in his arms. . . . Volodin was at his most spectacular, offering a type and standard of dancing not ever seen by this generation, and certainly not since Nijinsky. He is incredible, beyond technique, and indescribable! . . . They danced together with mythical ecstasy. The complete entity of their glamorous partnership is dazzling and moving, sending shudders down the spine, bringing tears to the eyes. . . . The opening-night audience responded with a 40-minute ovation."

Although Mariela had never raised the subject with Vladimir, there was no doubt in her mind that despite Dame Sybil's apparent devotion to her husband, Neville Wadmond-Woods, the eminent Member of Parliament, the incandescence and passion created onstage by Volodin and Parkinson were carried beyond the footlights.

After carefully applying her makeup, she slipped into a sleeveless emerald-green taffeta gown by Balmain, with a straight skirt, fitted bodice and high neckline, and freshened the beehive hairdo created for her that morning by Laurent of Alexandre's. A pair of diamond-and-pearl earrings was her only jewelry. Mariela slipped a navy-blue cape with a burgundy Peter Pan collar over her exquisite shoulders, wrapping the folds of the cloak protectively around her voluptuous body. The limousine was waiting when she swept from the hotel lobby into the street. A passerby stepped off the sidewalk to make room for her, while the liveried doorman solicitously helped her into the back seat. She planned to arrive at the restaurant before Vladimir, installing herself grandly at the table. Grandly—but was it grand to be early? Definitely not! Not this time. Not this last time. He *had* to remember her. This evening *had* to be special. Better to make a grand entrance than to wait grandly!

As the car turned out of the Rue de l'Amigo into the spectacular medieval Grand Place, she asked to be let out. The driver stopped with a screech of brakes. A frightened pedestrian started cursing bitterly in Flemish. "Gotverdoemine lulleke domkop!"

Mariela stepped into the thousand-year-old square and stood riveted, transfixed by its majestic beauty. The ornately carved stone and gold-leaf Gothic buildings, with their leaded windows, glittered like gold lace in the night illumination. The September wind was having its own gentle way with billowing clusters of delicately transparent jonquils, which provided an out-of-season, yellow-dappled spring in their huge concrete pots scattered throughout the vast historic area. The indulgent weather spread a purple-and-blue haze, wreathing her head loosely in wisps of lavender chiffon. Like a schoolgirl overcome with exhilaration, she wanted to rush off happily in every direction. She was awakened from her reverie by a cacophony of chimes—a clock began striking the hour and a myriad others were chiming their minutes.

Panic seized her. She had just stepped back in history, only to find herself propelled into the turmoil of the present! How would she explain it all to Vladimir? Did she have the strength? Or the generosity? A wintry shiver ran through her as she crossed the square and reentered the car.

The Chez Père Gautier, considered by gastronomy experts to be the best restaurant in the world, was just around the corner. In existence since 1690, it was a haven for impeccable foreign businessmen and diplomats, aristocratic ladies and elegant couples. Its name was modestly engraved on a small bronze plaque by the door. Immediately adjacent was another entrance, this one bearing no identification, which led into the establishment's discreet and famed Salons Particuliers—that marvelous European combination of luxurious private dining room and intimate lounge designed expressly for tête-à-têtes. *Definitely* not for sleeping! Gourmet food and the chance to be alone with each other! Sheltered from prying eyes. After all, man does not live by bread alone! The Salons Particuliers of the Père Gautier had been frequented at one time or another by every crowned head in the world, notably Edward VII, King Farouk, and more recently by the Shah of Iran, with various beauties.

Mariela rang the bell, which was surrounded by a discreet ring of polished brass. The door opened automatically into an entrance hall, a dizzying splendor of richness. Deep red velvet and soft muted oak reflected from the mirrored walls. Ancient gas fixtures, cleverly converted, flickered, casting creamy warmth. Mariela was immediately met by Madame Gautier, a woman of indeterminate age with a painted, time-eroded face on which the eyebrows were penciled arches drawn where the hairs had been savagely plucked. Her furrowed neck was long past hope of repair. Although she admitted to fifty, the loose skin and prominent veins on the slender hands revealed that Madame Gautier was probably nearing seventy.

"Oh, Lady Chelmsford!" she greeted Mariela in her guttural voice. "Ees such a pleasure seeing you again after so long a time! Madame mustn't punish us zis way." Her usually lackluster eyes lit up for a shining moment. "Monsieur Volodin, he ees *here!* Madame! Here! I trust madame had a good journey," she continued. Mariela's cape was removed with the assistance of Henri-Jacques, the maître d'hôtel, gloating with petty power, and passed to the cloakroom attendant.

"I'd forgotten how relaxing traveling by train could be," Mariela said perfunctorily, not listening to her own words, and added quickly, "I specifically requested an inconspicuous—"

"We've been able to give you zee Salon Balzac. It is private, madame, indeed—very private. As a matter of fact," she continued obsequiously, her manner infuriatingly confidential, "I saw monsieur perform on Thursday evening. He dances like a bird."

"Yes, yes, I—" The reference automatically made Mariela think of a "I hope your evening will be satisfactory."
plumed serpent. She wondered why. Perhaps because Vladimir always reminded her of a peacock. Heart pounding, head spinning, excitement and dread mounting, she squeezed polite words from her constricted throat and quickened her step. With an uncertain gait Madame Gautier led the way up the thickly carpeted stairs, coquettishly patting her reddish hair, which had lost its glint and was worn plastered to her skull in a semblance of style.

She turned around on the first-floor landing: "Everything has been arranged according to your instructions, Lady Chelmsford," and she laid her hand lightly on Mariela's bare arm.

"Good, good." Mariela swept by the woman into a small antechamber.

"Le Salon Balzac," said Madame Gautier, withdrawing in respectful haste.

Mariela knocked softly at the door and entered. Vladimir rose auto-cratically from the seat he was straddling. Princely and dashing, he wore purple velvet trousers, which flounced like a cavalier's into wide cuffed brown leather knee boots. His black crew neck sweater was belted with florins and crowns arranged alternately around his slender waist. Mariela, as if in the domineering presence of a Roman emperor or Renaissance pope, went rigid with fear, opening and closing her glossy lips in speechless awe. Vladimir strode impatiently toward her, bowed low, and turned her hand over, burying a passionate kiss in the depth of its palm. "My darling, my dushka," he whispered, his eyes fierce, adoring. "I was afraid maybe some-thing had gone wrong with your plans, Mariela. All evening I was worried."

"Vladimir!" She managed to speak his name, with undisguised joy. En-gulfed by something indescribable stirring in the depths of her being, she trembled from head to foot. He noticed a faint mist of perspiration clinging to her forehead and could not shut out the disturbing smell of black hair and white skin, the musky smell that dark women exude. Her smell. Abruptly, with electric fever, Vladimir grabbed Mariela by the waist, kissing her mouth avidly and passionately. She vibrated with pleasure. An urgent tightening between her legs. Gently his fingers cupped and followed the contours of her breasts. He took her hand and pressed it hard against the stiff bulge of his cock. "See what you do to me!"

"Wait, Vladimir, wait."

Her sultry gaze, touched with rapture, contained both challenge and hesi-tancy.

"I can't."

"Not now, please . . . please," she said, recoiling.

Vladimir looked at Mariela, baffled by her mysterious withdrawal.

For days he had longed to see her. So obsessive was his excitement that he had hardly been able to concentrate on anything else. Tonight, after the performance, he had actually run to the restaurant, arriving deliberately early in the childish hope that somehow his haste would make her mate-rialize sooner. Suddenly there she was, standing in the doorway in a blaze of flashing, speckled, colored light. But something was wrong—or so it seemed. But what?

He placed his hand on the small of her back. They moved toward an open fire, its reflection dancing mischievously on the dark walnut ceiling of the small room.

"How was the performance?" she asked, hoping to camouflage the anxiety that was swelling in her.

"Performance was all right. Orchestra all right." His full, sensuous mouth changed from a pout to a self-deprecating grin. "I could have been better."

She pulled away from him. "Vladimir, I've never known you to be happy with any of your performances. Never!" Mariela was satisfied with the emo-tionless tone she was able to sustain.

He admired her slow, swaying walk. The green gown was particularly becoming, its folds making pulsating, silky ripples against her crotch and buttocks.

"Have a seat, dushka." Vladimir pulled out a high-backed antique tapestry chair. They sat facing each other at an antique Flemish table. Silverware and linens had already been laid out for supper, as well as freshly baked baguette in a wicker basket, a pot of Normandy butter, an exquisite platter of *jambon du pays,* duck pâté de foie gras, and a Val St. Lambert crystal bowl brimming with juicy Changal pears and figs. Vladimir poured champagne ceremoniously from a bottle nestled in an ice-filled silver bucket. Mariela's hand holding the outstretched glass was quivering. She drank the pale liquid silently.

"Are you all right?"

"Yes, yes, yes," she said, staccato. "Why do you ask?"

"You seem so far away." He spoke in a soft voice that trailed. "We mustn't let so much time pass before we see each other again."

"What?" Mariela said.

"I beg your pardon?"

"I merely said, 'what?' "

"Oh . . . I was just saying that we mustn't let so much time come between us."

"No, Vladimir, you're . . . you're quite right. We mustn't." A fine sadness welled up as she repeated the convincing lie.

"You've never been more beautiful!" he whispered huskily.

Two candles in hurricane lamps flickered at one end of the heavy oak table, defining the perfect oval of her face and turning her irises opalescent.

Mariela was about to say something but lowered her lids and smiled mysteriously instead, having decided the evening should go exactly as planned, just like old times. After champagne and kisses she would surprise him with her bag of tricks. Passionate, violent, frightening, cruel. And final. He would leave, shocked and disgusted. The next day she would return to England, then America. Finis. The end of the affair.

Vladimir was speaking ebulliently now. ". . . I didn't dance with Sybil . . . audience . . . Veronica . . . bitch . . . too heavy . . . Veronica . . . next week . . ."

Mariela barely heard a word he said. She was just staring vacantly, mesmerized, immobile in his magnetic field. His golden laughter pierced her daze. How she was going to miss him! The thought of never seeing Vladimir again sent a spear of ice cleaving through her heart.

Vladimir's laughter dissolved. The gaiety in his eyes was extinguished. He lit a cigarette. The smoke created a blue, faintly iridescent halo. He stood up and refilled their glasses, then gently bent down and kissed her neck. His eyes fell to her breasts and hips and legs.

There was a knock on the door and an elderly, white-haired waiter, with a florid well-larded face, entered carrying a full tray.

"What's this, what's this?" Vladimir asked, turning in a swift half circle. "What kind of restaurant are we in? Are we not permitted to choose what we eat?"

"Vladimir, hush! I've already chosen!"

"How? . . . When? . . . Where? . . . He paused between words, stressing them like military taps.

"I telephoned Madame Gautier from Paris—"

"From Paris!" he interrupted, thunderstruck. "You've been here before?"

"I wanted to make sure everything would be—"

"You've been here before!" he repeated insistently.

"Yes, I have," she declared coolly. "Please, darling, come and sit down." Mariela signaled the waiter to begin serving. After polishing them, he placed a bowl and plate before each of them.

"And the flowers," continued Vladimir, moving to the dining table with fluid grace. "Those . . ." He sat down and drummed his fingers against a vase containing tiger lilies interspersed with coral and pink sprays of heather and deep green bracken, flown in especially for the occasion from the north of Scotland. "Those flowers! Whose idea was that?"

"Mine, of course." Impulsively she took his hand in hers. "You know I've always had a weakness for tiger lilies. I wanted to make sure everything would be"—she searched for the right word—"perfect."

Vladimir screwed his eyes to their smallest and most penetrating. "Do you always go to such trouble to make everything . . . *perfect* when you come here?"

"Whenever I entertain, Vladimir, I always seek perfection."

With schoolboy defiance, he removed the fingers that gripped his, stubbed the cigarette on the sole of his boot and flung its butt across the room.

The waiter poured a small quantity of wine into Vladimir's glass, waiting for him to taste it. "Let's cut the crap!" he said, throwing up his hands. "Just pour!"

"Vladimir, really! Your command of English improves daily," Mariela commented sarcastically.

The waiter filled both glasses uncertainly. When he was finished, Vladimir rudely grabbed the bottle from his hand and read the label. " 'Vin de la maison.' What kind of wine is this, Mariela?" he asked with belligerence. "Is this the wine you select when you . . . when you *entertain* in this place?" He slammed the bottle loudly on the table. "I've never heard of this label!"

"I can assure you that when one dines at Père Gautier, the best wine *is* the house wine," she stated uncompromisingly, "and this one is fine for me!"

"Waiter! Bring me a bottle of Batard-Montrachet 1938!" ordered Vladimir with theatrical importance. "Why should I drink shit house wine!" he sputtered. The waiter left the room awkwardly.

"Why is 1938 such a good year?" asked Mariela with mock aloofness.

"It's the year of my birth!" he said, laughing.

"It's also the year Hitler annexed Austria," retorted Mariela.

A huge and troubling lull filled the space. Vladimir made his table napkin crack like a whip as he unfolded it. Mariela, using a Delft ladle matching the tureen, served the soup. Thick, rich, creamy *potage* Crécy, with yellow melted butter and green freshly chopped parsley floating on its surface.

They ate in silence. The clatter of spoons muffled by the opulently draped walls and the rugs. The fire and candles, a mute corps of dancing amber figures, provided the only movement. Mariela sat rigid and uncomfortable, automatically raising the silver spoon to her lips, lowering it to the bowl, with the grace and precision of a prima ballerina, never permitting the cold, impervious stare to wander from the noble face.

The fear and uncertainty that had corroded Mariela's spirit at the prospect of meeting Vladimir gradually faded away and were now replaced by unadulterated disappointment. Was this the new urbane Vladimir she had read about, his success made vulgar by his flaunting it? She was appalled, fascinated—and unexpectedly pleased. This would make it easier for her later on. Much easier. But one look at Vladimir—the gleam of his teeth in his open mouth, the sight of his moist tongue between his full, pouting lips, the long shadows cast by his high cheekbones over his hollow cheeks, the sadness of his gray eyes, the electric force of his presence—and Mariela was anesthetized in spite of herself. All she could think of was being crushed in his arms.

The sommelier reappeared. He held the bottle of wine at an angle, permitting Vladimir to read its label. "Batard-Montrachet 1938! Now, that's more like it," Vladimir declared with a generous and captivating smile. "Don't you—"

"I'm sorry we've troubled you," Mariela said, turning to the sommelier apologetically. "Mr. Volodin has changed his mind and will have the house wine after all." She kept her spoon poised in midair, like a final punctuation. Stealthily the sommelier crept out, his expression wide-eyed and baffled. "As a . . . as your friend, I would like to know . . ." Mariela paused. Vladimir's eyelids arched into circumflex accents, questioning. "Why did you carry on about the wine like a spoiled brat?" she asked in exasperation.

Vladimir picked up his napkin abruptly and wiped the corners of his mouth. He studied Mariela. It could have been one minute or many. She was sitting across from him, radiant, lovely, his. And everything was all wrong! Slavic melancholy flooded his face. "Why do you bring me to a place you have already been with other men?"

She raised her head, scanning the face of her lover, and said softly, "When a woman of thirty—and in my case I should say *over* thirty—enters your life, Vladimir, or that of any man fifteen years her junior, remember that she carries with her a few suitcases, and if you want that woman you have to accept her, bag and baggage included." Her tone was icy, like that of the tiny Delft bell she tinkled between thumb and forefinger, alerting the staff she was ready for the next course. She made a nonchalantly graceful arabesque with her right fingers touching her hair. Slack flesh pulled at the back of her upper arm. She noticed it with bitter acceptance and quickly lowered her hand to her lap.

Two waiters responded to the summons. One cleared the table. The other put down a *civet de lièvre* sealed with pastry in a brown earthenware pot. When its heavy lid was removed, the rich aroma escaped, assailing their nostrils.

"I hope you don't expect me to eat all this—"

"Vladimir!" she said. "The Père Gautier is internationally famous for its food!"

"I didn't think it was famous for plumbing! Although, on second thought . . ." Unconsciously his eyes moved to the right corner of the room, where a wide couch, too large to be called a sofa and too small to be construed as a bed, stood invitingly. Behind it a carved wooden screen discreetly concealed a marble basin and bidet.

"Eating here is an experience," Mariela continued, grateful for the break that had dispelled the tension. "When in Belgium, do as the Belgians do. You know, here they eat rats too."

"Rats!" he exclaimed, incredulous.

"Yes, rats!" she answered. "There's a restaurant at Bruges—"

"You mean"—a mounting shadow of revulsion crossed his face—"the things . . . that . . . that crawl?"

"No, not like those. Here they are bred especially for human consumption and are considered quite a delicacy."

Turning to the waiters, who made no effort to conceal their mirth, Vladimir pointed suspiciously to the casserole and asked, "Are there rats in this dish?"

"No, but the animal is a member of the same family!" replied Mariela, suppressing a smile.

"Oh, God!" Vladimir sighed, holding his head. "What is it?"

"Jugged hare!" Mariela told him. "It's a national dish. And Madame Gautier tells me it's been hung for at least a week!"

"Hung? What do you mean hung? Hung how? It sounds Chinese or obscene!"

"Vladimir, they hang wild game to age it."

"Oh!" he replied. There was a small, awkward pause. "Well, whatever they do, it smells marvelous!" He spoke with the detachment of a stockbroker.

The waiters paused at the door, patches of perspiration from long hours of hard work showing under their arms. "My name is Marcel," said the heavier one. "We'll leave the remainder of the dinner in the dumbwaiter." He pointed to a small recess enclosed by a sliding panel. "You will find a selection of roquefort, *confiture de cerises,* bottles of cognac, vodka, champagne, as well as coffee and tea. Should you require anything else, do not hesitate to ring. I hope that everything has been satisfactory, Lady Chelmsford. Good night."

Now they were alone. Their eyes met. His were steely. "So it's Lady Chelmsford, is it?" Vladimir asked, intrigued. "Since it is not your *nom de plume,* is it your *nom de restaurant?*"

"Lady Chelmsford is my maiden name," Mariela stated flatly.

"Haven't you lost your title?"

"Lost my title, Vladimir? The daughters of English earls never lose their titles. They may lose everything else, including their peaches-and-cream complexions, but they never lose their titles! Come, Vladimir, let's eat. Our food is getting cold."

"Lady Chelmsford! It is quite beautiful. Why don't you use that title more often?" he asked.

"Because," she answered, "with my new name I acquired a new life. 'Mrs. Curtis Lodge' is fine with me. It's who I want to be."

"If that is who you want to be," he spat out contemptuously, "why don't you choose to spend more of your time with *Mr.* Curtis Lodge?"

He was right, of course, more than he realized. She *had* made a choice, and would soon be going back to it.

"Now, Vladimir . . ."

Vladimir slammed his glass on the table, its contents splashing onto his plate. He lurched from his chair toward the window, spewing forth furious little clucks and clicks in Russian. Then he whirled around. "In other words, Mrs. Curtis Lodge, I am your official stud?"

"You knew my situation from the start."

"What am I supposed to do when you are playing the role of Mrs. Curtis Lodge? Hide away from the world? Stay in closet until you decide you're tired of counting your money and it's time for me to get an airing? Or when you itch for a good fuck?" His raging words set the room ablaze.

Mariela sank back in her chair, stunned by the intensity of his emotions. "Stop it, Vladimir! What's come over you? I have never questioned you, and I've never questioned your personal life when you're not with me. I don't question you, because it's none of my business. And *that,* my dear Vladimir, cuts both ways." This was it. Too late to back off now, and so she continued the thought. "I run my life as I see fit. I'm sure you do the same with yours. Staying in a closet is not your style. And if you do stay in closets when I'm not around, you're a damn fool!" She took a swallow of wine to avoid his eyes.

Now it was Vladimir's turn to be stunned. He banged his hand against the silk moiré wall savagely, causing an etching to fall to the floor, its glass shattering. She had never seen him so incensed.

"Vladimir, you'll have to calm yourself," she pleaded, trying valiantly to bring her own emotions under control. "Please . . . come . . . you're spoiling this lovely dinner." This *last* lovely dinner, she might have said.

How ironic—that he should be voicing his jealousies now, at the end of the relationship. After all, it was the end!

Once again the room was plunged into stillness.

Vladimir returned to the table and sat down slowly, cradling her face between the palms of his hands. He looked at her gently. "Mariela, I'm sorry. I love you. But sometimes I wish . . . if only you were not . . ." His face finished the sentence. He was aflame with Mariela's nearness, and the hardness stretching the fabric of his pants made him focus once again on his unquenchable lust for her silky magnificence.

Tenderly she slid his hands from her face. "Vladimir, we really must eat. I planned this for you. So please . . . try to enjoy it."

Mariela ate slowly. Her appetite was gone. "Vladimir," she began. "I can't begin to tell you . . ." The sound of his plate noisily being pushed away from him interrupted her. "Don't you like the food, darling?" She could feel his antagonism mounting.

"No, I'm not eating rats. Nor hung rats! Nor family of rats!"

"Oh, Vladimir, why?"

"How can you ask . . . How can you have the . . . the audacity to tell me . . . to tell me that rats are the speciality at some restaurant I've never heard of in . . . Ghent . . . or Antwerp . . . or wherever in hell it was you mentioned! Mariela, during the war, in Leningrad, my mother, my brother and myself were forced to eat—" His voice broke. He sucked in his breath, setting his teeth on edge, and squeezed his eyes tightly shut to prevent the tears from welling up. "My mother was forced to hunt for. . . for rats, so we could eat—" Once again the voice was lost, but he caught it in the back of his throat. "We were *forced* to eat rats! Yes, goddammit, rats! And not because they were chic, Mariela, but because we were hungry. Starving!" He paused. "Can you understand that?"

"Yes, I *know* you had extreme wartime hardships. I—"

"Hardship!" he shouted. "*Extreme wartime hardship* you call it! There is no word in the dictionary for the kind of *wartime hardship* we suffered! Our story is beyond language. We lost twenty million men in *wartime hardship!* Three times population of fucking Belgium . . ."

"Oh, Vladimir, I am sorry. I didn't mean to be so . . . so insensitive. I apologize most humbly. Will you forgive me?"

He looked at her and let out a deep, weary sigh, annoyed with himself for having permitted anger and melancholy to flare so quickly and unexpectedly.

"Will you forgive me?" she repeated.

"I could forgive you anything, Mariela."

The candles melted lower and lower, the fire burned itself out on the grate in a heap of soft white ash. For one moment, for one mad, wonderful moment Mariela forgot the real purpose of tonight's meeting and reached across the table, taking one of his hands in hers, kissing and licking each of his fingers. Slowly. A prickling sensation spiraled from his groin throughout his nervous system. The floodgates were opened, letting the stream of desire flow betwen them once again.

She bit into an overripe pear, handing it to Vladimir. Back and forth the fruit was passed, its juices oozing from their lips and trickling down their chins in sticky rivulets. Mariela knew exactly what he was thinking of—the wetness between her pleasure-giving thighs. Vladimir knew exactly what she was thinking of—the massive manhood bursting in his trousers. They spoke of art, music, literature. Soon he would sink the full length of his blue-veined cock, hard, throbbing, rigid, into her pulsating and quivering flesh. Their discussion was punctuated by the names of Picasso, Pavlova, Stravinsky, Callas. Soon her cunt would grip it, sucking it into its depths. He amazed Mariela with his increasing knowledge of Byron, dazzling her with a short passage from *Childe Harold,* which he recited with crisp boyishness. Finally nothing but the core was left of the pear.

"Mariela, I can't wait—I'm hungry for you! Only for you . . ." With easy familiarity he put his hand underneath her skirt, caressing her thigh.

"Wait."

"Wait? Wait for what?"

"Vladimir . . . I must talk to you."

"Now?"

"Now." Deliberately, she shrank away from his touch.

"You came all the way to Brussels just to talk to me?"

"Yes—well, I only meant that . . . that I . . ." She floundered hopelessly.

"You only meant that you haven't had a good fuck since the last time you saw me." A chillingly sensual film blurred his features. He rose, walked slowly to the door and locked it. He turned around. Their eyes met. A message passed. He didn't move. He said nothing. His nostrils flared slightly. How well Mariela recognized the signal! He approached, touched her shoulders, then forced her face toward him, holding her by the hair.

"So you want to talk!" he said harshly. "Is that right? Get up!" Something new was in the air. Danger mingled with the odor of sex. This wasn't the script she had planned for this scene! Control gone! Vladimir in the driver's seat! In a dreamlike ecstasy Mariela obeyed him, trembling like someone about to meet God. She exhaled a small breath, which he caught with his mouth. She threw her head back, circling one arm around his neck like a paper streamer. They explored each other's tongues with the lust and urgency of the very first time.

Vladimir stood with his legs apart. Hands on hips. "Unfasten your dress and kneel down!" he commanded. Hunching over, she unzipped the green garment, lowering it to her waist. A sheer bra covered only the lower part of her breasts. He cupped the fullness beneath the stiff and hard nipples, surrounded by the large deep-colored areolas. Fluid welled in her vagina. Dropping to the floor, she closed her arms around his knees, feeling a curious mixture of numbness and excitement. Her hands touched the thrusting belly and felt the imprisoned penis. She unbuttoned his pants with unbridled voracity. "Take off my boots!" he rumbled as he held onto the wall. She all too willingly complied. He flung his trousers aside with his feet and ripped off his sweater. Naked, Vladimir was straddling her head, straining his legs farther apart. She reached for the large erect shaft. "Take it," he ordered imperiously. "Take it all!" She gasped and shuddered as Vladimir pressed his flesh firmly against the roof of her mouth. How she wanted that! Mariela parted her lips wider and wider, drawing the swollen penis farther and farther down her throat in deep sucking movements, gradually engorging the hugeness of his organ. Her breath rose and fell quickly with the rhythm of his breathing. She felt his hands caressing her shoulders. He nimbly unfastened her bra, and held the large, free-flowing breasts. She moaned softly as he pressed and twisted the nipples in his fingers, rolling them harshly again and again as if this moment in time depended on their hardness. He spoke in a low voice. In his tongue. In broken phrases. Words. Unintelligible words. His cock pulsed with the beat of his heart. She felt an abrupt increase in pressure around her tongue. She sucked and sucked at him, swirling at his life, feeling his internal glow. He wrenched her wrists behind her back cruelly, causing her to let out a cry of pain. "How do you like the roles being reversed, bitch! You wanted to talk, talk! Tell me, bitch! Did you ever see a bigger cock?" Her head leaned back as he started a slow rotation of his hips . . . increasing . . . stopping . . . inserting himself deeper and deeper. His hand pulled her closer to him. With a violent movement she tore herself away. Then she licked the soft mound of his flesh between the scrotum and anus, flicking her tongue in and out. She could barely tolerate the mounting anguish between her legs. He seized Mariela by her disheveled hair and forced her mouth back upon him. She arched her back. A hot flush erupted from deep within him. An explosion of molten lava spread outward. Warm and wet and metallic. The thick fluid ran out of her mouth, around the penis, over her face. His hips kept thrusting against her darting tongue. She waited for his surge of excitement to abate. It didn't. Mariela eased him out of her mouth, her face coated with the liquid of love.

Helping her from the floor, Vladimir caught the dress, clutched it, holding it at the waist. He kissed Mariela tenderly, letting his head roll from side to side, tasting himself on her wet lips.

"Put your arms up!" he growled, pulling her gown over her head. The ripe, full breasts looked as if they were being invisibly held up by the nipples. His hands danced magically over her velvety skin.

"Lean on the table!" he commanded with menacing savagery. She obeyed.

"Not that way! On your stomach!" Mariela gasped at his renewed wave of heat. "Spread your legs!" Stiffening her knees, she lowered her chest on the tabletop, pushing the remains of the meal out of the way. A wine glass toppled over, the red liquid running over her fingers like blood.

"Spread your feet wider!" She rose on the tips of her toes, embarrassed by the degree she was forced to bend her hips, and rested her cheek on folded arms. Expecting. Trembling. Excited past the point of no return. The probing fingers smoothed over her belly, reaching her crotch, pushing past the swollen lips, fingering her flesh. Lingering there. One . . . two . . . three . . . They slid in so rapidly, reaching so deeply inside her. The scream that wanted to erupt from her throat did not come out.

Vladimir entered Mariela with a fierce and unexpected force. She caught her breath sharply and screamed with tormented desire, losing herself in a boundless wave of ecstasy. There was no question of who was master. In and out, he rode her with a determined sense of possession, like a small boy on a carrousel horse. She talked to him through her body, directly into his blood stream. Standing, and supporting Mariela's buttocks with both hands, like two bands of fire, Vladimir moved near a mirror, watching with all-consuming excitement as Mariela writhed in wild abandon, lifting and lowered herself onto his entire length. The sound of their music rose further to inflame their passion, now borne along the same stream.

Exhausted, they fell into a chair. He took her in a sitting position, driving and pounding the air from her lungs. Nearing his second climax, Vladimir carried Mariela to the couch, her legs wrapped around his waist. They both soared, reaching the brink of heaven. Entering it at full speed. Fusing together. Exploding. He fell prostrate into her arms. They remained silent for several minutes on the sobering journey back from the demanding realms of love.

"Mariela, how can I stay so long without you? I cannot . . . I cannot," he murmured as he slipped to her side. "I love you . . . I'm proud of our love. It's so frustrating having to hide each time we meet. That's why—"

"Sh-h-h-h. Sh-h-h-h. Sh-h-h-h." She rested her head close to his shoulder. Her elaborate hairdo had long since wilted and her face was shiny, free of makeup, like a little girl's.

"You would never guess what I am thinking about," Vladimir said, flush with childish enthusiasm, his arm loosely around her.

"What?"

"It's crazy, just crazy, but listen to this: I'm thinking that we're having tea under mighty oak tree. You have spread a linen cloth on the myrtle-covered ground and we are about to eat watercress sandwiches from a wicker picnic basket. Like we did in Brighton. How does that sound to you?"

"Oh, Vladimir! You make it all sound so marvelous." He had painted an English country scene, and recollections of an early childhood in Britain flashed across her mind. That was before the war, when her grandfather, the old Earl of Chiselhurst, was still alive. Tea was served on the terrace, and she could picture the adjacent croquet green, with Nanny admonishing her, "Now, now, Lady Mariela! The guest always plays first! You know that!"

Vladimir continued jovially, "Especially if after picnic my dessert can be you!"

"Oh, Vladimir, you're . . . you're . . ." Her face remained pensive and downcast.

"Divine, yes?"

"Yes! Divine!"

Unexpectedly Mariela burst into a flood of silent tears.

"Now, now, now, what have we here?" He enveloped her in his arms. "Since when are you a little crybaby?"

Mariela was pale. Very pale. And he was genuinely concerned about her uncharacteristic fragility. She seemed vulnerable. Desperate, even. Swiftly she disengaged herself and turned her back to him.

"Mariela . . ."

She faced Vladimir once again. "Yes—what is it?" The voice was small. Detached. Numb. Sobbing.

Totally oblivious of his own naked beauty, Vladimir got up, walked majestically behind the screen and returned to Mariela bearing a tissue. "Here, dry your tears."

A towel concealed his hips. He offered to share it with her. Perspiration still lingered on her body. It glistened lushly. Like the overripe pear eaten earlier.

Vladimir was unaware of the phantoms that lurked in Mariela's mind. She didn't know where to begin, or how to begin. Vladimir would go through all the convolutions of persuading her to change her mind. She wouldn't. She couldn't. This was the end!

"Come on, dushka. I think it is getting very late. Let's dress and get out of here. I have matinee tomorrow." He touched her cheek, stood up, and started looking for his scattered clothes.

"The fact is, Vladimir"—she hesitated, pronouncing his name syllable by syllable as if poring over a precious relic—"I must talk to you *now*."

"Come on, darling, get dressed. Tell me story later. Because I can't wait to sleep next to you. It's the best part of love." He was easing into his cashmere sweater and pants.

"The fact is, as much as I . . ."

"Fuck!" Vladimir swore. "I can't find my other sock."

"As much as I *care* for you . . ." Mariela stressed the word, both grateful and annoyed that he wasn't paying attention.

"Ah, I've got it!" Vladimir waved the sock frantically.

"We cannot go on seeing each other like this," she said in a rush. "I mean," she added, stammering, "the way we have."

"What the hell are you talking about, Mariela?"

"Not so loud," she warned.

He paused and stood like a statue for a moment, then came back and sat once more on the couch. *"What* did you say?"

"Our relationship must . . . must end."

He could not quite believe what he was hearing.

"I can no longer see you," she blurted out. "I mean . . . Vladimir, I can no longer be your . . . your . . ." She was unable to finish the sentence.

"Lover? Is that what you're trying to say?"

"Yes." Grief flooded her whole body.

"Why not?" His tone was frigid. "Why not?" he repeated loudly.

"Vladimir, please," she implored. "Keep your voice down!"

"How very British," he sneered. "Don't get excited and keep your voice down!" He was shouting now. "Why must things change? Why?" Striding to the dumbwaiter, he poured himself a glass of vodka, downing it quickly as if to extinguish the fire of his anger.

"Well, in the first place, Vladimir," she continued, trying desperately to control the nervousness that threatened to paralyze her lips, "I'm a married woman." The minute she had said it, Mariela felt foolish.

"So what?" Vladimir bristled with impatient hostility. "You were a married woman when I met you! Didn't seem to bother you then! Why should it bother you now?" He laughed out loud with contempt.

"The whole thing seemed so innocent at first, so . . . so . . . inconsequential. I didn't realize I would—O God!"

"Enough of your goddamn God!" he shouted, tossing his glass into the fireplace.

"Don't raise your voice," she entreated.

"I'm surprised," Vladimir added acidly, "you didn't say I am *different*. Isn't that what women always say? Oh, darling, you are so different!"

"Well," she replied, taking a cigarette from a table by the couch, "it always *is* different."

"How am I different?" he raged. "Or is it *was?*"

"I've never felt for any man the way I feel about you."

"And how *do* you feel about me, Mariela?" His eyes were slits. Cruel! "How?" he rasped.

"You're very *dear* to me of course . . ."

"I'm very *dear* to you of course!" he mocked, a slight smile playing around the corners of his sensual mouth. "Is that all I am to you, Mariela—very dear?"

She ignored the question and was now curling up underneath the large towel, warm with the life of her body. "Come sit next to me, my darling," she said, holding her cigarette as if it were a magic wand that could bring him over. It did.

"Mariela," he asked, "are you trying to tell me there's . . . there's someone else?"

"Oh, Vladimir! Of course there isn't anybody else! There hasn't been anybody since I met you. And now that this is the hour of truth, I confess: there was never anyone before you. No one at all."

"Mariela, it's the same for me—so why can't we continue seeing each other? I'm sure—"

"No, Vladimir. Hear me out—without interrupting me. I really don't know how to start. . . . You know me, yet you don't know *about* me. But one thing you should know is that until I met Curtis in Zurich in 1954 my life had been a depraved and corrupt mess." Without wishing it, all the images returned: Ravenstein . . . Glover . . . Berger . . . Hamilton . . . blackmail . . . filth. And finally hearing with heaven-sent relief that Jack Hamilton had died of a heart attack, taking his warped mind with him—an unexpected wedding present. "At that point the only thing I wanted in the world was to build a new life—to get away, but most of all to have a new life. Curtis made that new life possible. I couldn't have done it by myself. There are many things I have kept hidden from him, things I could never bring myself to talk about and probably never will. Let's just say that I have gone through life slamming doors on various compartments of my past. But he believed in me blindly. And in a way his trust made me a new person. Now, lately, he has been spurred by great political ambition, and stands every chance of succeeding. What do you want me to do, Vladimir? Ruin the life of the man who restored mine? I cannot disappoint him. This goal means everything to Curtis, and I won't let him down. He needs me by his side for the campaign *and I will be there.*" She enunciated those words with painful clarity. "I owe him so much. As Mrs. Curtis Lodge, I was reborn. I owe him an enormous debt of gratitude. I must pay it. I want to pay it—you wouldn't respect me if I didn't."

"You speak of respect, Mariela." He stared deeply into her eyes. She had to force herself to return his scrutiny. "Your husband restored your life to *you. You* owe him a debt of gratitude for the rest of your life?" he asked with intensity and an edge of querulousness. "I'm sure you've done your duty."

"Being a dancer, and being Russian, you, more than anyone, understand duty. *Duty* is the rest of your life. Besides, Curtis and I are useful to each other."

" 'Useful to each other'!" he mimicked. "Nobody in the West ever does anything unless it's *useful* to them!"

"Let's not get into a political discussion, Vladimir! Things are far from perfect between Curtis and me—otherwise even you couldn't have swayed me. But it's a reciprocal arrangement, and it works. I like the security he offers me, and he likes my brains. We're soul mates."

" 'It works'!" he sneered. "Reciprocal! He likes your brains! Does he fuck your brains and suck your soul?"

"Why be so vulgar at a time like this? . . . Curtis matters a great deal." She paused to get her bearings. "I can't begin to tell you . . . how much this . . . upsets me! I'm almost demented at times! I often think of . . . of killing myself! Sometimes it seems death is the only way out!" Suddenly her face showed terror of a kind that was contagious, and it raced through every fiber of her body.

"Is that the only reason we should stop seeing each other?"

"Actually, no. There's a great deal more, much more." She sat straight on the divan, holding onto the towel. "When I was fifteen my parents enrolled me in a private girls' school outside Munich." The color drained from her face. "I met a young German officer. He was tall and blond and beautiful. We made love. It was the first time for me. . . . He died on the Russian front. When the war was over I was reunited with my parents. They were very shocked to discover they had a grandson!" Mariela laughed with bitterness. "They were intellectuals and eccentrics, but, I hasten to add, not liberal-minded people! To put it bluntly, Vladimir, my father threw me out."

"From the house on Belgrave Square?"

"No. But that's another story. The house on Belgrave Square, where you met me, used to belong to my family. But they lost everything, and Curtis bought it back for me as a wedding present."

Vladimir had been fussing with her hair with one hand, but now the hand did not move. "I didn't know you had a son. What happened to him?"

"Do you recall the picture of a young boy in my London house? I told you he was my nephew. I have no nephew, I was lying. . . . *That* was my son!"

"But what about the portrait you showed me, of your sister who passed away?"

"I've never had a sister." She looked at him. Unblinking. "The portrait was of me." Vladimir's eyes reflected surprise. "My son's name is Oliver. He's just graduated from military academy and lives with his grandparents in Germany. I don't see him very often. In fact, he doesn't even know I'm his mother. That makes me feel rather—rather dreadful. Actually, it makes me feel like hell! It's fun for him, I suppose, having a rich and beautiful English lady for a godmother! But all that is going to change soon. Oliver is going to enter college in America. Curtis has agreed to let him live with us, and to this day I've never told him Oliver is my son. I've never told anyone but you. . . . I carry such guilt. . . . I need Oliver. I want to do what is right for him. I must make a future for him. Curtis has no heir . . . and with him Oliver will have a future."

There was a great quietness. Vladimir stood up suddenly. The movement was so exaggerated in the stillness it seemed almost violent.

"And now . . . you and I, we must part?" His voice hovered perilously over an abyss of distress.

"Yes. It's also because I love you, because you are so young, be-cause . . . ," she stammered. "It would destroy us, Vladimir. I love you too much for that."

"Mariela, I love you too. I cannot live without you."

"Nowadays, Vladimir, nobody dies of love."

"Don't you believe I love you?" he asked, shaking her gently.

"I believe that you love me as much as you can love anyone."

"How would you call what I feel for you if it is not love?"

"Growing up," she answered as she fell back against the pillows with a look of anguish. Frantically Mariela ripped and tugged at the waist chain with its small scarab charm hanging loose around her naked hips. The thin gold links quickly gave way under the strain. She rolled it in her hands like a cherished rosary. In a tremulous, tear-stained voice she said, "I want you to have this and keep it always."

"Why would you give this to me now?"

"This was a symbol—my symbol. It was found in Tarutu's sarcophagus." She turned the scarab over, revealing the hieroglyphic inscription on its flat underside.

"What does it say?"

"*'I belong to me.'* But that has all changed. I love you, Vladimir," she whispered in unconditional surrender. "You're the only man I've ever loved. Ever."

He pressed his mouth hard on hers. But she drew away and continued: "Wherever you are, whatever you do, a part of me that no one has ever touched will always belong to you. And this chain will be the reminder." He took the chain and kissed it as if it were her body. She cradled his head tenderly. "The life you've chosen is all-consuming. I know dance comes before country, family, me—everything! Otherwise you would not be the genius you are." Her voice broke. "Everything else—like being with me right now—is icing on the cake. That's life. Your life! Cake becomes tedious if we eat it every day. You would resent the infringement of my demands on your time. No more romantic weekends in Brussels—I assure you of that, Vladimir." She looked at him gently. "We are both happy in the pursuit of unhappiness. It is our fate."

He lay next to her, holding her fiercely, furiously, desperately, with the same compulsion he held his past—a past buried in the roots of his ineffable and profound misery, made more intolerable by the fact that he had never been able to understand it. His life was a constant dance to the angry tune of unspoken and ill-defined regrets. He could lash out in despair. He could seek a semblance of love. He could pretend. But there was no solution, and he felt doomed. Adversity had never produced compassion in Vladimir. But now his body jerked about and a violent moaning rose in his throat, rose to his lips, and exploded. The voice that emerged was not his own but the whine of the helpless, wounded beast that had been caged deep within him for over twenty years. Vladimir sobbed unashamedly, not knowing if it was for her or for himself or for some long-forgotten experience.

"Think about what I've told you. You know I'm right," Mariela said soberly.

They looked at each other silently. The silence glided into understanding.

Now he too knew it was hopeless. "You'll keep in touch?" fingering the broken gold chain.

"Yes . . . of course."

"Every day? Will you telephone me every day?"

"Yes, every day. Whenever that is possible, Vladimir, I will phone you every day. I . . . promise."

"And always be my friend?"

"Always, Vladimir . . . always. I will be the best friend you have in life. The best! Friends last a lot longer than . . ." She couldn't bring herself to utter the word. "You know that." She took a deep breath.

"Mariela . . ."

"Yes, Vladimir, what is it?"

"Let's . . . let's hold each other close. Very close."

"Yes." Tears welled in her great liquid eyes, rolled down her cheeks, wetting his forlorn face, beading on her naked shoulders.

Mariela fell into a deep sleep. Once again she dreamed of Vladimir. This time they were to meet by a boathouse overlooking Lake Huron, in Michigan. It was a warm, sunny, carefree summer day, the cicadas singing in the trees, and with happy abandon she walked along the main road above the lake. She stopped under a Colonial portico. Excitedly, Mariela ran along a gravel path, bordered with petunias and pansies, to a flight of wooden steps, slippery with algae, that descended to the water's edge. There, lying on a seat in a rowboat, was a huge bouquet of tiger lilies. She looked around, but there was no sight of Vladimir. Bending down on the short pier, the blue water lucent through the wooden slats, she reached to pick up the flowers, but the rowboat, as if cut loose by unseen hands, started to drift away. Farther and farther.

Turning around, Mariela found herself standing, alone, on a copper-colored butte, the wind blowing savagely but noiselessly through her hair. Overcome by a sudden fearless calm, she walked without difficulty toward the edge of an arid desert stretching into the distance. There was a rustling in the tall grass behind her—she hesitated, then turned around. The noise had been made by an old shepherd with a gnarled cane. He appeared to be smiling kindly, and she walked toward him. However, as she got closer Mariela could see that his face was contorted with mocking cynicism. As she was drawn involuntarily toward him she watched the distorted features evolve gradually, almost imperceptibly, into those of VLADIMIR. VLADIMIR as an old man. Hollowed-eyed, hollow-cheeked, cadaverous, a toothless smile rocking with monstrous laughter. Seized with uncontrollable and devastating panic, she wrenched herself from the magnet that pulled her and fled with uncoordinated movements toward the precipice, falling, head and stomach turning somersaults, into a dark abyss.

Mariela screamed. Opening her eyes, she reached out to touch Vladimir for comfort. Before her hand came down to rest on the empty divan, she knew he was gone. Near the lace edge of the pillow there lay a pair of frayed dancing slippers, his oldest and most treasured.

Grief-stricken, she buried her face in the slippers and wept. Over and over again she repeated his name, crying and wailing, demented, with the empty victory of a woman who has achieved what she wanted.

⁂

DENISE/*Paris/Tuesday, September 18, 1962*

Denise was angry. Happiness was an emotion for other people. Denise never really understood it. Anger was something she did understand, and now she was being very understanding. Of herself. Not of Vladimir Volodin.

She had the picture in front of her. Right there in today's edition of *France-Soir*.

It showed the Russian ballet star coming out of a Brussels restaurant. Not any restaurant. This was Chez Père Gautier. You didn't go to the Père Gautier to be alone. That's why they had private rooms for rent. Privacy, so you could be by yourself with someone else.

The photo didn't show anyone else. It didn't have to. If you rented a room to have privacy for two, you didn't leave together to advertise the fact. Not when there was always the possibility of photographers hanging around. Photographers who could catch you coming out at two A.M., as someone had caught Vladimir Volodin. It was two A.M. The paper said so.

Vladimir had been there, and not with her.

She was furious. Who was it?

Denise stamped across her bedroom. She turned and stamped back, throwing the newspaper violently onto the bed.

Violence didn't help. The only thing that helps is action, she thought. If the Russian wasn't going to call her, she was going to find out whom he *did* call.

"Globeworld Investigative Agency, Inc. Brody and Briac. Offices worldwide." The card had been in her personal file ever since Denise had had Sinclair MacAlpine investigated to determine his potential as a suitable match.

Soon she was speaking to Jean Briac. It wasn't necessary to discuss a fee. He knew Denise would pay well for the information she wanted. Denise knew she would get it.

". . . I'll also want his complete itinerary, Mr. Briac, for the next two years. Leave nothing out."

She walked out toward the drawing room. She felt better.

Where there's a will, there's a way. Denise had the will. Hence she would have her way. With Vladimir, as with everyone else she had ever met.

The phone rang. She picked it up. It was Darvina. "Hello, hello, it's finally you! Where have you been?"

"Nowhere. I've been busy. You know how it is—luncheons, obligations. Why?" How easy it was, thought Denise, to lie when you are trusted implicitly.

"I've called so many times. Why didn't you at least let me know—something? I was waiting for you."

"Don't wait for me."

Silence followed.

"Can I see you? I'll come to your apartment after work. It's been so long, Denise."

"No . . . I need some air. I'll meet you at Fouquet's at five. No, make it six."

When Denise entered the Champs-Élysées café, Darvina saw at once that everything was not well with her.

Darvina was astonished at her drawn face and the gaunt, wiry look she had taken on. "Denise," she said, "what is it? What has happened to you?" She took her hand in sorrow. Darvina flinched at the energy with which Denise pushed her away.

Denise ordered hot chocolate and a piece of pastry. An old lady strolled into the café selling flowers. Darvina bought a white carnation and handed it to her friend.

Denise took it, smelling it delicately. Mute.

"Why have you been avoiding me?" Darvina asked.

"I've told you—I've been busy, I have obligations. Yesterday I had a frightful headache."

How things had changed, thought Darvina, remembering the happy times when Denise would call her in the middle of the night, when she didn't have all these social obligations, these luncheons, these headaches, these strange and sudden malaises that always seemed to arise when they were supposed to meet.

Darvina tried to shift the conversation, to lighten it, to distract Denise. But her words didn't ring true. She was cold. Cold from not being able to find the right phrase. "I remember when I was seven years old," she said dreamily. "I—but who cares about my childhood! Tell me about yours. What did—"

"I didn't have a childhood," Denise interrupted.

Another silence. Silence condensed in such a small space as to make it unbreathable.

"Am I boring you?"

"Not at all," Denise answered savagely.

"I love you," Darvina said without looking at her.

Denise wasn't answering.

Who said silence was golden? Leaden, yes! "Please, say something!"

"I didn't think it was a question."

"Denise, what *is* wrong?"

There was so much emptiness between the phrases.

"Darvina, I do not love you anymore," she said. "I have loved you very much. But the most violent passions have a way of ending abruptly." She would have wanted to shout, "NO! I HAVE NEVER LOVED YOU! WHY SHOULD I HAVE LOVED YOU?" But that would have demanded more conversation, more explanation.

"But at night . . ."

"What do you mean, 'at night'?"

Darvina was trying to understand what had happened, what was happening now. She knew only too well that a woman like Denise lost interest only when there was someone else. "Have you found another lover?"

"Yes."

"Who is she?"

"Why a she? Why should it be a woman! You're the dyke, remember?"

"But . . . you said you didn't like men."

"I'd never found the right man . . . before."

Darvina was in shock. "Why must you act like this with me?" She was crying. "You're so cruel and heartless. Must you break with me in this . . . awful way?"

"Stop shouting! Do you know of a good way to break?"

Darvina's thoughts of Denise were riddled with flashbacks and fast-forwards. Love awakened. Love fleeting. Love . . . suddenly gone. Despite everything, Denise still wore that noble mask, totally detached, that coldness. But that was when Darvina had discovered in her the most daring gestures, when she was at her most passionate. Darvina felt beaten and rejected. But she had to spend one more night with Denise. She was depending on the night, on her passion, waiting to see Denise's beautiful face thrown back in rapture, her body abandoned to Darvina's expert caresses. But in love, as in banking, one lends only to the rich. And right now Darvina felt poor.

"What are you thinking about?" asked Darvina.

"His mouth."

How she hated Denise's truthfulness. Was it at all possible that all these nights, these sighs, this passion . . . could end like this?

Denise was now more aloof than ever, and it had nothing to do with remorse. Already she was signaling for the check. In a hurry to leave.

"Must you?"

"Yes. I have an errand."

"Can I come along?"

"Suit yourself."

They entered Denise's limousine.

"There's a toy store I want to go to, Gerard," she said to her chauffeur. "I don't know the exact location. We passed it the other day, but it was closed. Just drive along the Rue Cambon, will you? I think I remember where it is."

Denise fiddled with the knob of the radio, and settled for Bobby Darin crooning "Mack the Knife."

She leaned forward toward Gerard. "I remember now. Cross over the intersection . . . turn left . . . It's in the middle of the block, just above the milliner's. . . . That's it, that's it—Le Jardin. Do you see it?"

The car came to a halt.

Darvina moved toward the door.

"Wait here," said Denise. "I'll only be a minute."

She approached Le Jardin, studied its window carefully, and entered resolutely. Shortly afterward, she stepped out carrying an enormous doll with long curly blond hair, and got into the car.

"Is it a present?" asked Darvina.

"Yes."

"I bet you looked just like that when you were a kid!"

"I know."

"Why didn't you have it wrapped?"

Denise didn't answer. Her eyes were fixed lovingly on the doll. "I finally have it. I finally have it," she repeated.

"I don't understand."

"You don't have to understand." The deep amber rays of the dimming September sun invaded the car through the windows.

"Have you seen the doll before?"

"Oh yes, I saw the doll twice before. Once sixteen years ago and again last week, but the store was closed." Darvina and Denise rode in painful silence. They were on the Avenue Kléber.

"Stop at this trash can, Gerard," she commanded abruptly.

Denise jumped from the car, lifted the cover off the can, dropped the doll in it unceremoniously, and came back. The solemnity was gone. Her luminous eyes were glittering wickedly and she began to laugh.

"Well, that's it, Gerard, let's go."

"Where to?"

"Home."

"Denise, what the hell did you do that for?" asked Darvina. "Why did you buy the doll if you didn't want it? Why not give it away to some needy child?"

"Oh, shut up. I *did* want it. Besides, this doll has always been mine," she said emphatically. "And with what is mine I do as I please." She stared straight ahead. The lids lowered, lowered, then closed.

※

It was December 1946. Denise and her mother were passing in front of Pooh's Corner in Prairie, Indiana. In the window, amidst the gaiety of the shiny toys ready for Christmas, was a spectacular doll almost as tall as Denise.

"Oh, Mama! Look at that beautiful doll! Do you think Santa Claus will bring me one like that?"

"Stop bein' foolish, Deeny. Ya know there ain't no Santa Claus!"

"Couldn't we just go inside?"

"Ain't no point, chile. I jist ain't got the money to buy a doll like that."

Denise pleaded with tears in her eyes. "Please, Mama, please! I ain't never seen anything so pretty in all my life. If I . . . if I could only just touch her!"

She pulled her mother by the arm, dragging her inside the crowded store. In her excitement she bumped into and ignored a big rocking horse with a real saddle, rhinestones in its eyes and a long yellow mane.

"I wanna see the doll in the window," said the lovely and surprisingly mature child.

"I know the one," replied the saleslady. "She looks just like you!" Noticing how Denise and her mother were dressed, she added with slight contempt, "Should I even bother taking it out? It's very expensive, you know, almost eight dollars!"

"Oh, please!" Denise lifted the irresistible blue eyes. Grudgingly the saleslady gave her the doll to hold.

Denise caressed the hair, the pretty dress, the face, the arms, the shoes, the legs, fingered the starched petticoat, thinking it was all a dream. The saleslady said condescendingly, "We have less expensive dolls, of course." She brought another. "This one, for instance, costs only two dollars."

"Look, Deeny," said Mrs. Cunningham, "Ah know ya got yer heart set on havin' a doll, so at Christmas Ah can git you the small one if—"

"No, Mama," Denise interjected strongly. "I don't want any doll really." She kissed her mother's hand. "I only wanted to hold the beautiful one, just hold it, that's all."

They left the store empty-handed. Denise never played with a doll again.

—※—

"Well, we're home," said Darvina, shaking Denise's arm. She searched her face for a sign of warmth, of invitation, and saw nothing. "Shall . . . I mean . . . am I . . . Shall I come up?" She smiled bravely.

"No, I have to sleep."

"Sleep," thought Darvina, ". . . the great refuge of love ended." She turned to chance once more, and whispered to Denise, "We could sleep together. Just one more time, please?"

"Gerard, take Miss Darvina home."

"Please, Denise, please . . . One day he will no longer love you . . . I will not love you . . . and you will be alone."

"I've always been alone." Denise slammed the door and disappeared inside. It was a little after seven. Carla handed her the evening's messages. The Marquis de la Rouchefolle, Madame Wilkinson, Jean Briac. . . .

Denise didn't bother to read any further. The investigator wouldn't have called unless he had something worthwhile. She went directly to her room and closed the door. The conversation with Jean Briac was brief. Denise's disillusionment was complete, yet somehow she wasn't surprised.

"Whore, whore, whore," she chanted. "Mariela the whore hanging on Lodge as if he were God on earth, shooting him those melting glances, behaving as if she really *cared*." Her mood rose from languor to ferocity, from sorrow to sarcasm, from confusion to callousness. The night Curtis threw his hat in the ring came to mind, particularly Mariela's speech: "I believe in this man not just because he's my husband but because *he* believes in this country, and I will stand beside him with pride and devotion every step of the way." Slimy anger was slapping her neck, slowly straightening the soft curls. "Oh sure," she muttered, "that bitch—she stands beside Curtis and sleeps with Vladimir Volodin. And to think Sinclair forced me to assist at this masquerade! Yes, *forced*—how blind everyone was! How could they be so blind!" Her breath caught in her throat. "That whore!"

Denise laid her plans. "What's that number? I hope I didn't misplace it." With the sweet excitement of anticipated revenge, she dialed Michigan.

The call was answered on the first ring. "Lodge-for-Governor Headquarters."

"Mr. Lodge, please. This is Mrs. MacAlpine, calling from Paris."

Curtis came to the phone. "Denise! Good to hear from you. What's up?"

"From what I'm told, you've got the election clinched. Congratulations!"

"Well, Denise, not quite. There's still a lot of ground to cover—"

"Sinclair says it's in the bag. Curtis, I should really be mad at you for not stopping in Paris on your way back from Brussels. . . ."

"Brussels? I haven't been to Brussels in ages."

"Oh, I thought— Well, never mind . . . I thought you'd gone to Brussels with Mariela. . . ."

He laughed. "Nope, neither of us has been to Brussels. I spoke to Mariela a couple of days or so ago. She was in London. What made you think we were in Brussels?"

Now came Denise's moment for acting. "Only that friends saw her in Brussels at Vladimir Volodin's performance of—Oh, well, if you say she wasn't there, then they must have been mistaken."

"Must be, Denise. Mariela's never been a fan of the ballet that I know of. That's your baby. . . ."

"Well, I've taken up enough of your time, Curtis. Just wanted to say how much we're rooting for you. Good luck with the election."

Curtis didn't answer right away.

From her cozy throne halfway around the world Denise could tell she had caught him totally off guard. A glint of victory flashed in her eyes.

354

At last he spoke. "Sure, Denise. . . . See you soon, I hope. Regards to Sinclair."

That night Denise MacAlpine found sleep at last.

⁕

VLADIMIR-MATTIE/*Palm Springs*/*Monday, December 31, 1962*

"Miss Maxwell?"

The sound of her name cut through Mattie's thoughts. She had just convinced herself that Vladimir's lips had been softer and more responsive than the scene had called for. She was certain, in retrospect, that he had been conveying something personal.

"Miss Maxwell?"

"What the hell is it now?" Mattie yelled at the young man standing at her trailer door. "Haven't we spent enough time under that fucking sun today? Where's my dresser? She's never around when I need her. I've got to unloosen this corset. It's killing me!"

They'd been filming in the desert outside of Palm Springs for the entire afternoon. Palm Desert, they called it. Bullshit! There weren't any palms. Only sun and sand and grubby sagebrush. Two days on location. Two miserable days out of the otherwise inoffensive three weeks she'd been on this film. They had an incredibly tight shooting schedule and were undergoing all the assorted agonies any large group experiences when far from home. The previous weeks had been bad enough, but at least the studio was air-conditioned. Even Hollywood hadn't figured out how to air-condition the desert.

They were doing *The Nightingale and the Eagle.* How could she be a nightingale in this heat? That was her part—the singer. The one obsessed with the eagle—a Russian dancer who falls in love with her. Almost enough to defect from his ballet troop. Almost, but not quite.

The New York singer and the Russian dancer. It barely called for acting, except the falling in love.

Vladimir danced. Danced and moved like an eagle. Like a majestic, powerful, driven creature. That's the way Mattie saw him. Leaping and soaring as he threw his hard muscular body into the air, performing as though he had wings hidden in those taut-sinewed arms and shoulders. She also saw his unmistakable ability to manage intimacy with a multitude, while remaining an aloof, isolated star.

How did he see her? They kissed for the cameras. They held each other for the cameras. The film faded out and implied that they made love. In reality, Vladimir remained coldly casual and faded away from her to his dressing room, or back beneath the umbrellas to wait for a retake or to argue with the director.

Between scenes Mattie disappeared into her own quarters or screamed at the grips to bring her more ice. Her trailer, which was moved to the working site each day, already was starting to take on the character of any cubicle Mattie occupied for more than fifteen minutes. Today's chicken salad sandwich, half-eaten at lunchtime, lay on the corner of her makeup stand, next to a celluloid kewpie doll, which was leaning against a purple stuffed duck with one yellow button eye hanging loosely by a thread. Resting on blue velvet in a sealed glass case was a most incongruous object, acquired by Mattie for an outrageous sum at auction at Christie's, in London, and which she never traveled without—Napoleon's mummified penis. A chaos of bottles and powder, lipstick and pancake pads covered the remaining surface of the table.

"They're going back to the hotel, Miss Maxwell. The limousine is waiting for you, if you're ready."

"Why the hell didn't you say so? Of course I'm ready. I've been ready to get out of this shithole since we got here." Ten minutes later Mattie, followed by her secretary, Virginia, her maid, Turid, and assorted flunkies, went out into the blazing sunlight. She negotiated the sand on her high heels and entered the spacious, air-conditioned limousine. She instructed Turid to draw a cool bath as soon as they got to the hotel. That and some weed would improve her mood!

That wasn't going to be the case, however. The lights and screens were already set up in the lobby when she arrived. The director was waiting for her.

"Dammit, Roger. One fucking thirty-second scene. It's the last day of the year. Can't we knock off?"

"Mattie, we're already running behind schedule, and we've just started. Vladimir's here. Change, and we can finish this up. It's simple. Come on, baby . . . we should get it in a couple of takes."

"We should get it in one take, if you know what you're doing," she snapped. Immediately she regretted her harsh words. "You know I was only kidding, Roger. You're the greatest!" She gave him an affectionate kiss and, with her dresser, headed toward the elevator.

Turid helped her switch costumes in her room. The makeup people made a couple of quick adjustments to compensate for the difference between the desert sunlight and the indoor kliegs. Mattie alternately fumed and sulked. It was supposed to be New Year's Eve. Why were they doing this shit on New Year's Eve?

"Turid, see if you can get Sylvia on the phone," she snapped.

Powder was applied to her makeup as she waited.

"There's no answer, Mattie," Turid said. "It's nine o'clock in New York now. She must be out."

"All right, then try Monty in L.A." Mattie took a couple of pills from a small box on her vanity table and washed them down with a glass of champagne.

Turid came back a few minutes later. "The butler at the house says Mr. Clift has a guest from New York, Libby Holman, and they're away until tomorrow night."

"Out. Everybody's out having a good time, damn them." Her pouting lips were sagging like wet wash on the line. She put a few joints and pills of several colors in her purse and went downstairs, followed by her entourage.

Back in the lobby, it took three takes. It also took an hour. The tension was high. The first two tries she was tight as a drum.

· Just before the third Vladimir whispered to her, "You feel like cactus."

"Wha . . . what?" she stammered. "Who feels like a Goddamned cactus?"

His eyes sparkled at her like lanterns. His lips curled in mocking laughter, illuminating his face and changing all the stern angles into curves.

"You come from desert. You feel like cactus. Stiff and sharp. Now we are in the oasis. You should be like a palm tree. Smooth and supple. Moving on the cool desert breeze blowing across clear water. Then we can finish this scene and I can try on costumes. Everyone can stop for your New Year. Move easy, beautiful. Like dance, like singing."

His powerful fingers rested on her arm, and the cactus lost its thorns. They did the last take and she did move like a palm tree. It was good. She knew it was good.

"Great!" Roger confirmed, kissing Mattie enthusiastically. "Great! Let's wrap it up for the holiday. Relax. Have a good New Year's. Enjoy yourselves. We've got to put it together again the day after tomorrow, so loosen up tonight. That last take was beautiful. Just beautiful!"

Mattie was still trying to understand how Vladimir's statement had affected her. A dancer, a fucking dancer, telling her how to act! *She* Mattie Maxwell, an Oscar-winning actress, and this foreigner told her how to relax! And it had worked! She stared across the set at him, and their eyes caught. The amusement was visible in his. Amusement, and something more. She could have read it as disdain, but she knew that wasn't right. Could it be interest?

The bustle around them changed character. Lights and cameras were disappearing. Grips hauled things away, hiding them wherever such things got hidden. Some of the people had vanished, going their own ways, but others appeared.

New Year's Eve was here, and the hotel was full of people looking desperately for something or someone to make the occasion memorable. For something to give significance to the artificial ritual that was about to be imposed upon the continuous passage of time. The ritual that would somehow magically turn 1962 into 1963.

Mattie Maxwell and Vladimir Volodin became part of the significance. The crowd moved in, pressing menus, napkins, envelopes—anything that could be written on—at them. Mattie found her thoughts chopped off again as she scribbled "To Betty," "To Uncle Harry," "To—," "To—," adding the famous signature.

Turid was trying to run interference for Mattie and handed her a piña colada. The drink sloshed between her fingers as Alan Persky, the producer, broke through the mob, inviting the remaining members of the cast and crew to a party in his suite. When he got to Mattie she was standing right next to Vladimir.

"Are you going to L.A., Mattie?"

"No. I've rented my house to Montgomery Clift, since we're going to be in New York for five or six weeks. I guess I'm stuck here."

"Then join the party," Alan Persky said effervescently. "We owe ourselves something after these last three weeks, and this town sure doesn't have much else to offer, unless you like signing autographs. Mattie, Vladimir, we need you there. You'll be our New Year stars."

"I have costume yet to worry about," Volodin replied. "I'll go later."

He looked into Mattie's eyes. If there had been amusement there before, it was gone. He just looked miserable.

Vladimir looked the way she felt. New Year's Eve again, and where was she? In the middle of nowhere, surrounded by strangers, and looking forward to more of the same tomorrow, and the next day, and more. Maybe a party would help. If she could only get back to her suite and get moving again. A couple more bennies and some champagne ought to help. Drinking and pills were merely the most accessible option. Scarcely even a choice.

Virginia was at her elbow. "This package just came for you," she said. "I thought you might want it."

Mattie received the parcel without being fully conscious that she had taken it. She spoke to Virginia. "I won't need you, darling. You and Turid find something else to do. Go to the party. And be sure to send a case of champagne to the crew—and one to the cast. I'll take care of myself." I've always taken care of myself, she thought miserably. Why should tonight be any different?

Vladimir spoke. Making it different. "Have dinner with me tonight. We will eat in my suite."

" 'Eat in my suite,' " she mimicked, letting out a short laugh on a breath. "You've become an English poet."

His face flared in a grin, and as quickly faded into disquiet. "The only English poet was Byron," he answered with an uncertain chuckle, shrugging. "Are you coming or not?"

He turned away and strode through the crowd of admiring eyes riveted on his awesome presence, leaving her standing there. His dresser responded to a Volodin gesture, draping a fur coat over the dancer's shoulders. Vladimir pulled the coat tight, as though the additional warmth would protect against some coldness deep inside.

Before Mattie knew what was happening, she was following him, pulled like steel after a magnet by the power generated in his wake. He moved commandingly toward an open elevator, making it his own.

She found herself in the elevator with Vladimir, and they rode up together. Mattie trailed in his force field as he swept into his suite.

"Let's get this costume fitting done," he yelled impatiently. "Where are the seamstresses?"

One appeared, holding a bolero over her arm. Without a thought Vladimir stripped the outfit he was wearing, revealing the hard, naked torso that was the instrument of his art. He slipped into the new costume and spun in front of the full-length mirror.

There was a long silence. Then: "What is this piece of shit?" He frowned.

"I beg your pardon . . . ?" the seamstress asked, dumbfounded.

"You heard me! Shit! What is this shit? Pizdah!"

"But Mister Volodin, it's the design you approved—"

"It is not! It isn't the same. I would never approve such shit! What are these?" he sneered, tearing at the beads on the bolero. "What are all these . . . these . . . shit beads? Beads are for circus horse!" His face was now a mask of anger. "These beads get in the way of dancing! Costume should be simple! So audience can see line, body, steps—not beads!"

They were both reduced to frozen stares. Mattie watched the contretemps in stunned fascination, as if she were watching a Ping-Pong match, her head swiveling back and forth between the protagonists. She'd thrown her own tantrums, but he was doing it with grace. With true style. Besides, he looked terrific, period.

"I am dancer, not circus horse. Not even in movie am I circus horse!" He removed the bolero and threw it to the floor.

"Get rid of shit beads!" he ordered, "and . . . and Happy New Year!" Vladimir slapped the youngest dresser on the backside with camaraderie and kissed the other two resoundingly.

One of the seamstresses picked up the garment and they left.

His anger vanished like cigarette smoke in a convertible.

"Where is my mail?" Volodin asked quietly. His dresser handed him a stack of letters and telegrams and left the room. The dancer whipped through them, glancing at the envelopes and discarding them on the floor until he came to one yellow Western Union missive. His face lit up and he tore open the envelope. Obvious disappointment replaced the smile as he scanned the words pasted on the page.

"HAPPY NEW YEAR. YOUR FANS IN PARIS MISS YOU. DALLAS ANXIOUSLY WAITING APRIL APPEARANCE. DENISE."

How strange that Denise would send him a wire. He had neither seen nor spoken to her since last summer.

He crumpled the sheet into a tight ball and threw it into the corner of the room.

"Bad news?" Mattie asked tentatively.

"Nothing. It is nothing." He wished to be in Paris too. He thought of Denise, her cool beauty and expensive soft skin. Just as quickly he dismissed the whole idea.

Mattie and Vladimir stared at each other, lost in separate loneliness.

"Why don't you open the package?" he asked quietly.

Mattie looked puzzled until she remembered the parcel still clutched in her hand. She looked down at it, and her face broke into a smile as she saw the return address. Vladimir's spirit seemed to bounce with hers.

"Gift from boyfriend?" he asked, laughing.

"*Your* boyfriend," she interjected. "*Your.*" Since the film had begun, Mattie had taken great delight in correcting Vladimir whenever he mispronounced a word or dropped a pronoun.

"All right, all right. Is it from *your* boyfriend?"

"Maybe," Mattie answered, half shyly, half swaggeringly. The Memphis address could belong only to Elvis Presley. Elvis had remembered her at the end of the year! With childish enthusiasm she ripped the brown mailing wrapping from the package, her chest rising in anticipation.

First a box appeared. She removed the lid and placed it beside her with graceful movements. Then she inserted her hand into the packing and deftly extracted an elongated shiny object which she held at arm's length. As she did, other objects followed rapidly, each matching the first in size and color and held together by a single string: eleven perfect link sausages.

"Ah!" Vladimir exclaimed. "A New Year's—what do you call it?—snack! A New Year's snack from a wealthy admirer."

"He *is* wealthy," Mattie replied. "Elvis has money to burn. He gives Rolls Royces and diamonds to all his girl friends. But sausages to me! I made the mistake of complimenting his mother's sausages at dinner one night at his home in Memphis. Since then, instead of Rollses and diamonds, he keeps me supplied with sausages. And I lied—I really don't like the damn things. I was just trying to be polite. I hate sausages! Just hate them!" She tried to laugh, but the tears in her eyes gave her disappointment away.

"Is it the same Elvis that—"

"Yes, the one and only, the king of rock 'n roll. I met him on the Sullivan Show in 1956."

"Yes, I know who is Elvis. I heard him in Leningrad on Radio Free Europe. I recall one song in particular, 'Keep Your Hands Off My Blue Suede Shoes.' To hell with sausages, Mattie. We will order a nice dinner. Something special, to celebrate." Vladimir was cheerful again.

"I can't eat like this. I still have all this makeup on, and I have to change out of my costume," said Mattie, looking helplessly at Vladimir. The man was powerful. His very presence was powerful. He had real, unconscious power. Not the studied presence of a . . . a Victor Mature, or a . . . an Alan Ladd, or even, she thought, of a Tony Rook.

"Costume does not matter," Vladimir replied, "and the makeup is easy."

He took her by the arms, one in each hand, and led her to a stool in front of the dressing table. He brushed a pair of tights from the seat onto the floor, sweeping them onto socks and ballet shoes that were already piled on top of each other. She perched tensely on the stool. Long, shapely limbs splayed out like a spider monkey.

Grabbing tissues and cold cream, his hands moved quickly. When they touched her, they were gentle. As gentle in their touch as he was strong in his presence. Nevertheless, when she looked at the image of his face in the mirror, she saw less than strength. She saw the same loneliness that was reflected in her own. She felt the isolation they found themselves in, stuck in this phony city in the middle of the desert, with people who were meaningless compared to the characters they were portraying for the cameras.

They had less meaning and less reality. Even her face wasn't her own. She saw it now, smeared with white goo, colors and form melting as the cream lifted and dissolved the unreality painted across its surface. The image wavered through a thin film of tears.

"You think of Elvis?" Vladimir asked.

"Of course not. He and I are good friends now."

"You no longer have your hands on his blue suede jacket?"

"They haven't been for a long time!" Her lower lip formed that familiar lopsided mischievous grin. "No. I was thinking of nobody. All the nobodies that aren't here. I want to call my father, but I don't even know where he's at." Mattie stared at herself through the moisture in her eyes. "My nose is too big," she said irrelevantly.

His fingers caressed the offending feature through the tissues as he wiped away the first layer of cream.

"It is a fine nose. A royal nose. It is needed to give contrast to those great dark eyes." His hands ministered to her eyes, wiping mascara from their edges, smoothing the eyelids as he lifted the cosmetics from their surface.

Somehow her eyelids felt cold. She felt the warm strength of his touch through them, letting it sink into her face, into her head. My nose *is* big, she thought.

"It's just right," Vladimir said aloud.

"Christ!" She almost jumped. "Are you a mind reader?"

"No," he laughed, "but my fingers read your face. You were twitching your nose. You must have been still thinking of it, the way your forehead furrowed at the same time."

As if to stop the thoughts, he smoothed her brow, wiping the cream over the skin in a slow massage. Her glistening eyes accentuated the translucent pallor.

The phone rang. Volodin leapt for it, as though it were going to run away if he gave it time for the second ring. He grabbed it, his entire body registering anticipation.

"Hello!" he cried. He stood there holding the black phone to his ear. The anticipation vanished in a descending veil of disappointment. "No. I don't care if it is a busy time. Keep trying." His cold cream-smeared hands had a hard time returning the unit to its cradle. It kept slipping from his fingers.

He came back and stroked Mattie's face again, pensively, almost absent-mindedly.

"I can't stand this fucking place," she said. "It's supposed to be a holiday season. We should have snow and slush in the streets. Not sun and sand."

Volodin was silent. He too was thinking of snow and the faraway place he loved and would probably never see again.

"Were you expecting a special call?" Mattie asked, flushed with childish jealousy.

"I've been trying to reach my mother in Leningrad and my brother in Kiev."

"I didn't know you had a brother."

"His name is Alexei Mikhailovich Volodin."

"Do they have phones in Kiev?"

Vladimir laughed. "Of course they have phones in Kiev. You think they communicate by smoke signals in Russia, like the American Indians did?"

Mattie's face reddened under his hands. "No, of course not. I just never thought about it before."

They didn't speak again for several moments. Vladimir lifted fresh tissues from the box on the table and carefully wiped away the last traces of Hollywood from Mattie's New York skin. He moved across the room and flipped on the radio, settling on a station that was blaring yesterday's music.

"I hope your brother calls," Mattie said softly. "And your mother."

"Do you have anyone to call?" Vladimir asked.

Mattie considered. She wished Sylvia had been home—or Monty! Or at least that they would have *called* her. She wished *anybody* would call her. Who the hell knew where she was? She wasn't even sure herself. It was just a goddamned stinking little town in a goddamned stinking, overgrown sandpit.

"I've never had anyone—not for long anyway," Mattie replied, half joking, half desperate, feeling the dark hole opening inside herself.

Vladimir's fingers stroked the underside of her chin, down her neck and across her shoulders, leaving trails of moist smoothness. They returned and repeated the motion, lingering longer at each point this time. Mattie leaned back, letting the tension fade from her neck and be absorbed into his hands. Her head tilted with abandon and rested against the hard muscles of his mid-section, behind the chair. She rolled her head in response to his touching, feeling those muscles through the cushion of her hair. Her imagination was making things happen between her legs. The cream felt cool and luxurious on her skin as her own hands came up and found his, following their movement and adding her own as she caressed the backs of his fingers. Her fingertips dipped into the spaces above his lower knuckles, exploring the vanishing tension there.

"I have no one either, not anymore. Nobody very close," Vladimir said in a voice as handsomely tuned as a fine violin.

His hands preceded him as he leaned forward, separating the fronts of her blouse, laying them aside and exposing her small, solid breasts. She opened her eyes and watched in the mirror, admiring the contrast of her dark nipples against the light skin of their smooth supporting mounds. Vladimir's palm moved over them as his body moved over a stage. Knowingly, expertly, exquisitely in tune and in rhythm with the music of her breathing. The slow manipulation of her nipples and breasts made her moan softly.

Mattie's fingers left his hands and undid the buttons below her breasts. She shrugged her shoulders and arms, to let the garment fall to her waist. One side fell. The other didn't. She shrugged again, but the sleeve was caught on her left elbow. Vladimir smiled at her in the reflecting glass as he slid the cloth over the obstacle. The image vanished as his inverted face came down across hers and his mouth entrapped her lower lip. He sucked it away from her teeth and teased it, nibbling the bottom edge. His lips left her mouth and worked their way into the hollow at the base of her throat, bending her head back against his naked shoulder. Her cheek tingled against the barely perceptible stubble of his late-evening whiskers. Her eyes closed and her breast heaved in response. The dark hole inside of her began to close up again, a little. She wanted to rise and press against him, press her long hard nipples against his bare chest, but she was trapped in the chair. The dancer controlled both their movements.

Volodin sensed the strain in her body. He stood, sweeping his hand over her arm, lifting her with him. Her auburn hair swirled behind as she was spun into his embrace. Her feet tangled and she clung to him for balance.

It was more than balance that she got. It was a body to hold and be held by. A superb body, rippling against her without seeming to move. Their mouths locked together this time, tongues exploring slippery nerve endings. Vladimir stroked down the straining arch of her back, wiping the remaining costume over her hips and letting it pile in a heap at their feet. The dress fell to the floor with the softness of the first snowfall of winter. His own trousers followed, and as they pressed together again, there was nothing left to intrude between them except the rigid pressure of his penis against her flanks.

The lonely world outside became a different universe, as remote from them as an undiscovered galaxy. They created their own universe. Its boundaries consisted first of the suite in which they clung to each other. Then it became the clean white sheets of Vladimir's bed, when he lifted Mattie effortlessly and placed her upon it. The bed moaned. Mattie looked for a cool place on the pillows, as if it would be the one spot where the bed would no longer moan. She found a pillow of hair. His hair. As sand absorbs water, her body was absorbing the light of his fingers. His tongue, his little flame, kissed her muscles, her flesh. A flower bloomed in each pore of her skin. Vladimir was taking her out of a world where she had never lived, hurling her into a world she was yet to live in. He was taking her down into the night. A night beyond the night of the room, beyond the night of the town, beyond any night she had ever known.

The dimensions of their private reality shrank further, limited to the confines of their touching and exploring. Crevices, folds, mounds. Skin on skin. Hair, and places hidden in hair. Moist, soft, warm places. A universe created for their entrance only. Created and occupied by no one else. Complete and sufficient unto itself.

There was much communication in that universe. Bittersweet communication, silently filtered through a language of tenderness and compassion, unencumbered by words, sung by touch and feel. Nerves and impulses, glands and hormones, need and fulfillment. Their own place, their own language, their own mysteries.

The cosmos was small. They made it that way, and let it grow through their own creation until tiny meteors began to appear. Meteors, and then comets. Small, whispering comets in erotic flashes. Larger, blazing comets, rising from the darkness and sweeping across their combined loneliness, tracing threads of each other and sweeping through their space. Blazing and concentrating when their pelvises finally joined in coupled rising rhythm, until the mass of their passion grew to the critical point and exploded in a nova of release.

Vladimir and Mattie, eagle and nightingale, lay together, letting the shrunken outside world slowly intrude again into their consciousness.

"I need a cigarete," Mattie said.

"A cigarette and dinner. I shall order." Vladimir, still slippery from cold cream, rose and found the phone, buried under Mattie's discarded costume.

He ordered with care, and they celebrated the coming of the new year with champagne and caviar. Mattie marveled at the idea that a hotel in the middle of a southern California desert should stock the tiny black fish eggs from a third of the way around the world. Vladimir accepted it as his right to have them on command.

Mattie also marveled at the body that lay naked next to hers. Alternately they giggled over the bubbling wine they tipped into each other's mouths and retreated into pensive, distant silence.

"Why do you run like this, Mattie?"

"Like—like what?" She turned toward him.

"Like—like me."

"It's a long story." She let out a sigh and brought her fingers to her face. She stared off, as if gazing into a distant mirror. "I knew I didn't want to be just another chick singer. I didn't want to go on playing Vegas for a bunch of drunkards and gamblers. I knew I couldn't go through life unnoticed. It would have been unbearable. I had to be the center of attraction—of the world. I had a unique talent and an unrelenting drive. And then—I guess I was tired of being poor. I wanted to buy everything I desired, whenever I felt the urge. It was a drive that was all-consuming. I wanted to be rich, famous and laid regularly. It's as simple as that. I wanted to become a legend. Fast. At any price."

"Did you pay the price?"

"Yes. I'm still paying—but it's normal. There are certain things you have to pass through in order to come out on the other side—alive." She sipped at her drink slowly and then put it down on the night table. "I woke up one morning and realized I was out of the romantic abyss, but had become madly, incurably in love with this ambitious, selfish dream I had been flirting with all my life. Success." She gave a small sigh. "And you, Vladimir? Why do you dance?"

"Somehow life tastes better when I dance."

"But why do you dance so much?"

"Pasternak, the great Russian writer, said: 'Sleep not, sleep not the artist. Do not give in to slumber. You are a hostage of the ages. You are a captive of time.' I too am a captive of my time, a captive of my life. By choice. But how can I explain, I'm still restless and unsatisfied. You may have discovered, Mattie, that we may not know where we are, but we generally know where we've been."

"What about love?" she interrupted.

"Dancing is my only true love. I gave up everything for it. I only hope it wasn't in vain. Not for me as much as for the people I've hurt pursuing it."

"How can you speak that way? How could it be in vain?"

"One never knows. I could break a leg tomorrow. Or die—making too much love to you." Playfully, with chillingly sensual, ravenous laughter, he brought her on top of him. They lay forehead to forehead.

They made love again. It was slower and more tender than the first time. The holes in their spirits took longer to fill, and they worked at it carefully. She wanted desire to flow incessantly. His words were insignificant, senseless—harsh words, foreign words, metallic, gentle, explosive, words squeezed together, words of now and tomorrow, words of forever and never, words rooted in the town of his birth. Words.

Once again all was quiet.

"I could love you, but I won't," Mattie said.

"Good," replied Vladimir. "It's better that way. Fewer problems."

Silence again.

"How do you say 'fuck' in Russian?" she asked.

"I never say it."

"Why?"

"I don't know," replied Vladimir. "Ever since I left . . . my country I am even unable to make love to a girl who speaks Russian. I can do it in English, French, German, English—but not Russian."

"A multilingual cock!" teased Mattie. "Why is it you can't say the word in Russian? God knows, you make enough use of it in English."

"It isn't the same. I have a mental block about it. Maybe nostalgia . . . respect . . . the motherland—I don't know. Besides, I can't imagine Vronsky saying to Anna Karenina, 'Come here and *fuck* me.' "

"Well, they surely did it," giggled Mattie. "What's the difference with English?"

"When I say it in English it's a release—a release from anger, frustration, many things. I don't even understand, and I don't really mean the word in its true sense. I could say 'table,' or 'sky'—it would really be the same."

"Anyway," announced Mattie, "one of my New Year's resolutions is to clean up my act."

"What does it mean, *clean up your act?*"

"I want to stop using all those fucking goddamn vulgar words. Whoops! Here I go again! I should have said those *table* vulgar words. Or those *sky* vulgar words."

They both laughed too loud and too long, hanging onto the delicious sounds, not wanting to lose this precious escape from melancholy.

"It's not nice for a girl to use such language. And all those pills I see you taking all the time—why do you do it?"

"Oh, Vladimir. It's so hard to explain. . . . I have a feeling that people *want* me to be like my mother—that they expect me to fail. You know how people watch car races with the unconscious wish that perhaps someone will get injured? Maybe I just don't want to let them down."

"Listen, Mattie. If you know that much about yourself, then it should be easy for you to cut all that bullshit out of your life. You have good head on your shoulders. Use it!"

"Oh, I know where I'm going."

"Then do it without crutches. You don't need pills. You don't need to smoke strange cigarettes. You don't need to use bad words to give you sense of security. Your talent is the biggest security you could possibly have."

"The language won't be so hard. But the rest . . . It's been ten years—but I will try." Her head nestled on his naked shoulder. "Oh, Vladimir. You're so wonderful. I promise I will try!'

"What would you like more than anything else in the world right now?" he asked.

"To see snow," she answered without hesitation.

"So do I. And we shall. Tomorrow morning."

"Are you going to order it from room service, like the caviar?"

"No, but we shall have it. Wait and see," he said, setting the alarm clock. "I have a surprise for you."

They fell asleep in each other's arms. The sudden ring of the telephone woke them abruptly.

"Morning already?" yawned Mattie, stretching lazily. "It still feels like night to me." She was right. The illuminated hands of the desk clock indicated 3:30.

"It must be Leningrad!" cried Vladimir, kicking away the covers while fumbling for the switch on the bedside lamp. A yellow glow outlined his sinuous shoulders and torso as he lifted the phone to his ear. "Hello, hello"— his voice quivered—"hello, I can hardly hear you. . . . Oh . . . no, no, Mariela. I am so glad to hear from you! It's just . . ." Vladimir sat upright on the edge of the bed, his back to Mattie. "It's just . . . that I was expecting a call from Leningrad, from my mother. . . . And a very Happy New Year to you too, dushka. I was wondering why you didn't call. . . . Naturally, I understand. What matters is that you *did* call. How was the party? . . . Oh, she's a very good actress, but we hardly speak," Vladimir said, and laughed uproariously.

Feeling like an intruder in a conversation not meant for her to hear, Mattie edged lower into the bed, pulling the sheets over her head, trying to make herself invisible. Her spiral of imagined rejection began.

". . . Oh yes, dushka, it has been a long time, but I will see you soon. If all goes well, the picture should be finished shooting in about six weeks. . . . Oh, that would be wonderful. . . . Yes, dushka, that's good. . . . No, of course not . . . Yes, that's good, that's very good. . . . Yes . . . no . . . of course . . . Of course I'm alone. What makes you think I'm not?" Vladimir turned slowly toward Mattie, slightly embarrassed about his lie. "When will I hear from you again? . . . That's wonderful. I hope all is well with you, Mariela. . . . I miss you . . . and a big kiss!"

He hung up quietly and looked at Mattie. Timidly she peeked from beneath the sheet, raising her chin toward him, to the place where their eyes could meet. Vladimir eased himself languidly back into the bed. Mattie inched closer to him, nuzzling her head on his shoulder, trying soundlessly, wordlessly, to squeeze away her insecurities through the mere feel of his body.

"It was just a friend, Mattie—a good friend."

"I didn't ask anything," she said sadly. And soon they were asleep again.

When the alarm sounded the dancer was as good as his word. At the crack of dawn he commandeered a sleepy and probably hung-over cab driver and ordered him to the base of San Jacinto Peak, ten miles from El Mirador Hotel and towering two miles above the desert floor.

"Your calls didn't come," Mattie said. "Didn't you want to wait for them?"

Vladimir's eyes hardened. "No, I wasn't really expecting anything," he replied, forcing his voice into a sardonic lower register. "I'll try again some other time. Besides, Russian New Year falls on the thirteenth of January."

Mattie detected the insincerity in the statement, but she let it pass. Instead she snuggled close to Volodin, trying to hold onto the feeling they had momentarily brought into each other's lives.

They rode the first cable car of the day, watching the rays of the sun pick their way through the jagged edges of the mountain during the twenty-minute ride to the top. The temperature dropped steadily. They were level with the first snow at the second cable-car station.

It was not only a journey to a different climate. They were also trying to turn it into a journey back to a different time. A different time for each of them. A time when there was something to enjoy that wasn't manufactured by producers, agents and publicity men.

For a few hours on top of the mountain they succeeded. They scrambled through the white crystals and talked of times past. They laughed and stared pensively from rock ledges at twenty miles of desert view spread all around below them. The silly little town they'd just left looked like a toy beneath them. Mattie found El Mirador, and it appeared like a dollhouse, as if it were seen through the wrong end of a telescope.

They continued walking, Vladimir cupping her elbow in his ungloved hand, their breath frosting the air. His grip tightened into a cuddly bear hug, but she broke free and sent him a few paces ahead, with strict orders not to turn around.

"Woman of mystery!" he teased, strolling off in compliance.

A few minutes later she called after him, "You can look now. This is *my* surprise!" He whirled around.

His name stretched four feet wide across the snow: "V-L-A-D-I-M-I-R V-O-L-O-D-I-N."

Brown stains interrupted some of the lines where dead pine needles were exposed by the twig Mattie had used to write his name in the soft white surface. It was a surface newly laid down the night before. A new surface for a new year, as yet untrampled by tourists' feet.

Mattie threw herself into the fresh powder, dragging Vladimir with her as her mind swept over the previous hours, savoring their perfume and attempting to embed them in her memory, to be stored there as a precious piece of jewelry. Jewelry that she could take out on special occasions and wear around the edges of her consciousness. She kissed him warmly, biting into summer on a wintry morning, perceiving the ecstasy, the boundless thrill of understanding hands pressing softly.

By turns charming and moody, ingenuous and deceitful, Vladimir was a mesmerizing enigma. A mesmerizing enigma that was slowly taking hold of Mattie.

Behind her, the large letters of his name were slowly disappearing, brushed by a sudden gust of wind.

—※—

MATTIE/*New York City*/*Tuesday, October 8, 1963*

On Sunday, June 2, 1963, Mattie Maxwell had sold out all 55,000 seats at Shea Stadium. People had been lining up for tickets to the concert weeks in advance.

Therefore it was easy to sell out the Winter Garden nightly for the entire run of her limited six-month engagement of *Jazz Age Clara*.

Mattie Maxwell's opening-night performance had been received as one of the greatest moments in the history of New York theater. Her dynamism, dramatic flair and incomparable voice breathed life into the frenzied years of the roaring twenties and its most sparkling symbol, the incandescent redhead—the "It" girl, Clara Bow.

How brilliantly Mattie portrayed Clara's rise to the top. How poignantly she recreated her slide over the edge in a series of nervous breakdowns.

The musical extravaganza that brought Mattie Maxwell to the Broadway stage was a tribute to the combined forces of imagination, flair, talent, and taste.

A perfect vehicle for the superstar.

Tuesday, October 8, 1963. *Jazz Age Clara* was in its fourth smash month. Mattie was exhausted but ecstatic. She mopped her brow with a large man's handkerchief, barely managing to catch her breath when the curtain went up for the fifth time in response to the continuing applause.

The packed auditorium rose to its feet as one body. Whistles. Cheers. A deafening ovation. Mattie was *their* "It" girl.

The huge cloth wall descended again, separating her from the accolades.

"Miss Maxwell! Miss Maxwell!" A stagehand appeared at her elbow. Mattie turned, expecting a bouquet, but instead she saw anxiety.

"Miss Maxwell. Your secretary's on the phone." His voice was urgent. "She says it's very important."

For a second Mattie was furious. "What can be so fucking important that Virginia should interrupt my curtain calls?"

"I don't know, Miss Maxwell. She insisted I get you at once."

Mattie found her way to the phone, wavering between pleasure at the audience's response and annoyance at having the response disturbed.

"Mattie?" Virginia queried.

"Of course."

"You'd better get home immediately—and don't say a word to anyone."

"Why?"

"The cops are here."

"The cops! What the hell are they doing?"

"Tearing the place apart!"

"Why?" the actress demanded.

"Let's not talk over the phone," replied Virginia. "You never know who's listening."

"Listening to *what?*" Mattie exploded. "I still don't know what you're talking about!"

"Mattie, trust me. Just get over here. Fast. Oh, and if you have anything in your purse—you know—pills or—get rid of them."

"What the hell are you . . . ? Oh, never mind. I'll be there!" She slammed the phone down and headed for her dressing room. She didn't take time to remove her makeup or costume. Thoughts began to piece themselves together: What was Virginia saying about pills . . . or . . . ? 'Get rid of them!' Mattie didn't have any. Suddenly she felt cold and grabbed a cape that was hanging in the corner. Shivering, she gathered the cape around her shoulders. What were the cops doing? Her next thought was of Vladimir. They were supposed to meet at her apartment after some ballet company he had gone to see—she didn't know which one or where—had no idea how to reach him—or what she would find when she got home, but knew that if there was going to be scandal, at all costs Vladimir had to be protected!

The scene was chaos. Everything was on the floor. All the drawers were empty. The paintings by Chagall, Dufy and Delacroix that usually hung on her suede walls were scattered everywhere. Even the plates on the electric switches had been unscrewed.

Virginia was there. So was Sylvia. Mark Ellis and Terry Gold, representatives from Mattie's public relations firm, were milling around and muttering with her attorney, Richard Weiss.

"Mattie, thank God you're here!" said Virginia. "You should have seen what this place looked like fifteen minutes ago—swarming with cops!"

There were no uniforms left. Only a plainclothes lieutenant.

"What the hell have you done to this place?" Mattie screamed.

"We have a warrant," the lieutenant said, holding out a piece of paper.

"Warrant? Fuck your warrant! What's the idea of destroying my home?"

"We . . . received information that you have drugs on the premises," he replied.

"What kind of information? Are you crazy? Who's going to clean up this mess?"

"I'm sorry." The lieutenant looked almost but not quite apologetic.

"Well, what did you find?" Mattie challenged hysterically. "Did you find anything?"

"No, Miss Maxwell. I'm glad for your sake that the place seems to be clean. Try to understand. We have a job to do. . . . This Lenny Bruce thing puts us under enormous pressure. We have orders to—"

"Who the hell and where the hell do you think you are? The secret police? Russia? I thought this was America! Who's the creep who fed you this . . . *information?* What sick nut would do such a thing to me?"

"I can't say who contacted us."

"Well, are you satisfied now? Have you ripped up everything you wanted to examine? Now do you believe there's nothing here?"

"I told you, Miss Maxwell, you're clean."

"Thanks a bunch. Now, if you're through with me, get the hell out of here! GET OUT OF MY HOME!"

He did. Just as Volodin arrived.

"What's happened? Are you moving?" Vladimir asked, nonplussed.

Mattie ran to him, sobbing.

Virginia and Sylvia filled him in on the details.

"Did they find anything?" he asked.

"I'm still here, aren't I! No, they didn't—but God, I wish I *had* something in the house!" Mattie was shaking uncontrollably.

"If you did, you'd be in jail now," Sylvia said. "You're lucky."

"Lucky, my ass! Look at this mess!" Mattie was on the verge of panic. "What am I going to do? What about all the bad publicity this is going to bring me? It will kill *Jazz Age Clara! And* probably my career!"

"Mattie?" It was her lawyer, Richard Weiss. "Mattie, I know this is a difficult time for you, but I can set your mind at rest about one thing. This *will not* make the papers. We've already taken care of it. Your reputation is perfectly safe. You are absolutely innocent—the unfortunate victim of some crackpot!"

Vladimir held her.

"Mattie, my little Mattie," he soothed.

He drew her face into the warm hiding place of his neck. "Sylvia's right. You were lucky that nothing was found."

They clung together. The Russian's hand softly stroked her auburn hair. He purred quietly in his throat, as though talking to a kitten. The shaking gradually subsided as they fell into a mutual silence. Behind Mattie's back, Vladimir gestured to the others to leave.

When at last the room emptied out, he broke the stillness. "Mattie, we must talk. . . ."

"Who the hell started this?" she whispered in a daze, ignoring him. "Who called the fucking cops?"

"Who called the cops is not important." He led her to a couch, put the slashed cushions back in position. "What *is* important is what you're doing to your life." His voice was heavy with concern. "You are still using all that crap! Now I know it. You are going to destroy your life if you don't STOP! Last year in Palm Springs you promised—"

"I *wanted* to stop but I *can't*," she said. "I need it. I really need it. . . .

I tried." Her voice was crackling with the high voltage of reality. "I couldn't bring myself to tell you I failed. . . . How can you understand, Vladimir? I may be the biggest star, but let's face it, I'm all alone!"

"Don't you think I too am all alone? But with all the misery I've gone through, I'm cleansed of human limitations, and I feel stronger for it! You don't see me using any crutches, do you?"

"You obviously don't need them. For me it's a different story. Getting to the top hasn't been easy. I didn't climb my way up, I *clawed* my way up." She was flushed and breathing shallowly. "It's an agony that's tough to forget."

"I know a little about agony myself, Mattie. Do you really believe that life was handed to me on a silver platter? Do you?"

She didn't answer, stood up, and went behind the bar. "In my kind of life it's so *easy* to lose your perspective on reality," she continued. "It's kept at arm's length from you by press agents, studio heads, hangers-on. Finally you believe your own publicity, slowly become that fantasy figure they have created for you. I know it. I know it all too well. I live it. I revel in it." She came back, handed him a drink, and sat down. "There is an anger that bursts inside you when you're on top, trying to get back at all the inhumanity you had to swallow to get there. I've always been afraid that suddenly . . . all of this will be taken away from me." She trembled and shook her head. "It's so . . . intoxicating . . . getting accustomed to the sweet smell of success."

"Don't you think I, too, have the realization that all gods can tumble?"

"Yeah . . . ?" Her voice trailed sadly.

"Coping with your insecurities with pills, booze, and whatnot—that's sweeping your problems under the rug. They still remain, Mattie." Vladimir turned her face toward his. "Do you need to take a pill to get an orgasm?"

She giggled. "No—that's one kick I get without them."

"Then why take pills to feel up or down or secure, just for a few hours? Can't you find the inner resources?"

Mattie flew up from the sofa, looking like a penniless waif. "Obviously I don't have . . . those inner resources."

"Mattie, you can if you want to." He pulled her back beside him. "I'm going to make a demand. Give up your crutches . . . give up your habits—your drugs—once and for all."

"Why?"

"For me—because I care."

"Damn it, Vladimir, I've tried. I want to do it—for you . . . for me . . . but I can't! I can't do it by myself!"

"If you need help, get it! There are hospitals for this, aren't there?"

"Yes, there's—What would I tell the press?"

"Just take off. Tell everyone you've earned a long vacation—say you're going on a world cruise."

"Vladimir . . . does it really matter . . . to you?"

"It matters *very* much!"

"Vladimir, what would my life be without you!" She hugged him fiercely and burst into tears. "This time—this time I promise. I *swear* I'll do it . . . for you!"

Meanwhile, as he climbed the steps to the station house, the drug squad lieutenant was still speculating as to who the very generous informant had been.

Denise hadn't used a return address.

❈

VLADIMIR-DENISE/*Riviera*/*Tuesday, July 7, 1964*

Knowing how bored and restless he got when not dancing, Vladimir had planned to remain only two days at the Château d'Antibes.

But this was his *fourth* day at the château and he was neither bored nor restless.

After the incident of the Fabergé egg, when he had taken Denise so brutally, she had made no direct effort to get in touch with him. Just as well. Vladimir had had no intention of ever seeing *her* again.

When the London Ballet Company was contracted to appear in Dallas in April of 1963 under the auspices of the MacAlpine Foundation, Vladimir was certain Denise would hound him, making his life impossible, taking her revenge.

She got her revenge. But she got it simply by ignoring him. From time to time she threw him a small ration of charm. The same dose she rationed to everyone. How he hated her then, with her cool, withering glances.

After his third performance, much to his surprise, Denise left town without saying goodbye.

The next February, following the premiere of *Don Quixote* at La Scala in Milan, Vladimir received a leaf-thin gold case filled with his favorite brand of Russian cigarettes, Avrora. Inside, an inscription: *September 12, 1962–? Denise*. With it a perfumed note: "Will you meet me for supper at Nepentha?" Not a question. A command. Intrigued, Vladimir canceled his plans for the evening and joined her. They had been lovers ever since.

And now, under a cloudless Mediterranean sky, Vladimir stretched like a languid tiger in the midday sun.

Denise was sleeping soundly beside him on the oversized Hermès beach towel, with one arm arching over her head. Naked. He raised himself on one elbow, looking into her face, marveling at the perfect symmetry of every feature, and savoring the smoothness of her body, its skin unmarred by fat or wrinkles. She seemed to be in suspended animation. He listened to the sounds of her breathing.

Her stillness maddened him. His hand went to her breast, caressing it, waiting for her to stir. Then he stroked her belly. Her eyes opened. She removed her sunglasses. Vladimir smiled. Her blond hair glistened. He buried his face in it, nuzzling through it until his lips found the soft spot on the nape of her neck. He blew softly to clear the last strands from his mouth, and his tongue caressed the pale skin.

"Oh, darling, I must have fallen asleep," she said apologetically. "How long has it been?"

"Too long. And I will punish you." Effortlessly Vladimir took Denise in his arms and ran across her small stretch of private beach toward the ocean.

Laughing, she struggled to free herself from his tight grip. "Oh, darling, don't! Don't, I beg you! I don't want to get my hair wet!"

"Everything will be wet! Everything!" He splashed with her into the cool sea. Vladimir played the shark to Denise's porpoise, attacking her playfully as she pushed him away. In such encounters it is usually the porpoise that wins. Their contest was a draw. In fact, it was better than a draw. Both of them were winning. Vladimir kissed her salty mouth until she could no longer breathe. Released her. They pushed each other under the water, then surfaced, letting the waves lap at their skin. The sea was placid and inviting.

Denise rolled gracefully on her back and floated. A verse from James Whitcomb Riley which her father used to recite, came to mind:

> "Oh! the ole swimmin'-hole! When I last saw the place,
> The scene was all changed, like the change in my face;
> The bridge of the railroad now crosses the spot
> Whare the ole divin'-log lays sunk and fergot."

Vladimir began to swim away. His powerful arms and shoulders cut through the water. He looked right at the sun, its glare hypnotizing him. After thirty yards his speed increased as he headed away from land. The land and the beach began to drift away from his consciousness. He heard Denise's cries of "Vladimir, Vladimir," but kept on going. Her voice grew smaller, diminished, and died away somewhere on the shore. He passed the coral reefs to his right. All thoughts of Denise disappeared from his mind. All thoughts disappeared. A detached, unencumbered sensation of absolute freedom invaded his body. It was ecstasy. Nothing existed—only himself, the shooting rays of the sun and the water.

The water grew cooler. Vladimir recalled the last vacation he had taken with the Kirov School, to Ushkovo on the Baltic Sea, when he was fifteen. Even then he had felt compelled to swim longer than anyone else. Those days were gone. Those long sun-filled days of being so young and filled with so many dreams were gone. Dreams are no longer dreams once they have been fulfilled. There was nothing to dream about anymore. He recalled boating through the lagoons at Ushkovo, followed by the picnics of kasha, tea and fruit compote. These thoughts filled Vladimir with a strange peacefulness as he swam farther and farther with strong, even strokes. He wanted to swim on forever. To escape. To be alone, never again to return to land.

Suddenly he snapped out of his trance and the pace slowed. Vladimir looked behind him. The distant beach seemed like a slash of uneven white paint, Denise a tiny stick figure waving its arms. He began to head back toward land, toward life, toward reality.

Twenty-five minutes later he reached Denise.

"What got into you?" she asked. "Didn't you hear me calling? I thought you were going to swim forever."

"I almost did."

"It's dangerous to go out that far!" she continued. "You could get run over by a speedboat!"

"Who cares?" he said, laughing, holding her little waist. "We all come from the sea. I can't think of a more glorious place to die than the sea."

"Aren't you tired?"

"A little. Let's go lie down."

Denise trotted out of the water. Vladimir followed and dried her gently with a fresh towel, then readjusted the large umbrella. Joyously they dropped to the soft sand.

They remained silent, almost not breathing, lying shoulder to shoulder. Her eyes took in the expanse of blue. It was impossible to distinguish between the sky and the color of the sea below. She blinked, closing out the view, allowing her thoughts to fill her mind.

Denise had never in her life been in love. And never thought she could be. But now she was. Now she knew real passion. And when real passion reigns, it is the salt of life. She couldn't do without salt. She knew that too.

Vladimir's voice broke her reverie. "Come back from wherever you are," he said, touching her high cheekbones. "You're very beautiful today, . dushka."

"I'm beautiful every day," she teased.

"Every day you're with me!" He paused. "What were you thinking?"

"I was thinking how long you made me wait for you," she confessed. "I've never waited so long for anything in my life!"

"Was it worth it?"

"Yes!" Her blue eyes gleamed their happiness.

She turned sideways, reached into her white canvas beach bag and pulled out a large Japanese parchment fan to shade her eyes from the sun. Her almost expressionless face, outlined against the fan, managed to convey a mixture of pathos, pride and childishness. She became silent again.

"*Now* what are you thinking about?"

"I was thinking about the day after tomorrow and how much I'm going to miss you."

"Then why don't you come with me to Berlin?" He lit a cigarette, letting the smoke curl slowly from his nostrils. "I'm dancing—"

"I can't!"

His eyebrows shot up in a question.

"I can't. I must go to Dallas and be with Sinclair."

"Why? I thought you could spend your time as you wish."

"Seven months of the year I spend as I wish. Five months I spend with him. Our marriage contract specifies—"

"A marriage contract!" Vladimir exploded, holding his head. "I've never heard of marriage contract! Can't you Westerners do anything unless it's on piece of paper?" he said sarcastically, springing to his feet. "Does it also spell out how often you make love and in what positions?"

Denise ignored his reaction and continued. "When a very rich man marries a beautiful woman thirty years his junior, it is understood that certain limitations and compromises must be accepted. Anyway, our interests are quite divergent. Sinclair is ninety-five percent business and I am—"

"Ninety-five percent pleasure?"

"I wouldn't say that." She cast him a look of reproach. "I have six homes to look after. The MacAlpine Foundation takes up a lot of my time. Anyway, for those five months, which do not even run consecutively, I receive an enormous allowance that permits me to indulge as I wish the other—"

"Am I an indulgence?"

"No, you are a personal desire whom *I* like to indulge. Now, my gorgeous Cossack. I must speak with you. Seriously."

He shifted and gracefully folded his body into a lotus position.

Denise turned over on her stomach, resting her chin on one hand. She looked straight ahead and spoke in an even voice. "Lincoln Center, in New York, will be finished in 1966. It will be the greatest complex of buildings for the arts in America. They're going to have the best of theater, the grandest of operas and the finest ballet company. Its gala opening is scheduled for September or October 1966." Denise leaned her head on his lap and continued, "How would you like to mount your own production of *Sleeping Beauty* for this event?"

"You mean the choreography?"

"Everything. The choreography, the supervision of casting, your choice of set designer, costumes—*your* production."

"Denise, of course I—what dancer could refuse such an offer? I have already restaged *Sleeping Beauty* for the Berlin Company."

"Yes, I know. That's why I suggested *Sleeping Beauty*."

"But, Denise, this would run into hundreds of thousands of dollars!"

"Well," she said very quietly, "I'm chairman of the board of trustees of

Lincoln Center, and my foundation—the Sinclair McAlpine Foundation—will finance many of its operatic and dance productions. Are you interested?" Her face was triumphant.

"It would be very good."

"Is that all you have to say—'*It would be very good*'?"

"Yes. It would be very good for Lincoln Center to have best dancer in the world appearing with their new ballet company."

"Well . . . I thought you would be ecstatic." Her smile had gone.

"I stopped being ecstatic years ago. Everything that must happen will happen." He began making patterns in the sand with his fingers. "There are many things I want to change in *Sleeping Beauty*. For example, how prologue should—"

"Consider it done." Slowly she sat up and put her arms around his neck. "In 1966 the Lincoln Center Ballet Company will open its season with *Sleeping Beauty*, choreography and production by Vladimir Volodin!" Denise ran her hands over the hard, muscled chest. "You make me so happy," she said.

"You too, my beautiful Denise. You make me happy. I never imagined you were such marvelous woman."

"You know so many marvelous women, Vladimir." Her fingers played with the gold chain he wore loosely knotted around his neck. "How marvelous am I?"

Vladimir was pensive for a moment before he answered. When he did answer, it was honest. As honest as he could be. "*Now*, you are the most marvelous."

"More than Mariela?" She was sorry she had said it, but Denise burned with jealousy as the brunette's image glowed in her mind.

"Who told you about Mariela? What do you know about Mariela?" Vladimir held her away from him. "What are you doing, spying on me?"

"No, but I recognize this," she said, fingering the chain again.

"How?"

"How many chains have an Egyptian scarab for a pendant?"

"So what?" said Vladimir, his expression hardening. "Why didn't you mention chain before? You've seen it for months."

"I was determined *never* to mention it. But you've worn it now four days in a row—"

"I wear it only when I'm not dancing, which happens to be very seldom."

"Could I ask you, what's the significance of this scarab?" She spoke in a rush.

"I've been told," he replied, "that it was found in a sarcophagus whose mummy was called Tarutu."

"Tarutu? Who was Tarutu?" she asked, feigning surprise.

"Tarutu," said Vladimir with a slightly mocking smile, "was a young girl who died because she couldn't be fulfilled. Her lover was—how you say?"

"Faithless?" Denise injected.

"Yes, faithless, and left a curse . . ."

"Which is?" she asked with an open challenge in her voice.

"Which is, Miss Nosy, that if for any reason her sarcophagus should break, evil and destruction will befall its owner."

"And what do the hieroglyphics on the back mean?" asked Denise, turning the scarab between her long fingers.

"They mean," replied Vladimir with a burst of laughter, "they mean that you are too curious." He threw her a quick, furtive look and shrugged at her questioning gaze. Silently he took her hands and brushed his lips on their soft skin. "Enough of Tarutu," he said. "Enough."

"I apologize for bringing it up. I couldn't control myself. What about Mariela?" she plowed on.

"We are good friends," Vladimir said, annoyed. "Just good friends—and I don't wish to speak about her. I never ask you about men in your life."

"Vladimir, if you wanted me to, I would leave Sinclair to become yours completely." She meant it.

Vladimir stared out over the sea. It was not an offer he had expected, but neither did it surprise him. "You are already mine," he finally said. "At least when we are together. Isn't that enough?"

"We have to keep it so secret. I would like to shout my happiness to the world!" Denise softened. "I am sorry, Vladimir. I'm afraid I'm very jealous." A somber feeling swept over her. She was determined to find out *everything* about the past of Mrs. Curtis Lodge III, alias Lady Mariela Chelmsford, and make sure Vladimir's desire would never stray.

"Jealous over me! Me, your gorgeous Cossack!" He lay back, pulling Denise over him. "The sun must bring out insanity."

"I'm insane about you," she said, laughing.

He stroked her soft, warm shoulders delicately. His fingers performed a slow, light dance across her skin as he looked deep into her blue eyes. He saw a softness there. A softness that seemed totally out of character with anything he had ever really noticed in Denise. It was a softness that *no one* had ever seen in Denise. A softness that had never been seen because it had never been there before.

"I love you," Denise said. She had said it before, many times. But this was the first man to whom she had spoken the words honestly. "I love you. I love you very much."

"You love me?" He sighed heavily. "Tell me about it. I want my own ballet with you right now."

He proceeded to devour her lips, her mouth, her breath. He rubbed his hands lovingly down her body. She pressed her legs together, trying to curb the hunger, the need, trying to prolong the sweet, painful waiting, yearning, stretching every second to a minute, every minute still longer. Yearning turned to ecstasy. Then she succumbed. And let go.

He knew well how her body felt against his. They both knew the feeling.

It was always good with them. This time it was *very good*. There on the beach, under the hot noon sun.

When their lovemaking was over, Vladimir was no longer serious. "I'm starved! Starved, starved!" he shouted playfully. "Are we going to have lunch, Denise? Call from the bathhouse. Get us something to eat! Food!"

"I don't think the servants would feel comfortable serving us in the nude," she giggled.

"They don't have to. They may wear whatever they want!"

"Vladimir! You're mad!"

He spun his naked body across the sand, then jumped in the air, twisted, and with a great leap was on her again. "Of course I'm mad! All Russians are mad! Didn't you know that! M-a-a-a-d!"

It was quite late in the afternoon before Denise called for lunch.

❊

MARIELA/*London/Thursday, October 15, 1964*

It was late at night when the First Lady of Michigan entered her Belgrave Square home. Tarutu's face, painted on the Egyptian sarcophagus, gazed inscrutably at Mariela from its post in the hallway. As she passed, its curse seemed to breathe a chill over her.

"Nonsense," Mariela whispered to herself. "Egyptian curses don't apply in 1964."

The evening had been very pleasant. The dinner celebrating the engagement of her son, Oliver, and Genevieve, was a resounding success. Warm and close. And they had laughed a lot in the posh surroundings of the Savoy Hotel ballroom. Mariela glowed with satisfaction when she thought about the upcoming marriage. Oliver would be assured of a future in Curtis' automotive empire; he would lead the good life. Also, he and Genevieve were very much in love.

Mariela had even managed to get past her nervousness over the presence of her houseguest, Denise MacAlpine. Fortunately that problem seemed to have solved itself immediately. Denise had to catch an eight o'clock plane in the morning and left the group early. Mariela bade her good night and goodbye with a suppressed sigh of relief. She also said goodbye to Curtis, who had to leave for Germany right after dinner.

Denise always had an unsettling effect on Mariela, and always would have. Somehow it struck Mariela from the first day they met, in 1956, on Sinclair's yacht that it was dangerous to be contented around Denise, in the same way it was dangerous to stand under the only tree in a field during a lightning storm. The impression never left her.

The house was quiet. All the servants were asleep. Mariela felt tired and went upstairs. The view from her bedroom windows was absolutely blank. The fog clung to the air like cotton candy. Big Ben tolled the time. Three o'clock in the morning.

The view in her mirror was better. Mariela was still a beautiful woman, and the mirror didn't have to lie to show her that. A little redness in the eyes, perhaps, but it had been a long evening. Sleep would take care of that. She could sleep late into the morning. There was nothing on her schedule.

She remembered that Vladimir, in Vienna, would still be awake, and on an impulse wanted to tell him all about the festivities, she put a call through to the Hotel Sacher.

As always, he was delighted to hear her voice. "You sound exhausted," Vladimir said.

"Exhausted, but in seventh heaven. I couldn't be happier for the children. By the way, guess who invited herself to spend the night?"

"A friend?"

"Funny you should put it that way—it's Denise MacAlpine. Came all the way from Texas! She asked a million questions about you and the scarab chain—oh, and she took an instant liking to Tarutu."

"Tarutu? Your mummy with the curse that—"

"Who else?"

"Whatever—" Vladimir interrupted himself. "Let's get serious. I'll be in Chicago in September. Can you join me for a couple of days? But don't tell Denise. She's insanely jealous—she'd never understand our friendship."

Mariela thought she heard a click on the phone, attributed it to a poor connection, said her farewells and rang off. As she did, the lighted button on Denise's extension phone went out as well.

Mariela turned off the lamp and rolled onto her side. It was a three-blanket night. "It would have been nice if Curtis were here with me," she thought. She stretched herself in her bed, but sleep didn't come that easily. Curtis was now on his way to Germany.

"On business" . . . he'd said.

Mariela didn't believe him. She knew he had several affairs going, an old habit he'd resumed sometime during the first year of their marriage. But then, Mariela felt so guilty that she had never found the courage to tell him that Oliver Leitung was *not* her nephew but her illegitimate son! Nevertheless she was very grateful to Curtis, and in her own way, loyal. She would stay with him as long as he wished.

She turned on her stomach and tried to force sleep to come. It didn't work.

"God, it's quiet!" she said to herself.

As if in response, something scraped in the silence. Did she hear foot-steps? Maybe Denise had gotten up. She listened intently. Something else clicked. Her senses came fully alert again. Nothing.

The house was old. All London houses are old, and they all have their noises.

Nothing to worry about, she thought.

Her eyelids finally settled heavily.

The crash that followed might well have been a bomb, considering the effect it had. Mariela screamed. Her hand knocked the lamp from its table as she fought to find the switch. She screamed again.

The servants were no longer asleep. Their footsteps echoed in the house, sounding to Mariela like the ride of the Valkyries. Her maid dashed into the room, throwing on the light.

Mariela sprang upright in the bed, her hands shaking as she held the sheet.

"What . . . who . . . ? What was that?" she yelled.

"I don't know," the maid replied. "Seems to have come from downstairs, ma'am."

"Find out!" Mariela demanded, trembling.

Before the maid has a chance to respond, the housekeeper stumbled into the bedroom, ashen and weak at the knees. "Mum, it's that coffin. 'E's . . . 'e's . . ."

"Coffin," Mariela repeated.

"That bloody coffin, mum. 'E's . . ." Her eyes grew and grew in terror until they seemed to fill her whole face. "That Egyptian thing!"

"You mean Tarutu! *What?* What *is* it?"

" 'E's fell down, mum!"

Mariela led the procession downstairs. She had to. She had to see for herself.

One look told all. It was true. What light there was illuminated harrow-ing patches of eye, and nose, and mouth. Twisted bits of ancient Egyptian wood were scattered across the hall.

The sarcophagus lay open, its lid snapped in two. One piece had bounced, turned over, and smashed into jackal-faced fragments. The other piece of the casket of the lady singer of Amun had fallen whole, as the centuries had left it. And Mariela felt the voice of the gods on her heart. It seemed to mouth its silent curse, over and over.

Mariela fainted, not having noticed that Denise hadn't bothered to come downstairs—not having noticed that the cord that held Tarutu to the wall had been deliberately cut.

※

VLADIMIR-MATTIE/*New York City/Wednesday, May 5, 1965*

It was always the same. However early Mattie planned to dress and make up, there was the scramble at the end, that last-minute rush, with scattered jewelry, spilled powder, crumpled gowns and a succession of maids unable to establish order in her inner sanctum, the ornate dressing room of her Central Park South duplex apartment.

Mattie was seated in front of a large black marble-topped vanity table with a chrome base studying her reflection in a three-way mirror surrounded by light bulbs. A collection of false eyelashes was stuck to the glass.

Turid, her personal maid, moved around nervously and, in an effort to appear busy, shifted clutter from one place to another.

Mattie surveyed the chaos. "God! What a mess! This place looks like a disaster area! I'll never change!"

Virginia, her secretary, peered around the corner. "It's California again. Morris Altman of Vista Films is on the phone," she whispered piously. "He wants to speak to you—*personally*. It's his fourth call, Mattie!"

If Virginia was impressed with Morris Altman, Mattie was not. Not anymore. "I haven't got time to talk to him, not now! Tell him . . . oh, tell him, uh . . . Tell him anything! Anyway, Virginia, you're better at making excuses than I am." She winked at the prim-looking secretary, a young woman whose granny glasses and pug nose emphasized her perennially surprised expression.

"But, Mattie . . ."

"All right, all right, I'll take it," Mattie said irritably, picking up the Art Deco telephone. "Hi, Morris!" she said casually. "Look, make it snappy! I've got to meet Volodin at the Met—"

"Is he dancing?"

"No, he's singing *La Bohème.* . . . Of course he's dancing!"

"Who's more important I'd like to know, your old Uncle Morrie or a twirling ballerina?"

"That's what I like about you, Morrie! You have a knack for putting things in a nutshell. A twirling ballerina, of course!" Raucous laughter could be heard in the phone as Mattie held it away from her ear. "Pass me the mascara, Turid. Look, Morrie. You haven't called me all the way from California to chat about Vladimir Volodin. So why don't you get to the point?" Clutching the phone between her shoulder and neck, she started applying colored eye cream.

Altman cleared his throat self-consciously. "I've been thinking about doing the movie version of *Jazz Age Clara,* and of course, Mattie, you'd be a natural for it." Altman's voice echoed thinly as if at the bottom of a rain barrel. "After all, you created the role on Broadway."

"And seeing as I own the property, Morris, I'd be *such* a *natural* for it that it won't be made without me!" she replied sarcastically. "As a matter of fact, I've formed a corporation to produce it myself."

"Well, that's what I want to talk to you about, Maxwell." His voice floated out rich and complacent. "Maybe we can make an arrangement with your corporation and—"

"The person to discuss that with is my manager," Mattie cut in. "You know Sylvia Rubins, don't you?"

"Of course, Maxwell, of course, but I wanted to mention it to you first. After all, kid, we've made four great films together. Why not five? What are old friends for?"

"I haven't been a *kid* for quite a few years, Morrie." She burlesqued a yawn for Turid's benefit. A phone rang in the bedroom. She held the phone away from her mouth. "Oh, it's my private line. Will you get that, Turid? I'm not in for *anyone!*"

"What did you say?" Morris Altman asked.

"I was talking to Turid."

"Ingrid? Ingrid who?"

"Ingrid Bergman, the maid, Morrie—the maid! I'm kidding. Her name is Turid, T-U-R-I-D. Ingrid is off today. Now, where were we?"

"When will you be back in California?"

"In about two weeks. We just wrapped up *By Strings Attached* this afternoon."

"Where can I reach Sylvia in the meantime?"

"She's staying at the Algonquin. Look, Morrie, I've got to run. I really do. Arthur's is opening tonight. You know, Sybil's new discothèque. Sybil Burton—Richard's ex."

"When are we going to—"

"Morrie, for Christ's sake, have a heart, will you? How can I put my mascara on and talk to you at the same time?" She took a deep breath. "Goodbye, Morris. Call Sylvia." Without waiting for a reply, she slammed the phone down. "As a matter of fact," she muttered under her breath, "I'm an expert at putting mascara on like that!"

Mattie got up, threw off her dressing gown and stepped into a pinkish beige lace baby doll dress. It stopped several inches above the knee. She spun around in front of the wall mirror. "Who'd dream I'd ever be going out looking like this? I was wearing more sophisticated clothes when I was ten years old!" she joked, admiring the effect. "Bill Blass says it's the latest fashion!"

Virginia stuck her head through the door. "The limousine's arrived. You should hurry if you want to pick up Mr. Volodin. It's nearly eleven o'clock."

The limousine crawled toward the stage door entrance of the Metropolitan Opera House on West Thirty-ninth Street. A group of fans were clustered at the door. Mattie leaned forward to the driver. "Jorge, do you see that lady with the ponytail standing near the curb?"

"Yes, Miss Maxwell."

"That's Melba, Mr. Volodin's dresser. Pull up beside her, and then will you and Melba see to it that Mr. Volodin makes it here without getting mauled?" Mattie leaned forward and slipped to the floor. "I don't want to create more commotion by being seen. Otherwise we'll be stuck here another hour!"

Jorge stopped the car and opened the rear door.

"Oh, hello, Melba." Mattie greeted the dresser sheepishly from her hiding place on the floor in the rear of the car.

"Hello, Miss Maxwell—what are you doing down there? Aren't you feeling well?"

"I'm feeling super!"

"Oh," said Melba simply, and turned around, baffled.

The crowd burst into a loud roar. "There he is now with Tiny!" Melba waved to get their attention.

The dashing figure of Volodin was shielded from the onslaught of admirers by his six-foot-seven-inch black bodyguard, nicknamed Tiny. The pair shoved their way toward Mattie's limousine. On reaching it, Volodin pushed Melba forcefully into the rear seat.

"What are you doing, Vladimir?" protested Melba.

"You're coming with us!"

"But, Vladimir, I have to wash your tights . . . I'm not dressed . . . I don't go to clubs."

"Well, Melba, it's never too late to start! Tonight's the night!" He spotted Mattie. "Hello, beautiful. What are you doing on your knees?" Vladimir exploded with laughter. "We can't do it in front of Melba."

He grabbed Mattie, helping her back onto the seat, and kissed her greedily.

"Vladimir, it's so-o-o good to see you. You don't know how hard I've worked on this film. I'm dead on my ass. Finally wrapped up the location shots for *By Strings Attached* this evening at eight. But I'll be at your performance Saturday night with bells on!"

"I'll arrange the tickets for you."

"That'll be great! Thank you!" She kissed him enthusiastically.

As Mattie's Cadillac turned up Third Avenue it was slowed almost to a halt in an enormous traffic jam. Two policemen with white gloves were directing on foot at the intersection of Fifty-fourth Street, while several others were on horseback. The sidewalks were crammed with pedestrians, some of them piling into the street, trying to get ahead by running alongside the idling cars. A number of vendors were selling hot dogs, ice cream and sodas from carts. A clown was carrying a large bouquet of red balloons, each one attached to a long string and bearing the single word *Arthur's;* he was giving the balloons away to delighted passersby.

"I don't think we're going to make it!" the driver warned, turning the corner.

"What do you mean by that, Jorge?" Mattie was apprehensive.

"Take a look for yourself, Miss Maxwell."

The street was blocked solid by a column of stationary vehicles. Colorfully dressed people were alighting from several of them. Trucks and vans from NBC, CBS, and ABC television were parked on both sides. A number of photographers and journalists were recognizable from their heavy bags of equipment and the tape recorders they carried.

"Why don't we just get out and walk?" Vladimir suggested impatiently. Mattie agreed.

"If I may say so," countered Jorge, "I think you're both making a terrible mistake! When this mob catches sight of the two of you, they'll tear you apart!"

"In that case," joked Mattie, "why don't we let Melba go first!" Melba looked aghast. "I was only joking, dear!" Mattie said, laughing. "You know we wouldn't do a thing like that!"

Jorge got out of the car and opened the back door. Vladimir led the way, pushing through the crowd. He was stopped as abruptly as if he had run into a brick wall. Mattie stepped into the street, holding Melba by the hand. "Hang onto me, Melba, or we'll lose you!"

"Look! It's Mattie Maxwell!" shouted a voice, followed by another, "Isn't that Mattie Maxwell?" News of her presence spread like wildfire through the crowd.

"Going out with you," Vladimir joked, "is an occupational hazard!"

"I'd rather be recognized than unrecognized, wouldn't you?" He mumbled something Mattie couldn't hear. The surging mob had descended on them like vultures on carrion. They picked Vladimir up, carrying him effortlessly on their shoulders.

"Vladimir, Vladimir!" they chanted. "It's Vladimir Volodin!"

Suddenly Mattie lost her grip, and Melba was swept off her feet. "Madonna mia!" she cried, crossing herself vigorously. "Che cosa ho fatto! Dio mio!"

"Who's that dago up in the air?" somebody yelled. "Is she some kinda movie star?"

"Yeah," a voice hollered. "Can't you tell from the mustache? It's Anna Magnani!"

Mattie did not feel the slightest fright at being lifted with pure blazing fervor above the heads of the throng. What struck her was how pretty and peaceful they all looked, with fresh flowers woven through their hair and colorful beads wrapped around their necks. From the front door of the site of the old El Morocco, a red carpet had been rolled out to the curb. Under the green awning, with *Arthur's* written across it in script, a small band played on the sidewalk. The musicians spotted Mattie and launched into a jazzy version of her latest hit. That was followed by the title song from her second Oscar-winning movie, *The Nightingale and the Eagle,* which she and Vladimir had made together in 1962. An army of photographers surrounded them, flashbulbs popping.

"Are you all right?" Mattie shouted to Vladimir.

"What did you say?"

"Never mind! Forget it!" Allowing all the resistance to drain from her body, she slumped backward onto the heads and shoulders of her bearers. At a distance she recognized and waved to Rock Hudson and Ross Hunter, who were making a desperate attempt to enter the club. Mattie, Vladimir and Melba were finally eased down on the black-and-white tile entrance hall of Arthur's. They could hear the pounding of music in the distance. John Springer, the publicist and the evening's organizer, greeted them, and several shots of Mattie and Vladimir were hastily arranged for the hungry paparazzi. Vladimir was visibly annoyed. Suddenly he broke away and moved on ahead, cursing.

Mattie ran and grabbed Vladimir by the arm. They made their way through the crowded corridor toward the swinging doors leading to the main room, where a small dance floor was surrounded by tables. The pulsating music of Jordan Christopher's combo, the Wild Ones, struck them like a blow. "There's Twiggy," said Mattie, but her words were drowned by the band's rendition of the Rolling Stones's current hit, "Satisfaction."

"Hi, there . . ." The rest of Mattie's words were swallowed in an upsurge of sounds. She looked like a mime mouthing in a void. The lights blinked inside Vladimir's skull. John Springer led them to Sybil Burton's table. With the exception of Melba, everyone knew one another.

The dance floor was a forest of pretty legs, topped by bodies so alluringly costumed that the impression went beyond total nakedness. Psychedelic contraptions lit up and blacked out the dancers' faces.

People abandoned themselves to the night. They were on a vast plain. Crowded! Empty! The music enveloped them in a cloud of animal sensuality. Its effect was mesmerizing, frenetic, terrifyingly visceral. The old wanted so to be young. The young were convinced they would never grow old. And everyone was involved. Everyone was there. Tall black men danced with short-skirted, blond-maned nymphets. Jaded roués shuffled and fading flashing queens swished. They played "A Hard Day's Night"—and it was. They played "I Wanna Hold Your Hand"—and no one did. No one touched—not the dancers of indeterminate ages in childlike costumes; not the handpicked, make-me-a-movie-star waiters beckoning in black turtlenecks and white aprons. Servicing rather than serving. Taking chances— and waiting for them. Watching, waving and waiting. Loneliness churned behind the pill-clouded façades. Buttons glittered mind-blowing messages.

"Profumo goes down. So does Christine Keeler." The phrase bounced on a bare breast. Beguiling. Three sexes—and no sex. Music—and no melody. Compulsive happiness. The bid for recognition. The furtive glances of the dancers. Flashes, glimpses of something vulnerable and alone. An impersonal togetherness. Eyes shut tightly as if to lock in fantasy, the better to visualize it. Strangers. Automatons. Did they see you? Know you? Were you real?

"Come on Vladimir, let's dance," Mattie begged. Vladimir stood, wearing the same outfit he had been photographed in helping Queen Elizabeth down the stairs at Covent Garden: a white stretch jump suit tucked into knee-high gray suede buccaneer boots. His presence froze the audience as he walked to the dance floor, tossing away the cigarette he hadn't lit.

The combination of Volodin, Mattie and the disco beat was a pulsating aphrodisiac for the crowd that opened slightly to watch them. Photographers surrounded them relentlessly while they danced. The captive air was thick with the sweet smell of pot. An exquisite, heavily made-up blond girl approached and tapped Mattie on the shoulder. "Do you mind?" purred the stunning stranger.

"Yes, I do, but go right ahead," Mattie replied good-naturedly. She returned to the table and observed the lovely platinum-haired creature in boots and thigh-high knitted dress gyrating suggestively with Vladimir. She bore a striking resemblance to the late Marilyn Monroe.

"Who's that pretty girl Vladimir's dancing with?" Mattie asked socialite C. C. Flynn, who was seated beside her.

"That pretty girl used to be a pretty boy," C. C. Flynn replied. "She's Candy Darling, an actress, part of Andy Warhol's retinue."

"Gosh . . . ! Yes . . . !" contributed Andy.

"Everybody's after Vladimir," Mattie said, marveling. "I've never seen anything like it! I've always told him that if he was a religion, I'd join it!"

Vladimir returned, and took a long swig of his drink, as if to quench a moody restlessness. Playfully he swept a protesting Melba from her seat, twirling her onto the floor.

Someone put a hand on Mattie's shoulder. She turned sharply. It was Tony Rook. Mattie felt a quick tremor. He had aged unbelievably. His hair was tousled, his eyes were bloodshot, and the sensual mouth had taken on a cruel edge. Tie askew, collar loose—he was no longer the fastidious dresser she once had known. Evidently he was smarting under a sense of failure; he had the eerie, wary look of a shell-shocked veteran.

"Tony! What a surprise!" Impulsively Mattie stood up, throwing her arms around him. Eleven years had passed since she had first met him. Now without a doubt Mattie Maxwell was the greatest female box office star in the world. He knew it. She knew it. Everyone knew it. "I didn't see you, Tony—although who could in this crowd! Where are you sitting?"

"I'm not—I'm not sitting anywhere. I'm at the bar." His sentences dragged into muddy bottom. "Oh, Mattie, how great to run into you tonight! How glamorous you are!" He gave her a deep, appraising look. "You are just fabulous! We haven't seen each other in ages. . . ."

"Yeah, I know. But the way you've been traveling and the way I travel now . . ." The man's smile brought back memories. "Wow, the last time I saw you was in . . . in London. You were still—" Mattie was about to say "married" but caught herself in time. "You were with Beverly. You both came to see me at the Palladium." Mattie vividly remembered the gold ring ornamented with a musical note which he wore that night. Strange how the mind focuses on some unimportant matter which is remembered long after with utmost fidelity.

"Oh, yes. How could I ever forget it! You had the audience on fire!" he said. "How long will you be in New York?"

"About two more weeks."

"Can I give you a call?"

"Would you believe I don't know my own number! Call my manager, Sylvia Rubins, at the Algonquin. She'll give it to you. Or else give me yours. Where are you staying?"

"I'm at the Americana," he answered uneasily. "But I don't know if I'll be there tomorrow, after . . . after what happened last night."

"What happened last night?" asked Mattie.

"Don't you read the papers? Don't you know that I bombed?"

"I'm sorry, Tony. I didn't know."

"Everyone knows it. Everyone." His voice rose. He saw Vladimir walking toward them. "Maybe we could have dinner or something," Tony said dimly.

"Maybe," she echoed. Tony left, his spirits visibly heightened.

Vladimir and Melba came back to the table. Between puffs and pants she exclaimed, "I don't understand why people do this for pleasure!"

C. C. Flynn was posturing as if a hundred cameras were focusing on her bland looks. "That was Tony Rook, wasn't it?" she asked in her arrogantly snobbish voice. Without waiting for an answer she went on. "I was at the Americana last night! The worst opening I've ever seen! What a disaster! He was drugged out of his mind and couldn't perform!"

"Gosh," pronounced Andy.

"What did the audience do?" asked Mattie, genuinely concerned.

"At first they were tolerant, even encouraging. But finally they lost patience. Apparently Tony couldn't remember the songs at all," C. C. Flynn continued loudly. "He was constantly off key and mumbled a lot of idiocy about peace, love and beauty. Then he fell flat on his face. He was simply awful, my dear, awful."

"Gosh," said Andy.

"Look," Vladimir whispered to Mattie. "Let's go. I've had enough gossip and noise for one night. I still prefer Bach to rock. I have an early class.

Why don't we simplify things and wake up together in the morning?" He looked at her, stroking her neck. "How does that sound to you?"

"Just great," she said warmly. "Your place or mine?"

"What's wrong with your place?"

"Nothing, and I can make tea for you in the morning."

"And I'll make love to you all night," he said, kissing her gently on the lips, oblivious to the clicking cameras.

"It's a deal," she exclaimed, standing up. "You know, I'm beginning to like this arrangement already."

"What are the chances of getting out of this place unnoticed?"

"Not very good, I'm afraid, but my car is waiting for us."

"You mean you kept the driver sitting out there all this time?" he asked in disbelief. "Mattie, that's inhuman, it really is!"

"Well, everybody does it," Mattie explained innocently.

"Well, everybody is wrong. At least you could have invited the driver in and let him have a good time too!"

"But, Vladimir, nobody invites a chauffeur in."

"Then *we* should have."

"Oh, you're wonderful, Vladimir, you really are. That's why I love you. But what's the point of having a car if it's not there for your convenience? You aren't nostalgic for Russia, you have a nostalgia for poverty!"

"Oh, shut up, Mattie! We could have gotten a taxi without any problem!"

"I'll tell you what," Mattie said impishly, taking his arm. "We'll invite the driver home with us. After all, why should I save it only for you? The poor driver is entitled to the same fun, don't you think?"

They made their farewells and collected Melba. On their way toward the door Mattie couldn't help scanning the bar for one final glimpse of Tony Rook. She couldn't see him anywhere.

"Whom are you looking for?" Vladimir asked.

"An old friend—Tony Rook."

"Yes, I saw you talking to him a little while ago. Your Waterloo, I believe."

"We all have one."

At that moment Mattie caught sight of a tired figure sitting alone at the bar, slumped over his drink. It was Tony.

"Come, on," Vladimir said with a roguish smile, taking Mattie by the waist. "Let's go!"

—※—

For Denise there was nothing extraordinary about the beginning of the day at Whitewillow Manor in Nassau. Today was like yesterday, and tomorrow would be like today. Routine. The hairdresser had come. The manicurist. The personal maid. Everyone fussing over her. Everyone always fussing over her. Now they were gone.

She and Sinclair were to give an outdoor luncheon for about seventy-five guests. A full-size symphony orchestra, flown in from Dallas, would provide the entertainment. But with fifteen people on staff, plus decorators, coordinators and additional secretaries hired for the occasion, things would take care of themselves, as they always did. Smoothly and with elegance.

Denise walked to a window of her three-story Tudor mansion. The hundred and thirty-seven acres of manicured lawns—dotted with gazebos, arches, lovely ponds and pools, banks of flowering shrubs, carefully pruned hedges—spread as far as the eye could see. Picnic tables had been set under the towering palm trees near the sea.

But the wealth and elegance seemed so meaningless to her now. No matter what she tried, what she purchased, where she traveled, her thoughts were with Vladimir. Always with Vladimir. The precious stolen days and weekends and weeks spent with him were a constant reminder of her voracious longings. Never before in all her jaded years had she fallen in love. The kind of love that life had thus far denied her, that she had denied herself. Denise had discovered that her soul, which had never surfaced, was brand-new. Ready to give all. Surrender. Surrender to one man. Volodin. Denise did not make him a divine plaything; she loved the divinity in him.

Now was her time to be with Sinclair. But why? There was really no reason to compromise any longer. She had everything. More money than could be spent in ten lifetimes. She had all. But she didn't have Volodin. So she *didn't* have everything. Not yet. Denise cherished the thought that now, at last, she had found love, a love for which she would gladly sacrifice all her riches if only Vladimir would ask her. But he hadn't. Why didn't he ever ask anything of her? Denise was suffering, and all that suffering was grist for her mill. Something would have to be done. Life without Vladimir was becoming unbearable.

The room was suddenly narrow. The walls were closing in on her. She felt as if a great wetness was seeping through the floors, surging through the rugs. Submerging her. She could have drowned in that deluge.

Sinclair entered the room. "Damn, you look good, Princess!" He whistled in appreciation. "Come sit by me on the sofa—let's you and I have a little chat."

She looked at him, unflappable, wondering what kind of little chat he had in mind.

"Oh, hell—" Sinclair fumbled in his pockets, looking for nothing in particular, biding his time. "Oh, hell, I might as well get to the point. Seems like the goddamned gods are not with me these days. Just now that I have you all to myself, I've got to go . . ."

Denise raised her eyes to him in sublime innocence.

"There's trouble down in Venezuela. Riots have broken out around our plants. Bad. Real bad! They're throwing stones. Setting fires. We may have to evacuate our staff." He laid his hand on her knee. "Goddammit," what can I say! I hope you can understand that I'm needed there. I'm so sorry, Princess."

Sorry? She wanted to spring from the sofa in sheer delight, but for now at least the façade had to be preserved. She swallowed hard and said hurriedly, "But Sinclair, I'd be only too glad to go with you." Denise had no such intentions and began counting the flowers on the cloisonné vase in front of her.

"As much as I would love to have you with me, it's not advisable. I wouldn't allow myself to endanger you."

"I'm sorry, Sinclair, truly sorry." His hand on her knee felt like a trap.

"I'll be back within a week—and I promise, when I return we'll go anywhere you say—you'll have only to name it. Just the two of us—like old times —anywhere in the world."

Anywhere? There was nowhere in the world Denise wanted to go with Sinclair MacAlpine. She just smiled.

". . . please convey my regrets to our friends at lunch." He held her close. "And be a good girl!"

"My thoughts will be with you, Sinclair—every minute. Just hurry back."

Without missing a beat, Denise called Carla and gave orders to cancel the luncheon.

She was flying high. Quickly she opened the drawer of her vanity table, double-checked Brody and Briac's latest report on Vladimir Volodin's schedule, and rang New York.

"Vladimir, it's me, Denise."

"Denise . . ." He sounded worried. "You're not in New York, are you?"

"No, I'm in Nassau."

He was silent.

"Vladimir . . . are you still there . . .? I can't hear you—Have I called at a bad time?"

Taking the phone from the bed table to the bathroom so as not to disturb his companion, Vladimir answered. "Don't be silly, you never call at bad time. I was getting a massage before class."

"I've got great news," she said eagerly. "I can meet you in Washington on Sunday!"

"How . . . ? I mean, how did you know I'd be in Washington?"

"Am I wrong? Aren't you performing at the White House for the President?"

"Yes—news certainly travels fast! It was finally decided only last night. I had to get out of another commitment . . ."

She wasn't listening, concentrating on what she would say next. "And after that, you have five free days. Wouldn't it be super if we could fly to your new house in Mougins? I think I ought to be your first houseguest—"

"Denise, how could you *possibly* know about Mougins?" He coughed in surprise. "I just bought that little windmill above Saint-Tropez a few days ago. I never even mentioned it to you."

She didn't lose a beat. "Of course you mentioned it to me. Don't you remember? Last time we spoke. How else would I know?"

"I suppose when I'm speaking to you I don't know what I'm saying." A few minutes earlier he had been deeply puzzled. Now he was shaking with laughter.

"It's all right, Vladimir. I'll settle for Washington!"

"Denise, you are truly amazing." He laughed again. Nothing escaped his overdeveloped sense of the ridiculous. "You know more about my schedule than I do."

She did. She also knew he was seeing Mattie and that Mattie would also be performing in the same star-studded program at the White House on Sunday.

At least, thought Denise, for the four or five days she would be with Vladimir, Mattie wouldn't be *performing* in his bed.

※

MATTIE/*New York City/Friday, May 7, 1965*

Mattie was seated on the floor, close to the fireplace, wearing a crushed velvet crimson dress, an antique Indian necklace of hammered gold set with diamonds and garnets circled her neck, rings were on all her fingers. A fire made of twigs leaped fitfully on the hearth washing her in colors for which there were no names.

Virginia entered the spacious but cozy living room. "The cook wants to know what time you'd like dinner served, Mattie."

"How late is it now, Virginia?"

"Nearly eight."

"Tony should be here any minute." She fidgeted with an earring, thinking. "Let's see now . . . Tell the cook we'll eat at nine sharp. Spencer should set up in the study—that's less formal than the dining room."

"I'll get it organized, Mattie. Have a good evening. I'll see you in the morning."

"Well, I might not see you till early afternoon." Mattie laughed, putting down a copy of John Lennon's *In His Own Write*.

The woman left Mattie to the solitude of the peaceful room. One thing was undeniable. It was well lit. Lamps! Lamps! Lamps! A Tiffany at each end of a blue sofa. An antique collection, with glass shades molded in the form of yellow daffodils and red tulips, intermingled their colored illumination with the fire's dancing patterns on the green plants and on the ceiling. Each lamp and piece of furniture reminded her of some special time, some special place. Mattie lit her cigarette in true Bette Davis style.

The doorbell rang.

Jumping to her feet, Mattie admired herself in a long mirror. It courted her. She looked good. She knew she looked good! She checked the champagne bottle in the silver ice bucket. There was a knock at the door.

"Come in," she said.

"Mr. Tony Rook," the butler announced.

"Show him in, Spencer." It was all going too fast. She was aware that her pulse was racing. Her composure was on the brink of disappearing.

They rushed into each other's arms, embracing like old friends.

"Boy, this is some pad you've got here, Mattie!" Tony exclaimed, walking about and looking all around him in unabashed wonder. His eyes settled on a portrait of Mattie by Andy Warhol hanging over the mantel on which two Oscars, a Tony and a Grammy stood at attention.

"Yeah," she said, laughing proudly. "It's a bit different from that pigsty on Fifty-third Street, isn't it?"

"Oh, I don't know, I kinda—"

"Yeah," she cut in, "so did I."

"So did you what?" he asked, clumsily putting his hands in his pockets.

"Kinda liked it!"

"Yeah, so did I!"

"Duck shit and all! It's such a long time ago! Wow! It's hard to believe that eleven years have gone by. Do you remember poor old Boris?" They were laughing and talking at the same time. Then their merriment subsided, swallowed by awkward silence.

"Mattie—" He abruptly took both her hands in his. "You look great, you really do!"

"So do you!" she lied. Wrinkles were etched deeply into his face. He looked tired, debauched. His clothes were shabby.

As if Tony had just read her thoughts, he looked down deprecatingly at his Levi's, worn-out blazer and sneakers. The lazy grin flashed.

Oh my, that grin still has magic, thought Mattie.

"Mattie—I almost didn't get up the courage to come over and say hello to you at Arthur's the other night," he said softly.

"Why, Tony?"

"Just that after my disastrous opening . . . You see, I hadn't performed in over five years. . . ."

"I understand, Tony. You don't have to explain."

"No, no, I want to explain," he said in broken tones of despair. "Well— I mean, what happened—well—I was awfully drunk . . . and . . . I'd taken a few pills to . . . I needed to boost my confidence—and, goddammit, I blew it! The bastards at the Americana canceled my contract! They wouldn't give me a second chance."

"Please, Tony!"

"But I know it will never happen again. I'm back on the scene, and for good! I'm in control now! I know it!"

"That's the attitude, Tony! You always were a great performer. And no one—"

"Should have taken it away from me. Is that what you were going to say?"

"Yeah."

"Baby, no one ever will! Never again!"

"Come on, Tony, no point crying over spilled milk—or should I say champagne?" She handed him a fluted crystal glass. "What was it that Albert Camus said?"

"I don't know, Mattie. What was it that Albert Camus said?"

" 'Today is the first day of the rest of your life.' Let's drink a toast to that." She lifted her glass. "To the rest of your life—and today."

He lifted his glass, clinking hers. "Here's to today," he whispered. "And to us, forever this time—and our future." Within an instant his mask of hushed melancholy, frustration and despair fell away. Another mask took its place: smiling, cocky, confident. But it didn't fit—any more than if it had been painted on by a blind artist. "And baby, *we* have a future!"

Mattie's eyes darkened. She felt uncomfortable. "Let's put some records on!"

"What do you have?"

"The Beatles of course."

"You and the rest of the world." They were on their hands and knees, Mattie dragging the albums out of a cabinet. "Don't you have any of mine?"

"Yes," she lied, "but they're all in California."

"How do you like living in that stinking snake pit?"

"Oh, well, what can I tell you? Sunshine—sunshine until you want to

394

shoot it! The only good thing about the place is that you can turn right on a red light—"

"But you can also turn wrong."

"Have you heard my latest yet?" Mattie asked, wanting to change the topic. "It's 'Live from Carnegie Hall.'"

"I'd love to hear it, Mattie. Put it on now."

"No sooner said than done!" She took the album out of its sleeve.

Tony rose suddenly and helped himself to another drink. "As Shakespeare once said, 'All's well that ends well,' and here the two of us are together again at last! . . . By the way, I'll bring you a stack of my albums tomorrow. They're just great, baby!"

She looked at him with blank amazement, lowering the arm onto the record. The silence in the room was broken by a burst of applause. "Ladies and gentlemen," a voice cried, "live from Carnegie Hall—Miss Mattie Maxwell!"

"Where do you hide the john, Mattie?"

"There's a powder room around the corner, right off the entrance hall. I'll show you the way."

"I wouldn't hear of it. You just stay right where you are."

Tony left the room. But why now? Hadn't he just asked to hear her album? What was so urgent about the john, she wondered, and why had he taken his shoulder bag with him? Such a strange thing to do. Oh well . . . Mattie got up from the floor, tucked herself cozily into a soft chair, and sank down, mesmerized by the soaring sound of her own voice singing "Strangers on the Shore."

Tony came back and sat opposite her. He was strangely sparkling. His complexion had altered visibly. "Mattie," he began, "I just can't get over how great it is seeing you again! Just like old times! And you don't look a day older! Just more beautiful!" His eyes walked into hers, but something about them made Mattie feel uneasy, sending waves of suspicion through her entire being. Getting up, he staggered and walked toward Mattie with jerky, uncoordinated steps, and attempted to put his arms around her. A medicinal smell, laced with alcohol, was overpowering. Giving him one of her marvelous smiles, she pushed him away gently and rose.

"Look, I have to check on the meal. You're hungry, right?"

"Aren't you having something sent in from the take-out Chinese restaurant?"

"Not everything is exactly as it was!" she said, looking at him ironically. "There's been a few improvements around here—like food that's fit to eat! I'll be right back."

"Do you mind if I make a phone call?" he shouted after her.

"Be my guest!" Passing the powder room, Mattie was about to switch off the light when she noticed a reddish trickle on the marbled wall. Bending down, she examined it more closely. It was blood. A broken hypodermic needle clumsily wrapped in tissue had been discarded in the waste-basket. Tony had mainlined. She shook her head sadly, feeling compassion for him.

As Mattie walked toward the kitchen the butler stopped her. "Oh, Miss Maxwell," he said, "I was looking for you. Mr. Georgio Sant'Angelo's on the telephone and wants to know your plans for tomorrow's fitting. Will you be seeing him at eleven in the morning or one?"

"That's all right," she said, "I'll take the call in the powder room."

Mattie closed the door and picked up a wall extension. She pushed an illuminated button. "Hello, hello . . ." There was no sound. She pushed another button. Also dead. The last button suddenly lit with a red glow. A conversation was in progress. She recognized Tony's voice and was about to hang up. But something within her told her to listen.

VOICE: ". . . can't you speak any louder, Tony?"
TONY: "No! And I can't talk too long either, so shut up and listen."
VOICE: "Okay, Tony, but my opinion is—"
TONY: "Sam, your opinions don't count! I don't pay you to give me opinions. I pay you to give me publicity, and I'm not missing this chance."
VOICE: "Okay, okay, shoot."
TONY: "Phone the papers. Give Earl a call. He's a good guy and likes me! Get in touch with AP and UP. Give them the scoop: Mattie Maxwell and Tony Rook are back together and can be seen dancing tonight around—around eleven at Arthur's. This ought to knock Beverly and her knight in shining armor right off the front pages. And give a buzz to *Life*—I bet they'll go for it!"
VOICE: "Tony, let's not get carried away!"
TONY: "Look, egghead, I know what I'm doing. Just get your ass to Arthur's to see that all goes smoothly. And, Sam, *please* stay in the background or she might—"

Mattie didn't want to hear any more. Putting the phone down softly and leaning against the door, she took a cigarette from a small porcelain dish on the hand basin. A chill raced through her body. She felt her arms and legs shaking. She was sick. An ache formed a ball in her belly. Gradually she regained her composure. The hazel eyes shone with a steely glitter. Resolutely Mattie strode toward the living room, feeling like a thoroughbred awaiting a race. She walked into the room. Tony was still on the phone.

When he saw her his voice shot up several decibels. "And listen, Milton, if the contracts are ready, I can be in your office tomorrow afternoon. . . . Great! See you at four then." Tony hung up. He was all smiles, verve and aplomb. "I was just talking to my agent, and guess what! Milton's got me Vegas! I used to be a big-money spinner there—and now I'm going to grab the world by the balls again!"

Mattie wasn't really following the words but she was listening closely to the voice. "What? Oh—I'm glad, Tony! In fact, why don't we drink another toast to it?"

"Fine, baby, fine! Shall I pour?"

"No, let me do it, Tony." Walking toward the champagne bottle, she stopped and turned around. "Tony, are you on drugs?" There was no enmity in her question. "I mean, hard drugs?"

"Isn't that a bitch! I wonder who could have spread a rumor like that!" He laughed hollowly. "You don't believe that, do you, Mattie baby? I take a few pills now and then, like you do, but none of the hard stuff for me."

"I'm only asking, Tony, because I found a broken needle in the bathroom a few minutes ago, and I'd hate to think my butler was shooting up. You know how high-handed servants can get when they're stoned." The champagne bubbled merrily as she poured.

"Oh, that!" He motioned with a wave of the hand, his look combining the coyness of a starlet just asked her age and the stubbornness of a hit man pleading the fifth. "I've—I've started taking vitamin B-12 shots. You ought to try it! It's fantastic! My doctor put me on it." Tony was making it worse.

"To Las Vegas!" she declared with affected bonhomie, raising her glass.

"To Las Vegas!" he repeated. "And don't forget *us!* To us too!"

"How can I forget us, Tony?"

"Then do it."

"Do what?" Her head was a jumble of thoughts.

"Raise your glass and say it."

She forced herself to go through with the charade. "To us, Tony, to us!" He leaned toward Mattie. "When is Beverly getting married?" she asked.

The question shocked him. He flinched visibly. "As soon as Sir Gregory's divorce from Cecily Vivian is final. Divorce is more difficult in England."

"And then Beverly will be a lady—at last." Mattie's voice oozed sarcasm. He missed it. "Tony," she whispered, opening her knowledgeable eyes wide, "all that's in the past now. You have the future to think about and—I've gotten quite good at telling fortunes! You didn't know that, did you?" She closed her eyes theatrically. "And your immediate future involves a great French meal. How does that sound?"

"That sounds terrific."

"So why don't I just lead the way!"

"I'm ready." Unsteadily Tony rose to his feet and followed her up the thickly carpeted stairs. "Look, Mattie, I've got a great idea. . . . Uh . . . after dinner, why don't we go to Arthur's?"

"Fab, Tony!" she exclaimed, feigning surprise. "Leave it to you to come up with the unexpected!"

When she reached the top of the stairs Mattie saw Spencer standing with English dignity at the study door, incongruous under a black-and-white Jackson Pollock.

"Spencer," she said, "would you ask Jorge to have the car ready? We'll be going to Arthur's after dinner."

"Should I make a reservation, Miss Maxwell?"

"Yes, but under your name, Spencer," she answered slyly. "We can do without the press. I'm sure you feel the same way, don't you, Tony? This evening belongs to the two of us."

"You're absolutely right, Mattie, I wouldn't want *anything* to spoil it!"

As Mattie and Tony entered Arthur's, photographers descended on them like misery on the world.

"Where did all these photographers come from?" asked Mattie mischievously. "How did they even know I would be here tonight?"

"Beats me," Tony said, shrugging uneasily.

The paparazzi had a field day. The superstar posed graciously with Tony but refused any comment.

Tony did all the talking. And there was quite a lot of talking to be done!

"Are you and Miss Maxwell happy to have found each other again?" a reporter quizzed.

"We never really left each other. Sometimes it takes getting away from someone to discover what you've really lost, and that's what we've done." He gave Mattie a loving glance.

"Will you and Miss Maxwell be working together?" asked a gangly stringer.

"Well . . . uh . . . I haven't given it a thought. It's the last thing I have on my mind! Now enough, boys!" Tony winked charmingly—or so he thought. He had once seen Clark Gable wink the same way on screen—it had to be effective!

"We haven't heard from you, Miss Maxwell."

"Oh, you will," Mattie promised. "You will." Boy, will they ever! she thought. Tony wants publicity, he'll get it. Wait, just wait! Another loving glance.

It was past two o'clock in the morning when Tony and Mattie left the sweaty crowd at Arthur's.

Back in the limousine: "Where to?" asked Jorge.

Tony was confident. "To Miss Maxwell's."

They crossed the park. Tony was feeling better and better. His hand inched across the seat, up under Mattie's dress, along her thigh, into the crevice—not noticing its dryness. Her face tightened as if in pain.

He saw no danger signal. "Oh, Mattie, how could I have been such a fool! You were always the only one for me. I'm still the same old Tony. Some people drink. Some smoke. Me, I fuck all night." She gazed at him steadily. "And if you're still the same old Mattie, you know what I'm talking about!" He moved more ardently now, beneath the cloth, expressing desire. His mouth edged to her nipple.

She was rigid with anger. "The chauffeur—please, Tony!"

"What do I care!" he tossed off in a slightly inebriated voice. "After all these years he must have seen a thing or two in the old back seat, eh, Mattie girl?"

She shrank back, disgusted and barely in control.

Undeterred, Tony reached for her again.

"Tony, stop it! Stop it—please!" As if accidentally, her elbow collided with his testicles. He retreated. The car arrived at its destination and pulled to a stop. Tony grabbed the handle, ready to alight.

Mattie's hand settled firmly on his arm. "My dearest Tony," she cooed, getting out of the car, "you don't know how much I'm dying to make love to you, but . . . ah, I'll have to take a rain check. Someone is waiting for me upstairs. I'm sure you'll understand."

He stopped. Looked at her in amazement. "You mean . . . you have . . . I thought that . . ."

"Yes?"

"I thought . . . Well, at least let me walk you to the elevator, Mattie, then your car can drop me—"

"Sorry, darling, I suggest you get a cab. The driver's going home to the West Side and it would really take him out of his way."

Tony eased out of the car, watched it disappear, and stood on the sidewalk. Immobile. The street light found his face and hit it harshly with an unflattering beam of greenish color. The color of deception.

"Let's say goodbye here, honey. I'm in a hurry." Mattie kissed him.

"Good night." Tony stretched the word out to make it last a second longer. Mattie walked away. "I left my tote bag upstairs," he said quietly, catching up with her at the door.

"Oh, forget it, Tony," she said, dismissively. "You can get it tomorrow. Yeah—why not tomorrow? I'll call you. Where are you staying?"

"At the Gotham."

"Of course. You've always stayed at the Gotham. Still the same old Tony!" She veered around and looked at him. Seeing *him* for the first time. The chaos of his life spilled out before her like raindrops whipped into a frenzy by the wind. The stiffness of his silence told her how painfully humiliated he was. The same old Tony? No, it was not the same old Tony. The cocky attitude was gone. And gone too was the gambler's smile and the outlaw's wit. She saw him as he really was—poor, neglected, alone. Vanquished by solitude, by failure. A loser.

His big eyes turned on her, reflecting undisguised anguish. An anguish veiled with the same softness Mattie had found in the eyes of a stray white cat she had taken home years ago. The shock of Tony's tragedy overwhelmed Mattie, engulfing her in a wave of pity. She felt ashamed of the easy game she'd been playing with this man ravaged by his devastating downfall. This man without defenses. Defeated. A weak man. A man whose infinite sadness had rendered him almost invisible. But a man she had once loved. A faint mist of perspiration beaded his forehead—the sweaty teardrops of his misery.

"Tony, come on up," she heard herself saying softly.

His face registered both joy and suspicion. "But I thought you had someone upstairs?"

"I was kidding—you know me."

"Baby, I must admit, you really had me fooled," he said as they entered the building. "What an actress! No wonder you won an Oscar!"

"Two," said Mattie, squeezing his arm.

In the elevator Mattie watched the little movements of his shoulders as he bent forward at the mirror intently scrutinizing some shadows on his face. He found them all.

Once again they were in Mattie's apartment. The carpeted, high-ceilinged living room had taken on a late-night quality—a certain foreboding quietness, a great wave of emptiness. In the fireplace, flames were flickering their last gasps, licking the logs, casting strange shadows that rounded off all the edges in the room.

Tony walked toward the terrace door and stared at the brilliant city with a fixed, grim expression. "What a view you've got from here, baby!" Abruptly changing moods, he rubbed his hands buoyantly and went to the bar. "Well, I think I'll make myself a nightcap. What can I fix you?" He poured a straight shot of whiskey and drained it.

"Nothing for me right now, thank you."

He raised his head in bafflement. "Did I hear you right? Did you say *no* to booze? What's happened?"

"Oh, I still drink, but very little." Mattie sat on the floor amidst a pile of embroidered cushions from North Africa festooned with tiny beads and mirrored glass. She stared at the dying embers.

"Good God! I remember—" Tony interrupted himself with his own laughter. "I remember when you could drink me under the table! Do you want a bennie instead? I got some in my bag. Oh—and I've got something else you might like, it's—"

"I don't take pills anymore, Tony."

"You *what?*" He was dumbfounded. "Come on, come on—seriously. Have you joined some religious order—the Christian Scientists or something?"

"No, Tony, nothing like that."

"What, then?" He poured his third whiskey and came toward Mattie, glass in hand.

"It's a long story." She sighed. "The result is that I've learned to love a very worthy human being."

"Who?" Tony asked, a tremor in his voice.

"Me."

"Shit, you had me worried again." Relieved, Tony dropped into an armchair partially covered with a silver fox throw. Casually he spread his legs wide apart.

Mattie didn't want to look at his crotch, but she did. It was as tight as she remembered it. With a fond, quiet smile, she recalled how this familiar position of his always stirred her blood and made her want him desperately. This time her blood didn't stir. It never would again. Never for him. Mattie was forever unshackled from her distorted memory of their times gone by.

"What are you smiling at?" he asked, setting his empty glass on the coffee table.

"Nothing."

"Well, then"—he beckoned, arms reaching out—"how about coming over here and sitting by your man?" Mattie got up and went over to Tony, kneeling on the floor next to him.

"Baby, I've got a great idea." His confidence was surfacing. "I'm footloose and fancy-free. Let's travel to the Coast together. I still have a lot of things to get settled there. In fact—"

"Tony, stop this game!" Mattie took his hands gently away from her shoulders.

"What the hell are you talking about, Mattie? What game?"

"The 'get Mattie to fall into the trap' game. Shall I get you another drink? It's Scotch on the rocks, isn't it?" She rose and walked behind the bar.

"Mattie, I don't understand . . . I don't understand . . . I don't understand . . ." He kept repeating the words like a damaged robot in a science fiction movie.

"What don't you understand, Tony? It's really very simple." She handed him his glass and resumed her position at his feet. "Accidentally I overheard your telephone conversation with Sam." Tony lurched forward, trying to get up. Mattie held his arms firmly. "No, please, Tony, sit down. Let me finish." His head hung low, like a flower suddenly gone limp. "I went along with the game, swearing I would take my revenge in some way. I felt angry and belittled. But you see . . ." Mattie put her hand under his chin, forcing him to raise his head and look at her. Again she saw the green eyes, dull, defeated, begging her to stop. ". . . you see, Tony, I'm incapable of hurting you."

"Mattie, I wish I could . . . explain everything . . . make you understand . . ."

"Oh, Tony, I understand. That's why I couldn't possibly hurt you." Tony was silent, sweat dripping down his forlorn face. "Take your jacket off, Tony, you'll be more comfortable." She went behind the chair and helped him.

"Don't you still love me, Mattie?" His voice was flat, like a poker player's.

"No, Tony, I don't. For so long I thought I did. There was always that sliver of hope that perhaps one day—oh, I don't know—one day we could make it, especially after your breakup with Beverly. But it was simply a delusion. I haven't loved you for years."

"I'm so alone, Mattie." He was kneading his hands. "People are avoiding me because I'm nobody again! It's the most humiliating—"

"There's only one way to get even with them."

"What is it?"

"By becoming somebody again." She paused. "But you can't do it carrying a monkey on your back."

A glint of pride tinged with defiance shone in the lackluster eyes. "What are you talking about, a monkey on my back?"

"Roll up your sleeves, Tony." She bent down, reaching for the button of his slightly frayed cuff.

"No! Don't!" he shouted in panic, bolting from his chair.

"Do it, Tony, do it!"

He was lost in his grief. Abruptly he rolled up his sleeves. "Yes, I am a junkie. Yes. *A junkie!*" he shouted. "You wanted to see it! Did you ever see what it looks like? Here!" He grabbed Mattie forcibly, shoving his bare arm under her eyes. "Look! Look at it! Take a good look!" Black-and-blue track marks, ugly bruises and scabs edged their way up his arm, each vein a road to his despair, each puncture a crater in his tortured soul. "This is what life has done to me!" he screamed in a frenzy. "Life has done it to me . . . LIFE!"

"Life doesn't do that to you, Tony. You do it to yourself," Mattie said sharply. "Stop this self-pity! Whether it's booze or drugs, that's the easy way out! If that's the way you choose, take a gun and get it over with! At least you'll save the people who care for you a lot of grief!"

In a burst of sheer desperation, he moved toward his tote bag, snatching at the clasp. She took both his arms. "No, Tony. Not now. Please." The bag dropped. Mattie guided him to the couch. They sat together, hands clasped. The only sounds were the crackling embers and Tony's uncontrolled sobbing.

Mattie broke the silence. "Last year—I don't know if you saw it or not—there was a lot of publicity about a four-month trip I took around the world."

"How was it?" he asked feebly.

"The trip around the world took me as far as the Whitney Clinic, right here in New York."

"What was wrong with you?"

"I had become an addict. Pills. Booze. You name it. Slowly but surely I was following in my mother's path."

His eyes narrowed. His voice croaked. "What . . . what gave you the willpower . . . to stop? I've tried. What made it possible for you to stop?"

"Vladimir."

"Vladimir Volodin?"

"Yes. We met each other during the filming of *The Nightingale and the Eagle* and became very close. He was an inspiration." Involuntarily her eyes drifted to a framed photograph of Vladimir resting on a chrome-and-glass console.

"Do you love him?"

"Yes, I do. Now I'm sure of it. I've finally lifted my head out of the sand." Mattie lit a cigarette. "Tony . . . I want to repay a debt I owe you."

"A debt? What debt?"

"Everything that happened to me was part of a chain of events. Talent alone doesn't do it. One has to be in the right place at the right time, and, purely by accident, you put me there."

"How?"

"Think of it. If Jeremy hadn't died, you would not have left me. Oh—I think you would have, but perhaps not so suddenly. Then I wouldn't have been on the Jack Paar show or done the Sullivan show—see what I mean?"

Tony lifted his large tear-filled eyes.

"This is what I'm proposing to you," Mattie went on, with great sensitivity and dignity. "I'm not offering you a meal ticket. I'm not gonna play nurse. But I will find you a hospital and get you well again." She rested her head gently on his lap. "Now, please don't cry, Tony . . . please."

He ran his fingers gently through her hair. "I'm bankrupt, Mattie."

"Shhh—don't think about money. I'll take care of your hospital bills." She straightened herself up. "I won't let you down if *you* don't let *me* down."

He dropped to his knees, clutching her ankles. "Will you ever forgive me? Please forgive me! When I think of all the pain I must have caused you . . ."

"All the pain was good. It gave me the necessary push. I was determined to show you—determined to show the world what I was capable of doing!"

"And you did. . . . Oh, Mattie, please, please don't leave me tonight!"

"Tony, I won't." She helped him up from the floor and they held each other tightly. She could taste the saltiness of his tears as they wet her cheek.

"I haven't slept in three days."

"Well, you'll sleep tonight."

They walked slowly up the stairs, Tony leaning on Mattie. "Remember what Camus said?" she asked.

"No, Mattie. I—I don't remember what Camus said. What did he say?"

"Today is the first day of the rest of your life."

Tony answered with a great sob—a great sob of happiness.

—✳—

MARIELA/*Grosse Pointe/Tuesday, September 20, 1966*

"The party's going well, very well indeed," Curtis said, kissing Mariela proprietarily on the cheek. "With a wife like you, and your genius for organizing these affairs," he continued admiringly, "I bet I'll raise over half my reelection funds here tonight!" Curtis was cheerful, exulting in the challenge his grueling campaign swing was making to his strength and vitality.

"Thank you, darling, but let's not minimize the support of the four richest gentlemen in Michigan," she said, raising her Baccarat glass in a toast to the four men standing across the room. Curtis immediately followed Mariela's example, and the tycoons raised their glasses in a return toast.

"In fact, beautiful," said Curtis under his breath, "I think I'll go to work on guaranteeing their maximum support right this minute!"

As her husband sauntered over to them Mariela looked around. Yes, she thought, the party is going very well indeed. She had managed everything with imagination, skill, taste and attention to detail. Emery was serving champagne from a silver tray. Uniformed maids were circulating inconspicuously among the guests with hors d'oeuvres. Masses of tiger lilies were arranged in precious Oriental vases. Buffets heaped with sumptuous food and several plentifully stocked bars were strategically placed throughout the immense and richly appointed formal reception room. A room big enough to accommodate the elegant and brilliant throng assembled to ensure the reelection of their governor, Curtis Lodge III.

Through the open French doors, across the crowded grand terrace and beyond the well-lighted pool could be seen the last of the hundred or so guests arriving at the thirty-five-room Lodge mansion in Grosse Pointe, Michigan. Five hundred dollars a head, thought Mariela, and most would contribute ten times that much. Holding hands, their faces shining with happiness, Genevieve and Oliver passed by, smiling at her warmly. She spotted Pete Conrad, the astronaut who, with Richard Gordon, had in the past week achieved the first in-orbit docking with Gemini II. Smoothing her Balenciaga black velvet off-the-shoulder gown, she walked over to him.

"Mariela," he said, a glad smile lighting his face, "it's so good to see you."

"Dear Peter." She held both his hands. "Thank you for doing us the honor of being here with us and bringing glamour to our party."

"The glamour is *you*, Mariela."

"Now, now, don't be modest. Everyone is dying to meet you." She took his arm. "You should be congratulated for setting the record last week—it's fascinating! Just think: no one has ever been as high before!"

"I'm not so sure about that, but thanks anyway! I take it this is not a sculpture of Night Sanctuary," he said with a twinkle in his eye, pointing to an exquisite figure of a horse standing on a Louis XV tulipwood table.

"Hardly." She laughed, holding his arm tightly. "That's one of a much older horse, from the T'ang Dynasty, and I doubt this one ever won the Derby."

Photographers were hemming them in, clicking away. The five-piece band began the familiar strains of "California Dreamin'."

"Can I have this dance, Mariela?" asked Peter Conrad. "Those flashbulbs are blinding me!"

Mariela was following him onto the dance floor, which had been laid down for the occasion, when Walter Chase, one of Curtis' campaign aides, came toward her. "Excuse me for interrupting," he said, "but *Time* magazine would like a picture of you and Governor Lodge together."

She apologized to Peter. As she made her way toward Curtis she counted three copies of the new see-through blouses from Yves St. Laurent—one woman wore a flesh-colored leotard under hers; another, countless strings of beads covering her breasts; and the third had pinned two large "Reelect Lodge" buttons in strategically located places.

Curtis was exchanging quips and inside jokes with the press. Mariela took her husband's arm, cameras started flashing. A red-faced reporter from UPI called out "Governor Lodge, could you make a statement about the increased number of race riots this year?"

"I'll repeat what I've already said in Grand Rapids, Saginaw, Bay City and Port Huron. They are deplored by most people, black as well as white, but will probably cause a white backlash in the gubernatorial elections, which will hinder the civil rights movement—the most deplorable result of all." They were hanging on his every word now. When Curtis spoke he was passionate and convincing. "And I want to add that I certainly don't agree with the Moynihan Report on the cause for black unrest. And I—" The cheers from the guests drowned out the remainder of his speech.

"Mrs. Lodge," called out a woman reporter wearing a paper dress, "do you agree with the Moynihan Report that 'the very essence of the male animal, from the bantam rooster to the four-star general, is to strut'?"

Mariela didn't hesitate: "The essence of the male animal as well as of the female is to dance, and strutting is just one dance of many."

"Could we have a picture of you alone, Mrs. Lodge, under this magnificent painting?"

"I leave Mariela to you," said Curtis with a wink to the press. "I can see the fourth estate has good taste and appreciates beauty." Mariela moved under the sixteenth-century portrait by Vecchio, "La Bella," representing a woman, probably a Venetian courtesan, sumptuously coiffed and draped in scarlet and deep green. It dominated the entire room. Curtis graciously backed away, whispering in her ear, "You're the best, darling—keep it up!"

"The portrait looks amazingly like you, Mrs. Lodge!" said a photographer.

"I suppose it does in some ways," Mariela replied, "and that's the reason the governor purchased it from the Thyssen Collection." The cameraman took about ten pictures, thanked her and said, "Look in the people section of *Time* magazine next week and you'll see yourself, Mrs. Lodge—not that publicity will be a novelty to you!"

"To tell you the truth, I didn't expect all this celebrity when my husband became governor, but I'm getting quite used to it," said Mariela. "Why don't you interview Senator Dirksen over there, in the blue suit?" she suggested to the reporters, "and ask him why he's rejecting this year's civil rights bill after accepting the bills of the last two years."

Someone tapped her on the shoulder.

She turned around. It was Sinclair MacAlpine, her husband's lifelong friend and one of his largest campaign contributors. Perhaps his most loyal supporter, since, as an out-of-state contributor, he expected to receive no benefits other than the gratitude of someone he truly admired.

"Well, well," said Mariela, bussing him on both cheeks, "if it isn't the big man himself. What a marvelous surprise! Curtis will be thrilled to know you're here. Is Denise with you?"

"No, she's in New York checking up on the ballet our foundation is sponsoring—*Sleeping Beauty*, it's called—or *Sleeping Queen,* or something like that." His voice boomed in the oath-thundering accent of his native Texas.

"Will you be attending its premiere? I'm going. It should be a memorable evening. I hear Lincoln Center is nothing short of spectacular."

"Naa—I'm not interested in seeing Comrade Vlad-rag flying through the air. That's Denise's department. She's nuts about ballet! She must be nuts about something—we surely don't see much of each other these days. . . . The Dallas Philharmonic Orchestra is my baby. Anyway, I'll be flying through the air myself in a couple of days. I'm piloting my own jet to the Orient for some business meetings." He looked around. "Where's your spouse, Mariela? I wanted to have a few words with him."

"I don't know," said Mariela. "I haven't seen him in a while. But don't move too far away, Sinclair. I'll find him and tell him you're here."

Where was her husband? He seemed to have disappeared, and Mariela couldn't find him as she wandered through the tangles of political conversation and topical gossip.

"That damned Ralph Nader legislation is going to cost the auto companies a fortune unless—"

"Do you know that workers are demanding a dollar forty an hour instead of a dollar-twenty-five?"

"That man over there—he'll be the new governor of Maryland—his name's Spiro T.—"

"Premarital intercourse has increased sixty-five percent over the last—"

"My daughter comes home from college and starts riding her bike barefoot in the snow—she must be taking this LSD they"—

"Did you read *Valley of the Dolls* yet? In a strange way it's a lot like *The Agony and the Ecstasy,* but more—"

Once again Walter Chase approached her. "Governor Lodge is waiting for you in the blue room. He would like to speak to you privately."

"Oh, good!" said Mariela. "I was looking for him everywhere." Her heels clicked down the long marble corridor. The sounds of laughter and conversation drifted out to her as she passed by room after room. Finally she reached the library. The door was closed. She opened it and walked in. Curtis was alone. He was standing, rubbing his fingers across his forehead. His back was turned and he didn't look at her as she entered. He was gazing at the portrait that Alice Neel had done of them for their first anniversary; its heavy black outlines now seemed somehow ominous to Mariela.

"What are you doing here, darling? Everyone's asking for you. Sinclair MacAlpine has arrived and he—"

Suddenly Curtis whirled around on her. His face was gray and his lips bloodless.

"You poor darling," said Mariela, holding both his arms, "you look so exhausted. It's been such a long day—"

"No, please!" It was a panicked cry. He jerked himself free of her hands. "I just received a phone call from campaign headquarters, Mariela. Did you ever hear of . . . Lord and Lady Chiselhurst?"

Mariela's mind stopped. She just stood there, unable to think, thinking only that she couldn't think. Finally she managed to say, "Who, dear? I'm sorry, I was still thinking about the party, somebody had said something about Martin Luther King and—"

"Lord and Lady Chiselhurst," Curtis repeated without changing his voice.

Her face became impassive and her eyes met his unflinchingly. "Has it got something to do with the campaign?"

"Nothing! Absolutely nothing!" he burst out. "It has to do with *you,* Mariela."

"I'm afraid I don't know what you're talking about, Curtis." Her heart began to beat so loudly she thought he would hear it.

"You know very well what I'm talking about, Mariela! Lord and Lady Chiselhurst!"

Gradually she became filled with a strange terror. "I never heard of them," she persisted. She turned her back on Curtis, and from a dark-blue tooled-leather end table she picked up a framed photograph of Oliver and Genevieve on their wedding day. "What have this lord and lady done to make you so upset?"

Curtis crossed the room abruptly, snatched the photograph out of her hand, and threw it against a Korean lacquered screen. Her terrified green eyes shifted from the pieces of broken glass to his face. All his composure was gone. Curtis appeared shattered. "Lord and Lady Chiselhurst, Mariela, have . . . they have—" Curtis was tripping over words. "Lord and Lady Chiselhurst have been found in the south of France, savagely murdered."

Mariela remained immobile, frozen, like a scared rabbit in the middle of the highway, not sure which way to jump to avoid disaster.

Curtis stalked toward the window, framed with heavy blue taffeta drapes, and turned around slowly. "Investigation into their murder, Mariela, reveals that Lord Chiselhurst was head of the Nazi party in England and had to flee to Vichy in 1939. It reveals that he was prevented from ever going back to his homeland and was condemned to death *in absentia* for his collaboration with the enemy during the war. Furthermore, it reveals that they had a child, an only child, a daughter who happens to be your age, who is Lady Chelmsford, and . . . and . . . who is married to the well-known industrialist and governor of Michigan. And . . . and this information has been released to *News of the World* in England as well as to the American wire services. It's only a matter of hours before headlines will break in this country!" he shouted harshly and uncontrollably. "Do you still not know who Lord and Lady Chiselhurst are?" His eyes suddenly cruel with wounded vanity, he came leaping across the room—his big body throwing a giant shadow—grabbed Mariela by the hair, jerked her arm away from his shoulder, and pushed her down brutally into a chair. He went on furiously, "LORD AND LADY CHISELHURST ARE YOUR PARENTS, MARIELA!" Curtis was pacing up and down, walking around the room, muttering to himself, darting frantic looks as if stricken of mind. "The investigation also reveals that Oliver, your supposed nephew, is actually your illegitimate son by a German soldier, and . . . and that, thanks to your high connections, you were spared arrest as accessory to the murder of Karl Ravenstein following one of his orgies in 1954!"

Mariela felt as if little bits of herself were being chipped off.

"Do you still not know what I'm talking about?" Curtis was close to real hysteria, his eyes blazing. Without waiting for a reply, he went on. "The press has irrefutable proof that, under the name of Mariela Koenig, you were a highly paid call girl in New York! The demons you harbor can never be silenced. It is too late! By noon tomorrow every voter in Michigan will also be aware of this gruesome story, and I can kiss my chances of reelection goodbye!" He lifted Mariela from the chair and flung her aside so violently that she slammed against a pearwood chess set, scattering its carved pieces all over the floor. Her eyes remained fixed on Curtis. Mariela knew she was facing her own past.

Finally she whispered, "Do you believe all this?"

"Shut up!" Curtis said under his breath. "You don't even have the grace to be ashamed of yourself!"

She swayed, holding onto the chair for support.

He clawed at her, savagely ripping the priceless necklace encircling her throat: twenty-five bronze-black pearls that Curtis had given her as a pre-wedding present on Sinclair MacAlpine's yacht in 1956. The jewels scattered on the floor like hailstones.

"What are you doing?" she gasped.

"I bought them like I bought you! I'll do with them what I want!"

Mariela found herself on her knees picking up the irreplaceable beads. He brought his foot down on her hand, viciously, grinding it into the floor, forcing her to release the pearls. She let out a small cry of pain and fell sideways on the blue carpet, covering her face with her hands.

"Why didn't you tell me the truth from the start, Mariela? Why did I have to find out in this . . . in this goddamned way and have my whole life break apart by losing all my chances for reelection!"

She waited for the next onslaught. His silence was now a greater challenge to Mariela than his rage. She stood up with difficulty and sat on the divan, tears streaming down her face. "I couldn't risk losing you . . . I just couldn't."

"Bullshit, you—"

"You've already judged me, before hearing my defense."

He walked slowly toward her, took her wrist, and held it in a fierce grip. She couldn't move. "Don't waste your breath with denials. I have tangible proof of everything!"

"What you have said is true." Her words came out choked with emotion. "But what I told you when we met is true as well. I told you my parents were recently killed. For me they have been dead for a long time. I haven't seen or spoken to them in over twenty years. As for Oliver—his father died before he was born. I thought it best for his future to give him a respectable past. For me, from the moment I saw you, that first day in Zurich, 'Mariela Koenig' also died, along with her past. I wanted to be the wife you deserved and expected."

"I should have paid more attention to Denise's innuendos all these years," Curtis said with callous satisfaction, flinging her arm away. "She was trying to spare my feelings, but now I have no doubt whatsoever that you were carrying on a sordid affair with that Russian dancer who is living in the limelight of promiscuity and art."

"As for my affair with the . . . with the Russian dancer—there was *nothing sordid*. I . . . I . . . ." Mariela's eyes filled with tears. "You had resumed your indiscretions. I felt alone. He was a young man I loved. I gave him up, knowing you needed me by your side to further your political ambitions. I could have left you then. But I made my decision. I wanted to help you. Nothing else mattered. I still see him. We are friends, but we haven't been lovers in four years." She reached toward a lapis lazuli box and nervously took out a cigarette. "I tried to make you happy. I *wanted* to make you happy. I purposely closed my eyes to the many affairs you were flaunting— *brazenly!* I could have mentioned that girl you've been keeping in Dearborn for the past two years."

"What girl?"

"The one who is supposedly cataloging your art collection."

Curtis looked at her in surprise. "But she does work . . . ah . . . she *is* on my staff," he faltered painfully.

"I shouldn't even have brought this up. I realize this is not the issue," Mariela said hurriedly.

"Mariela, the divorce begins as of this moment," Curtis said grimly. "I want you *out* of this house tonight and *out* of the country immediately or I'll have you deported. As far as I'm concerned, you're dead! Mrs. Curtis Lodge is dead!"

"What about . . . about Oliver?"

"I don't know what I will do, because hurting him would also hurt Genevieve, which is something I want to avoid at all costs. She is my daughter and an innocent victim."

"But where am I . . . to go?" Mariela asked fearfully.

"I'll let you use the house in Aruba until you've made further plans. You have thirty days."

Walter Chase entered the room. The telephone rang and he picked it up. "No, please, you don't have to—" Walter sputtered, hanging up immediately.

"Who is it?" asked Curtis.

"Another dogcatcher."

"What the hell do you mean by dogcatcher?"

"I'm sorry, Governor. It's the fifth time someone has called in the last ten minutes to say he wouldn't vote for you for dogcatcher!" Now he spoke urgently to Lodge. "I've just finished talking with headquarters, Governor, and they say maybe all is not lost. If you separate yourself officially from *her* as soon as possible, we can publicize that angle. They say few people re-

"What's this got to do with Walter Jenkins?" Lodge interrupted. member the Walter Jenkins scandal of last year—"

"Nothing. Except it blew away almost as fast as it blew up," he said, referring to the scandal surrounding the presidential aide arrested for homosexual practices in a public rest room. "The political analysts say it didn't lose the President any votes, because people aren't so shocked by such things anymore and also because more urgent national problems helped the public forget. So maybe we'll be lucky and get some big crises to help the voters forget your unfortunate association with this sordid revelation." They both turned toward Mariela and regarded her contemptuously.

Mariela could hardly believe what she was hearing. In the space of fifteen minutes she had turned from being "the best" to an inanimate object discarded like an empty beer can. Now her husband had his arm around his obsequious secretary, talking eagerly about "courage," "responsibility" to the voters, and the "charisma of principle" as they both walked out of the room without looking back at her.

Mariela took three gasping breaths. She was lost now, but she had been lost before. It was a familiar feeling, not unlike meeting an old friend. She stood up. How had she been so accurately linked with the death of her parents? How had the investigation led to such a thorough exposé of her past? A past that had been so successfully concealed. Who stood to benefit? Her thoughts were whirling. And Vladimir? When did Denise first speak to Curtis about Vladimir? The jagged pieces of the puzzle began to fit, one into the other. A picture emerged hazily. Blond, willowy—and deadly.

In slow-motion bitterness she took a sip of champagne from the glass Curtis had left behind. It tasted sour. Like vinegar on a sponge. She had to speak to Vladimir. She had to. She wanted to. Now!

Mariela walked out of the blue room for the last time.

—⁂—

Denise was luxuriating in a bath Yvette had prepared. Steaming water with a temperature of exactly 120 degrees, as indicated on a hand-carved wooden thermometer. With bubbles frothing up to her neck, she eased farther into the tub as if reclining on a cloud, her vanilla-blond hair wrapped in a turkish towel.

Vladimir would be here shortly. At last! Their meetings, even the most casual, had become rarer and rarer. She had been waiting for over a week to see him alone. His excuses were always the same. An early rehearsal. A matinee. A strained ankle. There was always an excuse. Tonight there would be no excuse. It was Wednesday. Vladimir was not performing.

Where were the days when his yearning for her love was so acute that he wouldn't even take time to remove his makeup before rushing to her? When had Vladimir stopped loving her? Had he ever loved her? Could he have duped her into believing that he did? She would have known. Those things cannot be faked by a man. Or could they?

Denise could endure making love to someone she didn't love; the thought of being made love to by someone who didn't love her was intolerable. But all that was academic. She and Vladimir had not been intimate in over a month.

Denise knew she was sharing him now, but with whom? The papers were full of a renewal of his affair with Mattie Maxwell. Obviously one of his cheap sexual flings—what else could it be? After all, what was Mattie Maxwell compared to her! Nonetheless she smarted whenever she remembered that it was Mattie Maxwell whom Vladimir had escorted to the party she gave for him at the Four Seasons after his gala opening at Lincoln Center only a week ago. Why Mattie, when Denise had been his sponsor, his angel—his lover?

Denise was determined not to let *anyone* break up their affair. She had too much of herself invested in it. And if someone as highly placed as Mariela had proved defenseless against her, Mattie Maxwell didn't stand a chance. The drug bust had failed. But she could be dealt with once again. This time no slipups. This time her career would be dealt the final blow. Money and power have a language of their own.

She thought of Mariela. Mariela's letter to Vladimir—which she had read in his dressing room opening night at Lincoln Center—had shattered Denise. Taken her heart away. With every publication singing nothing but Vladimir's praise for the past week, and just when Vladimir should have been filled with nothing but gratitude, it was obvious he was ignoring her and that, despite everything, he planned to meet Mariela on the ninth of October in Aruba. No, she would never forget the letter. Never forgive it.

Memories of the quiet times she had spent with Vladimir glided, perfumed, into her mind. Oh yes, of course there had been the excitement of the beginning—the telephone, the commotion of laughter, the glitter of rendezvous, the sweetness of faraway places—but it was the calmness of the days she had spent with him that left its imprint in the depths of her emotion.

Denise was certain of one thing: If she could get him alone, Vladimir would be hers once again, as before. Hadn't she always gotten what she wanted? Why should this time, of all times, be different?

Her dependence on Vladimir had grown beyond physical gratification. Never had she felt like this. She was in love. It was a love definitive and absolute. Darvina had been sacrificed to it. Her marriage was nearly over. She couldn't have cared less! Nothing mattered to her but Vladimir. He was her sole preoccupation.

Drying herself voluptuously with a thick white towel, Denise admired her reflection in the full-length mirror. Her mirror! It never tired. It took, it gave! Love! Always love! She splashed Night Sanctuary over her soft skin and ascended a few steps to the dressing room. It didn't take long to do her face; she wore practically no makeup. As a final touch the full lips were liberally covered with gloss. They shone. Though unmistakably a woman, she created the illusion that she was a child. Was she really thirty-four or merely fifteen?

Denise slipped into a white crepe de chine dress by Givenchy and a pair of white high-heeled sandals. She eased the seventy-five-carat Junker diamond onto her ring finger, fastened the treasured black and white Vanderbilt pearls around her neck, and went downstairs.

Once again she thought of the special language of money and power. And what a language it was! Its nuances brought a smile to her lips. A twisted smile—bitter, grotesque, savoring the ecstasy of revenge.

She picked up the phone. The number she dialed was listed in her book next to a single name—Brody. The detective answered. "Mr. Brody, I am expecting Mr. Volodin shortly. When he leaves my house I want him tailed. Report back to me as soon as possible. And by the way, that Chiselhurst-Lady Chelmsford matter was handled beautifully. I hope you were satisfied with the bonus."

Denise felt in control again. For Mrs. MacAlpine it was almost the equivalent of happiness.

She walked across the living room to an elegant silver serving cart inlaid with mother of pearl. The vodka was chilled, the caviar surrounded by chopped onions and the grated yolk of egg. "Yvette, please," she said autocratically, "my guest does not like onions! How long will it take you to remember that?" It was rare that Denise exerted herself for anyone beyond a momentary whim. But today she was concerned that everything should be faultless. She spoke to her maid in French—the kind of French learned on the expensive pillows of the best resorts.

It was precisely three in the afternoon when the butler answered the intercom and returned to say, "Mr. Vladimir Volodin is on his way up."

"Show him in, please," Denise instructed, her hand weaving an elegant web of gesture. "I'll be right back." She left the room with the assurance of a woman for whom yachts had always materialized, doors of the best suites of the finest hotels had been flung open, and planes had been held for her departure.

Vladimir Volodin, clad in a beige stretch jumpsuit, entered the staggeringly luxurious blue and white room overlooking Fifth Avenue and threw his cap onto a chair.

With a proprietary air he walked toward the serving tray and helped himself from an iced crystal decanter. He drank the vodka, not at ease.

All the furniture, rare books, precious paintings, the rugs surrounding him, seemed like a *mise-en-scène* from a play in which he felt terribly miscast. A photograph of a sprawling mansion, framed in lapis lazuli, caught his eye. Suddenly the French doors opened and Denise appeared, a glass of champagne in her hand.

"Good afternoon, my dear," Vladimir said, intoning "my dear" in a way that chilled her. He approached and kissed the pale, velvety cheek perfunctorily.

"Is it such a chore to kiss me?" She modulated her voice carefully.

"You know better than that, Denise. We Russians kiss as easily as Americans shake hands."

"Don't lose that habit."

"Is this a new acquisition?" he inquired, bored, pointing to the photograph on the table.

"Yes," she said hesitantly. "As a matter of fact—"

"Where is it?" he cut in. "California?"

"No, Palm Beach, Florida," she said in her haughty, doesn't-everybody-have-one, rich-girl drawl. "Would you believe that I haven't even slept in it yet—and the final papers were signed weeks ago!"

"How many houses does that make now, Denise? An even dozen?"

"Let's not exaggerate, Vladimir! There's no need to play the Bolshevik with me!" There was a faint irritation in the golden voice.

"No point getting excited, Denise. In other words, I was right!"

"What do you mean?"

"It *is* an even dozen!" he teased.

"Six actually—just six." She avoided his eyes nervously and abruptly brought the sparring to an end. "I see you've already helped yourself to vodka! But I have a concoction for you I know you'll like even more!" Denise's hand rested familiarly on his shoulder. "I've heard you've switched your poison to rum punch!"

"Who told you that?"

"Suzy's column."

"How does she know what I drink!"

"Whatever you do, whatever you wear, whomever you see—even when you fuck, it's in the public domain and reported in the press!" She handed him a tall, expertly made drink topped with a mint leaf and cherry. "I don't seem to get it from the horse's mouth anymore," she added matter-of-factly.

He gave her one of his long, hard looks and remarked to himself how her seeming fragility contrasted so interestingly with her fierce determination.

She returned his gaze, taking notice of his eyes. Eyes that had seen so much and were seeking—God only knew what! His physical presence was overwhelming. Vladimir was all panther grace, fueled by vibrant sexuality.

He sipped his drink. "It's great, one of the best rum punches I've had. Denise, you would have made a great courtesan!"

"Courtesans cater to men. I have always had men catering to me. You are the sole exception." Denise batted her lashes. "Do you have to go to the bathroom?" she said, trying to be cheerful, knowing cheerfulness is a trap.

"No!" He was puzzled. What silly question was this? A child's game.

"Come anyway." She pulled him along to the upper floor.

Vladimir, not easily impressed by opulence, stared in disbelief. Bathroom, had she said? Ah, no, a palace! An Egyptian palace! Furnished by Cecil B. De Mille in shining technicolor. There stood King Tut. Pure gold! His life-size barge, pure onyx! He looked to Vladimir the very image of Tarutu. Vladimir recalled June 1960, London—the first time he had seen that authentic sarcophagus at Mariela's home. And now this? Was there no end to woman's need for symbols? Especially here in the bathroom? And the aura. The splendor of it all. For what? Americans were preoccupied with bathrooms. Plumbing! Junk food, he thought. Eating and excreting. Watched by Tut as you wash your tit? Tit for Tut? This is getting ridiculous. Marble everywhere—floors, walls, vaulted ceiling, columns decorated in rich enamel. The sunken mosaic-and-gold tub a huge square, as large as an average swimming pool. Up a few steps, behind a partition, a sauna, bidet, whirlpool, and a solid onyx toilet. A black hole! Everywhere inlaid friezes of precious jewels creating a traditional Egyptian pattern far more splendid than any Nile king must have known. Was there no end to Denise's extravagance? She was trying to prove something. Money was no object. He was looking around him as though he had been forced to watch an indecent act.

"How do you like it?" she breathed expectantly. "Harrods of London did it. It's a duplicate of the one I have in Dallas."

"You're well toilet-trained, Denise," Vladimir told her, gazing disgustedly at the solid gold snakes that masqueraded as faucets. "You cannot discern function from fire," he said cryptically.

"What do you mean?" She was thrown off-balance.

"Lack of soul, feeling, mood. Can't you see it? A mistaken notion that

414

embellishing the exterior will somehow compensate for bare interior. If you feel empty inside, Denise, buying an extra piece of gold plumbing won't help. Look at the way civilizations that were purely ornamental have died out. They had no soul, Denise. The soul is what lives after you die, whether you are a nation, a people, or—" For some unaccountable reason Vladimir was suddenly sexually excited by his own rage and frustration. "Or a beautiful woman," he finished.

"All I wanted to do was show you my new bathroom!" Denise responded in amazement. "I wasn't expecting a sociological harangue!"

His face was aflame. "It is excesses like these that breed revolutions. They pinpoint inequity. Truly this is a room for waste! For it. Of it. In it. A shit room if ever I saw one!" He turned on his heel sharply. Contemptuously.

They walked down to the living room. Vladimir looked at her calmly, sipping at his rum punch.

"Why do you look at me that way? You frighten me."

"I must say, Denise, you have the right attitude for your kind of life. A girl shouldn't marry until she meets the right amount."

She looked at him with almost ferocious disdain, put down her champagne and slowly returned to her seat.

"You speak about money and power as if they were sins," said Denise in a voice that commanded attention. "I must express myself clearly, Vladimir. It's true. I adore power and everything it brings. I don't feel I have to excuse myself for it. And no one had to teach me this cult. It's dictated by nature. Isn't it natural to love oneself?" she demanded fiercely. "To worship what really wishes us well? And nobody wishes me better than I wish for myself! I'm sure *you*, Vladimir, would have no trouble giving lessons on the same subject!" She turned her head sharply in a gesture of impatience and continued. "You criticize the rich and all their appurtenances, but every time I see your picture in the paper, there you are with the beautiful people— meaning the rich people! Greek shipowners. Heiresses. Highly publicized actresses. Politicians and politicians' *wives!* You don't fraternize with your doorman that I know of. You have less patience than anyone I've ever seen with people who serve you. And you're not grateful to *anyone* who helps you, ever! And that includes me!" She was losing herself in her words, spoken with an expression of cruelty.

"If you are trying once again to remind me of *Sleeping Beauty* production and what it has cost, may I say that if you believe in your conceited and warped mind that you can buy me as you do bathroom or Palm Beach mansion, I then must tell you I feel grossly underpaid! I am not for sale! As for relationship with doorman, I cannot help what the press reports. They want to photograph me with celebrity, no? Besides, these people you mention are not just rich. They offer taste, intellect, quality, integrity, talent. They are people of accomplishment. You are just rich. And that is too poor for me!" He looked at her coldly. "I have known squalor and poverty such as you have never imagined. Not that I wish you to commiserate with me about it.

Can't you understand that wealth alone does not interest me? But why continue this talk? You cannot understand!"

Oh yes, she understood. How well she understood. Her poverty-ridden youth and its bitter privations were still vivid memories. "Acquaintance with poverty and squalor is always an accident of fate. Like a disease, it is unwanted, and it is commendable and normal to try to recover from it."

He looked at her curiously. "What do you know about poverty?"

Her smile was enigmatic. "I know."

Languidly he lowered himself into a beige-cushioned armchair near the window, melting into the seat like a chameleon onto a branch. Denise opened a rosewood box containing his favorite Russian cigarettes, Avroras, and offered one to him. Vladimir lit it and smoked pensively.

She prepared two plates of caviar and toast, handed him one, and nibbled at hers in slow motion without taking her eyes off Vladimir, who was staring silently through the window pane. "What is wrong?" She sounded as if expecting the worst.

Vladimir spoke slowly. Without turning. "A friend of mine has died."

"Oh," she cried, "I'm dreadfully sorry. Was it a close friend?"

"Yes, a very good friend. Gennady Liepka. We were about the same age . . . went to the Kirov together . . . graduated at the same time. He was gentle, generous, extremely talented. Gennady joined the Bolshoi Company. I saw him in Paris only last June when they appeared at the Palais du Congrès. . . . I found out today he killed himself. It is very sad."

"Why did he . . . ?"

"No apparent reason—but perhaps he too had a deep dissatisfaction within himself and was projecting into the future. A dancer's life span is very short —very short. Something must have snapped. I can understand it. One has to be a dancer to understand. It could have happened to me. Who knows? Maybe it will. It is sometimes hard to survive. Those who do are *golden nuggets*." He sighed. "I wish I had more words to express myself. I can only dance my feelings."

"At least you can dance them. Not all of us have such an outlet for our sentiments!"

His mood swung abruptly and he thrust out his glass and cheerfully said, "Any more of this bullshit drink? It's very good."

"As much as you want." Denise took his glass. She returned with his drink and sat on the edge of his chair. She slipped her hand protectively behind his neck. "I really want to help you."

"What is it with women and their mania of wanting to help and protect?"

"You want to be the heroic, isolated sufferer," she said patronizingly. "It is so Slavic!"

"Maybe."

She moved to another chair. "Vladimir, I was worried. It's so good to have you to myself again. Why did it take you so long to see me alone?"

"Well . . . I do have . . . very tight schedule . . ."

"Yes—yes, I know. You've always had a tight schedule, it is nothing new, but this is the first time that . . . that . . ." She hesitated momentarily. "I feel . . . I feel you're trying to avoid me." She looked at him for a response. There was none. He continued staring straight ahead out of the window. She attempted another tack. "Vladimir," she said, slowly uncrossing her legs, "what has changed between us?"

He inhaled deeply, not bothering to disguise his exasperation, and turned toward her. "Denise, why must you . . . why must you give me . . . mudn'yeh!"

"What does that mean?"

"It means a . . . hassle . . . pain in the ass!"

"I'm not trying to hassle you. I'm merely trying to clarify the situation."

"Why does situation need clarifying? It should be pretty clear by now. You aren't the only woman in my life."

"Yes . . . yes . . . ," she faltered. "I'm finally realizing that."

"The others aren't demanding clarification. Why you?"

"I . . . I was under the impression our relationship was special."

"Special? Special? Why special?"

"But . . . but . . . the way we made love . . . surely that was special?"

"What was special about it?"

"It was special to me, and I thought—"

"Well, you thought wrong. It was special to you perhaps, but not to me! I always make love like that."

"You mean to say . . . you've never loved me?"

"No!" he said emphatically. "I know that a woman claimed by passion can fall in love . . ."

"And a man?"

"What can I say? A man can make love with sentimental indifference. You're a woman of the world, Denise. You ought to know that!" Her eyes misted over and she turned her lovely back on him. "Denise . . . for me you do not wear well. You are not part of my world. Unfortunately you must dominate or you cannot function at all. I cannot, could never be in love with you. Not now, Not ever." She lowered her head. He could see that she had been stricken by his words and he regretted his abruptness. "Denise, I have been enchanted by you," he continued, tempered by guilt rather than real feeling. "I love your femininity. Your breeding. Your beauty. What you represent to me as a woman . . . Who knows? Perhaps it's all my fault. Maybe I'm not able to love."

"But . . . but . . ." She was agitated. "You did everything in your power to make me fall in love with you!"

"Don't be ridiculous! I did nothing of the sort! That's a romantic fantasy you've built up in your mind, and I'm incapable of living up to it!"

"You're conveniently discovering you don't love me after . . . after your production of *Sleeping Beauty* has been paid for! You had no qualms about accepting my money. What a heartless game!"

"I never asked you for anything, Denise. And *you* are the one who's the master at playing games!"

"I can have any man in the world I want."

"Have them! I'm not in competition with any of them!" His eyes followed a sparrow hopping on the windowsill.

"Vladimir . . . I love you."

"Only because you can't have me."

"Perhaps—but it doesn't diminish the strength or the validity of my emotions. I have not played with love . . . I have not played with emotion. I've held onto it like a miser. Now that I'm ready to let go completely . . . you are the one who lets me down. With you I wasn't playing a game. I have never loved anyone in my life. . . . I love *you* from the bottom of my soul."

"I'm sorry."

"You are incapable of all emotion, least of all being sorry."

"Oh, for heaven's sake, Denise, shut up! You're incapable of loving *anything* except what you have purchased. I'm not one of your possessions. And as for your soul! There's a hole in it so big no amount of cock is ever going to fill it!" His words spattered and dripped like an egg thrown forcefully against the wall.

"Please do me a favor and save your vulgarities for Mattie Maxwell!" The blood ran to her face, then drained away just as quickly.

"I was wondering how long it would take for you to get to her!"

"Despite your busy schedule, how strange that you still have time for that alley cat!"

"I wouldn't expect you to understand what I see in Mattie. You detest everything and everyone who gets close to me. You're so goddamned self-centered!"

"What about you?" she retorted with venom. "You have an insatiable craving for admiration! You pursue love with the desperation of hate—afraid of commitment—afraid . . . afraid of missing something around the corner—and must fuck everything in sight!"

"And I can add to that," stated Volodin calmly. "I'm also cruel, malicious, egotistical and selfish. But that doesn't negate the fact that you don't appeal to me any longer." He placed the glass on the end table beside him, and pushed it away. "I want to bring our relationship to a conclusion. I hope to finish it amicably."

Her face flushed once again. "You . . . you don't want to make love to me anymore. Is that it?"

"That's it! I couldn't!"

"How could I have been so naive?" Her anger was mounting. "Do you know, Vladimir, I've even thought of divorcing for you!"

"That would be positively absurd! Don't burn your bridges behind you. One day you may find yourself out of bridges to burn. I don't know why you would ever want to leave Sinclair. You have . . . good thing going for you. Very good business . . ."

"It isn't business!" she snapped.

"What do you call it then? Pleasure?—with a man thirty years older than yourself!"

Denise felt stripped of her power to charm. "I don't see what concern it is of yours."

"Then it *is* business."

She got up, fuming, refusing to answer. She took his glass and walked to the portable bar. The silence in the room was deafening. She mixed another rum punch and placed it on the table in front of him.

Vladimir savored the beverage. "You make the best rum punch in town, Denise," he said with appeasing gentleness.

"Will you give me a reference?"

"Sure," he promised, "anytime."

"Your friend Mariela must be feeling dreadful." There was a hint of spiteful glee in her voice. "Of course her husband's political ambitions are ruined. And so is she!"

"Don't sound so cheerful when you say that."

"Please, Vladimir, let's stop quarreling."

"I've known Mariela for as long as I've been in the West." He pressed his fingertips to his temples. "She's my closest friend. I want to help her, and I will."

Talk about playing games! Denise thought. What a liar Vladimir was! When she had first mentioned Mariela to him in Paris, he had assured her they were the most *casual* of friends, had met only once, "ever so accidentally." Of course she knew better now, and now it was all too clear, despite everything, that Vladimir was still ready to stop the world for Mariela. Yet he could not spare Denise even one more hour of his love.

"Have you seen today's papers?" Without waiting for a reply, Denise reached over to a wicker basket for the *Times* and threw it in his lap. It landed with the hollow sound of a dead bird.

"I've already seen it!" he snarled, throwing it on the floor. The headline was splashed across it in large letters over a photograph of Mariela hiding her face: DAUGHTER OF BRITISH PEER, WIFE OF U.S. TYCOON, FLEES COUNTRY.

"Vladimir, she had a baby by—"

"She was fifteen, Denise—and it was twenty-five years ago. You Americans thrive on hearsay and gossip. Why would anyone willfully destroy another human being?"

"I feel sorry for poor Curtis Lodge."

"Why? He may not have a political career to look forward to, but he still has his millions and automobile factory too! You don't have to feel sorry for him, Denise. He'll be okay!"

"Even so . . ."

"American newspapers are so destructive!" His voice trailed off reflectively. "What was the purpose of raking all this up?"

"If a man's going into politics, he'd better make sure there aren't any skeletons hanging around his closets!" Denise said. "The blame is entirely Mariela's. She must have known her past would eventually be dragged up, and she should have warned Curtis. Anyway, all's well that ends well. The papers are happy. It sells copies."

"For a minute there, Denise, I underestimated you! You should have been a newspaper woman! You have nose for a good story!" It took all of his willpower not to remind her what a *good story* Denise MacAlpine's restored virginity would have made. "Anyway, Mariela's staying at her home in Aruba," he said.

"I know, but the way I hear it, her husband has given her thirty days to get out!"

"And when she does, I've made all the arrangements for her to stay at *my* place in Mougins, in the south of France, for as long as she wishes!"

"But—"

"But nothing! How do you happen to know so much about her? Why do you insist on talking about her misfortunes? It depresses me. Anyway, I plan to visit her soon."

"When your engagement is finished?" Denise hoped her voice had not betrayed her.

"No. Next weekend. I'm going down after the matinee on Sunday, and I'll be back in time for Tuesday night's performance. That's confidential of course!" He sank into the depths of the chair's soft cushions, propping his feet on the windowsill, his hands clasped behind his head, bringing to a conclusion any further discussion of Mariela. Vladimir paused before he spoke. "How strange life is," he pronounced with melancholy. "I have achieved the impossible and still I don't feel good about myself. I don't know why I keep abusing my body, my feelings. I guess there is always a toll to pay. To live for one's libido is infantile, but—who knows—perhaps I'll be forever infantile.

"There are wounds inflicted on a child that time can't heal." His eyes appealed poignantly to Denise. "My only salvation is to return to my art with recharged fervor—learn new techniques, new ballets, with the same violent love I had at the very beginning. Otherwise I might as well never have left my country. I must do it to vindicate myself and the harm I've done my family."

"What is this sudden spiritual spasm all about?" she asked nastily.

"Denise, I am what they laughingly call a legend—*a living legend!* That's dangerously difficult to live up to. I'm always expected to surpass myself. I'm twenty-seven years old—which leaves only five or six years of important dancing ahead of me. . . . Then . . ."

"Then what?"

"Oh—then perhaps I'll be ready for one woman . . . maybe."

"Why not me?" Denise implored.

"Oh, Denise, if there could only be something more humane about you, if you had ever struggled even a little bit, or suffered, or occasionally failed . . . As it is, I can be *with* you but not part of your kind of life. Your soul could never reach into my soul. . . . I was hoping that I could speak with you as a friend." Denise stood up and paced the floor. "That is possible, isn't it?"

She sniffed nervously. "I . . . I . . . I don't think so."

He could see she was distraught. "Well, in that case I'd better . . . I should leave."

"Please don't," she said a little desperately.

"Look . . ." He was uncomfortable. "What time it is?"

"Five—why?"

"I have a rehearsal with Murray Taylor at six—"

"Today?" she interrupted. "But I took it for granted that we'd be having dinner!"

"I didn't realize . . ."

"You didn't realize!" she snapped. "I've invited a few people I knew you'd enjoy!"

"Well, that's just too bad!"

"What am I going to look like in front of my friends?"

"Frankly, Denise"—he hurled defiance at her, losing his patience once more—"I don't give a monkey's fuck what you're going to look like in front of your friends!"

"I've gone to a lot of trouble on your account!"

"Denise, what you mean to say is that you've gone to a lot of trouble on your *own* account. Please don't do me any favors." She sat down abruptly. They stared, eyes swearing at each other in silence. "I'm sorry," he said.

She paid no attention. "Murray Taylor," she repeated slowly, enunciating each syllable. "But that's a modern dance company, with hardly any financial backing. How can they afford you, the highest-paid dancer ever?"

"They can't, but I'd be willing to pay for the privilege of dancing with them. In fact, I'm going to give four free performances," Vladimir added rapidly. "I don't care about money. When will you get that through your head? I can put all my possessions in two suitcases. I'm not like you and your friends. I'm just a Russian peasant. I come from nothing. That's something no one can comprehend unless one has experienced it firsthand."

Denise whirled around in her chair. "Vladimir . . . I have experienced it firsthand."

He raised his eyes to her in mock astonishment.

"We are very much alike," Denise began. She was biting her lips to fight back the tears.

"How can you say that?" he broke in. "Your life is so—so trite. It has no —merit." He smiled a nonsmile, a grimace that said, "I don't like you."

"Merit?" she queried. "Merit? Is your success due to merit, or is it due to talent, a talent you were lucky enough to be born with? Well, I was born with something too. I was born with beauty. And I didn't want to go through life being a beauty in a coal-mining town, a veritable Cinderella. . . ."

"Coal mine? What . . . ?"

"I *use* my beauty as you *use* your talent. And why is one better than the other? Has either one of us ever *earned* these gifts? No, but we can use them. And *not* using them is a crime. Most successful Americans flaunt the banner of the poverty they overcame. *I* hid it! I was ashamed of my family, my life, my clothes, my house—but not my beauty. Should I have wasted it? I was poor, Vladimir. Wretchedly poor. Surprised? Oh yes—and it hurts even more because I lived in a country where others were *rich!* At least you were poor living among the poor. If it was an untenable state, it was an expected state. In my case, the violent shock of my childhood, the early neglect, was a shock that destroyed my capacity for feeling anything except resentment. Yes, and ambition!" She was shouting now. Her breasts heaved. Her nails dug into the palms of her hands. "I was unwilling to rot or starve. I like the good things—caviar tastes as good on my lips as on yours! I use my gift for pleasing men, and it is *a gift!* I can see your unhappiness and hostility in every word you utter, in every action you take, in your face, in your eyes. You have climbed to the top of the hill, and what do you see? *Nothing, absolutely nothing!* At least I give something in return. What do you give?

"I have given my whole life to dancing! I give everything, probably more, to public. What is left for me?"

"Your ego!" She was contemptuous. Her anger had hardened into ice.

"No, it is a compulsion," he replied forcefully. "I must dance."

"The same thing! You make love to forget you are not dancing—and you dance to forget you are incapable of love!"

"Denise, listen to me. I need time to reappraise myself. I'm like a man walking in a powerful gale with my back against the wind, and no matter what I try, I find myself at the starting line. Do you understand?"

Her fists clenched and unclenched reflexively. "No, I don't understand. The only error I made was falling in love with you!"

"I am sorry," Vladimir said, barely audible.

"You are my life!" She burst into tears, explosive, uncontrollable, leaving her chair to perch herself tentatively on Vladimir's lap.

Momentarily he was abashed. He opened his arms to her and cradled her head between his hands. Her tears fell on his neck like stabbings of guilt. He squirmed, imagining the teardrops a watery noose.

"You talk about merit," she said, jerking away from him viciously, commandeering new strength. "Let me tell you about *my* father. This honest

422

man knew nothing but the futility of merit. Life was nothing but unjust for him, and he died crushed by it. The memory of my father will forever prevent me from believing in anything the least bit humane. Merit, you say? My brother discovered merit by dying in Korea in a town whose name he could not even spell, for a reason he never understood. Well, I understand my reasons. I've always known my battle lines, and I knew all along I wasn't going to end up as an unknown soldier. Who are you to judge me?"

Vladimir stared. "I'm sorry, Denise. I wish we could be friends. I am not a faithful lover, but I can be a loyal friend."

She was sobbing. He was striding toward the door. "Don't leave me now!" Denise threw herself bodily against Vladimir. She was holding a man without arms. Blind. Deaf.

His foot held open the heavy door. She sobbed even louder. "Don't leave me . . . !"

"I must, Denise. Yes, I'm leaving—can you stop me?"

"I guess not." Her voice was barely a whisper. "Let me see you again, please."

Vladimir's face revealed nothing. "I'll think about it," he said.

For the first time in her life, a door was closing on Denise.

⁕

VLADIMIR-MATTIE/*New York City/Wednesday, October 5, 1966*

Vladimir Volodin left Denise's apartment shortly after five. His rehearsal was not scheduled until eight. He had lied. Lied because it was easier than explaining to Denise he was meeting Mattie at six at the Russian Tea Room.

Vladimir wanted to walk. Walk and think. He realized that the cruel, blind ambition he found so ugly in Denise was not so far from his own. He was disturbed by some of the things she had said. Disturbed because they were true.

Briskly Vladimir strode down Fifth Avenue, went up Fifty-ninth Street, made a left on Seventh Avenue, another left on Fifty-seventh Street.

His anger and frustration began to fade.

He passed Carnegie Hall and stopped under the red canopy of the Russian Tea Room. A quick glance at the large peacock diorama in its front window inopportunely reminded him of Denise. It brought a smile to his lips. He pushed through the etched glass revolving doors and entered. A waiting line had already formed. The captain recognized Vladimir and immediately waved him to his customary table toward the back of the room. He edged his way into a lipstick-red-leather and bronze-tooled banquette, and once again noticed the enormous blue-and-gray ballet canvas to his right, as well as the autographed pictures of Artur Rubinstein, Franco Corelli, Leopold Stokowski, and Kukla, Fran and Ollie.

A waiter, dressed Cossack-style in a pale-green tunic with braided gold trim and black trousers, handed Vladimir a huge, glossy menu with lively and colorful Russian patterns ornamenting its front and a glossary of Russian dishes on the back. Vladimir placed it, unopened, beside his plate.

"I'm not ready to order yet," he said in Russian. "I'm waiting for a friend. Have you seen Mattie Maxwell?"

"Huh?" said the waiter.

Vladimir scowled good-naturedly and spoke to him, again in Russian, repeating his question.

Reddening slightly, the waiter looked around nervously but did not reply.

Vladimir threw his hands into the air and switched to English. "I'm in the Russian Tea Room, speaking to a Russian waiter, in Russian, and I get no reply! Why don't you answer me?"

"I don't understand Russian, Mr. Volodin," said the waiter.

Vladimir pointed to the name tag over his pocket. "Feodor is a Russian name!"

"My name is Theoso. I'm Greek. I'm replacing a friend who's sick. I'm from Brooklyn."

"I'm from Russia, but I speak Brooklynese," Volodin stated, mangling the accent almost beyond recognition. "Anyway, pleased to meet you, Theo," said Vladimir, extending his hand. The waiter smiled. The dancer laughed. Now Vladimir was obviously in a good mood.

"Can I get you anything from the bar, Mr. Volodin?"

"Yes. I would like a rum punch."

"Something to eat as well?"

"But I just told you . . ." He smiled, remembering that his conversation had been entirely one-sided. "Not yet."

"Okay, Mr. Volodin, I'll come back later."

"Do that. Then we can discuss the old country. I'll reminisce about Leningrad, you can talk of Sheepshead Bay."

The waiter left with a grin.

The back room was filled with this year's ingenues accompanied by last year's producers, child stars with mothers, opera groupies and ballet students, press agents, and out-of-towners pointing discreetly at the celebrities. By the green proscenium arch Leonard Bernstein and Beverly Sills were sipping dark, aromatic tea in glasses, served from a silver samovar. They noticed Vladimir first and waved.

Vladimir searched the room with eyes that spoke anticipation. They fixed themselves on the approaching figure of Mattie Maxwell. He signaled enthusiastically, pushed out the table, and, with an exaggerated flourish, motioned her to sit beside him.

"Mattie, my lovely one, welcome to the Brooklyn Tea Room," he announced.

"What the hell are you talking about?" she retorted.

"The Brooklyn Tea Room, where the Russian waiters have been exiled to the cold regions of Brooklyn."

"You're a crazy man again today," she replied.

"Me crazy? This country is crazy! Only in America do they have a Russian Tea Room with Greek waiters living in the depths of Brooklyn. But I shall make up for the loss. I'll be their token Russian for the day."

"I would rather keep you as *my* token Russian," Mattie said softly. "I'm glad to see you are so happy."

"I am happy with you. Once again my joy is compounded by your presence." He shifted from flamboyant joy to concerned tenderness. "Why are you not smiling? Come, baby. Cast a glittering flash of radiant beauty upon your private Russian."

"I'm afraid I'm not exactly in a glittering mood today." Mattie fidgeted with the flamingo-pink napkin. "Vladimir, I'd like a drink." Before he had a chance to raise his hand for the waiter she added, "No, make it two. I need a double." Her eyes were downcast.

"What's the matter, Mattie?" He took her hands. They were cold. Icy cold. "Well," he began, "if you want to eat, we'd better order now. I have a rehearsal at eight."

"I'm not hungry."

"Please, tell me what is wrong, Mattie. You look as if you've lost your best friend."

"I probably have," she said in the enigmatic Mattie Maxwell voice that evoked both tears and laughter.

"Did someone . . . die?"

"Yes . . . the fucking rabbit died."

"Rabbit? Rabbit! What rabbit? I know about your ducks. Since when have you started keeping rabbits?"

"I don't keep rabbits," she said, smiling bravely. "This is a *special* rabbit. Come on, Vladimir. Be serious."

"All right," he said, sighing dramatically. "We have a special dead rabbit. What does this indicate?"

"This rabbit died in a laboratory. What it indicates is"—it had been a long time since Mattie had lived a moment so full of anxiety—"that I am pregnant." She turned away so that Vladimir would not see the tears beading her lashes.

Volodin settled deliberately into his seat. The glitter in his eyes became a serious glint. Real this time. The tenderness did not leave his face. It deepened as he stared at Mattie.

"You—you are pregnant?"

"That's right," replied Mattie. "I'm afraid you have initiated a case of fatherhood." She smiled weakly at her feeble attempt at a joke.

"Fatherhood! Ohtets!" The words were alien to Vladimir. For all the years of wild oats he had sown, it was a conversation he'd never had before. Fatherhood . . . Father . . . Not yet! No visions of a little Vladimir or a little Mattie rose in his mind. He felt only that something irreversible had happened to someone he cared for.

"You see," said Mattie, stifling her sadness, "I will probably lose you completely now. Losing you is not only losing the man I love. But when you asked me a moment ago if I had lost my best friend—well, you were right, losing you *is* losing my best friend." Her trembling hands reached for his, then released them suddenly in a gesture of infinite resignation.

"Are you certain?" asked Vladimir.

"Certain that I'm pregnant or certain that you're the father?" She paused. "You've been my only lover for the past two years—there hasn't been anyone else."

"I see." Volodin was quiet for several moments. When he finally spoke he said, "Marriage is not something that I contemplate at this point."

"I know," she replied. "It's not something I'm contemplating either."

Vladimir reached for her hand and stroked her fingertips softly. It made Mattie's heart beat faster and glow.

"What are you going to do about—about the child?" Vladimir asked.

"I'm going to have it of course."

"Do you want to?"

"Certainly. It's *your* child, and I want to have *your* child." She spoke low because of the pain in her heart. "Is there anything wrong with that?"

"No," Vladimir answered, "no. . . . It's just that it's another one of those things that I . . . have never contemplated."

"Well, you will have another seven and half months to contemplate it before the actual event," Mattie said, smiling faintly. "I really love you, Vladimir, and I want this. But please understand—and I swear it—I don't want to obligate you. I know your life . . . and you don't owe me a thing. I only wish you could be happy with it also."

"Mattie, I must be away next weekend, for a couple of days—"

"Where are you going?"

"Please . . . no questions. I have lots of things on my mind right now. I am full of many thought—"

"I'm full of *thoughts*," she corrected him.

"That's what I *said*. I am full of many thought. But I promise you, when I come back we will talk about this, and . . . and you have not lost me as a friend. Just give me time to get used to the idea of being a father." His eyes glittered again. "Ah, happiness! This is a situation that calls for *serious* happiness."

They both laughed. The Brooklyn waiter decided it was safe to come back to the table and take their order.

"Waiter!" Vladimir bellowed. "We'll have hot borscht, beluga and Malossol caviar, nalistniki, blini, and eggplant à la Russe."

He whispered in Mattie's ear, *"And* don't give me that *not hungry* bullshit! You're eating for two now!"

A short, unremarkable man who had been sitting at a center table just in front of Mattie and Vladimir paid his check and slipped away to the phones. There, in front of a big, white painting of a Russian winter carnival, he dialed seven digits.

"Hello? Hello? Mrs. MacAlpine? No, just tell her Jim Brody is calling. . . . Thank you. . . . Mrs. MacAlpine? Brody here. I'm in the Russian Tea Room. I thought you'd be interested to know that . . ."

✻

VLADIMIR/*New York City/Wednesday, October 5, 1966*

It was nearly midnight when Vladimir entered his Park Avenue hotel. He picked up his mail and got into the elevator. The rehearsal had lasted longer than expected, yet had left him elated. To dance—that was always his answer, cathartic and exhilarating.

He was barely inside his room when the phone rang.

"Vladimir." Denise was all honey and sugar. "I've come to agree with you. I want to apologize for my outburst, and I promise not to push you anymore. I won't demand anything. . . . Please, Vladimir, please let's be friends. I want you to be happy any time you can be."

"Denise, what is this?" Vladimir was caught off guard. "You have as many façades as one could have wigs. And you must have twenty of those!"

Denise laughed with forced gaiety. "Do you still plan to go to see Mariela next weekend?"

"Yes, of course," he said. "I've told you that. In fact, I've told no one else."

"Then I have an idea," she began. "See what you think of this. As I told you, I have a new house in Palm Beach. Next Sunday, after your matinee, we can travel in my plane—"

He interrupted. "To Aruba?"

"Wait, Vladimir," she continued. "The plane would drop me in Palm Beach, and you could go on to Aruba. On Tuesday morning the plane would wait for you, then pick me up in Palm Beach, and we could come back to New York together. How does that sound to you?"

"How could I say no to such an offer? I appreciate it and I thank you."

"When may I speak to you to arrange the details?" Denise asked.

"You know my number and by now you know my hours."

"I'm going to do my best to forget them," she said with a laugh, "and that's a promise. Let's be friends. I think I'd like that! I'd like that very much!"

"Yes. So would I. I told you I can be a loyal friend." The thought of being the father to Mattie's baby flashed across his mind, as it had so often in the past few hours, each time more pleasurably than the last. How he wished he could confide in Denise. He knew he *would* tell Mariela. *She* would understand. But Denise? The abruptness of her *volte-face* made him hold his tongue.

"Then I'll see you Sunday?"

"Sunday, yes. I can't think of a better way to launch our new friendship."

✳

VLADIMIR/*New York City/Sunday, October 9, 1966*

"Have a good evening, Mr. Volodin. Nasty weather, isn't it! Feels like winter!"

Vladimir ignored the doorman's greeting and open umbrella as he stepped from his hotel to the sidewalk. His hand tightened the silk scarf under his black leather coat; he drew the sable collar snugly under his chin and pulled his Dutch cap lower on his head.

The wind churned through the Park Avenue canyon, clinging against the buildings and driving the raindrops into the slush underfoot. Vladimir cursed the wet assault as he strode to the shelter of Denise's limousine at the curb.

The chauffeur took his shoulder bag and Vladimir slid into the spacious passenger compartment.

It was empty.

The sliding glass panel separating him from the driver was open, and he leaned forward as the chauffeur settled behind the wheel.

"Where's Mrs. MacAlpine?" he demanded.

"She's waiting for you on the telephone, Mr. Volodin," the chauffeur replied.

The cover to the cabinet containing the bar was open. Next to the neatly arrayed bottles and glasses the mobile phone lay off its hook. Vladimir loosened his collar and raised the receiver against his ear.

"Hello, Denise, where are you? Why are you calling me in the car?"

"I tried your room several times, but you weren't answering."

"Yes . . . that's right. That's right. I was running late coming back from the theater and didn't pick up the phone. Where are you?"

"Vladimir!" The voice on the phone was choked with emotion. "I'm afraid something terrible has happened." She halted. "Sinclair was in San Diego on business, and apparently he's had a stroke. I don't believe it is a serious one, but I'm going to have to fly out. I'm sure you can understand. I'm expecting another call from San Diego any moment."

"Does that mean your plane can't take me to Aruba?"

"No, dearest, not at all! It means you will have to fly to Aruba by yourself. I wouldn't dream of changing your plans at the last minute. I know how much it means to you."

"What about you? Won't you need your plane to go to San Diego?"

"One of Sinclair's corporate jets will fly me out. You must excuse me, Vladimir. I'm terribly upset. Don't worry about me, dearest. Just make yourself a drink and relax. I'll call you at the airport before your departure. I have to go now. The other phone is ringing. It must be San Diego. Goodbye, darling."

"I'm so sorry, Denise, I really am. Thank you."

Vladimir replaced the dead phone in its cradle and settled back into the soft leather seat. The news didn't bother him. After all, he didn't know Sinclair. Now he wouldn't have to endure Denise's conversation on the trip. Mariela was occupying his thoughts. And Mattie.

The rain had stopped as the limousine worked its way through the traffic to the F. D. R. Drive. The world outside still felt gray and cold. So did Vladimir. Actually, the air was clear—clearer than normal for New York. The city lights were bright and sharp through the oval rear window as the limousine crossed the Triborough Bridge.

The final glow of the sun vanished behind the jagged skyline. Commuter traffic was picking up a little. The trip to LaGuardia was shorter than he had expected—probably because of his preoccupation with Mariela. If only he didn't have to sit through the damned plane flight before he could see her. Comfort her. Help her. Let her know that all was not lost. That he was her friend and would prove it.

The car passed Astoria Boulevard, crossed back over Grand Central Parkway, and turned left on the service road toward the main entrance of the Marine Air Terminal. It was devoid of other vehicles. The silence in the plush automobile was broken by the roar of massive jet engines. A commercial flight left the runway and fought for altitude directly over the limousine. Takeoff patterns were to the south that evening. The racket from the planes did nothing to eliminate the butterflies flitting in Vladimir's stomach.

The car stopped in front of a small terminal at the west end of the field. Vladimir again buttoned his collar as he walked to the glass entrance doors. The liveried chauffeur proffered his bag and, accepting it without acknowledging the man's presence, he entered the building.

There was little activity. The circular waiting room was broken at its periphery by unattended ticket counters and a closed magazine stand. To his right a set of glass doors was painted with the Butler Aviation sign. Vladimir could see through them and view the large cluster of planes, from single-engine craft hardly big enough for a pilot and passenger to the baby jets with their corporate logos painted on jutting stabilizers.

A tall, curly-haired man, outfitted in a blue uniform cut to fit his athletic frame, was leaning against the counter, talking to a young woman behind it. He casually toyed with the brimmed cap in his hand, facing her at an angle calculated to reveal his rugged profile and confident smile.

He's not talking about the weather, Vladimir mused to himself as he stalked through the door. The truth of his observation revealed itself in the momentary grimace of annoyance that flashed across the man's face when their eyes met. It was replaced immediately by a professional smile as he returned his cap to its proper position.

"Mr. Volodin?" The voice echoed with the practiced resonance that is *de rigueur* over an aviation radio. "I'm Captain Carpenter. We're ready to take off when you are."

"Has Mrs. MacAlpine called?" Vladimir inquired.

As if in response to his query, a telephone rang behind the counter. The young woman picked it up, then turned toward him. "Mr. Volodin? It's for you."

It was Denise. "Darling, I hope all will be well on your trip," she said with concern. "As you know, the plane will wait for you in Aruba and bring you back to New York on Tuesday as planned."

"How's Sinclair?"

"I'm afraid his situation is serious. Much more serious than originally thought, and I'll be leaving shortly." There was a short pause. Her voice mellowed. "I am deeply disappointed, Vladimir, that I won't be making this trip with you, even if it's only to Palm Beach."

Vladimir was careful to restrict his tones to those of mild disappointment. "I'm going to miss your company—I hope things work out for the best. Call me Tuesday in New York and let me know about your husband."

"I will, Vladimir. And think a little of me during your trip if you can."

"I shall," he lied. "I know how terribly upset you must be."

"Oh, I am, Vladimir—I'm so worried for my dear Sinclair. Good night, darling."

"Good night." He hung up and walked to the outer door.

"What are we waiting for?" he snapped at Carpenter. "Let's get going."

He raced across the tarmac. Mariela was waiting for him in Aruba and he wanted to get there. Soon. The sooner the better. Both because she was there and because he wanted to get off this damned airplane as quickly as possible. Where was it, anyway? The butterflies were dancing violently. The wind rose in a wail and lapped at his face.

Denise's plane rested at the far side of the parking area. Its fifty-nine-foot fuselage and eighty-foot wingspan were too large to be threaded through the smaller craft dotted around the tarmac. The Lockheed Jetstar loomed over the others like a mother hen in a nest of chicks. Its all-white surface was broken only by the registry numbers painted in large black symbols on the stabilizer. Light shone from the five windows on the side facing him.

As Vladimir and the pilot neared the ship an opening appeared in the side, just aft of the cockpit. The door vanished inside and a set of steps thrust out and down. Vladimir vaulted in, to be greeted by another blue uniform draped smartly on another trim male figure.

"Good evening, Mr. Volodin. I'm your copilot and steward. I won't be of much use to you until we're aloft, but after that please feel free to ask for anything you may want. My name is Craig. I can't guarantee three unlimited wishes, but we are well enough stocked to supply any reasonable need, and probably a few unreasonable ones." He broke into an expectant smile. It was a phrase the man had obviously used before, calculated to provoke a relaxing chuckle. It didn't work.

"My needs are always unreasonable. The main one will be to get back on ground as soon as possible. When do we take off?" Vladimir demanded curtly.

The man maintained his smile and continued. "Immediately, Mr. Volodin. Our flight plan is filed. We should be in Aruba in five hours. We have to cover two thousand twenty nautical miles cruising at four hundred forty knots—"

"I'm not interested in details I don't understand," Vladimir interrupted, brushing past the man.

"There'll be a stop in Miami to refuel, Mr. Volodin, which should take no more than thirty minutes." The smile was gone. The man walked toward the cockpit.

Vladimir's disposition improved as he settled into the luxurious cabin while the pilot and copilot/steward fired up the four engines. There was a mild rumble from the rear of the plane, where the engines were mounted in tandem, just in front of the tail, two on each side. The noise was tolerable. The ship was superbly soundproofed.

It was obviously Denise's plane. Unlike the cabin configuration normally used in a Jetstar for corporate travel, this plane was designed to carry very few people in maximum comfort. Its usable interior was twenty-five feet long and seven feet wide. There was room for Vladimir to stand at his full height in the center, although he had no desire to do so at the moment. He was quite satisfied to collapse into one of the soft plush lounging chairs and let himself be distracted by the artwork with which Denise had decorated her flying living room.

Vladimir wondered if the small Degas on the starboard wall was her own choice for its esthetic value or whether it was there as some sort of tribute to his own artistry. If it was, he was disappointed. The soft ballerina did not express his feelings of the drama and driving control he liked to bring to the stage. There were no male dancers represented. The other works were rather eclectic. The Vidal-Quadras did not hang well with a Miró and a Cézanne.

His personal art critique was interrupted by the sudden pressure of the seat against his body as the jet started on its accelerating rush down the runway. The plane left the ground and began its swift climb to the south. The air was sharp and clear, as it so often is just after a rain flurry. The lights of Queens lay below him, yellow and hearthlike, in contrast to the multicolored gleam of Manhattan visible through the starboard windows. The vibrancy of the city, glistening and sparkling below, seemed to project itself into the heavens themselves.

Like dancers behind a falling curtain, the blazing panorama vanished as the Jetstar climbed through an unexpected cloud layer. The plane was buffeted slightly in the dense clouds. Vladimir swallowed, fighting nervousness that was for him an inescapable element of flying. The buffeting ceased as the dark layer dropped below. Now the cloud tops emerged, glowing in soft patterns of black and indigo, illumined by the sudden appearance of a stark, awesome full moon.

Craig, the steward, came back from the cockpit and opened the top of a long ivory lacquered cabinet resting against the white velvet wall. A turn of the dial and the air was filled softly with the strains of Tchaikovsky. Ensconced in his seat, Vladimir watched with little interest as the man performed his duties. A minor ritual: lifting the glass higher than necessary, inspecting it, wiping it ostentatiously with a towel, holding it like a precious jewel. Setting it down on the exposed bar, he proceeded to mix rum with another concoction. The rattling of the ice added discordant notes to the diffused music.

"Rum punch, I believe," the steward said, offering Vladimir a full glass on a silver tray.

"Excellent," replied Vladimir. "I hope there's more in that shaker." Half the drink vanished in two quick swallows.

"Plenty more. And I can always mix another batch. Does the music suit you?"

"It doesn't matter. I want something to read. What do you have?"

"The library's in the back," the man answered, pointing to a door. "Shall I pick something or do you want to browse?" The first rum punch had already disappeared. The steward refilled Vladimir's glass.

"I'll find what I want." The dancer stood up and moved in the direction indicated. He opened the door. The rear of the plane was occupied by a round bed, surrounded by smoked mirrors. Several dozen books were displayed behind a grilled panel. There was a whole section of Byron. Denise had indeed anticipated his wishes. Vladimir picked up a volume at random.

It opened to the haunting short poem Byron had written to his friend Thomas Moore during the annual carnival in Venice in 1816.

So, we'll go no more a roving.
  So late into the night,
Though the heart be still as loving,
  And the moon be still as bright. . . .

Outside the window the moon was still bright. Vladimir returned to his seat with his book and stared at the clouds, now many thousands of feet below. It was no longer possible to see any lights on the land. Was it still land or were they now over water, he wondered. He turned to ask the steward, but he had disappeared into the cockpit.

While gulping the remains of his drink Vladimir idly contemplated the old question he had pondered since his youth of whether or not Byron had been the lover of his half sister Augusta. His conclusion was still that he had. It fitted Vladimir's own sense of romantic integrity to believe it—and no one could prove otherwise anyway! Vladimir returned to a half attentive reading of the other short poems in the book on his lap. Craig reappeared and mixed a fresh pitcher of rum punch. He refilled Vladimir's glass.

"We're making good time, Mr. Volodin," he said cheerfully. "There's a healthy tail wind. It'll cut half an hour from our flight."

Half an hour sooner he would step onto solid land! Half an hour sooner he would be able to soothe Mariela. The world had deserted her, but he, Vladimir Volodin, would not. How vulnerable she was! And frightened.

Words came back to him now, inexplicably haunting.

He and Mariela were having dinner in Chicago. "You remember Tarutu?" she had said. "My Egyptian sarcophagus? You were always making fun of it. Well, it broke—fell—toppled over into a thousand pieces—frightened me to death. It happened in the middle of the night, after the engagement party for Genevieve and Oliver, in London. Remember London? Where *we* happened? You don't suppose there's such a thing as a mummy's curse, do you?" She hadn't seemed quite convinced that there wasn't.

Now, two years later, Tarutu's curse was being fulfilled.

He could imagine her now, tears in her beautiful eyes. Perhaps there was something to this superstition. Volodin was Russian after all, and mysticism was no stranger to him. Nor was tragedy.

The rum was having its effect. In fact, it was having more than its usual effect. They were flying at 37,000 feet. The Jetstar was pressurized to an altitude of 10,000 feet. At 10,000 feet, however, alcohol has twice the effect it has at sea level. Vladimir found it harder than ever to concentrate on Byron and decided he definitely didn't like the Degas!

It seemed only moments before the steward reappeared. What now? Why the hell didn't the world leave him alone? He wanted to be free to think. Of Mattie . . . of Mariela . . . Soon he would be there to help. To try to help. To try . . .

"Remain where you are, Mr. Volodin, and fasten your seat belt, please."

(Where did this clown think he was going anyway?) "We'll be landing to refuel." (So let them. Who cares?)

The descent into Miami was smooth. The cloud layer had been left behind somewhere over South Carolina. It was warm enough on the ground to force Vladimir to remove his coat. The Dutch cap remained on his head.

His senses cleared somewhat with the increased air pressure but not enough for him to venture from the plane during the short stopover. He was well on his way to being drunk. Quite well on his way. Maybe that's why he thought the steward and pilot seemed less smiling and professionally cheerful as they settled in for the takeoff on the final leg across the Caribbean. Maybe it was simply his imagination. Anyway, he really didn't give a damn!

As the jet once again climbed into the moonlit sky, his ears popped with the dropping pressure. The steward reappeared. "Would you like to see the ocean from the cockpit, Mr. Volodin? It's beautiful out there tonight."

"No. I don't want to see anything until we land."

"Another rum punch, then?" The steward answered his own question by thrusting a full glass into Vladimir's hand. Vladimir grasped it with difficulty.

"Thank you." The words slurred. "Thank you," he repeated, consciously controlling his lips and tongue to make the phrase come out distinctly. His ears were still bothering him. "Is the pressure all right in here?" Vladimir growled.

"It should be fine. Would you like some chewing gum?" the steward offered. "That helps clears the ears."

"It's a disgusting habit!" Vladimir mumbled.

"As you wish, sir, but it does usually work."

"I'll be all right." Vladimir was decidedly drunk. His head lolled against the back of the chair. Despite his efforts to keep his eyes open his eyelids drooped. He willed himself once more to concentrate on Mattie. He still could not comprehend what a child would mean to him—only that he wanted it . . . a child . . .

The steward entered the cockpit. He took his position next to Captain Carpenter and pulled down the overhead oxygen mask. He breathed deeply several times. The captain already had a mask strapped to his face. "Damn it! It's sure hard to breathe back there with the pressurization off," the copilot said.

"How's our passenger?"

"He's fine. He's out, or nearly so." The copilot's head turned sharply toward the cabin. "I haven't had anything to drink and I damned near passed out myself."

They remained silent for a few moments. "I guess we'd better get on with it then," Carpenter said.

"I guess so."

Carpenter throttled back all four jets. The plane slowed to 130 knots, just above its stalling speed. He activated the altitude hold button on the autopilot and adjusted the trim to compensate for the slower speed. The plane settled under its control. Carpenter locked the direction to the Port-au-Prince OMNI station. He removed his hands from the wheel. The plane flew itself.

Carpenter and Craig took a dozen deep breaths from the masks, got up and stepped through the cockpit door into the cabin. Vladimir had collapsed limply in his seat.

Carpenter lifted the handle of the sliding cabin door. The door moved inward as the handle snapped up. A blast of air tugged at him. He pulled the door in farther and slid it inside the wall. A roaring, gaping hole, black and malevolent, was open to the sea, 20,000 feet below.

"Carpenter, are you sure about all this? I mean, can we get away with it?"

"Goddammit, Craig, what crappy timing for your idiotic doubts! I've never been more sure of anything in my life. Just think—our own airline, even if it's in a banana country. Besides," he said maliciously, "Mrs. MacAlpine is one well that will never run dry!"

"Huh?"

"Trust me, Craig. Come on, let's go."

Vladimir stirred from the sudden increase in sound and the abnormal pitching of the plane as the autopilot contended with the change in flying resistance.

He regained a measure of consciousness as the two men lifted him roughly from his seat. The heavy-lidded eyes opened slowly. In a state halfway between awareness and coma, Vladimir thought at first he was dreaming. Some resistance within him, some ancient instinct for survival, rose from his subconscious. "What—what's going on?" he slurred, clawing at the stationary seat legs with his feet.

"Just relax and take it easy, Mr. Volodin," the pilot coaxed. "It'll all be over before you can say Anna Pavlova."

"What—what are you doing?" He tried to pull his arms free, but to no avail.

"Take it easy, Mr. Volodin." The copilot held on tighter to his calf and upper arm. "We're nearly there. Easy does it."

Their voices reached his ears seemingly from a great distance, hollow-sounding, like an echo from some long-forgotten part of his past.

In an instant Vladimir realized the awfulness of what was happening and felt that terrible sensation of falling often experienced on awaking from a deep sleep. Only there would be no more awakening! They were trying to kill him! But who were they? And why were they doing it? He wasn't sure if he had spoken aloud, so mindless was his terror.

Vladimir was being half carried, half dragged toward the open door. He knew what was out there: nothingness and death. "Oh no!" he screamed. The wind blew the words away. "Oh no, no, no, no!" It was getting harder and harder to breathe. "Why—why are you doing this?" he begged, panic-stricken. "What—what have I ever done to you . . . ? I . . . I don't even know who you are . . . .!"

"But we know who *you* are, don't we, Mr. Volodin—and that's what counts!"

In his terror Vladimir had no time to reason. Mustering all his strength, he flailed about violently, scarcely knowing why he fought, only that he had to. His power increased with the knowledge. The beautiful white even teeth snapped at the hands that held him. The heel of a boot raked a shin. An elbow thrust into an eye. The legs thrashed. Oh yes, he was a true swan, both beautiful and vicious. "Now, now, Mr. Volodin, let's try and behave with a little dignity, shall we!"

"You told me he was completely out!" said Carpenter.

"He was! How am I supposed to know a ballet dancer has the strength of a horse!"

The door was only a few feet away. "I don't want to die!" Vladimir cried. "Not this way!"

"We have no other way to accommodate you, Mr. Volodin," the pilot replied cruelly. "There *is* no other way!"

"No, no, no, no, no . . . !" In a last desperate effort Volodin tried to overpower his captors. Kicking and scratching and cursing. His befuddled mind confused his thoughts. He didn't want to die! He couldn't die! There was so much left to do! Or was there? Perhaps he'd done it all! Everyone dies alone, but he would die *more alone*. Would he disappear, dissolve into space? Where would he land? In a tree or in water?

They were now by the open door. He could see the opaque hole staring at him. His tortured mind hurled into dementia. A beautiful creature was about to die, a swan caught in a swan song.

His drunken, oxygen-starved body was flung into black space. The 130-knot wind grabbed Vladimir in violent embrace, slapping out the scream that tried to rise from his laboring lungs. His lithe body twisted and spun like a rag doll in a clothes dryer.

Vladimir's cry of stark terror finally managed to surface, only to be instantly swallowed by the empty sky above the Caribbean. He was plunging toward her waters at 180 feet a second. The wind and fear forced a massive rush of adrenaline through his system, clearing the alcoholic fog. Instinctively his dancer's body moved to counterbalance the spinning and twisting. He found the spread-eagle arched position that stabilized his fall. His arms extended like those of a man on a cross.

His legs locked in resistance to the air pouring past him, toes pointed in a frozen *gambade*. His back held in a smooth curve, projecting his abdomen in a salute to the water below. Each movement of arm or leg turned him like a rudder. He flew.

Fear was a chaotic ally of exhilaration as his entire being sailed, flying and turning with a freedom he'd never attained on the hard surface of a stage. A freedom he would never be able to try for again. At the same time as his body gloried in the fantastic freedom of unrestrained flight his mind worked furiously at the realization that this was now his final dance. A dance choreographed by—whom? His mind flashed a six-letter word like an obscenity. Denise! Denise plotting, manipulating, arranging—for if she could not have Vladimir, no one would! Denise had transformed her inconceivable arrogance into a matchless wickedness. So there had been nothing wrong with her husband after all. There had been no stroke! There was no emergency! She had wanted Vladimir on this plane. Alone. And what Denise wanted she invariably got. He knew that now, knew too late she had succeeded in initiating the legend of the *late* Vladimir Volodin. They say one's mind clears in the last moments before death. It was certainly so for Vladimir Volodin.

Was it for this his mother had suffered shame? Labeled throughout Leningrad as the relative of a defector? Dying broken-hearted and never understanding. His brother in Kiev. What of him? Alexei had never understood either. Now he surely would not! People he would not see again. Thoughts he would not think again. So he was not a survivor after all. So he was not one of the *golden nuggets!* No regrets really. Nothing left undone. Could it be so terrible to die? After all, was it so terrible not to live? He *had* accomplished something. He *was* a phenomenon. Why, then, this total terror of repetition that had pervaded his life? Why this feeling of nihilism? He had lived with an expectancy of achievement that was at once impossible and possible. For he had recognized no limits but one. And here it was now. What tawdry irony that it should have come about through the grasping connivance of a petty, revenge-obsessed dilettante. How unlike Mattie she was! Mattie with whom he had so wanted a child. There would be no child. No blessing. Just a curse . . . Tarutu . . . Mamushka . . . Lucinka . . . .

The thought was never completed. Vladimir Mikhailovich Volodin made his final bow at 120 miles an hour against water harder than any floor he'd ever grand-jetéed across. The Gulf Stream carried the diffusing patch of red to the senses of her cruising sharks.

At last a great stillness.

⸸

Mariela looked out of the southern window of the large bedroom, down over the hills and shoreline cliff to the sea a couple of kilometers away.

The traffic on the Route Napoléon was almost all in the northerly direction. Late-summer vacationers, their luggage and water skis racked on the roofs of their cars, their boats in tow behind, wending their way home from the lazy life of St. Tropez, Ramaturelle, Mougins, and the surrounding areas.

Vladimir Volodin's house in Mougins wasn't very close to the road, but Mariela seemed unusually aware of the traffic sounds today. Probably because she was making the effort. The season was ending. There were no other sounds to listen to.

The house *was* quiet. The old Russian servant woman, Nadya, who had been with the house—a small converted old mill—since Vladimir bought it in 1965, had remained after her husband passed away. Nadya wasn't home—probably out shopping. Or perhaps she was at the village square watching the old men enjoying their daily *jeux de boules* on the carefully smoothed sandlot. They were there every day, and they all looked much alike. The scene varied only when they changed their clothes with the seasons. Fall was definitely here: they wore dark sweaters and had heavy caps on.

Mariela turned away from the window. The same massive Russian furniture and the six-foot-high wrought-iron candelabra still occupied the three main rooms. Vladimir's things were still piled about at random. There were stacks of photos from all his various performances, which he had probably never bothered to look at: Volodin in *Le Corsaire,* Volodin in *La Fille Mal Gardée,* Volodin with Béjart, Volodin . . . Volodin . . . Volodin . . .

Posters from his appearances in Paris, Berlin, New York, Los Angeles, Dallas, everywhere, were still rolled up. He had meant to send them to his family in Russia eventually. They remained unsent.

Books lay on heavy side tables and shelves. *Vladimir Volodin: The Man and His Art, Vladimir Volodin and Sybil Parkinson, Volodin and—,Vladimir Volodin: The——.* Books on Nijinsky, Diaghilev, Pavlova, Ulanova. Books on Egyptian, Iranian, Moslem art, ballet books, special editions of Byron's works, books in Russian, books in French, books, books, books . . .

Original Bakst sketches, set designs by Rouben Ter-Arutunian, costume drawings by Erté, leaned against the wall, never hung, never displayed . . .

His records were still stacked carelessly about, never played. His ballet slippers, untouched. Mariela, convinced that the ghost of the dancer moved through his house, had done nothing to make him feel a stranger. Nadya dusted from time to time—that was all. More than that might chase the ghost away.

It had been *his* house, without a touch of femininity anywhere to be seen. Now Mariela's things were there. They had to be, of course. You can't live somewhere for two years without having your own things around. But they disappeared among the remnants of the true owner. Now even the owner had disappeared. His ghost wasn't moving anymore.

It was surprising how such a small house could have such large rooms, Mariela thought disconnectedly.

Mariela was still beautiful. Her tall body, perhaps a little fuller, had lost none of its firmness. At the corners of her green eyes only very few wrinkles appeared when she laughed or when she frowned. But the eyes no longer flashed fire. They no longer glowed with determination. If they expressed anything, it was fatigue. Not the fatigue of rising too early after a late party. She didn't party anymore. Not the fatigue of a battle fought and won, or even a battle fought and lost. She no longer fought those battles. It was just fatigue. Permanent, unrelenting fatigue. But one had to look hard to see it.

There was no one there to look. No one but her, and she didn't need a mirror to tell her what she already knew would be there. Mariela no longer had to explain it to herself. But she did have to explain it to Oliver, if she could.

She had tried. She walked to the desk and sat down, picked up an envelope and addressed it:

Mr. Oliver Leitung
17 Belgrave Square,
London, England

She unfolded the letter and read it once more:

My dearest Oliver,

    Some things are far easier to say in a letter than in person or over the telephone. They are easier only because they are so hard to say under any circumstances. At least putting them down on paper requires organizing everything into some sort of coherence.

    I love you. I've always loved you. That's one thread that runs unbroken through our history from the time you were born. I'm proud of you. You've done well with your life. I believe that in some measure I was able to contribute to that. Maybe it will serve to balance some of the pain you hold me responsible for.

You are a fighter. You couldn't be otherwise, for you are, after all, my son. Perhaps that will help you understand my own life. I make no apologies for what I have done. I've gotten what I want, usually when I wanted it. I hope you won't judge me for what I've done or what I am about to do. People do what they can, and judgment is not ours to make. If you can't help judging, then at least please try to forgive.

I've spent two years thinking about myself. They've been difficult years. I'm tired, and I'm satisfied. I don't see anything more to do. I don't *want* to do anything more.

That's why life is no longer possible for me. The rewards are not there to sustain the effort, and the effort is too great. I hope you can understand. My decision has not been a rash one. No decision that takes two years to make could be described as rash.

Be good to Genevieve—she is very special and human and always believed in you—and it is so rare to find such people.

I wish both of you a good life. Think of me kindly, please. I love you, Oliver.

Your mother

Mariela folded the later carefully. She put it in the envelope and sealed it. She walked to the post office and made sure it got started on its way to London.

The traffic was still moving north. Everything has its end, whether it be summers, loves, or lives.

—❋—

MATTIE/*New York City*/*Wednesday, October 9, 1968*

"Mike, stop it!" The stern tone of Mattie's voice was belied by the gleam in her eyes as she retrieved her son from the pile of music manuscripts he had just tossed across the floor and laid him down on the sofa.

"Just like his father," Sylvia said. "Fortunately he's still cute enough to get away with it."

"So was Vladimir," Mattie answered. The gleam changed to a flicker of sadness. Today marked the second anniversary of Vladimir Volodin's death. Mattie stared at his portrait on the wall directly over the piano. She often imagined she was singing to him when practicing on the lower floor of her duplex. Whether that helped her or hindered her was a question that still couldn't be answered. Probably a little of both.

"Come on, Mattie," Jerry Sterling said, "let's try this one." The producer from RCA handed her a long sheet. She took it absentmindedly, smiling into the baby's face.

"Don't you think he's going to look very much like Vladimir?" mused Mattie. "Have you noticed the high cheekbones? You can already see them. And the—"

"Could we please stop talking about Mike?" said Jerry impatiently. "If we're going to the studio by Monday, we'd better get cracking!"

"Yeah, yeah, Jerry . . ." Her mind drifted, as it often did—though less often than it used to—over the year and a half she had spent at the Payne Whitney Clinic. It was a year and a half that was, for the most part, lost to her. A horrible year and a half. The breakdown had been complete. It wasn't so much the loss in her own life that she regretted. It was the loss of a crucial period in her life with Mikhail—the tiny baby that, throughout her ordeal, she couldn't remember.

Well, that was over. Mattie had been to the depths, there wasn't any place lower to go. But now it was all behind her, and the time had come for people to hear again, in a positive way, about Mattie Maxwell. The time had come to take hold of things—for both of them. The pulse of life was surging inside her. She was ready.

The news media hadn't been kind. It was the sixties and one expected a bit more tolerance, but famous people who had children out of wedlock were still fair game for the supercilious moralists and pseudomoralists, who had nothing better to do than make noise about the tragedies in other people's lives. And Mattie Maxwell was more than fair game—she was big game.

Of course Mattie didn't consider Mikhail part of her tragedy. She considered him a positive joy.

"The song, Mattie!" Jerry interrupted her train of thought. "The song! Please!"

"Yes, right, the song, I'm sorry. Let's go. I'm ready."

Mikhail Vladimir Maxwell let out a tremendous howl.

"We just can't work around here with a baby crying his head off," Ed Sturrock, the pianist-conductor, said.

"Well, if I hold him, he'll be all right."

"Can't you just put him in his room?"

"No, not today, Ed. I must have him with me." Mattie picked up the baby and gave him his favorite toy, a yellow-and-orange velvet duck. Mikhail fell asleep almost instantaneously. "By the way, I hope we have all winners on this album. I don't want to make a comeback with half-assed material."

"Come on, Mattie, you know I've never given you anything but the greatest material," Sammy Cahn assured her. "Believe me, I've transferred all your feelings into words. Besides, Mattie, *you* can turn any song into a hit."

"I just hope I'm still that great."

"Listen to her, she's looking for compliments." It was Sylvia this time. "Of course you're still great, and you're still beautiful."

"Come on, Sylvia. My vision isn't impaired. I can see what's in the mirror as well as anyone. Maybe better. I'm no sex goddess anymore. I look like a mother."

"Sex goddess? When the hell were you a sex goddess? You look like a mother. A beautiful mother. There's nothing wrong with that. Your Carnegie Hall concert is already a sellout, and this new album should be better than anything you've ever done before."

"Nothing's going to sell if we don't get it on tape." That came from another of the RCA men. *"Please,* can we try?"

"Sure," Mattie replied. "The *beautiful* thirty-three-year-old mother is going to try."

"Give me Mike," said Sylvia. "I'll hold him."

Mattie sat down at the piano. Her fingers worked across the keys, laying the base for an unleashing of the talent she hoped—she prayed—was still there.

She ran through the melody first, then added some of the left-hand counterpoint. It was a good song. Sammy was right. The words *were* her feelings. She knew she could do something with it. Ed Sturrock took her place and Mattie stood up.

She smiled at little Mikhail and opened her mouth. Her lungs filled. The sound came out clear, hard, and intense.

> *The night is a sanctuary*
> *Where you bring your heart,*
> *A place you can always run to*
> *When the mem'ries start . . .*

Every word she sang was catapulted from her musical heart. Her own soaring voice uplifted her, and all the anguish suddenly vanished.

The awesome talent once more vibrated with the atmosphere of the big time. She looked up at Vladimir's picture. Her dependency on him was over. So was the self-pity.

Mattie Maxwell had come to life again.

❋

DENISE/*New York City/Wednesday, October 9, 1968*

Denise MacAlpine got off at the sixty-fifth floor of 30 Rockefeller Plaza. She was immediately surrounded by photographers. Wearing her dazzling smile easily, unconsciously, with her charm in full bloom. She posed graciously while continuing to walk, and entered the Rainbow Room, working her way toward the head table.

The huge crowd at the "private" gala had been willing to spend a thousand dollars each for the honor of supporting the Lincoln Center Ballet Company and the privilege of rubbing elbows with each other. Denise smiled politely at everyone. The view from the window was unusually clear. One saw nothing but lights—street lights, bridge lights, office and apartment lights—millions of them. It was the kind of view that, before the night was over, would move a young man to say to his girl, "One day, darling, such a view will be ours."

Denise found her seat next to Yuri Zakharov. The dancer still had traces of makeup visible just beneath his hairline. It was obvious that Yuri had rushed to the dinner after his starring performance in *Giselle*.

Yuri Zakharov didn't have the look of the traditional dancer. His sharp features and black, unruly hair made him seem more like a hippie. Only his dark eyes projected something poetic, yet threatening. He radiated untamed violence. His total dedication and brilliance were unanimously hailed. Onstage he could propel himself by sheer will into anything he wanted to be, and at twenty-three, his technique was the best of any male dancer the Bolshoi had to offer. Since his defection in San Francisco six months before, Zakharov had astonished the American public with his bold, explosive dancing.

Someone was remarking on the shape of the table—large and round. "It's perfect. Nobody has a better seat than anyone else. I don't know why Averell can't persuade the North Vietnamese to use this shape in Paris."

"Because they won't sit with the South no matter what the shape of the table," someone else ventured, "and Li Duc Thieu won't take a separate table."

"Maybe the *gook* didn't tip the head waiter," a third voice quipped, causing a small ripple of chuckles.

The Chicago convention was still a hot topic of conversation. Humphrey was just beginning to try to disentangle himself from President Johnson's policies. The consensus was that he wasn't doing too good a job of it.

Denise offered her own opinions in the manner of someone who knows exactly what she thinks on every subject and couldn't possibly be wrong. She did it with such charm that her comments could be safely ignored or accepted without affecting the respect and good feeling everyone felt toward her. She smiled, she spoke, she was loved. She was deliciously seductive and acutely aware of her effect. Turning to Yuri Zakharov, who clearly hung on her every word, she said, "Mr. Zakharov, you were splendid tonight—positively splendid—!"

"You are very . . . very krasiva," he said. "Do you know what it means?"

"Yes, it means 'beautiful.' Thank you." She gave him an unyielding stare. "I'm so pleased to hear that next month you'll be dancing at the Palais des Sports in Paris. Paris is also very . . ."

"Krasiva," said Yuri Zakharov.

They laughed and, unconsciously, she put her hand over his. "I'm going to be in Paris at the same time. I will give a dinner party for you."

"I don't like parties," he replied, "but perhaps—"

"Do you like the art of Fabergé?" she interrupted, somewhat discomfited.

"Yes, it's quite magnificent."

"Then I'm sure you'll like to see my Fabergé Easter egg. It's something really unique. Very special. It's a musical box as well. The—"

A speaker stepped to a microphone on a large podium and addressed the noisy group. The chatter slowly subsided ". . . And, of course, we have with us the one person who has done more than any other to assure the continuity and excellence of the ballet in our city. I know I speak for all of us when I ask her to say a few words. Let me introduce to you the chairman of this evening's event. The floor, indeed, the whole room is yours—Mrs. Denise MacAlpine."

An enthusiastic flow of applause accompanied Denise to the microphone. She was as beautiful as ever. At thirty-six she didn't look thirty. Those sitting very close could, if they had wanted to, see the first evidences of not-quite-so-tight skin at the corners of her eyes, or the very minute creases that appeared just below them when she smiled, but no one looked for such imperfections.

She beamed a smile at the assemblage, that syrupy smile that could send a diabetic into coma, then let it fade into seriousness. The noise died with the smile. She had everyone's attention. "Today marks the passing of the second year since the unexplicable tragedy that took from us one of the greatest dancers in history. Vladimir Volodin soared across our lives and our hearts as he soared across our stages and our art. He brought the power of an enormous personality and an enormous talent to our world. It was a treasure that his country lost and the free world gained and embraced with all its being. Then, as it rocketed toward its ascendancy, it was tragically stolen from us by his untoward death. I was . . . I was . . ." She swallowed hard. "It was a great honor indeed for the Sinclair Mac-Alpine Foundation to bring him for the first time to our splendid Lincoln Center stage, and"—her fingers tugged at the jeweled strap of her white gown—"fate took him away from that same stage. There is no way to measure the effect of his death on his worldwide admirers. His loss . . ." Denise paused and glanced down, her eyes filled with tears. For a moment it seemed that a great emotion had gained complete possession of her. "However, tonight we are very fortunate indeed. We have another superb dancer from the same school that gave us Volodin. You have seen him perform in all his magnificence. I appreciate—all of us appreciate—your support . . ."

Two figures entered. They strode toward her, standing close to the podium.

Denise surveyed the room face to face. Victorious. And halted at the latecomers. She clutched the microphone as she recognized Sinclair! Sinclair—it was Sinclair! What had brought him to town?

". . . the support that allows us to maintain the greatness of our ballet company and to enjoy the grace, the youth, the beauty, the grace, the youth . . ." She caught herself repeating her words. Stopping abruptly, she veiled her big, limpid eyes, lowered her lids, and stared intently at her husband and his companion. Who *is* the man with Sinclair? Who is he? The face is vaguely familiar. She proceeded. ". . . and the talent—Vladimir's talent—I mean Yuri—Yuri's talent—" Her feelings of apprehension became intolerable. Suddenly, like a match being struck in the dark, she recognized the man with Sinclair! Denise mouthed his name silently, her lips forming, gaping the syllables in disbelief. "Carpenter . . . !"

The audience shifted uncomfortably, whispering to one another.

Carpenter, the pilot! Carpenter with Sinclair! Carpenter—Aruba! Dazed, she made a tremendous effort to collect herself. "We cannot hope to overcome—" The hollow voice broke. Her hands shot to her ears in a desperate effort to shut out the music that only she could hear. Music rising, surging in periodic waves.

The entire room sat mute, watching in total bewilderment as Denise lifted her arms toward the ceiling, fluttering them lightly like delicate wings, one arm, then the other, fanning them like a peacock, gracefully, fingers rippling the air. Now she was hearing more than music. What were those shouts, those moans? They stopped. The glorious night became a sanctuary. Waiting. Waiting for her. Only for her. And then a thousand violins erupted in unison, invading every part of her consciousness with the sounds of the "Blue Danube."

Compelled, she started waltzing while humming in tune to the haunting strains. "La, la, la, la-la, LA-LA, LA-LA . . ." The music was louder now. Harsher. She too sang more loudly and harshly—"La, la, la, la-la"—and danced faster and faster. She could hear life shrieking at her inside, but still the music played. And still she danced—pivoting, whirling—faster and faster. The fluid movements abruptly changed to a grotesque mechanical parody, punctuated by hysterical high-pitched laughter.

Gently, ever so gently, she was led from the podium. Her arms were still flailing about. And the folds of her chiffon sleeves, billowing with each movement, made her look like a great bird in flight. Her world was now a black cave. It was over.

Over—before Denise had ever come to the realization of the enormity of what she had done.

About the Author

MONIQUE VAN VOOREN was born in Brussels, the only child of well-to-do parents. As a young girl, she studied music, ballet, and drama, and was the Junior Figure Skating Champion of Belgium. She came to the United States on a Fulbright Scholarship to study philosophy at New York University.

But not long after her arrival in New York, she began getting Broadway offers and supper club engagements, and she launched an energetic show business career. Ms. van Vooren has acted in over thirty plays (comedy-dramas such as *Born Yesterday, Rain,* and *Cactus Flower,* as well as musicals including *Can Can, Irma La Douce, Kismet,* and *Damn Yankees*), and has appeared in over twenty movies (she starred in Carlo Ponti's production of *Andy Warhol's Frankenstein*). She has sung in such prestigious supper clubs as the Persian Room, the Empire Room, La Maisonette, and the Rainbow Grill in New York; the Americana in Miami, the Palmer House in Chicago, the Riviera in Las Vegas, and the Queen Elizabeth in Montreal. She has headlined galas in Cannes, Monte Carlo, Rio de Janeiro, Buenos Aires, and other cities around the world. Her television career includes appearances on all the major talk shows and variety programs, as well as her own hour-and-a-half television special, *Friends of Monique* (which was nominated for an Emmy Award).

Ms. van Vooren also writes for several major publications in America and Europe, and is Contributing Editor of *Interview, Cosmopolitan* and *Forum* magazines. She is proficient (speaking and writing) not only in her native French and Flemish, but in English, Italian, Spanish, Dutch, and German as well.

Monique van Vooren is now separated from her third husband, and has one son. She lives alone in her Manhattan apartment with her two Burmese cats, Vladimir II and Kismet, and summers at her home in Sardinia.